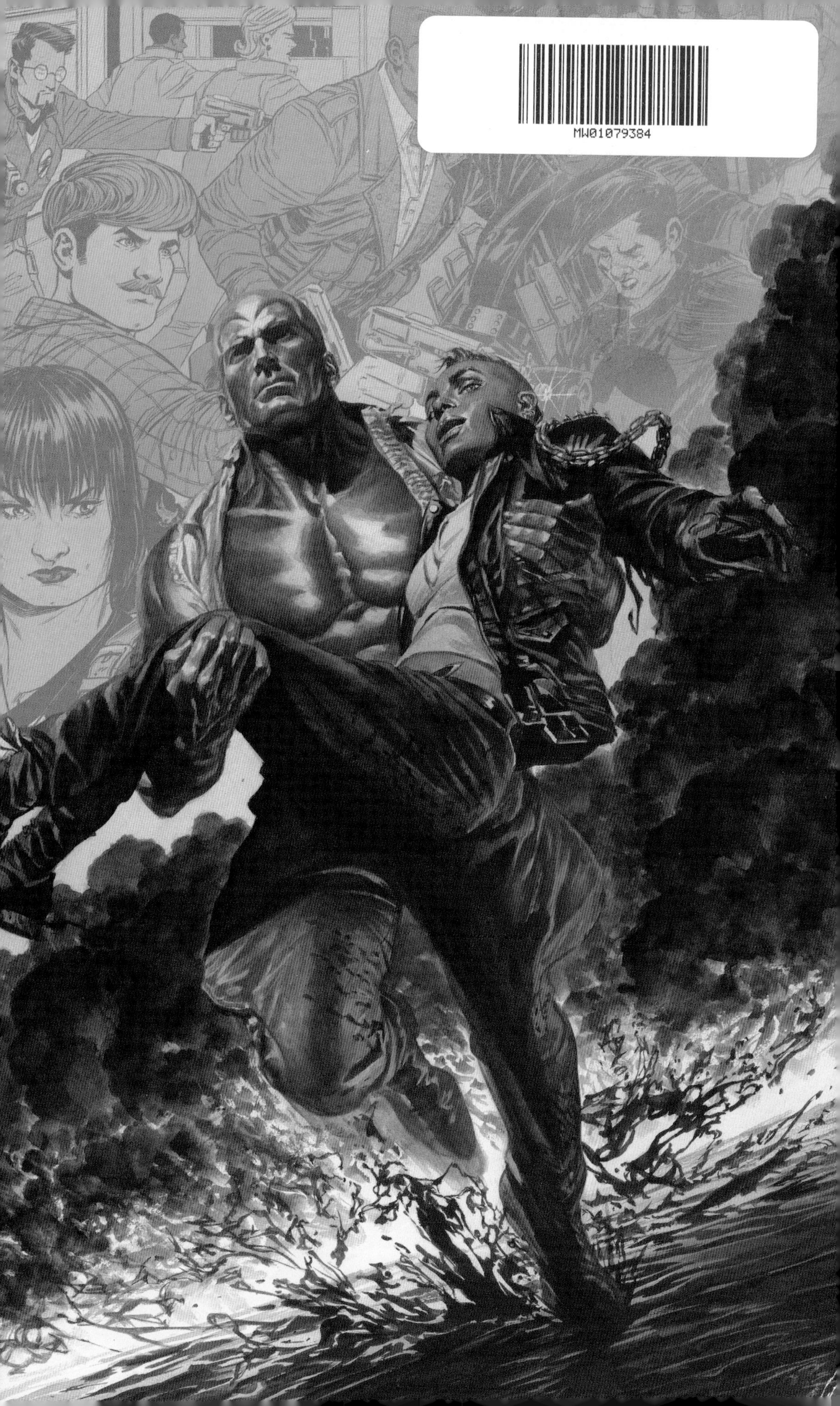

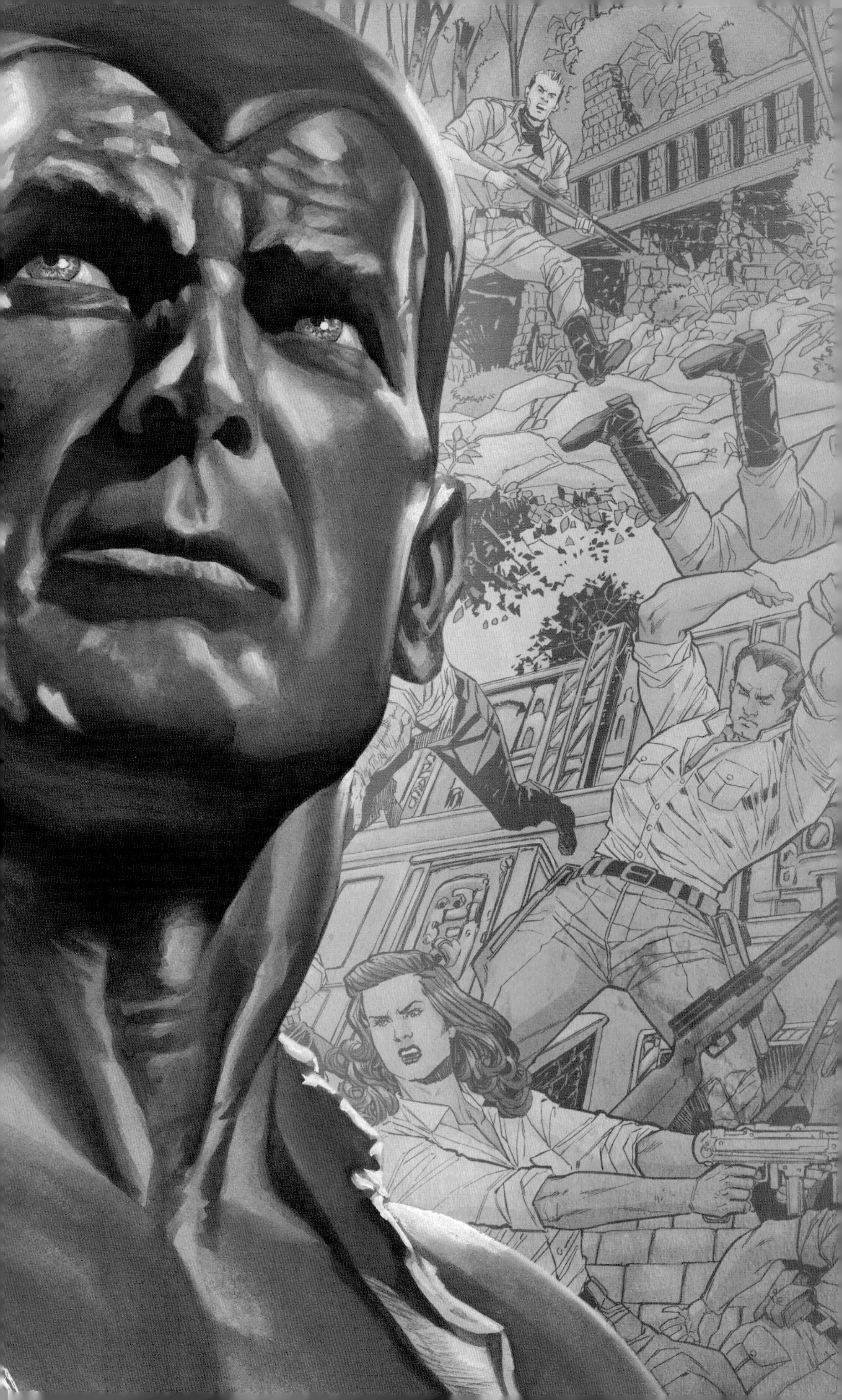

THE MAN OF BRONZE
DOC SAVAGE

OMNIBUS VOLUME ONE

written by: **CHRIS ROBERSON** issues 1-8
SHANNON ERIC DENTON 2014 annual

art by: **BILQUIS EVELY** issues 1-8
ROBERTO CASTRO 2014 annual

colors by: **DANIELA MIWA** issues 1-8
INLIGHT STUDIOS 2014 annual

letters by: **ROB STEEN**

cover by: **ALEX ROSS**

design by: **JASON ULLMEYER**

This volume collects issues #1-8 of the Dynamite Entertainment series Doc Savage as well as the Doc Savage 2014 Annual.

DYNAMITE®

 Visit us online at **www.DYNAMITE.com**
Follow us on Twitter @dynamitecomics
Like us on Facebook **/Dynamitecomics**
Watch us on YouTube **/Dynamitecomics**

ISBN-10: 1-60690-583-X
ISBN-13: 978-1-60690-583-8
First Printing
10 9 8 7 6 5 4 3 2 1

Nick Barrucci, CEO / Publisher
Juan Collado, President / COO
Rich Young, Director Business Development
Keith Davidsen, Marketing Manager

Joe Rybandt, Senior Editor
Hannah Elder, Associate Editor
Molly Mahan, Associate Editor

Jason Ullmeyer, Design Director
Katie Hidalgo, Graphic Designer
Chris Caniano, Digital Associate
Rachel Kilbury, Digital Assistant

DOC SAVAGE® OMNIBUS, VOLUME 1. First printing. Contains materials originally published in Doc Savage #1-8 and the Doc Savage 2014 Annual. Published by Dynamite Entertainment. 113 Gaither Dr., STE 205, Mt. Laurel, NJ 08054. Doc Savage ® and © Condé Nast. Used under license. Dynamite, Dynamite Entertainment & its logo are ® 2014 Dynamite. All Rights Reserved. All names, characters, events, and locales in this publication are entirely fictional. Any resemblance to actual persons (living or dead), events or places, without satiric intent, is coincidental. No portion of this book may be reproduced by any means (digital or print) without the written permission of Dynamite Entertainment except for review purposes. The scanning, uploading and distribution of this book via the Internet or via any other means without the permission of the publisher is illegal and punishable by law. Please purchase only authorized electronic editions, and do not participate in or encourage electronic piracy of copyrighted materials. Printed in China.

For media rights, foreign rights, promotions, licensing, and advertising: marketing@dynamite.com

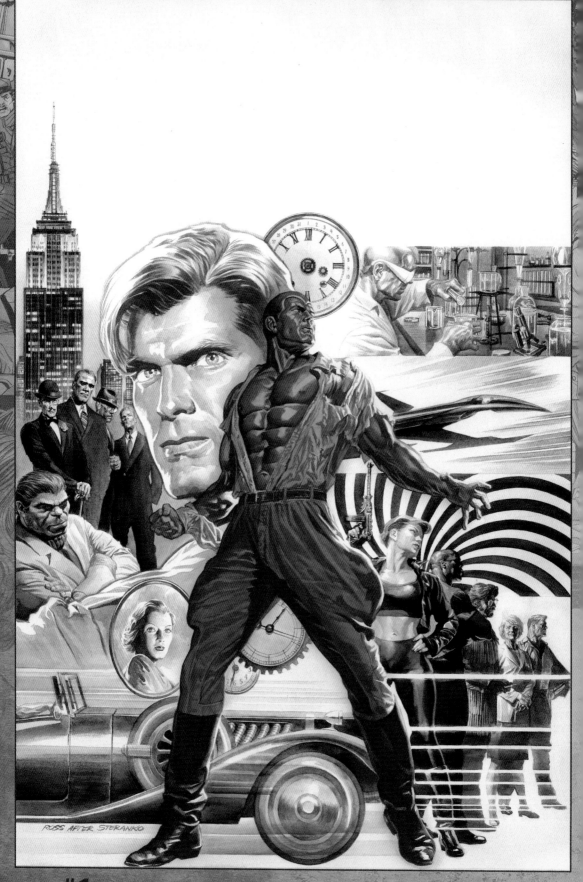

ISSUE **#1** COVER
art by **ALEX ROSS**

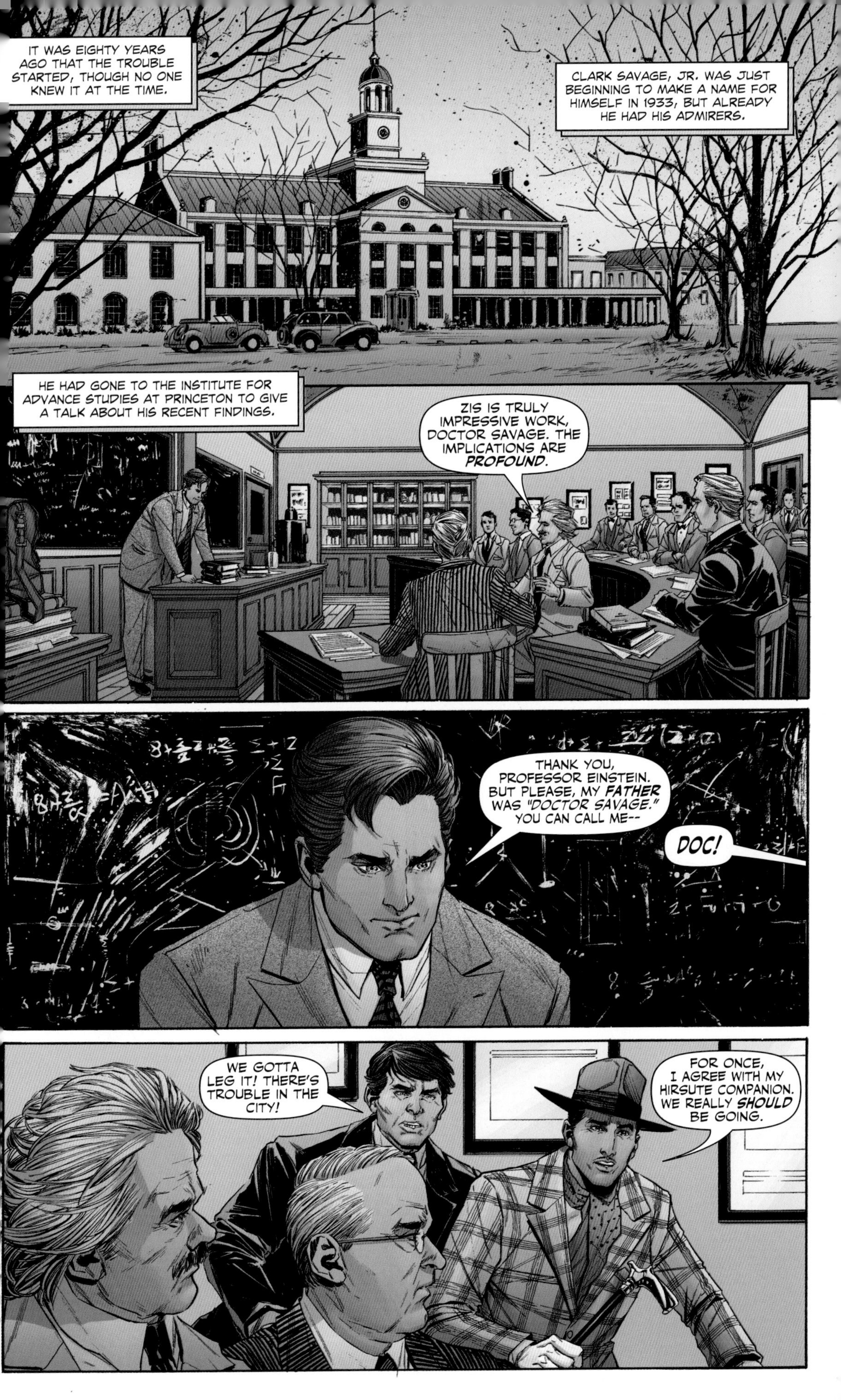
IT WAS EIGHTY YEARS AGO THAT THE TROUBLE STARTED, THOUGH NO ONE KNEW IT AT THE TIME.
CLARK SAVAGE, JR. WAS JUST BEGINNING TO MAKE A NAME FOR HIMSELF IN 1933, BUT ALREADY HE HAD HIS ADMIRERS.
HE HAD GONE TO THE INSTITUTE FOR ADVANCE STUDIES AT PRINCETON TO GIVE A TALK ABOUT HIS RECENT FINDINGS.
ZIS IS TRULY IMPRESSIVE WORK, DOCTOR SAVAGE. THE IMPLICATIONS ARE PROFOUND.
THANK YOU, PROFESSOR EINSTEIN. BUT PLEASE, MY FATHER WAS "DOCTOR SAVAGE." YOU CAN CALL ME--
DOC!
WE GOTTA LEG IT! THERE'S TROUBLE IN THE CITY!
FOR ONCE, I AGREE WITH MY HIRSUTE COMPANION. WE REALLY SHOULD BE GOING.

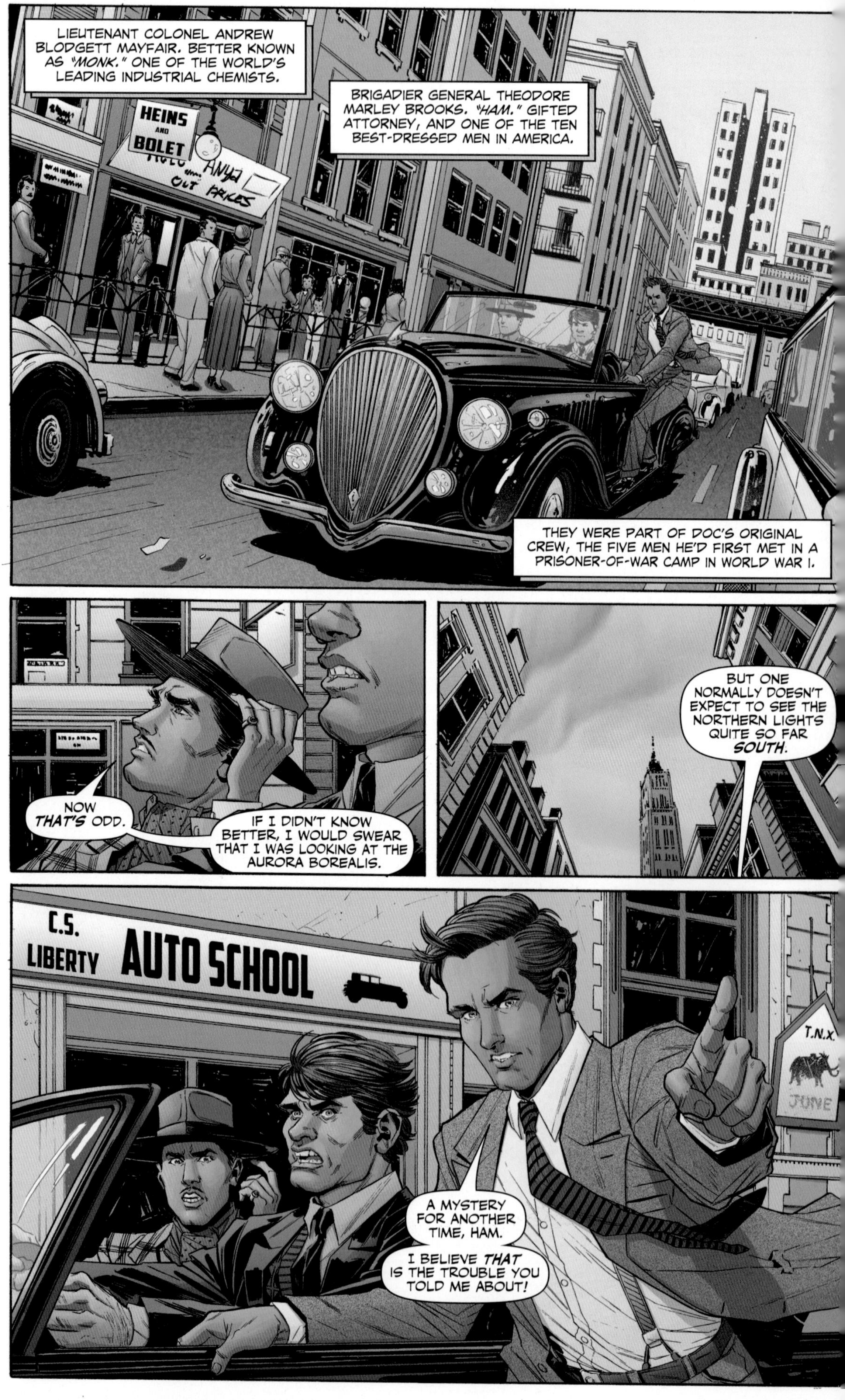
LIEUTENANT COLONEL ANDREW BLODGETT MAYFAIR. BETTER KNOWN AS "MONK." ONE OF THE WORLD'S LEADING INDUSTRIAL CHEMISTS.
HEINS AND BOLET
BRIGADIER GENERAL THEODORE MARLEY BROOKS. "HAM." GIFTED ATTORNEY, AND ONE OF THE TEN BEST-DRESSED MEN IN AMERICA.
THEY WERE PART OF DOC'S ORIGINAL CREW, THE FIVE MEN HE'D FIRST MET IN A PRISONER-OF-WAR CAMP IN WORLD WAR I.
NOW THAT'S ODD.
IF I DIDN'T KNOW BETTER, I WOULD SWEAR THAT I WAS LOOKING AT THE AURORA BOREALIS.
BUT ONE NORMALLY DOESN'T EXPECT TO SEE THE NORTHERN LIGHTS QUITE SO FAR SOUTH.
C.S. LIBERTY AUTO SCHOOL
T.N.X.
JUNE
A MYSTERY FOR ANOTHER TIME, HAM.
I BELIEVE THAT IS THE TROUBLE YOU TOLD ME ABOUT!

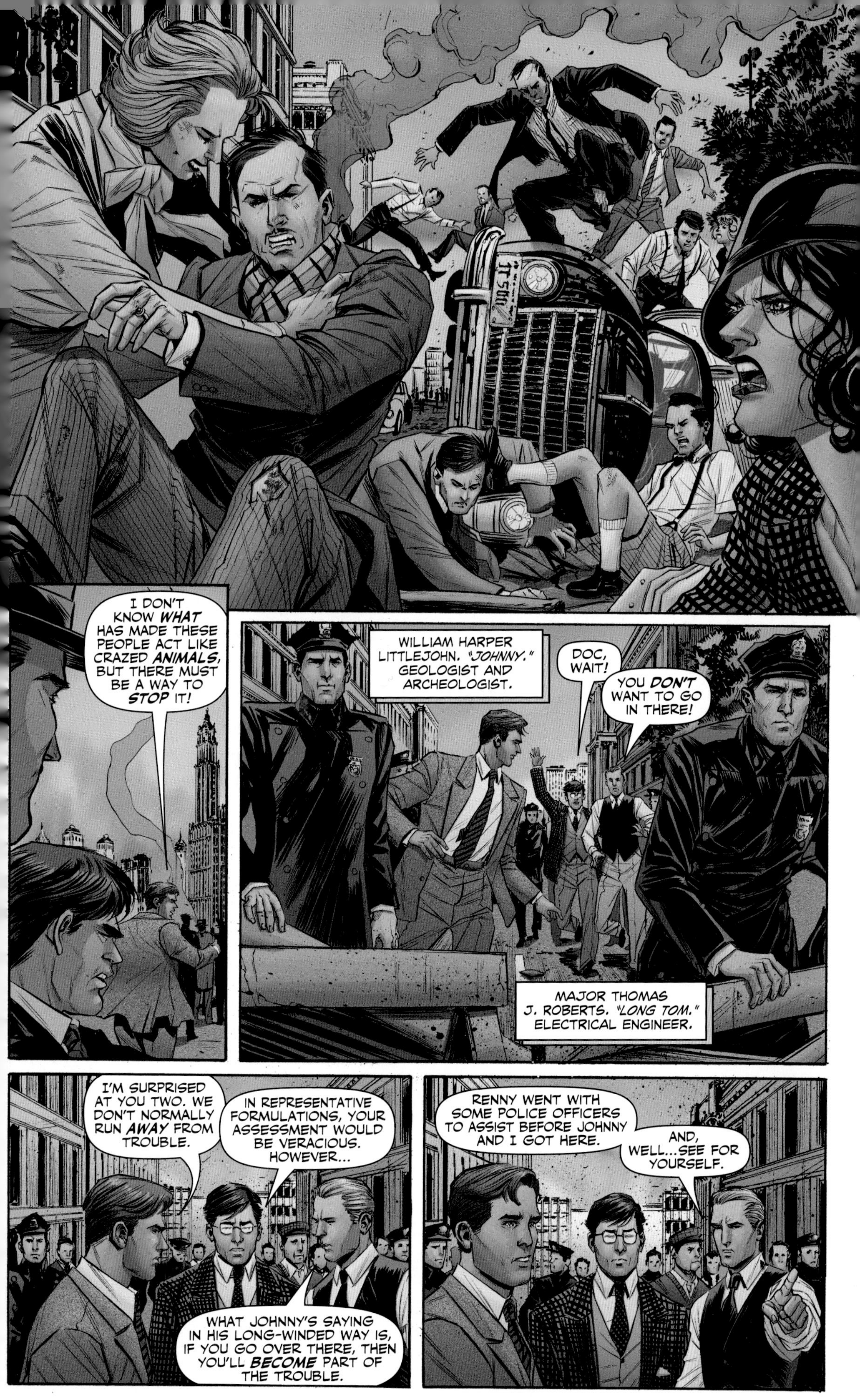
I DON'T KNOW *WHAT* HAS MADE THESE PEOPLE ACT LIKE CRAZED *ANIMALS*, BUT THERE MUST BE A WAY TO *STOP* IT!
WILLIAM HARPER LITTLEJOHN. *"JOHNNY."* GEOLOGIST AND ARCHEOLOGIST.
DOC, WAIT!
YOU *DON'T* WANT TO GO IN THERE!
MAJOR THOMAS J. ROBERTS. *"LONG TOM."* ELECTRICAL ENGINEER.
I'M SURPRISED AT YOU TWO. WE DON'T NORMALLY RUN *AWAY* FROM TROUBLE.
IN REPRESENTATIVE FORMULATIONS, YOUR ASSESSMENT WOULD BE VERACIOUS. HOWEVER...
WHAT JOHNNY'S SAYING IN HIS LONG-WINDED WAY IS, IF YOU GO OVER THERE, THEN YOU'LL *BECOME* PART OF THE TROUBLE.
RENNY WENT WITH SOME POLICE OFFICERS TO ASSIST BEFORE JOHNNY AND I GOT HERE.
AND, WELL...SEE FOR YOURSELF.

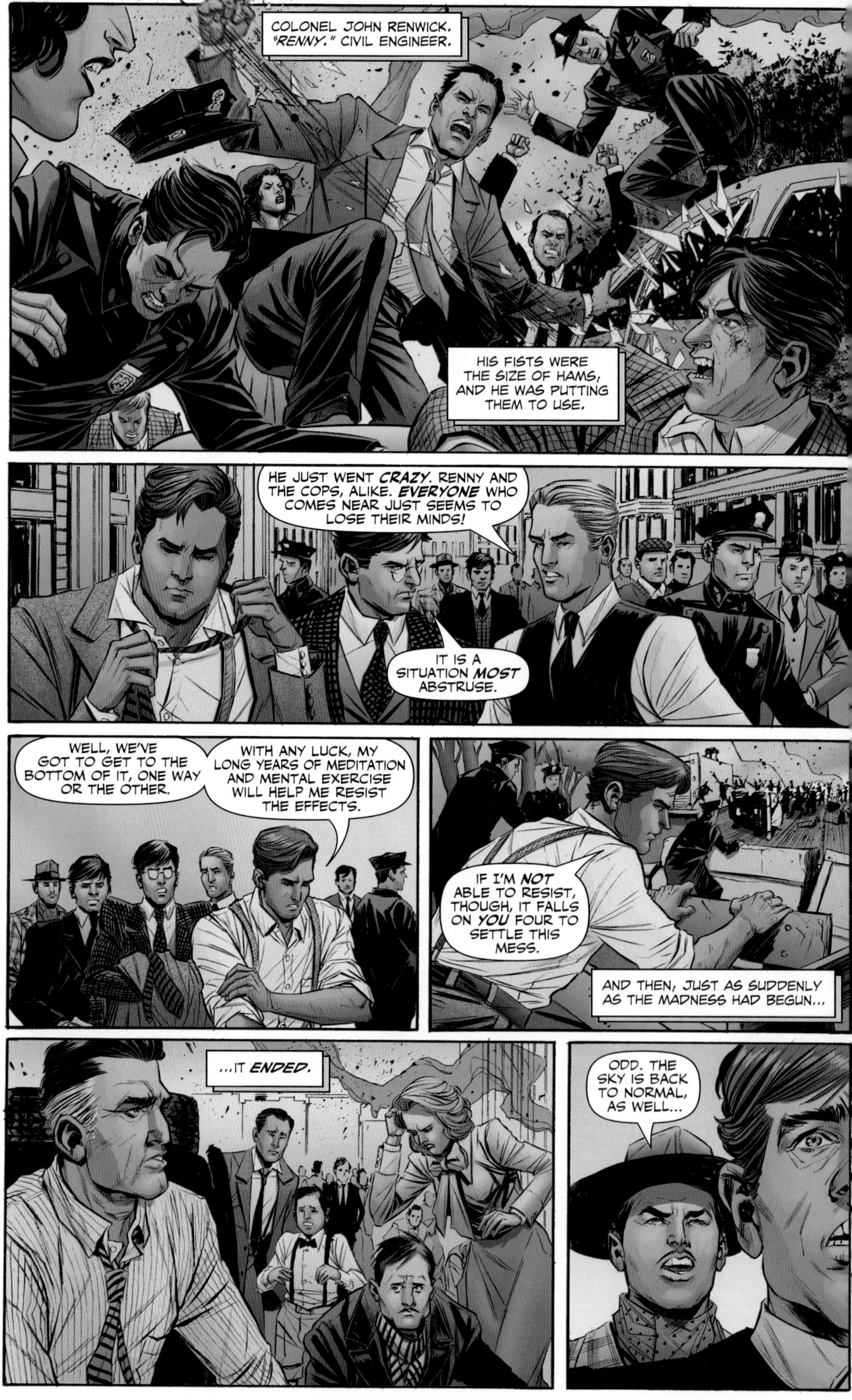
COLONEL JOHN RENWICK. "RENNY." CIVIL ENGINEER.
HIS FISTS WERE THE SIZE OF HAMS, AND HE WAS PUTTING THEM TO USE.
HE JUST WENT *CRAZY*. RENNY AND THE COPS, ALIKE. *EVERYONE* WHO COMES NEAR JUST SEEMS TO LOSE THEIR MINDS!
IT IS A SITUATION *MOST* ABSTRUSE.
WELL, WE'VE GOT TO GET TO THE BOTTOM OF IT, ONE WAY OR THE OTHER.
WITH ANY LUCK, MY LONG YEARS OF MEDITATION AND MENTAL EXERCISE WILL HELP ME RESIST THE EFFECTS.
IF I'M *NOT* ABLE TO RESIST, THOUGH, IT FALLS ON *YOU* FOUR TO SETTLE THIS MESS.
AND THEN, JUST AS SUDDENLY AS THE MADNESS HAD BEGUN...
...IT *ENDED*.
ODD. THE SKY IS BACK TO NORMAL, AS WELL...

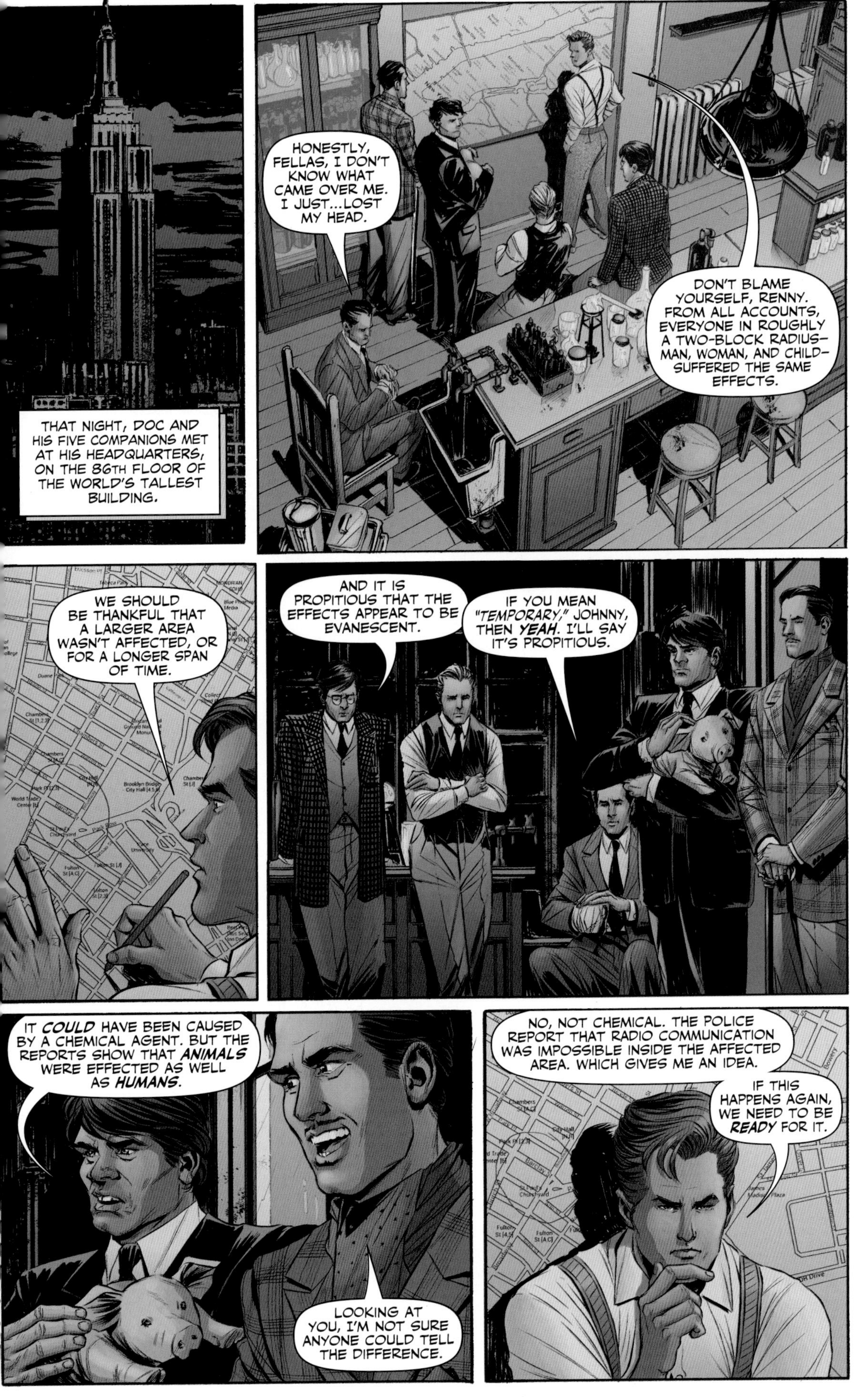

THAT NIGHT, DOC AND HIS FIVE COMPANIONS MET AT HIS HEADQUARTERS, ON THE 86TH FLOOR OF THE WORLD'S TALLEST BUILDING.
HONESTLY, FELLAS, I DON'T KNOW WHAT CAME OVER ME. I JUST...LOST MY HEAD.
DON'T BLAME YOURSELF, RENNY. FROM ALL ACCOUNTS, EVERYONE IN ROUGHLY A TWO-BLOCK RADIUS—MAN, WOMAN, AND CHILD—SUFFERED THE SAME EFFECTS.
WE SHOULD BE THANKFUL THAT A LARGER AREA WASN'T AFFECTED, OR FOR A LONGER SPAN OF TIME.
AND IT IS PROPITIOUS THAT THE EFFECTS APPEAR TO BE EVANESCENT.
IF YOU MEAN "*TEMPORARY*," JOHNNY, THEN *YEAH*. I'LL SAY IT'S PROPITIOUS.
IT ***COULD*** HAVE BEEN CAUSED BY A CHEMICAL AGENT. BUT THE REPORTS SHOW THAT ***ANIMALS*** WERE EFFECTED AS WELL AS ***HUMANS***.
LOOKING AT YOU, I'M NOT SURE ANYONE COULD TELL THE DIFFERENCE.
NO, NOT CHEMICAL. THE POLICE REPORT THAT RADIO COMMUNICATION WAS IMPOSSIBLE INSIDE THE AFFECTED AREA. WHICH GIVES ME AN IDEA.
IF THIS HAPPENS AGAIN, WE NEED TO BE *READY* FOR IT.

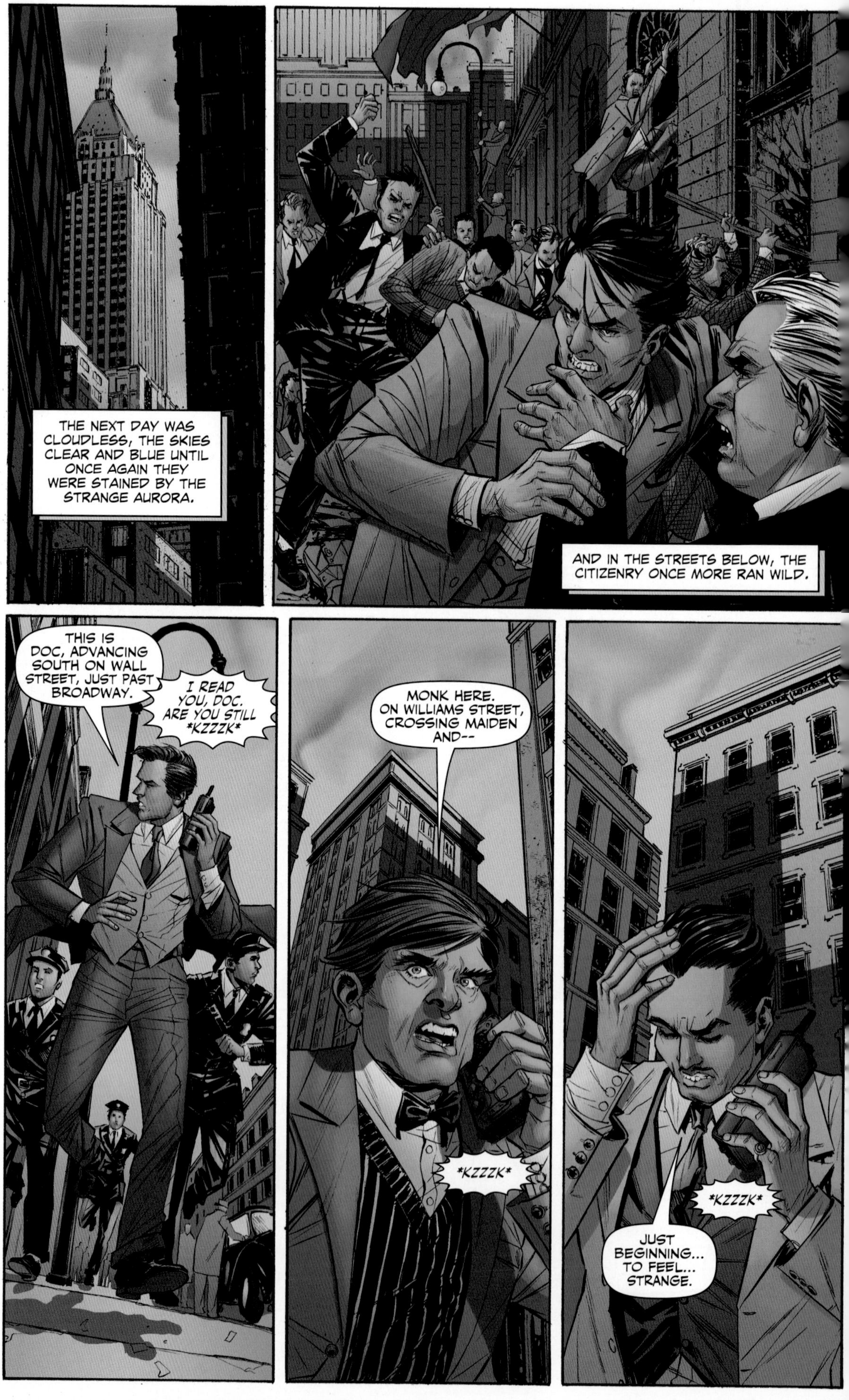
THE NEXT DAY WAS CLOUDLESS, THE SKIES CLEAR AND BLUE UNTIL ONCE AGAIN THEY WERE STAINED BY THE STRANGE AURORA.
AND IN THE STREETS BELOW, THE CITIZENRY ONCE MORE RAN WILD.
THIS IS DOC, ADVANCING SOUTH ON WALL STREET, JUST PAST BROADWAY.
I READ YOU, DOC. ARE YOU STILL *KZZZK*
MONK HERE. ON WILLIAMS STREET, CROSSING MAIDEN AND--
KZZZK
KZZZK
JUST BEGINNING... TO FEEL... STRANGE.

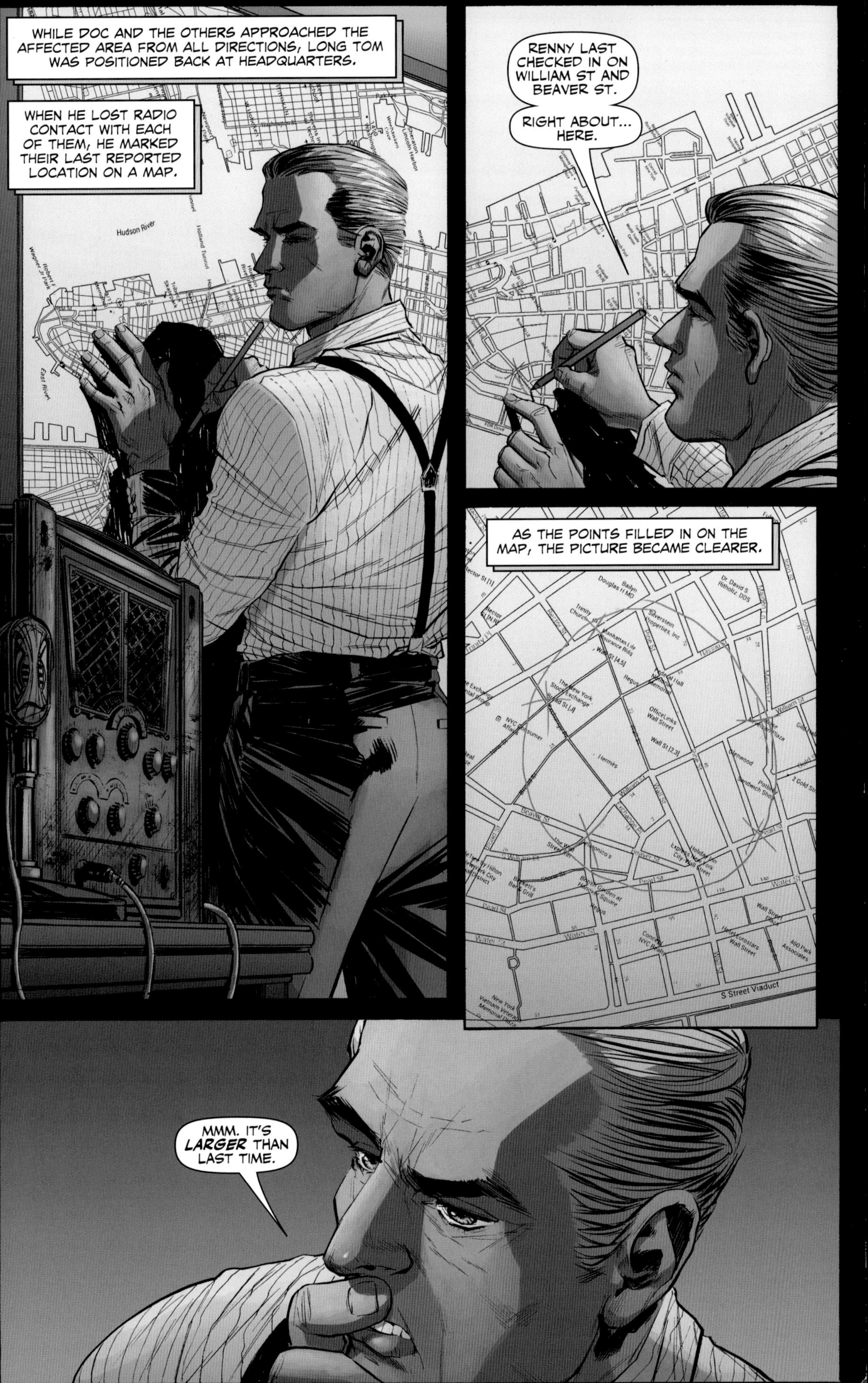
WHILE DOC AND THE OTHERS APPROACHED THE AFFECTED AREA FROM ALL DIRECTIONS, LONG TOM WAS POSITIONED BACK AT HEADQUARTERS.
WHEN HE LOST RADIO CONTACT WITH EACH OF THEM, HE MARKED THEIR LAST REPORTED LOCATION ON A MAP.
RENNY LAST CHECKED IN ON WILLIAM ST AND BEAVER ST.
RIGHT ABOUT... HERE.
AS THE POINTS FILLED IN ON THE MAP, THE PICTURE BECAME CLEARER.
MMM. IT'S *LARGER* THAN LAST TIME.

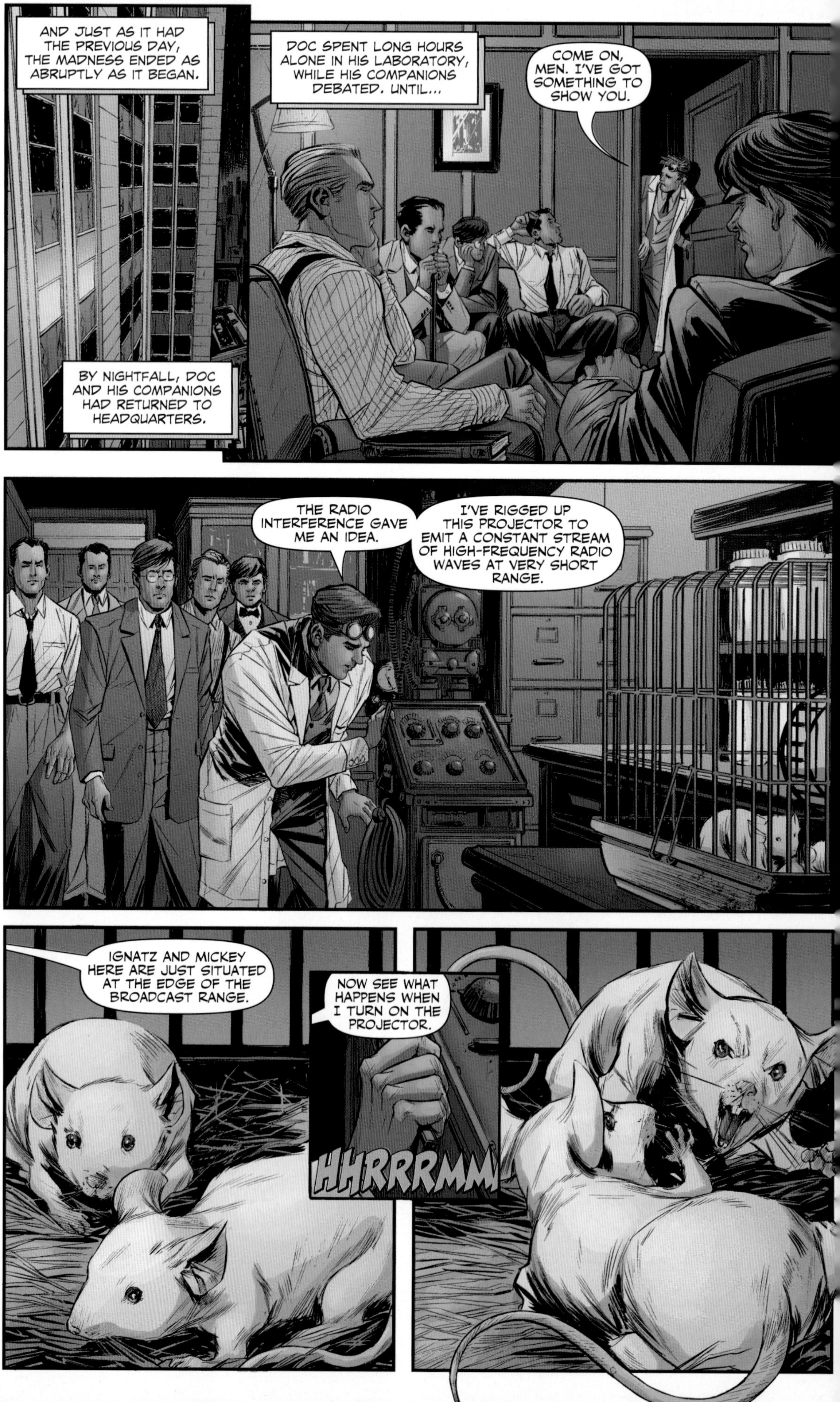

AND JUST AS IT HAD THE PREVIOUS DAY, THE MADNESS ENDED AS ABRUPTLY AS IT BEGAN.
BY NIGHTFALL, DOC AND HIS COMPANIONS HAD RETURNED TO HEADQUARTERS.
DOC SPENT LONG HOURS ALONE IN HIS LABORATORY, WHILE HIS COMPANIONS DEBATED. UNTIL...
COME ON, MEN. I'VE GOT SOMETHING TO SHOW YOU.
THE RADIO INTERFERENCE GAVE ME AN IDEA.
I'VE RIGGED UP THIS PROJECTOR TO EMIT A CONSTANT STREAM OF HIGH-FREQUENCY RADIO WAVES AT VERY SHORT RANGE.
IGNATZ AND MICKEY HERE ARE JUST SITUATED AT THE EDGE OF THE BROADCAST RANGE.
NOW SEE WHAT HAPPENS WHEN I TURN ON THE PROJECTOR.
HHRRRMM

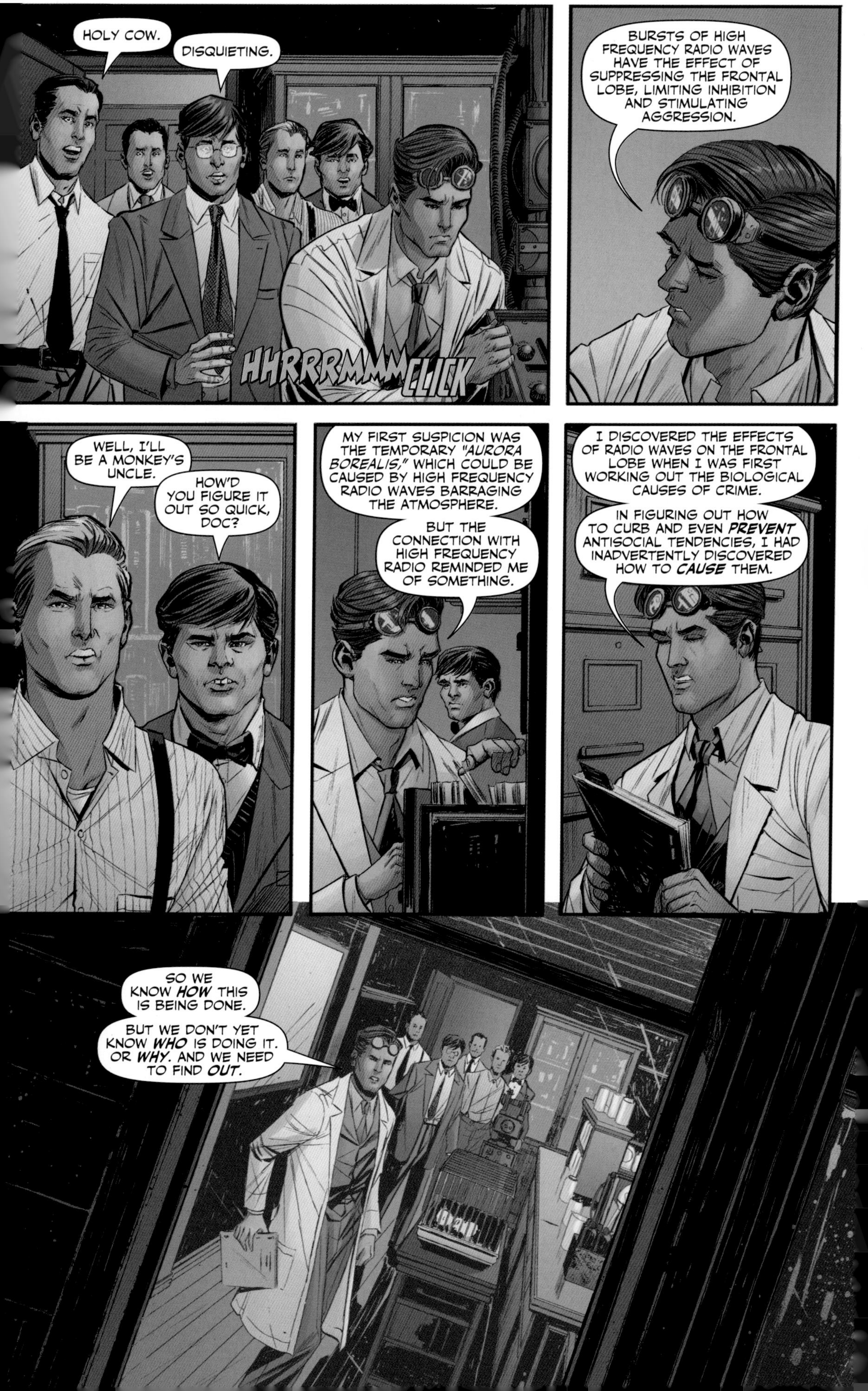
HOLY COW.
DISQUIETING.
HHRRRMMMCLICK
BURSTS OF HIGH FREQUENCY RADIO WAVES HAVE THE EFFECT OF SUPPRESSING THE FRONTAL LOBE, LIMITING INHIBITION AND STIMULATING AGGRESSION.
WELL, I'LL BE A MONKEY'S UNCLE.
HOW'D YOU FIGURE IT OUT SO QUICK, DOC?
MY FIRST SUSPICION WAS THE TEMPORARY "AURORA BOREALIS," WHICH COULD BE CAUSED BY HIGH FREQUENCY RADIO WAVES BARRAGING THE ATMOSPHERE.
BUT THE CONNECTION WITH HIGH FREQUENCY RADIO REMINDED ME OF SOMETHING.
I DISCOVERED THE EFFECTS OF RADIO WAVES ON THE FRONTAL LOBE WHEN I WAS FIRST WORKING OUT THE BIOLOGICAL CAUSES OF CRIME.
IN FIGURING OUT HOW TO CURB AND EVEN PREVENT ANTISOCIAL TENDENCIES, I HAD INADVERTENTLY DISCOVERED HOW TO CAUSE THEM.
SO WE KNOW HOW THIS IS BEING DONE.
BUT WE DON'T YET KNOW WHO IS DOING IT. OR WHY. AND WE NEED TO FIND OUT.

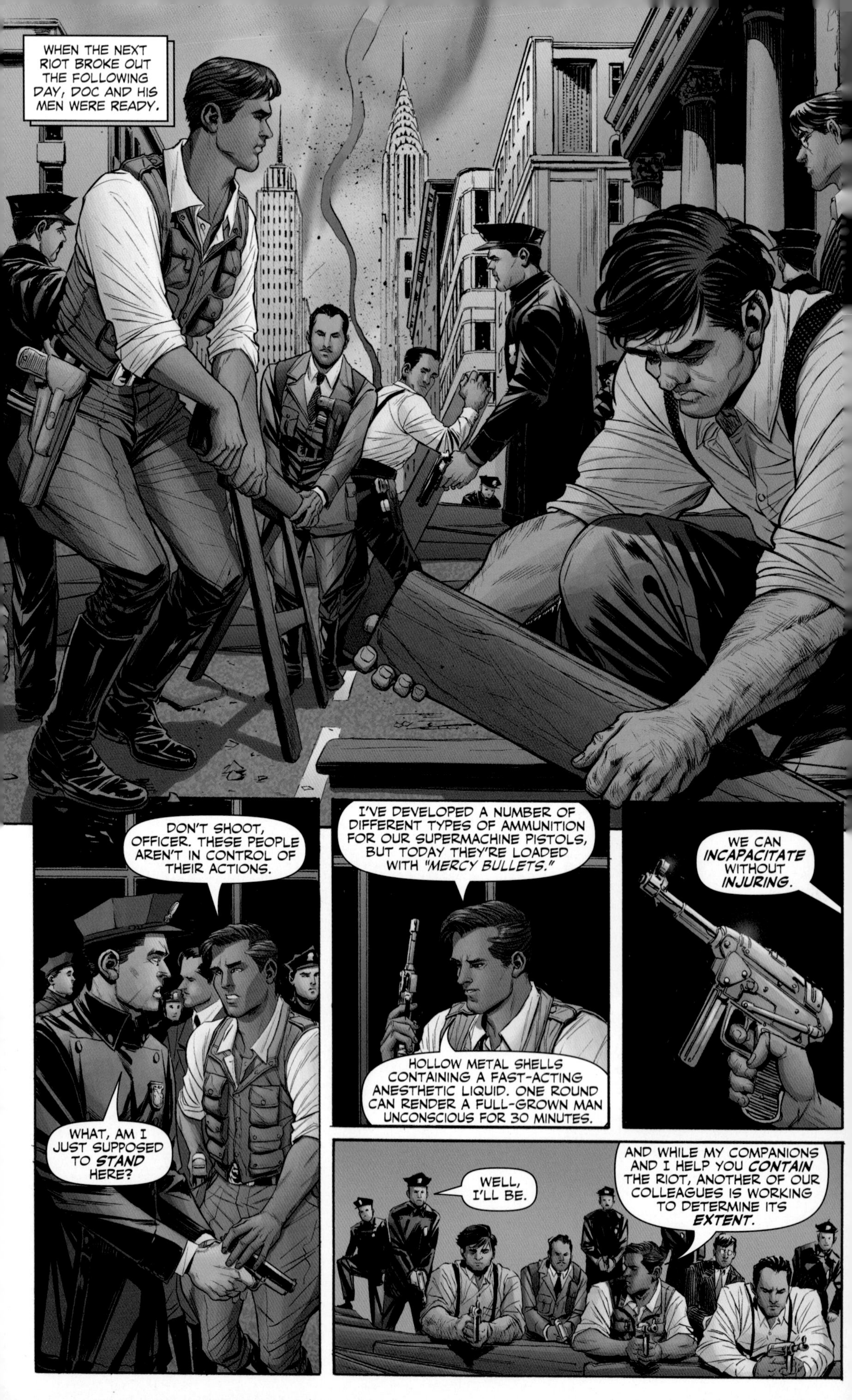
WHEN THE NEXT RIOT BROKE OUT THE FOLLOWING DAY, DOC AND HIS MEN WERE READY.
DON'T SHOOT, OFFICER. THESE PEOPLE AREN'T IN CONTROL OF THEIR ACTIONS.
WHAT, AM I JUST SUPPOSED TO STAND HERE?
I'VE DEVELOPED A NUMBER OF DIFFERENT TYPES OF AMMUNITION FOR OUR SUPERMACHINE PISTOLS, BUT TODAY THEY'RE LOADED WITH "MERCY BULLETS."
HOLLOW METAL SHELLS CONTAINING A FAST-ACTING ANESTHETIC LIQUID. ONE ROUND CAN RENDER A FULL-GROWN MAN UNCONSCIOUS FOR 30 MINUTES.
WE CAN INCAPACITATE WITHOUT INJURING.
WELL, I'LL BE.
AND WHILE MY COMPANIONS AND I HELP YOU CONTAIN THE RIOT, ANOTHER OF OUR COLLEAGUES IS WORKING TO DETERMINE ITS EXTENT.

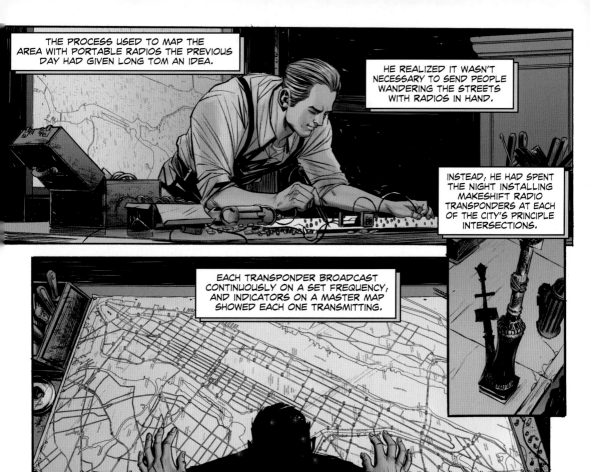

THE PROCESS USED TO MAP THE AREA WITH PORTABLE RADIOS THE PREVIOUS DAY HAD GIVEN LONG TOM AN IDEA.

HE REALIZED IT WASN'T NECESSARY TO SEND PEOPLE WANDERING THE STREETS WITH RADIOS IN HAND.

INSTEAD, HE HAD SPENT THE NIGHT INSTALLING MAKESHIFT RADIO TRANSPONDERS AT EACH OF THE CITY'S PRINCIPLE INTERSECTIONS.

EACH TRANSPONDER BROADCAST CONTINUOUSLY ON A SET FREQUENCY, AND INDICATORS ON A MASTER MAP SHOWED EACH ONE TRANSMITTING.

IF CONTACT WITH ANY OF THE TRANSPONDERS WAS LOST, THE INDICATOR WENT DARK. AND THE DARKENED LIGHTS SHOWED THE EXTENT OF THE EFFECT.

LARGER STILL, TODAY.

COVERING MOST OF TURTLE BAY.

BUT WHERE IS IT *COMING* FROM...?

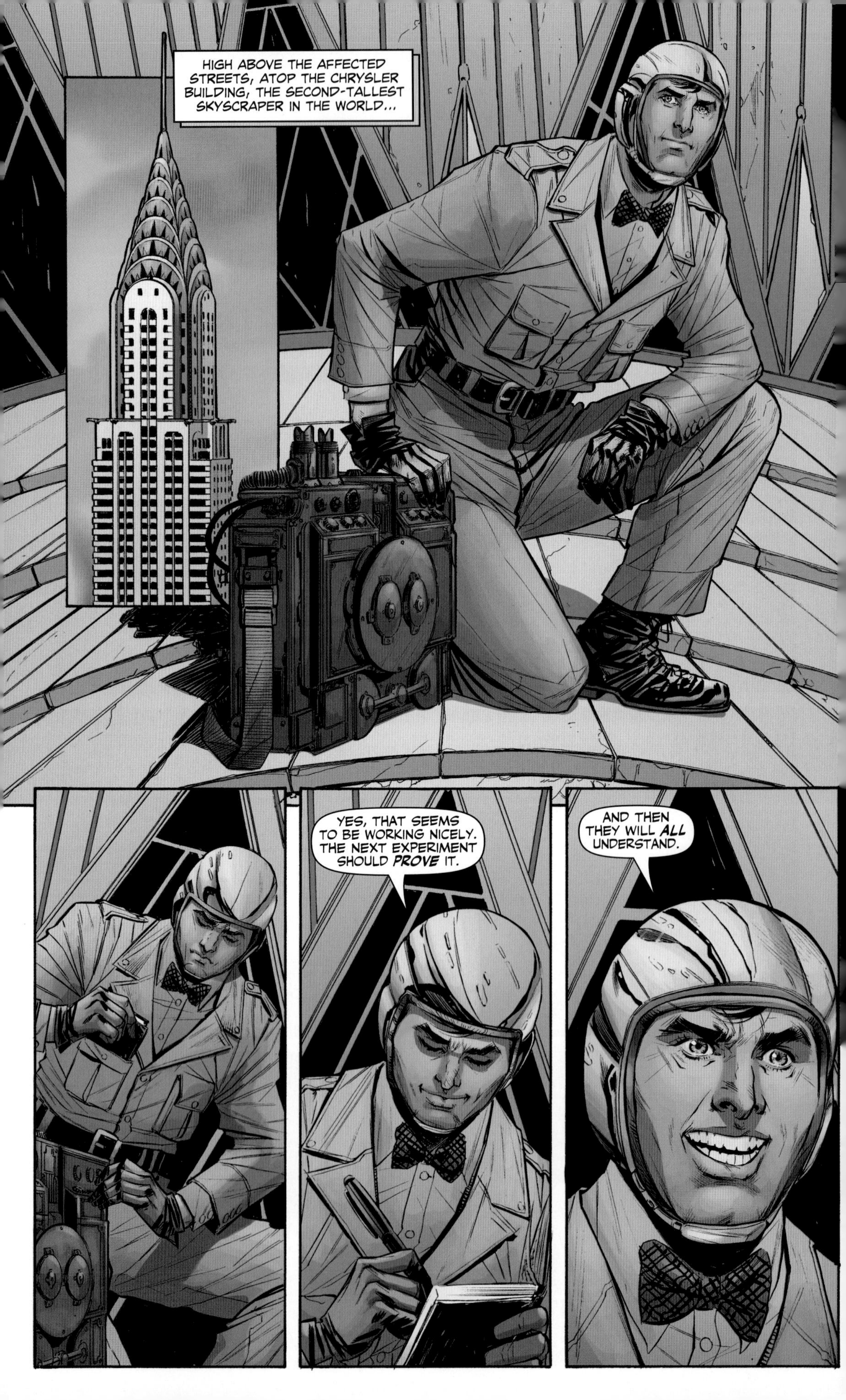
HIGH ABOVE THE AFFECTED STREETS, ATOP THE CHRYSLER BUILDING, THE SECOND-TALLEST SKYSCRAPER IN THE WORLD...
YES, THAT SEEMS TO BE WORKING NICELY. THE NEXT EXPERIMENT SHOULD *PROVE* IT.
AND THEN THEY WILL *ALL* UNDERSTAND.

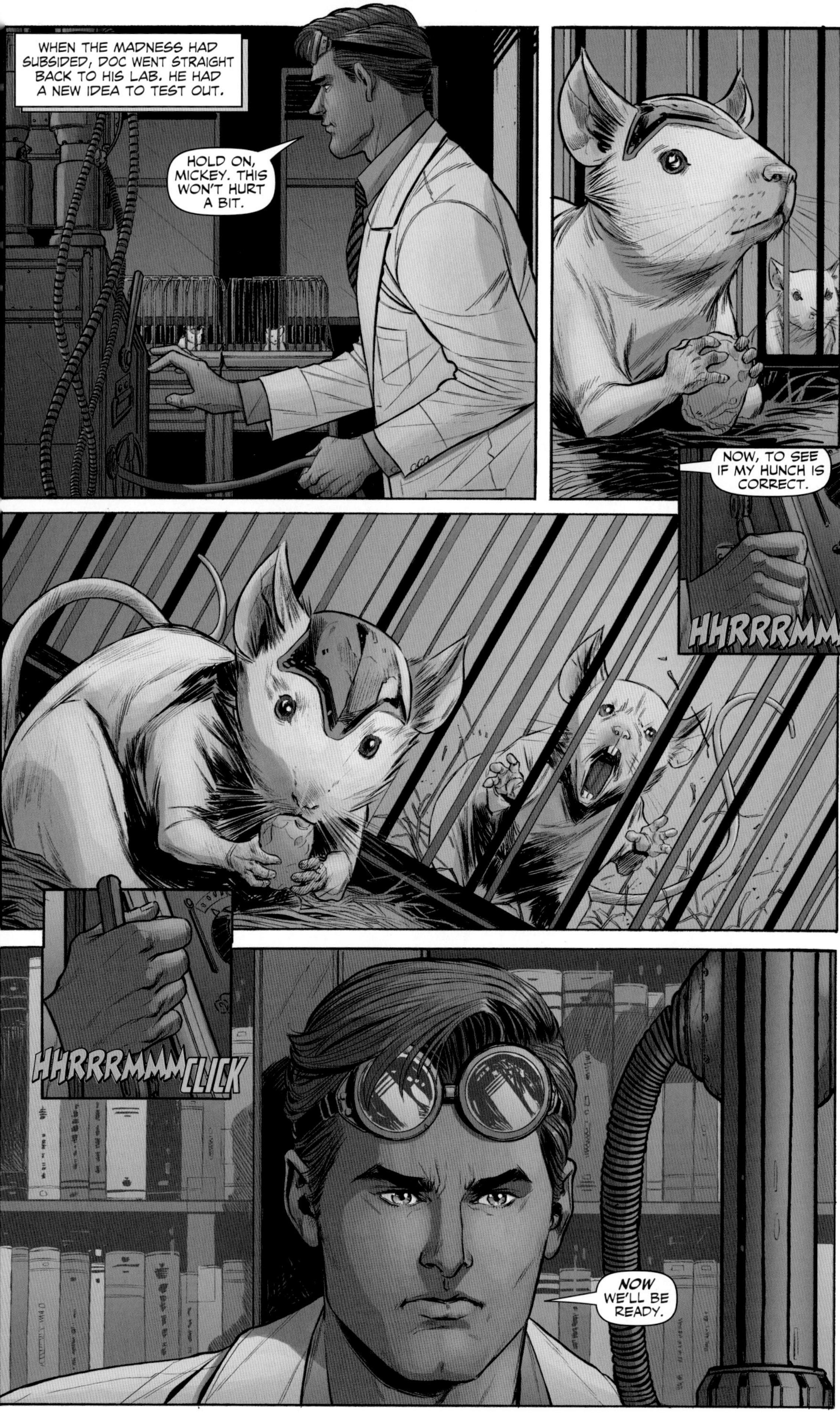
WHEN THE MADNESS HAD SUBSIDED, DOC WENT STRAIGHT BACK TO HIS LAB. HE HAD A NEW IDEA TO TEST OUT.
HOLD ON, MICKEY. THIS WON'T HURT A BIT.
NOW, TO SEE IF MY HUNCH IS CORRECT.
HHRRRMMM
HHRRRMMM CLICK
NOW WE'LL BE READY.

THE NEXT DAY, THE SKIES WERE ONCE MORE CLOUDLESS AND BLUE.

UNTIL...

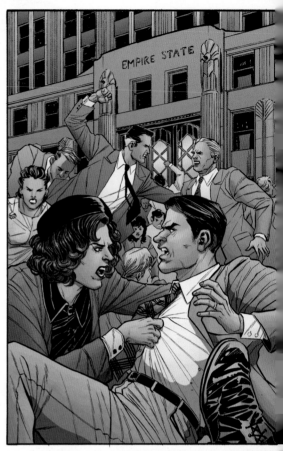

EMPIRE STATE

INTERESTING. I CAN ALMOST *FEEL* THE VIBRATIONS IN MY TEETH.

BUT THE METAL CAP SEEMS TO BE PROOF AGAINST THE MADDENING EFFECTS OF THE RADIO WAVES.

NOW COME ON, MEN. WE HAVE *WORK* TO DO.

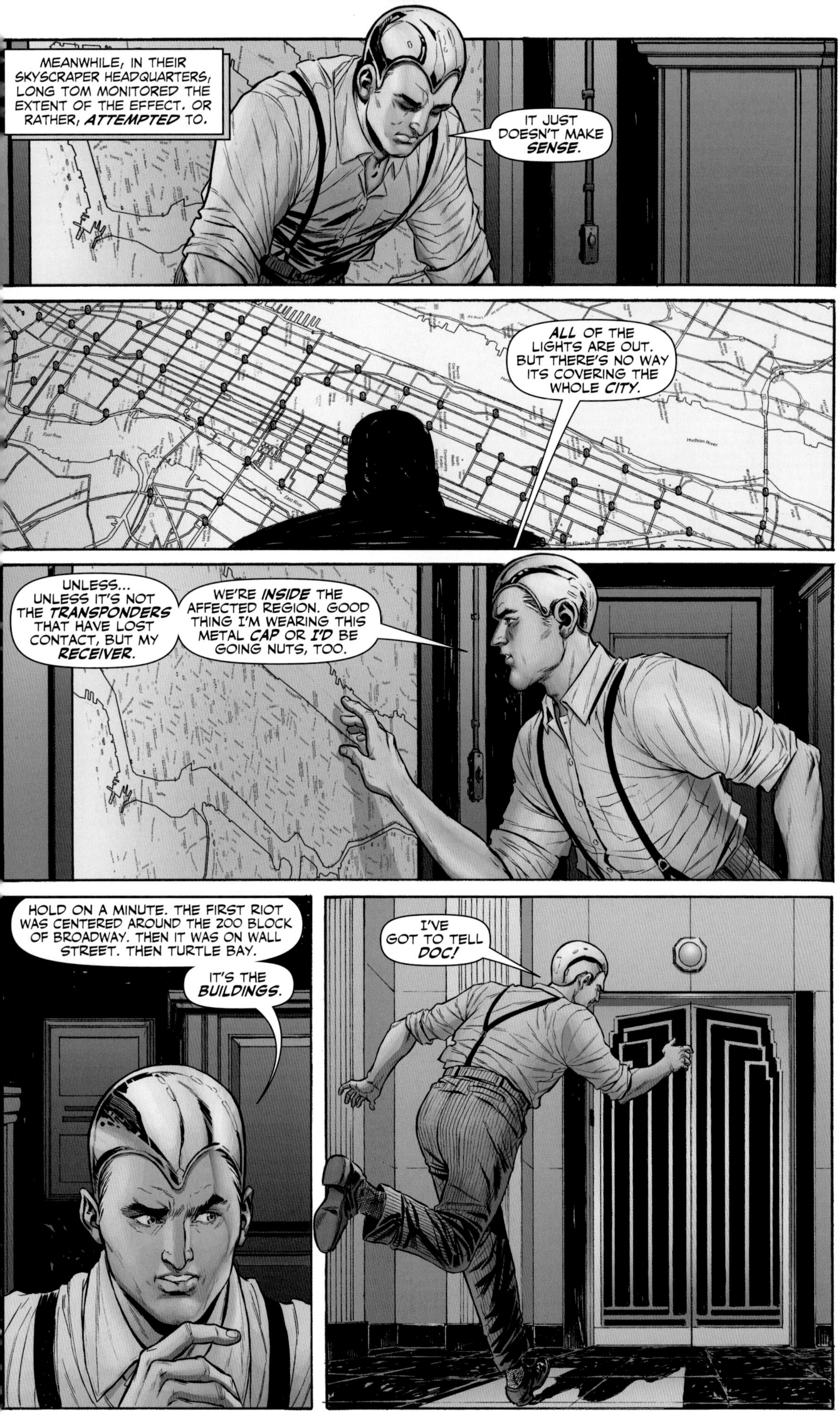

MEANWHILE, IN THEIR SKYSCRAPER HEADQUARTERS, LONG TOM MONITORED THE EXTENT OF THE EFFECT. OR RATHER, ATTEMPTED TO.
IT JUST DOESN'T MAKE SENSE.
ALL OF THE LIGHTS ARE OUT. BUT THERE'S NO WAY ITS COVERING THE WHOLE CITY.
Hudson River
East River
UNLESS... UNLESS IT'S NOT THE TRANSPONDERS THAT HAVE LOST CONTACT, BUT MY RECEIVER.
WE'RE INSIDE THE AFFECTED REGION. GOOD THING I'M WEARING THIS METAL CAP OR I'D BE GOING NUTS, TOO.
HOLD ON A MINUTE. THE FIRST RIOT WAS CENTERED AROUND THE 200 BLOCK OF BROADWAY. THEN IT WAS ON WALL STREET. THEN TURTLE BAY.
IT'S THE BUILDINGS.
I'VE GOT TO TELL DOC!

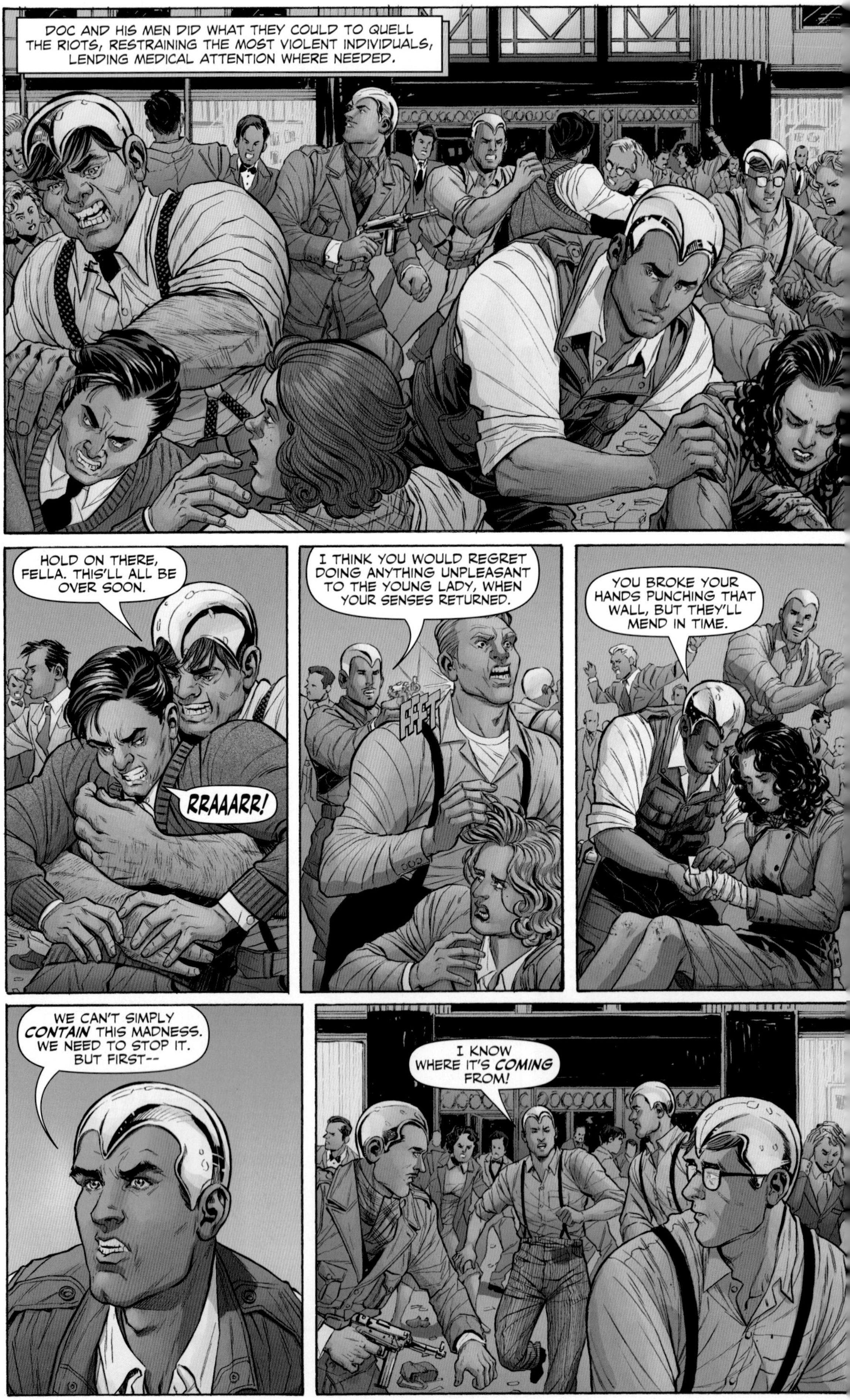

DOC AND HIS MEN DID WHAT THEY COULD TO QUELL THE RIOTS, RESTRAINING THE MOST VIOLENT INDIVIDUALS, LENDING MEDICAL ATTENTION WHERE NEEDED.
HOLD ON THERE, FELLA. THIS'LL ALL BE OVER SOON.
RRAAARR!
I THINK YOU WOULD REGRET DOING ANYTHING UNPLEASANT TO THE YOUNG LADY, WHEN YOUR SENSES RETURNED.
YOU BROKE YOUR HANDS PUNCHING THAT WALL, BUT THEY'LL MEND IN TIME.
WE CAN'T SIMPLY *CONTAIN* THIS MADNESS. WE NEED TO STOP IT. BUT FIRST--
I KNOW WHERE IT'S *COMING* FROM!

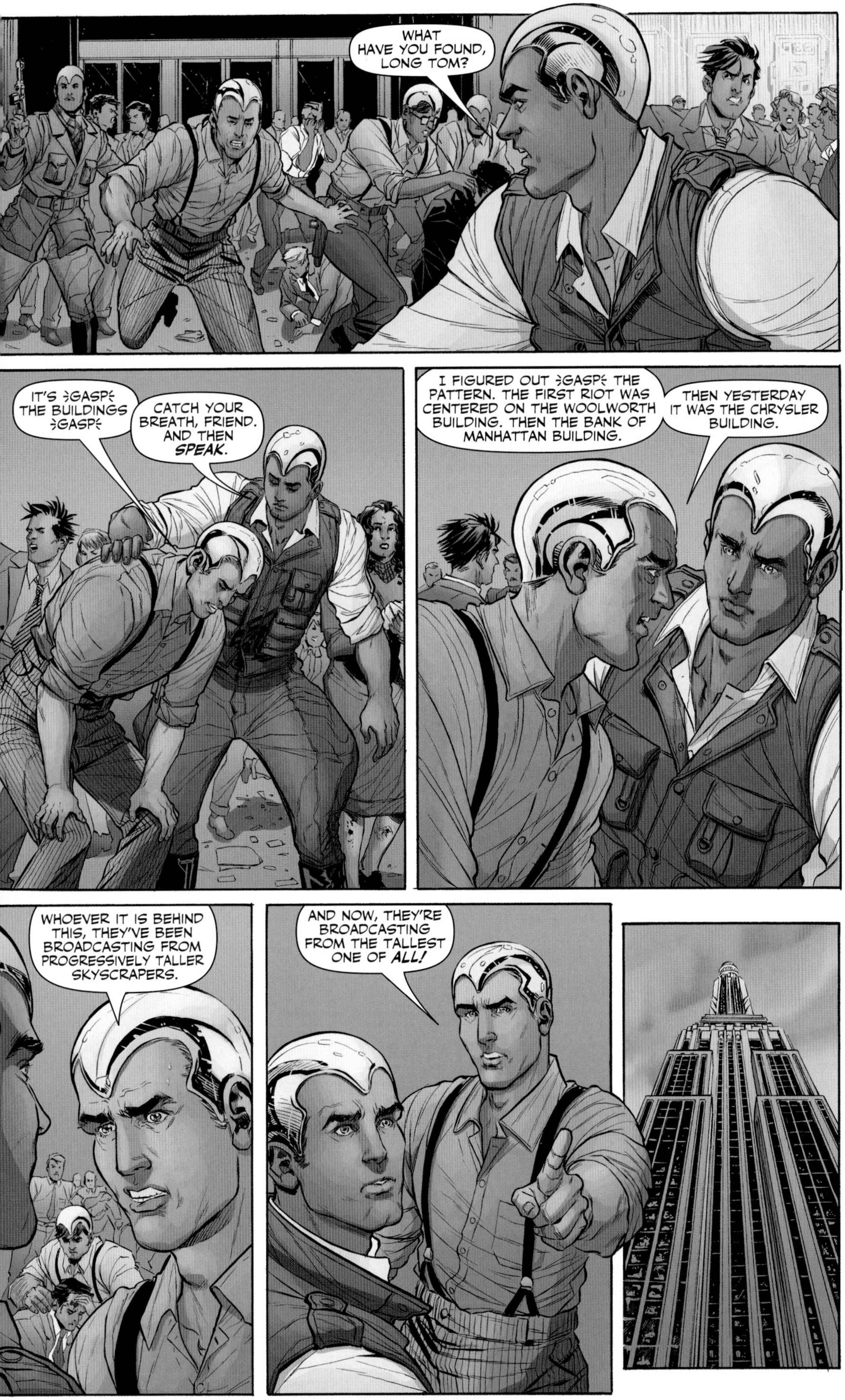
WHAT HAVE YOU FOUND, LONG TOM?
IT'S ⋛GASP⋚ THE BUILDINGS ⋛GASP⋚
CATCH YOUR BREATH, FRIEND. AND THEN *SPEAK*.
I FIGURED OUT ⋛GASP⋚ THE PATTERN. THE FIRST RIOT WAS CENTERED ON THE WOOLWORTH BUILDING. THEN THE BANK OF MANHATTAN BUILDING.
THEN YESTERDAY IT WAS THE CHRYSLER BUILDING.
WHOEVER IT IS BEHIND THIS, THEY'VE BEEN BROADCASTING FROM PROGRESSIVELY TALLER SKYSCRAPERS.
AND NOW, THEY'RE BROADCASTING FROM THE TALLEST ONE OF *ALL!*

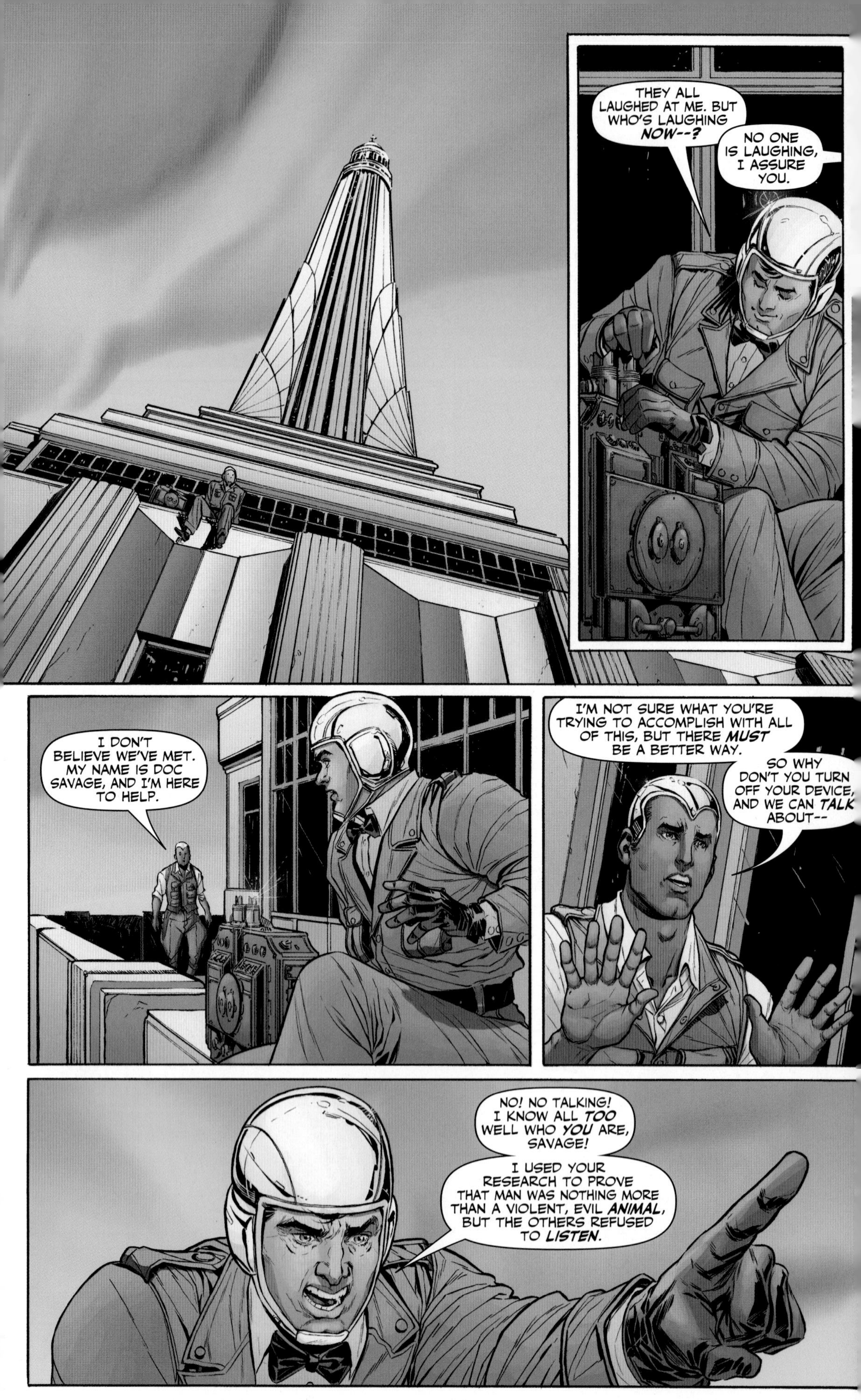

THEY ALL LAUGHED AT ME. BUT WHO'S LAUGHING *NOW--?*
NO ONE IS LAUGHING, I ASSURE YOU.
I DON'T BELIEVE WE'VE MET. MY NAME IS DOC SAVAGE, AND I'M HERE TO HELP.
I'M NOT SURE WHAT YOU'RE TRYING TO ACCOMPLISH WITH ALL OF THIS, BUT THERE *MUST* BE A BETTER WAY.
SO WHY DON'T YOU TURN OFF YOUR DEVICE, AND WE CAN *TALK* ABOUT--
NO! NO TALKING! I KNOW ALL *TOO* WELL WHO *YOU* ARE, SAVAGE!
I USED YOUR RESEARCH TO PROVE THAT MAN WAS NOTHING MORE THAN A VIOLENT, EVIL *ANIMAL*, BUT THE OTHERS REFUSED TO *LISTEN*.

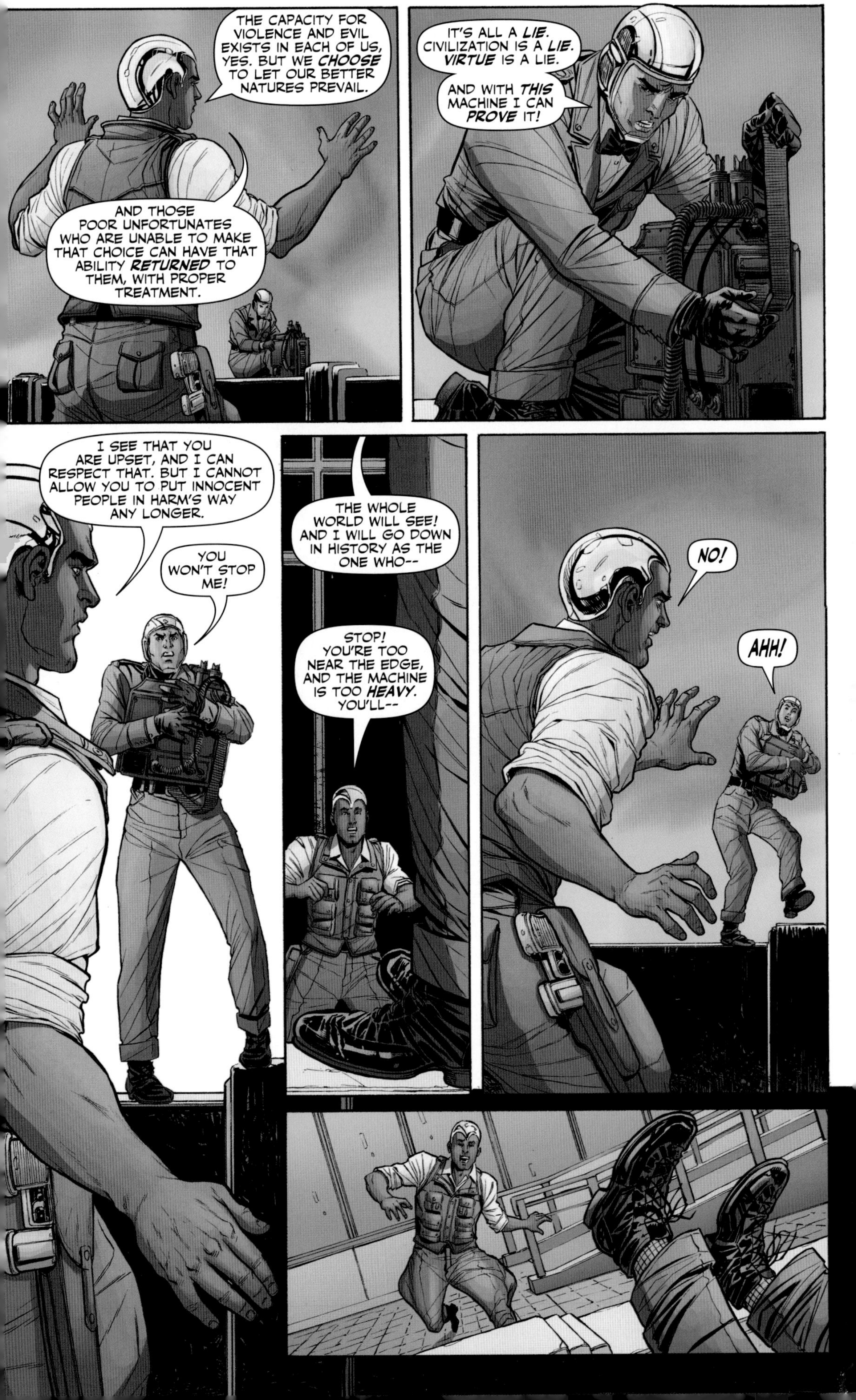
THE CAPACITY FOR VIOLENCE AND EVIL EXISTS IN EACH OF US, YES. BUT WE *CHOOSE* TO LET OUR BETTER NATURES PREVAIL.
AND THOSE POOR UNFORTUNATES WHO ARE UNABLE TO MAKE THAT CHOICE CAN HAVE THAT ABILITY *RETURNED* TO THEM, WITH PROPER TREATMENT.
IT'S ALL A *LIE*. CIVILIZATION IS A *LIE*. *VIRTUE* IS A LIE.
AND WITH *THIS* MACHINE I CAN *PROVE* IT!
I SEE THAT YOU ARE UPSET, AND I CAN RESPECT THAT. BUT I CANNOT ALLOW YOU TO PUT INNOCENT PEOPLE IN HARM'S WAY ANY LONGER.
YOU WON'T STOP ME!
THE WHOLE WORLD WILL SEE! AND I WILL GO DOWN IN HISTORY AS THE ONE WHO--
STOP! YOU'RE TOO NEAR THE EDGE, AND THE MACHINE IS TOO *HEAVY*. YOU'LL--
NO!
AHH!

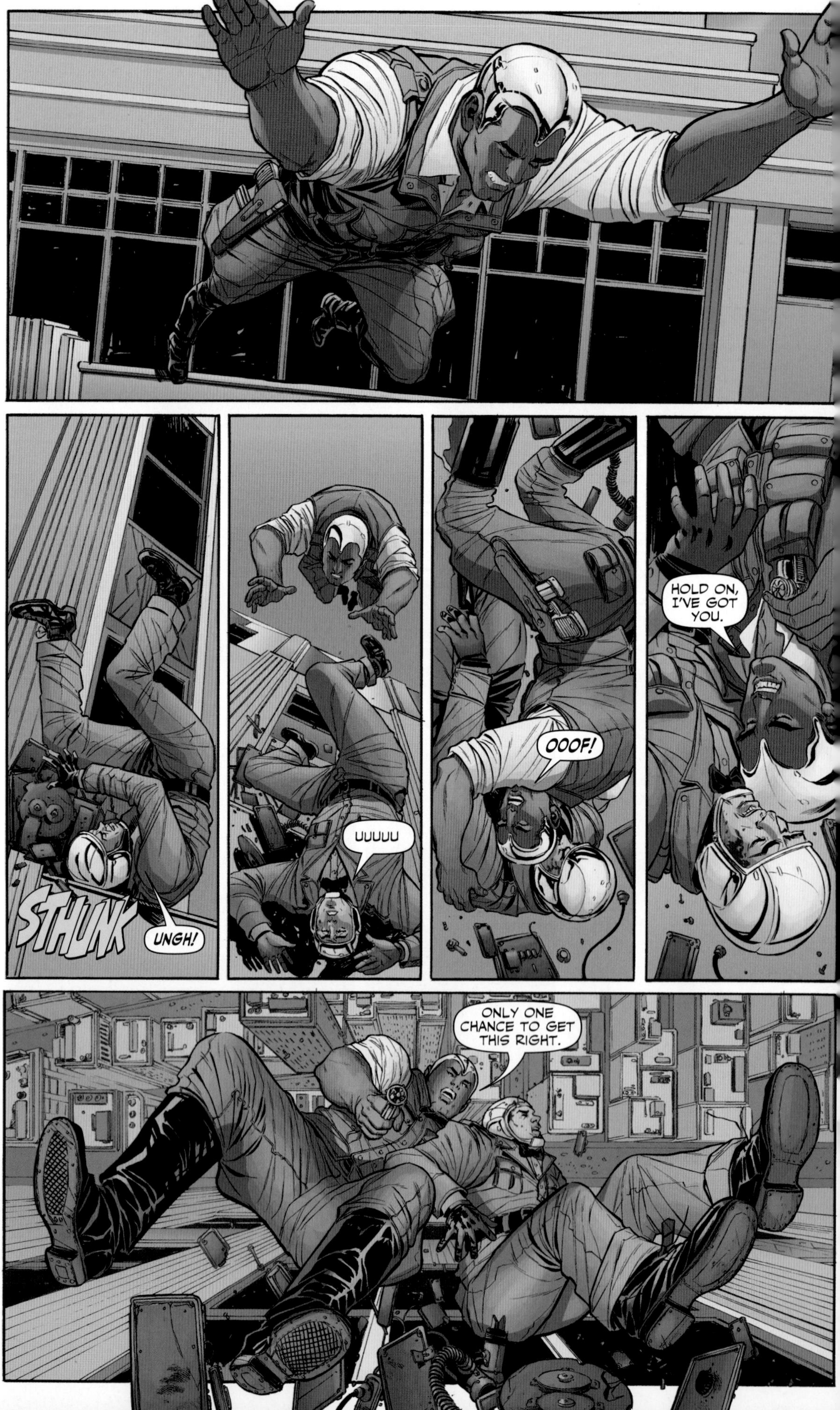
STHUNK
UNGH!
UUUUU
OOOF!
HOLD ON, I'VE GOT YOU.
ONLY ONE CHANCE TO GET THIS RIGHT.

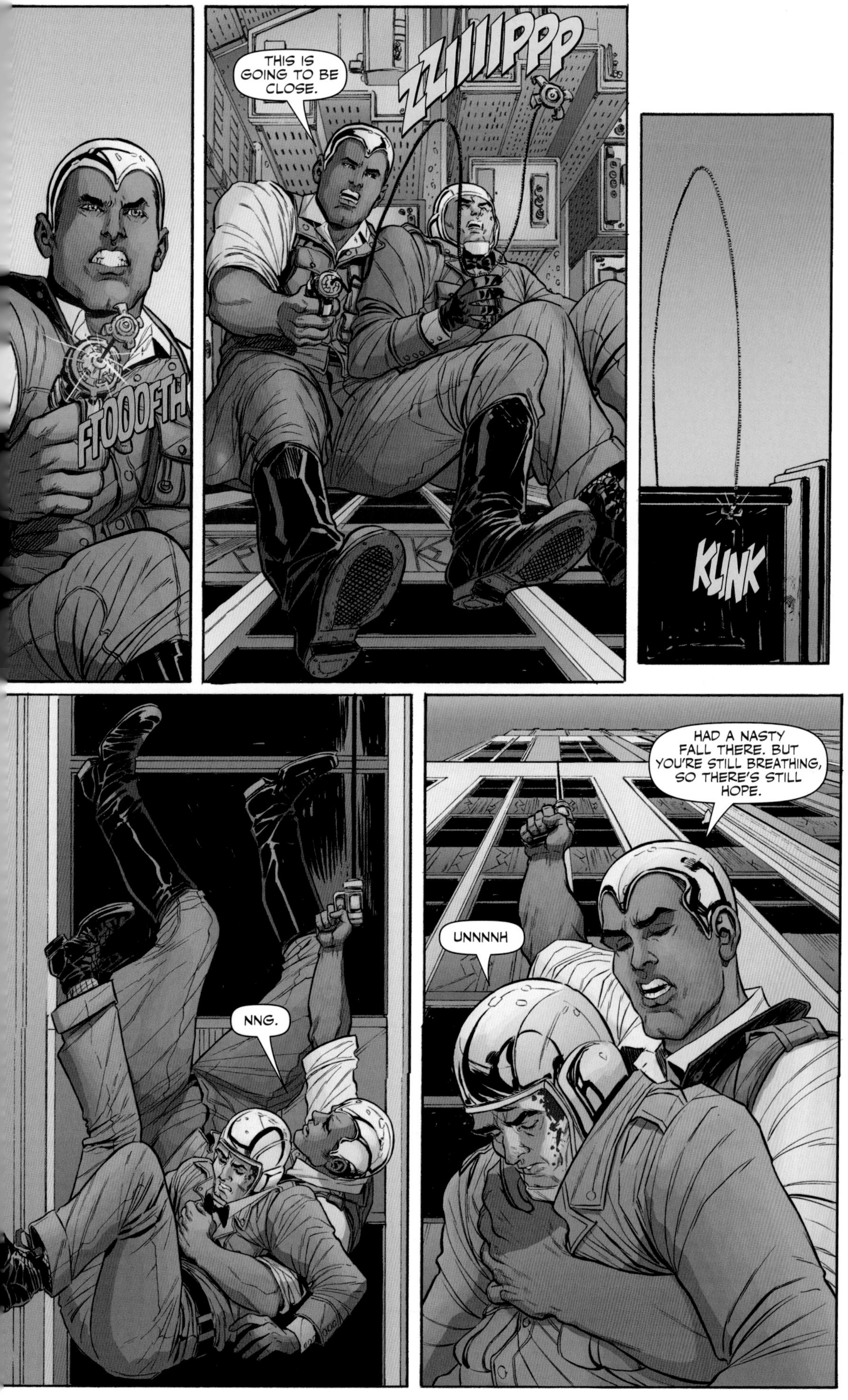
FTOOOFTH
THIS IS GOING TO BE CLOSE.
ZZIIIIPPP
KLINK
NNG.
HAD A NASTY FALL THERE. BUT YOU'RE STILL BREATHING, SO THERE'S STILL HOPE.
UNNNNH

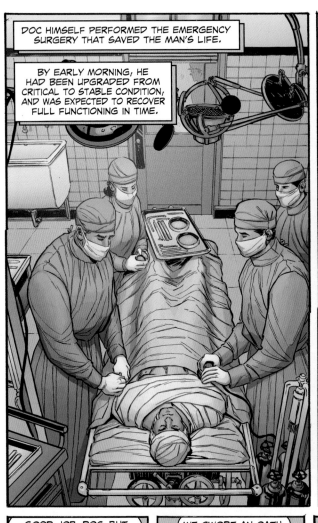

DOC HIMSELF PERFORMED THE EMERGENCY SURGERY THAT SAVED THE MAN'S LIFE.

BY EARLY MORNING, HE HAD BEEN UPGRADED FROM CRITICAL TO STABLE CONDITION, AND WAS EXPECTED TO RECOVER FULL FUNCTIONING IN TIME.

HAD THE MAN BEEN APPREHENDED IN LESS PUBLIC CIRCUMSTANCES, HE WOULD HAVE BEEN TRANSFERRED TO DOC'S UPSTATE FACILITY FOR *"TREATMENT."*

BUT AS IT WAS, HE WOULD BE HANDED OVER TO THE AUTHORITIES TO STAND TRIAL. DOC PREFERRED TO AVOID THE LEGAL SYSTEM, IF AT ALL POSSIBLE.

GOOD JOB, DOC. BUT SERIOUSLY, WHY'D YOU RISK YOUR OWN NECK? IF YOU'D MISSED WITH THE HOOK, YOU'D HAVE BEEN A *PANCAKE.*

LOATHE AS I AM TO AGREE WITH THIS PARTIALLY-SHAVED APE TWICE IN ONE WEEK, I CONCUR. WAS IT WORTH *YOUR* LIFE TO SAVE *HIS?*

WE SWORE AN OATH, GENTLEMEN.

"LET ME THINK OF THE RIGHT, AND LEND MY ASSISTANCE TO THOSE WHO NEED IT, WITH NO REGARD FOR ANYTHING BUT JUSTICE."

WE HELP *ALL* THOSE WHO NEED OUR ASSISTANCE. JUST BECAUSE A MAN COMMITS A CRIME DOESN'T MAKE HIM ANY LESS DESERVING.

IF ANYTHING, IT MAKES HIM *MORE* DESERVING. BECAUSE CRIME IS A *DISEASE* FOR WHICH WE HAVE THE *CURE.*

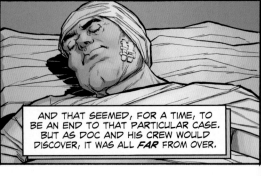

AND THAT SEEMED, FOR A TIME, TO BE AN END TO THAT PARTICULAR CASE. BUT AS DOC AND HIS CREW WOULD DISCOVER, IT WAS ALL *FAR* FROM OVER.

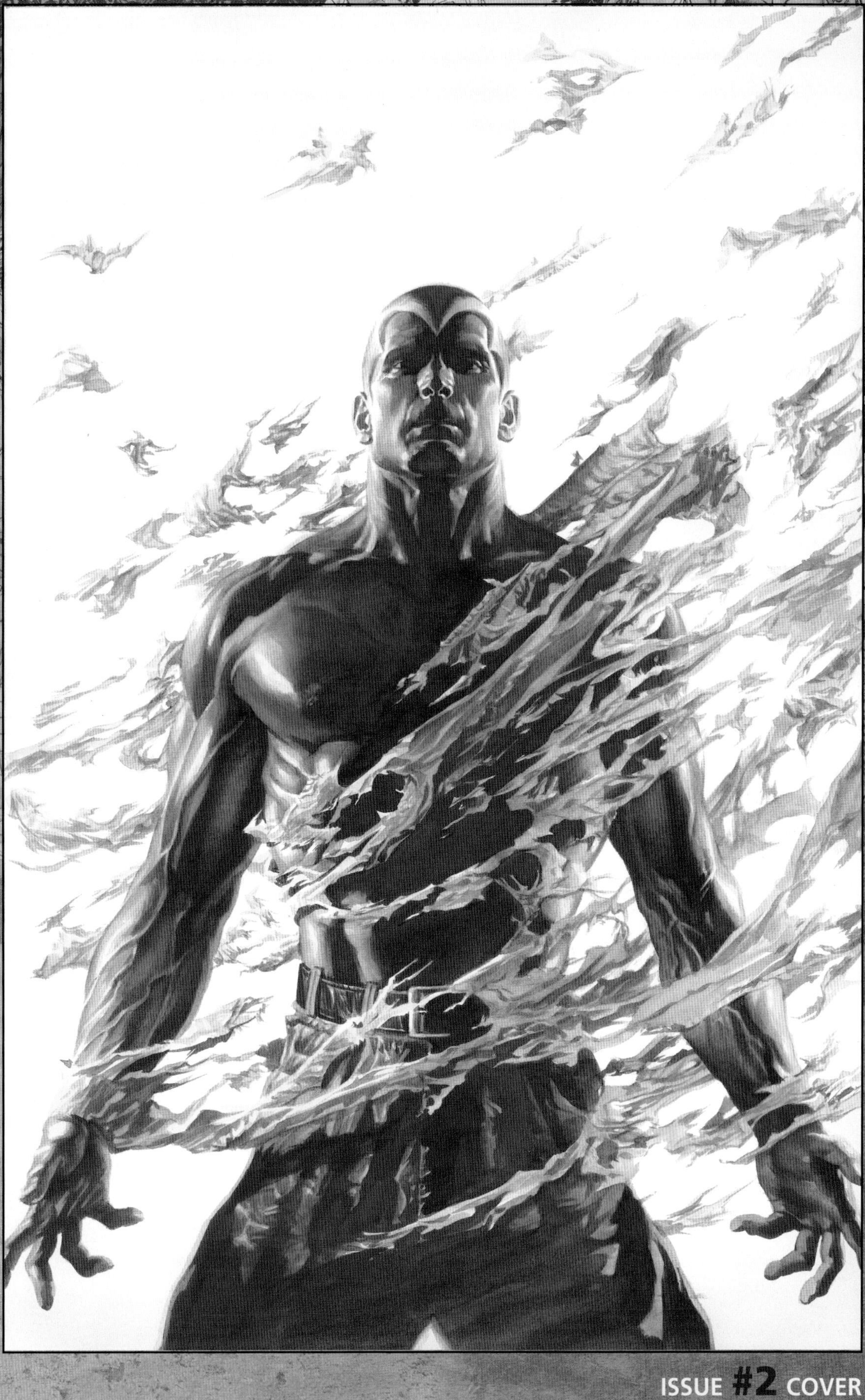

ISSUE #2 COVER
art by ALEX ROSS

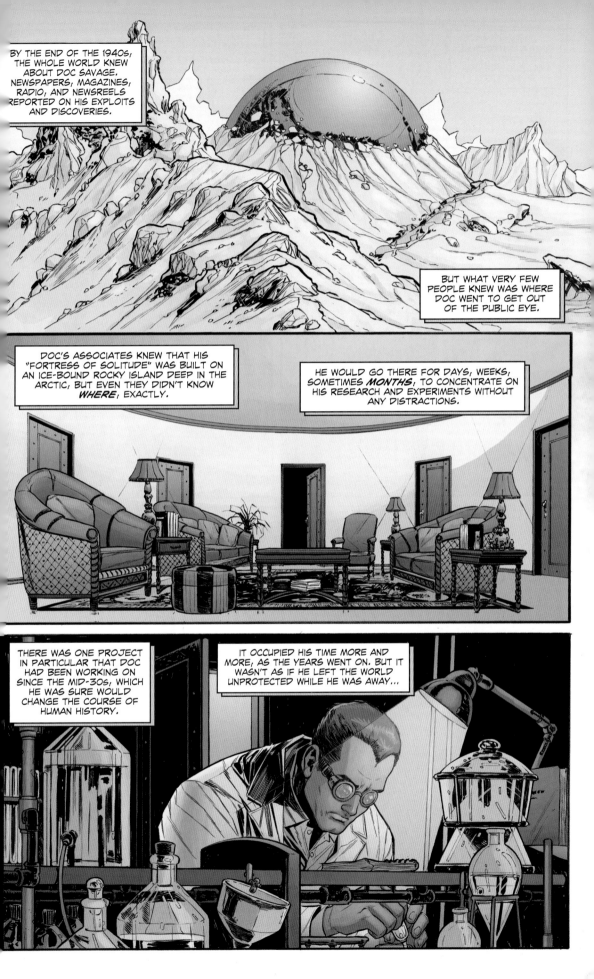

BY THE END OF THE 1940s, THE WHOLE WORLD KNEW ABOUT DOC SAVAGE. NEWSPAPERS, MAGAZINES, RADIO, AND NEWSREELS REPORTED ON HIS EXPLOITS AND DISCOVERIES.

BUT WHAT VERY FEW PEOPLE KNEW WAS WHERE DOC WENT TO GET OUT OF THE PUBLIC EYE.

DOC'S ASSOCIATES KNEW THAT HIS "FORTRESS OF SOLITUDE" WAS BUILT ON AN ICE-BOUND ROCKY ISLAND DEEP IN THE ARCTIC, BUT EVEN THEY DIDN'T KNOW *WHERE*, EXACTLY.

HE WOULD GO THERE FOR DAYS, WEEKS, SOMETIMES *MONTHS*, TO CONCENTRATE ON HIS RESEARCH AND EXPERIMENTS WITHOUT ANY DISTRACTIONS.

THERE WAS ONE PROJECT IN PARTICULAR THAT DOC HAD BEEN WORKING ON SINCE THE MID-30s, WHICH HE WAS SURE WOULD CHANGE THE COURSE OF HUMAN HISTORY.

IT OCCUPIED HIS TIME MORE AND MORE, AS THE YEARS WENT ON. BUT IT WASN'T AS IF HE LEFT THE WORLD UNPROTECTED WHILE HE WAS AWAY...

...WHICH WAS FORTUNATE, BECAUSE THERE WAS ALWAYS TROUBLE BREWING SOMEWHERE.

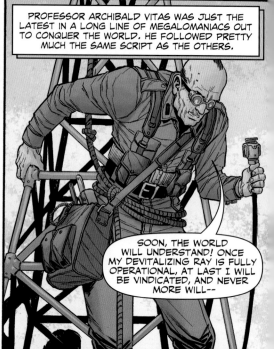

PROFESSOR ARCHIBALD VITAS WAS JUST THE LATEST IN A LONG LINE OF MEGALOMANIACS OUT TO CONQUER THE WORLD. HE FOLLOWED PRETTY MUCH THE SAME SCRIPT AS THE OTHERS.

SOON, THE WORLD WILL UNDERSTAND! ONCE MY DEVITALIZING RAY IS FULLY OPERATIONAL, AT LAST I WILL BE VINDICATED, AND NEVER MORE WILL--

OH, SHUT UP, ALREADY.

THWONK

I DON'T SEE WHY YOU NEED A "DEVITALIZING RAY," BUSTER. YOU COULD *TALK* SOMEONE TO DEATH.

PATRICIA SAVAGE WASN'T JUST DOC'S YOUNGER COUSIN. SHE WAS AN ADVENTURER IN HER OWN RIGHT, WITH HER OWN TEAM OF AIDES THAT OPERATED AS "PATRICIA, INCORPORATED"...

...BUT SHE FILLED IN FOR HER COUSIN WHEN HE WASN'T AROUND.

WE TOOK CARE OF THESE YAHOOS AND THEIR RAY-THINGEE.

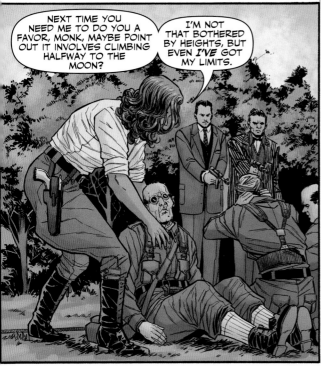

NEXT TIME YOU NEED ME TO DO YOU A FAVOR, MONK, MAYBE POINT OUT IT INVOLVES CLIMBING HALFWAY TO THE MOON?

I'M NOT THAT BOTHERED BY HEIGHTS, BUT EVEN I'VE GOT MY LIMITS.

I DON'T BELIEVE IT FOR AN INSTANT. IT LOOKED TO ME AS THOUGH YOU WERE HAVING THE TIME OF YOUR LIFE.

AW, SAVE THE SOFT-SOAPING, HAM. YOU KNOW PAT'S ONLY GOT EYES FOR ME.

AW, YOU FELLAS ARE CUTE, BUT I'M NOT REALLY THE MARRYING KIND.

NOW, LET'S GET VITAS AND HIS GOONS TO THE COLLEGE, AND WE CAN WRAP THIS ONE UP.

THE FORTRESS WASN'T THE ONLY PLACE THE PUBLIC DIDN'T KNOW ABOUT, OF COURSE. BUT DOC SHARED THE SECRET OF THE "CRIME COLLEGE" WITH HIS ASSOCIATES.

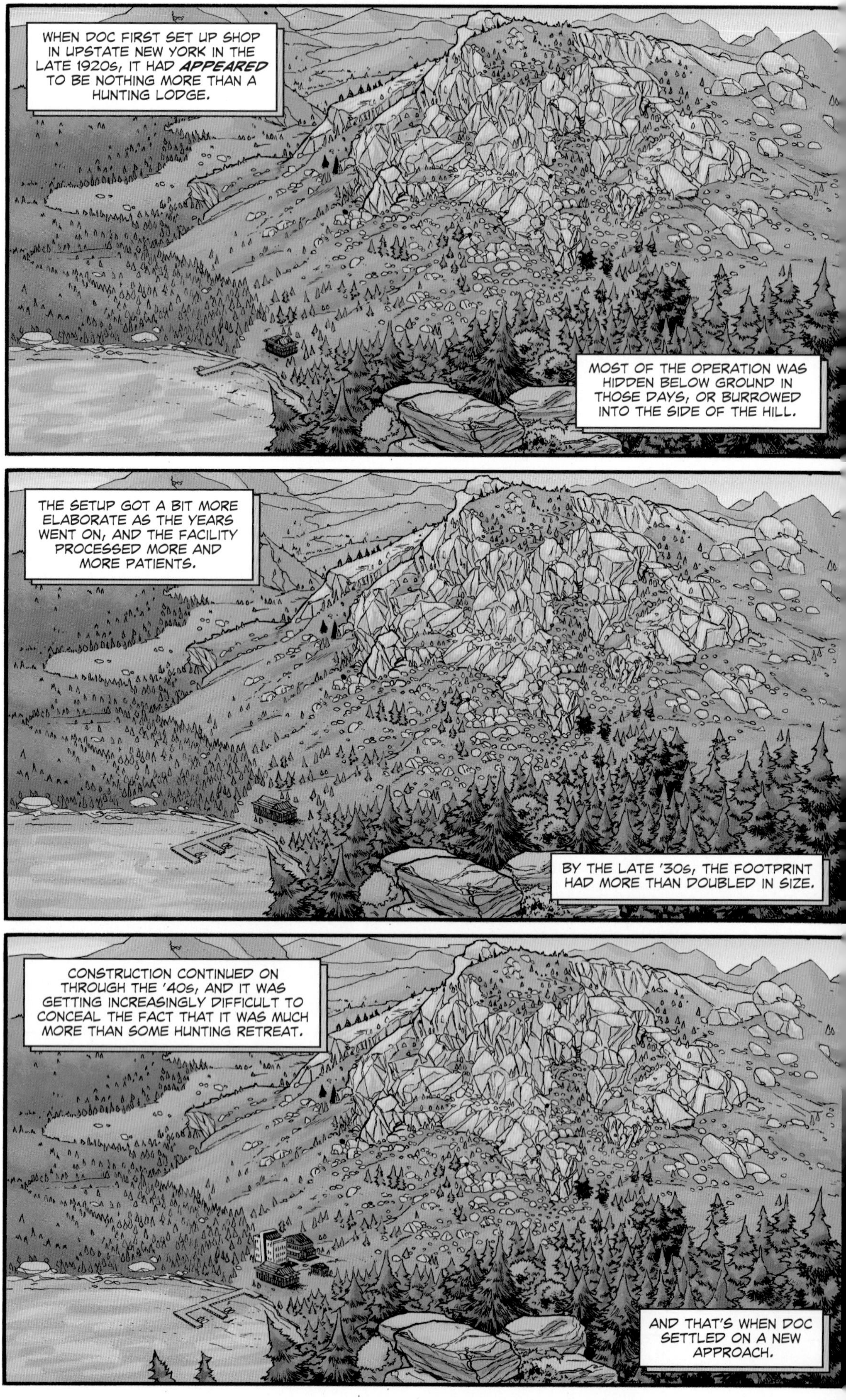
WHEN DOC FIRST SET UP SHOP IN UPSTATE NEW YORK IN THE LATE 1920s, IT HAD ***APPEARED*** TO BE NOTHING MORE THAN A HUNTING LODGE.
MOST OF THE OPERATION WAS HIDDEN BELOW GROUND IN THOSE DAYS, OR BURROWED INTO THE SIDE OF THE HILL.
THE SETUP GOT A BIT MORE ELABORATE AS THE YEARS WENT ON, AND THE FACILITY PROCESSED MORE AND MORE PATIENTS.
BY THE LATE '30s, THE FOOTPRINT HAD MORE THAN DOUBLED IN SIZE.
CONSTRUCTION CONTINUED ON THROUGH THE '40s, AND IT WAS GETTING INCREASINGLY DIFFICULT TO CONCEAL THE FACT THAT IT WAS MUCH MORE THAN SOME HUNTING RETREAT.
AND THAT'S WHEN DOC SETTLED ON A NEW APPROACH.

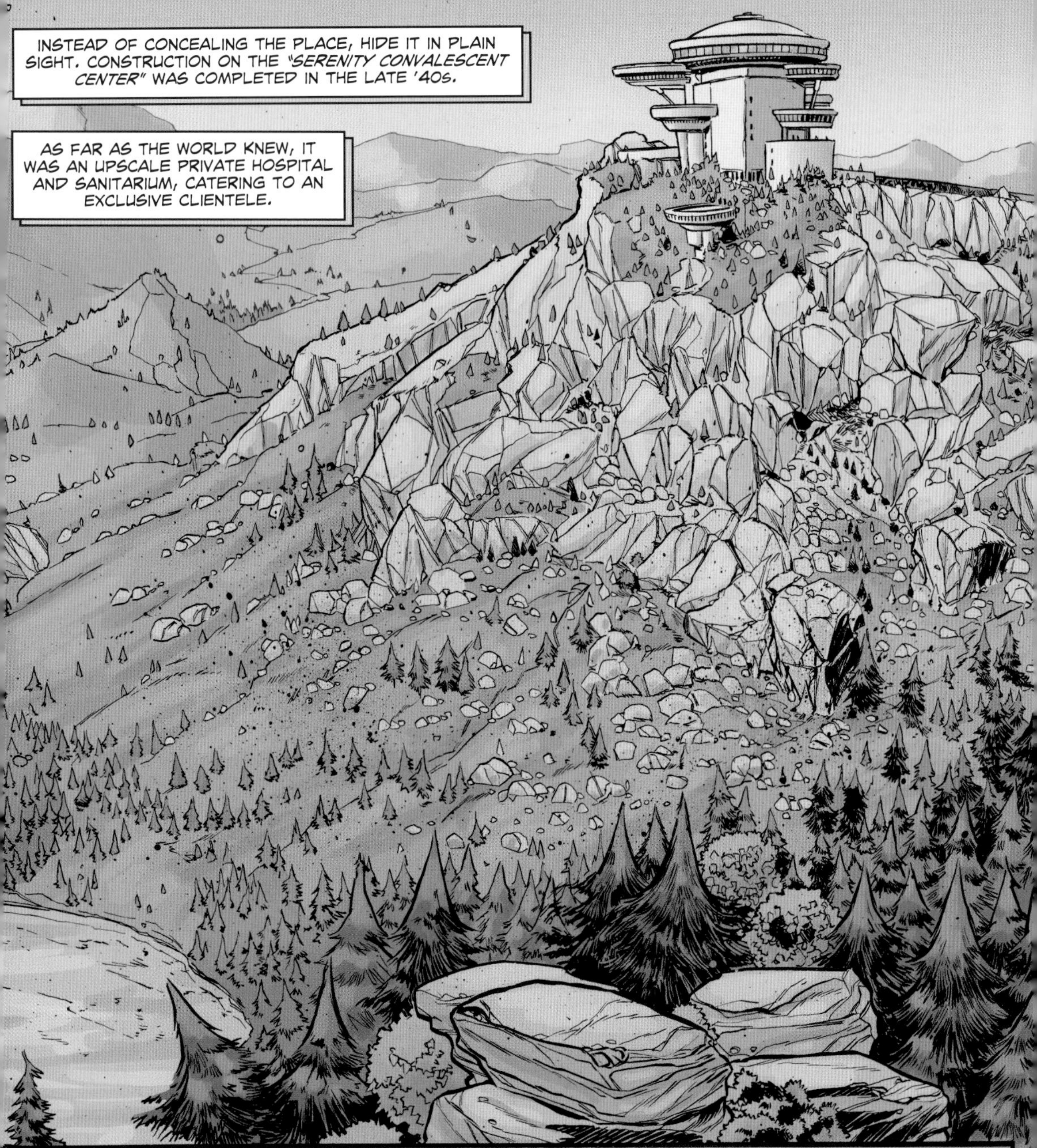
INSTEAD OF CONCEALING THE PLACE, HIDE IT IN PLAIN SIGHT. CONSTRUCTION ON THE *"SERENITY CONVALESCENT CENTER"* WAS COMPLETED IN THE LATE '40s.
AS FAR AS THE WORLD KNEW, IT WAS AN UPSCALE PRIVATE HOSPITAL AND SANITARIUM, CATERING TO AN EXCLUSIVE CLIENTELE.

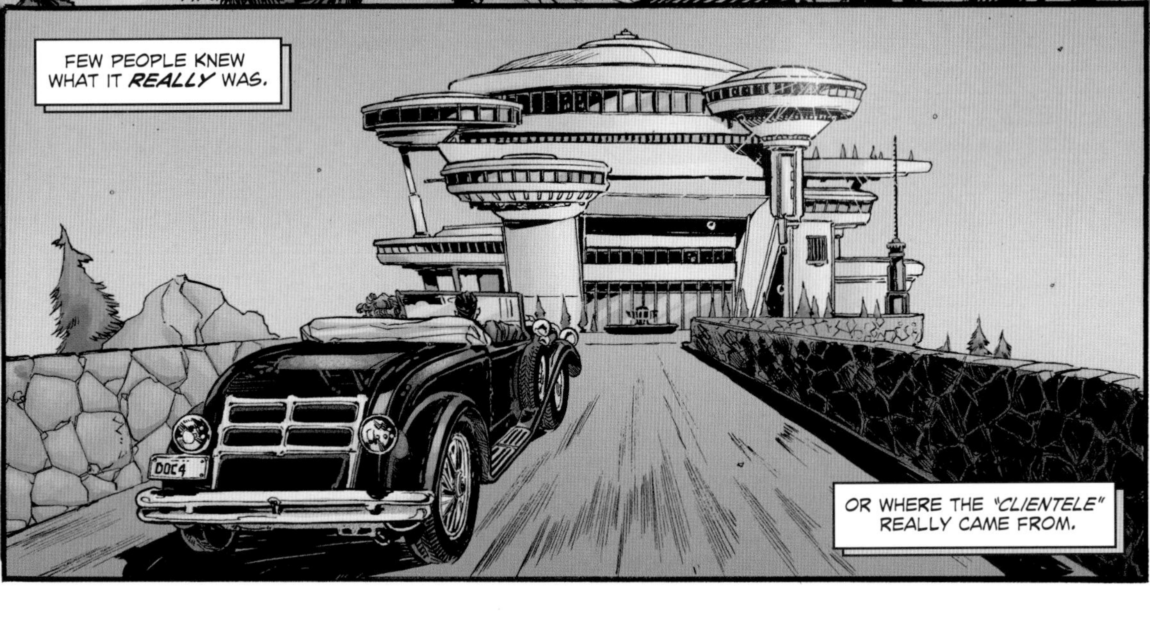
FEW PEOPLE KNEW WHAT IT ***REALLY*** WAS.
DOC4
OR WHERE THE *"CLIENTELE"* REALLY CAME FROM.

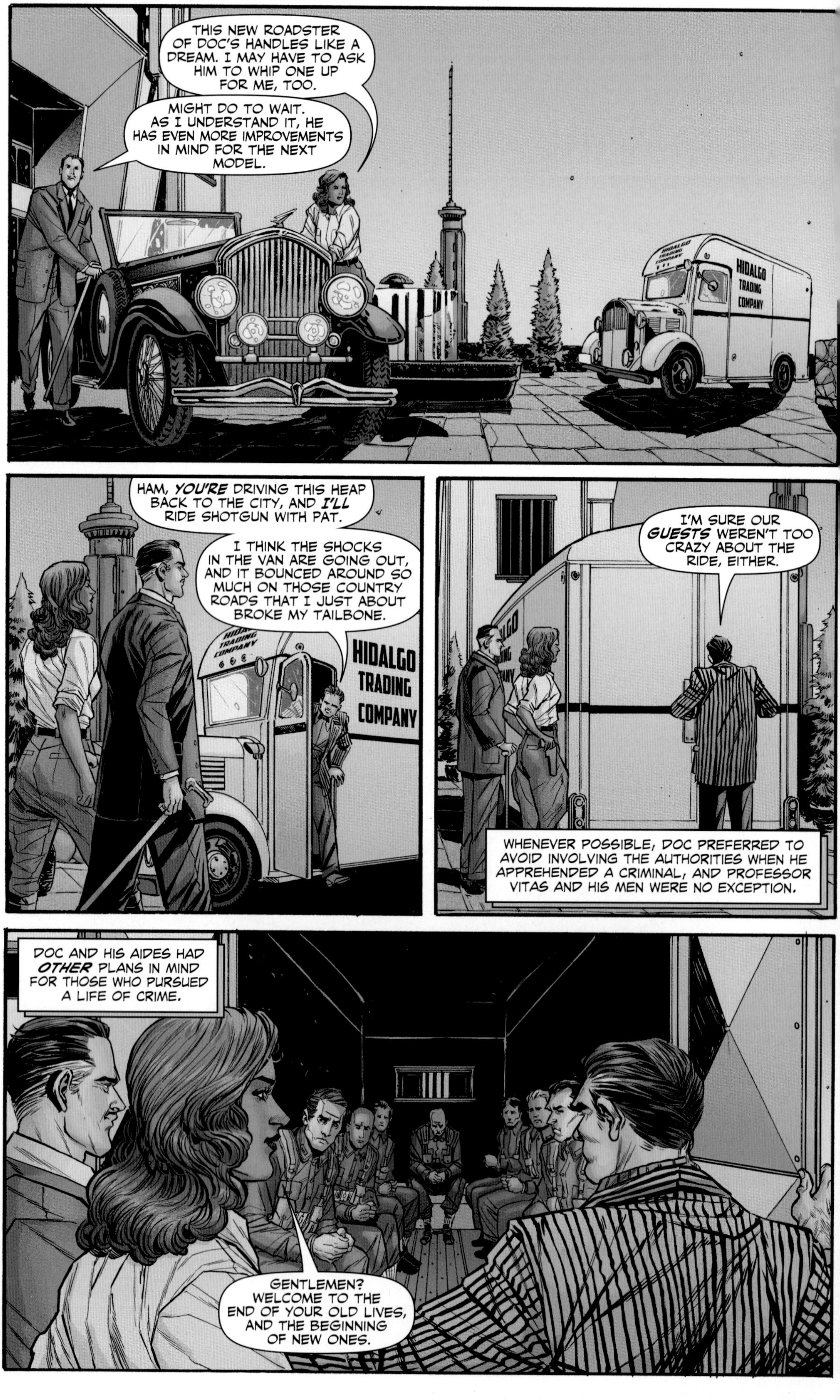
THIS NEW ROADSTER OF DOC'S HANDLES LIKE A DREAM. I MAY HAVE TO ASK HIM TO WHIP ONE UP FOR ME, TOO.
MIGHT DO TO WAIT. AS I UNDERSTAND IT, HE HAS EVEN MORE IMPROVEMENTS IN MIND FOR THE NEXT MODEL.
HIDALGO TRADING COMPANY
HAM, *YOU'RE* DRIVING THIS HEAP BACK TO THE CITY, AND *I'LL* RIDE SHOTGUN WITH PAT.
I THINK THE SHOCKS IN THE VAN ARE GOING OUT, AND IT BOUNCED AROUND SO MUCH ON THOSE COUNTRY ROADS THAT I JUST ABOUT BROKE MY TAILBONE.
HIDALGO TRADING COMPANY
I'M SURE OUR *GUESTS* WEREN'T TOO CRAZY ABOUT THE RIDE, EITHER.
WHENEVER POSSIBLE, DOC PREFERRED TO AVOID INVOLVING THE AUTHORITIES WHEN HE APPREHENDED A CRIMINAL, AND PROFESSOR VITAS AND HIS MEN WERE NO EXCEPTION.
DOC AND HIS AIDES HAD *OTHER* PLANS IN MIND FOR THOSE WHO PURSUED A LIFE OF CRIME.
GENTLEMEN? WELCOME TO THE END OF YOUR OLD LIVES, AND THE BEGINNING OF NEW ONES.

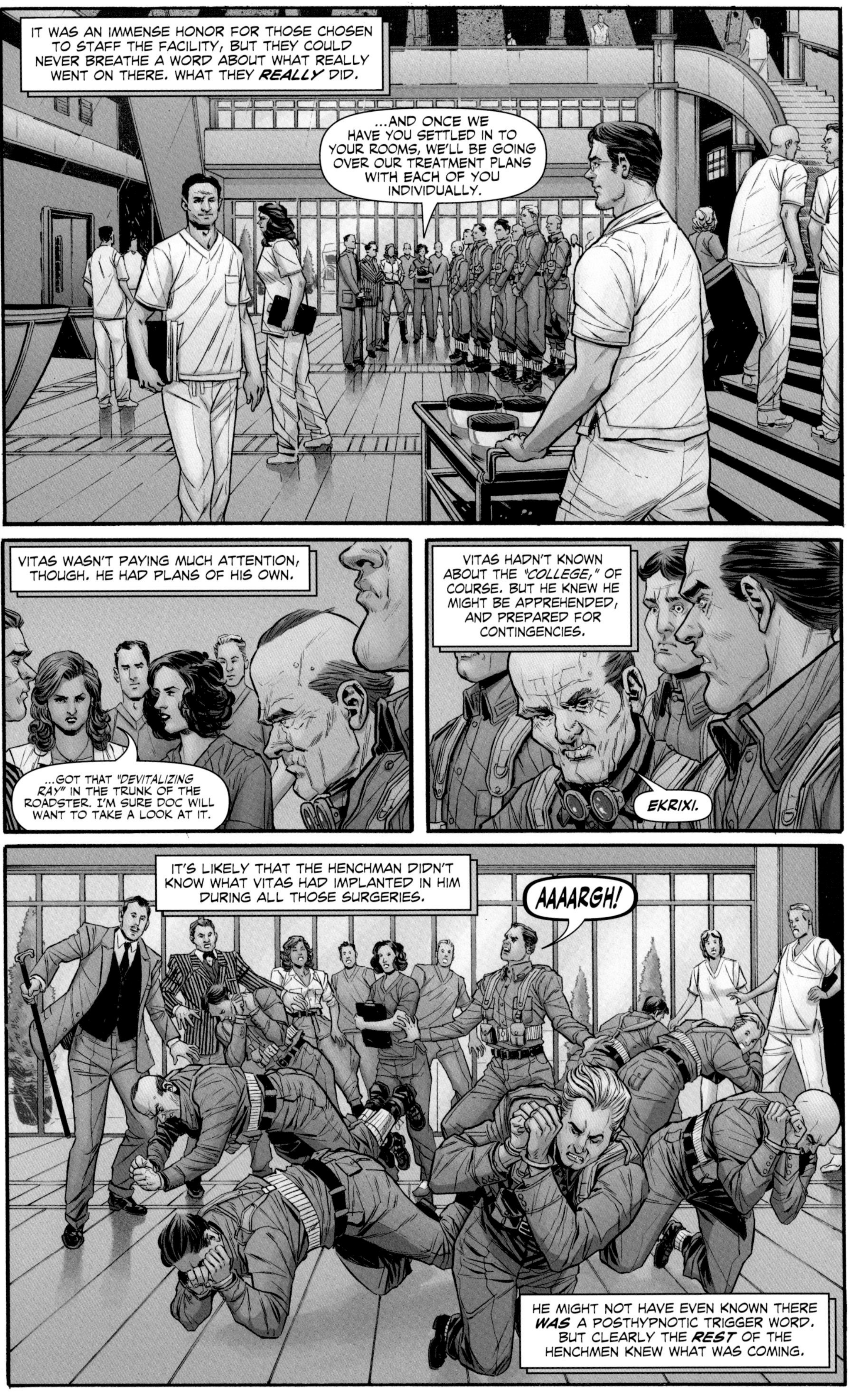
IT WAS AN IMMENSE HONOR FOR THOSE CHOSEN TO STAFF THE FACILITY, BUT THEY COULD NEVER BREATHE A WORD ABOUT WHAT REALLY WENT ON THERE. WHAT THEY *REALLY* DID.
...AND ONCE WE HAVE YOU SETTLED IN TO YOUR ROOMS, WE'LL BE GOING OVER OUR TREATMENT PLANS WITH EACH OF YOU INDIVIDUALLY.
VITAS WASN'T PAYING MUCH ATTENTION, THOUGH. HE HAD PLANS OF HIS OWN.
...GOT THAT "DEVITALIZING RAY" IN THE TRUNK OF THE ROADSTER. I'M SURE DOC WILL WANT TO TAKE A LOOK AT IT.
VITAS HADN'T KNOWN ABOUT THE "COLLEGE," OF COURSE. BUT HE KNEW HE MIGHT BE APPREHENDED, AND PREPARED FOR CONTINGENCIES.
EKRIXI.
IT'S LIKELY THAT THE HENCHMAN DIDN'T KNOW WHAT VITAS HAD IMPLANTED IN HIM DURING ALL THOSE SURGERIES.
AAAARGH!
HE MIGHT NOT HAVE EVEN KNOWN THERE *WAS* A POSTHYPNOTIC TRIGGER WORD. BUT CLEARLY THE *REST* OF THE HENCHMEN KNEW WHAT WAS COMING.

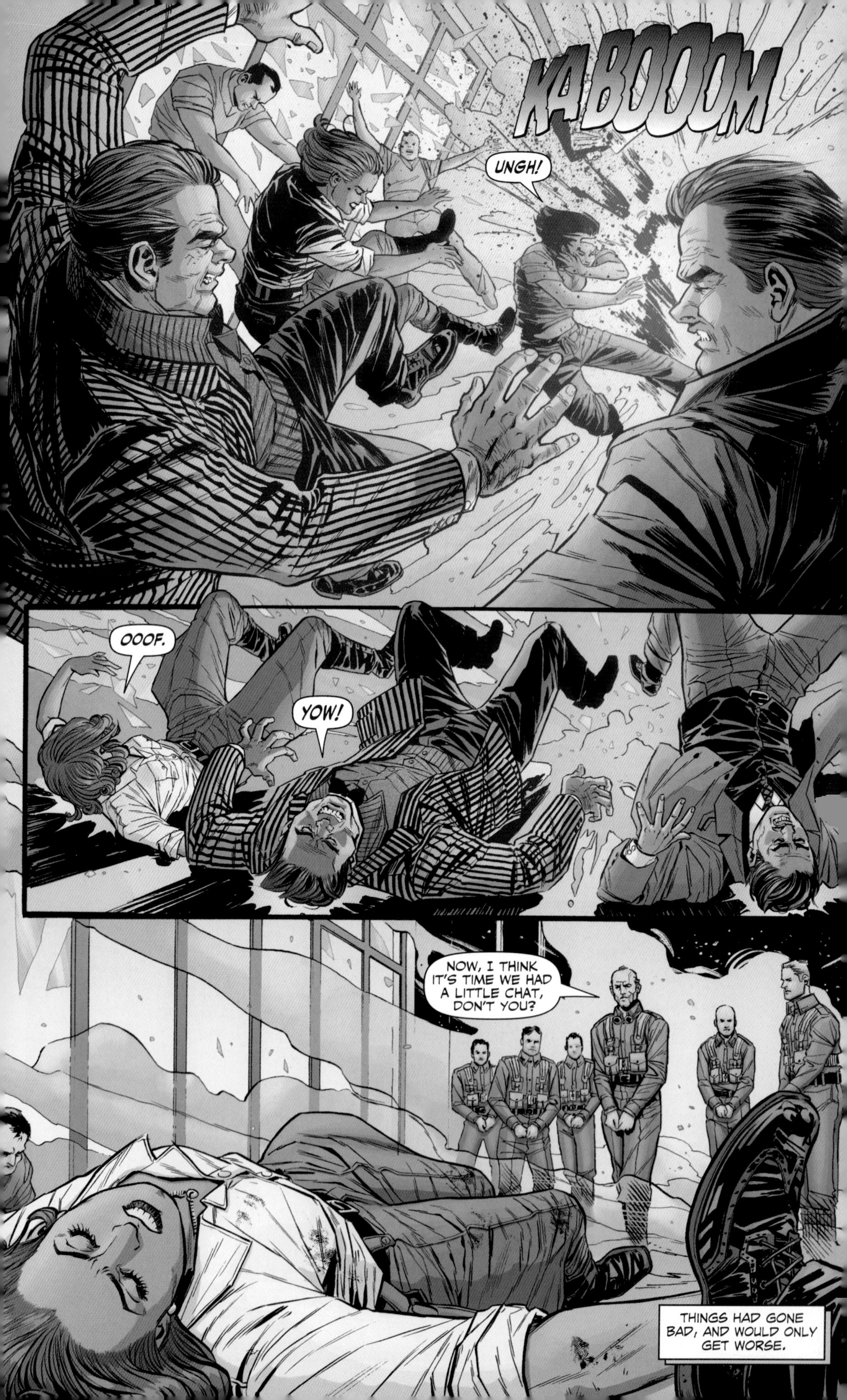
KABOOOM
UNGH!
OOOF.
YOW!
NOW, I THINK IT'S TIME WE HAD A LITTLE CHAT, DON'T YOU?
THINGS HAD GONE BAD, AND WOULD ONLY GET WORSE.

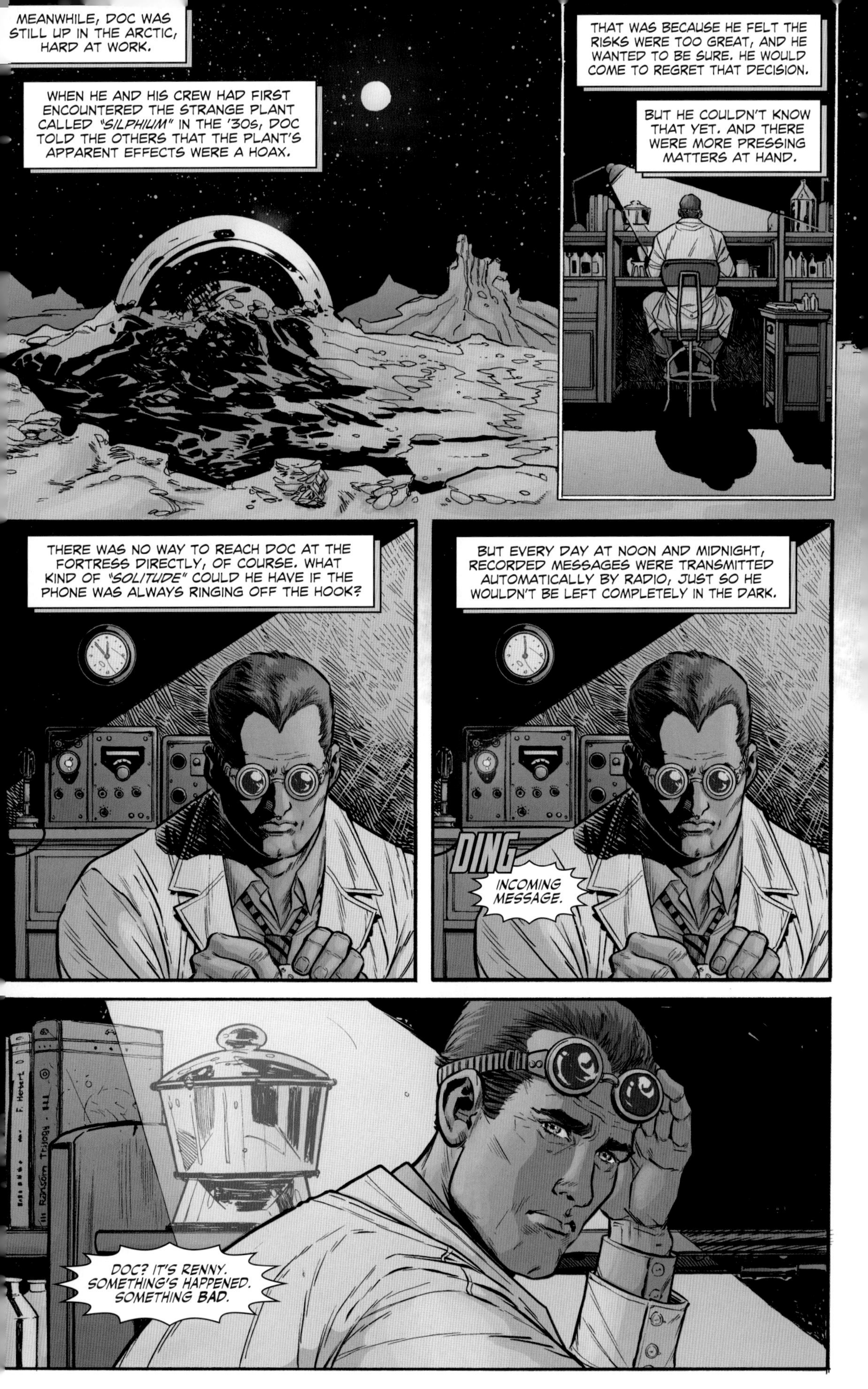
MEANWHILE, DOC WAS STILL UP IN THE ARCTIC, HARD AT WORK.
WHEN HE AND HIS CREW HAD FIRST ENCOUNTERED THE STRANGE PLANT CALLED "SILPHIUM" IN THE '30s, DOC TOLD THE OTHERS THAT THE PLANT'S APPARENT EFFECTS WERE A HOAX.
THAT WAS BECAUSE HE FELT THE RISKS WERE TOO GREAT, AND HE WANTED TO BE SURE. HE WOULD COME TO REGRET THAT DECISION.
BUT HE COULDN'T KNOW THAT YET. AND THERE WERE MORE PRESSING MATTERS AT HAND.
THERE WAS NO WAY TO REACH DOC AT THE FORTRESS DIRECTLY, OF COURSE. WHAT KIND OF "SOLITUDE" COULD HE HAVE IF THE PHONE WAS ALWAYS RINGING OFF THE HOOK?
BUT EVERY DAY AT NOON AND MIDNIGHT, RECORDED MESSAGES WERE TRANSMITTED AUTOMATICALLY BY RADIO, JUST SO HE WOULDN'T BE LEFT COMPLETELY IN THE DARK.
DING
INCOMING MESSAGE.
DOC? IT'S RENNY. SOMETHING'S HAPPENED. SOMETHING BAD.

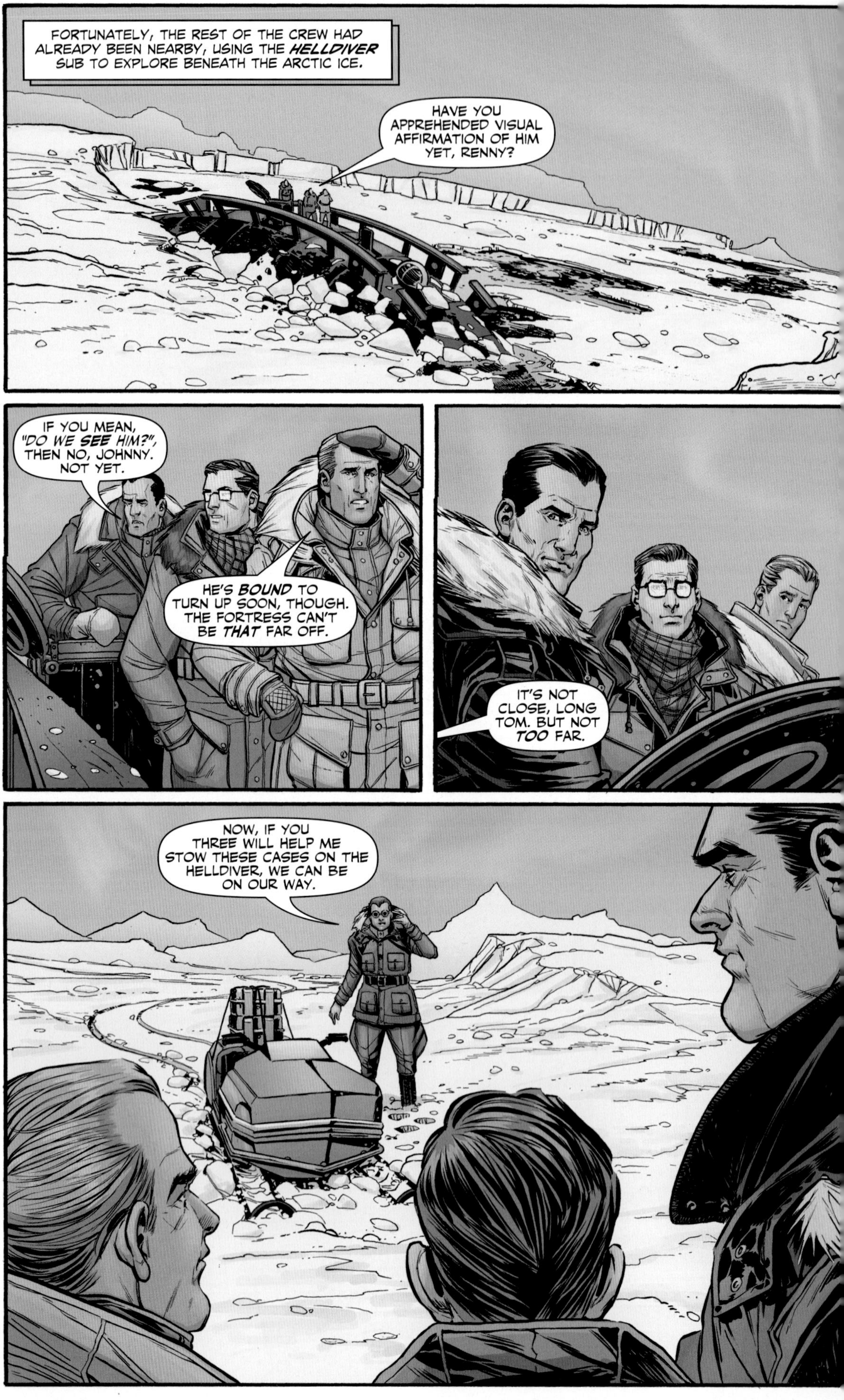
FORTUNATELY, THE REST OF THE CREW HAD ALREADY BEEN NEARBY, USING THE HELLDIVER SUB TO EXPLORE BENEATH THE ARCTIC ICE.
HAVE YOU APPREHENDED VISUAL AFFIRMATION OF HIM YET, RENNY?
IF YOU MEAN, "DO WE SEE HIM?", THEN NO, JOHNNY. NOT YET.
HE'S BOUND TO TURN UP SOON, THOUGH. THE FORTRESS CAN'T BE THAT FAR OFF.
IT'S NOT CLOSE, LONG TOM. BUT NOT TOO FAR.
NOW, IF YOU THREE WILL HELP ME STOW THESE CASES ON THE HELLDIVER, WE CAN BE ON OUR WAY.

THE HELLDIVER WAS ESPECIALLY DESIGNED TO TRAVEL BENEATH POLAR ICE, BUT IT COULD MOVE AT A FAST CLIP IN OPEN WATERS.

WE SHOULD REACH THE NEW YORK COAST BY MORNING.

NOW, HAS THE SITUATION CHANGED SINCE YOUR LAST REPORT?

ANY WORD FROM THE COLLEGE?

ASIDE FROM THE HEAD NURSE WHO WAS KILLED IN THE EXPLOSION, NO ONE ELSE HAS DIED YET, BUT I'M NOT SURE FOR HOW MUCH LONGER.

I'VE BEEN ABLE TO TAP IN REMOTELY TO THE INTERCOM SYSTEM IN THE FACILITY, SO WE'VE BEEN EAVESDROPPING ON WHAT'S GOING ON INSIDE.

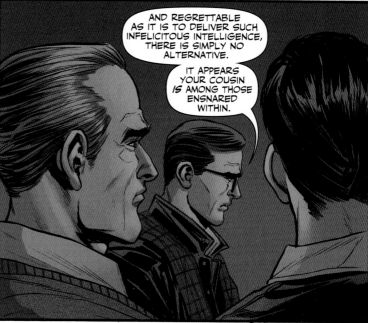

AND REGRETTABLE AS IT IS TO DELIVER SUCH INFELICITOUS INTELLIGENCE, THERE IS SIMPLY NO ALTERNATIVE.

IT APPEARS YOUR COUSIN *IS* AMONG THOSE ENSNARED WITHIN.

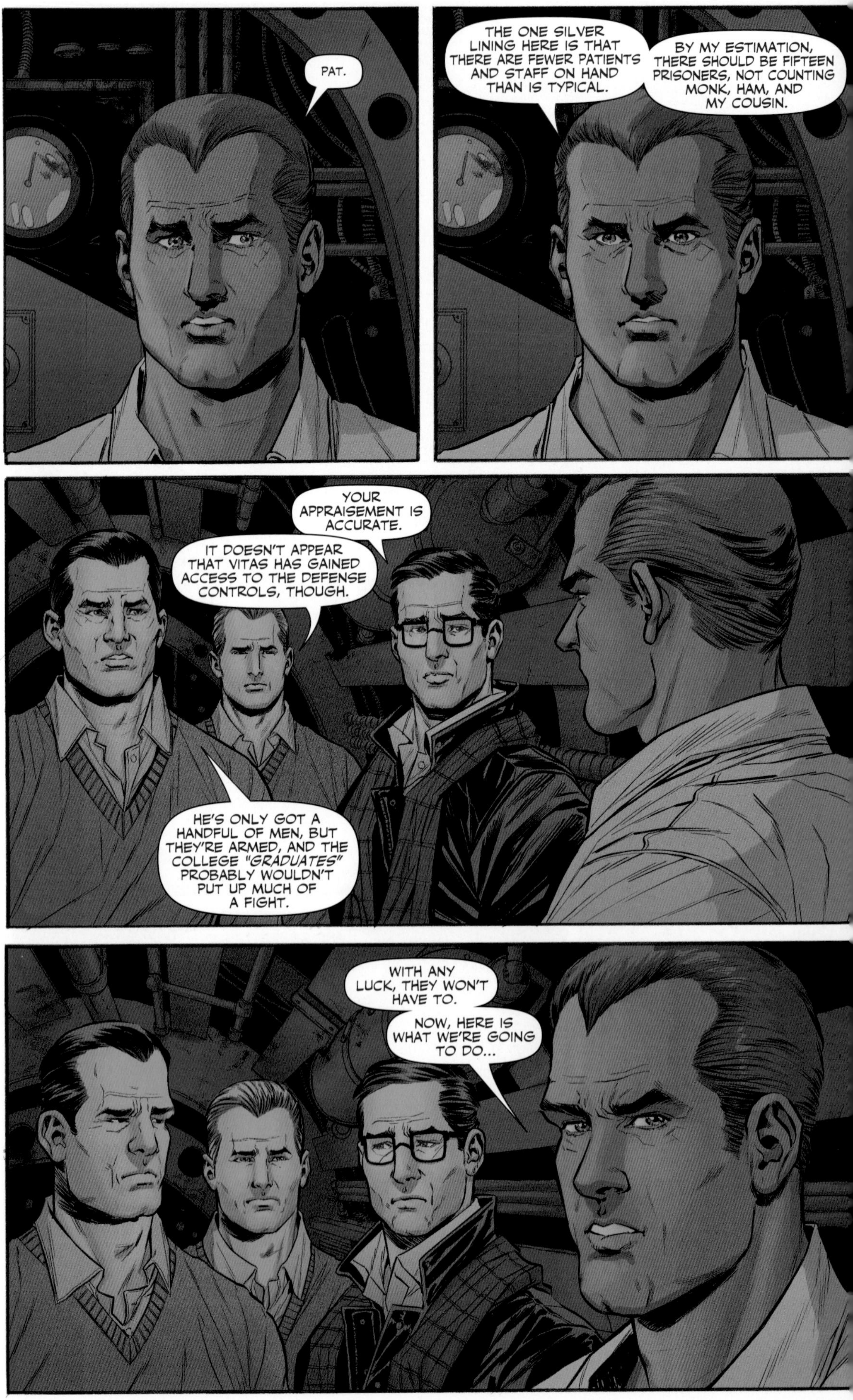
PAT.
THE ONE SILVER LINING HERE IS THAT THERE ARE FEWER PATIENTS AND STAFF ON HAND THAN IS TYPICAL.
BY MY ESTIMATION, THERE SHOULD BE FIFTEEN PRISONERS, NOT COUNTING MONK, HAM, AND MY COUSIN.
YOUR APPRAISEMENT IS ACCURATE.
IT DOESN'T APPEAR THAT VITAS HAS GAINED ACCESS TO THE DEFENSE CONTROLS, THOUGH.
HE'S ONLY GOT A HANDFUL OF MEN, BUT THEY'RE ARMED, AND THE COLLEGE "GRADUATES" PROBABLY WOULDN'T PUT UP MUCH OF A FIGHT.
WITH ANY LUCK, THEY WON'T HAVE TO.
NOW, HERE IS WHAT WE'RE GOING TO DO...

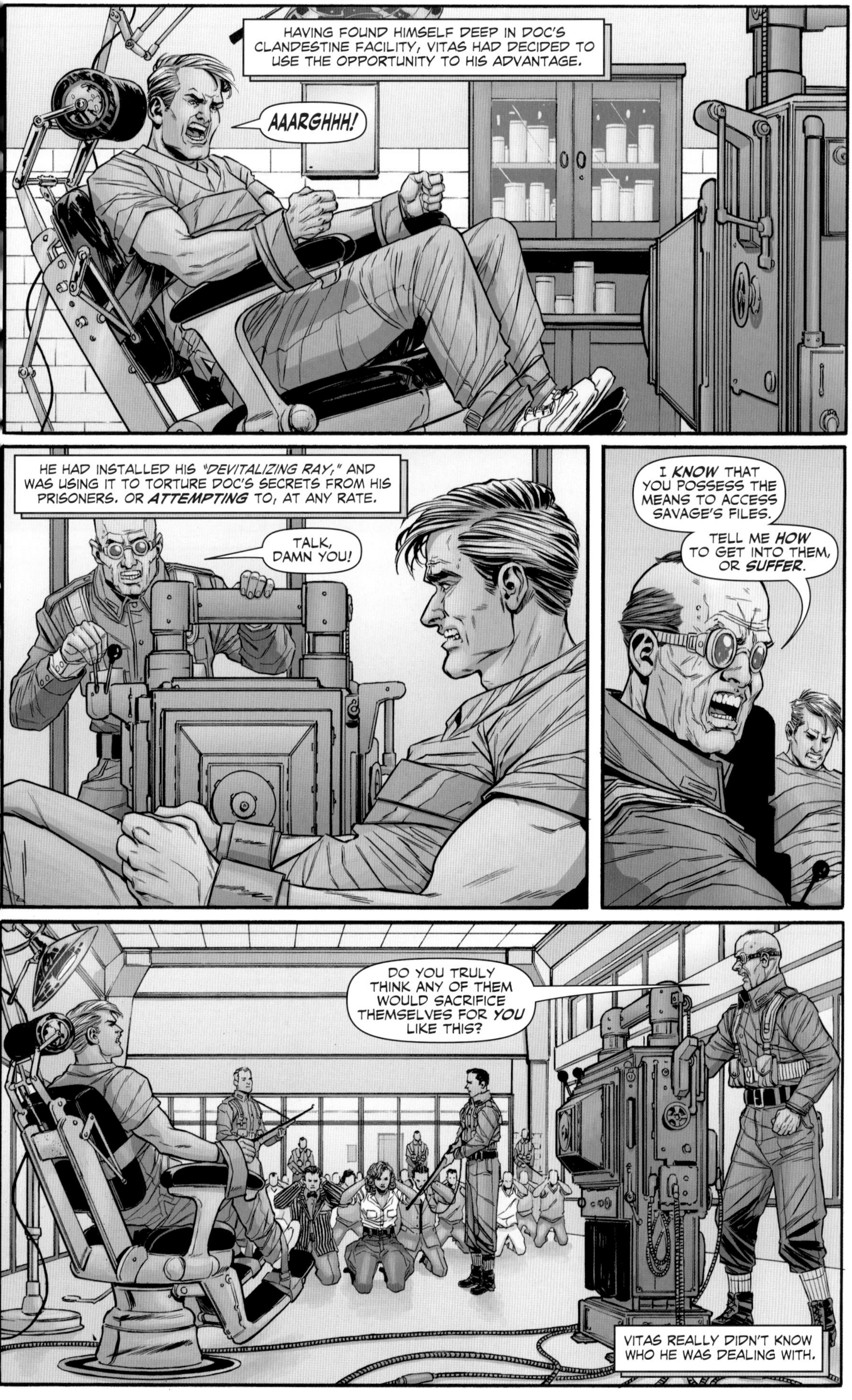
HAVING FOUND HIMSELF DEEP IN DOC'S CLANDESTINE FACILITY, VITAS HAD DECIDED TO USE THE OPPORTUNITY TO HIS ADVANTAGE.
AAARGHHH!
HE HAD INSTALLED HIS "DEVITALIZING RAY," AND WAS USING IT TO TORTURE DOC'S SECRETS FROM HIS PRISONERS. OR ATTEMPTING TO, AT ANY RATE.
TALK, DAMN YOU!
I KNOW THAT YOU POSSESS THE MEANS TO ACCESS SAVAGE'S FILES.
TELL ME HOW TO GET INTO THEM, OR SUFFER.
DO YOU TRULY THINK ANY OF THEM WOULD SACRIFICE THEMSELVES FOR YOU LIKE THIS?
VITAS REALLY DIDN'T KNOW WHO HE WAS DEALING WITH.

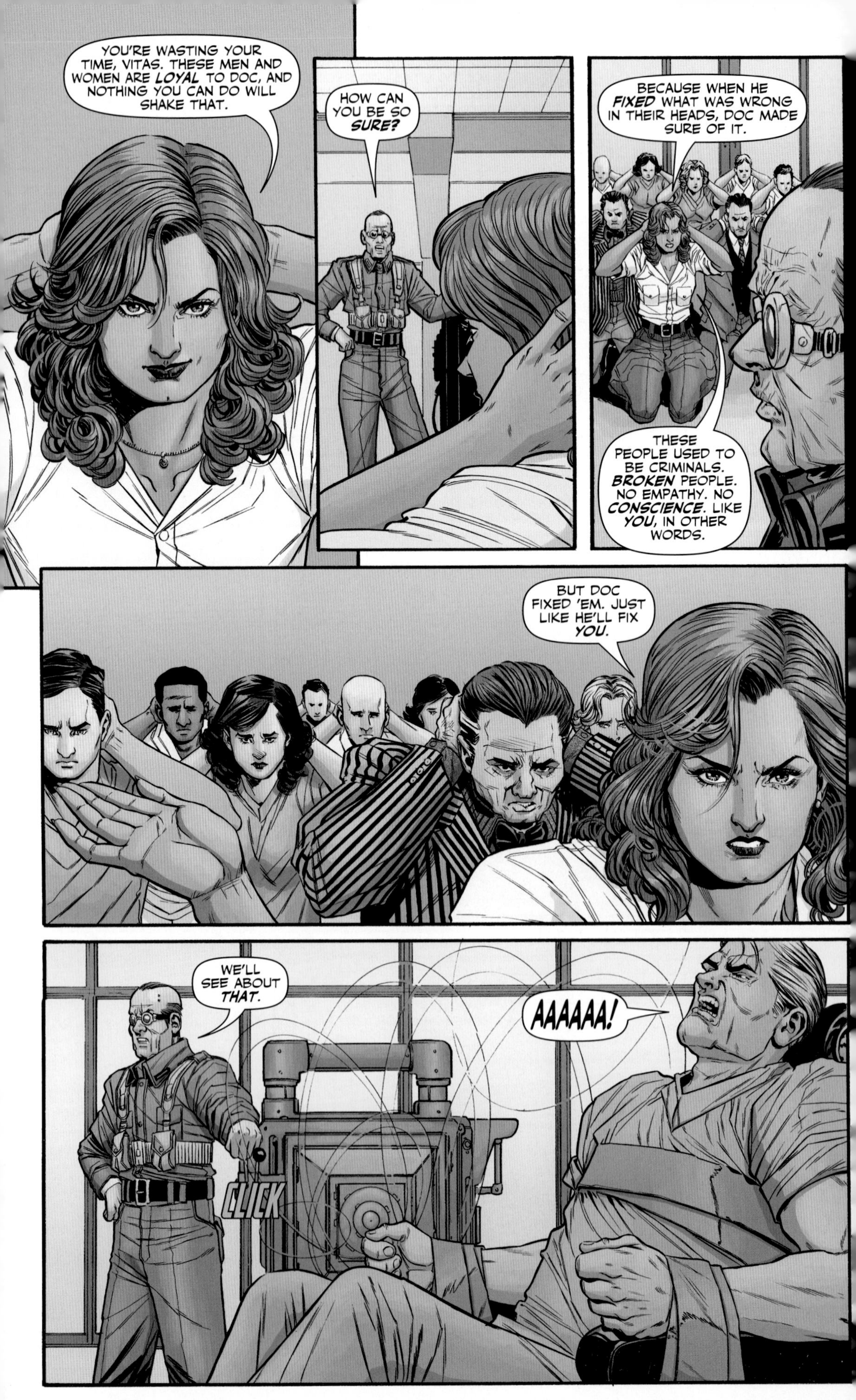
YOU'RE WASTING YOUR TIME, VITAS. THESE MEN AND WOMEN ARE *LOYAL* TO DOC, AND NOTHING YOU CAN DO WILL SHAKE THAT.
HOW CAN YOU BE SO *SURE?*
BECAUSE WHEN HE *FIXED* WHAT WAS WRONG IN THEIR HEADS, DOC MADE SURE OF IT.
THESE PEOPLE USED TO BE CRIMINALS. *BROKEN* PEOPLE. NO EMPATHY. NO *CONSCIENCE*. LIKE *YOU*, IN OTHER WORDS.
BUT DOC FIXED 'EM. JUST LIKE HE'LL FIX *YOU*.
WE'LL SEE ABOUT *THAT*.
AAAAAA!
CLICK

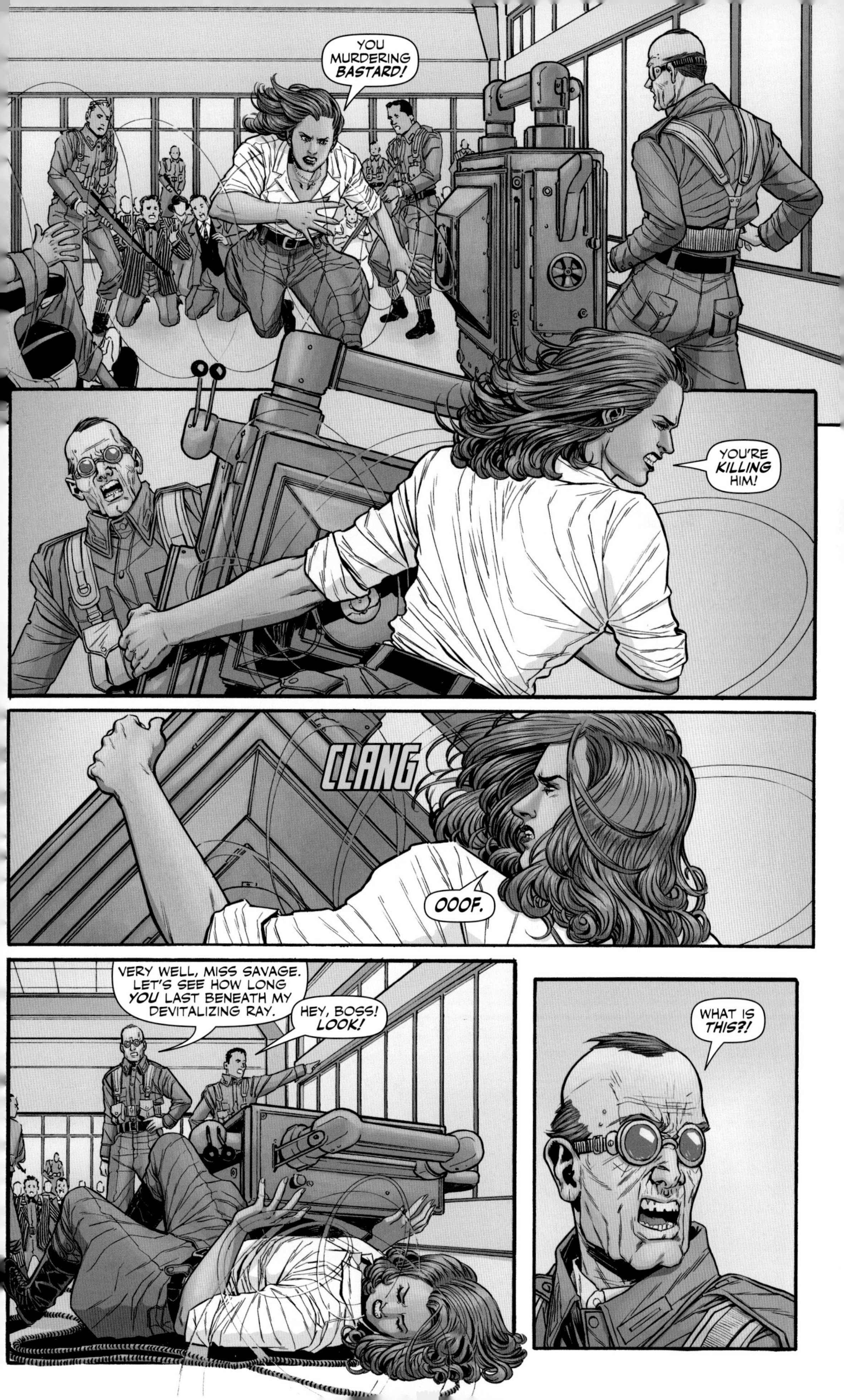
YOU MURDERING BASTARD!
YOU'RE KILLING HIM!
CLANG
OOOF.
VERY WELL, MISS SAVAGE. LET'S SEE HOW LONG YOU LAST BENEATH MY DEVITALIZING RAY.
HEY, BOSS! LOOK!
WHAT IS THIS?!

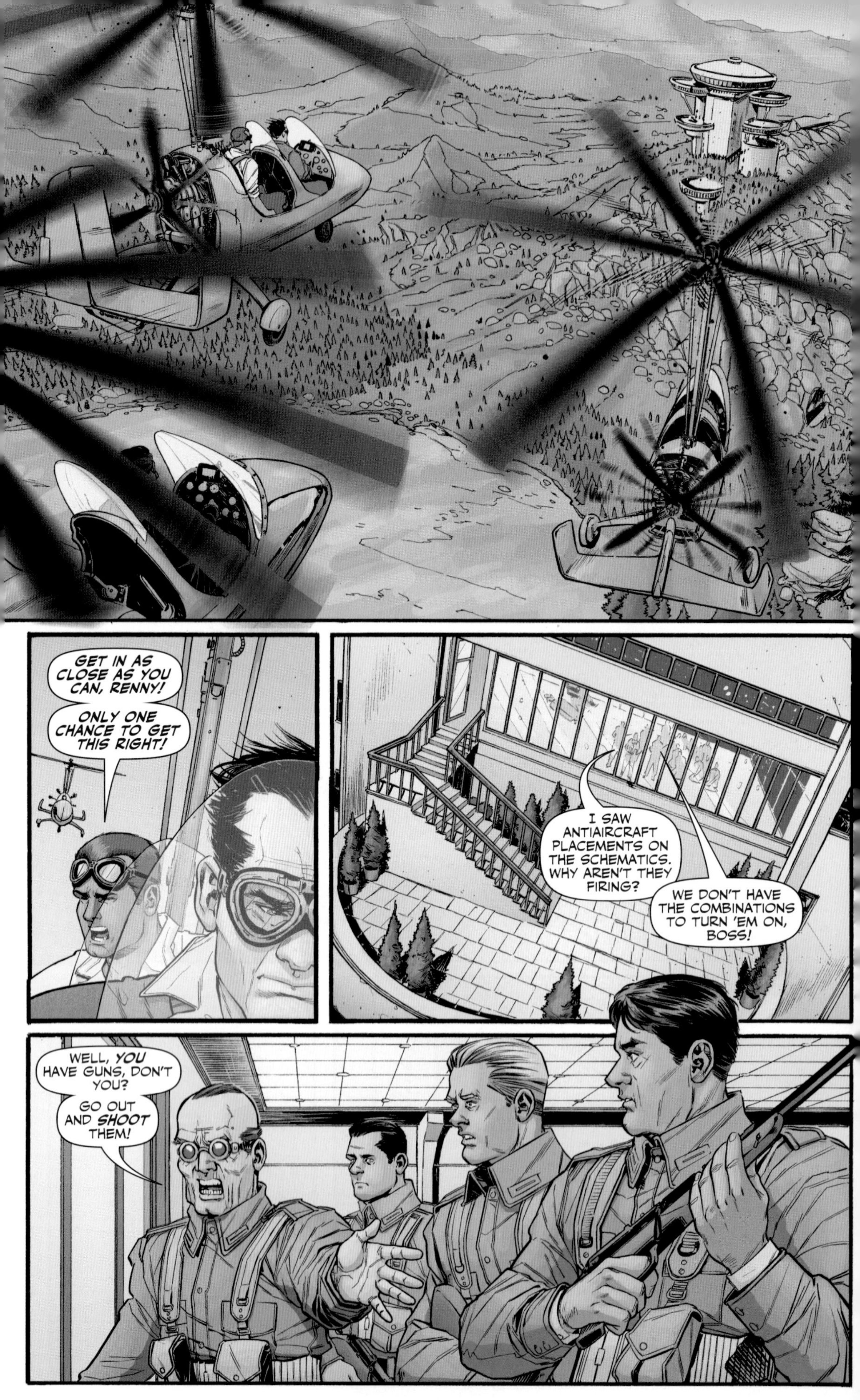
GET IN AS CLOSE AS YOU CAN, RENNY!
ONLY ONE CHANCE TO GET THIS RIGHT!
I SAW ANTIAIRCRAFT PLACEMENTS ON THE SCHEMATICS. WHY AREN'T THEY FIRING?
WE DON'T HAVE THE COMBINATIONS TO TURN 'EM ON, BOSS!
WELL, YOU HAVE GUNS, DON'T YOU?
GO OUT AND SHOOT THEM!

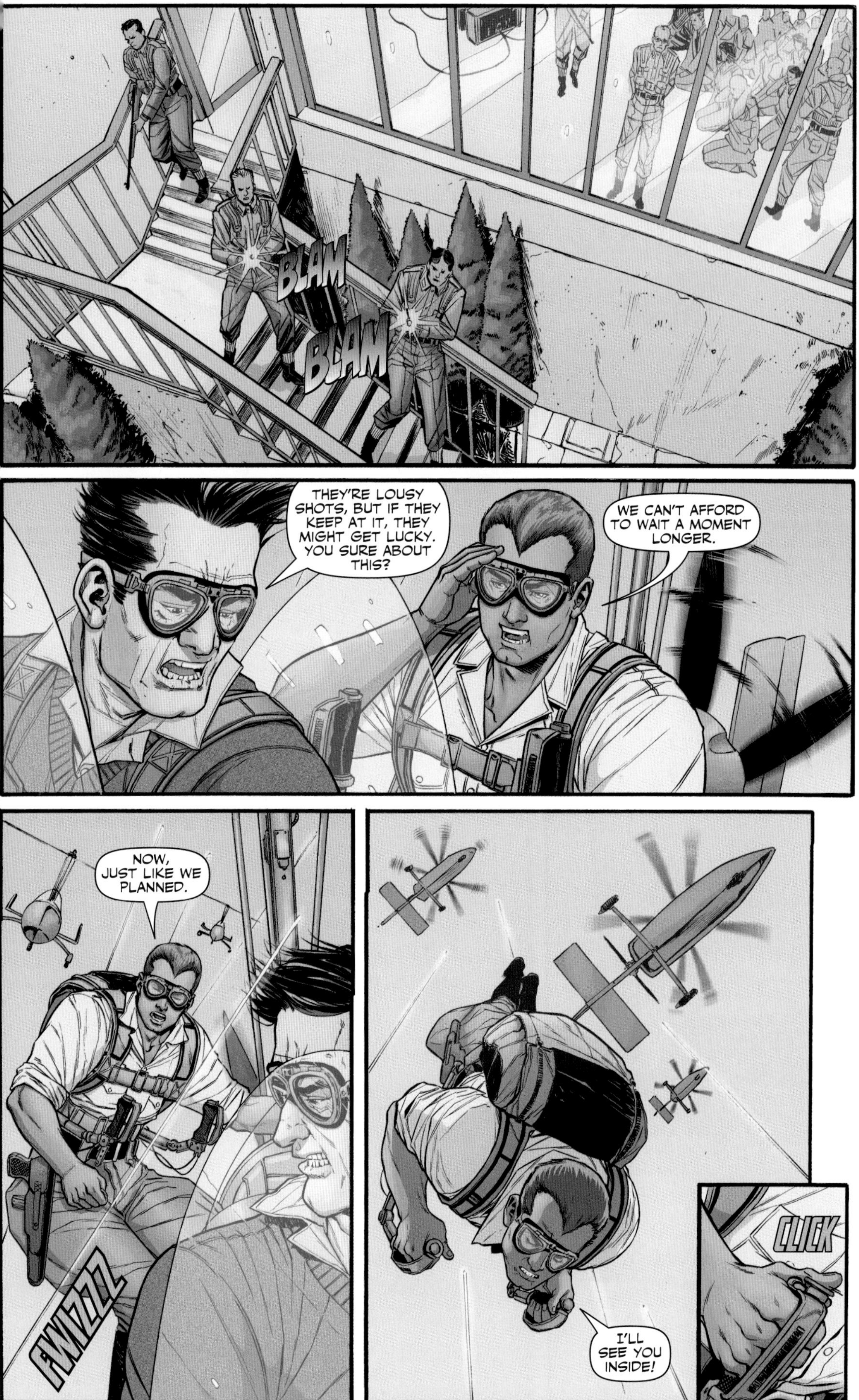
BLAM
BLAM
THEY'RE LOUSY SHOTS, BUT IF THEY KEEP AT IT, THEY MIGHT GET LUCKY. YOU SURE ABOUT THIS?
WE CAN'T AFFORD TO WAIT A MOMENT LONGER.
NOW, JUST LIKE WE PLANNED.
FWIZZZZ
I'LL SEE YOU INSIDE!
CLICK

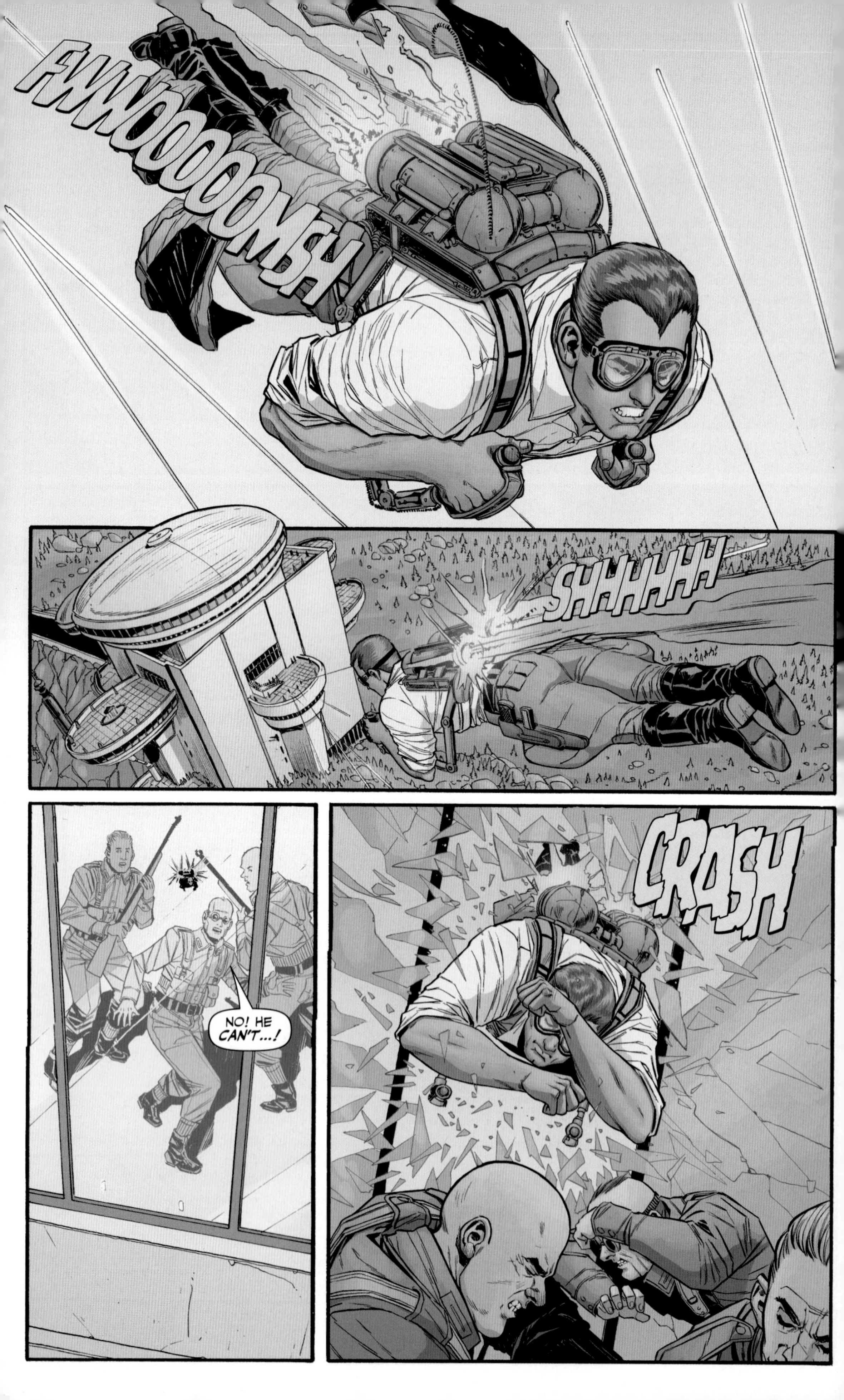
FWOOOOOOMSH
SHHHHHH
NO! HE CAN'T...!
CRASH

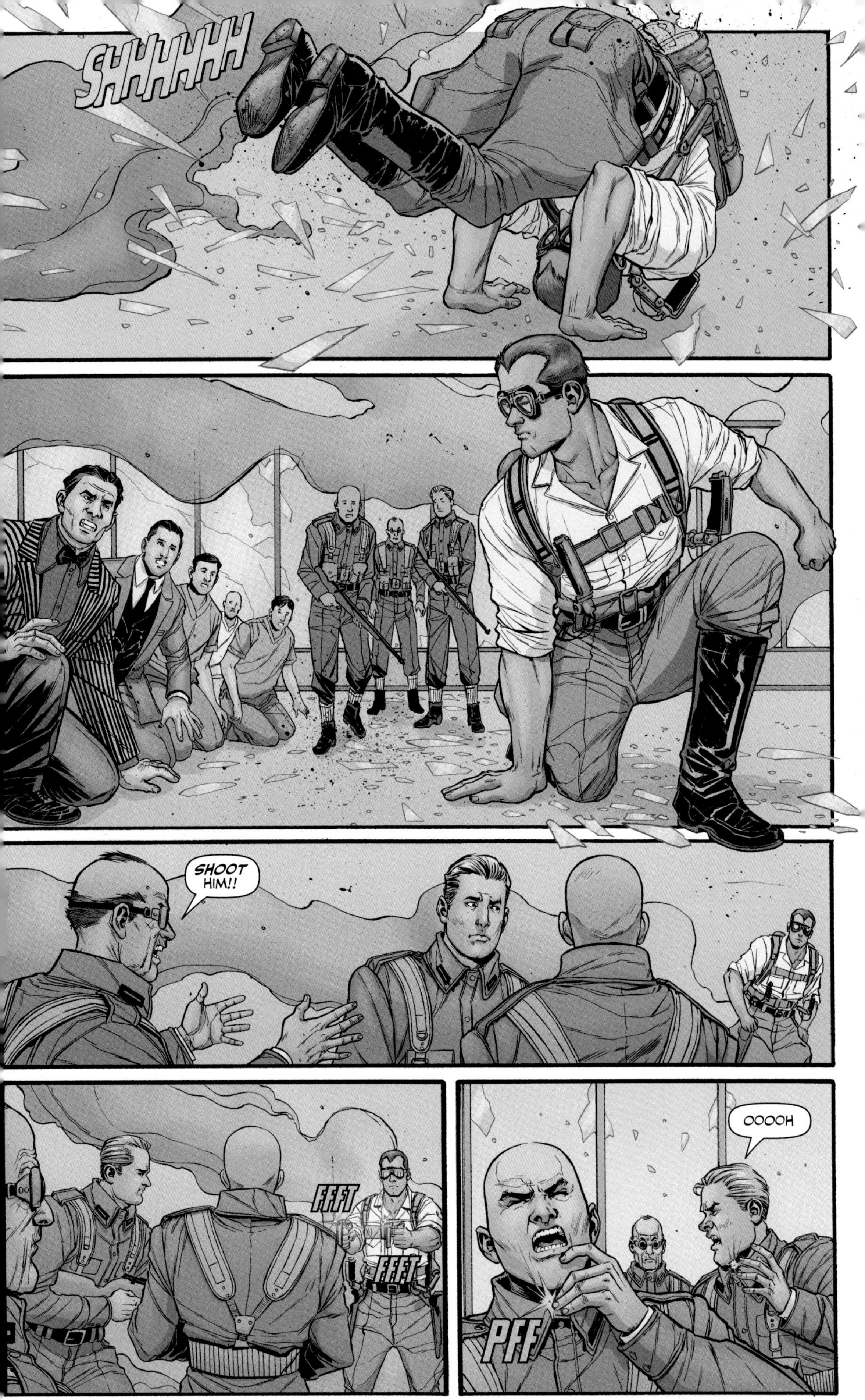
SHHHHHH
SHOOT HIM!!
FFFT
FFFT
PFF
OOOOH

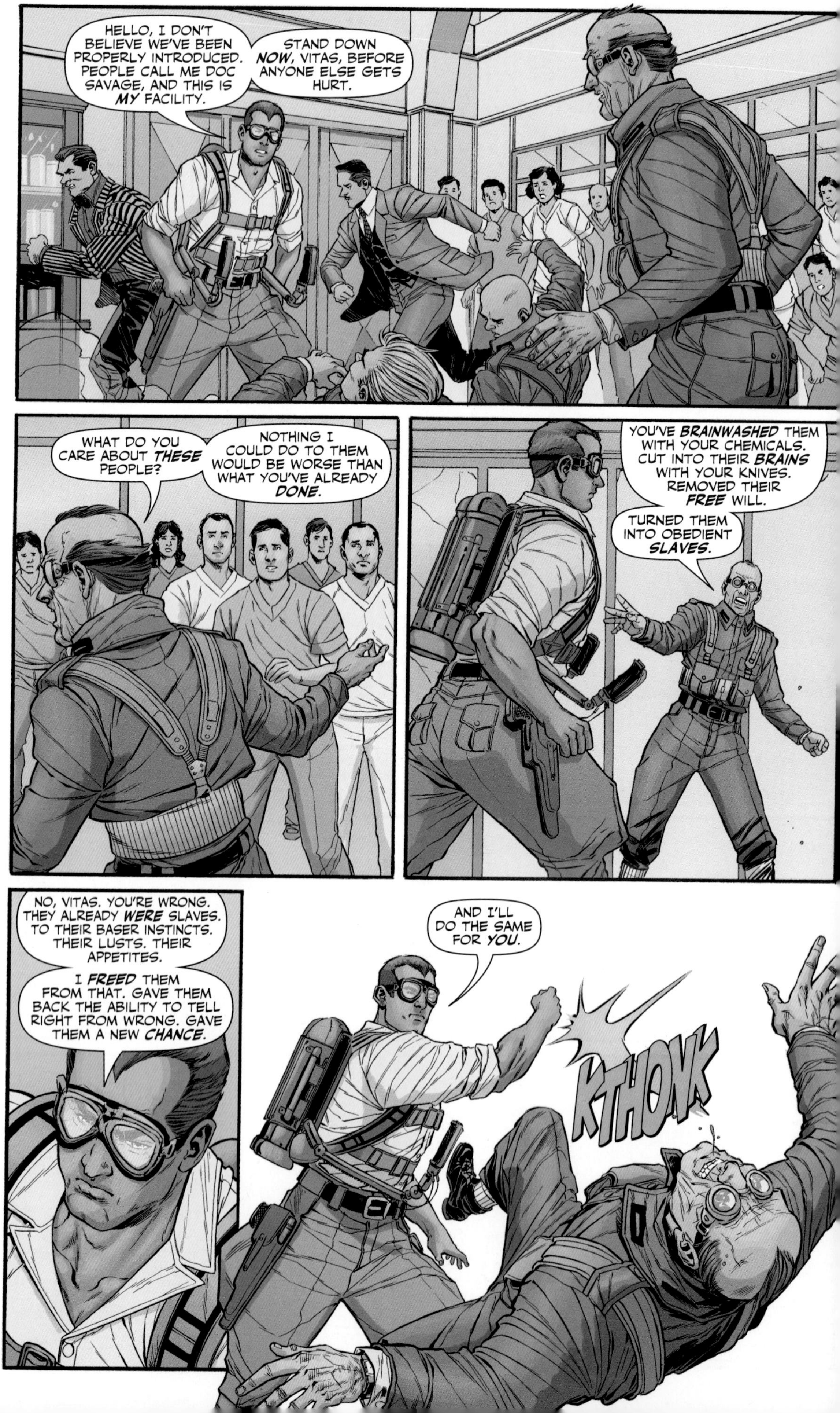
HELLO, I DON'T BELIEVE WE'VE BEEN PROPERLY INTRODUCED. PEOPLE CALL ME DOC SAVAGE, AND THIS IS *MY* FACILITY.
STAND DOWN *NOW*, VITAS, BEFORE ANYONE ELSE GETS HURT.
WHAT DO YOU CARE ABOUT *THESE* PEOPLE?
NOTHING I COULD DO TO THEM WOULD BE WORSE THAN WHAT YOU'VE ALREADY *DONE*.
YOU'VE *BRAINWASHED* THEM WITH YOUR CHEMICALS. CUT INTO THEIR *BRAINS* WITH YOUR KNIVES. REMOVED THEIR *FREE* WILL.
TURNED THEM INTO OBEDIENT *SLAVES*.
NO, VITAS. YOU'RE WRONG. THEY ALREADY *WERE* SLAVES. TO THEIR BASER INSTINCTS. THEIR LUSTS. THEIR APPETITES.
I *FREED* THEM FROM THAT. GAVE THEM BACK THE ABILITY TO TELL RIGHT FROM WRONG. GAVE THEM A NEW *CHANCE*.
AND I'LL DO THE SAME FOR *YOU*.
KTHONK

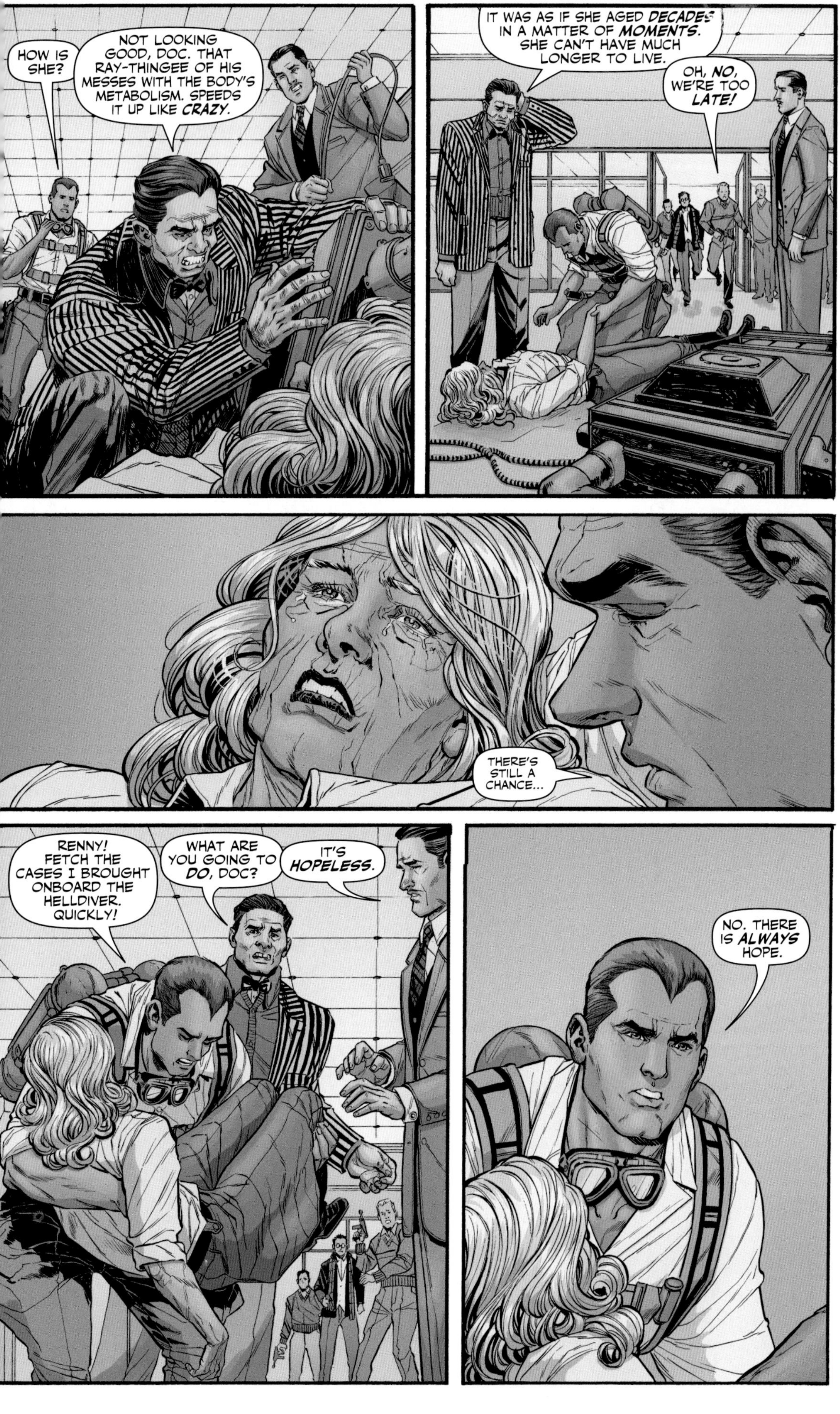
HOW IS SHE?
NOT LOOKING GOOD, DOC. THAT RAY-THINGEE OF HIS MESSES WITH THE BODY'S METABOLISM. SPEEDS IT UP LIKE CRAZY.
IT WAS AS IF SHE AGED DECADES IN A MATTER OF MOMENTS. SHE CAN'T HAVE MUCH LONGER TO LIVE.
OH, NO, WE'RE TOO LATE!
THERE'S STILL A CHANCE...
RENNY! FETCH THE CASES I BROUGHT ONBOARD THE HELLDIVER. QUICKLY!
WHAT ARE YOU GOING TO DO, DOC?
IT'S HOPELESS.
NO. THERE IS ALWAYS HOPE.

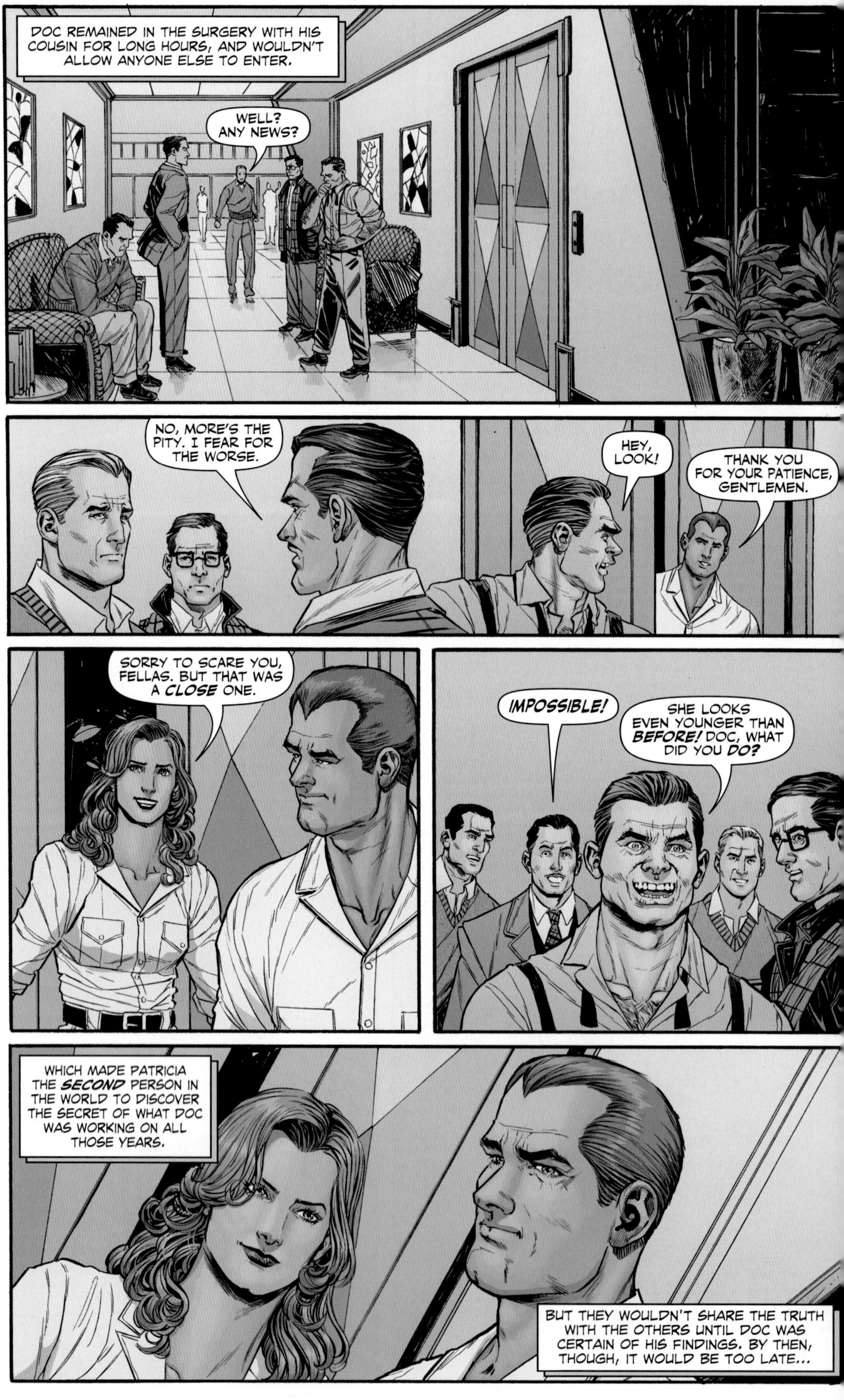

DOC REMAINED IN THE SURGERY WITH HIS COUSIN FOR LONG HOURS, AND WOULDN'T ALLOW ANYONE ELSE TO ENTER.
WELL? ANY NEWS?
NO, MORE'S THE PITY. I FEAR FOR THE WORSE.
HEY, LOOK!
THANK YOU FOR YOUR PATIENCE, GENTLEMEN.
SORRY TO SCARE YOU, FELLAS. BUT THAT WAS A CLOSE ONE.
IMPOSSIBLE!
SHE LOOKS EVEN YOUNGER THAN BEFORE! DOC, WHAT DID YOU DO?
WHICH MADE PATRICIA THE SECOND PERSON IN THE WORLD TO DISCOVER THE SECRET OF WHAT DOC WAS WORKING ON ALL THOSE YEARS.
BUT THEY WOULDN'T SHARE THE TRUTH WITH THE OTHERS UNTIL DOC WAS CERTAIN OF HIS FINDINGS. BY THEN, THOUGH, IT WOULD BE TOO LATE...

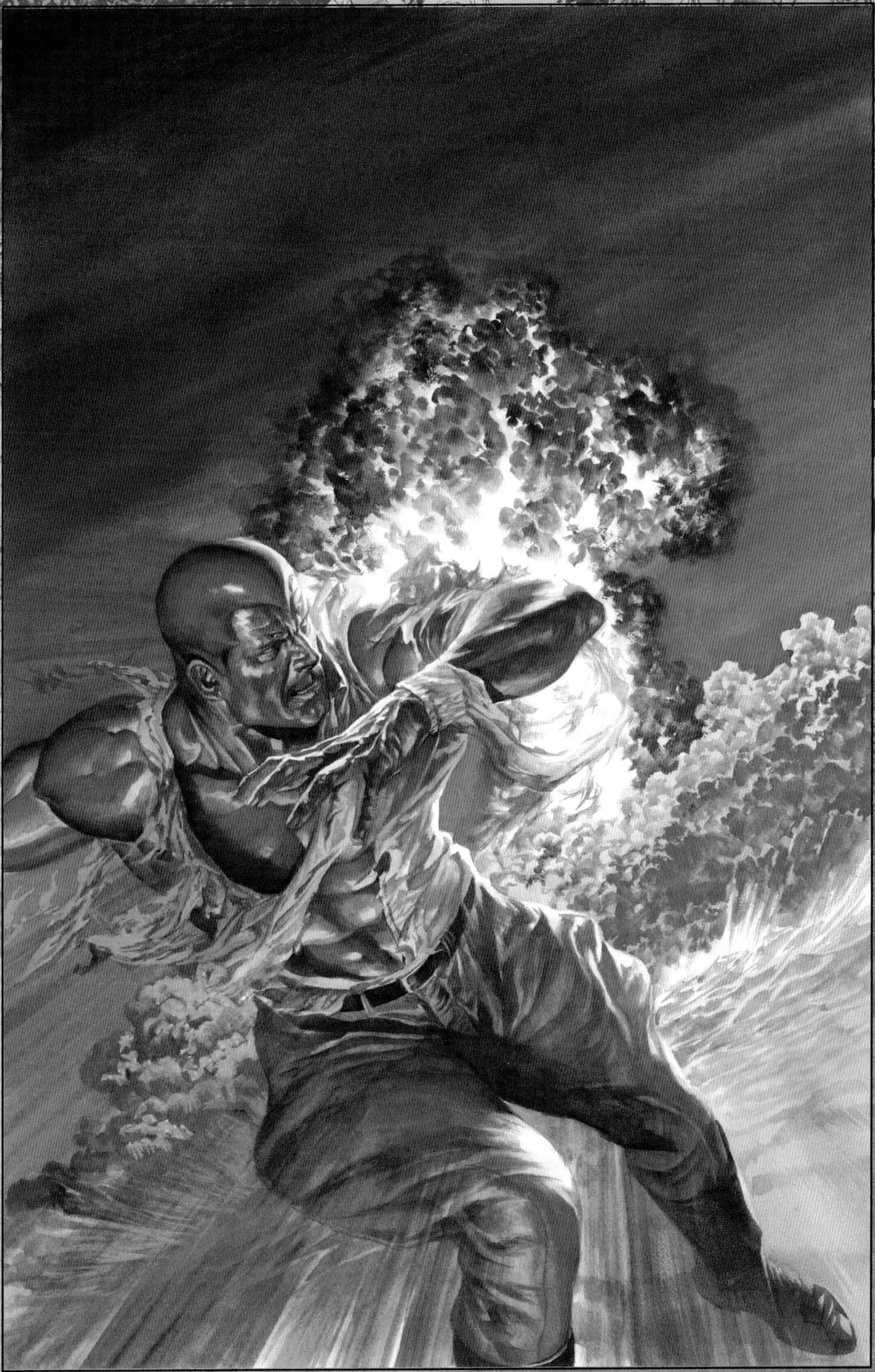

ISSUE #3 COVER
art by **ALEX ROSS**

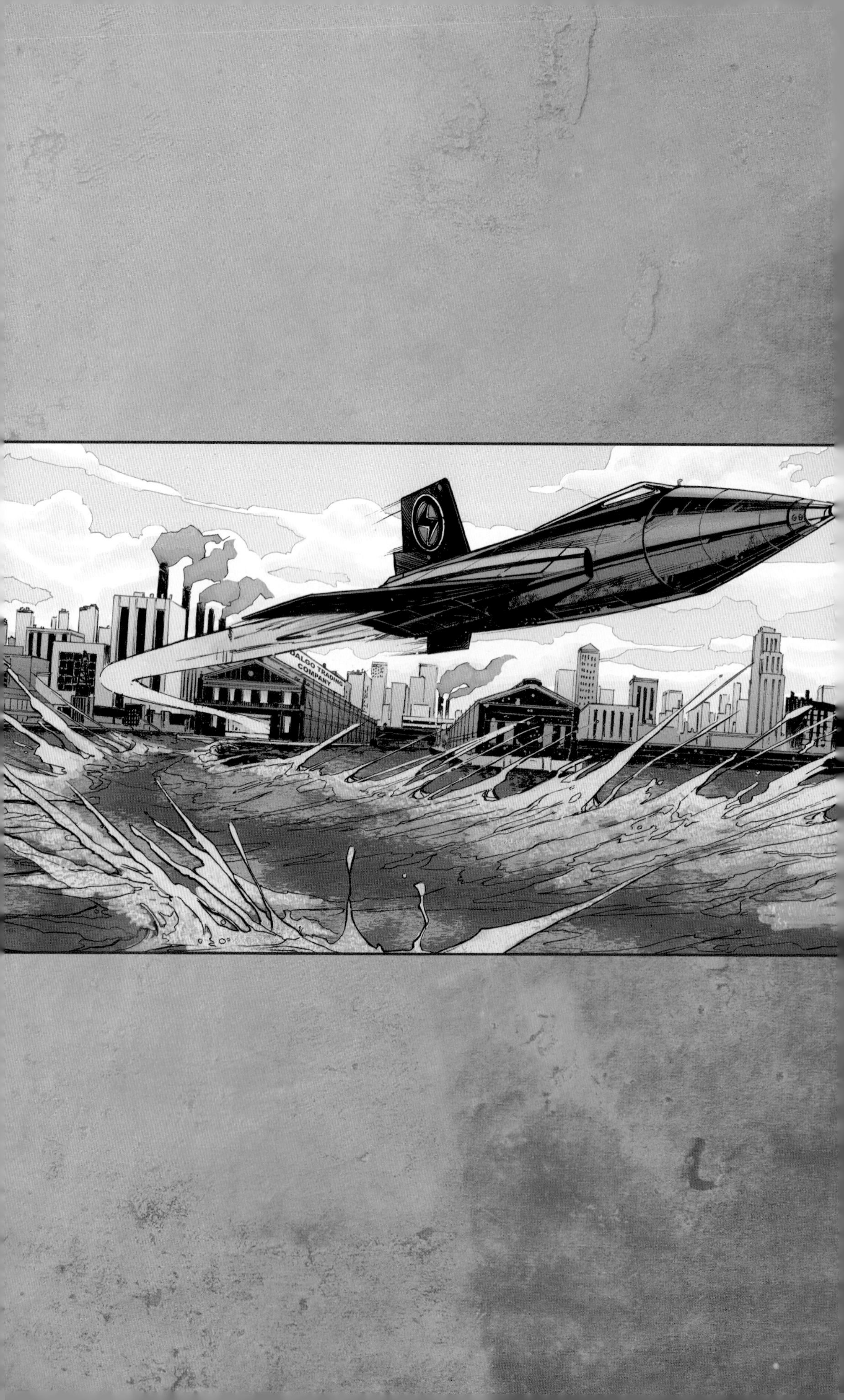
TRADING COMPANY

IN THE SPRING OF 1961, DOC SAVAGE DECIDED IT WAS FINALLY TIME TO REVEAL TO THE WORLD THE SECRET PROJECT HE'D BEGUN IN THE '30S.

THE PRESIDENT AND HIS CABINET WERE THE FIRST OUTSIDE OF DOC'S IMMEDIATE CIRCLE TO HEAR THE NEWS. THEY WERE UNDERSTANDABLY SKEPTICAL, AT FIRST.

WELL, AH, THIS IS A LITTLE HARD TO SWALLOW, SAVAGE. ARE YOU PUTTING US ON?

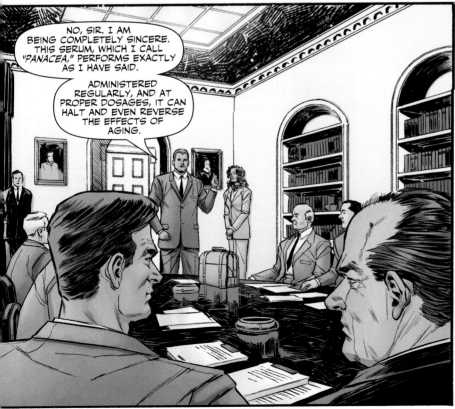

NO, SIR. I AM BEING COMPLETELY SINCERE. THIS SERUM, WHICH I CALL *"PANACEA,"* PERFORMS EXACTLY AS I HAVE SAID.

ADMINISTERED REGULARLY, AND AT PROPER DOSAGES, IT CAN HALT AND EVEN REVERSE THE EFFECTS OF AGING.

IT IS, IN ESSENCE, IMMORTALITY IN A BOTTLE.

IT IS A COMPOUND EXTRACTED FROM SILPHIUM, A PLANT WHICH ONLY GROWS ON THE ISLAND FORMERLY KNOWN AS FEAR CAY, NOW CALLED ORION STATION.

I HAVE CONDUCTED EXTENSIVE TRIALS ON MYSELF, SINCE I COULD NOT PUT ANOTHER PERSON AT RISK AS A TEST SUBJECT, AND I AM NOW CONFIDENT THAT THERE ARE NO DANGEROUS SIDE EFFECTS.

AT ORION STATION WE HAVE AMASSED QUANTITIES OF THE SERUM, WHICH WE WILL SOON BEGIN DISTRIBUTING FREE OF CHARGE TO HOSPITALS AROUND THE WORLD.

SOME GREETED THE ANNOUNCEMENT NOT WITH SKEPTICISM, BUT WITH CRITICISM.

IN ALL MY LIFE I'VE NEVER HEARD OF ANYTHING SO *IRRESPONSIBLE*.

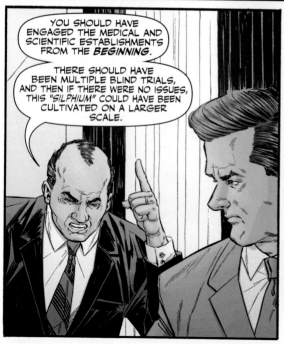

YOU SHOULD HAVE ENGAGED THE MEDICAL AND SCIENTIFIC ESTABLISHMENTS FROM THE *BEGINNING*.

THERE SHOULD HAVE BEEN MULTIPLE BLIND TRIALS, AND THEN IF THERE WERE NO ISSUES, THIS *"SILPHIUM"* COULD HAVE BEEN CULTIVATED ON A LARGER SCALE.

I'M SORRY, BUT I HAD TO BE *CERTAIN* THAT I WAS NOT PUTTING ANYONE ELSE'S LIFE AT RISK. THE STAKES WERE SIMPLY *TOO* HIGH.

OF *COURSE* NOW THAT THIS IS BEING MADE PUBLIC, WE CAN BEGIN THE PROCESS OF TRANSPLANTING SILPHIUM TO OTHER LOCATIONS FOR CULTIVATION.

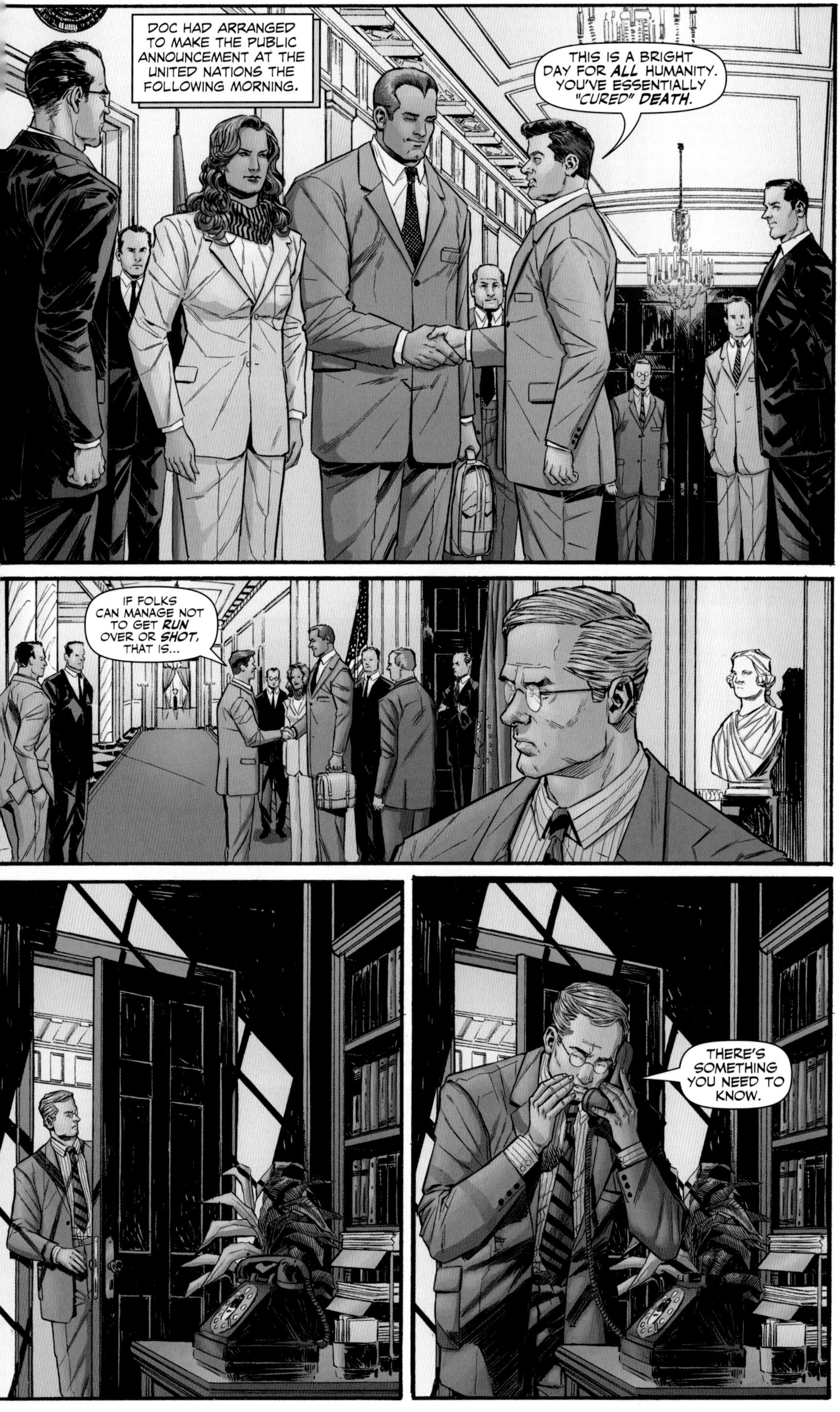
DOC HAD ARRANGED TO MAKE THE PUBLIC ANNOUNCEMENT AT THE UNITED NATIONS THE FOLLOWING MORNING.
THIS IS A BRIGHT DAY FOR ALL HUMANITY. YOU'VE ESSENTIALLY "CURED" DEATH.
IF FOLKS CAN MANAGE NOT TO GET RUN OVER OR SHOT, THAT IS...
THERE'S SOMETHING YOU NEED TO KNOW.

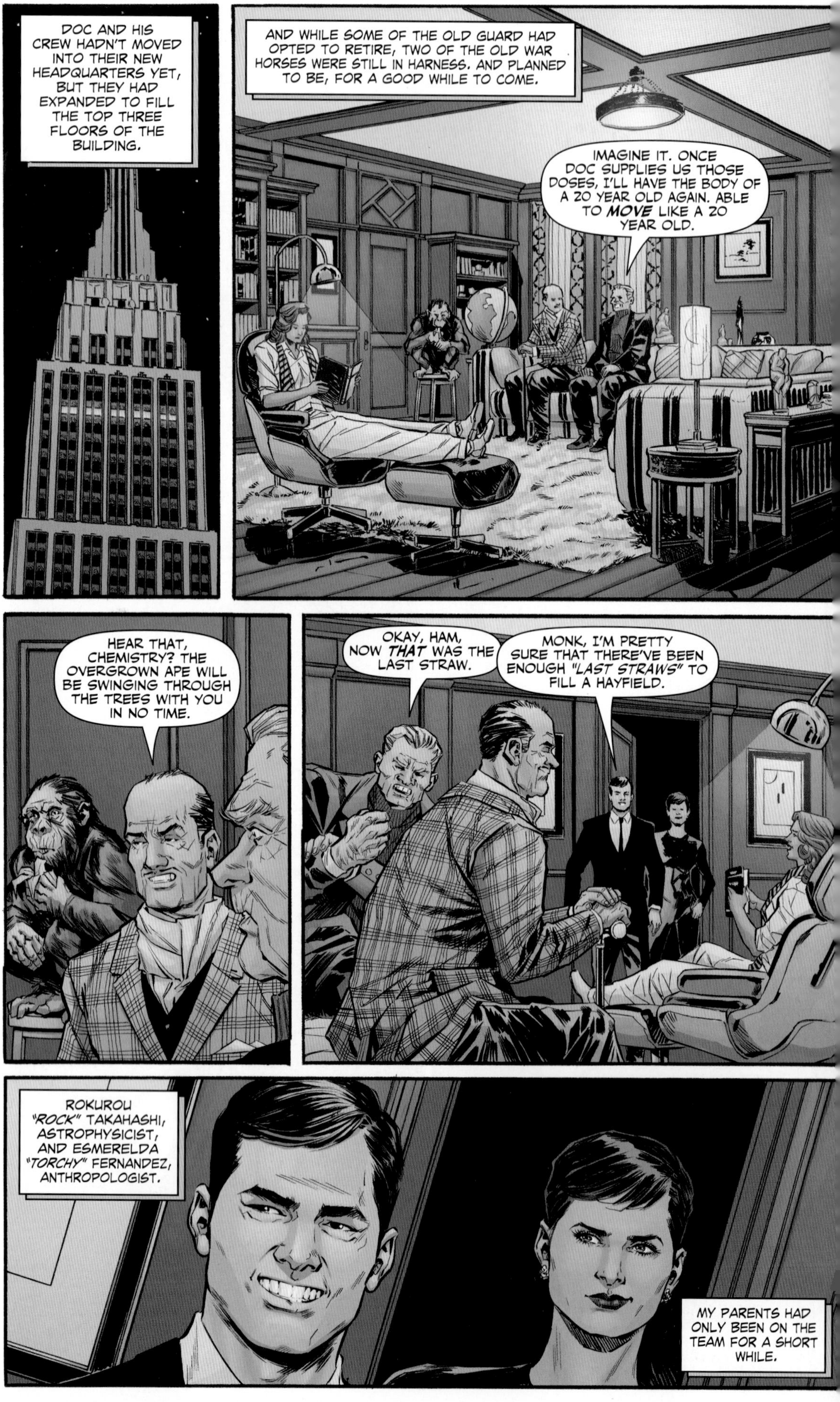

DOC AND HIS CREW HADN'T MOVED INTO THEIR NEW HEADQUARTERS YET, BUT THEY HAD EXPANDED TO FILL THE TOP THREE FLOORS OF THE BUILDING.
AND WHILE SOME OF THE OLD GUARD HAD OPTED TO RETIRE, TWO OF THE OLD WAR HORSES WERE STILL IN HARNESS. AND PLANNED TO BE, FOR A GOOD WHILE TO COME.
IMAGINE IT. ONCE DOC SUPPLIES US THOSE DOSES, I'LL HAVE THE BODY OF A 20 YEAR OLD AGAIN. ABLE TO *MOVE* LIKE A 20 YEAR OLD.
HEAR THAT, CHEMISTRY? THE OVERGROWN APE WILL BE SWINGING THROUGH THE TREES WITH YOU IN NO TIME.
OKAY, HAM, NOW *THAT* WAS THE LAST STRAW.
MONK, I'M PRETTY SURE THAT THERE'VE BEEN ENOUGH *"LAST STRAWS"* TO FILL A HAYFIELD.
ROKUROU *"ROCK"* TAKAHASHI, ASTROPHYSICIST, AND ESMERELDA *"TORCHY"* FERNANDEZ, ANTHROPOLOGIST.
MY PARENTS HAD ONLY BEEN ON THE TEAM FOR A SHORT WHILE.

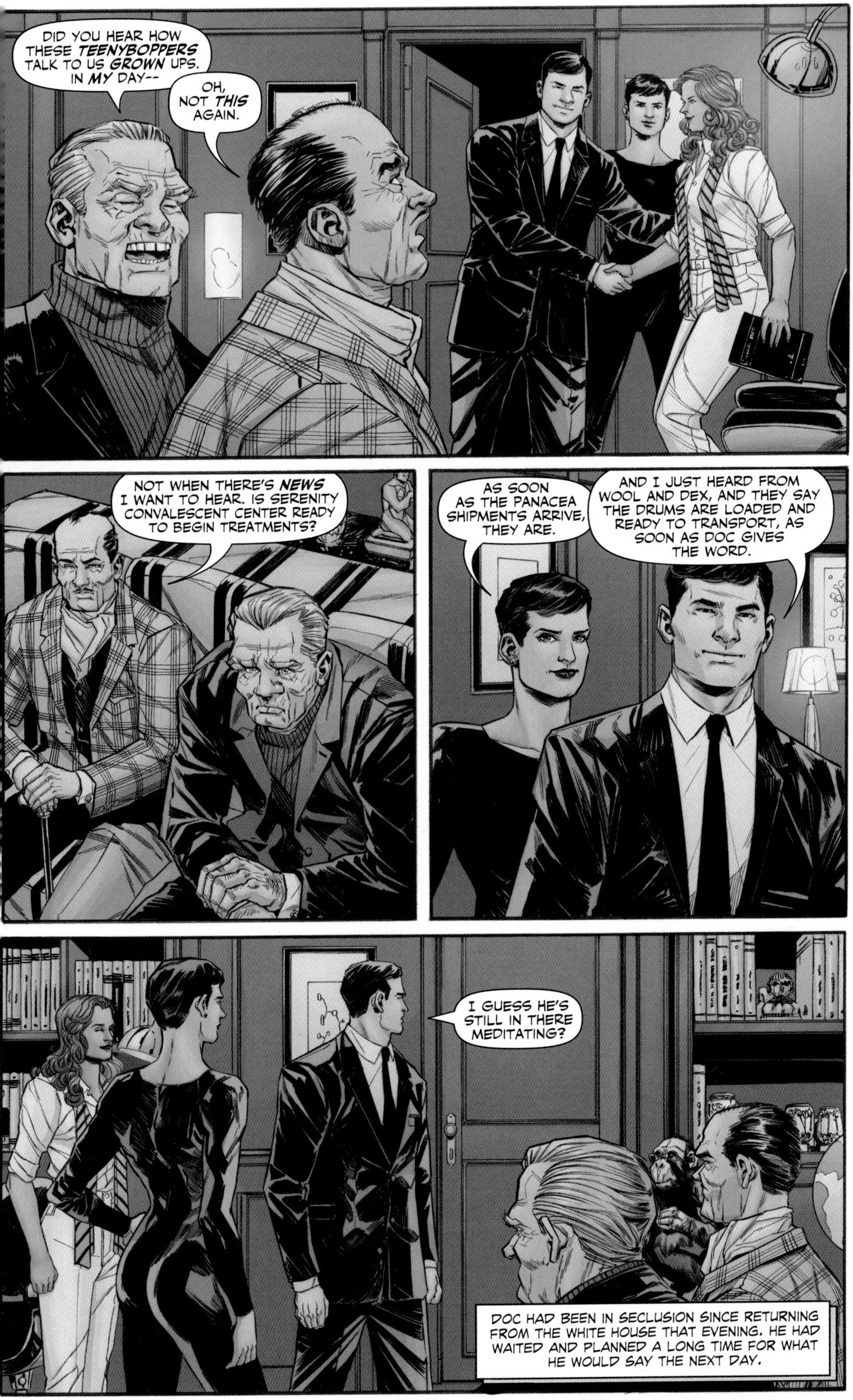
DID YOU HEAR HOW THESE *TEENYBOPPERS* TALK TO US *GROWN* UPS. IN *MY* DAY--
OH, NOT *THIS* AGAIN.
NOT WHEN THERE'S *NEWS* I WANT TO HEAR. IS SERENITY CONVALESCENT CENTER READY TO BEGIN TREATMENTS?
AS SOON AS THE PANACEA SHIPMENTS ARRIVE, THEY ARE.
AND I JUST HEARD FROM WOOL AND DEX, AND THEY SAY THE DRUMS ARE LOADED AND READY TO TRANSPORT, AS SOON AS DOC GIVES THE WORD.
I GUESS HE'S STILL IN THERE MEDITATING?
DOC HAD BEEN IN SECLUSION SINCE RETURNING FROM THE WHITE HOUSE THAT EVENING. HE HAD WAITED AND PLANNED A LONG TIME FOR WHAT HE WOULD SAY THE NEXT DAY.

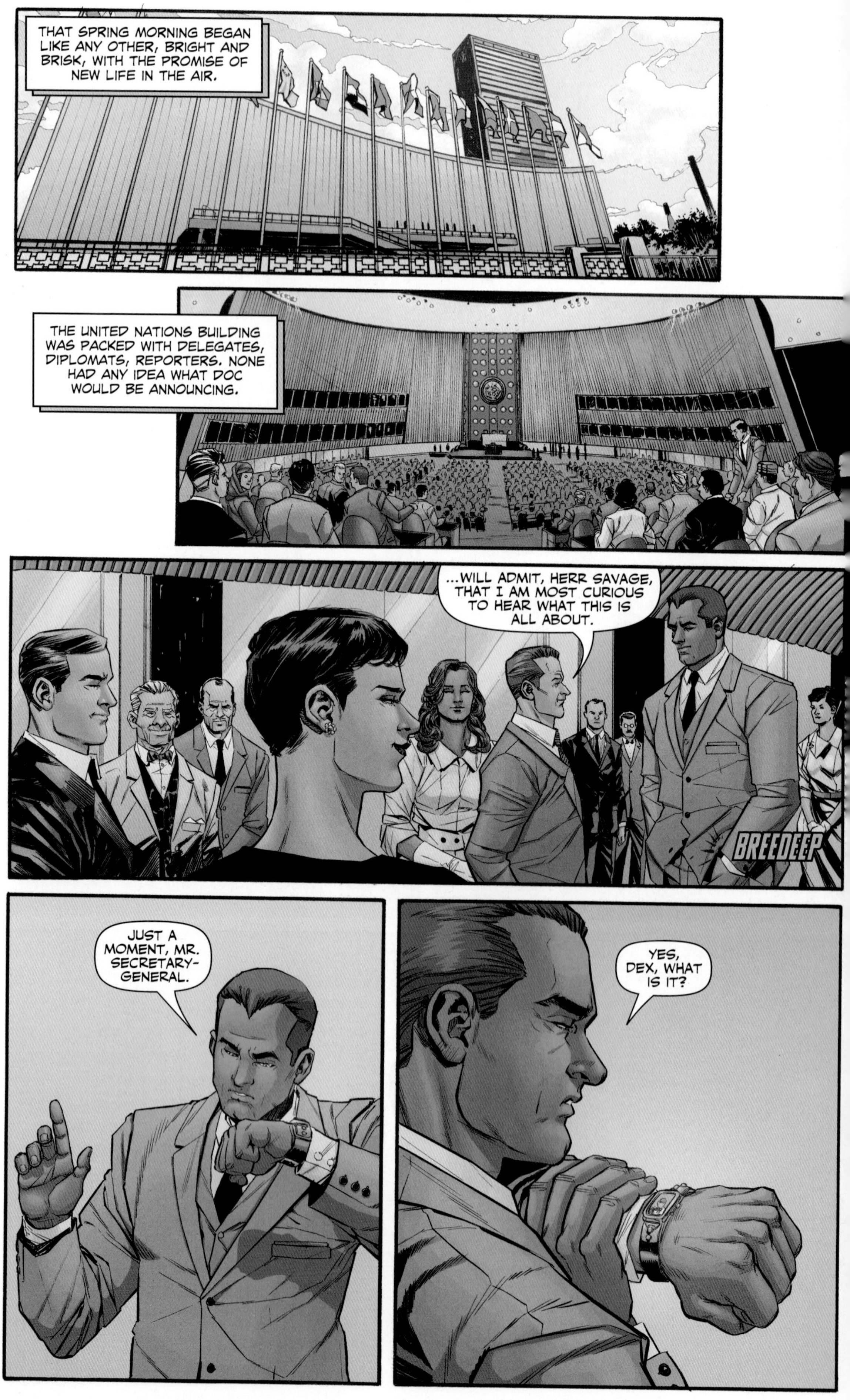
THAT SPRING MORNING BEGAN LIKE ANY OTHER, BRIGHT AND BRISK, WITH THE PROMISE OF NEW LIFE IN THE AIR.
THE UNITED NATIONS BUILDING WAS PACKED WITH DELEGATES, DIPLOMATS, REPORTERS. NONE HAD ANY IDEA WHAT DOC WOULD BE ANNOUNCING.
...WILL ADMIT, HERR SAVAGE, THAT I AM MOST CURIOUS TO HEAR WHAT THIS IS ALL ABOUT.
BREEDEEP
JUST A MOMENT, MR. SECRETARY-GENERAL.
YES, DEX, WHAT IS IT?

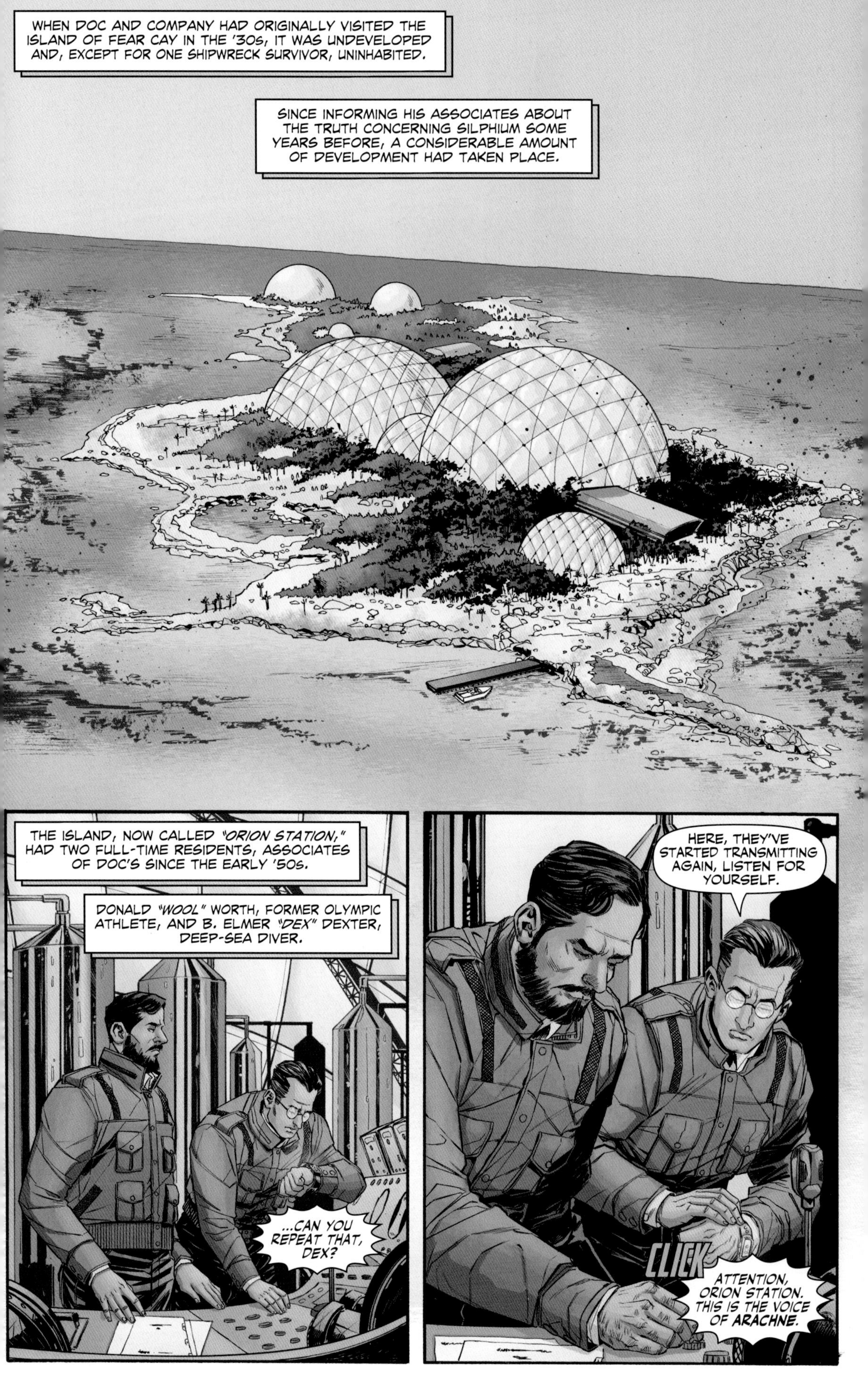
WHEN DOC AND COMPANY HAD ORIGINALLY VISITED THE ISLAND OF FEAR CAY IN THE '30s, IT WAS UNDEVELOPED AND, EXCEPT FOR ONE SHIPWRECK SURVIVOR, UNINHABITED.
SINCE INFORMING HIS ASSOCIATES ABOUT THE TRUTH CONCERNING SILPHIUM SOME YEARS BEFORE, A CONSIDERABLE AMOUNT OF DEVELOPMENT HAD TAKEN PLACE.
THE ISLAND, NOW CALLED "ORION STATION," HAD TWO FULL-TIME RESIDENTS, ASSOCIATES OF DOC'S SINCE THE EARLY '50s.
DONALD "WOOL" WORTH, FORMER OLYMPIC ATHLETE, AND B. ELMER "DEX" DEXTER, DEEP-SEA DIVER.
...CAN YOU REPEAT THAT, DEX?
HERE, THEY'VE STARTED TRANSMITTING AGAIN, LISTEN FOR YOURSELF.
CLICK
ATTENTION, ORION STATION. THIS IS THE VOICE OF ARACHNE.

BY SUNSET, YOU WILL DELIVER TO US ALL AVAILABLE QUANTITIES OF THE SUBSTANCE KNOWN AS "PANACEA."

IF YOU DO NOT, WE WILL LAUNCH A BALLISTIC MISSILE ARMED WITH A NUCLEAR WARHEAD AT NEW YORK CITY.

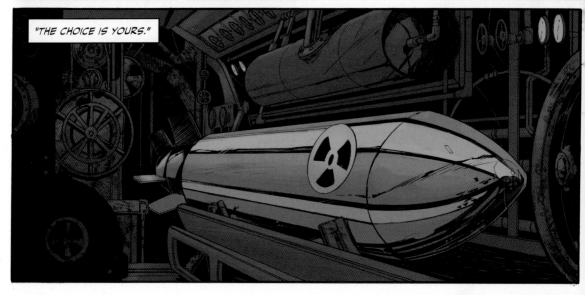

"THE CHOICE IS YOURS."

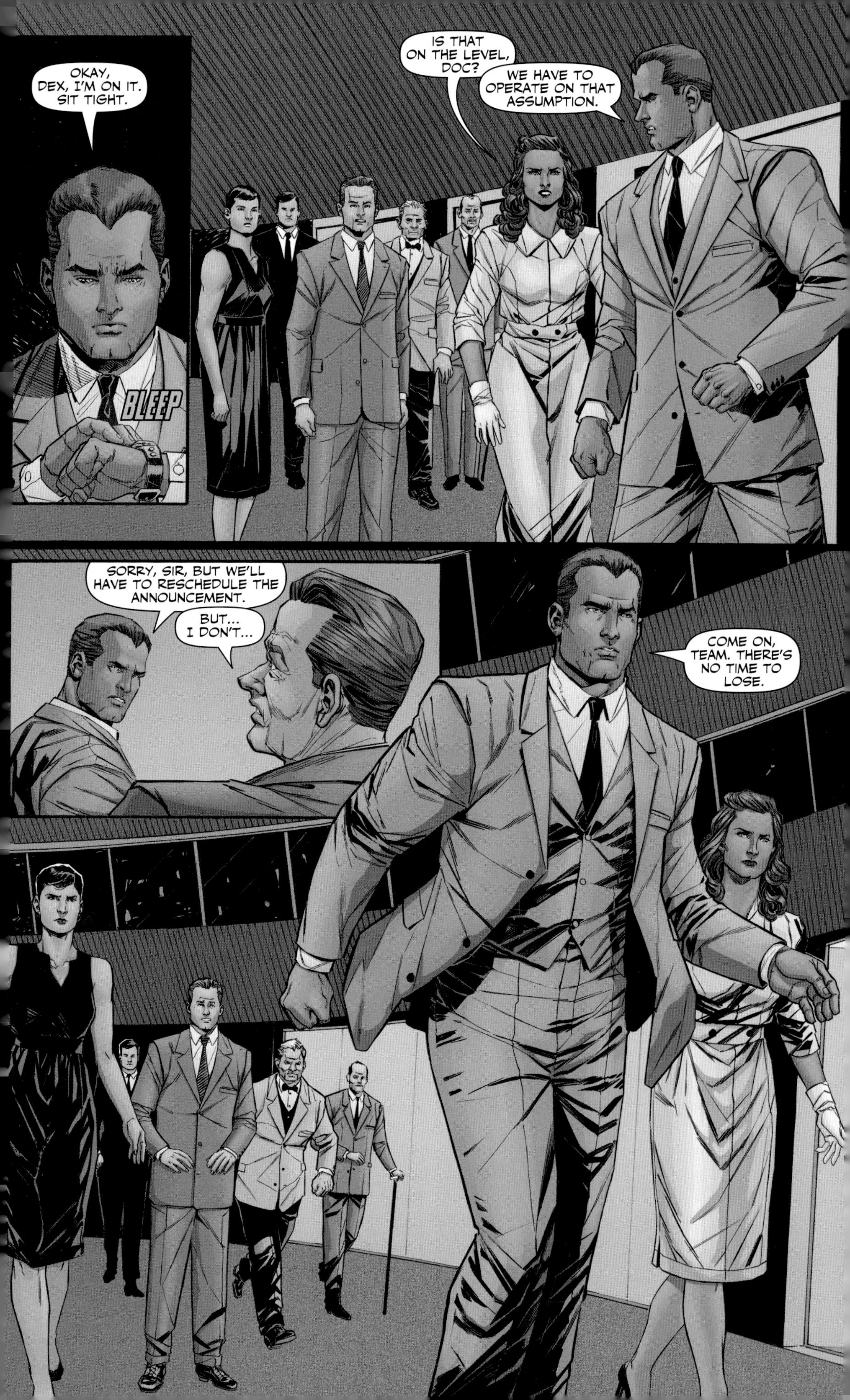
OKAY, DEX, I'M ON IT. SIT TIGHT.
BLEEP
IS THAT ON THE LEVEL, DOC?
WE HAVE TO OPERATE ON THAT ASSUMPTION.
SORRY, SIR, BUT WE'LL HAVE TO RESCHEDULE THE ANNOUNCEMENT.
BUT... I DON'T...
COME ON, TEAM. THERE'S NO TIME TO LOSE.

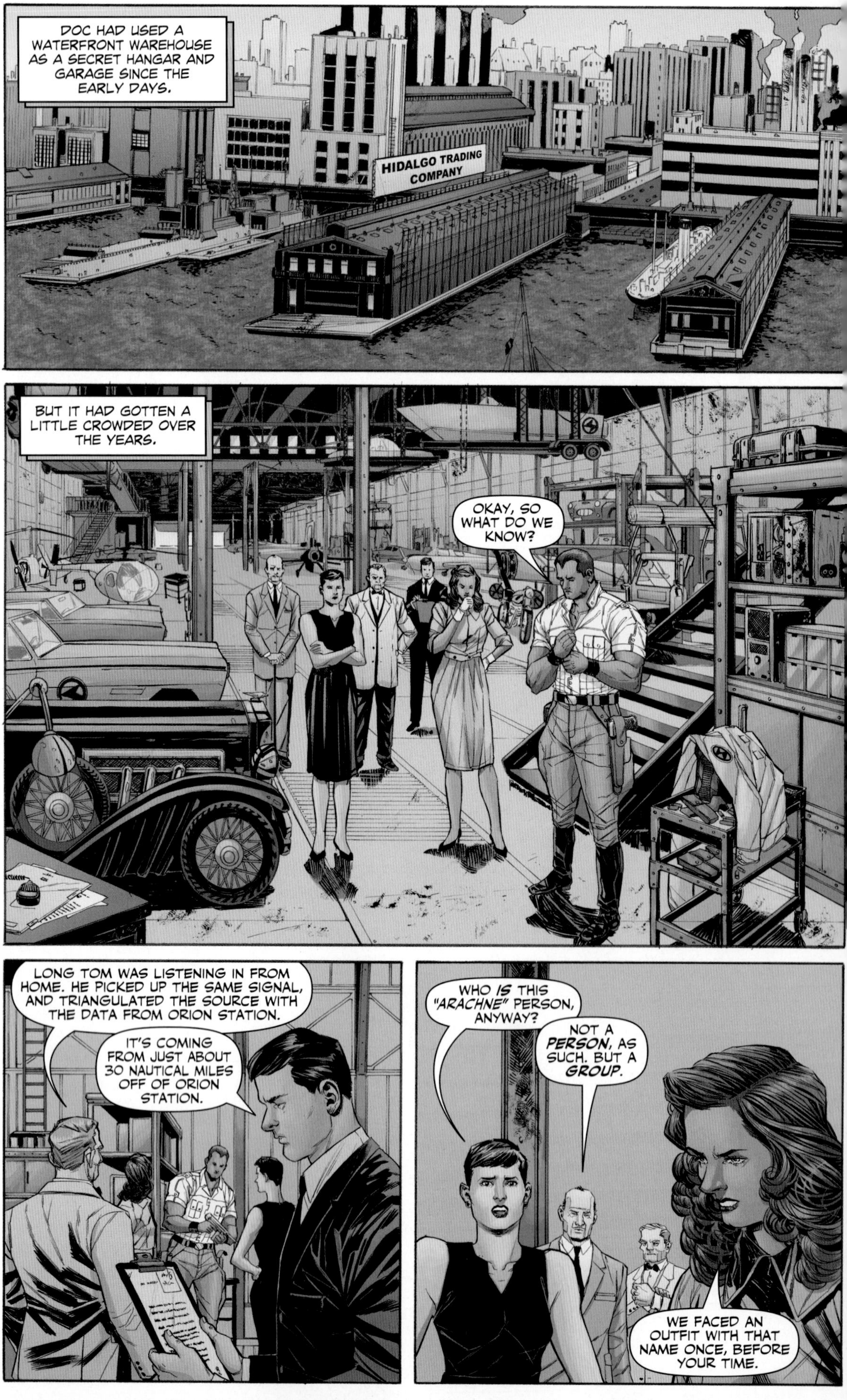
DOC HAD USED A WATERFRONT WAREHOUSE AS A SECRET HANGAR AND GARAGE SINCE THE EARLY DAYS.
HIDALGO TRADING COMPANY
BUT IT HAD GOTTEN A LITTLE CROWDED OVER THE YEARS.
OKAY, SO WHAT DO WE KNOW?
LONG TOM WAS LISTENING IN FROM HOME. HE PICKED UP THE SAME SIGNAL, AND TRIANGULATED THE SOURCE WITH THE DATA FROM ORION STATION.
IT'S COMING FROM JUST ABOUT 30 NAUTICAL MILES OFF OF ORION STATION.
WHO *IS* THIS "*ARACHNE*" PERSON, ANYWAY?
NOT A *PERSON*, AS SUCH. BUT A *GROUP*.
WE FACED AN OUTFIT WITH THAT NAME ONCE, BEFORE YOUR TIME.

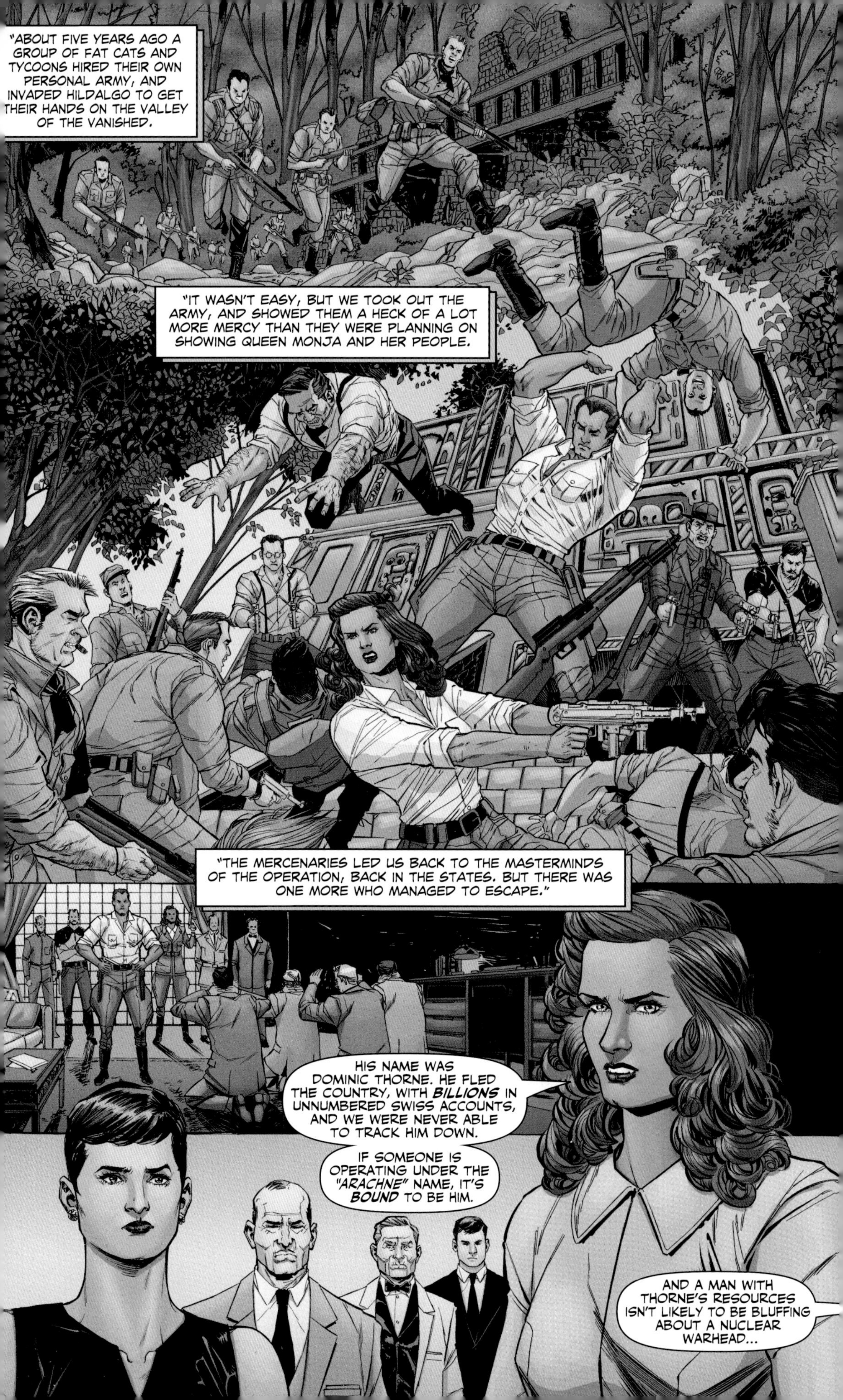
"ABOUT FIVE YEARS AGO A GROUP OF FAT CATS AND TYCOONS HIRED THEIR OWN PERSONAL ARMY, AND INVADED HILDALGO TO GET THEIR HANDS ON THE VALLEY OF THE VANISHED.
"IT WASN'T EASY, BUT WE TOOK OUT THE ARMY, AND SHOWED THEM A HECK OF A LOT MORE MERCY THAN THEY WERE PLANNING ON SHOWING QUEEN MONJA AND HER PEOPLE.
"THE MERCENARIES LED US BACK TO THE MASTERMINDS OF THE OPERATION, BACK IN THE STATES. BUT THERE WAS ONE MORE WHO MANAGED TO ESCAPE."
HIS NAME WAS DOMINIC THORNE. HE FLED THE COUNTRY, WITH BILLIONS IN UNNUMBERED SWISS ACCOUNTS, AND WE WERE NEVER ABLE TO TRACK HIM DOWN.
IF SOMEONE IS OPERATING UNDER THE "ARACHNE" NAME, IT'S BOUND TO BE HIM.
AND A MAN WITH THORNE'S RESOURCES ISN'T LIKELY TO BE BLUFFING ABOUT A NUCLEAR WARHEAD...

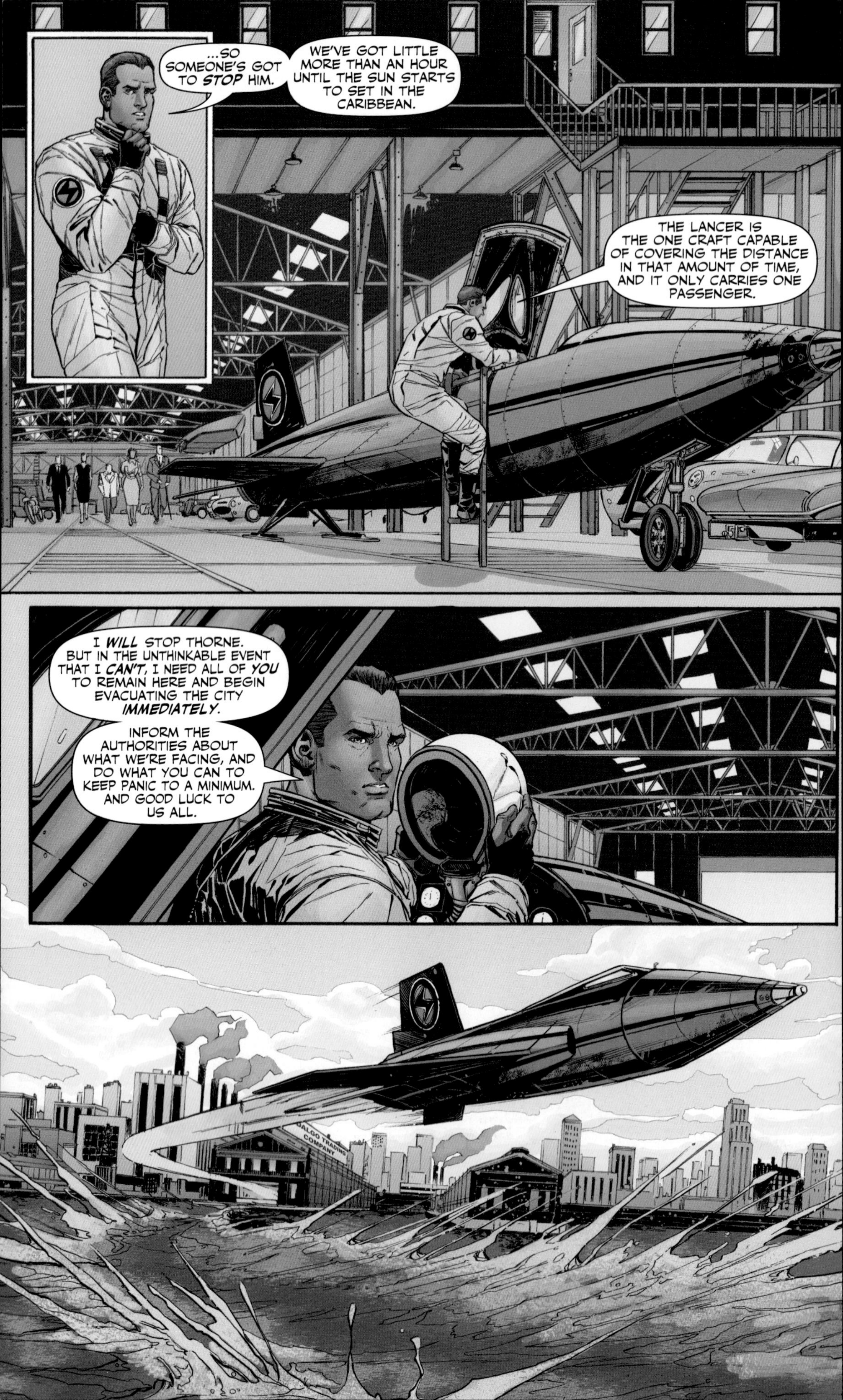
...SO SOMEONE'S GOT TO STOP HIM.
WE'VE GOT LITTLE MORE THAN AN HOUR UNTIL THE SUN STARTS TO SET IN THE CARIBBEAN.
THE LANCER IS THE ONE CRAFT CAPABLE OF COVERING THE DISTANCE IN THAT AMOUNT OF TIME, AND IT ONLY CARRIES ONE PASSENGER.
I WILL STOP THORNE. BUT IN THE UNTHINKABLE EVENT THAT I CAN'T, I NEED ALL OF YOU TO REMAIN HERE AND BEGIN EVACUATING THE CITY IMMEDIATELY.
INFORM THE AUTHORITIES ABOUT WHAT WE'RE FACING, AND DO WHAT YOU CAN TO KEEP PANIC TO A MINIMUM. AND GOOD LUCK TO US ALL.

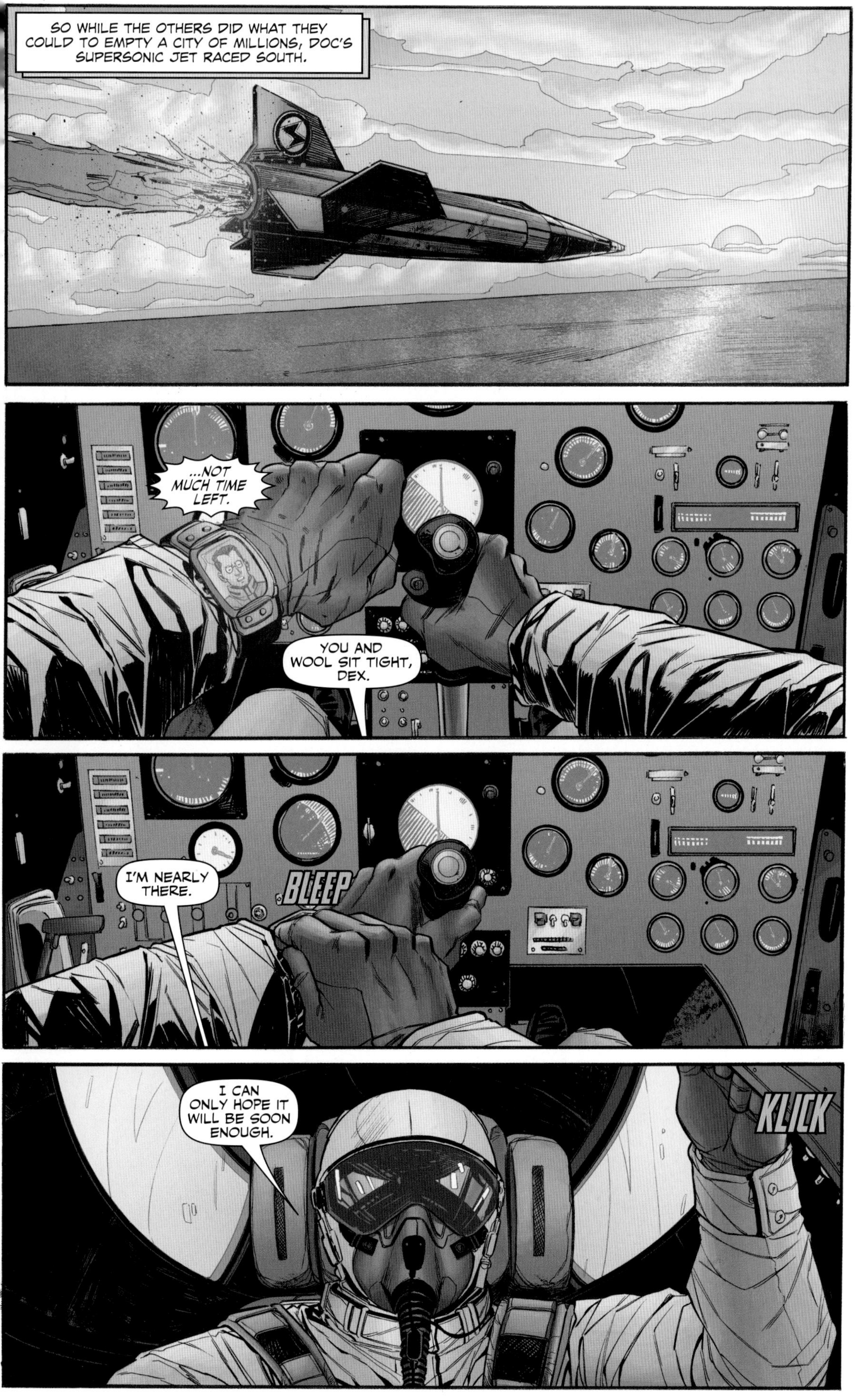
SO WHILE THE OTHERS DID WHAT THEY COULD TO EMPTY A CITY OF MILLIONS, DOC'S SUPERSONIC JET RACED SOUTH.
...NOT MUCH TIME LEFT.
YOU AND WOOL SIT TIGHT, DEX.
I'M NEARLY THERE.
BLEEP
I CAN ONLY HOPE IT WILL BE SOON ENOUGH.
KLICK

DOC HAD BASED THE LANCER ON THE X-15 DEVELOPED BY NASA AND THE US AIR FORCE A FEW YEARS BEFORE...

RRRRRVVVT

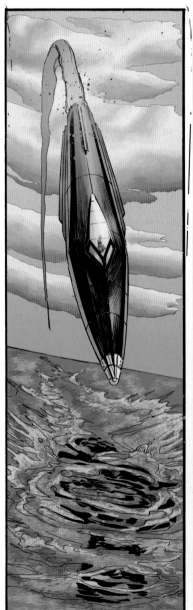

SPLASH

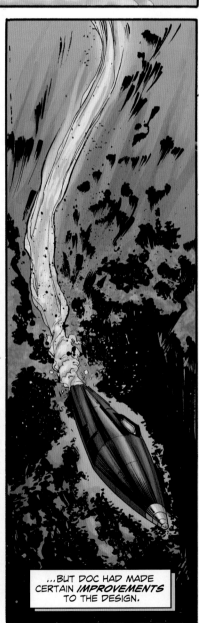

...BUT DOC HAD MADE CERTAIN *IMPROVEMENTS* TO THE DESIGN.

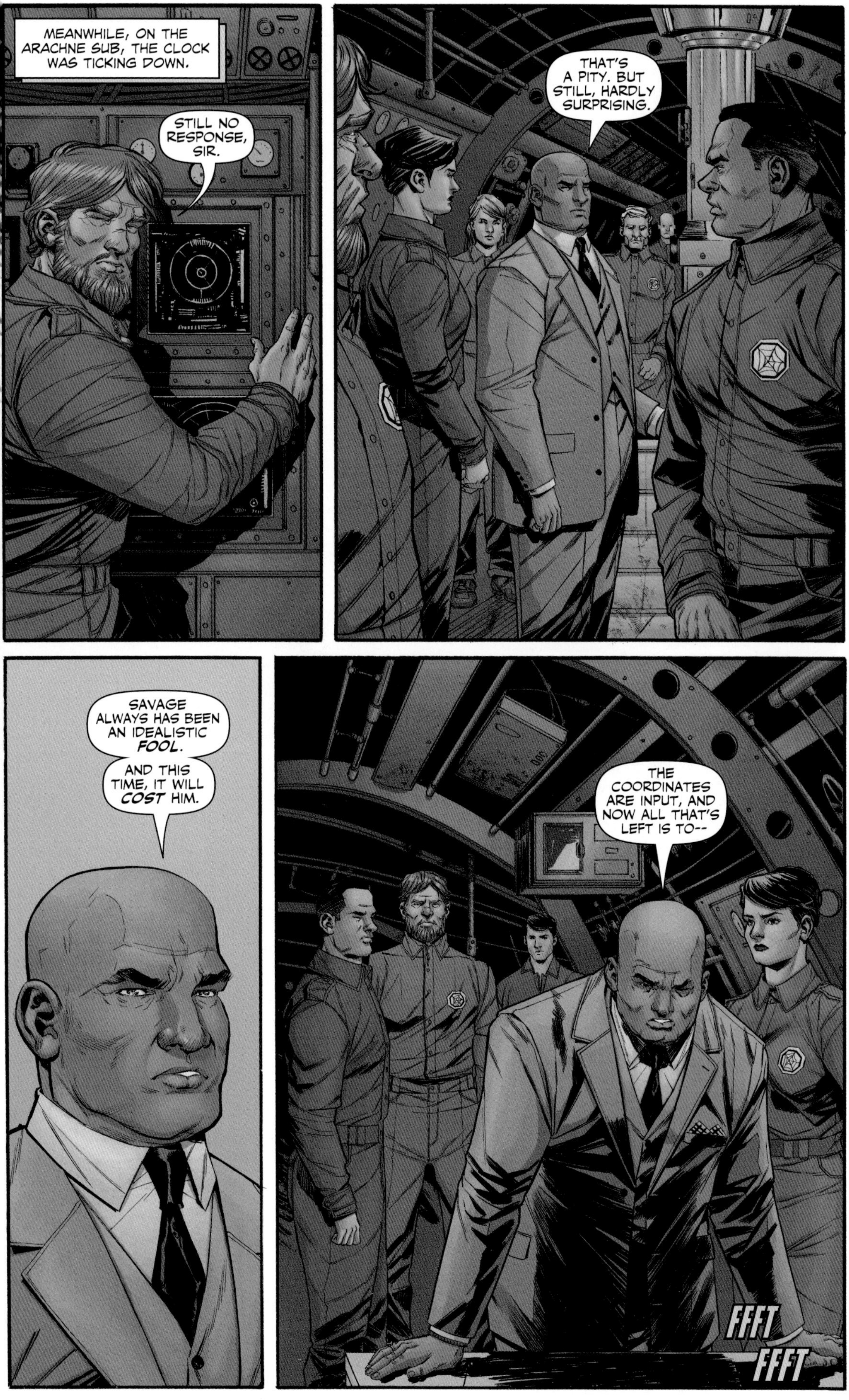
MEANWHILE, ON THE ARACHNE SUB, THE CLOCK WAS TICKING DOWN.
STILL NO RESPONSE, SIR.
THAT'S A PITY. BUT STILL, HARDLY SURPRISING.
SAVAGE ALWAYS HAS BEEN AN IDEALISTIC FOOL.
AND THIS TIME, IT WILL COST HIM.
THE COORDINATES ARE INPUT, AND NOW ALL THAT'S LEFT IS TO--
FFFT
FFFT

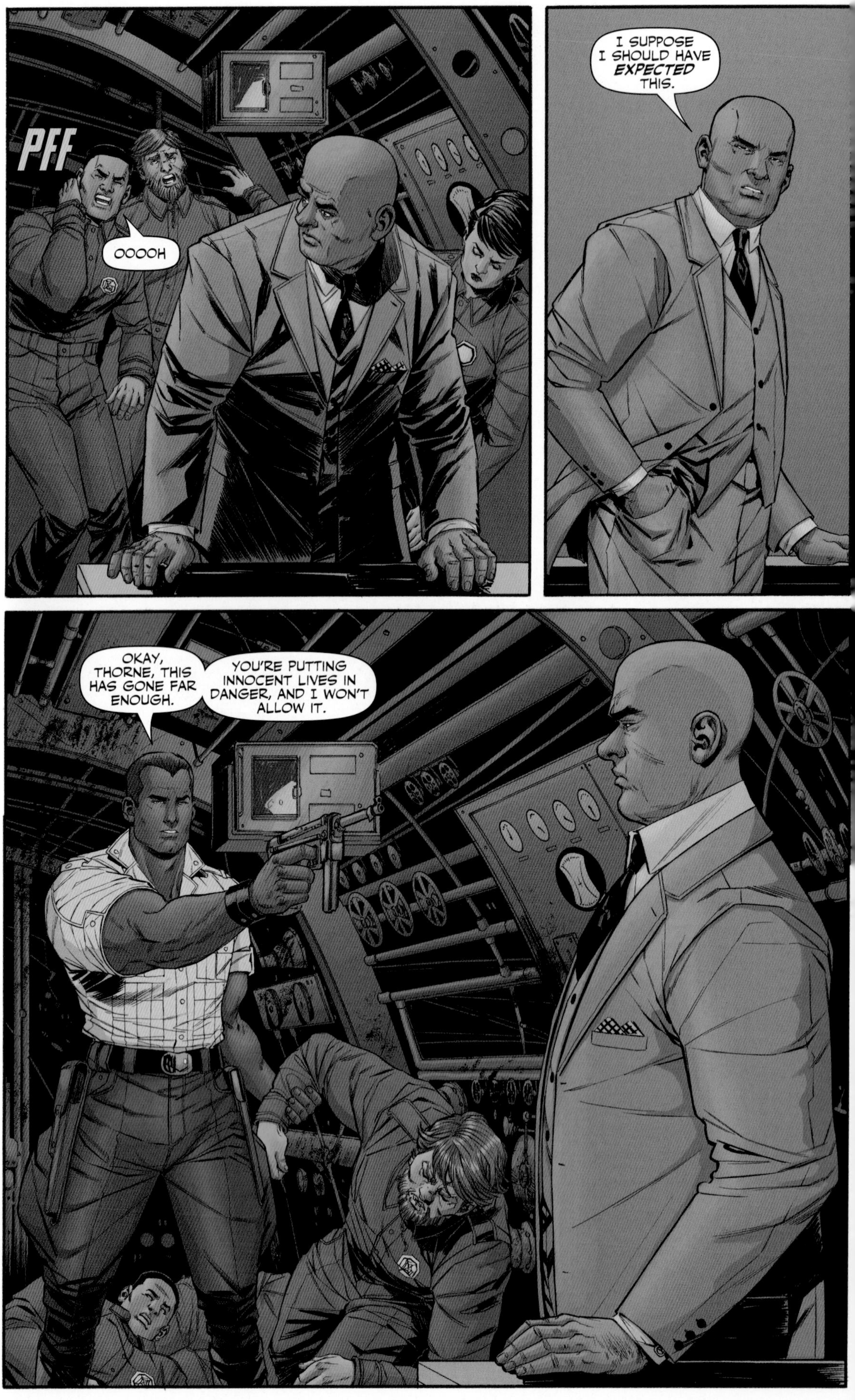
PFF
OOOOH
I SUPPOSE I SHOULD HAVE EXPECTED THIS.
OKAY, THORNE, THIS HAS GONE FAR ENOUGH.
YOU'RE PUTTING INNOCENT LIVES IN DANGER, AND I WON'T ALLOW IT.

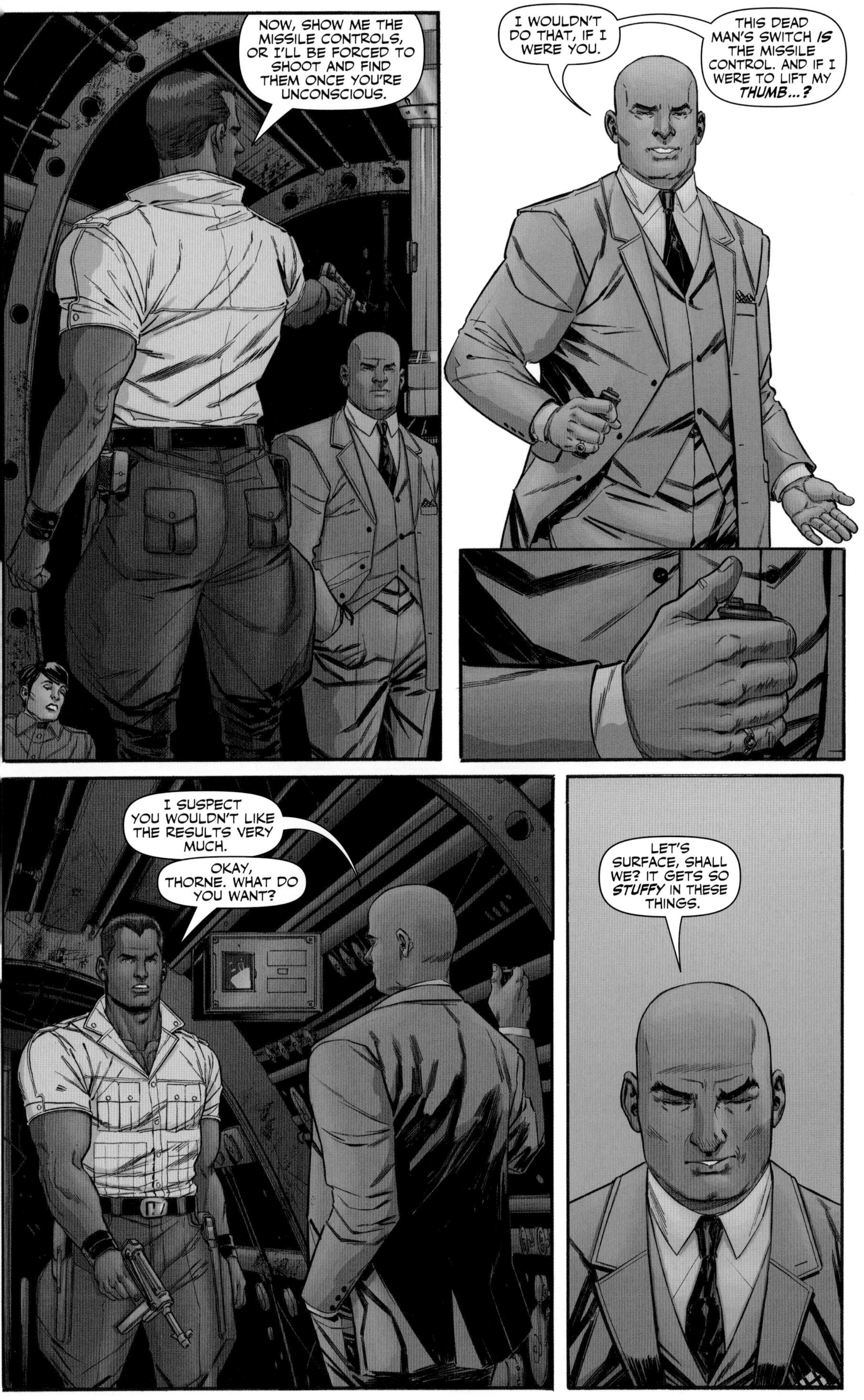
NOW, SHOW ME THE MISSILE CONTROLS, OR I'LL BE FORCED TO SHOOT AND FIND THEM ONCE YOU'RE UNCONSCIOUS.
I WOULDN'T DO THAT, IF I WERE YOU.
THIS DEAD MAN'S SWITCH *IS* THE MISSILE CONTROL. AND IF I WERE TO LIFT MY *THUMB*...?
I SUSPECT YOU WOULDN'T LIKE THE RESULTS VERY MUCH.
OKAY, THORNE. WHAT DO YOU WANT?
LET'S SURFACE, SHALL WE? IT GETS SO *STUFFY* IN THESE THINGS.

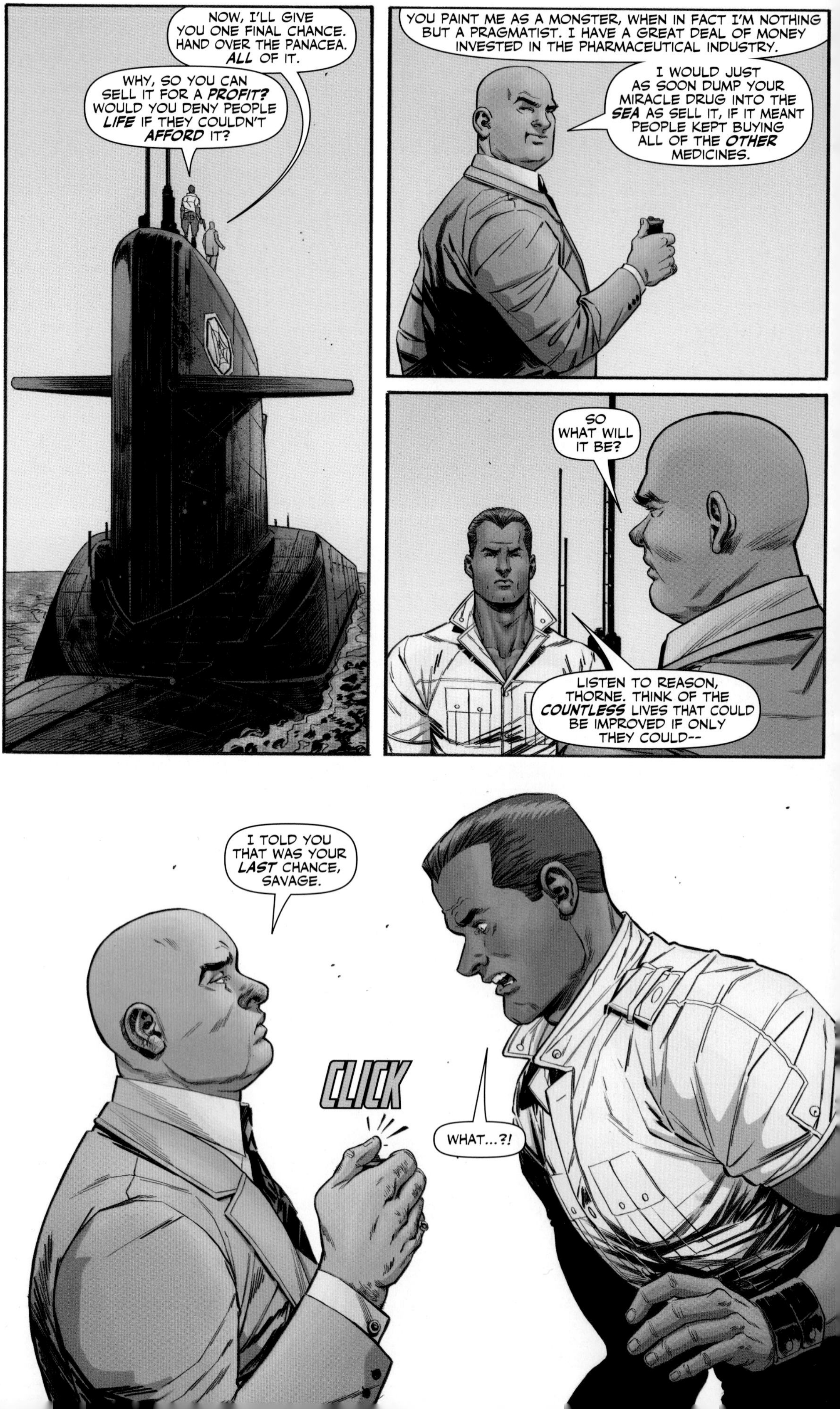

NOW, I'LL GIVE YOU ONE FINAL CHANCE. HAND OVER THE PANACEA. ALL OF IT.
WHY, SO YOU CAN SELL IT FOR A PROFIT? WOULD YOU DENY PEOPLE LIFE IF THEY COULDN'T AFFORD IT?
YOU PAINT ME AS A MONSTER, WHEN IN FACT I'M NOTHING BUT A PRAGMATIST. I HAVE A GREAT DEAL OF MONEY INVESTED IN THE PHARMACEUTICAL INDUSTRY.
I WOULD JUST AS SOON DUMP YOUR MIRACLE DRUG INTO THE SEA AS SELL IT, IF IT MEANT PEOPLE KEPT BUYING ALL OF THE OTHER MEDICINES.
SO WHAT WILL IT BE?
LISTEN TO REASON, THORNE. THINK OF THE COUNTLESS LIVES THAT COULD BE IMPROVED IF ONLY THEY COULD--
I TOLD YOU THAT WAS YOUR LAST CHANCE, SAVAGE.
CLICK
WHAT...?!

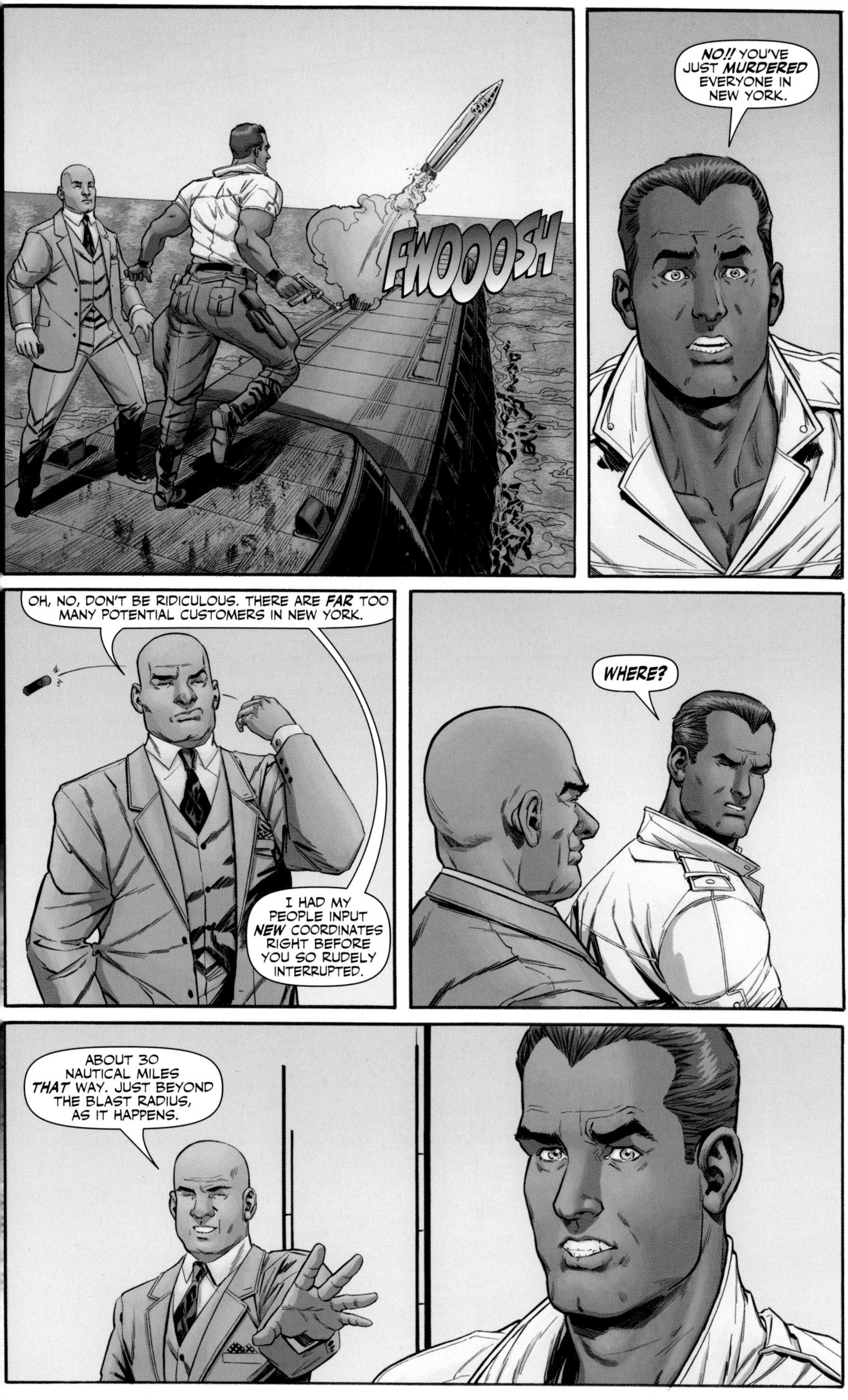
FWOOOSH
NO!! YOU'VE JUST MURDERED EVERYONE IN NEW YORK.
OH, NO, DON'T BE RIDICULOUS. THERE ARE FAR TOO MANY POTENTIAL CUSTOMERS IN NEW YORK.
I HAD MY PEOPLE INPUT NEW COORDINATES RIGHT BEFORE YOU SO RUDELY INTERRUPTED.
WHERE?
ABOUT 30 NAUTICAL MILES THAT WAY. JUST BEYOND THE BLAST RADIUS, AS IT HAPPENS.

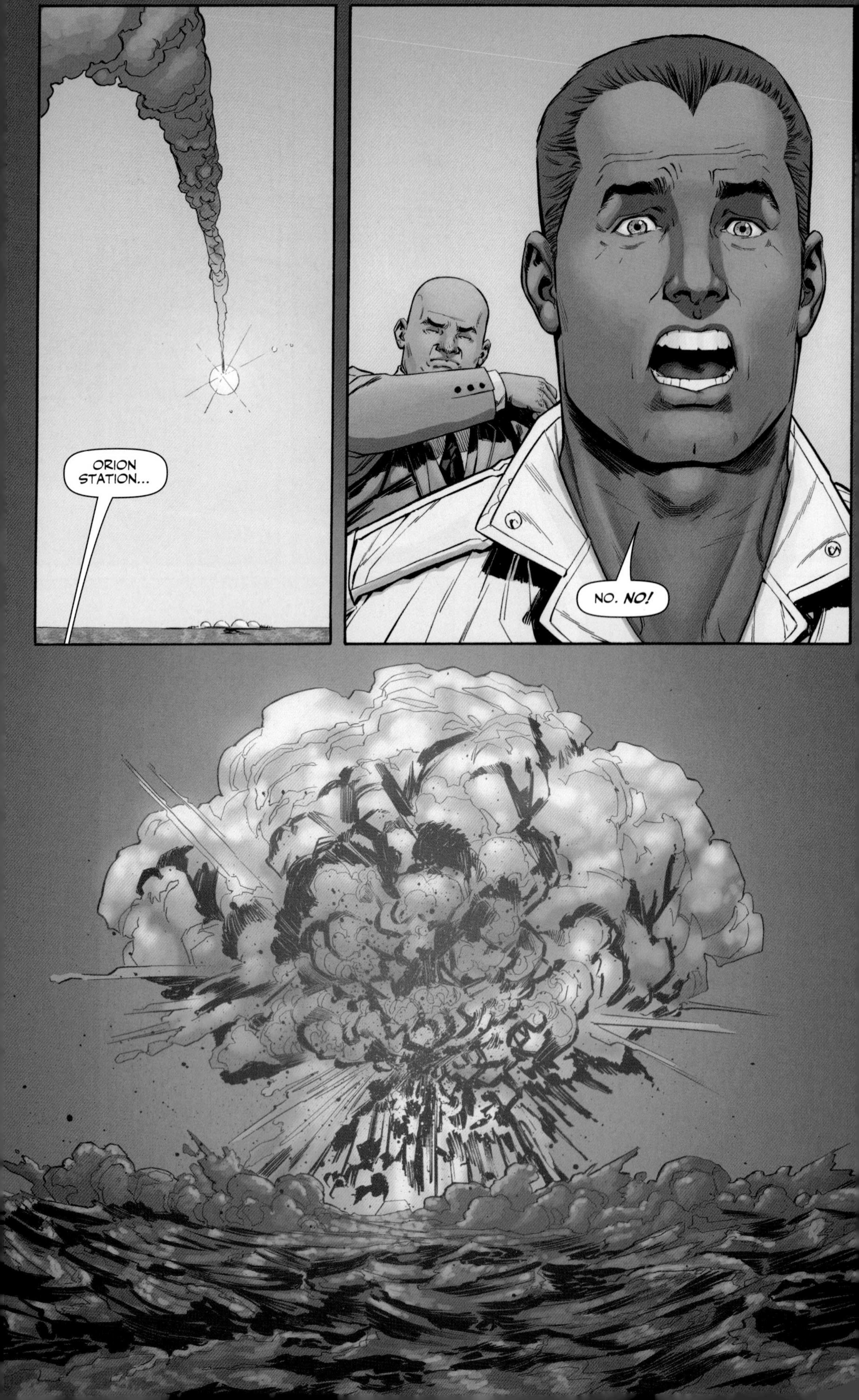
ORION STATION...
NO. NO!

DEX... WOOL...

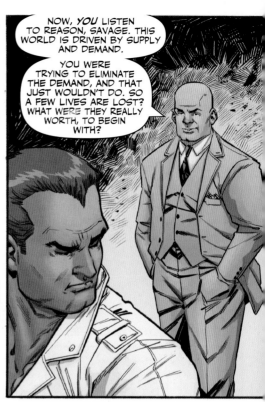

NOW, *YOU* LISTEN TO REASON, SAVAGE. THIS WORLD IS DRIVEN BY SUPPLY AND DEMAND.

YOU WERE TRYING TO ELIMINATE THE DEMAND, AND THAT JUST WOULDN'T DO. SO A FEW LIVES ARE LOST? WHAT WERE THEY REALLY WORTH, TO BEGIN WITH?

YES, TWO GOOD MEN JUST DIED. AND THOSE DEATHS ARE ON YOUR HEAD.

BUT BECAUSE OF YOU THERE ARE *COUNTLESS* PEOPLE THAT WILL NEEDLESSLY SUFFER OLD AGE AND DISEASE AND *DEATH*.

YOU'VE DOOMED THEM *ALL*.

NO ⟩COFF⟨ *YOU* DID.

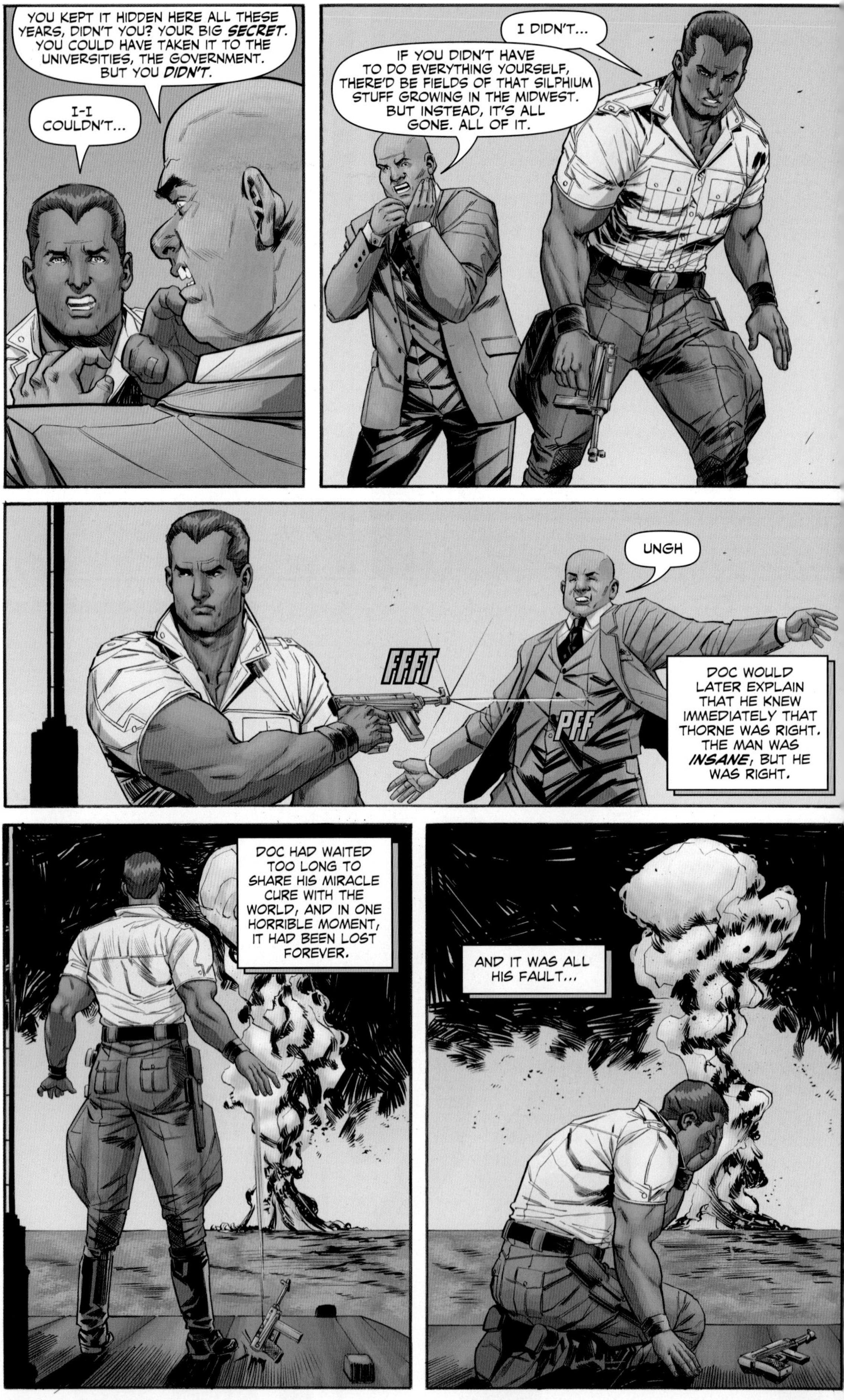

YOU KEPT IT HIDDEN HERE ALL THESE YEARS, DIDN'T YOU? YOUR BIG SECRET. YOU COULD HAVE TAKEN IT TO THE UNIVERSITIES, THE GOVERNMENT. BUT YOU DIDN'T.
I-I COULDN'T...
I DIDN'T...
IF YOU DIDN'T HAVE TO DO EVERYTHING YOURSELF, THERE'D BE FIELDS OF THAT SILPHIUM STUFF GROWING IN THE MIDWEST. BUT INSTEAD, IT'S ALL GONE. ALL OF IT.
UNGH
FFFT
PFF
DOC WOULD LATER EXPLAIN THAT HE KNEW IMMEDIATELY THAT THORNE WAS RIGHT. THE MAN WAS INSANE, BUT HE WAS RIGHT.
DOC HAD WAITED TOO LONG TO SHARE HIS MIRACLE CURE WITH THE WORLD, AND IN ONE HORRIBLE MOMENT, IT HAD BEEN LOST FOREVER.
AND IT WAS ALL HIS FAULT...

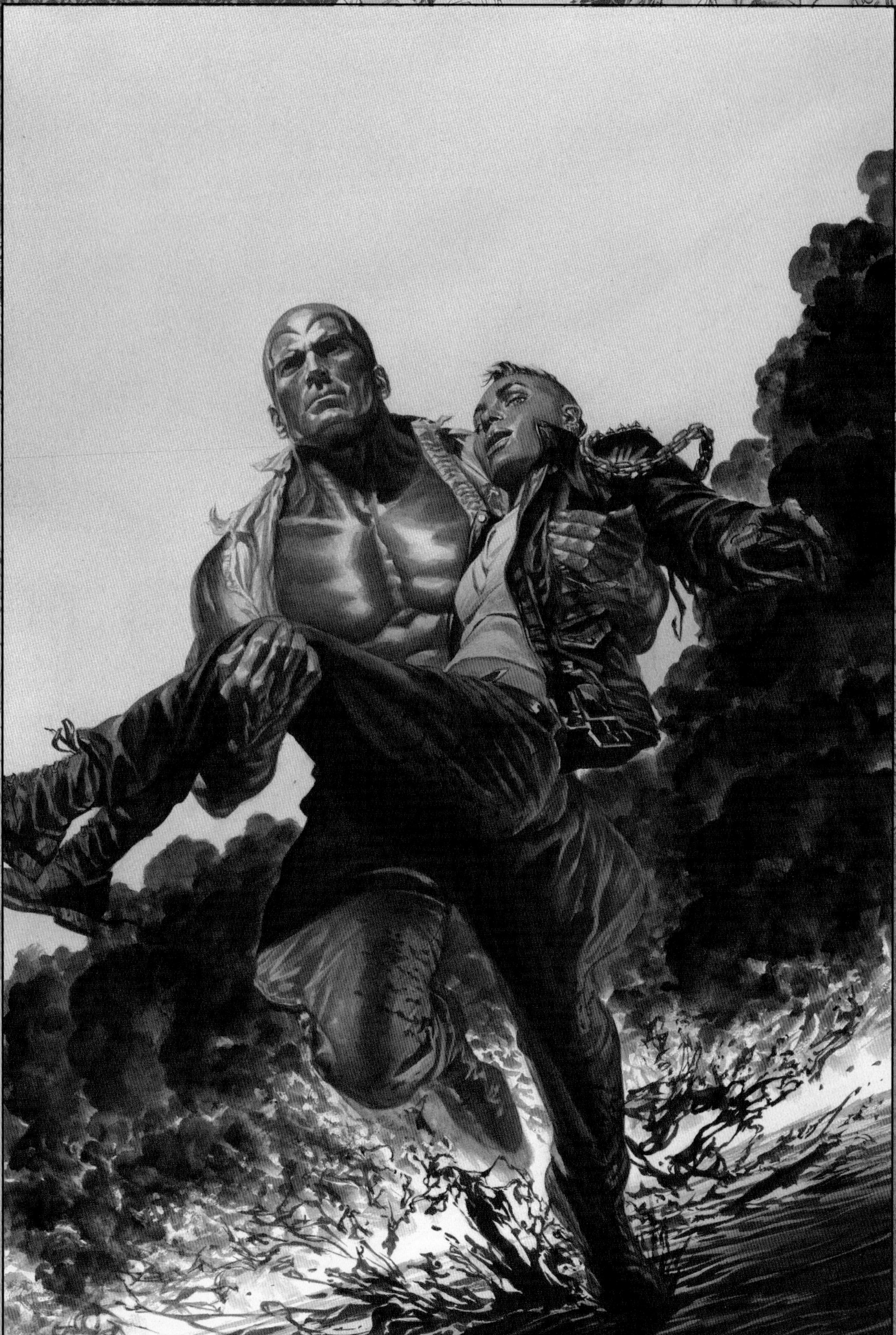

ISSUE #4 COVER
art by ALEX ROSS

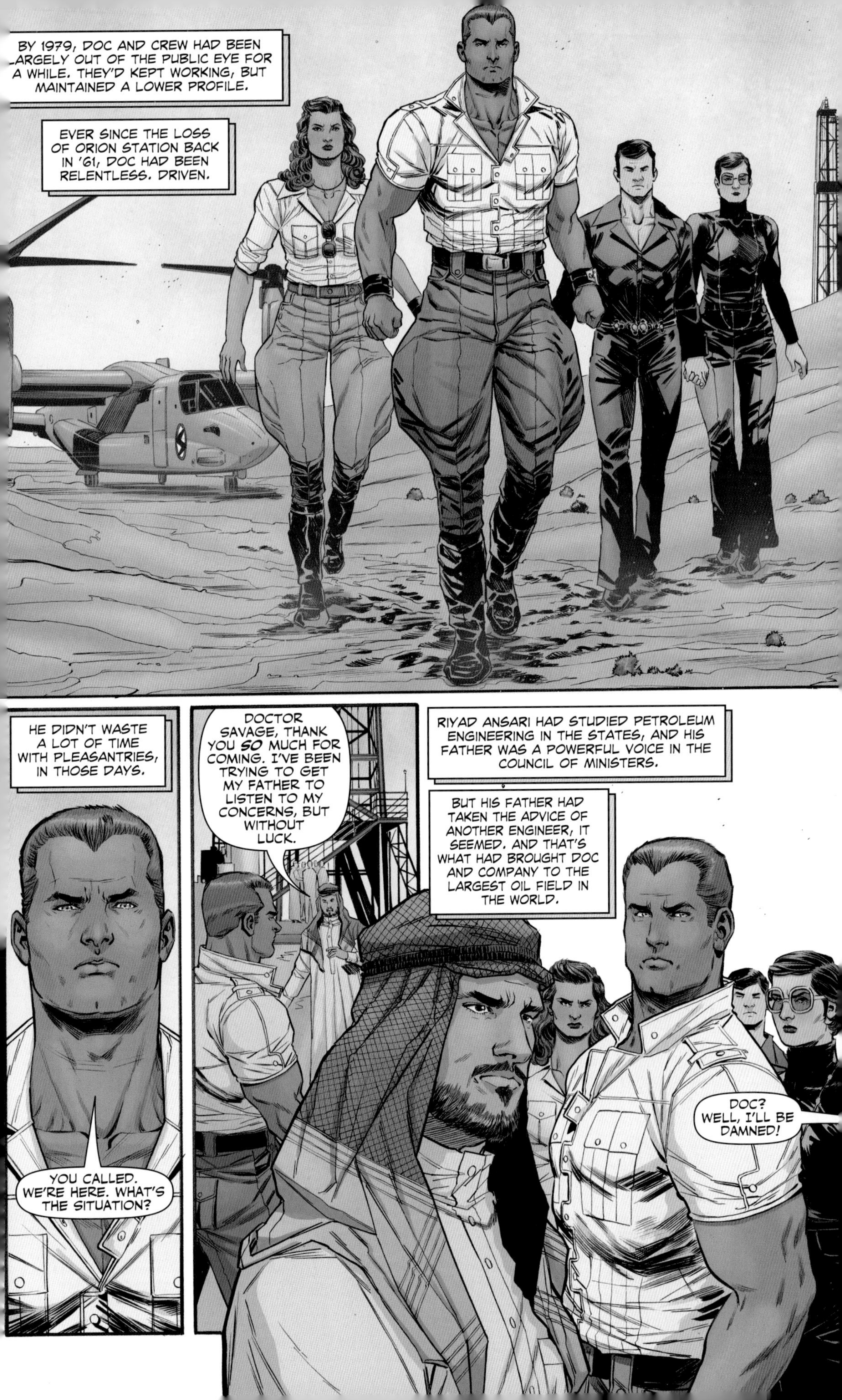
BY 1979, DOC AND CREW HAD BEEN LARGELY OUT OF THE PUBLIC EYE FOR A WHILE. THEY'D KEPT WORKING, BUT MAINTAINED A LOWER PROFILE.
EVER SINCE THE LOSS OF ORION STATION BACK IN '61, DOC HAD BEEN RELENTLESS. DRIVEN.
HE DIDN'T WASTE A LOT OF TIME WITH PLEASANTRIES, IN THOSE DAYS.
YOU CALLED. WE'RE HERE. WHAT'S THE SITUATION?
DOCTOR SAVAGE, THANK YOU *SO* MUCH FOR COMING. I'VE BEEN TRYING TO GET MY FATHER TO LISTEN TO MY CONCERNS, BUT WITHOUT LUCK.
RIYAD ANSARI HAD STUDIED PETROLEUM ENGINEERING IN THE STATES, AND HIS FATHER WAS A POWERFUL VOICE IN THE COUNCIL OF MINISTERS.
BUT HIS FATHER HAD TAKEN THE ADVICE OF ANOTHER ENGINEER, IT SEEMED. AND THAT'S WHAT HAD BROUGHT DOC AND COMPANY TO THE LARGEST OIL FIELD IN THE WORLD.
DOC? WELL, I'LL BE DAMNED!

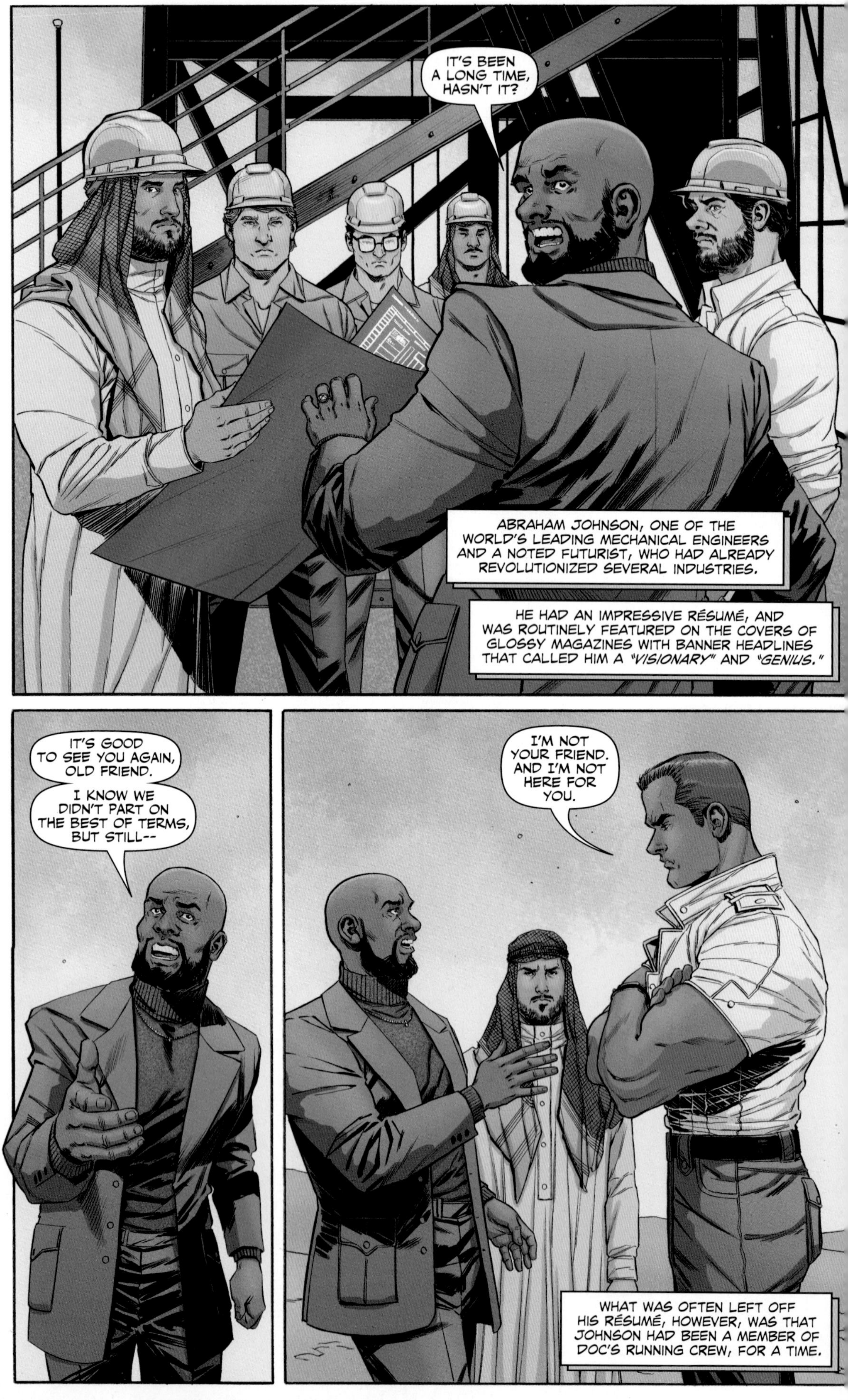
IT'S BEEN A LONG TIME, HASN'T IT?
ABRAHAM JOHNSON, ONE OF THE WORLD'S LEADING MECHANICAL ENGINEERS AND A NOTED FUTURIST, WHO HAD ALREADY REVOLUTIONIZED SEVERAL INDUSTRIES.
HE HAD AN IMPRESSIVE RÉSUMÉ, AND WAS ROUTINELY FEATURED ON THE COVERS OF GLOSSY MAGAZINES WITH BANNER HEADLINES THAT CALLED HIM A "VISIONARY" AND "GENIUS."
IT'S GOOD TO SEE YOU AGAIN, OLD FRIEND.
I KNOW WE DIDN'T PART ON THE BEST OF TERMS, BUT STILL--
I'M NOT YOUR FRIEND. AND I'M NOT HERE FOR YOU.
WHAT WAS OFTEN LEFT OFF HIS RÉSUMÉ, HOWEVER, WAS THAT JOHNSON HAD BEEN A MEMBER OF DOC'S RUNNING CREW, FOR A TIME.

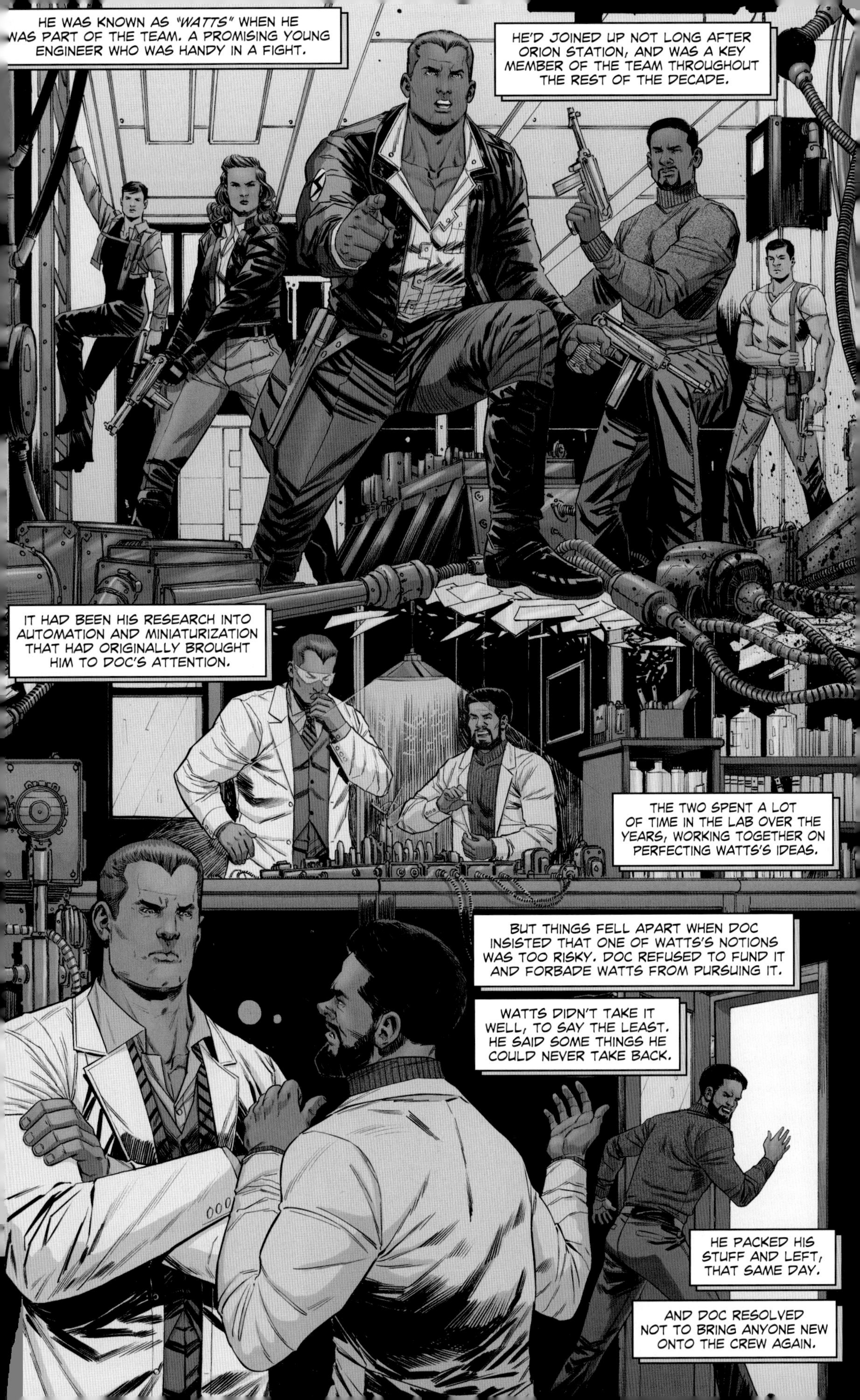
HE WAS KNOWN AS *"WATTS"* WHEN HE WAS PART OF THE TEAM. A PROMISING YOUNG ENGINEER WHO WAS HANDY IN A FIGHT.
HE'D JOINED UP NOT LONG AFTER ORION STATION, AND WAS A KEY MEMBER OF THE TEAM THROUGHOUT THE REST OF THE DECADE.
IT HAD BEEN HIS RESEARCH INTO AUTOMATION AND MINIATURIZATION THAT HAD ORIGINALLY BROUGHT HIM TO DOC'S ATTENTION.
THE TWO SPENT A LOT OF TIME IN THE LAB OVER THE YEARS, WORKING TOGETHER ON PERFECTING WATTS'S IDEAS.
BUT THINGS FELL APART WHEN DOC INSISTED THAT ONE OF WATTS'S NOTIONS WAS TOO RISKY. DOC REFUSED TO FUND IT AND FORBADE WATTS FROM PURSUING IT.
WATTS DIDN'T TAKE IT WELL, TO SAY THE LEAST. HE SAID SOME THINGS HE COULD NEVER TAKE BACK.
HE PACKED HIS STUFF AND LEFT, THAT SAME DAY.
AND DOC RESOLVED NOT TO BRING ANYONE NEW ONTO THE CREW AGAIN.

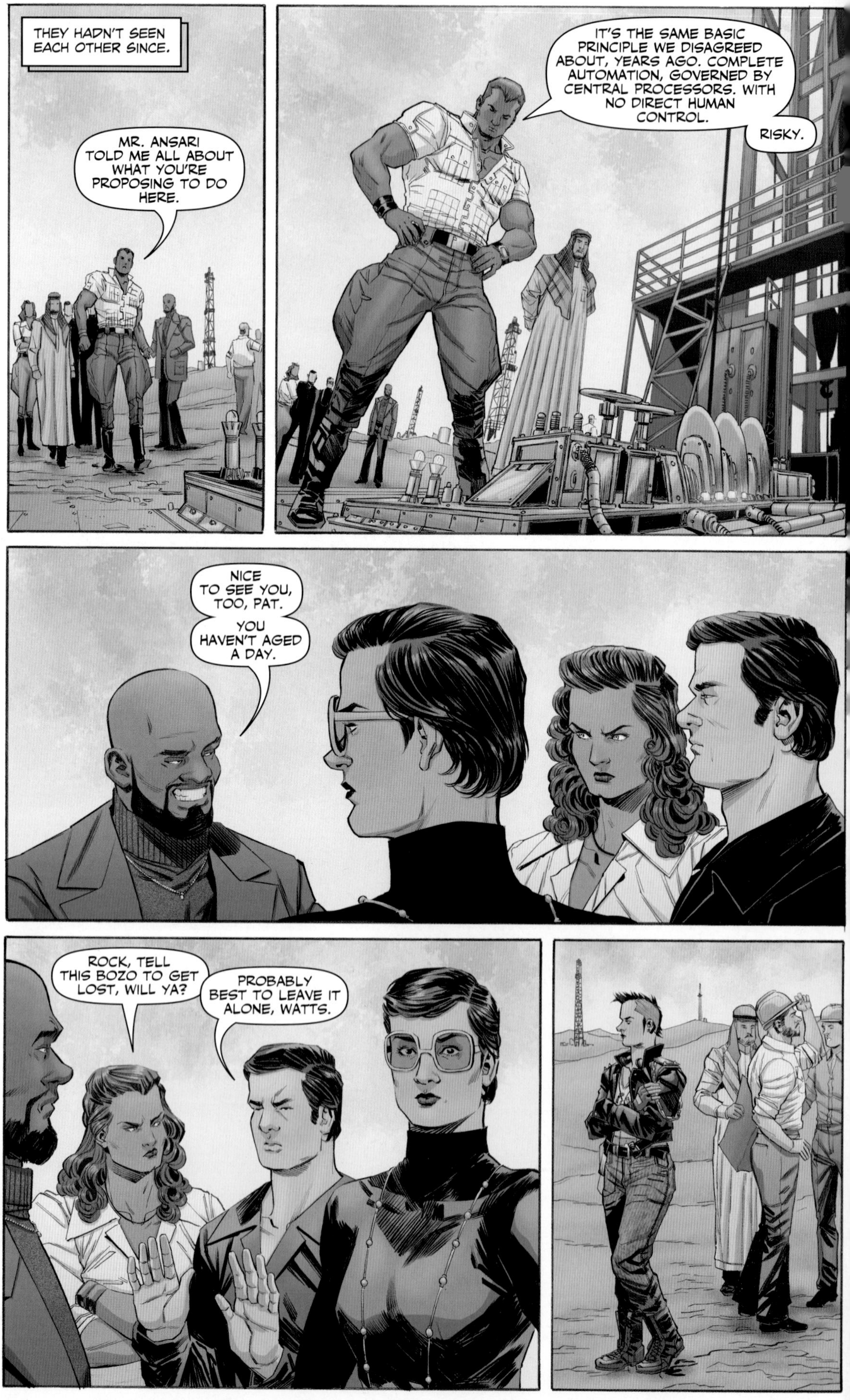
THEY HADN'T SEEN EACH OTHER SINCE.
MR. ANSARI TOLD ME ALL ABOUT WHAT YOU'RE PROPOSING TO DO HERE.
IT'S THE SAME BASIC PRINCIPLE WE DISAGREED ABOUT, YEARS AGO. COMPLETE AUTOMATION, GOVERNED BY CENTRAL PROCESSORS. WITH NO DIRECT HUMAN CONTROL.
RISKY.
NICE TO SEE YOU, TOO, PAT.
YOU HAVEN'T AGED A DAY.
ROCK, TELL THIS BOZO TO GET LOST, WILL YA?
PROBABLY BEST TO LEAVE IT ALONE, WATTS.

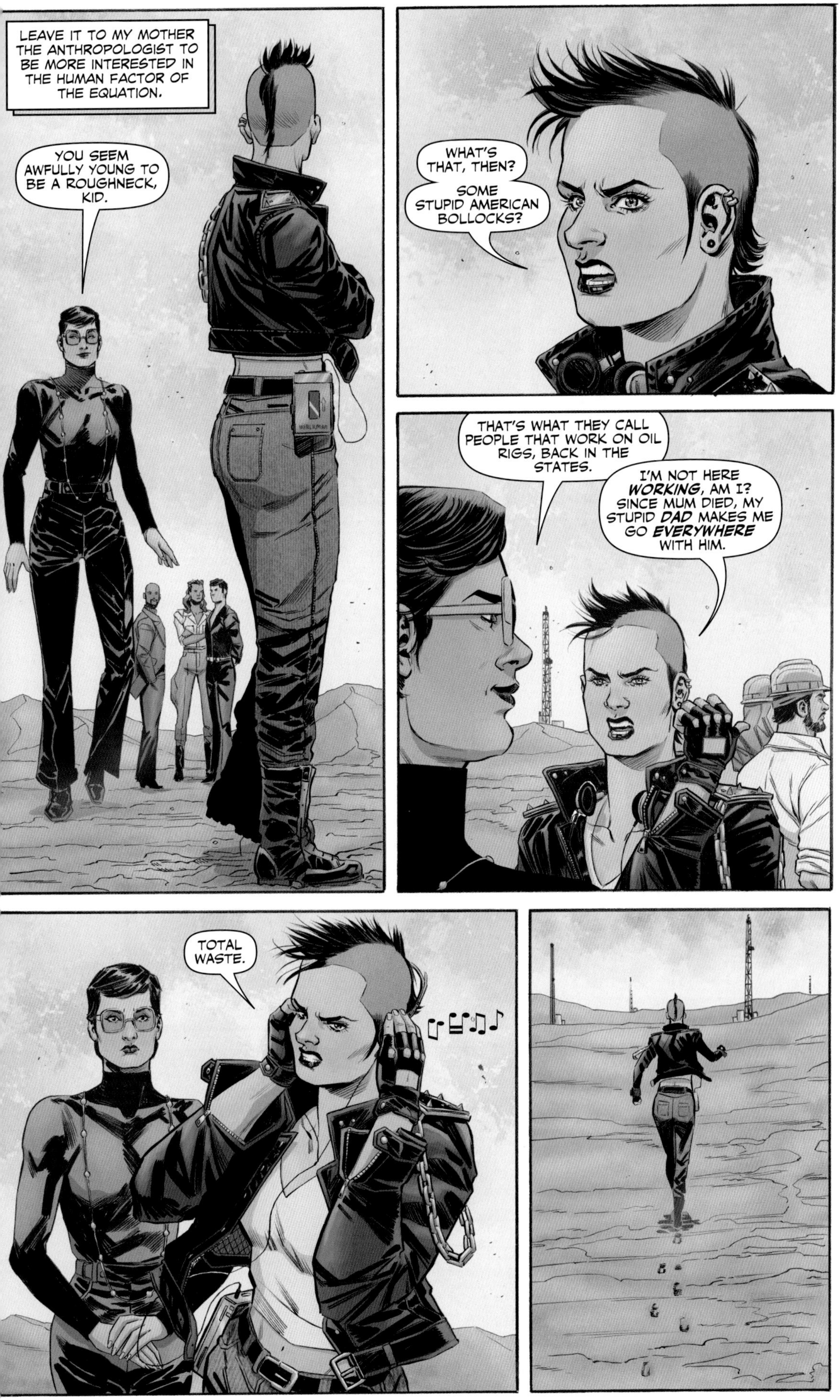
LEAVE IT TO MY MOTHER THE ANTHROPOLOGIST TO BE MORE INTERESTED IN THE HUMAN FACTOR OF THE EQUATION.
YOU SEEM AWFULLY YOUNG TO BE A ROUGHNECK, KID.
WHAT'S THAT, THEN?
SOME STUPID AMERICAN BOLLOCKS?
THAT'S WHAT THEY CALL PEOPLE THAT WORK ON OIL RIGS, BACK IN THE STATES.
I'M NOT HERE WORKING, AM I? SINCE MUM DIED, MY STUPID DAD MAKES ME GO EVERYWHERE WITH HIM.
TOTAL WASTE.

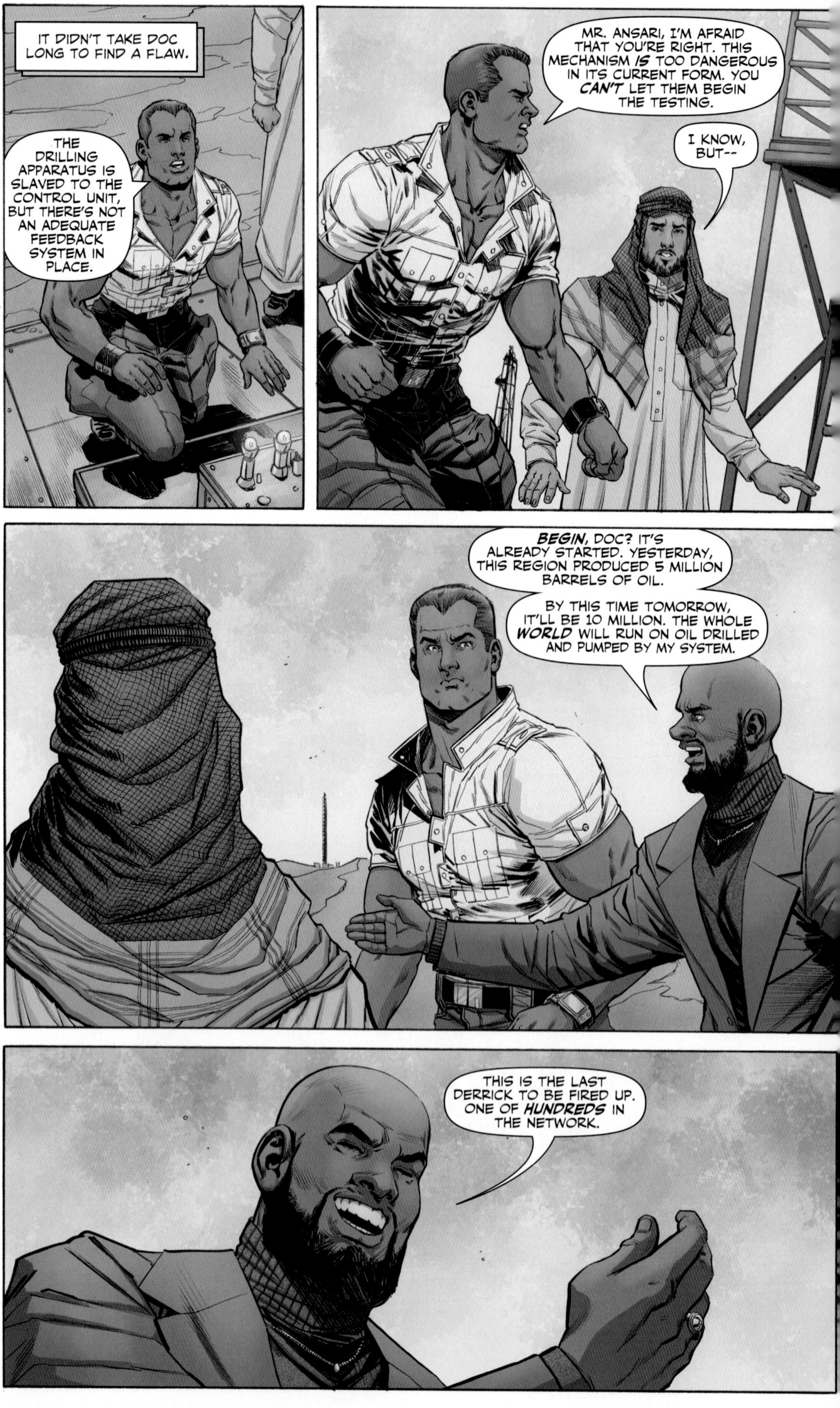
IT DIDN'T TAKE DOC LONG TO FIND A FLAW.
THE DRILLING APPARATUS IS SLAVED TO THE CONTROL UNIT, BUT THERE'S NOT AN ADEQUATE FEEDBACK SYSTEM IN PLACE.
MR. ANSARI, I'M AFRAID THAT YOU'RE RIGHT. THIS MECHANISM IS TOO DANGEROUS IN ITS CURRENT FORM. YOU CAN'T LET THEM BEGIN THE TESTING.
I KNOW, BUT--
BEGIN, DOC? IT'S ALREADY STARTED. YESTERDAY, THIS REGION PRODUCED 5 MILLION BARRELS OF OIL.
BY THIS TIME TOMORROW, IT'LL BE 10 MILLION. THE WHOLE WORLD WILL RUN ON OIL DRILLED AND PUMPED BY MY SYSTEM.
THIS IS THE LAST DERRICK TO BE FIRED UP. ONE OF HUNDREDS IN THE NETWORK.

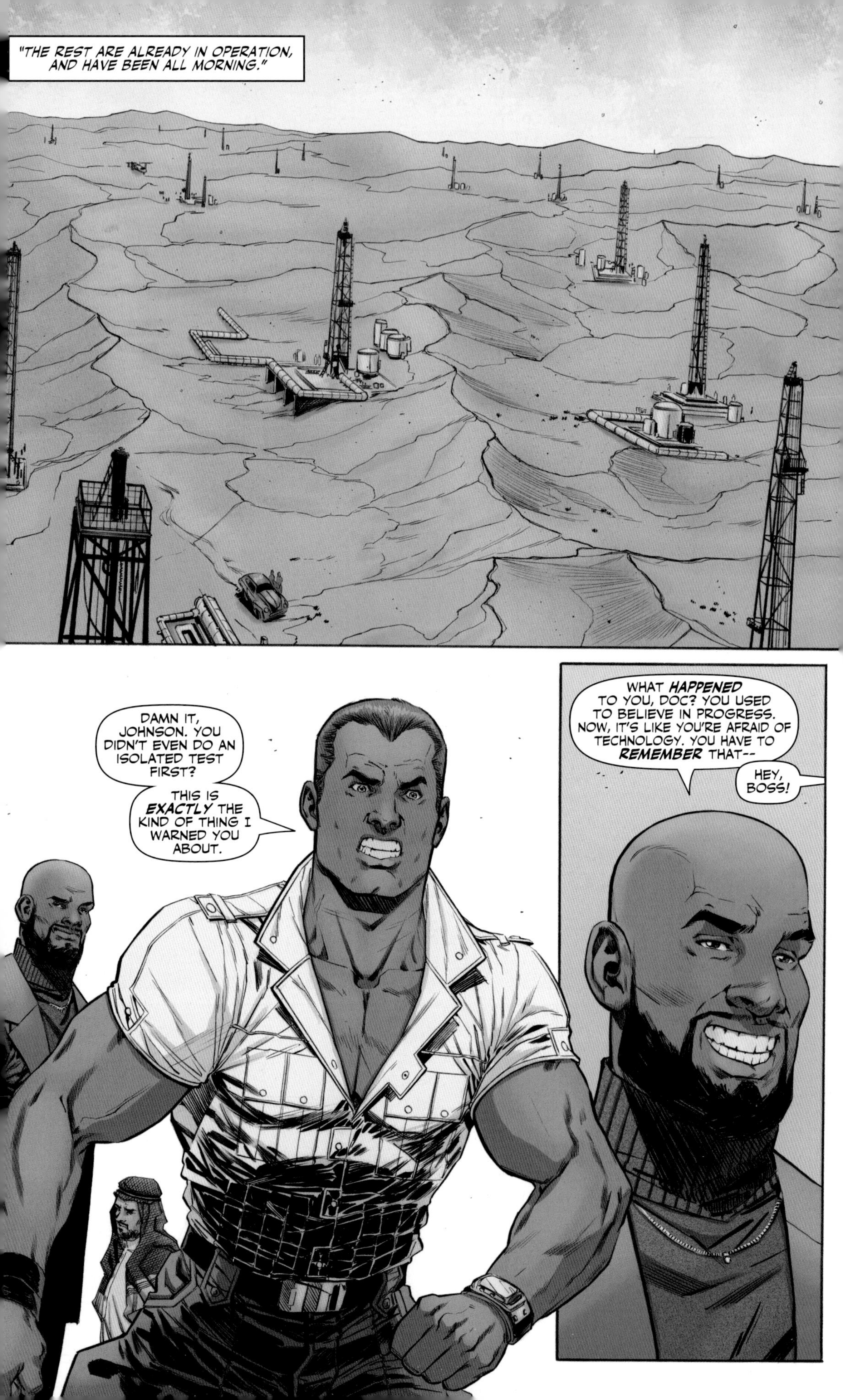
"THE REST ARE ALREADY IN OPERATION, AND HAVE BEEN ALL MORNING."
DAMN IT, JOHNSON. YOU DIDN'T EVEN DO AN ISOLATED TEST FIRST?
THIS IS EXACTLY THE KIND OF THING I WARNED YOU ABOUT.
WHAT HAPPENED TO YOU, DOC? YOU USED TO BELIEVE IN PROGRESS. NOW, IT'S LIKE YOU'RE AFRAID OF TECHNOLOGY. YOU HAVE TO REMEMBER THAT--
HEY, BOSS!

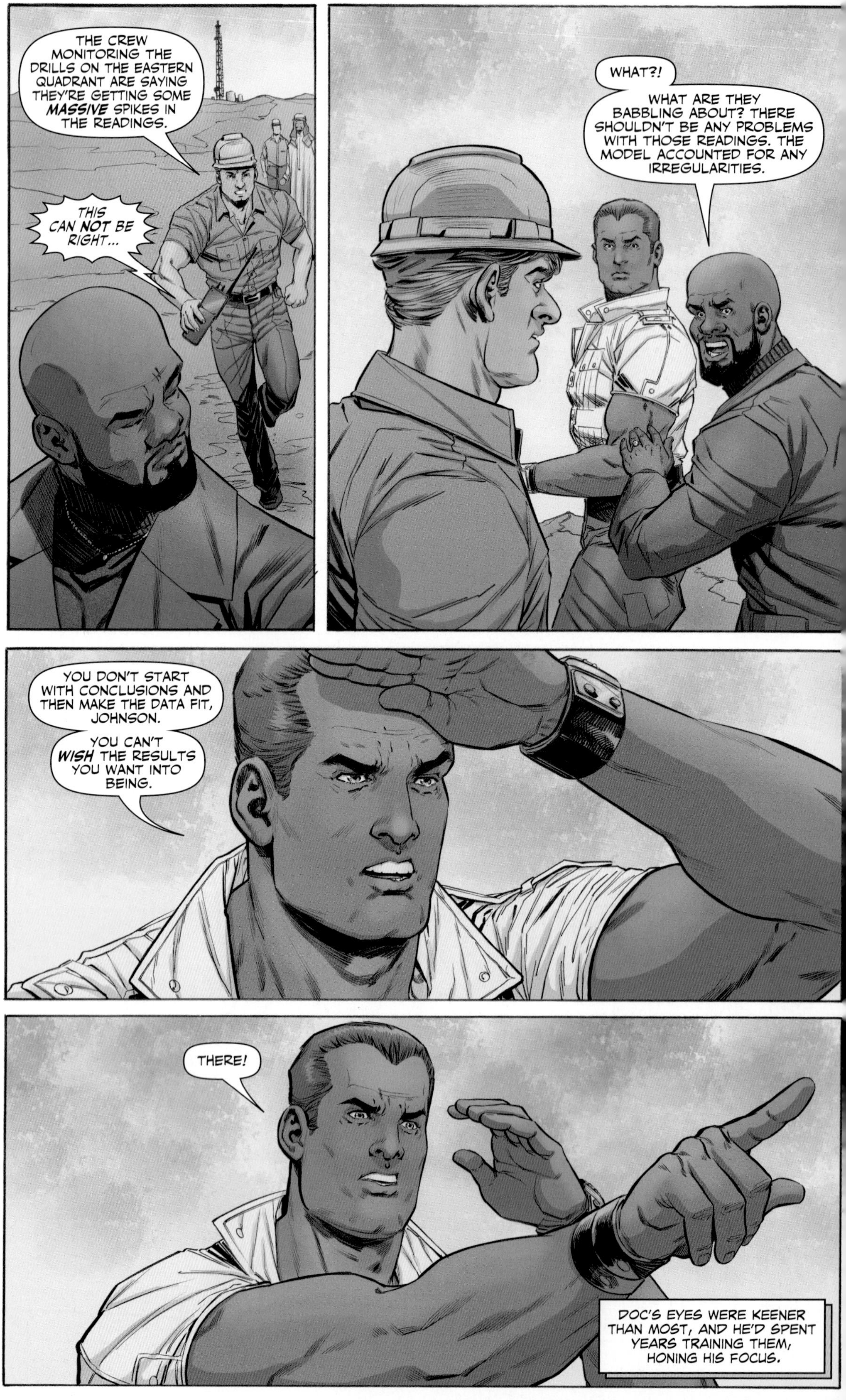
THE CREW MONITORING THE DRILLS ON THE EASTERN QUADRANT ARE SAYING THEY'RE GETTING SOME *MASSIVE* SPIKES IN THE READINGS.
THIS CAN ***NOT*** *BE RIGHT...*
WHAT?!
WHAT ARE THEY BABBLING ABOUT? THERE SHOULDN'T BE ANY PROBLEMS WITH THOSE READINGS. THE MODEL ACCOUNTED FOR ANY IRREGULARITIES.
YOU DON'T START WITH CONCLUSIONS AND THEN MAKE THE DATA FIT, JOHNSON.
YOU CAN'T *WISH* THE RESULTS YOU WANT INTO BEING.
THERE!
DOC'S EYES WERE KEENER THAN MOST, AND HE'D SPENT YEARS TRAINING THEM, HONING HIS FOCUS.

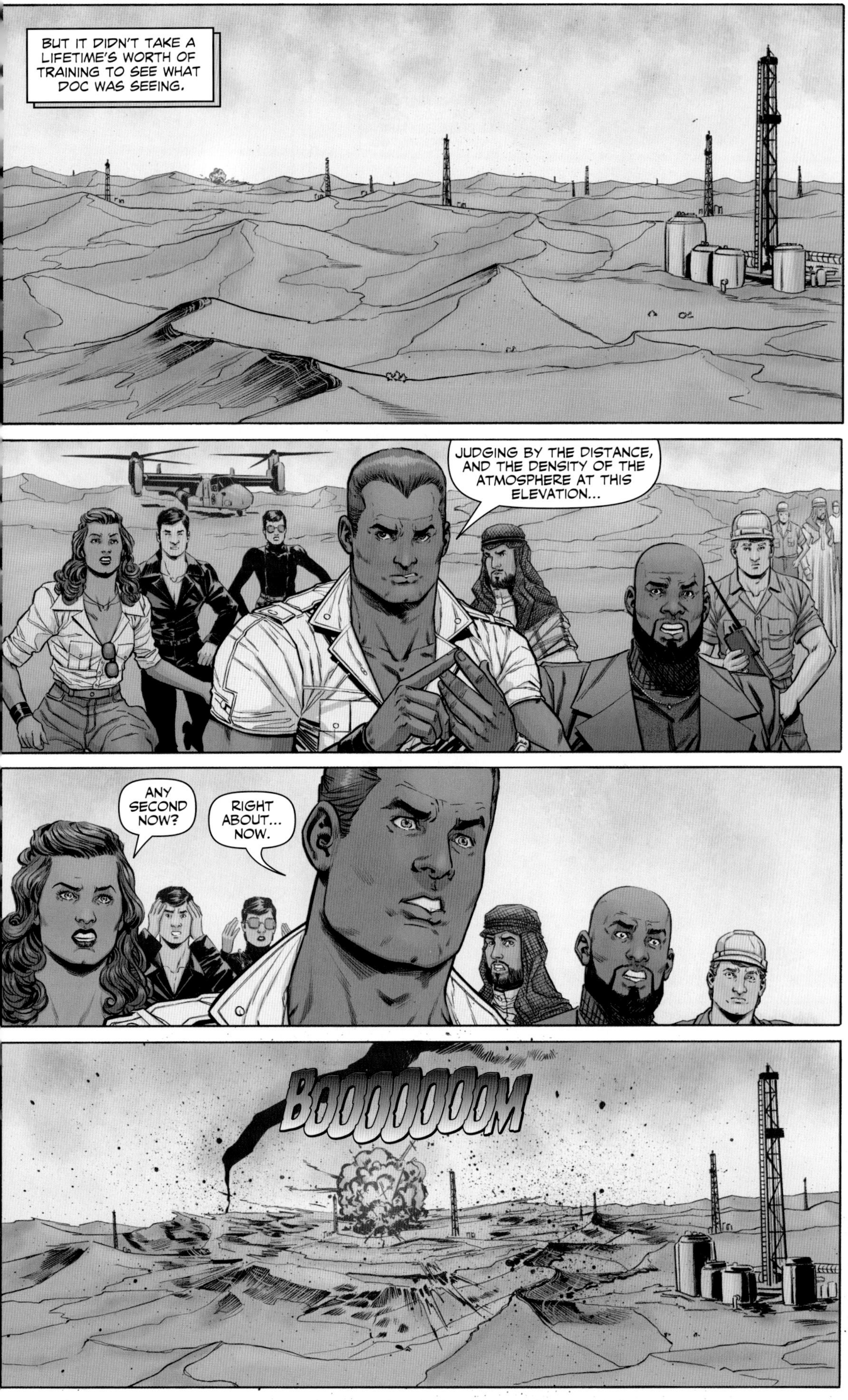
BUT IT DIDN'T TAKE A LIFETIME'S WORTH OF TRAINING TO SEE WHAT DOC WAS SEEING.
JUDGING BY THE DISTANCE, AND THE DENSITY OF THE ATMOSPHERE AT THIS ELEVATION...
ANY SECOND NOW?
RIGHT ABOUT... NOW.
BOOOOOOOM

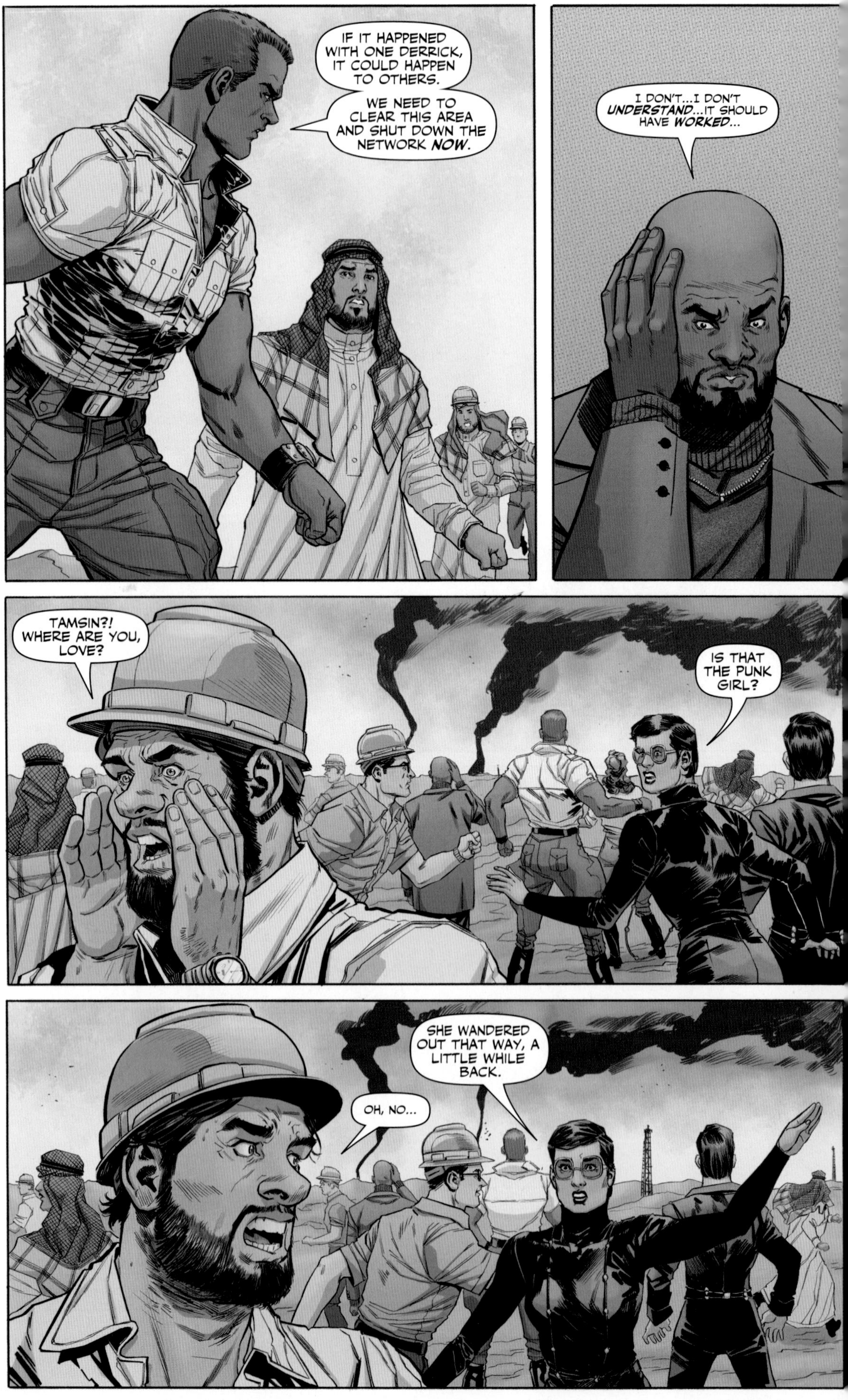
IF IT HAPPENED WITH ONE DERRICK, IT COULD HAPPEN TO OTHERS.
WE NEED TO CLEAR THIS AREA AND SHUT DOWN THE NETWORK NOW.
I DON'T...I DON'T UNDERSTAND...IT SHOULD HAVE WORKED...
TAMSIN?! WHERE ARE YOU, LOVE?
IS THAT THE PUNK GIRL?
SHE WANDERED OUT THAT WAY, A LITTLE WHILE BACK.
OH, NO...

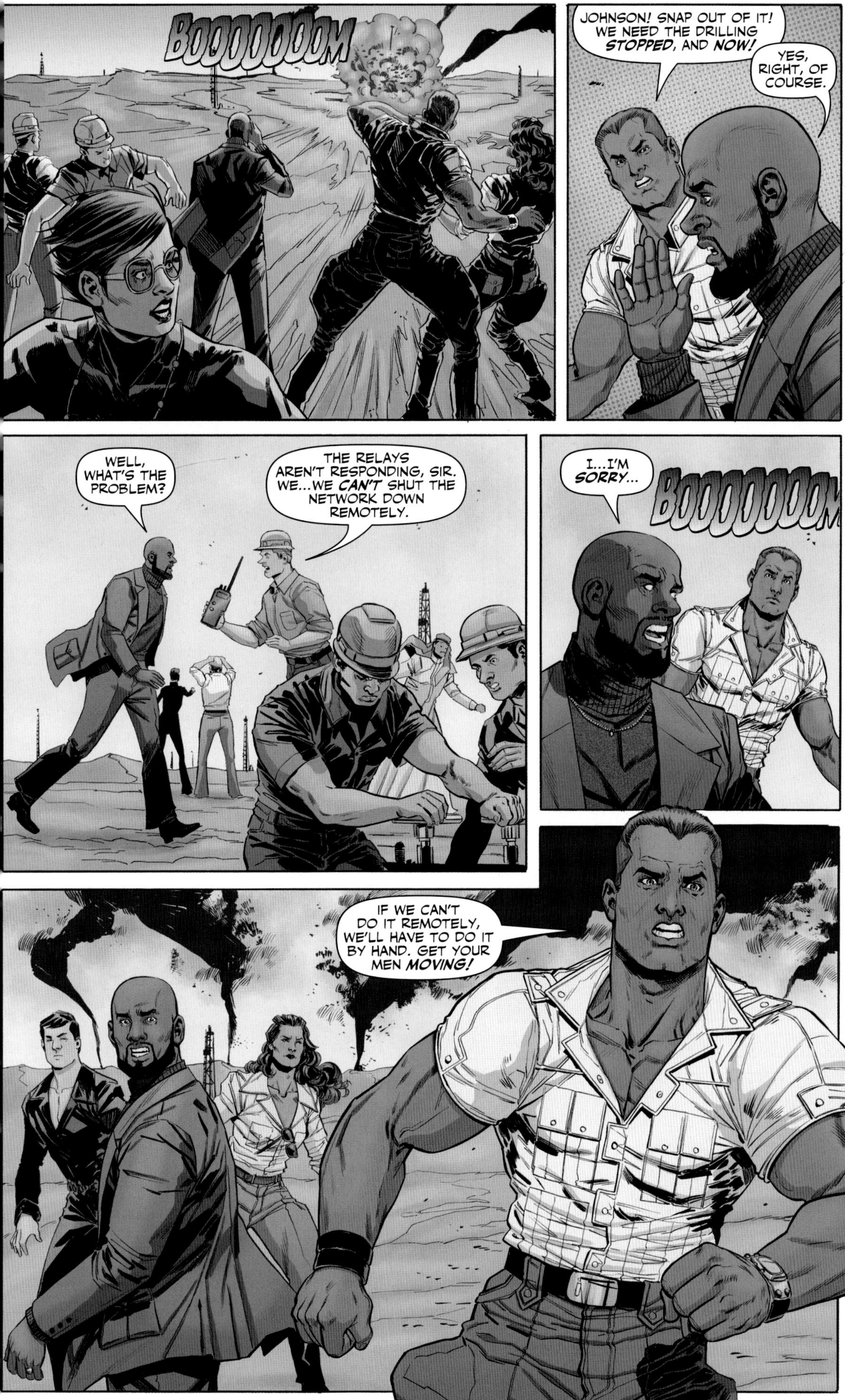
BOOOOOOOM
JOHNSON! SNAP OUT OF IT! WE NEED THE DRILLING STOPPED, AND NOW!
YES, RIGHT, OF COURSE.
WELL, WHAT'S THE PROBLEM?
THE RELAYS AREN'T RESPONDING, SIR. WE...WE CAN'T SHUT THE NETWORK DOWN REMOTELY.
I...I'M SORRY...
BOOOOOOOM
IF WE CAN'T DO IT REMOTELY, WE'LL HAVE TO DO IT BY HAND. GET YOUR MEN MOVING!

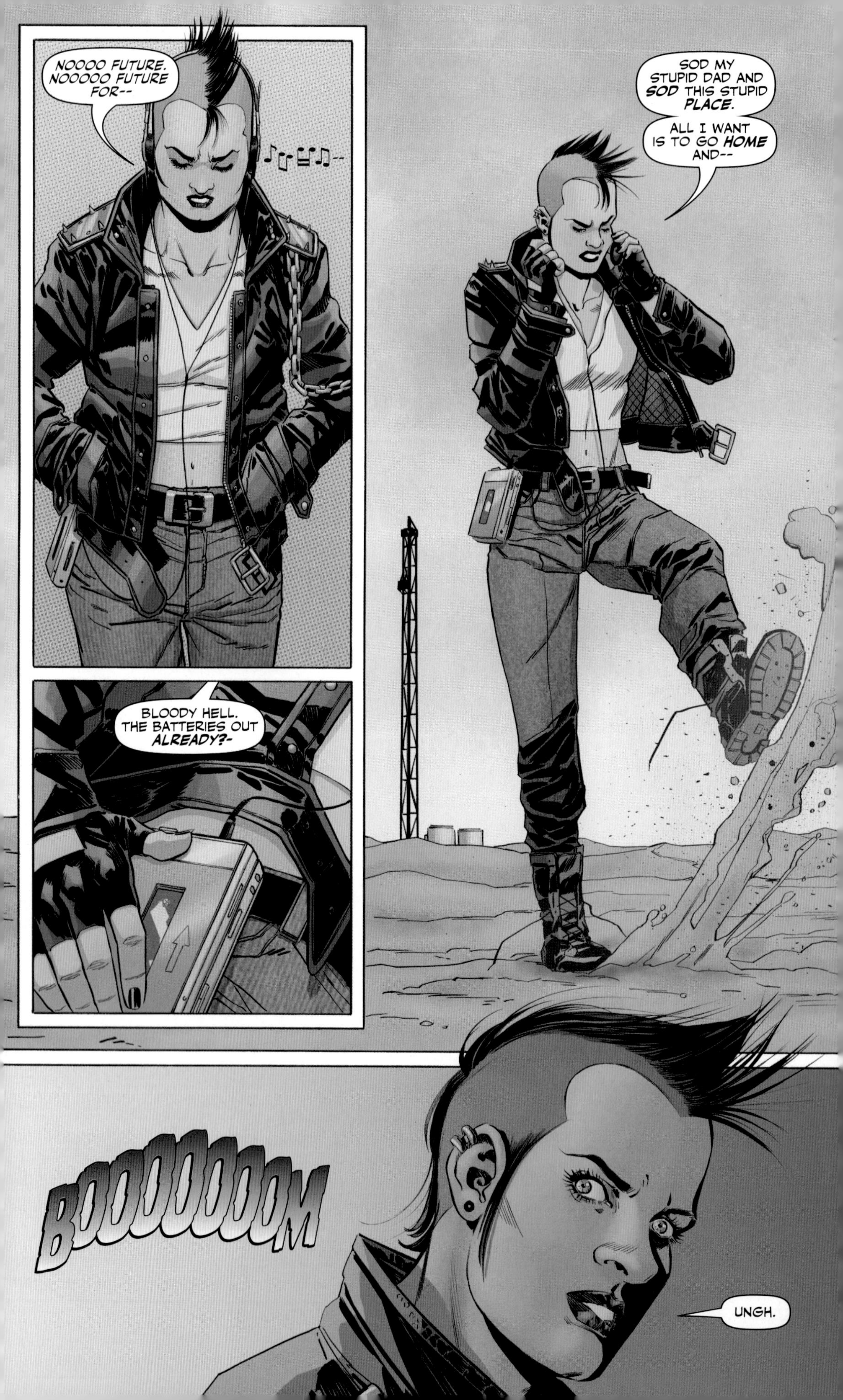
NOOOO FUTURE. NOOOOO FUTURE FOR--
BLOODY HELL. THE BATTERIES OUT ALREADY?-
SOD MY STUPID DAD AND SOD THIS STUPID PLACE.
ALL I WANT IS TO GO HOME AND--
BOOOOOOOM
UNGH.

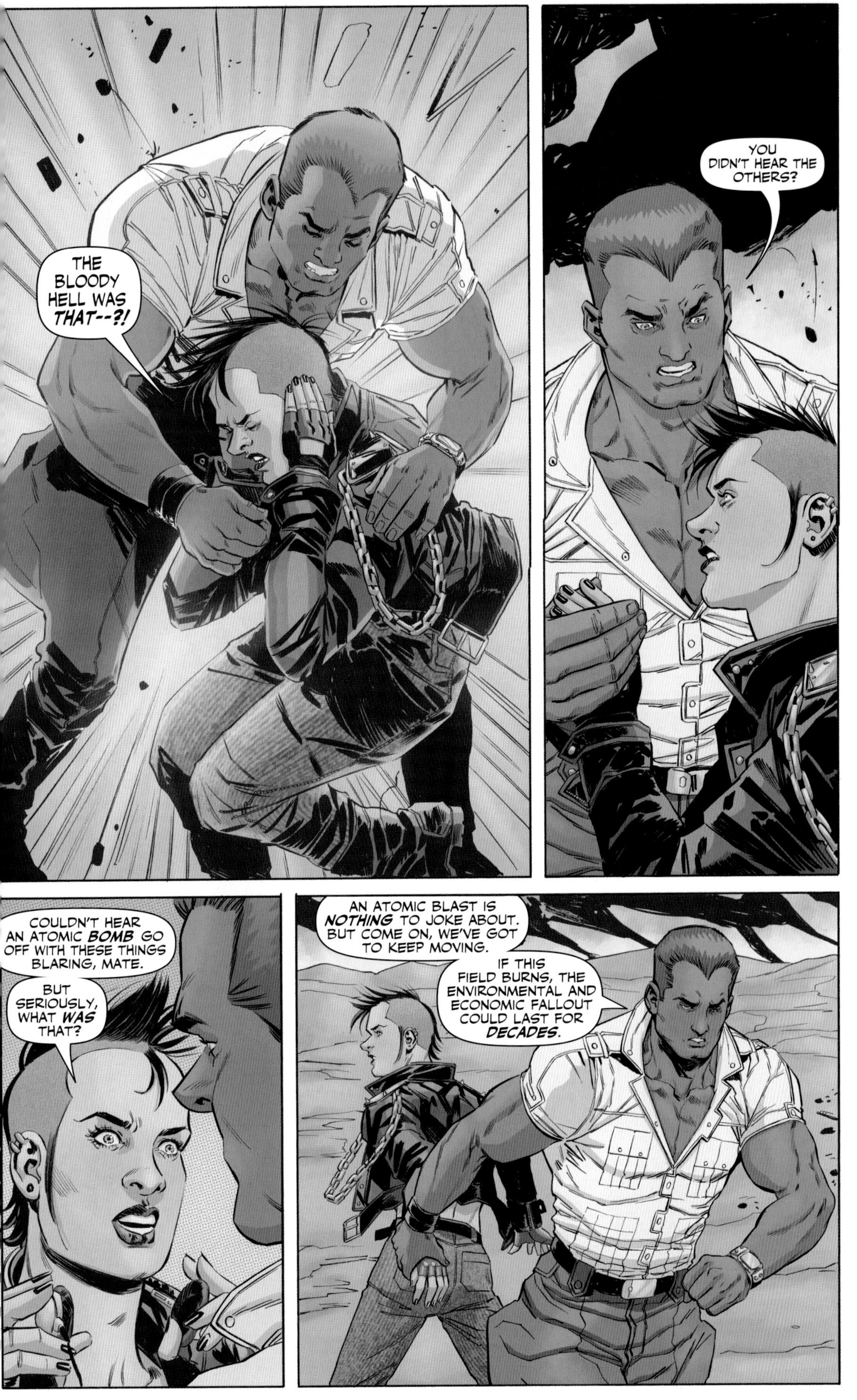

THE BLOODY HELL WAS *THAT--?!*
YOU DIDN'T HEAR THE OTHERS?
COULDN'T HEAR AN ATOMIC ***BOMB*** GO OFF WITH THESE THINGS BLARING, MATE.
BUT SERIOUSLY, WHAT ***WAS*** THAT?
AN ATOMIC BLAST IS ***NOTHING*** TO JOKE ABOUT. BUT COME ON, WE'VE GOT TO KEEP MOVING.
IF THIS FIELD BURNS, THE ENVIRONMENTAL AND ECONOMIC FALLOUT COULD LAST FOR ***DECADES***.

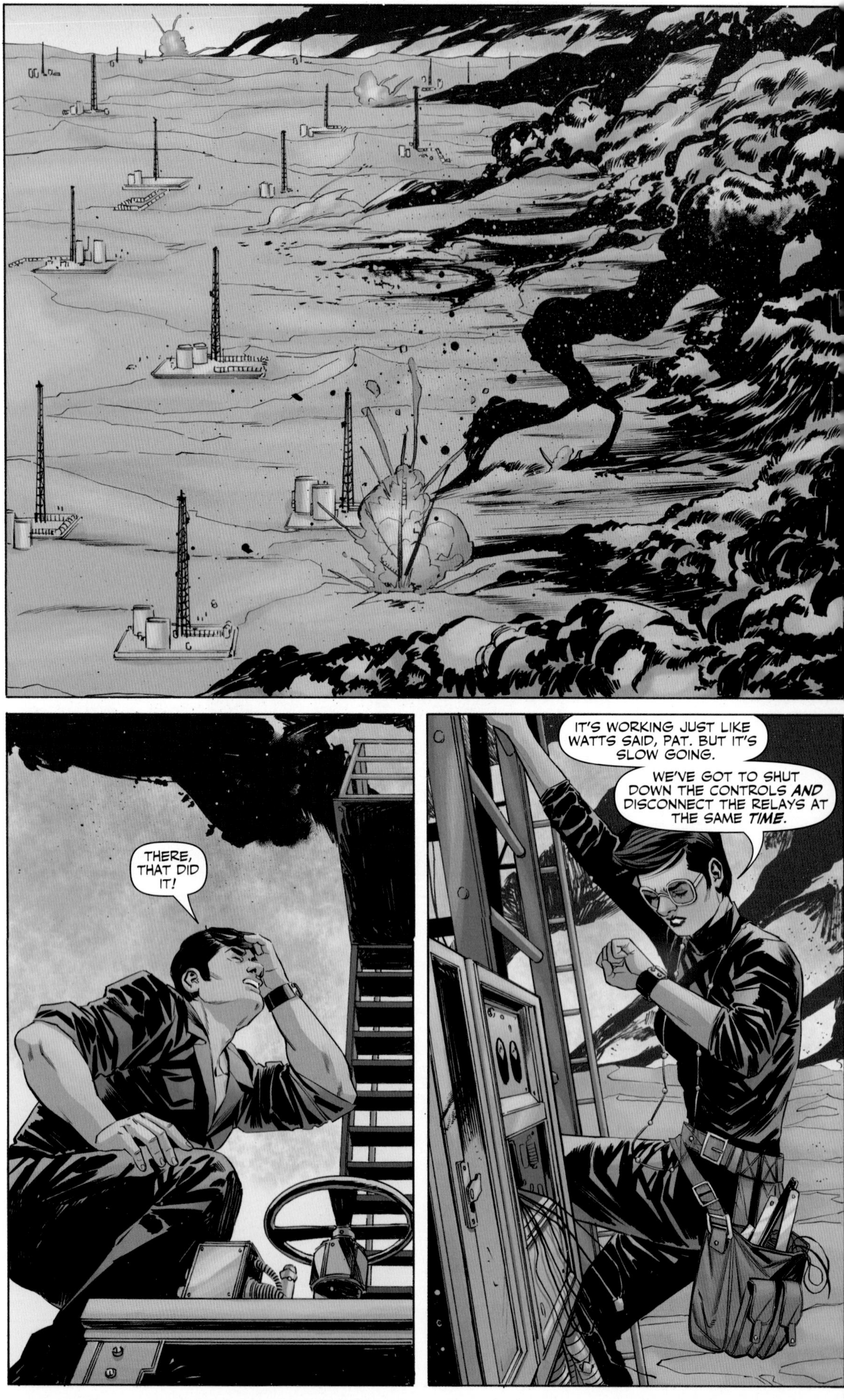
THERE, THAT DID IT!
IT'S WORKING JUST LIKE WATTS SAID, PAT. BUT IT'S SLOW GOING.
WE'VE GOT TO SHUT DOWN THE CONTROLS *AND* DISCONNECT THE RELAYS AT THE SAME *TIME*.

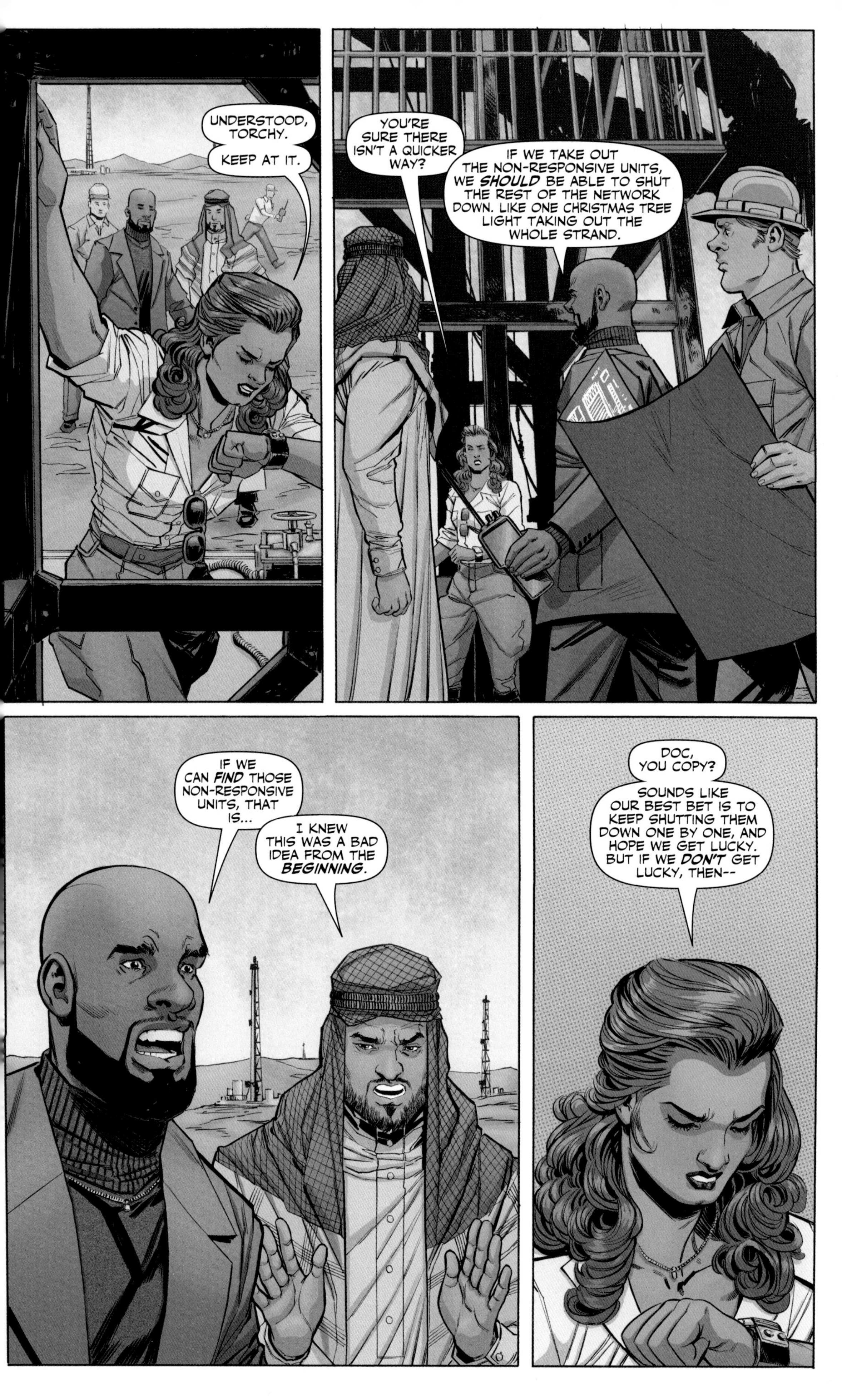
UNDERSTOOD, TORCHY.
KEEP AT IT.
YOU'RE SURE THERE ISN'T A QUICKER WAY?
IF WE TAKE OUT THE NON-RESPONSIVE UNITS, WE *SHOULD* BE ABLE TO SHUT THE REST OF THE NETWORK DOWN. LIKE ONE CHRISTMAS TREE LIGHT TAKING OUT THE WHOLE STRAND.
IF WE CAN *FIND* THOSE NON-RESPONSIVE UNITS, THAT IS...
I KNEW THIS WAS A BAD IDEA FROM THE *BEGINNING*.
DOC, YOU COPY?
SOUNDS LIKE OUR BEST BET IS TO KEEP SHUTTING THEM DOWN ONE BY ONE, AND HOPE WE GET LUCKY. BUT IF WE *DON'T* GET LUCKY, THEN--

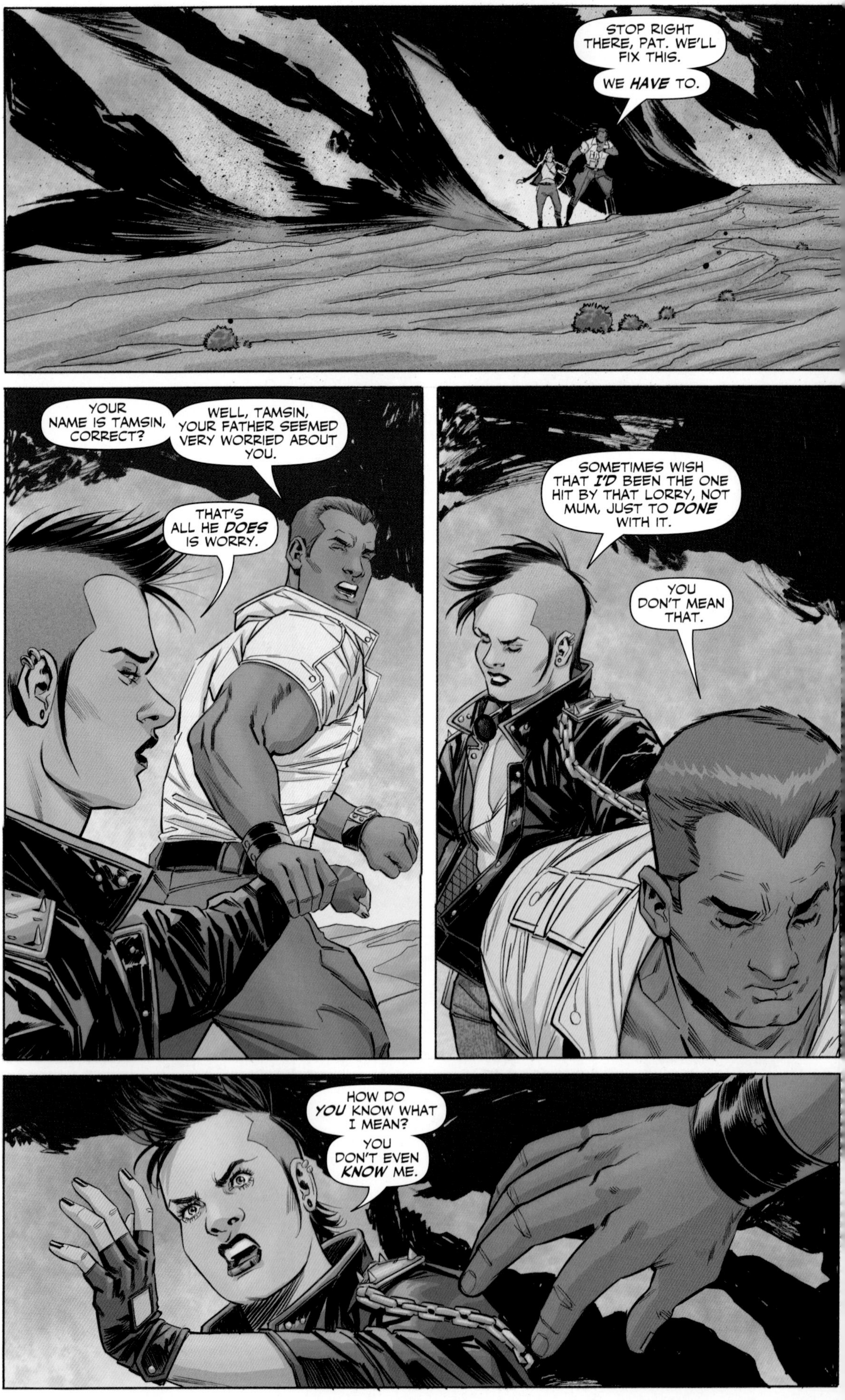
STOP RIGHT THERE, PAT. WE'LL FIX THIS.
WE *HAVE* TO.
YOUR NAME IS TAMSIN, CORRECT?
WELL, TAMSIN, YOUR FATHER SEEMED VERY WORRIED ABOUT YOU.
THAT'S ALL HE *DOES* IS WORRY.
SOMETIMES WISH THAT *I'D* BEEN THE ONE HIT BY THAT LORRY, NOT MUM, JUST TO *DONE* WITH IT.
YOU DON'T MEAN THAT.
HOW DO *YOU* KNOW WHAT I MEAN?
YOU DON'T EVEN *KNOW* ME.

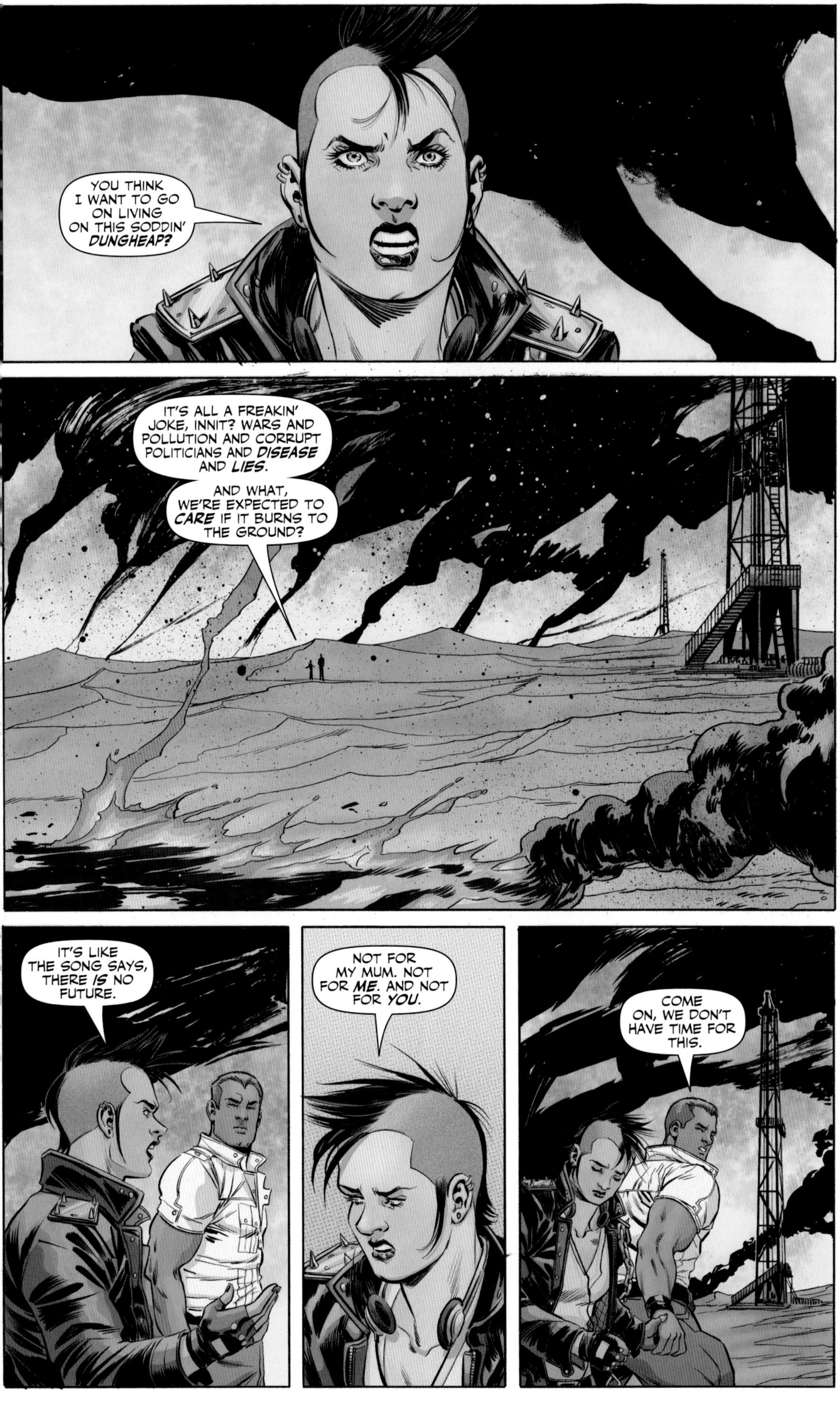
YOU THINK I WANT TO GO ON LIVING ON THIS SODDIN' *DUNGHEAP?*
IT'S ALL A FREAKIN' JOKE, INNIT? WARS AND POLLUTION AND CORRUPT POLITICIANS AND *DISEASE* AND *LIES*.
AND WHAT, WE'RE EXPECTED TO *CARE* IF IT BURNS TO THE GROUND?
IT'S LIKE THE SONG SAYS, THERE *IS* NO FUTURE.
NOT FOR MY MUM. NOT FOR *ME*. AND NOT FOR *YOU*.
COME ON, WE DON'T HAVE TIME FOR THIS.

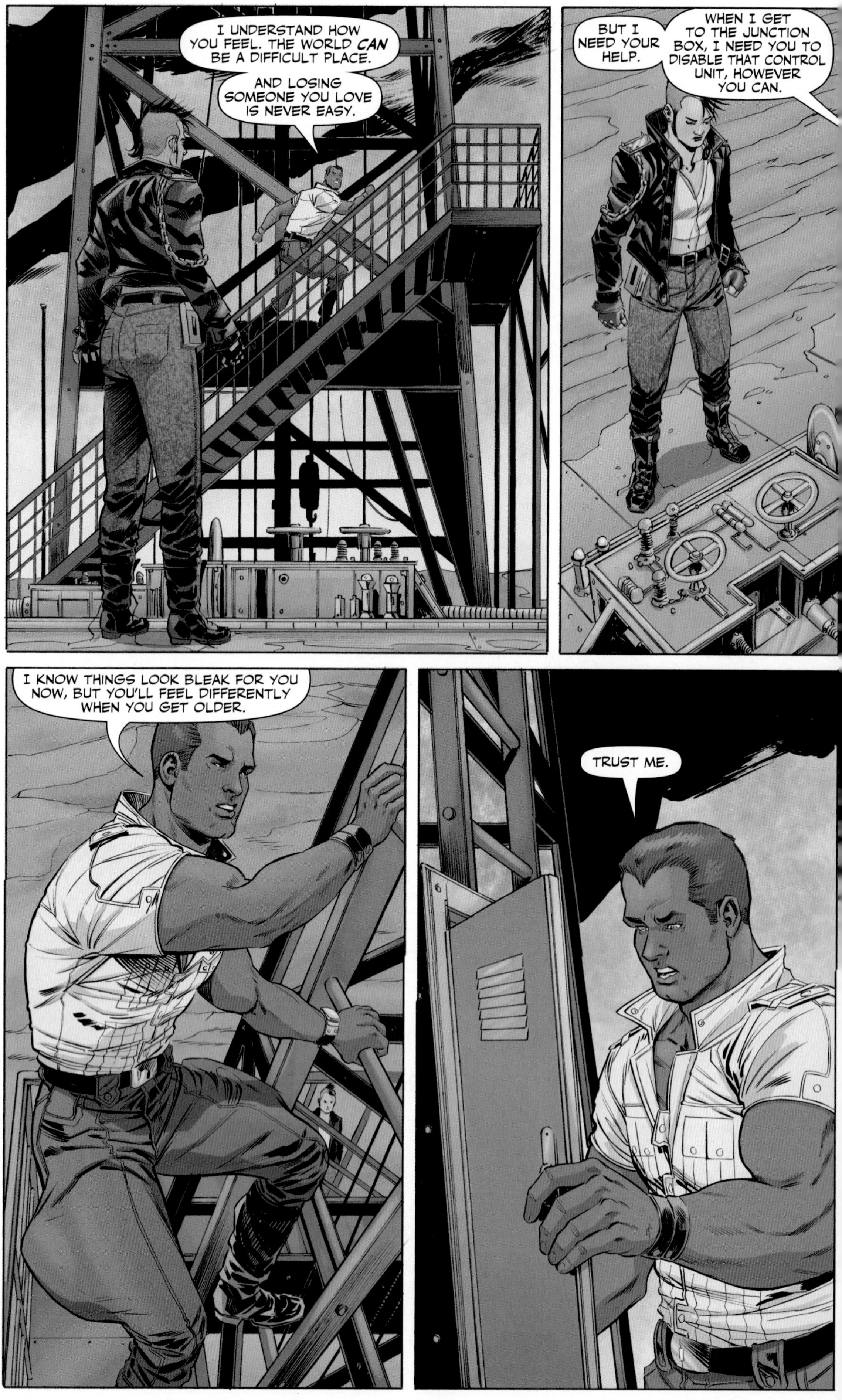

I UNDERSTAND HOW YOU FEEL. THE WORLD *CAN* BE A DIFFICULT PLACE.
AND LOSING SOMEONE YOU LOVE IS NEVER EASY.
BUT I NEED YOUR HELP.
WHEN I GET TO THE JUNCTION BOX, I NEED YOU TO DISABLE THAT CONTROL UNIT, HOWEVER YOU CAN.
I KNOW THINGS LOOK BLEAK FOR YOU NOW, BUT YOU'LL FEEL DIFFERENTLY WHEN YOU GET OLDER.
TRUST ME.

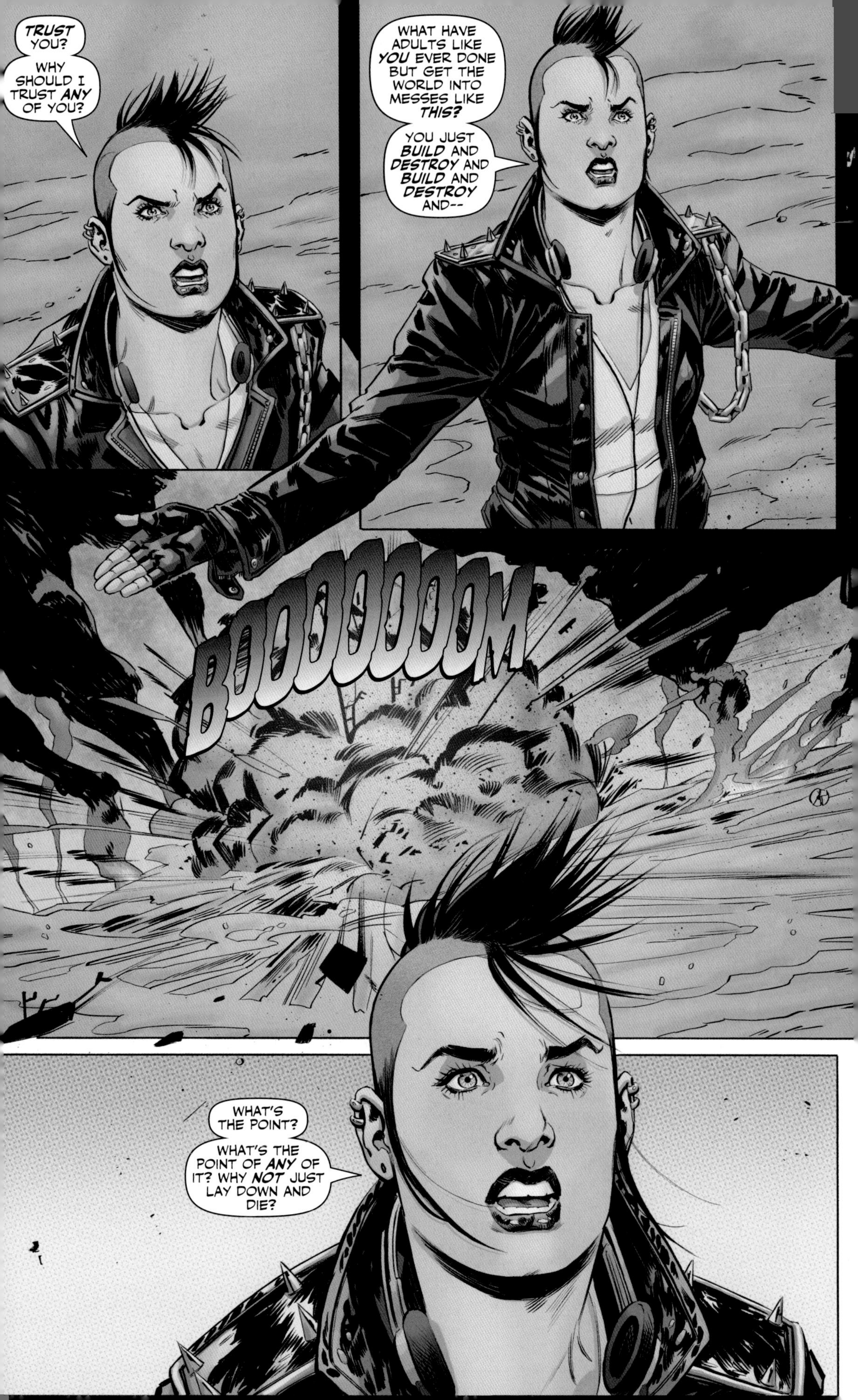
TRUST YOU?
WHY SHOULD I TRUST ANY OF YOU?
WHAT HAVE ADULTS LIKE YOU EVER DONE BUT GET THE WORLD INTO MESSES LIKE THIS?
YOU JUST BUILD AND DESTROY AND BUILD AND DESTROY AND--
BOOOOOOOM
WHAT'S THE POINT?
WHAT'S THE POINT OF ANY OF IT? WHY NOT JUST LAY DOWN AND DIE?

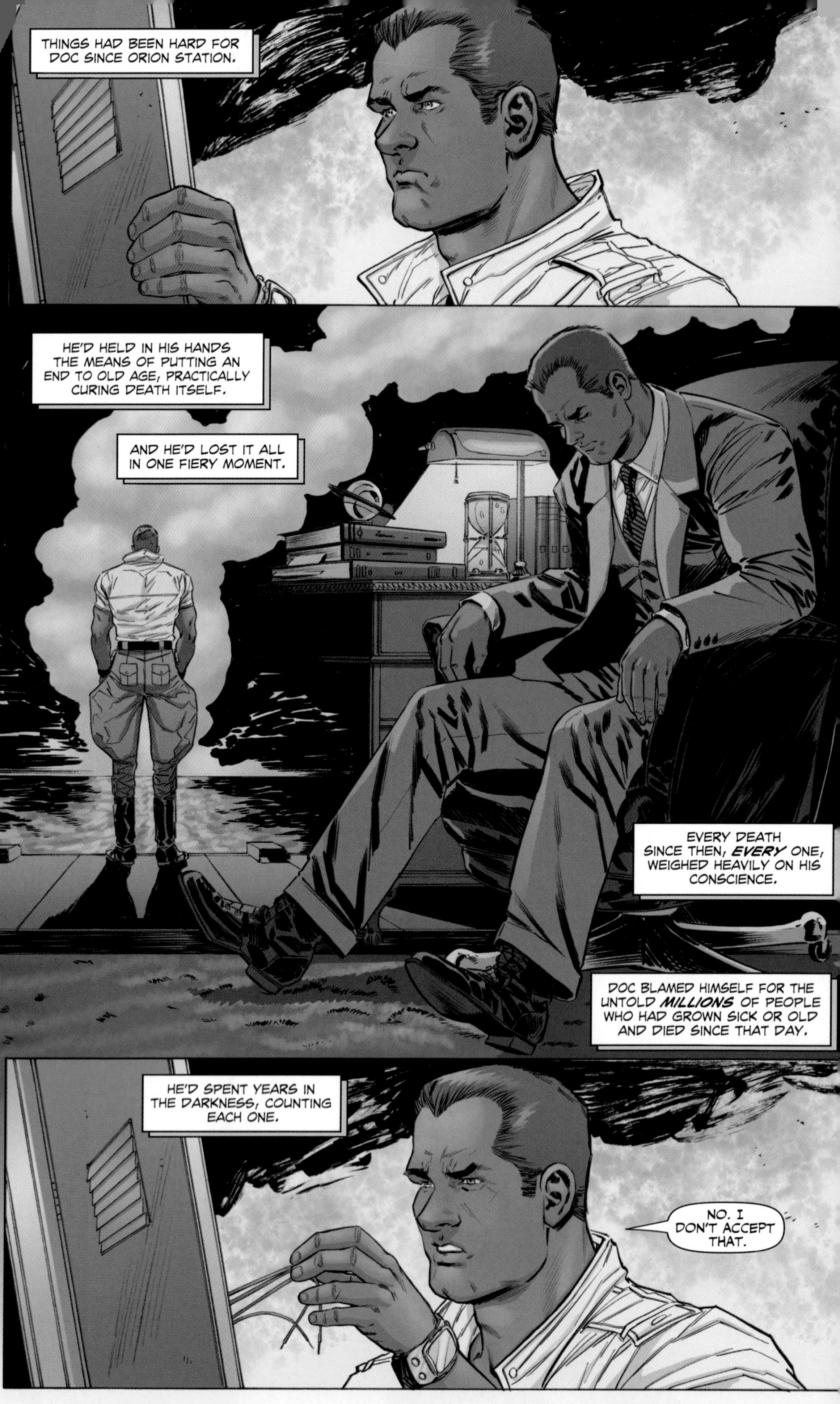
THINGS HAD BEEN HARD FOR DOC SINCE ORION STATION.
HE'D HELD IN HIS HANDS THE MEANS OF PUTTING AN END TO OLD AGE, PRACTICALLY CURING DEATH ITSELF.
AND HE'D LOST IT ALL IN ONE FIERY MOMENT.
EVERY DEATH SINCE THEN, EVERY ONE, WEIGHED HEAVILY ON HIS CONSCIENCE.
DOC BLAMED HIMSELF FOR THE UNTOLD MILLIONS OF PEOPLE WHO HAD GROWN SICK OR OLD AND DIED SINCE THAT DAY.
HE'D SPENT YEARS IN THE DARKNESS, COUNTING EACH ONE.
NO. I DON'T ACCEPT THAT.

THE FUTURE IS COMING, WHETHER WE LIKE IT OR NOT. IT'S UP TO US WHAT *KIND* OF FUTURE IT'LL BE.
BOOOOOOOM
WILL IT BE ***BETTER*** THAN TODAY, THE ***SAME***, OR ***WORSE?*** WE HAVE TO DECIDE.
BOOOOOOOM
WE HAVE TO ***CHOOSE*** TO HOPE. CHOOSE TO KEEP GOING. WE HAVE TO ***MAKE*** THE FUTURE.

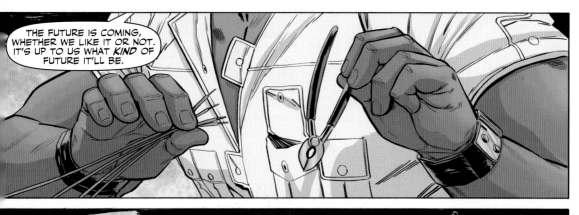

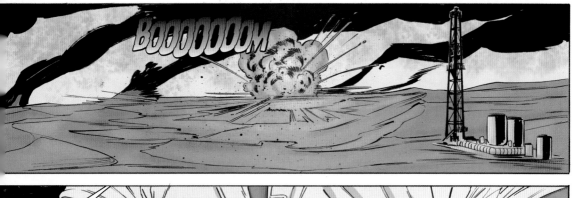

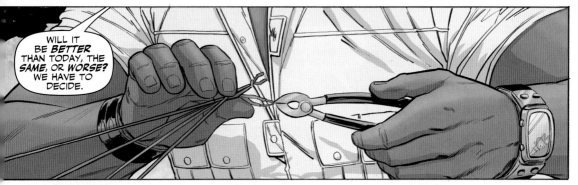

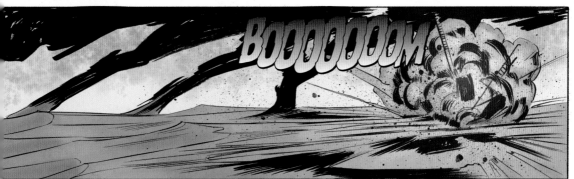

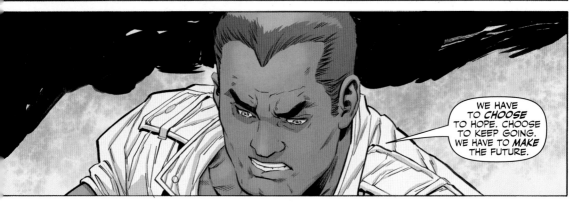

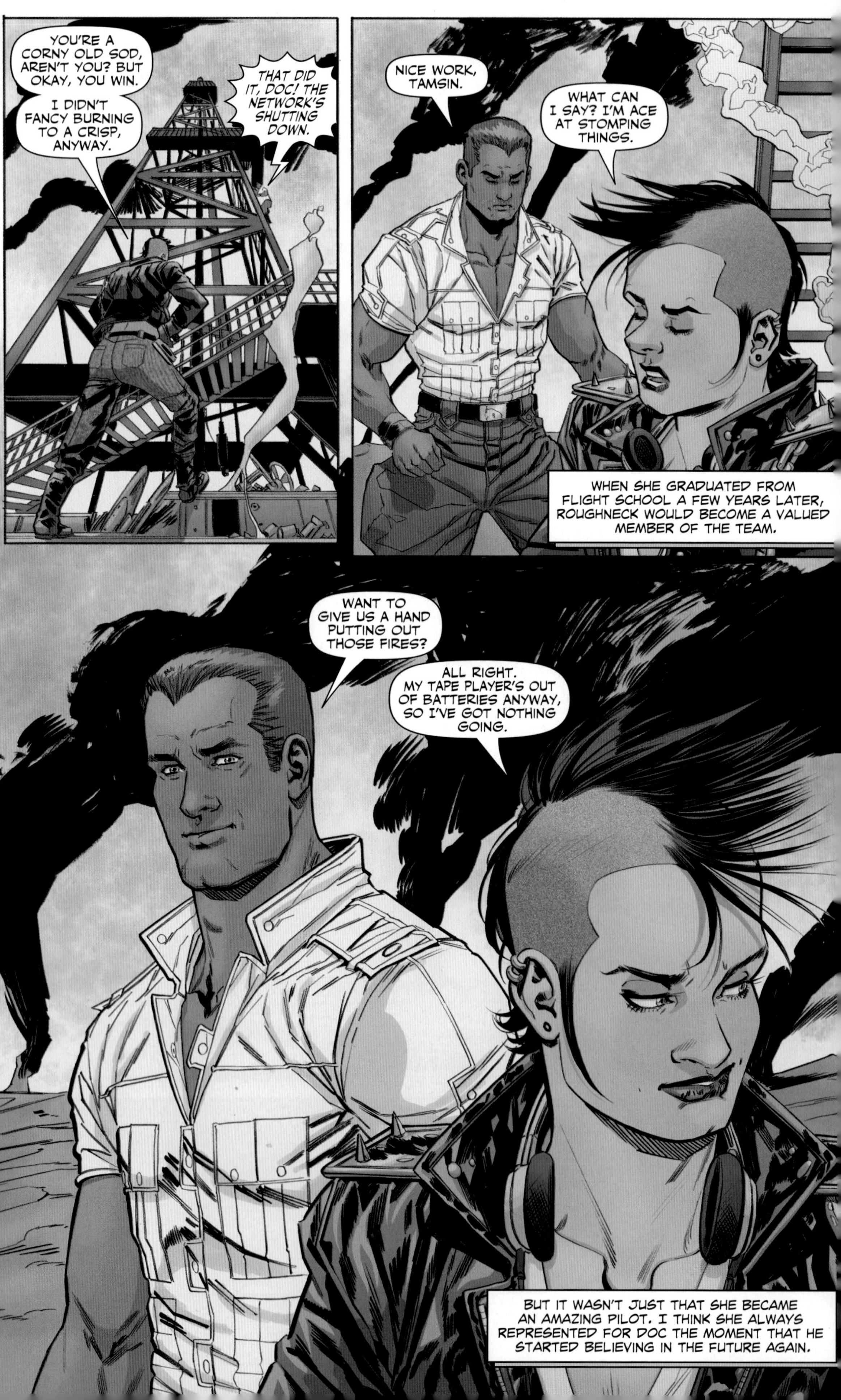
YOU'RE A CORNY OLD SOD, AREN'T YOU? BUT OKAY, YOU WIN.
I DIDN'T FANCY BURNING TO A CRISP, ANYWAY.
THAT DID IT, DOC! THE NETWORK'S SHUTTING DOWN.
NICE WORK, TAMSIN.
WHAT CAN I SAY? I'M ACE AT STOMPING THINGS.
WHEN SHE GRADUATED FROM FLIGHT SCHOOL A FEW YEARS LATER, ROUGHNECK WOULD BECOME A VALUED MEMBER OF THE TEAM.
WANT TO GIVE US A HAND PUTTING OUT THOSE FIRES?
ALL RIGHT. MY TAPE PLAYER'S OUT OF BATTERIES ANYWAY, SO I'VE GOT NOTHING GOING.
BUT IT WASN'T JUST THAT SHE BECAME AN AMAZING PILOT. I THINK SHE ALWAYS REPRESENTED FOR DOC THE MOMENT THAT HE STARTED BELIEVING IN THE FUTURE AGAIN.

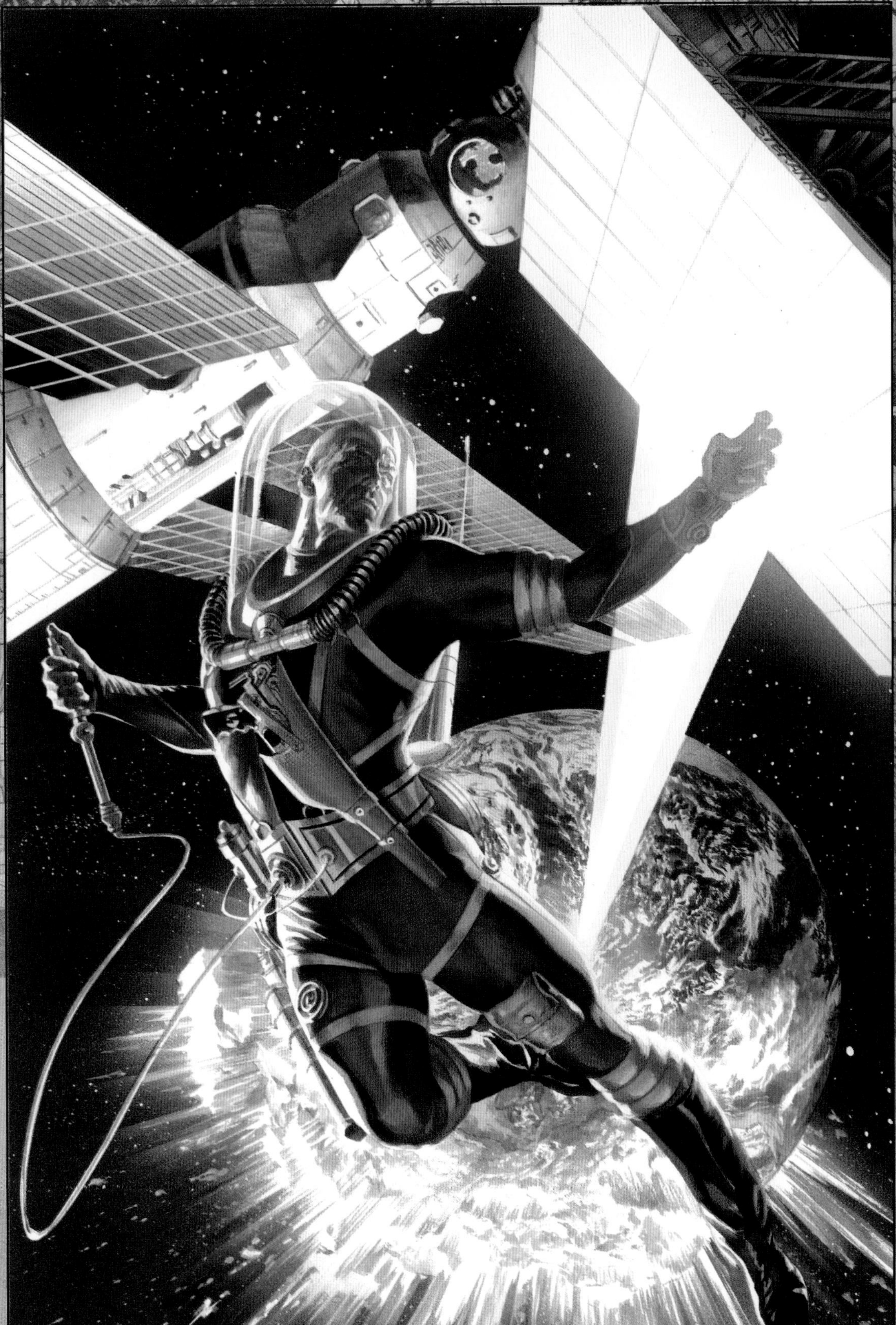

ISSUE **#5** COVER
art by **ALEX ROSS**

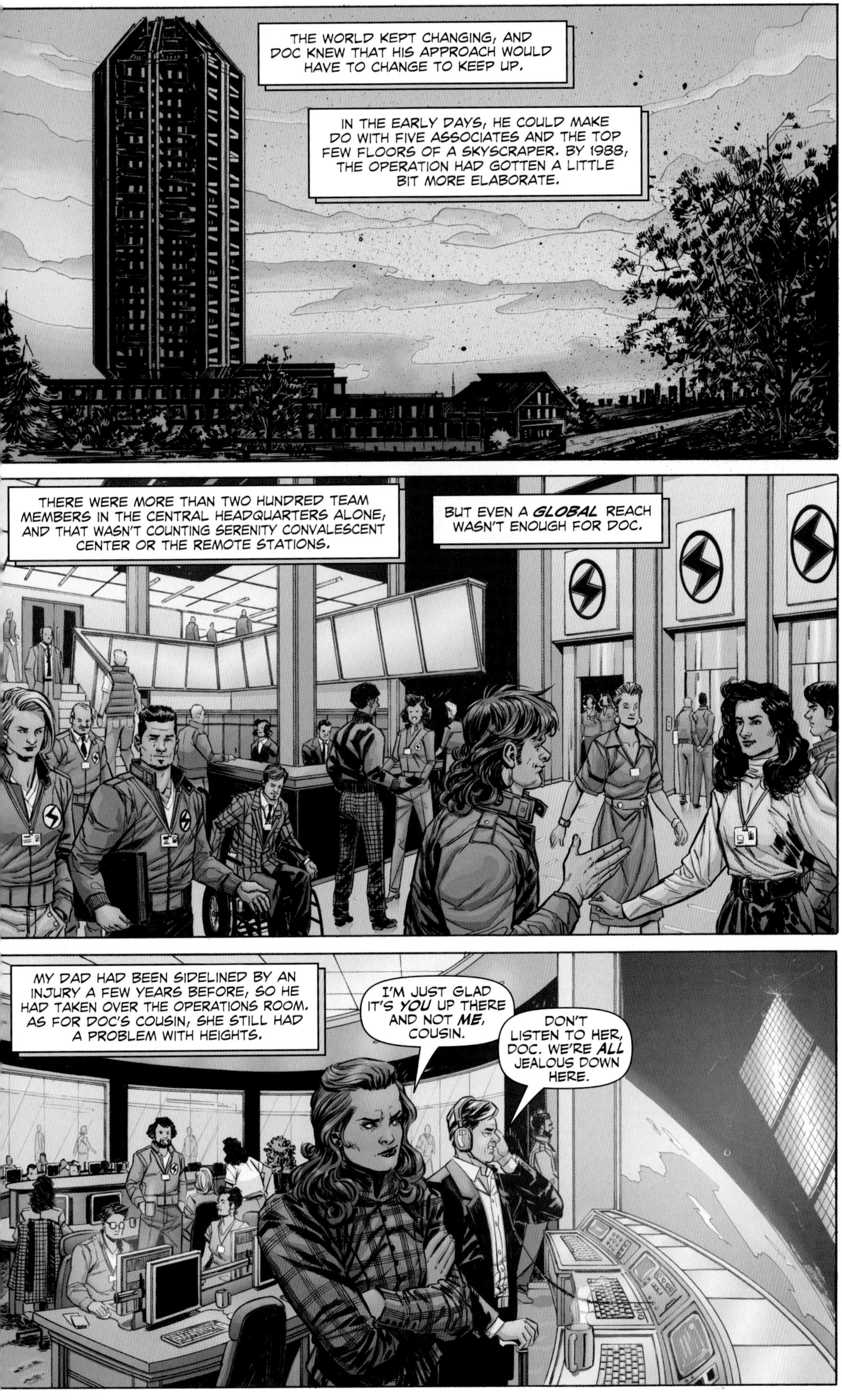
THE WORLD KEPT CHANGING, AND DOC KNEW THAT HIS APPROACH WOULD HAVE TO CHANGE TO KEEP UP.
IN THE EARLY DAYS, HE COULD MAKE DO WITH FIVE ASSOCIATES AND THE TOP FEW FLOORS OF A SKYSCRAPER. BY 1988, THE OPERATION HAD GOTTEN A LITTLE BIT MORE ELABORATE.
THERE WERE MORE THAN TWO HUNDRED TEAM MEMBERS IN THE CENTRAL HEADQUARTERS ALONE, AND THAT WASN'T COUNTING SERENITY CONVALESCENT CENTER OR THE REMOTE STATIONS.
BUT EVEN A *GLOBAL* REACH WASN'T ENOUGH FOR DOC.
MY DAD HAD BEEN SIDELINED BY AN INJURY A FEW YEARS BEFORE, SO HE HAD TAKEN OVER THE OPERATIONS ROOM. AS FOR DOC'S COUSIN, SHE STILL HAD A PROBLEM WITH HEIGHTS.
I'M JUST GLAD IT'S *YOU* UP THERE AND NOT *ME*, COUSIN.
DON'T LISTEN TO HER, DOC. WE'RE *ALL* JEALOUS DOWN HERE.

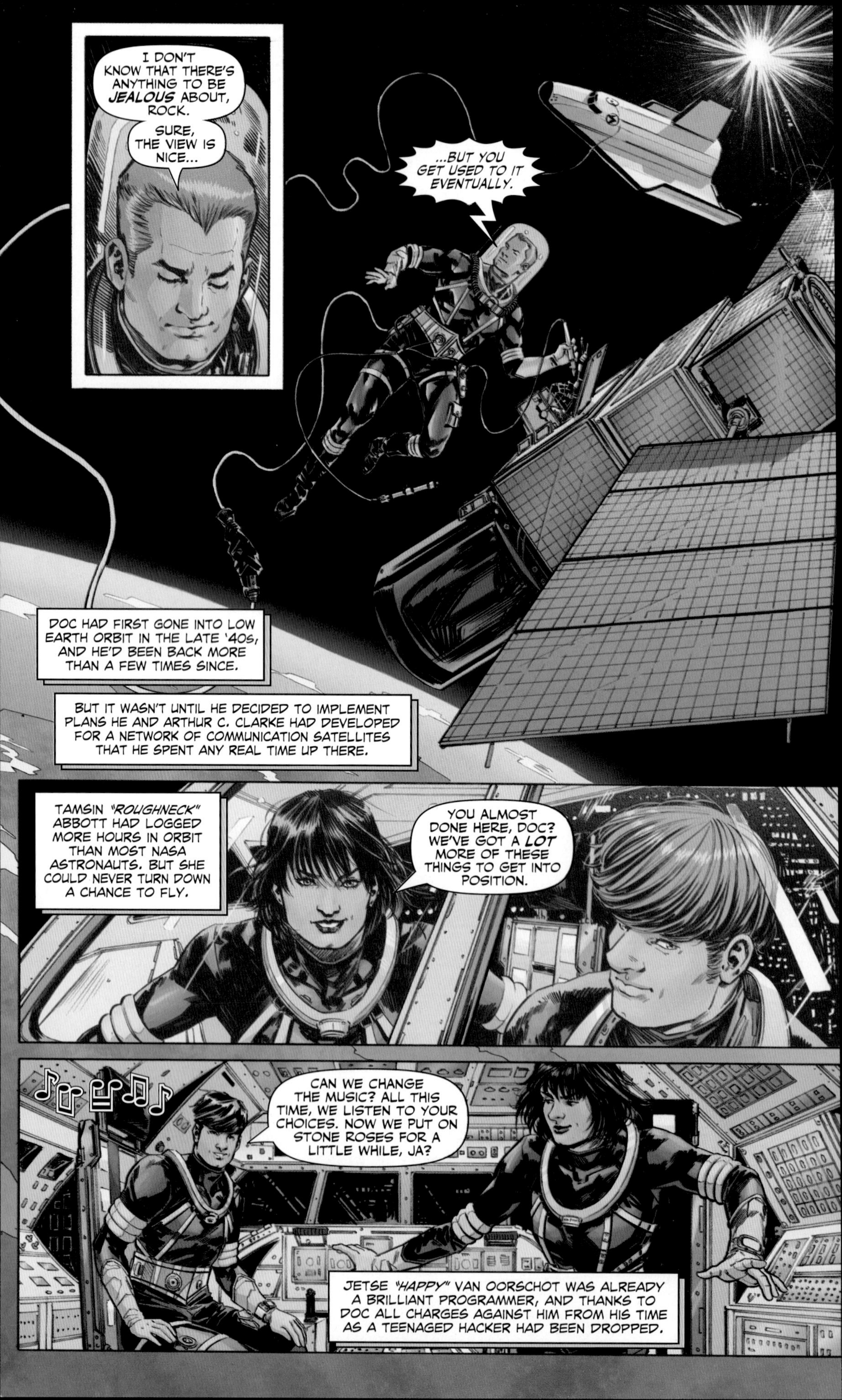
I DON'T KNOW THAT THERE'S ANYTHING TO BE JEALOUS ABOUT, ROCK.
SURE, THE VIEW IS NICE...
...BUT YOU GET USED TO IT EVENTUALLY.
DOC HAD FIRST GONE INTO LOW EARTH ORBIT IN THE LATE '40s, AND HE'D BEEN BACK MORE THAN A FEW TIMES SINCE.
BUT IT WASN'T UNTIL HE DECIDED TO IMPLEMENT PLANS HE AND ARTHUR C. CLARKE HAD DEVELOPED FOR A NETWORK OF COMMUNICATION SATELLITES THAT HE SPENT ANY REAL TIME UP THERE.
TAMSIN "ROUGHNECK" ABBOTT HAD LOGGED MORE HOURS IN ORBIT THAN MOST NASA ASTRONAUTS. BUT SHE COULD NEVER TURN DOWN A CHANCE TO FLY.
YOU ALMOST DONE HERE, DOC? WE'VE GOT A LOT MORE OF THESE THINGS TO GET INTO POSITION.
CAN WE CHANGE THE MUSIC? ALL THIS TIME, WE LISTEN TO YOUR CHOICES. NOW WE PUT ON STONE ROSES FOR A LITTLE WHILE, JA?
JETSE "HAPPY" VAN OORSCHOT WAS ALREADY A BRILLIANT PROGRAMMER, AND THANKS TO DOC ALL CHARGES AGAINST HIM FROM HIS TIME AS A TEENAGED HACKER HAD BEEN DROPPED.

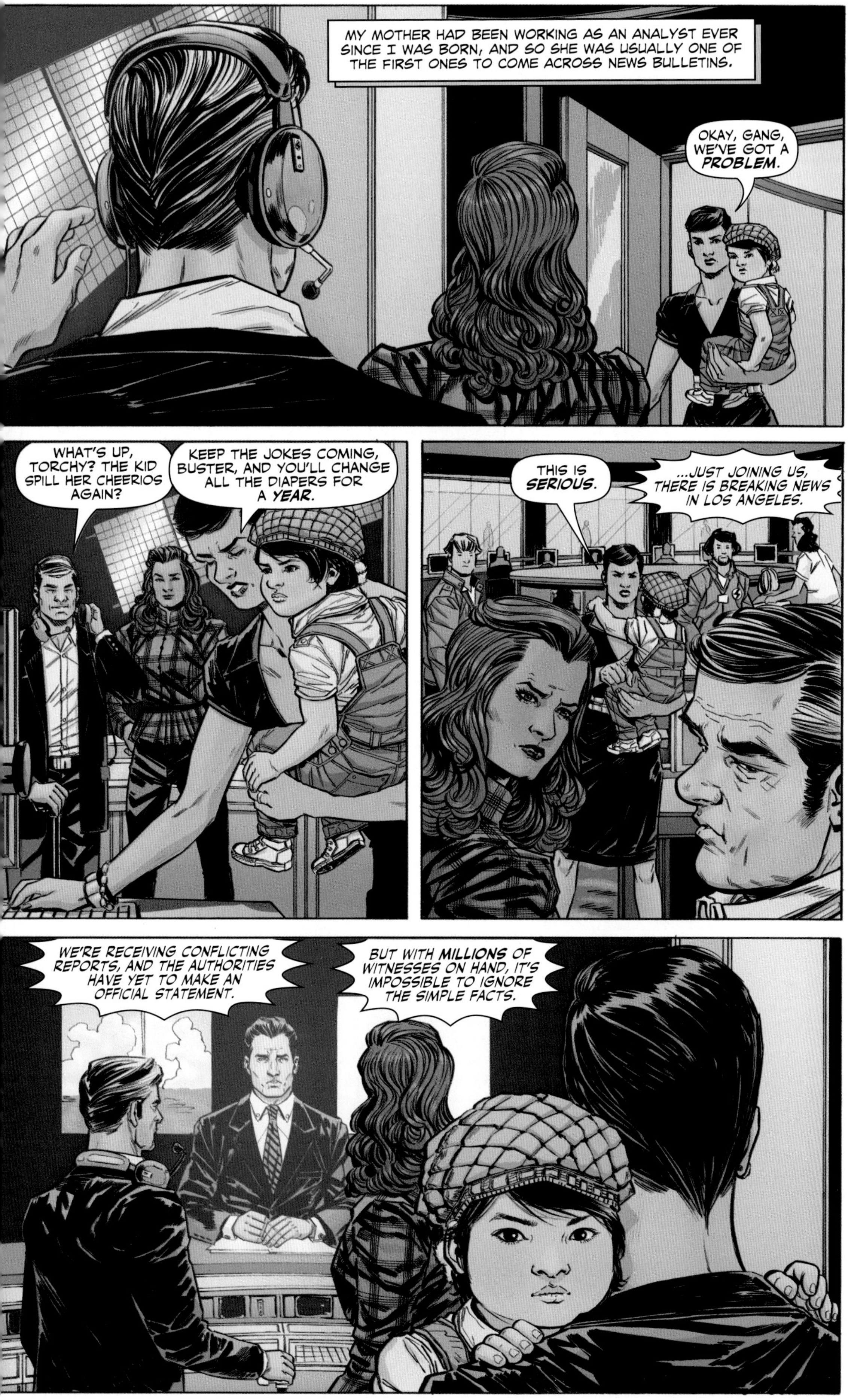
MY MOTHER HAD BEEN WORKING AS AN ANALYST EVER SINCE I WAS BORN, AND SO SHE WAS USUALLY ONE OF THE FIRST ONES TO COME ACROSS NEWS BULLETINS.
OKAY, GANG, WE'VE GOT A *PROBLEM*.
WHAT'S UP, TORCHY? THE KID SPILL HER CHEERIOS AGAIN?
KEEP THE JOKES COMING, BUSTER, AND YOU'LL CHANGE ALL THE DIAPERS FOR A *YEAR*.
THIS IS *SERIOUS*.
...JUST JOINING US, THERE IS BREAKING NEWS IN LOS ANGELES.
WE'RE RECEIVING CONFLICTING REPORTS, AND THE AUTHORITIES HAVE YET TO MAKE AN OFFICIAL STATEMENT.
BUT WITH **MILLIONS** OF WITNESSES ON HAND, IT'S IMPOSSIBLE TO IGNORE THE SIMPLE FACTS.

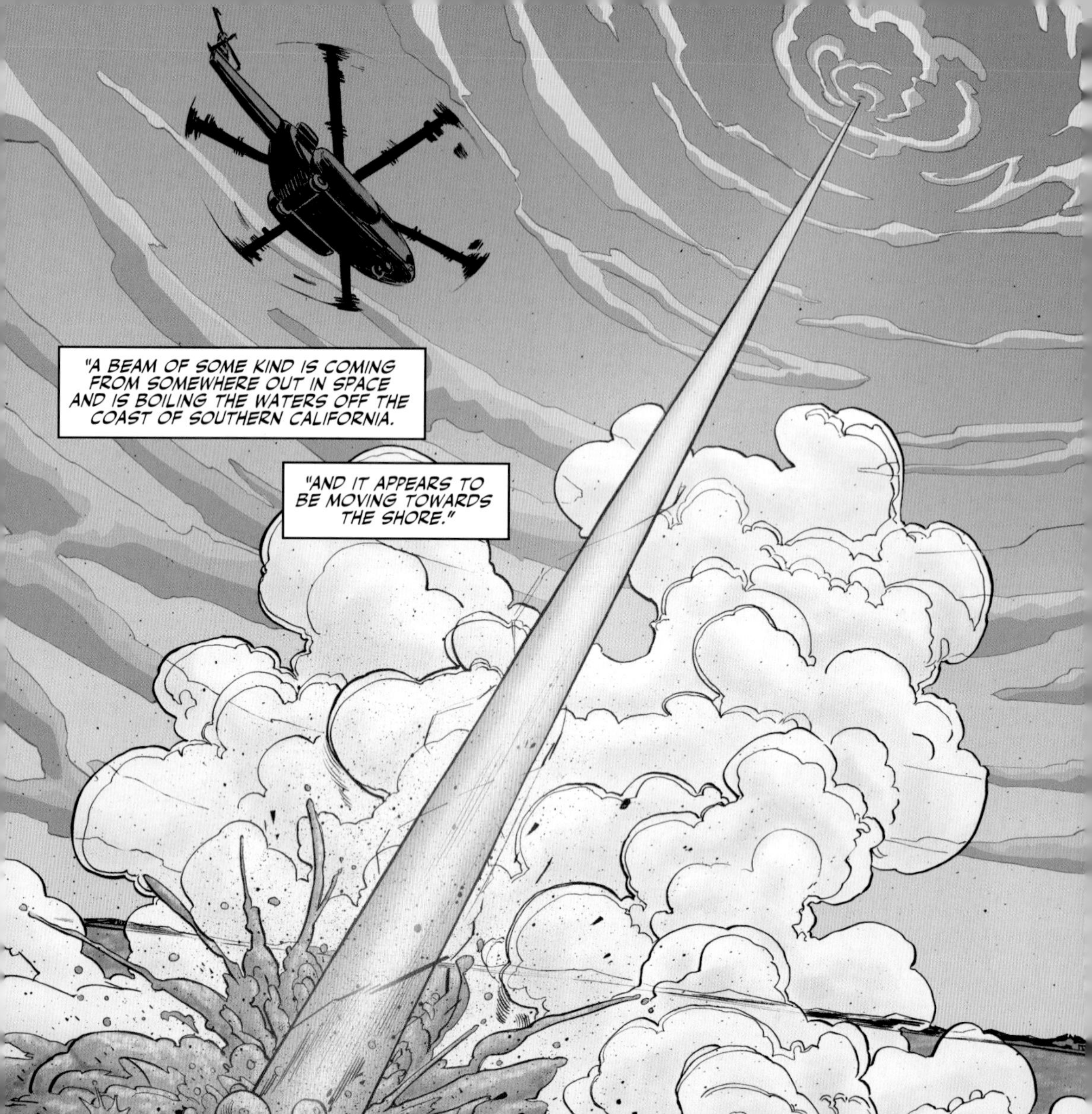
"A BEAM OF SOME KIND IS COMING FROM SOMEWHERE OUT IN SPACE AND IS BOILING THE WATERS OFF THE COAST OF SOUTHERN CALIFORNIA.
"AND IT APPEARS TO BE MOVING TOWARDS THE SHORE."

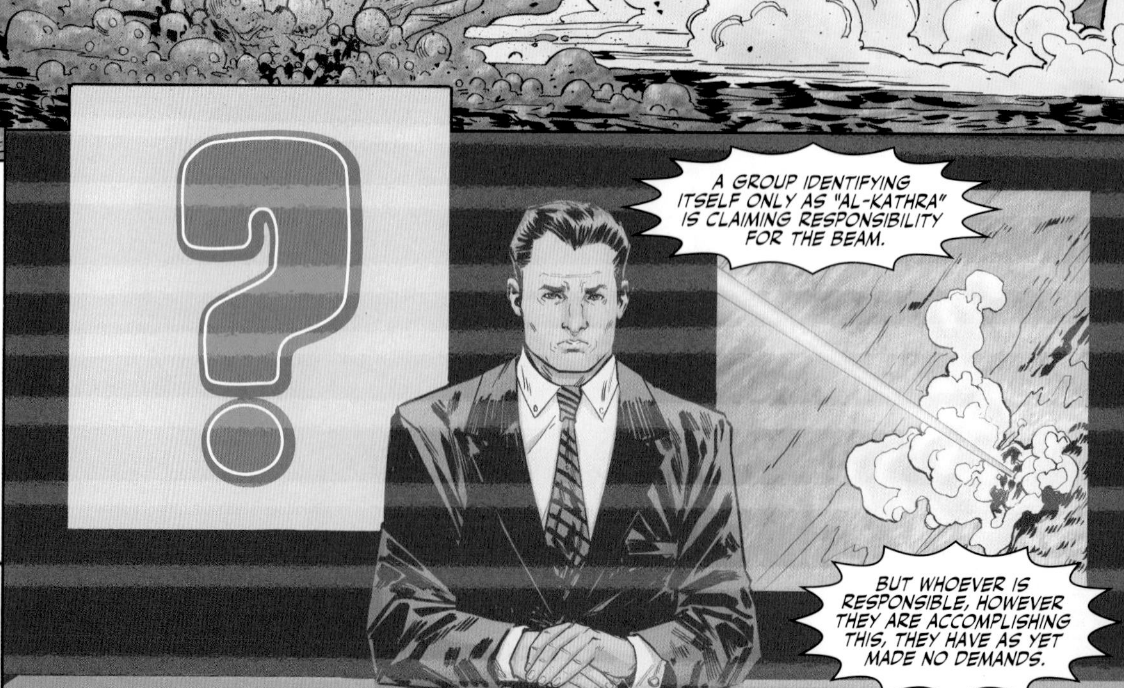
A GROUP IDENTIFYING ITSELF ONLY AS "AL-KATHRA" IS CLAIMING RESPONSIBILITY FOR THE BEAM.
BUT WHOEVER IS RESPONSIBLE, HOWEVER THEY ARE ACCOMPLISHING THIS, THEY HAVE AS YET MADE NO DEMANDS.

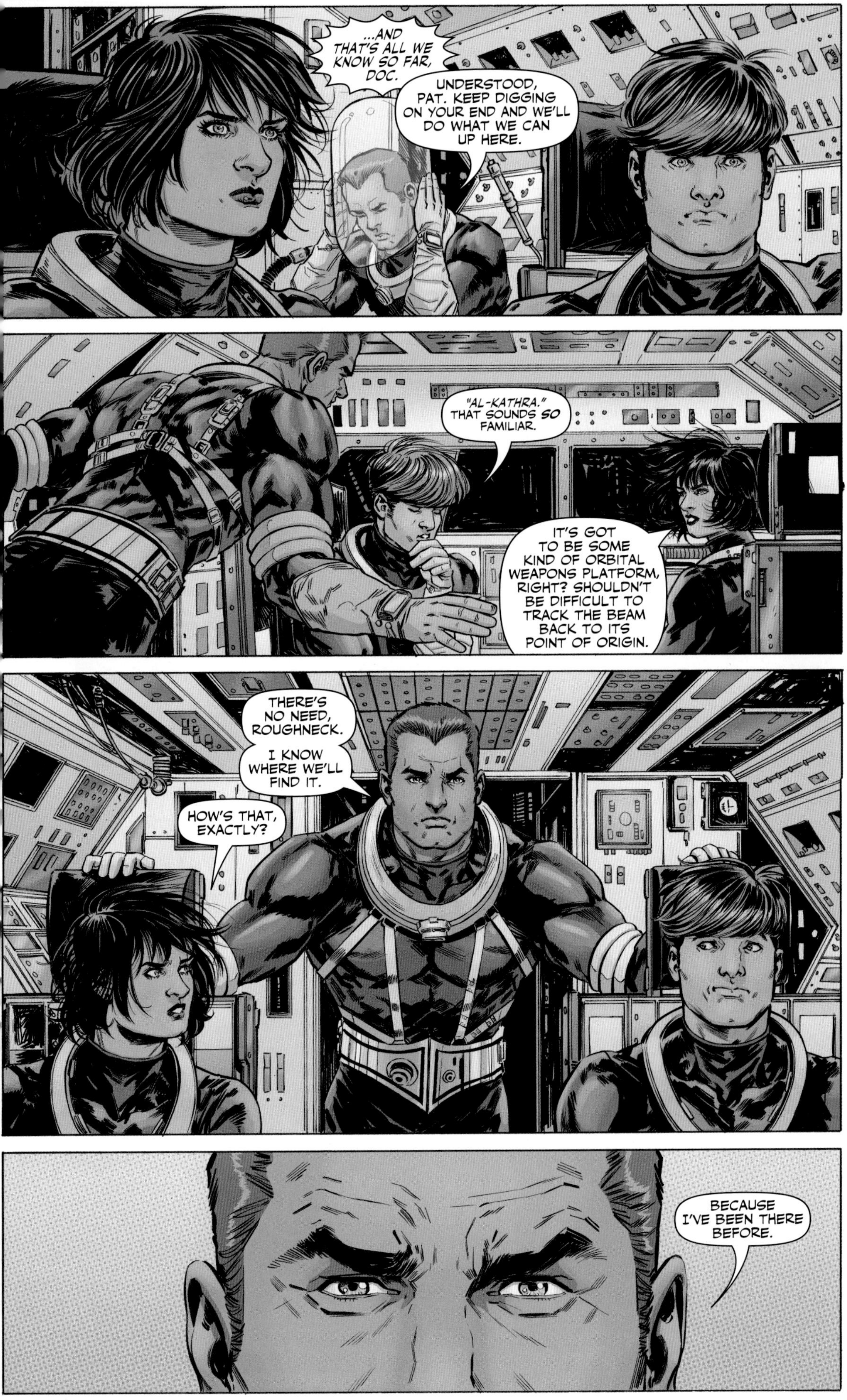
...AND THAT'S ALL WE KNOW SO FAR, DOC.
UNDERSTOOD, PAT. KEEP DIGGING ON YOUR END AND WE'LL DO WHAT WE CAN UP HERE.
"AL-KATHRA." THAT SOUNDS SO FAMILIAR.
IT'S GOT TO BE SOME KIND OF ORBITAL WEAPONS PLATFORM, RIGHT? SHOULDN'T BE DIFFICULT TO TRACK THE BEAM BACK TO ITS POINT OF ORIGIN.
THERE'S NO NEED, ROUGHNECK.
I KNOW WHERE WE'LL FIND IT.
HOW'S THAT, EXACTLY?
BECAUSE I'VE BEEN THERE BEFORE.

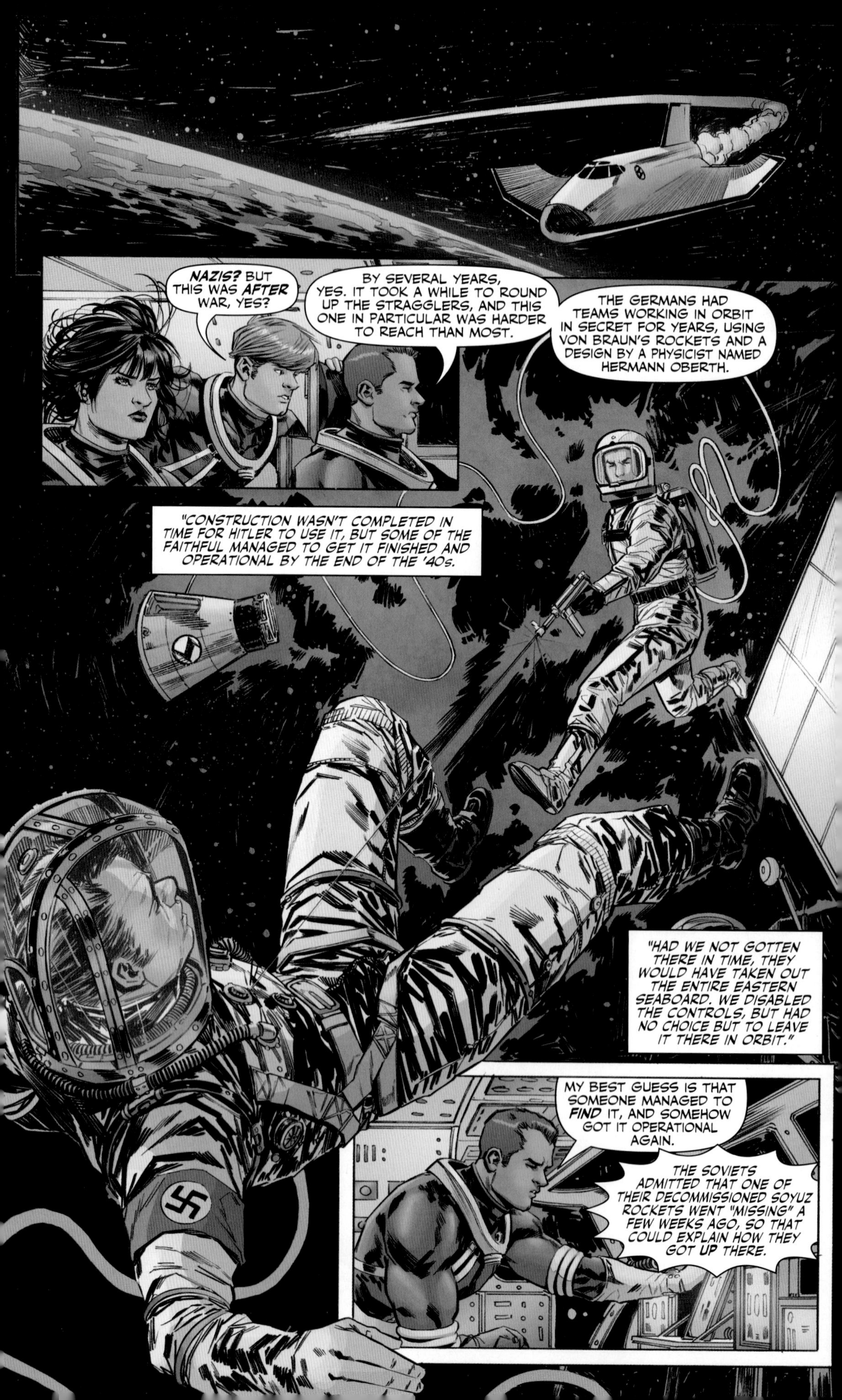

NAZIS? BUT THIS WAS AFTER WAR, YES?
BY SEVERAL YEARS, YES. IT TOOK A WHILE TO ROUND UP THE STRAGGLERS, AND THIS ONE IN PARTICULAR WAS HARDER TO REACH THAN MOST.
THE GERMANS HAD TEAMS WORKING IN ORBIT IN SECRET FOR YEARS, USING VON BRAUN'S ROCKETS AND A DESIGN BY A PHYSICIST NAMED HERMANN OBERTH.
"CONSTRUCTION WASN'T COMPLETED IN TIME FOR HITLER TO USE IT, BUT SOME OF THE FAITHFUL MANAGED TO GET IT FINISHED AND OPERATIONAL BY THE END OF THE '40s.
"HAD WE NOT GOTTEN THERE IN TIME, THEY WOULD HAVE TAKEN OUT THE ENTIRE EASTERN SEABOARD. WE DISABLED THE CONTROLS, BUT HAD NO CHOICE BUT TO LEAVE IT THERE IN ORBIT."
MY BEST GUESS IS THAT SOMEONE MANAGED TO FIND IT, AND SOMEHOW GOT IT OPERATIONAL AGAIN.
THE SOVIETS ADMITTED THAT ONE OF THEIR DECOMMISSIONED SOYUZ ROCKETS WENT "MISSING" A FEW WEEKS AGO, SO THAT COULD EXPLAIN HOW THEY GOT UP THERE.

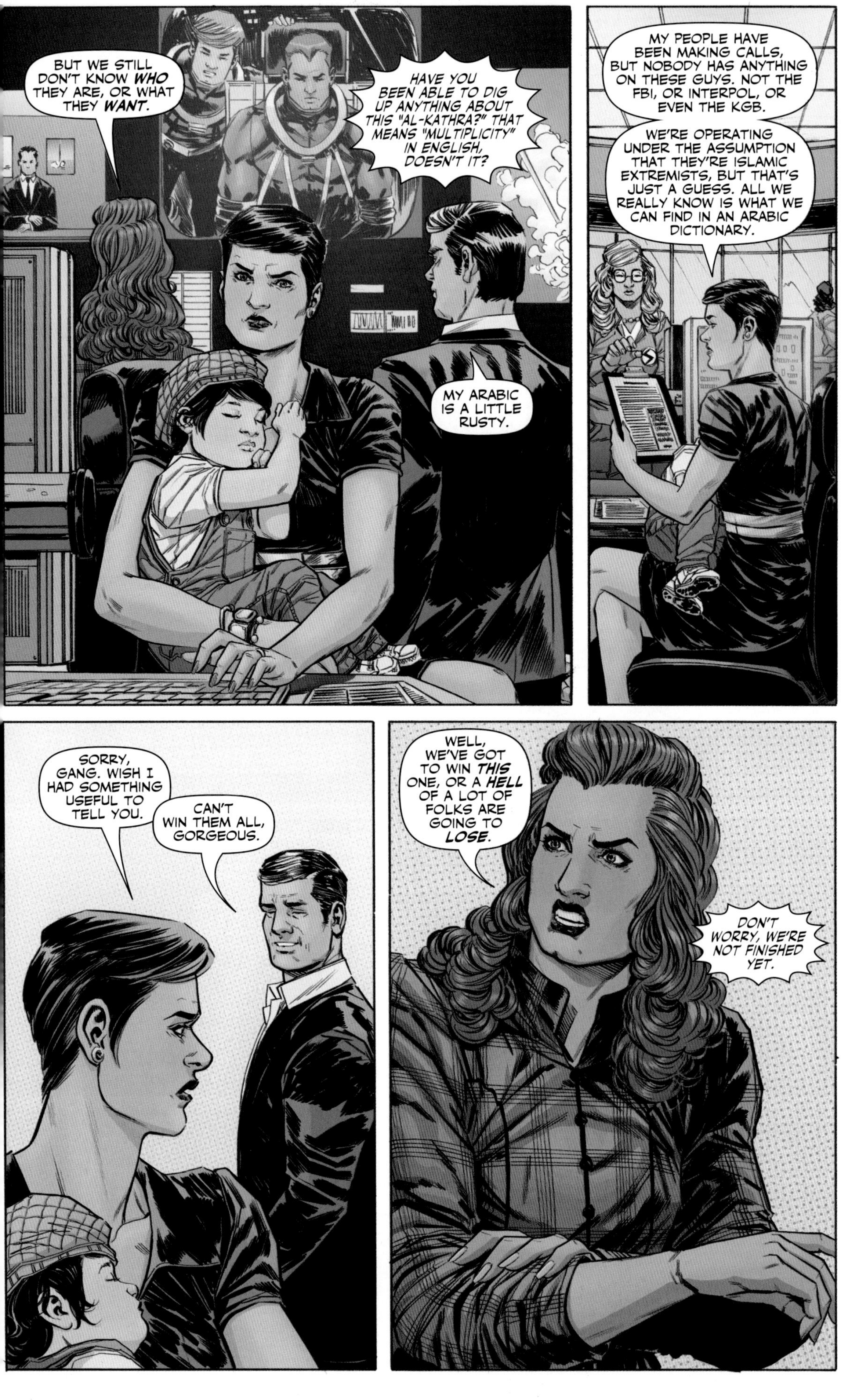

BUT WE STILL DON'T KNOW *WHO* THEY ARE, OR WHAT THEY *WANT*.
HAVE YOU BEEN ABLE TO DIG UP ANYTHING ABOUT THIS "AL-KATHRA?" THAT MEANS "MULTIPLICITY" IN ENGLISH, DOESN'T IT?
MY ARABIC IS A LITTLE RUSTY.
MY PEOPLE HAVE BEEN MAKING CALLS, BUT NOBODY HAS ANYTHING ON THESE GUYS. NOT THE FBI, OR INTERPOL, OR EVEN THE KGB.
WE'RE OPERATING UNDER THE ASSUMPTION THAT THEY'RE ISLAMIC EXTREMISTS, BUT THAT'S JUST A GUESS. ALL WE REALLY KNOW IS WHAT WE CAN FIND IN AN ARABIC DICTIONARY.
SORRY, GANG. WISH I HAD SOMETHING USEFUL TO TELL YOU.
CAN'T WIN THEM ALL, GORGEOUS.
WELL, WE'VE GOT TO WIN *THIS* ONE, OR A *HELL* OF A LOT OF FOLKS ARE GOING TO *LOSE*.
DON'T WORRY, WE'RE NOT FINISHED YET.

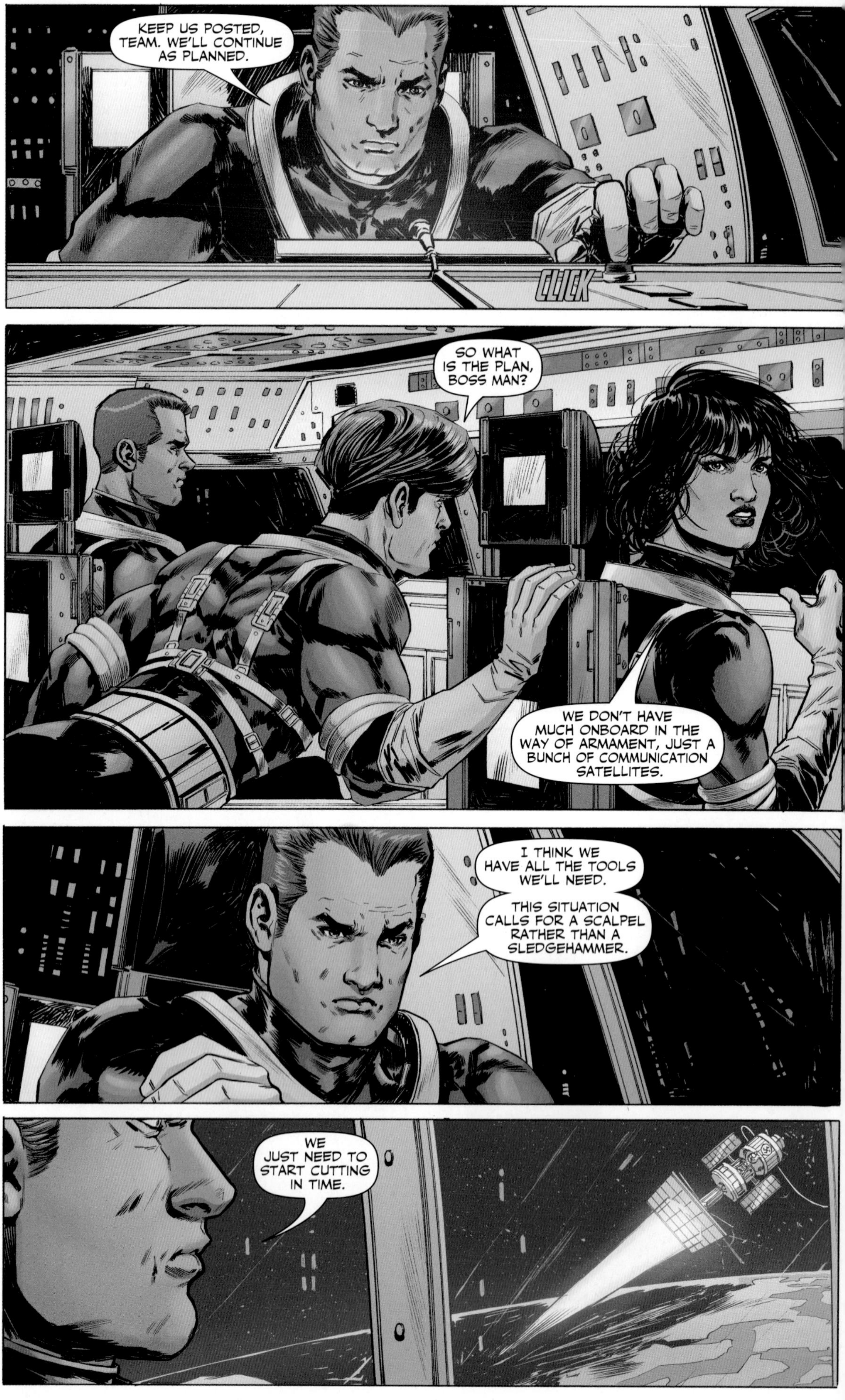
KEEP US POSTED, TEAM. WE'LL CONTINUE AS PLANNED.
CLICK
SO WHAT IS THE PLAN, BOSS MAN?
WE DON'T HAVE MUCH ONBOARD IN THE WAY OF ARMAMENT, JUST A BUNCH OF COMMUNICATION SATELLITES.
I THINK WE HAVE ALL THE TOOLS WE'LL NEED.
THIS SITUATION CALLS FOR A SCALPEL RATHER THAN A SLEDGEHAMMER.
WE JUST NEED TO START CUTTING IN TIME.

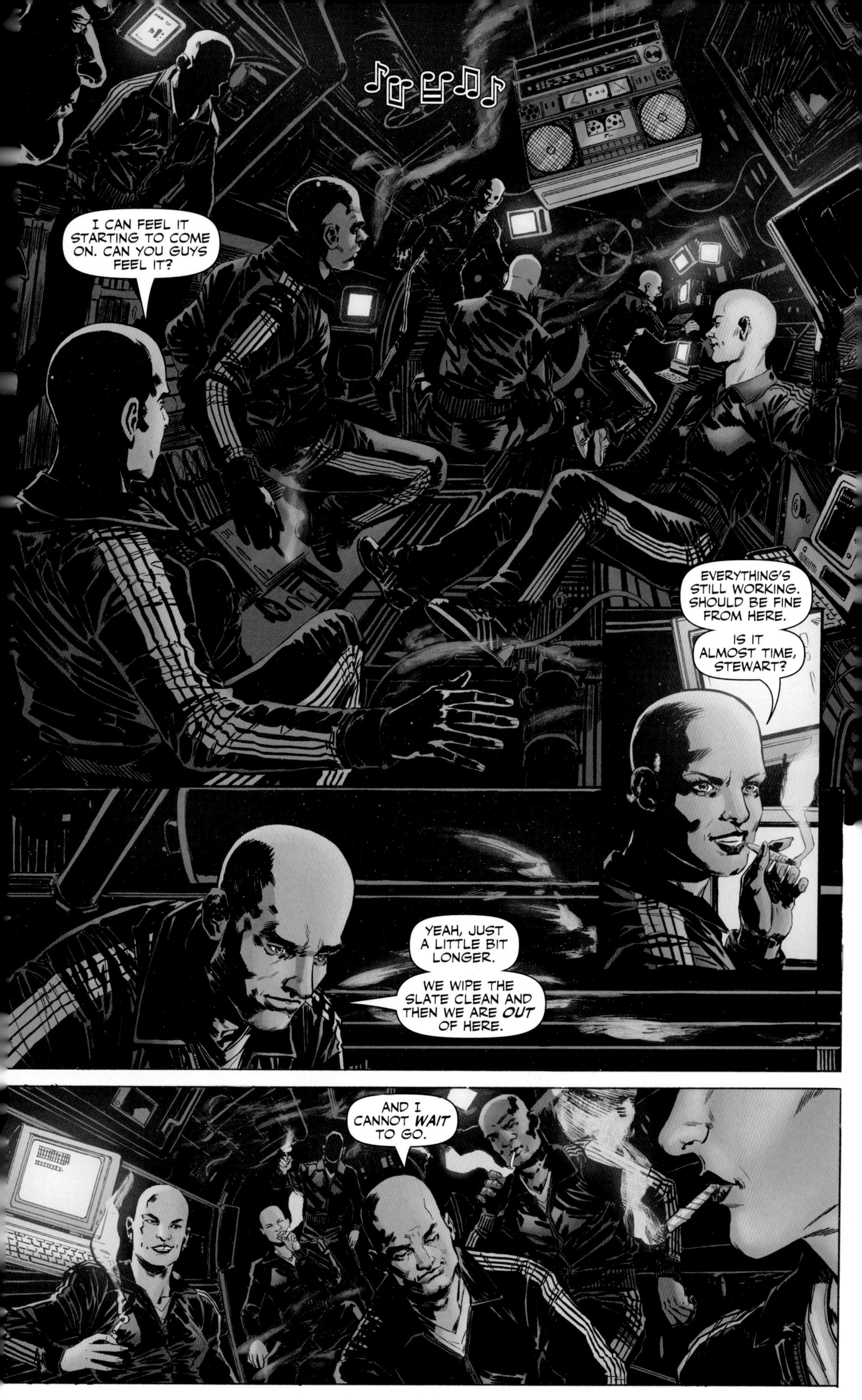
I CAN FEEL IT STARTING TO COME ON. CAN YOU GUYS FEEL IT?
EVERYTHING'S STILL WORKING. SHOULD BE FINE FROM HERE.
IS IT ALMOST TIME, STEWART?
YEAH, JUST A LITTLE BIT LONGER.
WE WIPE THE SLATE CLEAN AND THEN WE ARE *OUT* OF HERE.
AND I CANNOT *WAIT* TO GO.

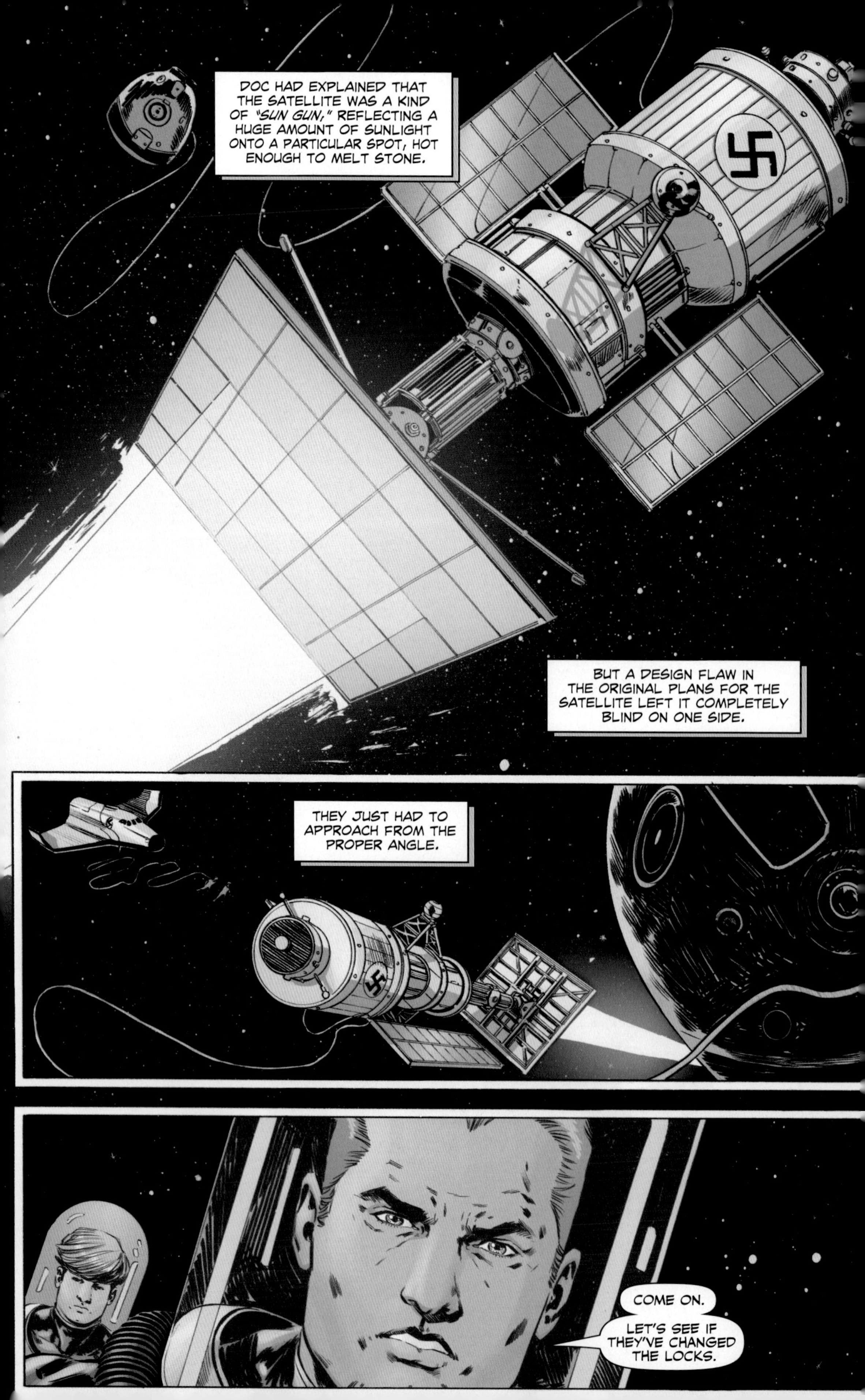
DOC HAD EXPLAINED THAT THE SATELLITE WAS A KIND OF "SUN GUN," REFLECTING A HUGE AMOUNT OF SUNLIGHT ONTO A PARTICULAR SPOT, HOT ENOUGH TO MELT STONE.
BUT A DESIGN FLAW IN THE ORIGINAL PLANS FOR THE SATELLITE LEFT IT COMPLETELY BLIND ON ONE SIDE.
THEY JUST HAD TO APPROACH FROM THE PROPER ANGLE.
COME ON.
LET'S SEE IF THEY'VE CHANGED THE LOCKS.

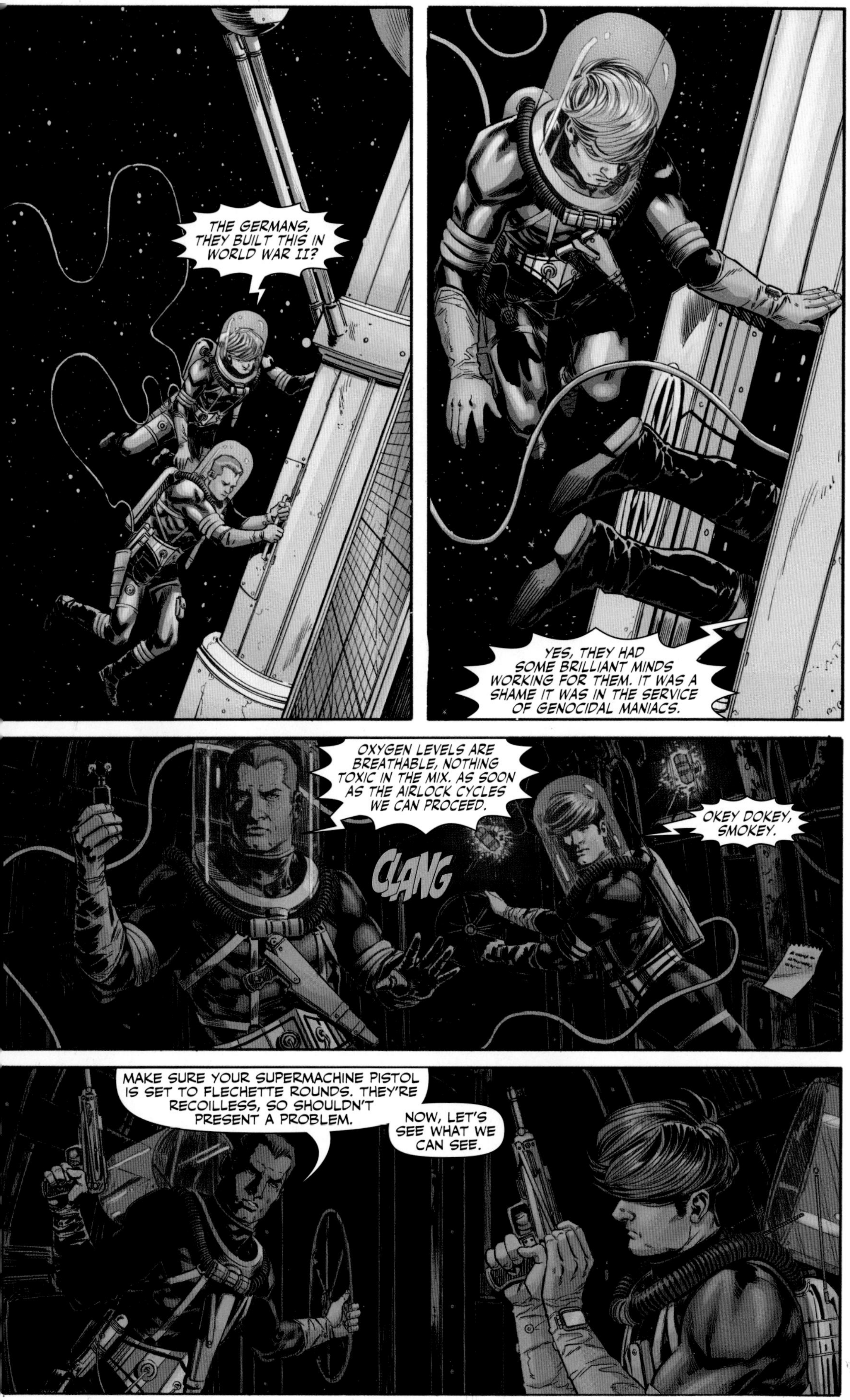
THE GERMANS, THEY BUILT THIS IN WORLD WAR II?
YES, THEY HAD SOME BRILLIANT MINDS WORKING FOR THEM. IT WAS A SHAME IT WAS IN THE SERVICE OF GENOCIDAL MANIACS.
OXYGEN LEVELS ARE BREATHABLE, NOTHING TOXIC IN THE MIX. AS SOON AS THE AIRLOCK CYCLES WE CAN PROCEED.
OKEY DOKEY, SMOKEY.
CLANG
MAKE SURE YOUR SUPERMACHINE PISTOL IS SET TO FLECHETTE ROUNDS. THEY'RE RECOILLESS, SO SHOULDN'T PRESENT A PROBLEM.
NOW, LET'S SEE WHAT WE CAN SEE.

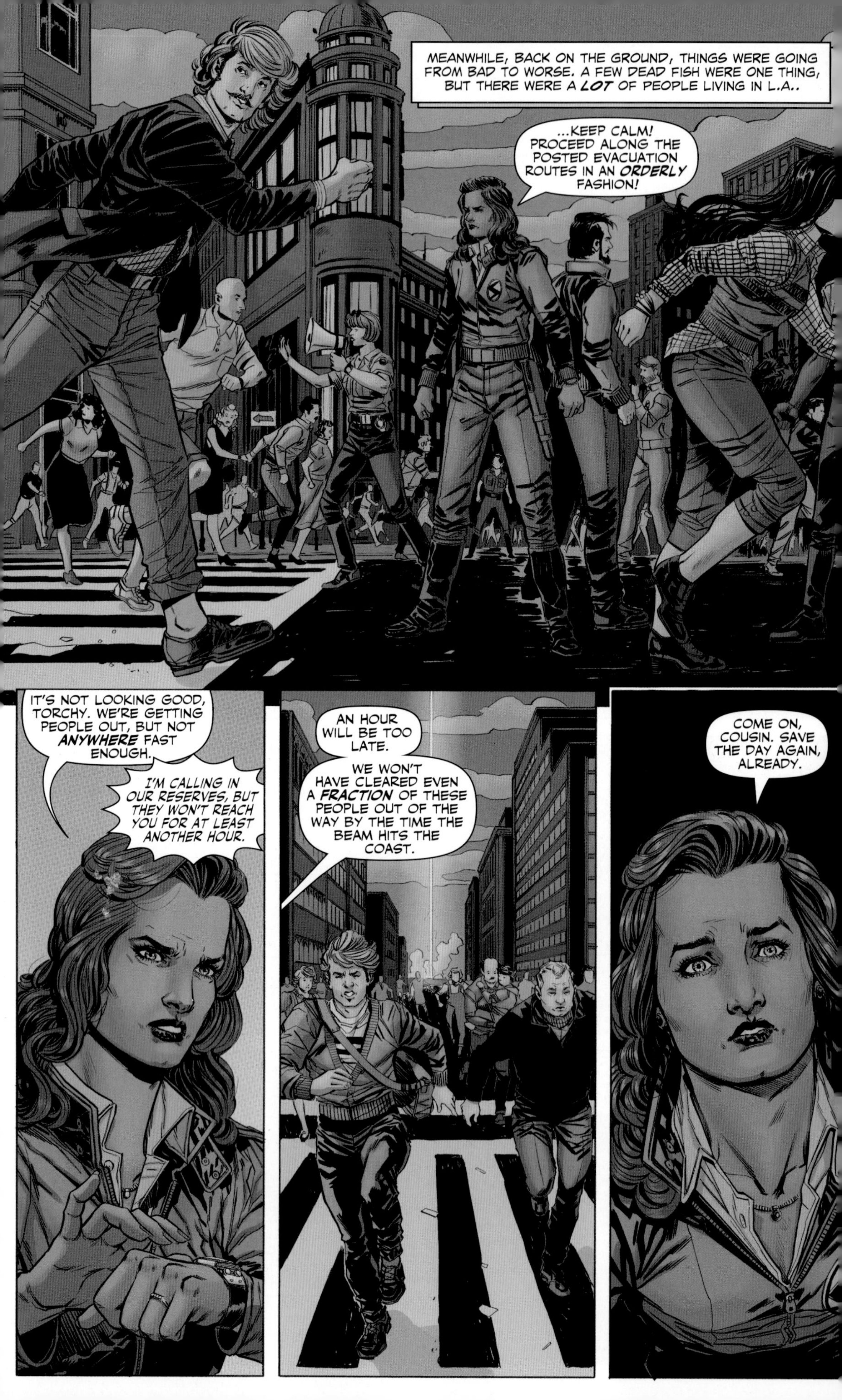
MEANWHILE, BACK ON THE GROUND, THINGS WERE GOING FROM BAD TO WORSE. A FEW DEAD FISH WERE ONE THING, BUT THERE WERE A LOT OF PEOPLE LIVING IN L.A..
...KEEP CALM! PROCEED ALONG THE POSTED EVACUATION ROUTES IN AN ORDERLY FASHION!
IT'S NOT LOOKING GOOD, TORCHY. WE'RE GETTING PEOPLE OUT, BUT NOT ANYWHERE FAST ENOUGH.
I'M CALLING IN OUR RESERVES, BUT THEY WON'T REACH YOU FOR AT LEAST ANOTHER HOUR.
AN HOUR WILL BE TOO LATE.
WE WON'T HAVE CLEARED EVEN A FRACTION OF THESE PEOPLE OUT OF THE WAY BY THE TIME THE BEAM HITS THE COAST.
COME ON, COUSIN. SAVE THE DAY AGAIN, ALREADY.

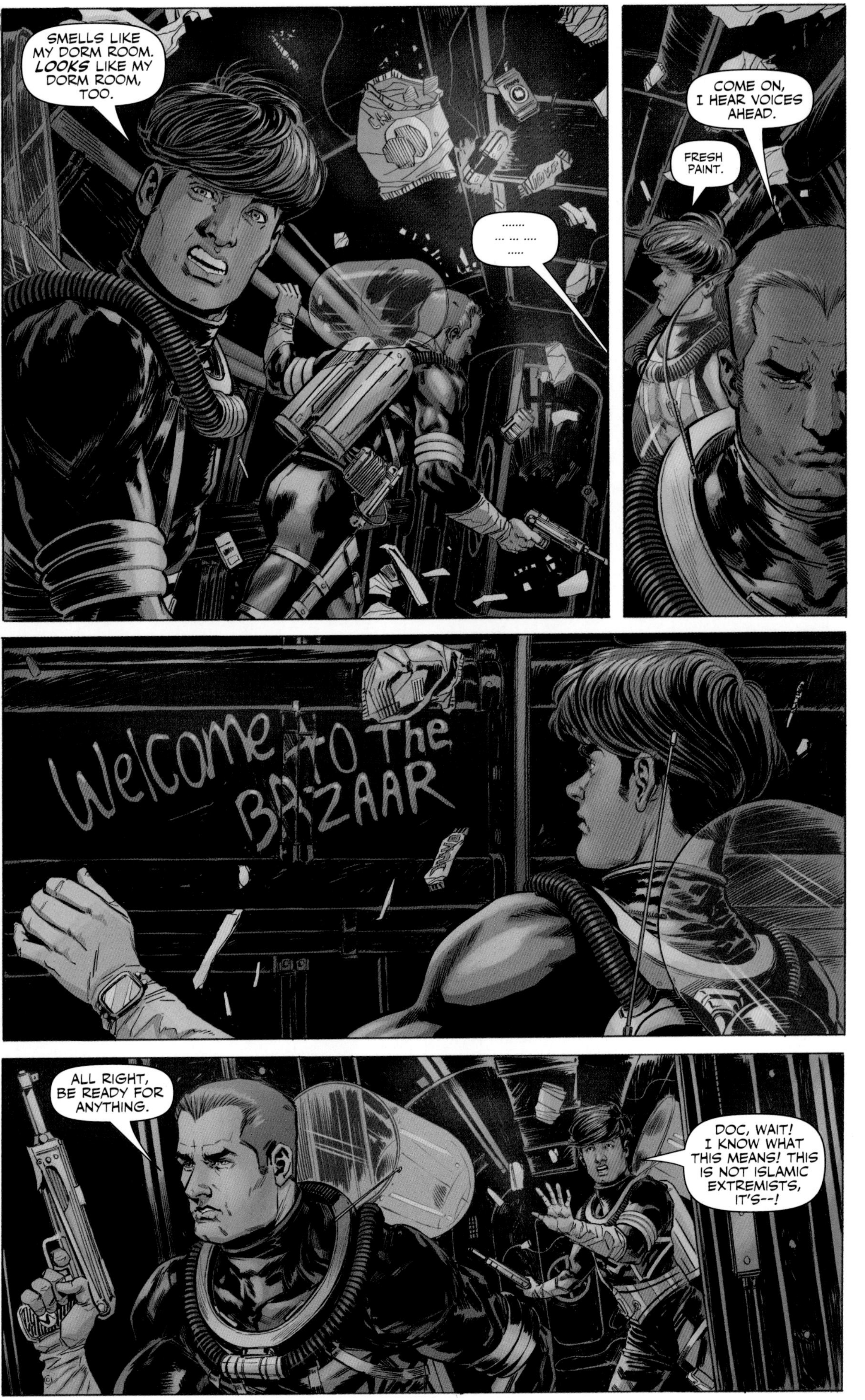

SMELLS LIKE MY DORM ROOM. LOOKS LIKE MY DORM ROOM, TOO.
....
COME ON, I HEAR VOICES AHEAD.
FRESH PAINT.
Welcome to The BAZAAR
ALL RIGHT, BE READY FOR ANYTHING.
DOC, WAIT! I KNOW WHAT THIS MEANS! THIS IS NOT ISLAMIC EXTREMISTS, IT'S--!

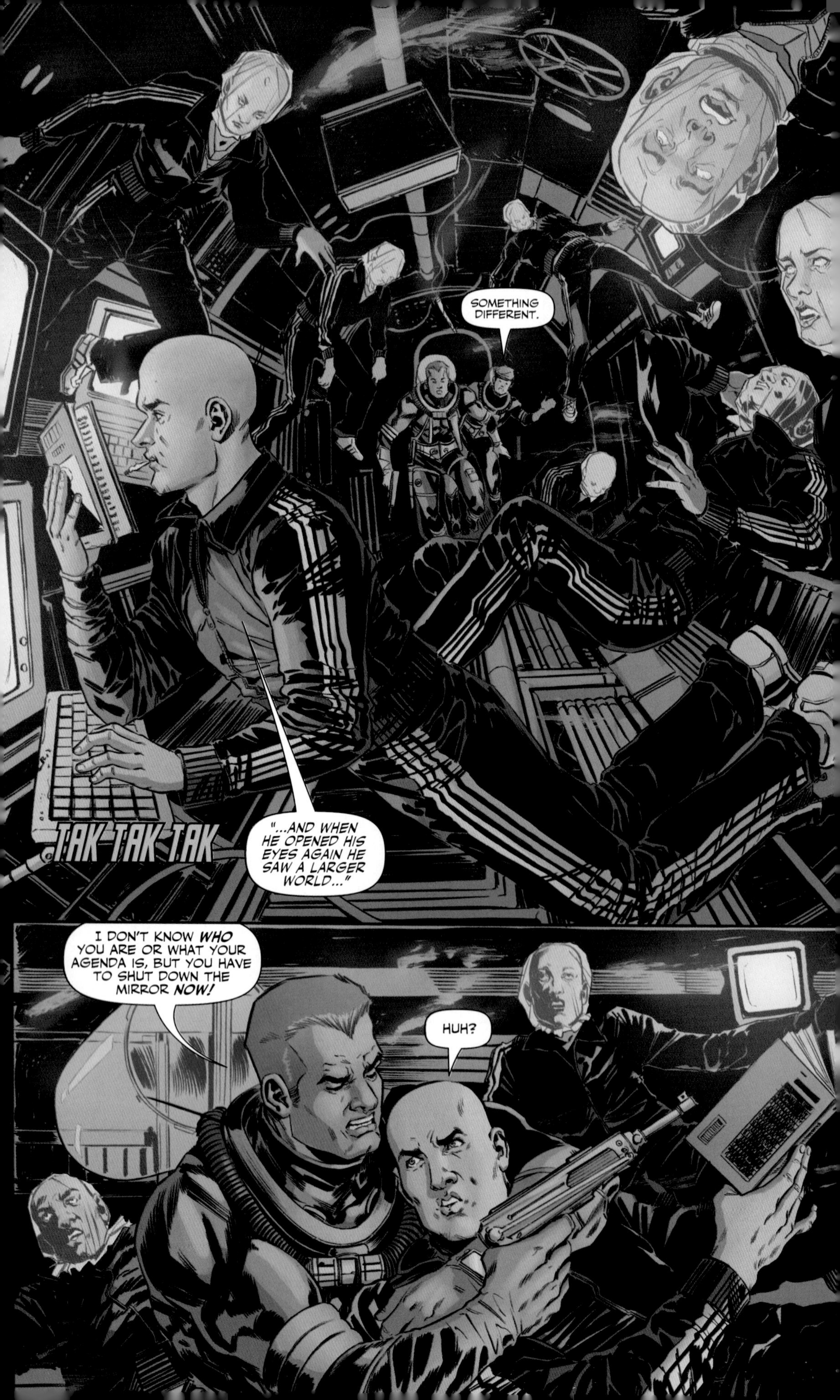
SOMETHING DIFFERENT.
TAK TAK TAK
"...AND WHEN HE OPENED HIS EYES AGAIN HE SAW A LARGER WORLD..."
I DON'T KNOW **WHO** YOU ARE OR WHAT YOUR AGENDA IS, BUT YOU HAVE TO SHUT DOWN THE MIRROR **NOW!**
HUH?

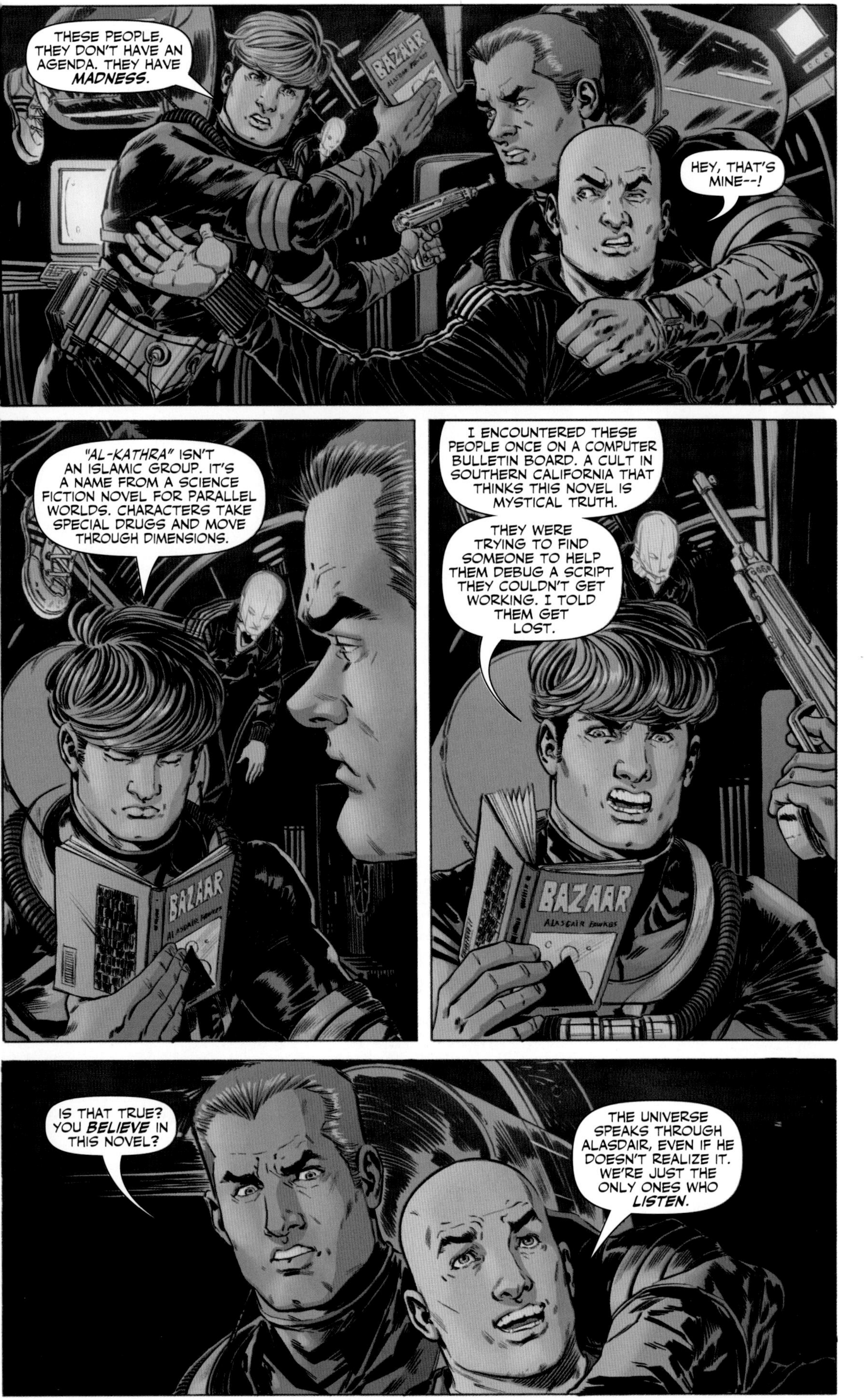
THESE PEOPLE, THEY DON'T HAVE AN AGENDA. THEY HAVE *MADNESS*.
BAZAAR
HEY, THAT'S MINE--!
"*AL-KATHRA*" ISN'T AN ISLAMIC GROUP. IT'S A NAME FROM A SCIENCE FICTION NOVEL FOR PARALLEL WORLDS. CHARACTERS TAKE SPECIAL DRUGS AND MOVE THROUGH DIMENSIONS.
BAZAAR
I ENCOUNTERED THESE PEOPLE ONCE ON A COMPUTER BULLETIN BOARD. A CULT IN SOUTHERN CALIFORNIA THAT THINKS THIS NOVEL IS MYSTICAL TRUTH.
THEY WERE TRYING TO FIND SOMEONE TO HELP THEM DEBUG A SCRIPT THEY COULDN'T GET WORKING. I TOLD THEM GET LOST.
BAZAAR
ALASCAIR FOWKES
IS THAT TRUE? YOU *BELIEVE* IN THIS NOVEL?
THE UNIVERSE SPEAKS THROUGH ALASDAIR, EVEN IF HE DOESN'T REALIZE IT. WE'RE JUST THE ONLY ONES WHO *LISTEN*.

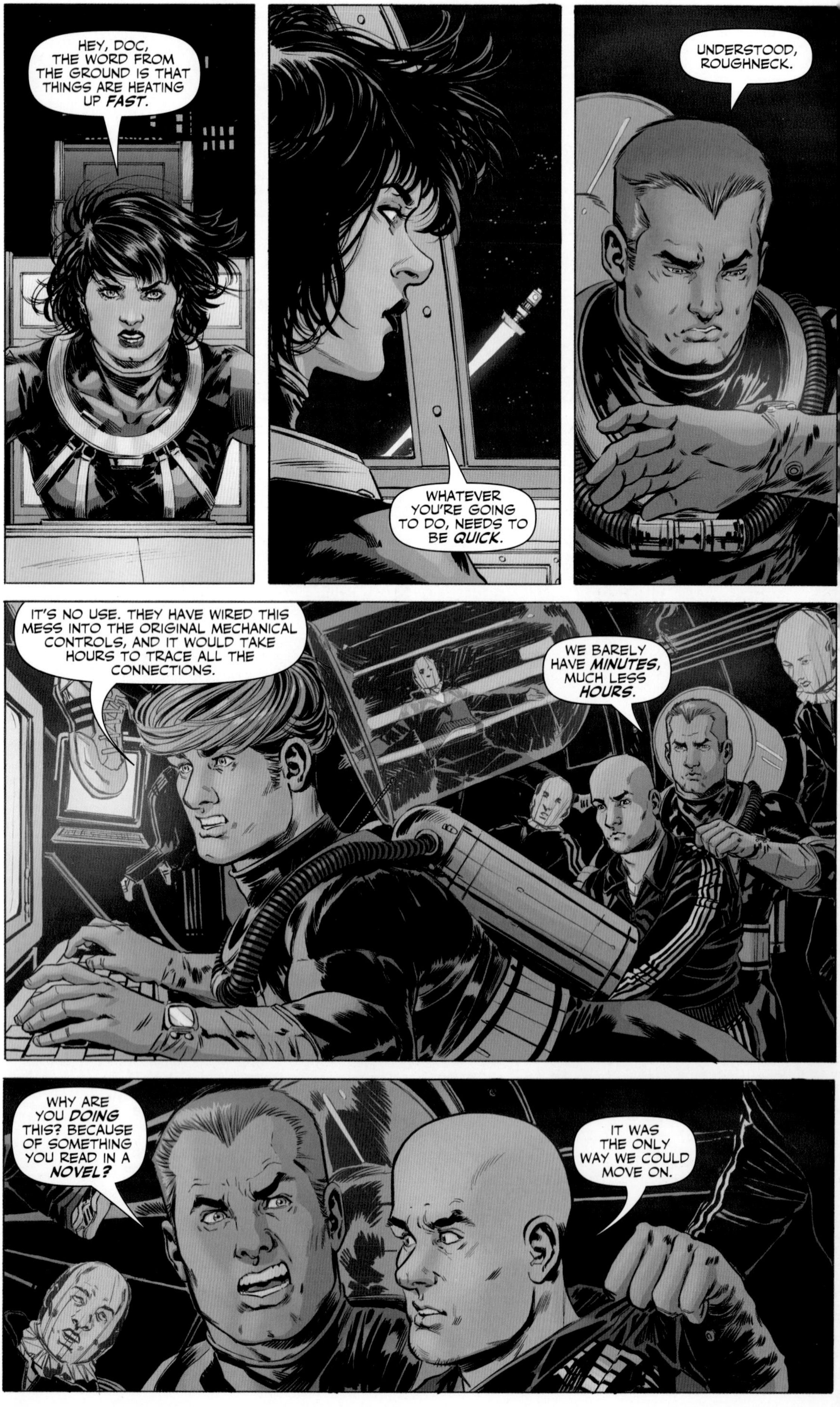

HEY, DOC, THE WORD FROM THE GROUND IS THAT THINGS ARE HEATING UP *FAST*.
WHATEVER YOU'RE GOING TO DO, NEEDS TO BE *QUICK*.
UNDERSTOOD, ROUGHNECK.
IT'S NO USE. THEY HAVE WIRED THIS MESS INTO THE ORIGINAL MECHANICAL CONTROLS, AND IT WOULD TAKE HOURS TO TRACE ALL THE CONNECTIONS.
WE BARELY HAVE *MINUTES*, MUCH LESS *HOURS*.
WHY ARE YOU *DOING* THIS? BECAUSE OF SOMETHING YOU READ IN A *NOVEL?*
IT WAS THE ONLY WAY WE COULD MOVE ON.

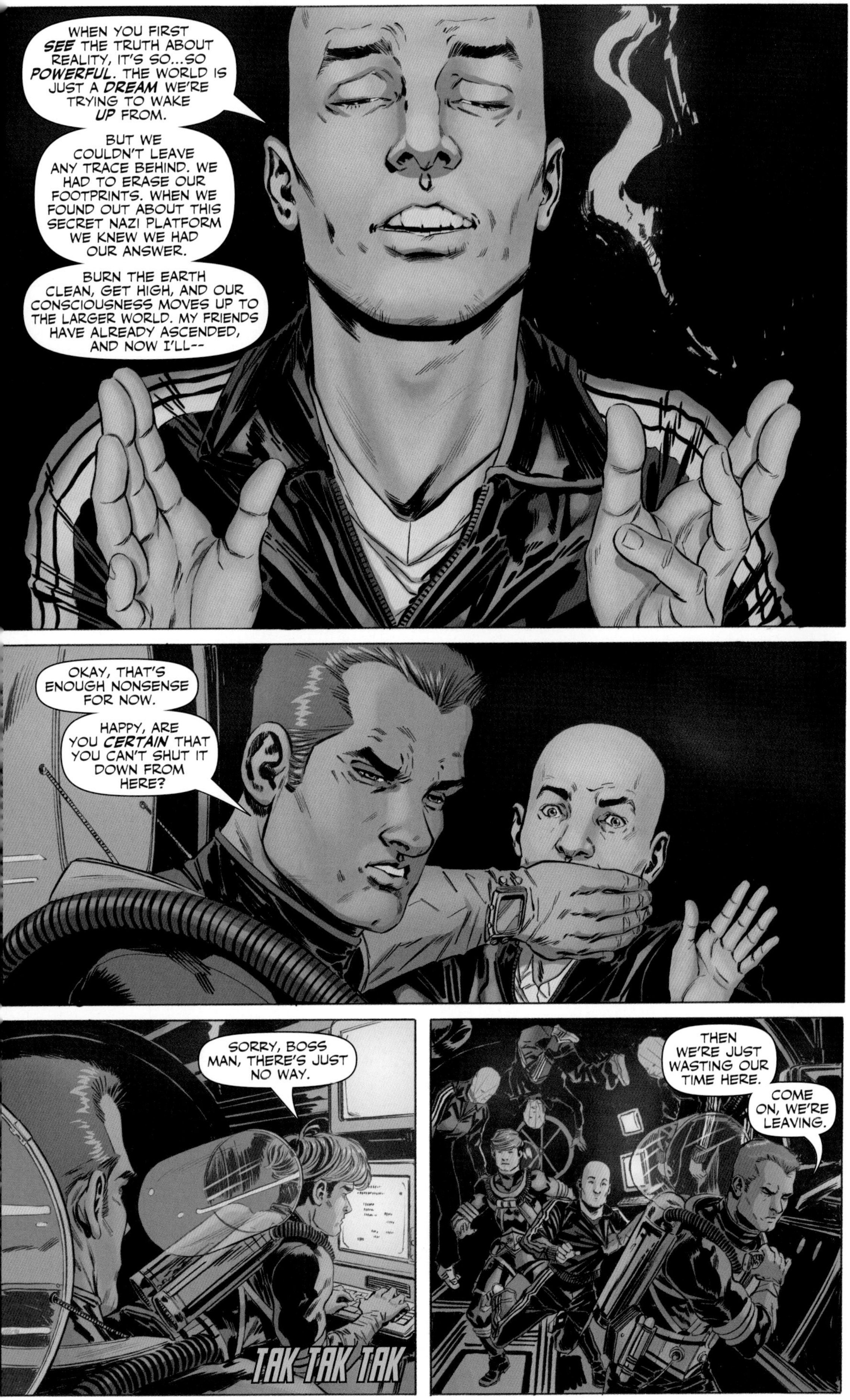
WHEN YOU FIRST SEE THE TRUTH ABOUT REALITY, IT'S SO...SO POWERFUL. THE WORLD IS JUST A DREAM WE'RE TRYING TO WAKE UP FROM.
BUT WE COULDN'T LEAVE ANY TRACE BEHIND. WE HAD TO ERASE OUR FOOTPRINTS. WHEN WE FOUND OUT ABOUT THIS SECRET NAZI PLATFORM WE KNEW WE HAD OUR ANSWER.
BURN THE EARTH CLEAN, GET HIGH, AND OUR CONSCIOUSNESS MOVES UP TO THE LARGER WORLD. MY FRIENDS HAVE ALREADY ASCENDED, AND NOW I'LL--
OKAY, THAT'S ENOUGH NONSENSE FOR NOW.
HAPPY, ARE YOU CERTAIN THAT YOU CAN'T SHUT IT DOWN FROM HERE?
SORRY, BOSS MAN, THERE'S JUST NO WAY.
TAK TAK TAK
THEN WE'RE JUST WASTING OUR TIME HERE.
COME ON, WE'RE LEAVING.

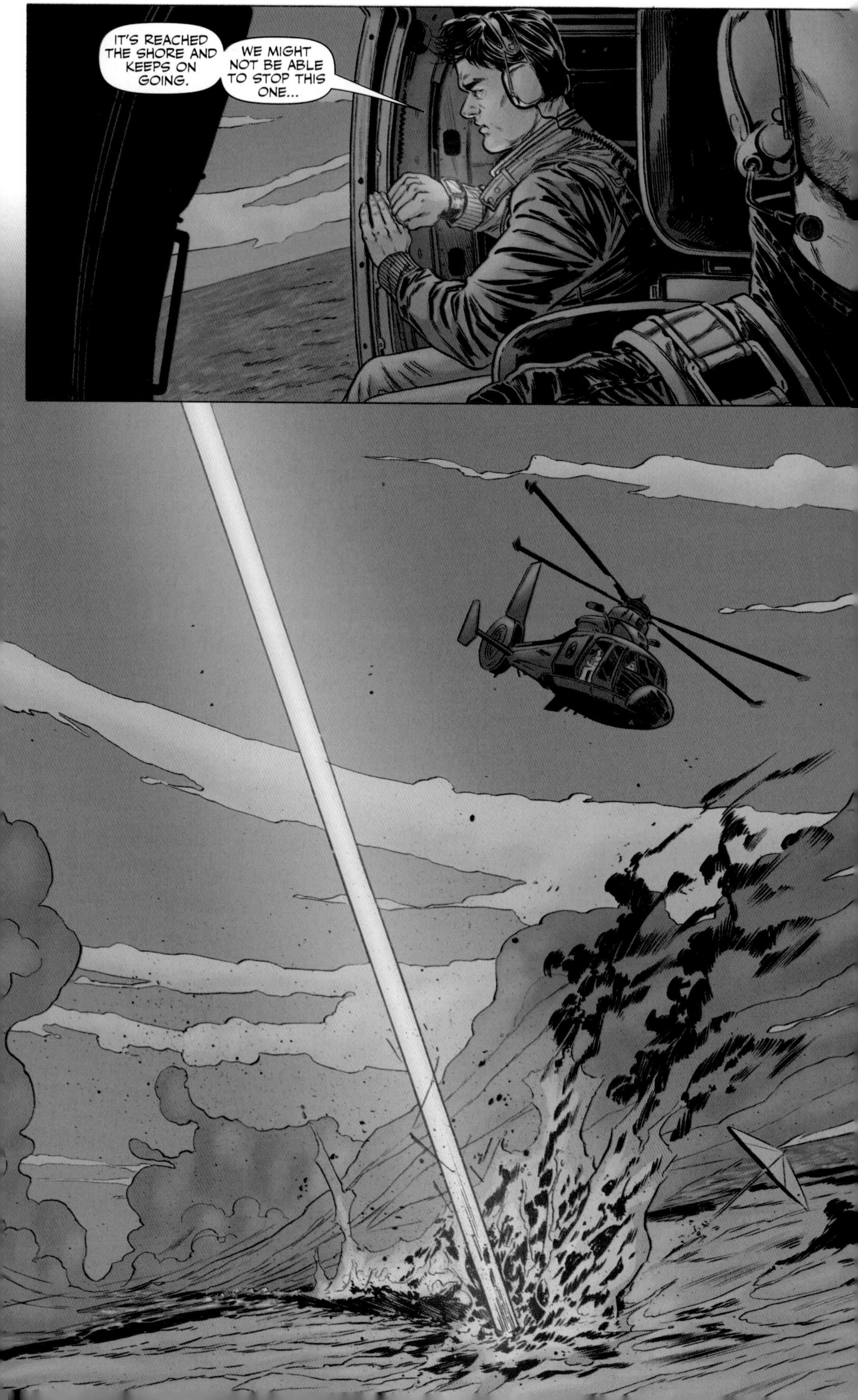
IT'S REACHED THE SHORE AND KEEPS ON GOING.
WE MIGHT NOT BE ABLE TO STOP THIS ONE...

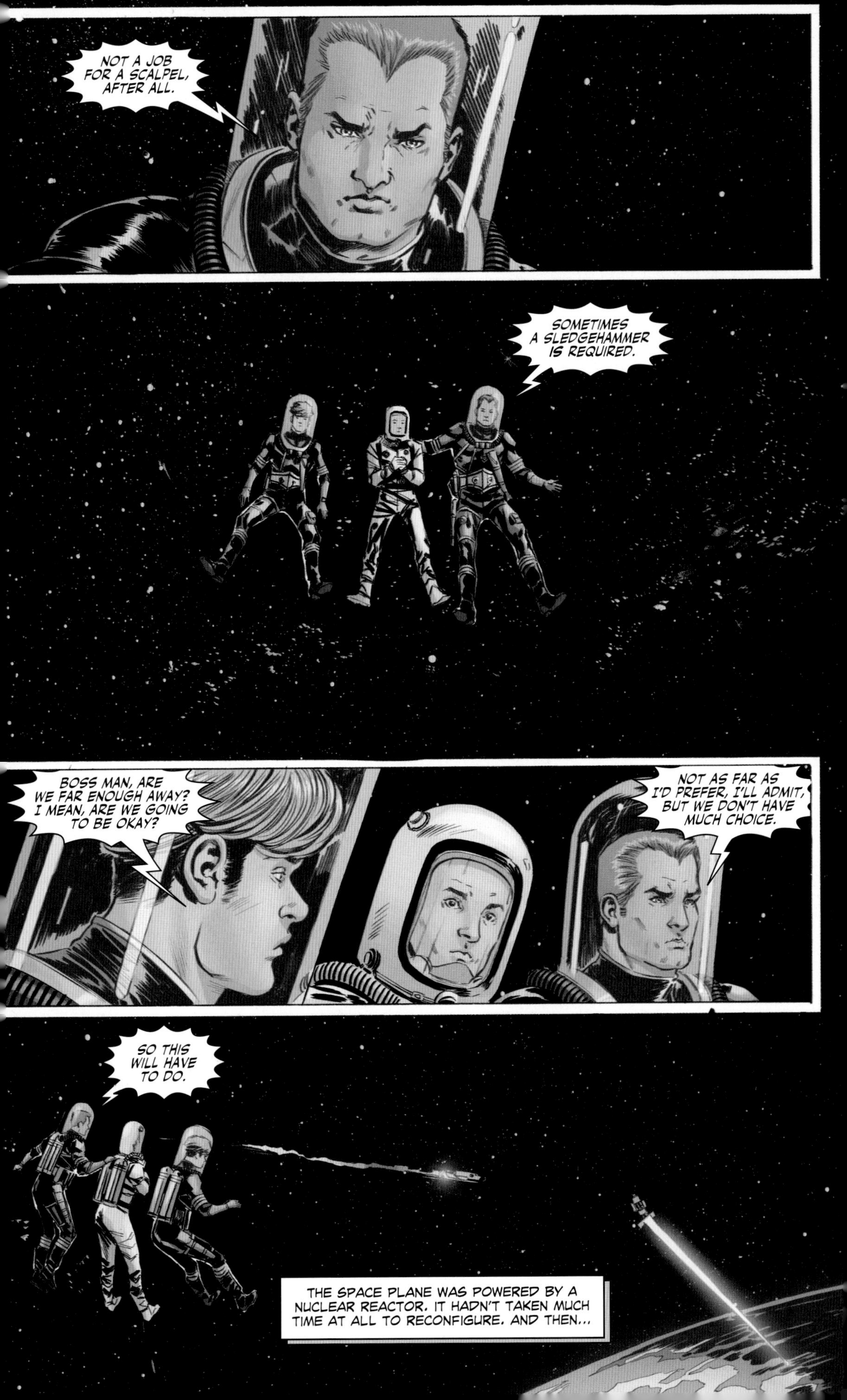
NOT A JOB FOR A SCALPEL, AFTER ALL.
SOMETIMES A SLEDGEHAMMER IS REQUIRED.
BOSS MAN, ARE WE FAR ENOUGH AWAY? I MEAN, ARE WE GOING TO BE OKAY?
NOT AS FAR AS I'D PREFER, I'LL ADMIT, BUT WE DON'T HAVE MUCH CHOICE.
SO THIS WILL HAVE TO DO.
THE SPACE PLANE WAS POWERED BY A NUCLEAR REACTOR. IT HADN'T TAKEN MUCH TIME AT ALL TO RECONFIGURE. AND THEN...

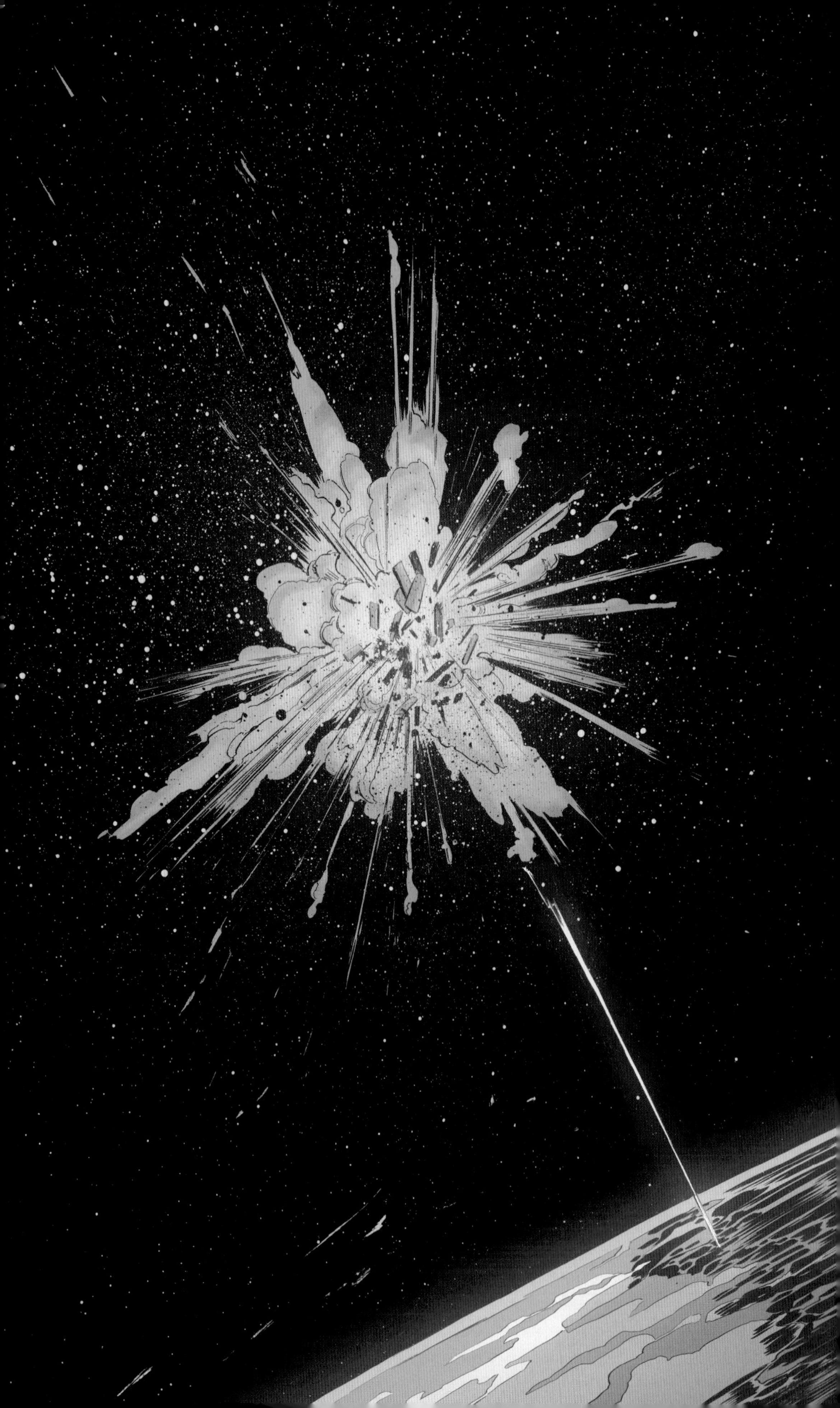

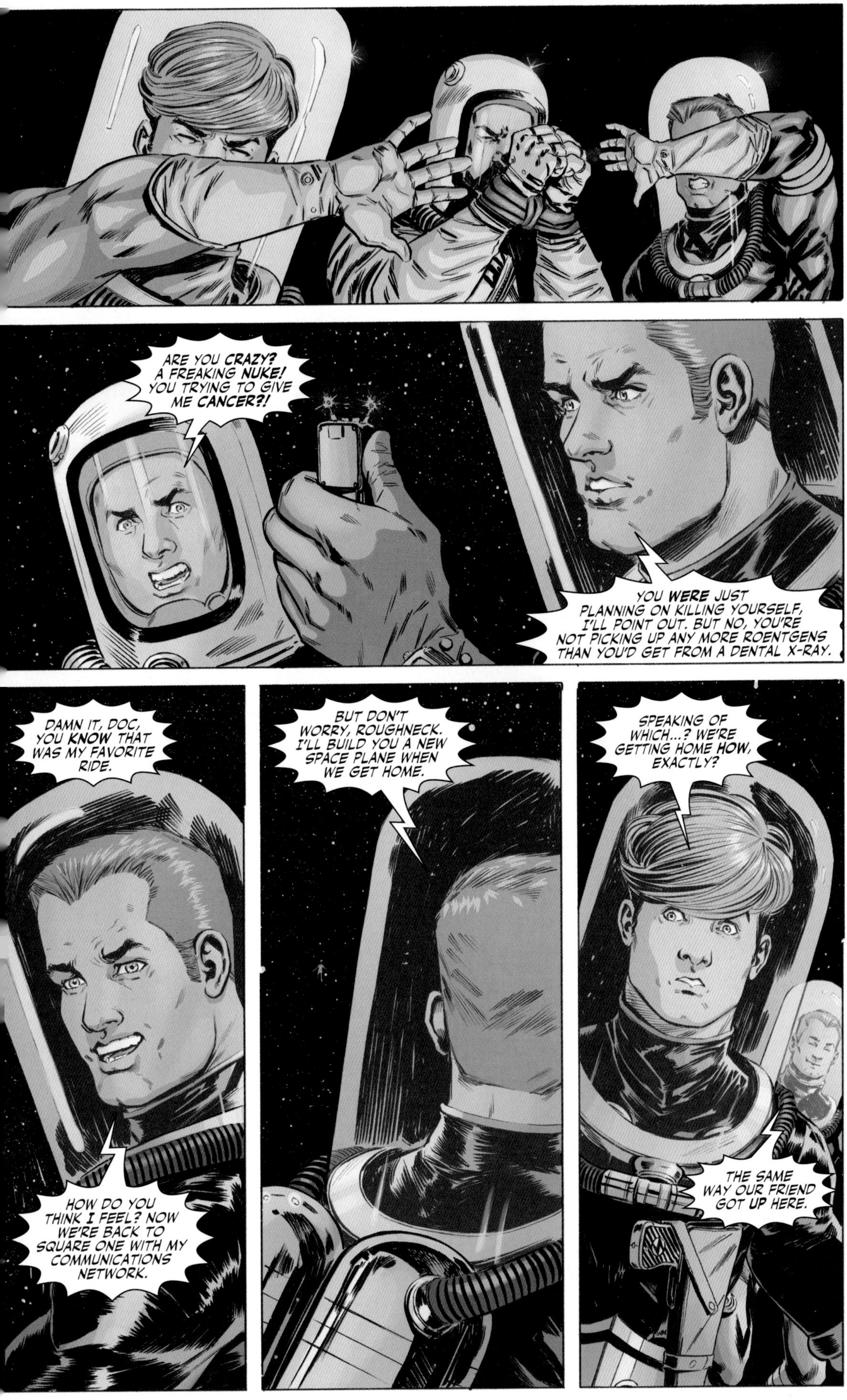
ARE YOU CRAZY? A FREAKING NUKE! YOU TRYING TO GIVE ME CANCER?!
YOU WERE JUST PLANNING ON KILLING YOURSELF, I'LL POINT OUT. BUT NO, YOU'RE NOT PICKING UP ANY MORE ROENTGENS THAN YOU'D GET FROM A DENTAL X-RAY.
DAMN IT, DOC, YOU KNOW THAT WAS MY FAVORITE RIDE.
HOW DO YOU THINK I FEEL? NOW WE'RE BACK TO SQUARE ONE WITH MY COMMUNICATIONS NETWORK.
BUT DON'T WORRY, ROUGHNECK. I'LL BUILD YOU A NEW SPACE PLANE WHEN WE GET HOME.
SPEAKING OF WHICH...? WE'RE GETTING HOME HOW, EXACTLY?
THE SAME WAY OUR FRIEND GOT UP HERE.

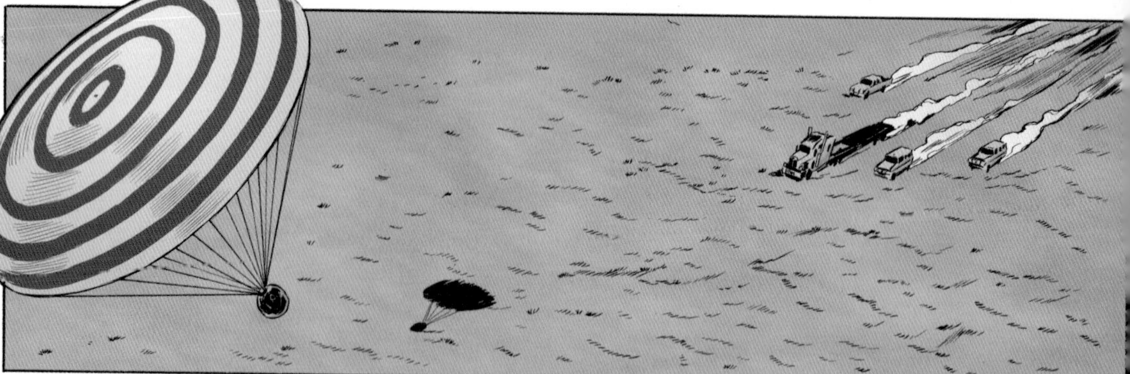

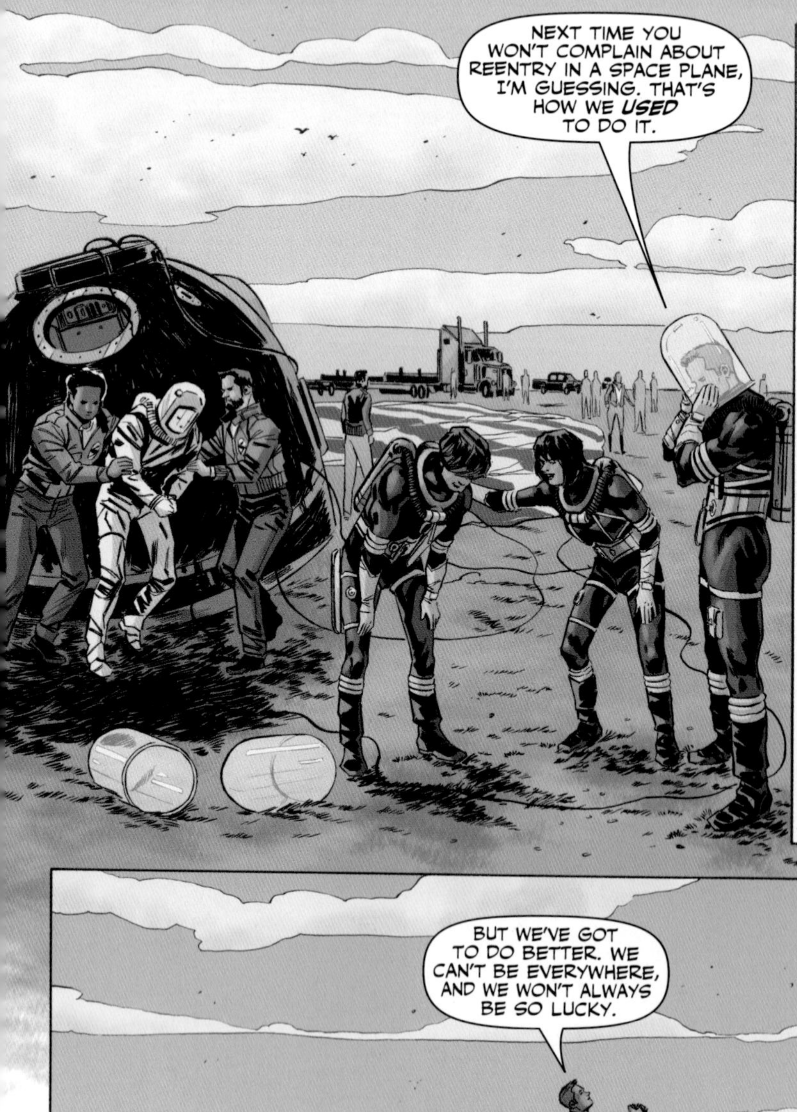
NEXT TIME YOU WON'T COMPLAIN ABOUT REENTRY IN A SPACE PLANE, I'M GUESSING. THAT'S HOW WE *USED* TO DO IT.

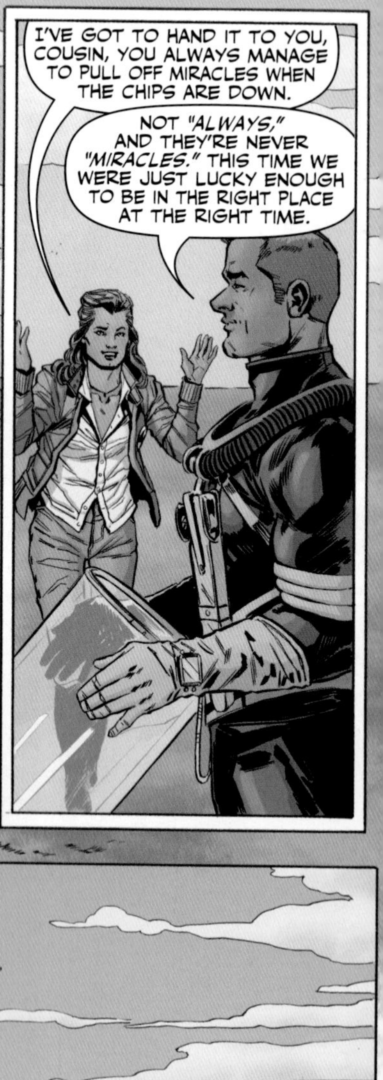
I'VE GOT TO HAND IT TO YOU, COUSIN, YOU ALWAYS MANAGE TO PULL OFF MIRACLES WHEN THE CHIPS ARE DOWN.
NOT *"ALWAYS,"* AND THEY'RE NEVER *"MIRACLES."* THIS TIME WE WERE JUST LUCKY ENOUGH TO BE IN THE RIGHT PLACE AT THE RIGHT TIME.

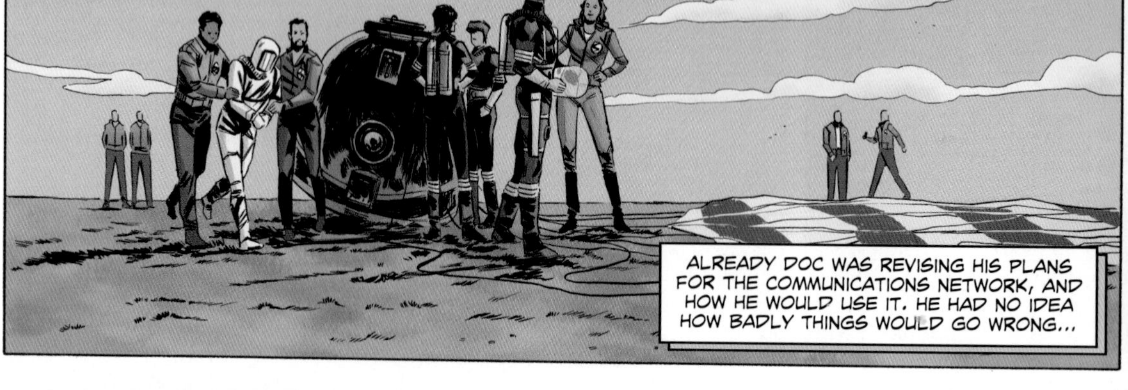
BUT WE'VE GOT TO DO BETTER. WE CAN'T BE EVERYWHERE, AND WE WON'T ALWAYS BE SO LUCKY.
ALREADY DOC WAS REVISING HIS PLANS FOR THE COMMUNICATIONS NETWORK, AND HOW HE WOULD USE IT. HE HAD NO IDEA HOW BADLY THINGS WOULD GO WRONG...

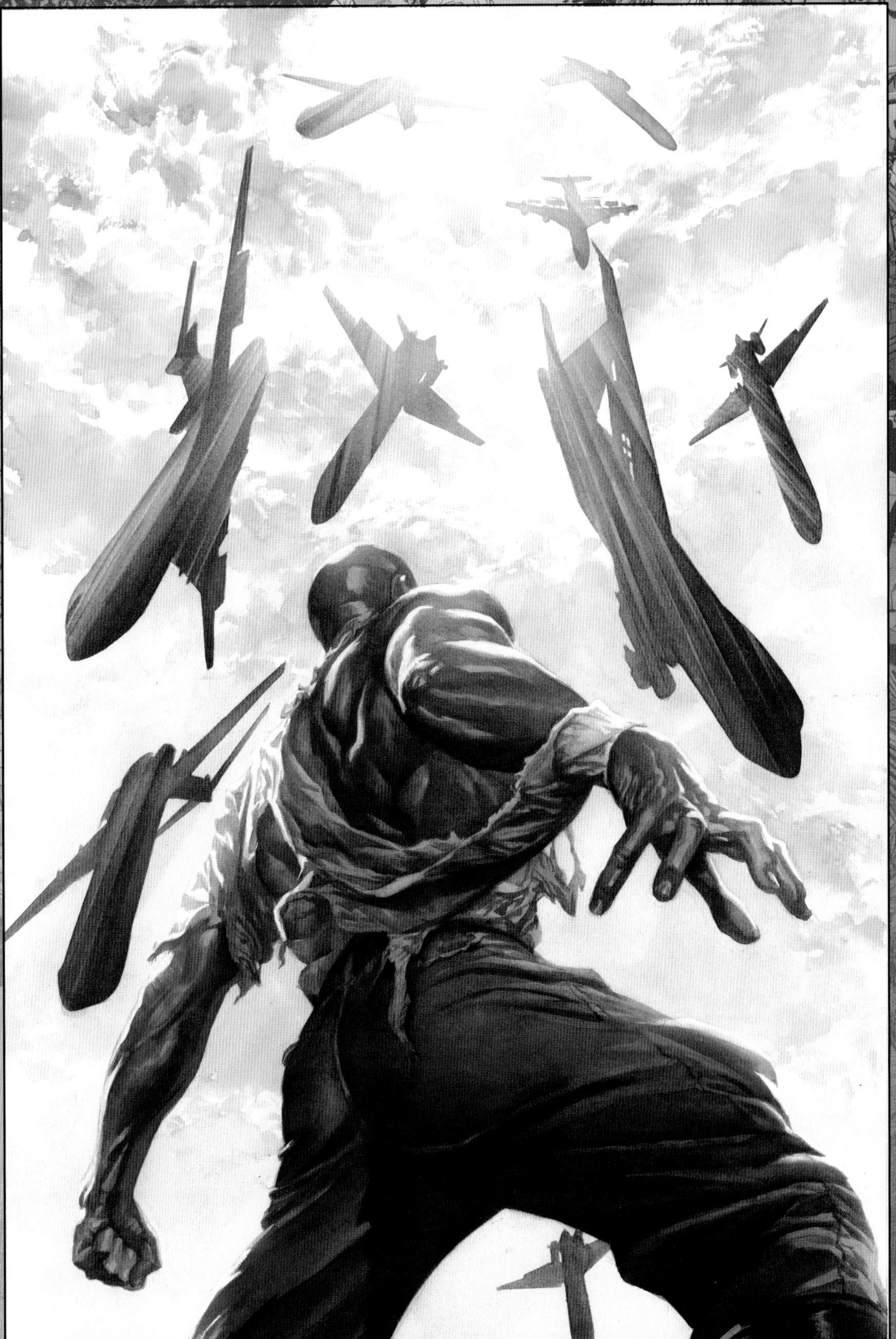

ISSUE #6 COVER
art by ALEX ROSS

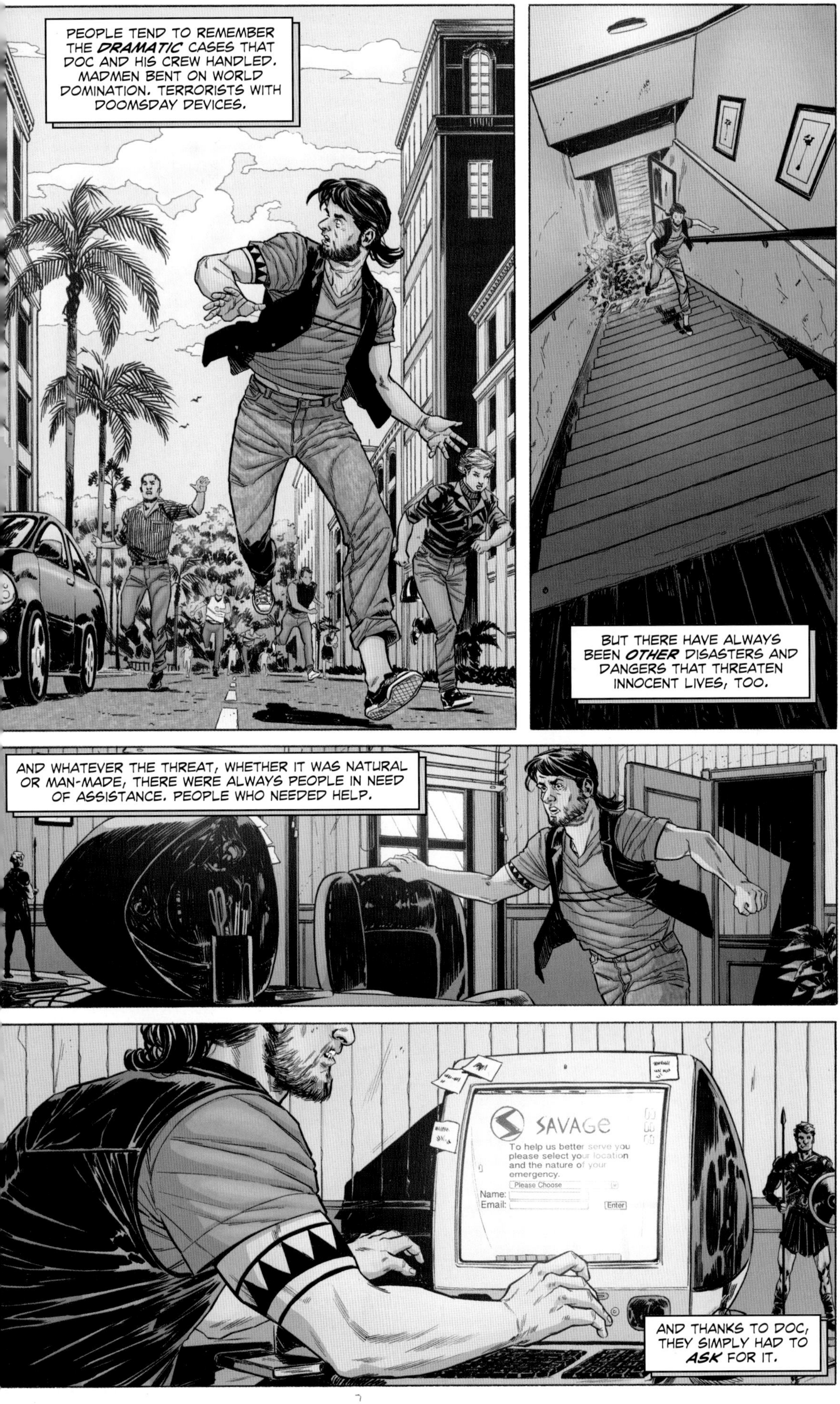
PEOPLE TEND TO REMEMBER THE DRAMATIC CASES THAT DOC AND HIS CREW HANDLED. MADMEN BENT ON WORLD DOMINATION. TERRORISTS WITH DOOMSDAY DEVICES.
BUT THERE HAVE ALWAYS BEEN OTHER DISASTERS AND DANGERS THAT THREATEN INNOCENT LIVES, TOO.
AND WHATEVER THE THREAT, WHETHER IT WAS NATURAL OR MAN-MADE, THERE WERE ALWAYS PEOPLE IN NEED OF ASSISTANCE. PEOPLE WHO NEEDED HELP.
SAVAGE
To help us better serve you please select your location and the nature of your emergency.
Please Choose
Name:
Email:
Enter
AND THANKS TO DOC, THEY SIMPLY HAD TO ASK FOR IT.

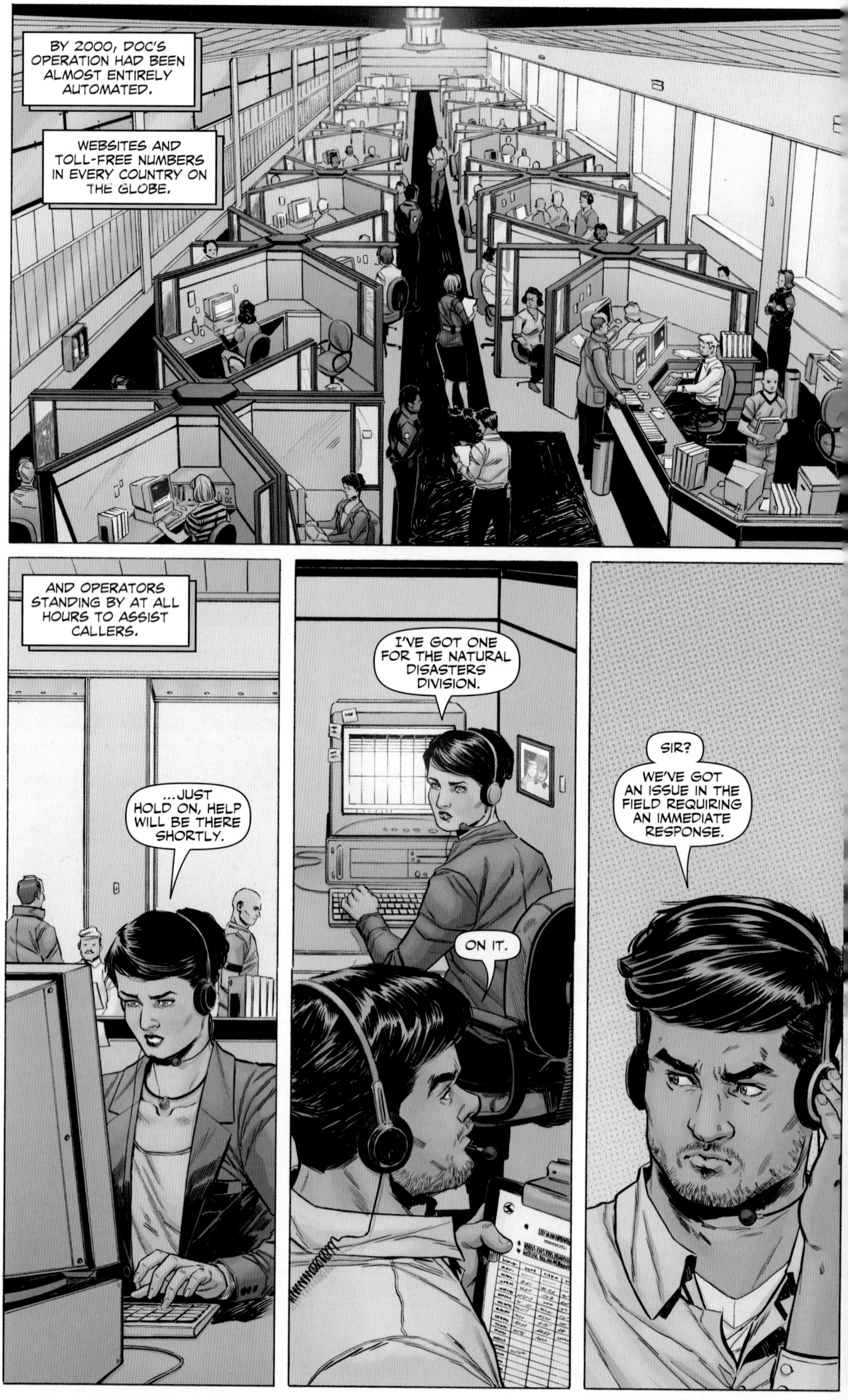
BY 2000, DOC'S OPERATION HAD BEEN ALMOST ENTIRELY AUTOMATED.
WEBSITES AND TOLL-FREE NUMBERS IN EVERY COUNTRY ON THE GLOBE.
AND OPERATORS STANDING BY AT ALL HOURS TO ASSIST CALLERS.
...JUST HOLD ON, HELP WILL BE THERE SHORTLY.
I'VE GOT ONE FOR THE NATURAL DISASTERS DIVISION.
ON IT.
SIR?
WE'VE GOT AN ISSUE IN THE FIELD REQUIRING AN IMMEDIATE RESPONSE.

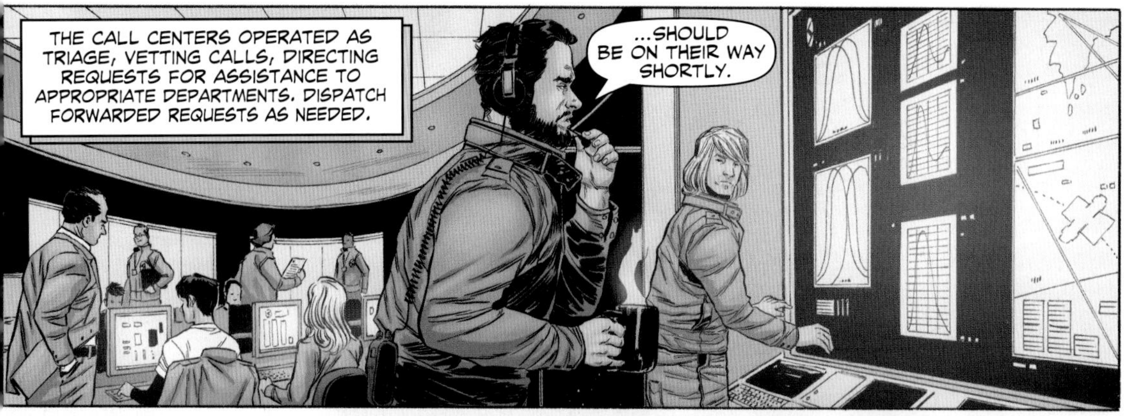
THE CALL CENTERS OPERATED AS TRIAGE, VETTING CALLS, DIRECTING REQUESTS FOR ASSISTANCE TO APPROPRIATE DEPARTMENTS. DISPATCH FORWARDED REQUESTS AS NEEDED.
...SHOULD BE ON THEIR WAY SHORTLY.

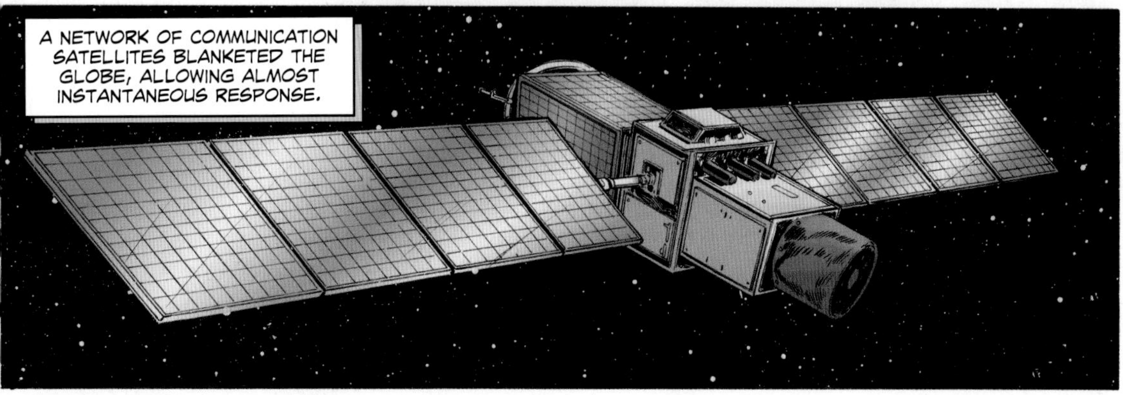
A NETWORK OF COMMUNICATION SATELLITES BLANKETED THE GLOBE, ALLOWING ALMOST INSTANTANEOUS RESPONSE.

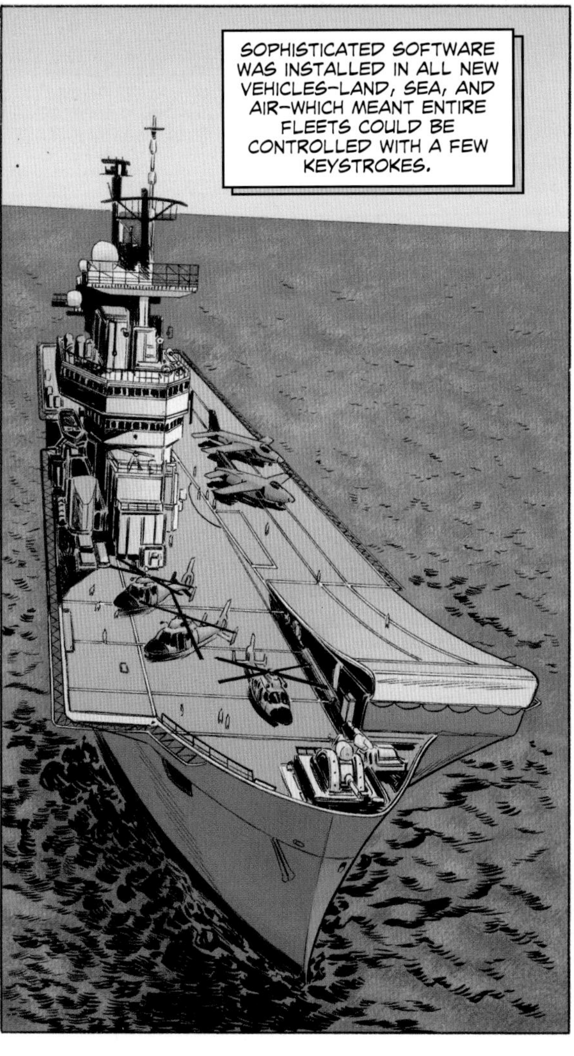
SOPHISTICATED SOFTWARE WAS INSTALLED IN ALL NEW VEHICLES–LAND, SEA, AND AIR–WHICH MEANT ENTIRE FLEETS COULD BE CONTROLLED WITH A FEW KEYSTROKES.

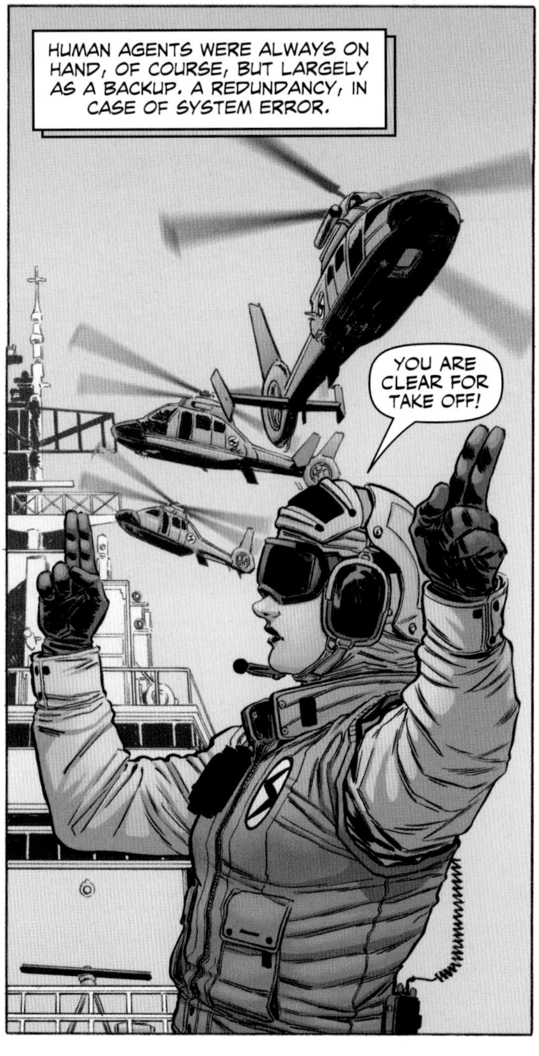
HUMAN AGENTS WERE ALWAYS ON HAND, OF COURSE, BUT LARGELY AS A BACKUP. A REDUNDANCY, IN CASE OF SYSTEM ERROR.
YOU ARE CLEAR FOR TAKE OFF!

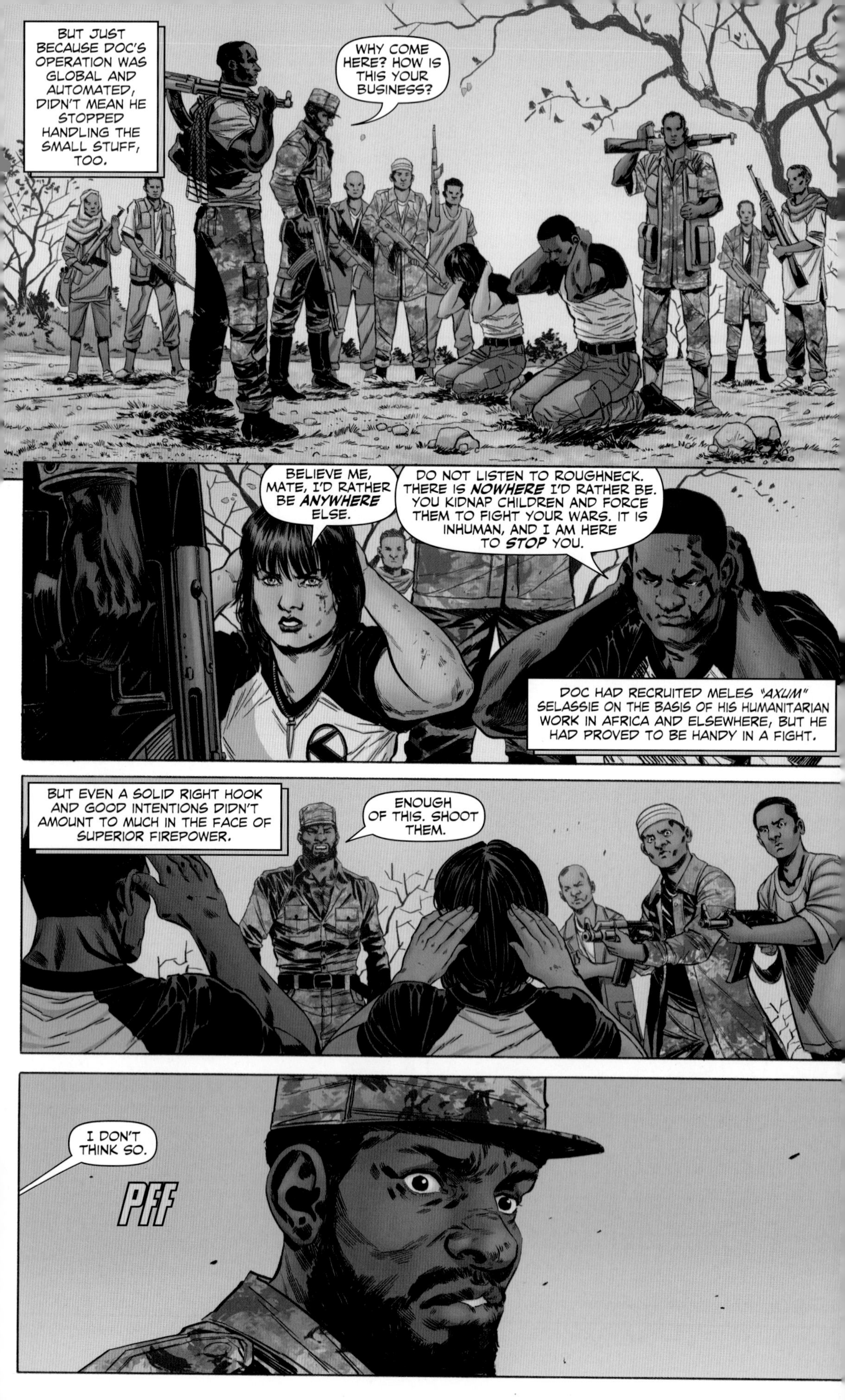

BUT JUST BECAUSE DOC'S OPERATION WAS GLOBAL AND AUTOMATED, DIDN'T MEAN HE STOPPED HANDLING THE SMALL STUFF, TOO.
WHY COME HERE? HOW IS THIS YOUR BUSINESS?
BELIEVE ME, MATE, I'D RATHER BE ANYWHERE ELSE.
DO NOT LISTEN TO ROUGHNECK. THERE IS NOWHERE I'D RATHER BE. YOU KIDNAP CHILDREN AND FORCE THEM TO FIGHT YOUR WARS. IT IS INHUMAN, AND I AM HERE TO STOP YOU.
DOC HAD RECRUITED MELES "AXUM" SELASSIE ON THE BASIS OF HIS HUMANITARIAN WORK IN AFRICA AND ELSEWHERE, BUT HE HAD PROVED TO BE HANDY IN A FIGHT.
BUT EVEN A SOLID RIGHT HOOK AND GOOD INTENTIONS DIDN'T AMOUNT TO MUCH IN THE FACE OF SUPERIOR FIREPOWER.
ENOUGH OF THIS. SHOOT THEM.
I DON'T THINK SO.
PFF

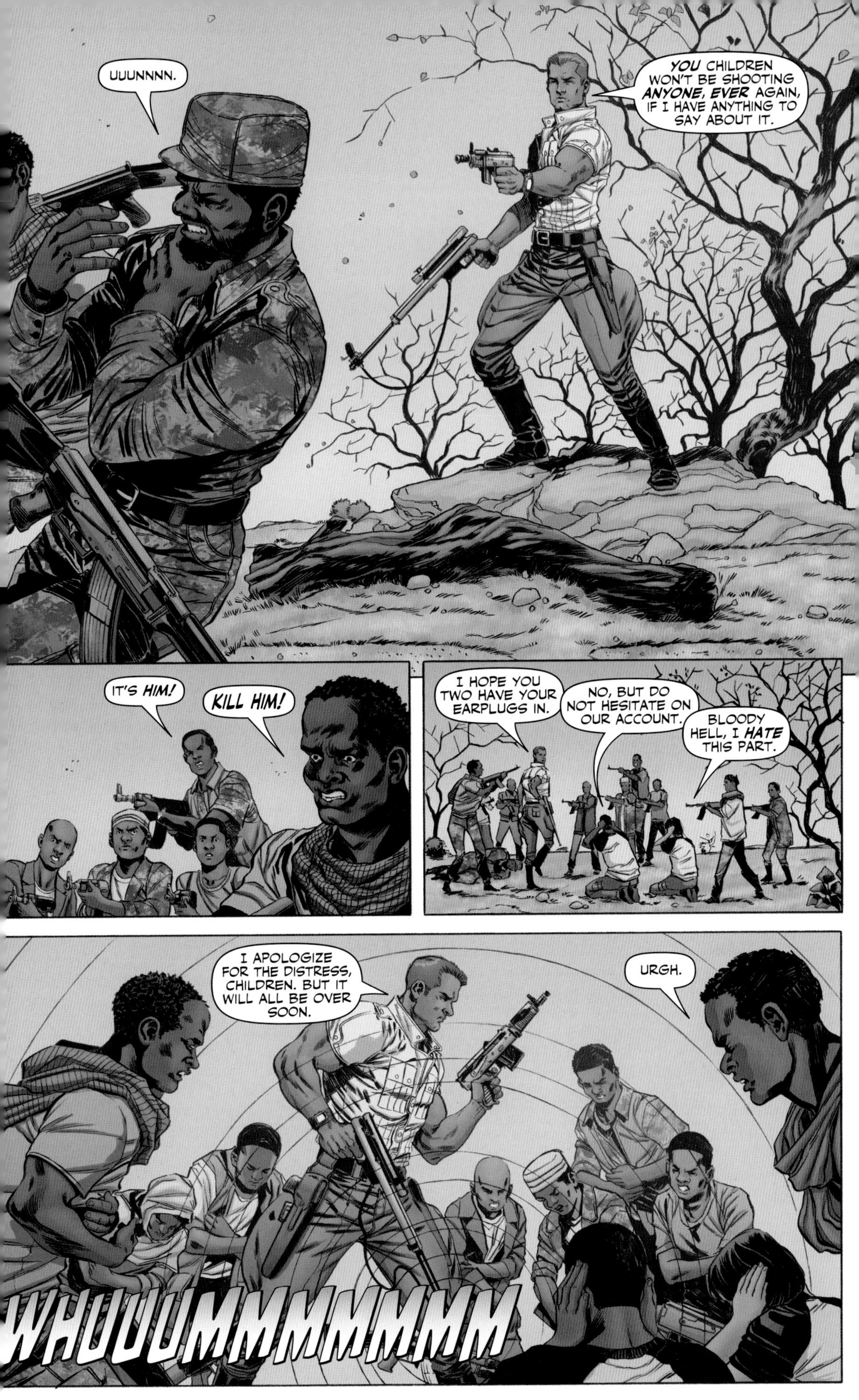
UUUNNNN.
YOU CHILDREN WON'T BE SHOOTING ANYONE, EVER AGAIN, IF I HAVE ANYTHING TO SAY ABOUT IT.
IT'S HIM!
KILL HIM!
I HOPE YOU TWO HAVE YOUR EARPLUGS IN.
NO, BUT DO NOT HESITATE ON OUR ACCOUNT.
BLOODY HELL, I HATE THIS PART.
I APOLOGIZE FOR THE DISTRESS, CHILDREN. BUT IT WILL ALL BE OVER SOON.
URGH.
WHUUUMMMMMMMM

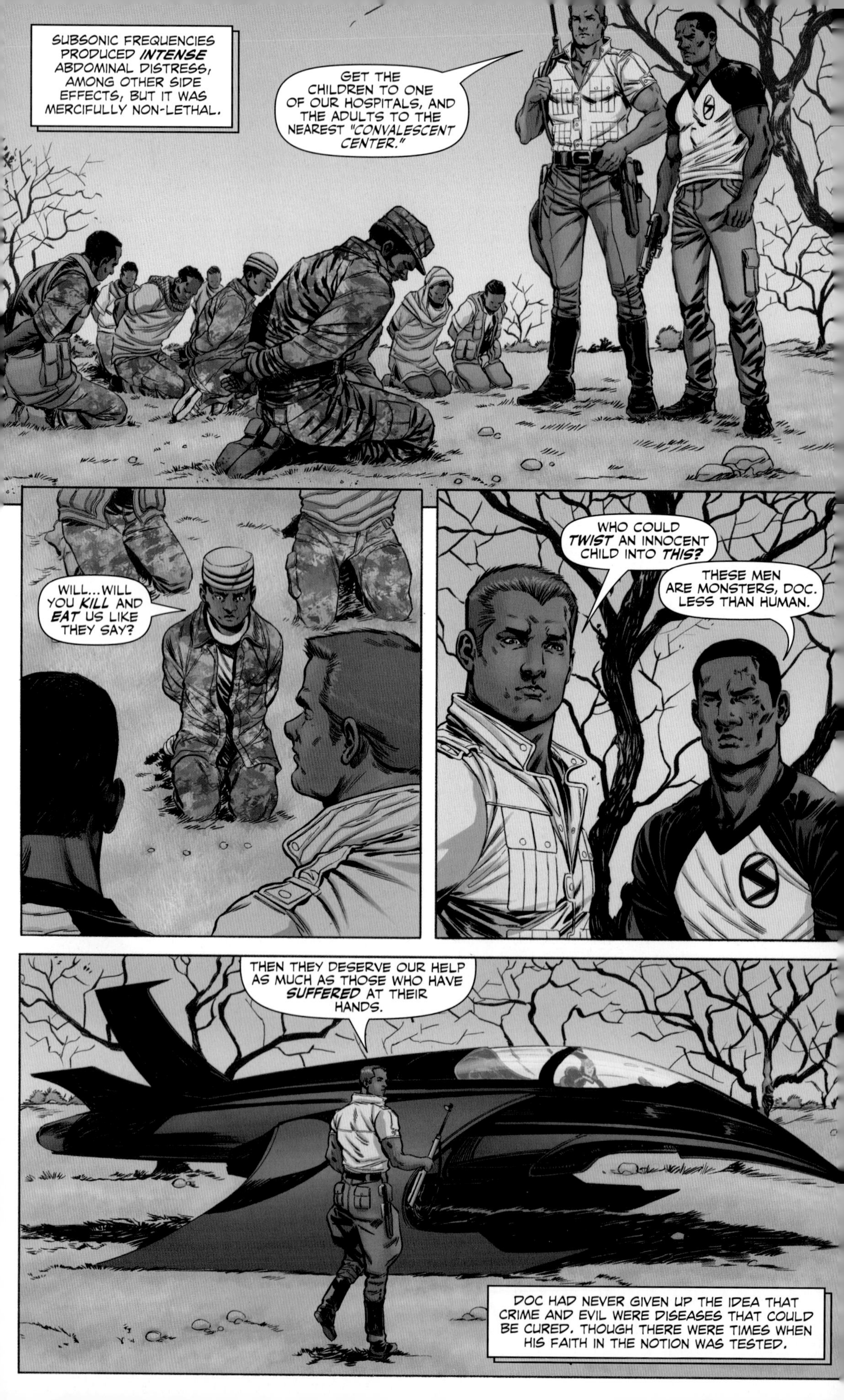
SUBSONIC FREQUENCIES PRODUCED INTENSE ABDOMINAL DISTRESS, AMONG OTHER SIDE EFFECTS, BUT IT WAS MERCIFULLY NON-LETHAL.
GET THE CHILDREN TO ONE OF OUR HOSPITALS, AND THE ADULTS TO THE NEAREST "CONVALESCENT CENTER."
WILL...WILL YOU KILL AND EAT US LIKE THEY SAY?
WHO COULD TWIST AN INNOCENT CHILD INTO THIS?
THESE MEN ARE MONSTERS, DOC. LESS THAN HUMAN.
THEN THEY DESERVE OUR HELP AS MUCH AS THOSE WHO HAVE SUFFERED AT THEIR HANDS.
DOC HAD NEVER GIVEN UP THE IDEA THAT CRIME AND EVIL WERE DISEASES THAT COULD BE CURED. THOUGH THERE WERE TIMES WHEN HIS FAITH IN THE NOTION WAS TESTED.

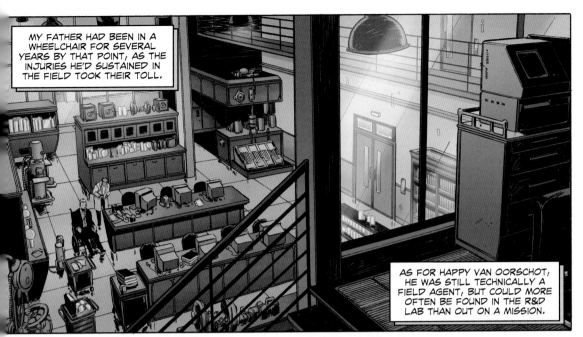

MY FATHER HAD BEEN IN A WHEELCHAIR FOR SEVERAL YEARS BY THAT POINT, AS THE INJURIES HE'D SUSTAINED IN THE FIELD TOOK THEIR TOLL.

AS FOR HAPPY VAN OORSCHOT, HE WAS STILL TECHNICALLY A FIELD AGENT, BUT COULD MORE OFTEN BE FOUND IN THE R&D LAB THAN OUT ON A MISSION.

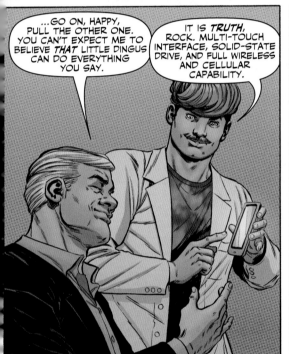

...GO ON, HAPPY, PULL THE OTHER ONE. YOU CAN'T EXPECT ME TO BELIEVE *THAT* LITTLE DINGUS CAN DO EVERYTHING YOU SAY.

IT IS *TRUTH*, ROCK. MULTI-TOUCH INTERFACE, SOLID-STATE DRIVE, AND FULL WIRELESS AND CELLULAR CAPABILITY.

WITHIN A MATTER OF YEARS, MATERIAL COSTS WILL DROP LOW ENOUGH THAT THE COST WILL BE VIRTUALLY *NIL*.

HEY, DAD. HEY, UNCLE HAPPY.

CAN I USE THE COMPUTER IN HERE? HOUSEKEEPING IS CLEANING YOUR OFFICE, DAD.

SURE, SWEETIE. JUST DON'T *WRECK* ANYTHING, WILLYA?

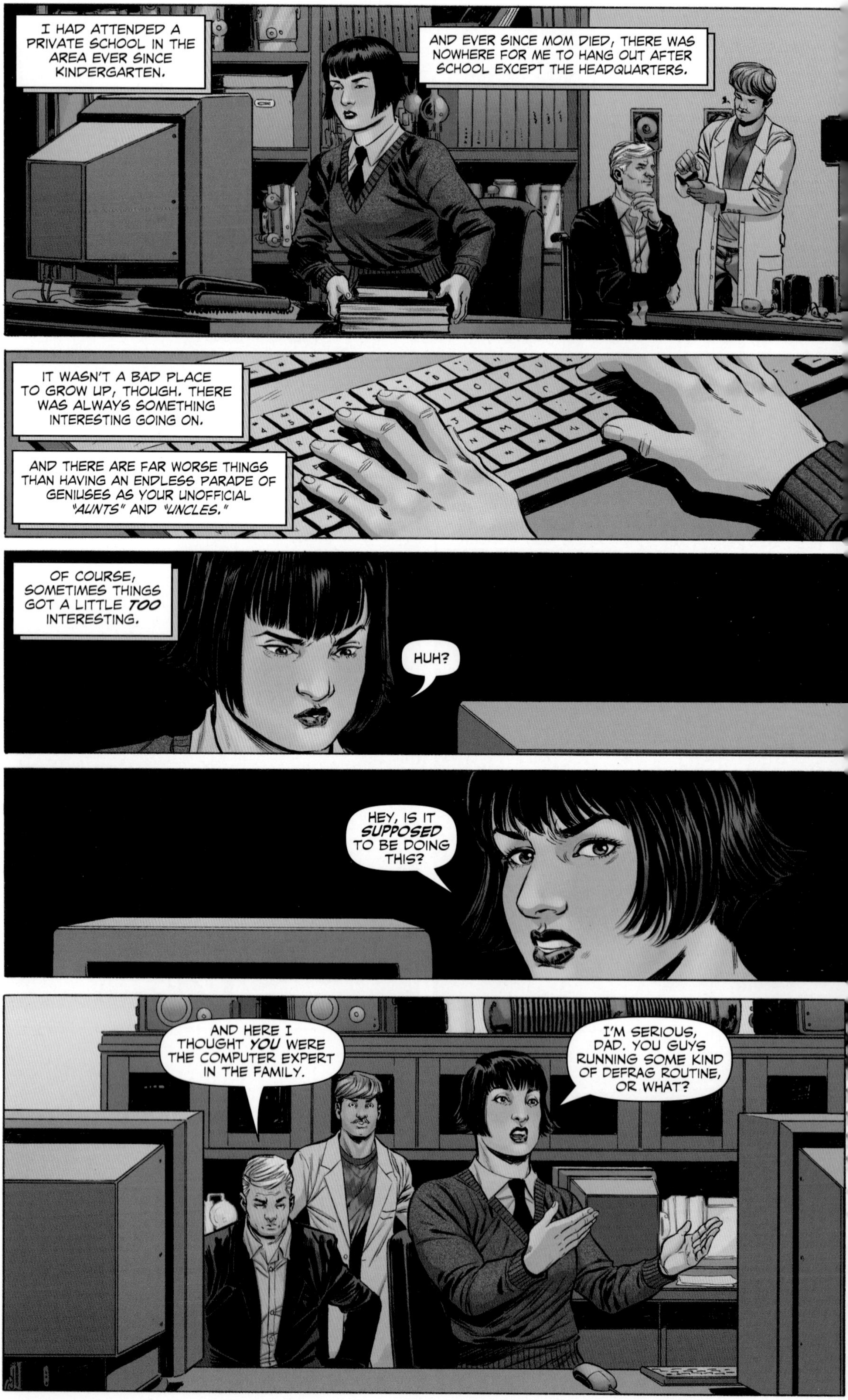

I HAD ATTENDED A PRIVATE SCHOOL IN THE AREA EVER SINCE KINDERGARTEN.
AND EVER SINCE MOM DIED, THERE WAS NOWHERE FOR ME TO HANG OUT AFTER SCHOOL EXCEPT THE HEADQUARTERS.
IT WASN'T A BAD PLACE TO GROW UP, THOUGH. THERE WAS ALWAYS SOMETHING INTERESTING GOING ON.
AND THERE ARE FAR WORSE THINGS THAN HAVING AN ENDLESS PARADE OF GENIUSES AS YOUR UNOFFICIAL *"AUNTS"* AND *"UNCLES."*
OF COURSE, SOMETIMES THINGS GOT A LITTLE ***TOO*** INTERESTING.
HUH?
HEY, IS IT ***SUPPOSED*** TO BE DOING THIS?
AND HERE I THOUGHT ***YOU*** WERE THE COMPUTER EXPERT IN THE FAMILY.
I'M SERIOUS, DAD. YOU GUYS RUNNING SOME KIND OF DEFRAG ROUTINE, OR WHAT?

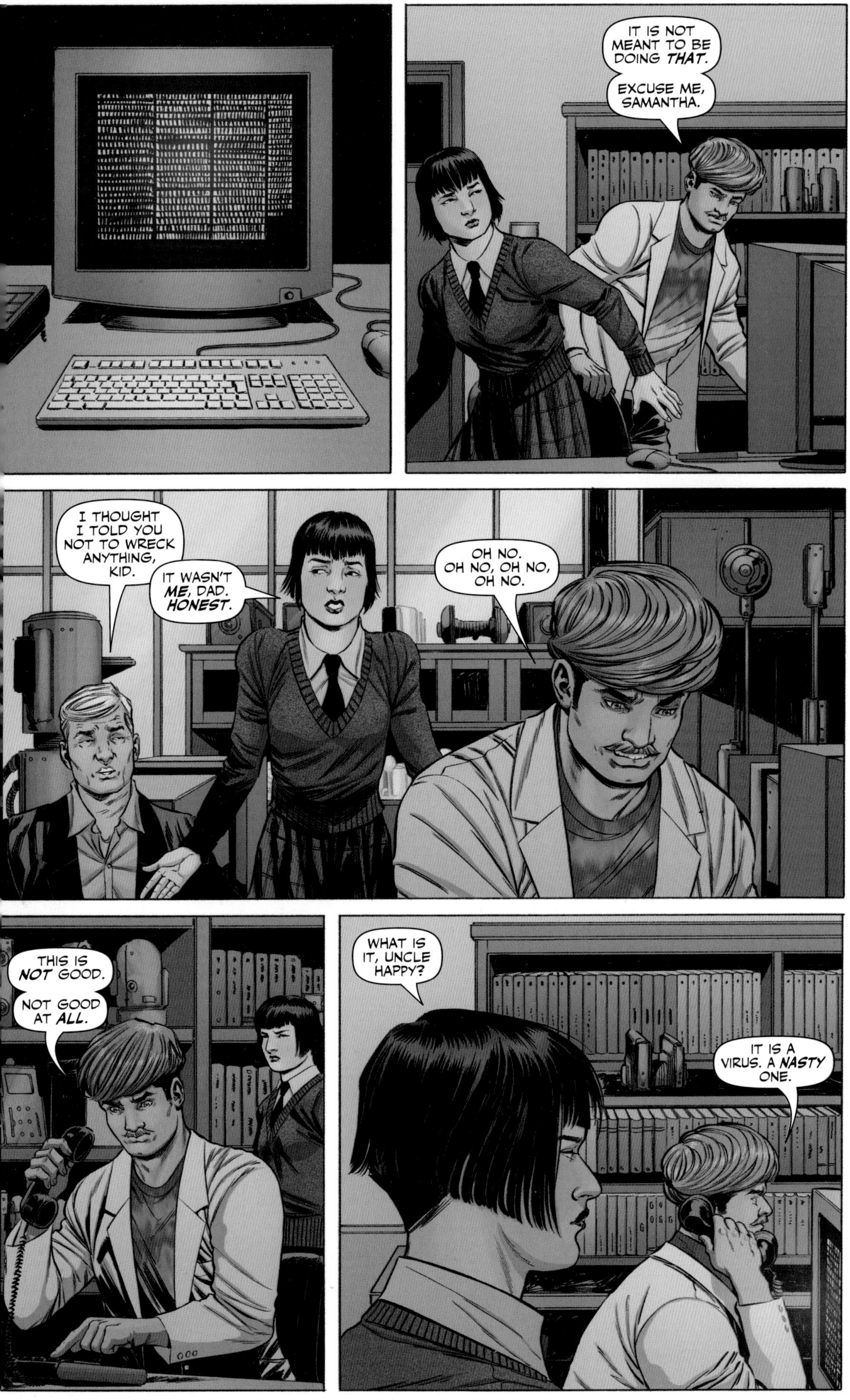
IT IS NOT MEANT TO BE DOING *THAT*.
EXCUSE ME, SAMANTHA.
I THOUGHT I TOLD YOU NOT TO WRECK ANYTHING, KID.
IT WASN'T *ME*, DAD. *HONEST*.
OH NO. OH NO, OH NO, OH NO.
THIS IS *NOT* GOOD.
NOT GOOD AT *ALL*.
WHAT IS IT, UNCLE HAPPY?
IT IS A VIRUS. A *NASTY* ONE.

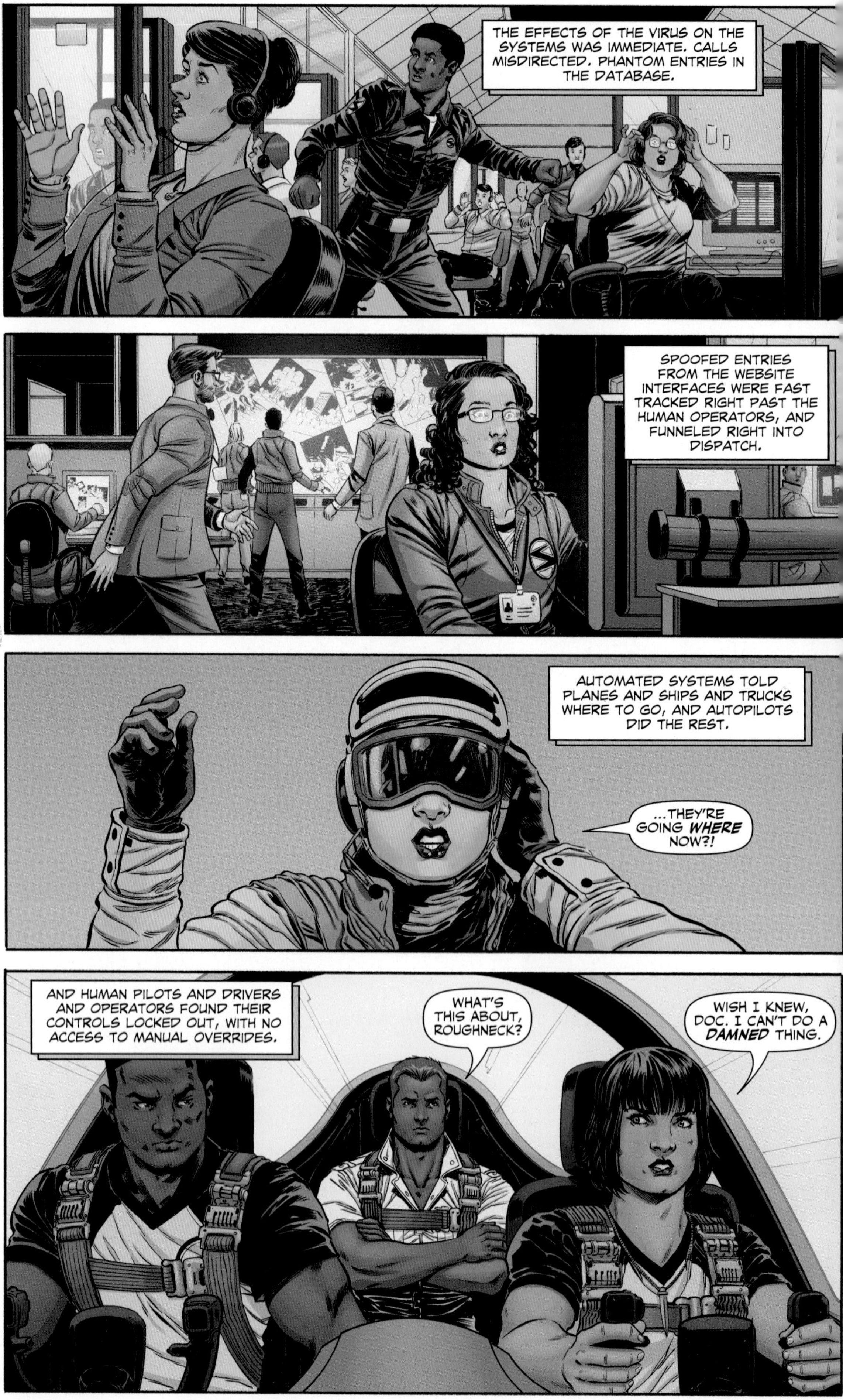
THE EFFECTS OF THE VIRUS ON THE SYSTEMS WAS IMMEDIATE. CALLS MISDIRECTED. PHANTOM ENTRIES IN THE DATABASE.
SPOOFED ENTRIES FROM THE WEBSITE INTERFACES WERE FAST TRACKED RIGHT PAST THE HUMAN OPERATORS, AND FUNNELED RIGHT INTO DISPATCH.
AUTOMATED SYSTEMS TOLD PLANES AND SHIPS AND TRUCKS WHERE TO GO, AND AUTOPILOTS DID THE REST.
...THEY'RE GOING *WHERE* NOW?!
AND HUMAN PILOTS AND DRIVERS AND OPERATORS FOUND THEIR CONTROLS LOCKED OUT, WITH NO ACCESS TO MANUAL OVERRIDES.
WHAT'S THIS ABOUT, ROUGHNECK?
WISH I KNEW, DOC. I CAN'T DO A *DAMNED* THING.

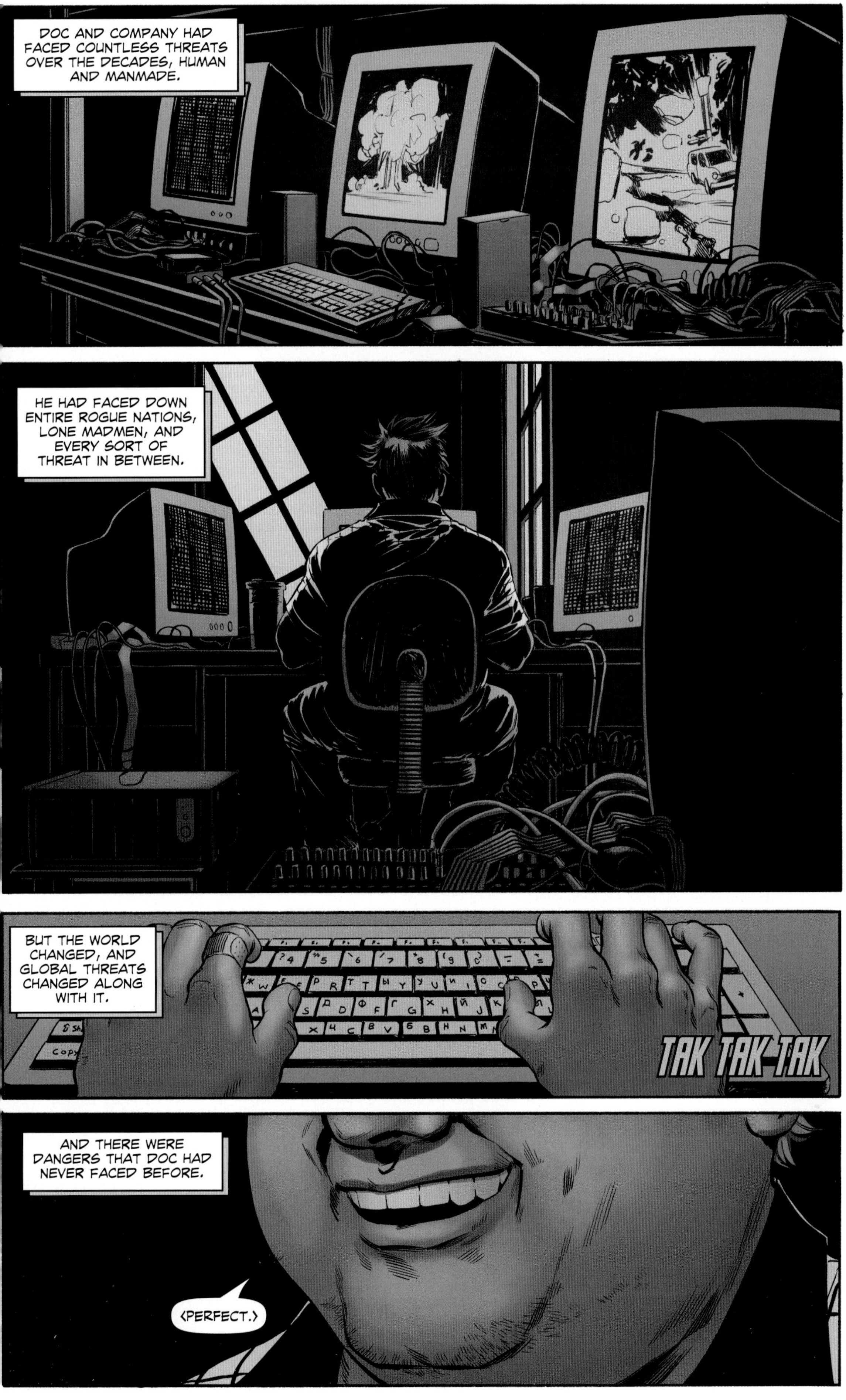

DOC AND COMPANY HAD FACED COUNTLESS THREATS OVER THE DECADES, HUMAN AND MANMADE.
HE HAD FACED DOWN ENTIRE ROGUE NATIONS, LONE MADMEN, AND EVERY SORT OF THREAT IN BETWEEN.
BUT THE WORLD CHANGED, AND GLOBAL THREATS CHANGED ALONG WITH IT.
TAK TAK TAK
AND THERE WERE DANGERS THAT DOC HAD NEVER FACED BEFORE.
‹PERFECT.›

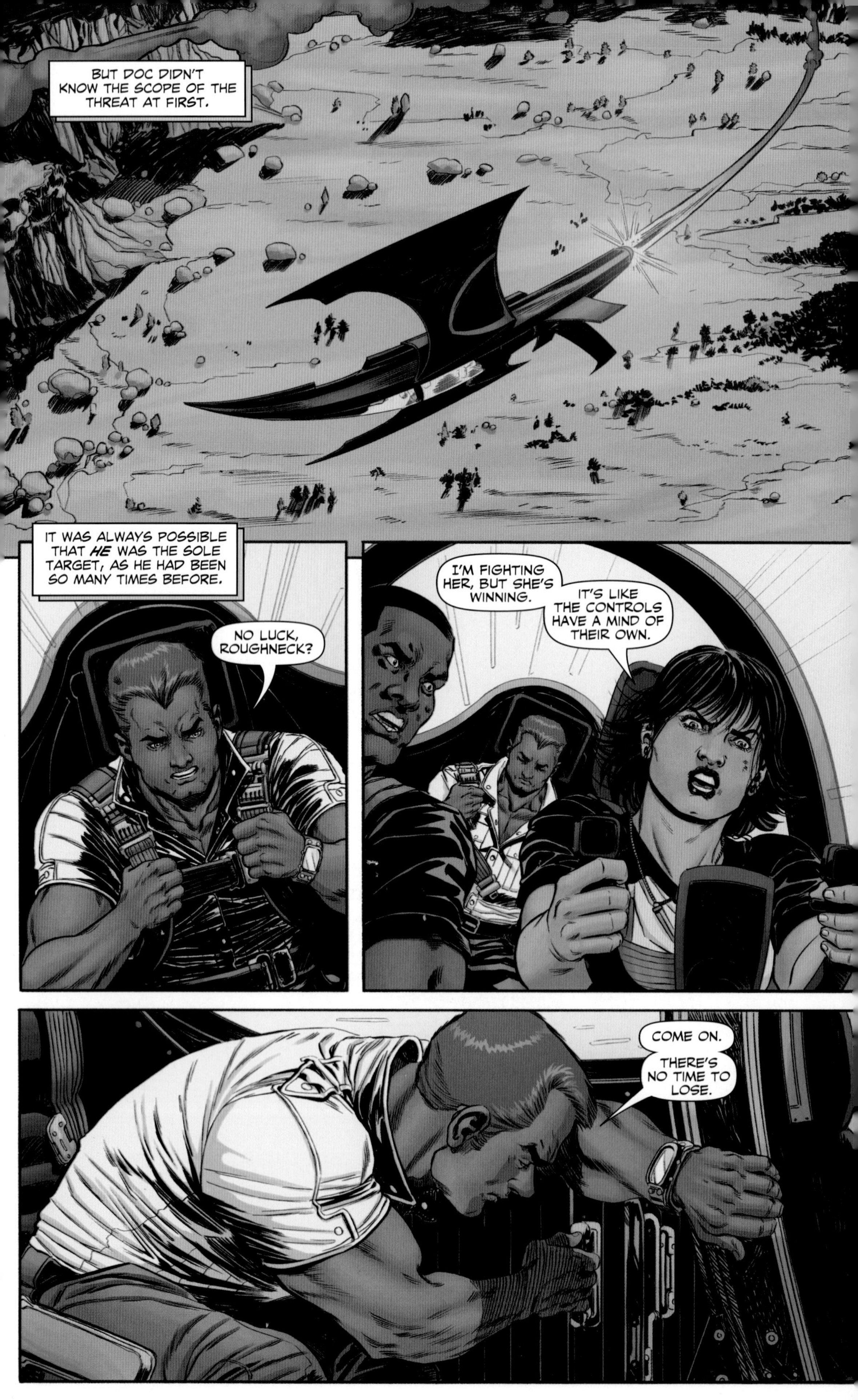
BUT DOC DIDN'T KNOW THE SCOPE OF THE THREAT AT FIRST.
IT WAS ALWAYS POSSIBLE THAT HE WAS THE SOLE TARGET, AS HE HAD BEEN SO MANY TIMES BEFORE.
NO LUCK, ROUGHNECK?
I'M FIGHTING HER, BUT SHE'S WINNING.
IT'S LIKE THE CONTROLS HAVE A MIND OF THEIR OWN.
COME ON.
THERE'S NO TIME TO LOSE.

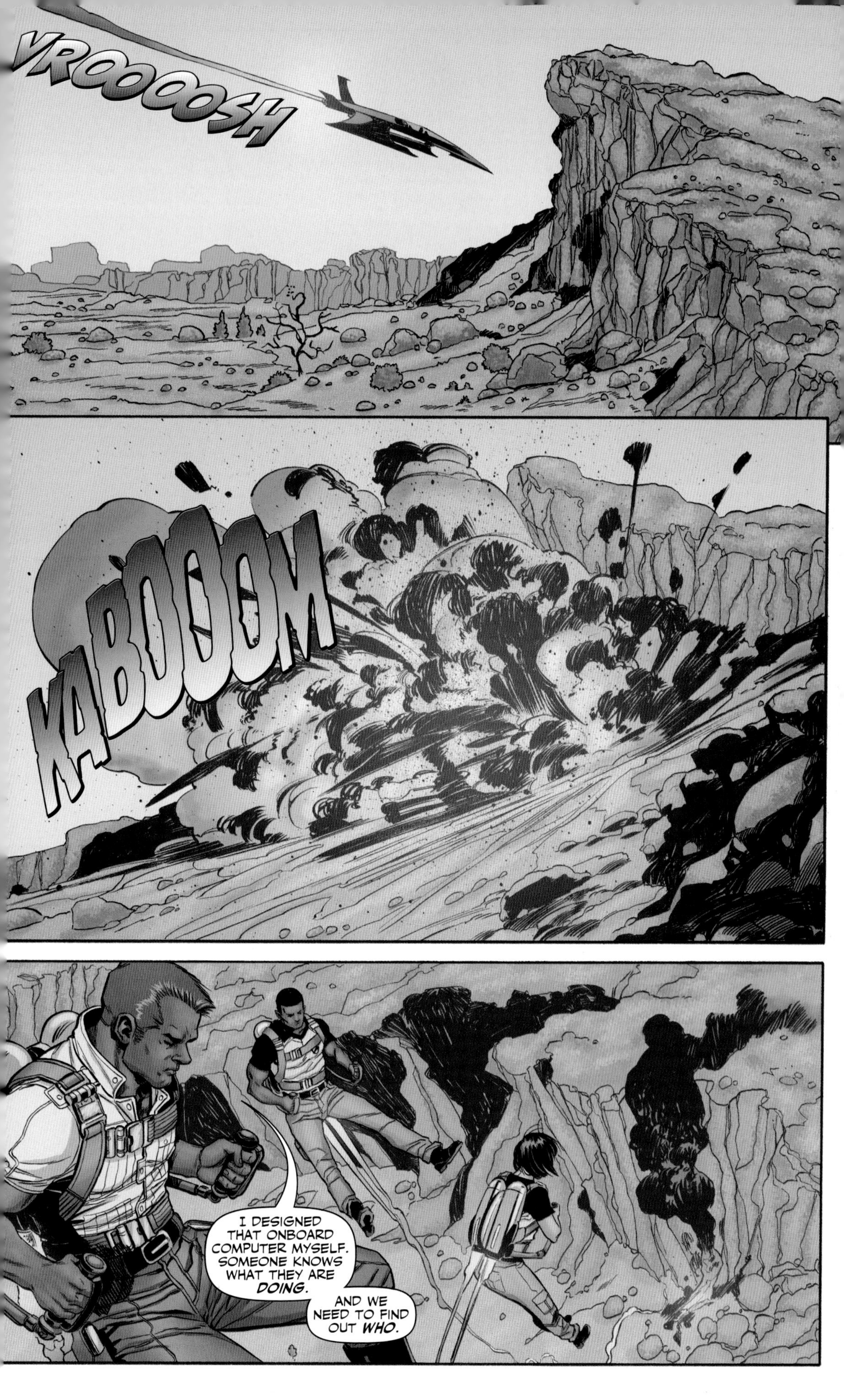
VROOOOOSH
KABOOOM
I DESIGNED THAT ONBOARD COMPUTER MYSELF. SOMEONE KNOWS WHAT THEY ARE DOING.
AND WE NEED TO FIND OUT WHO.

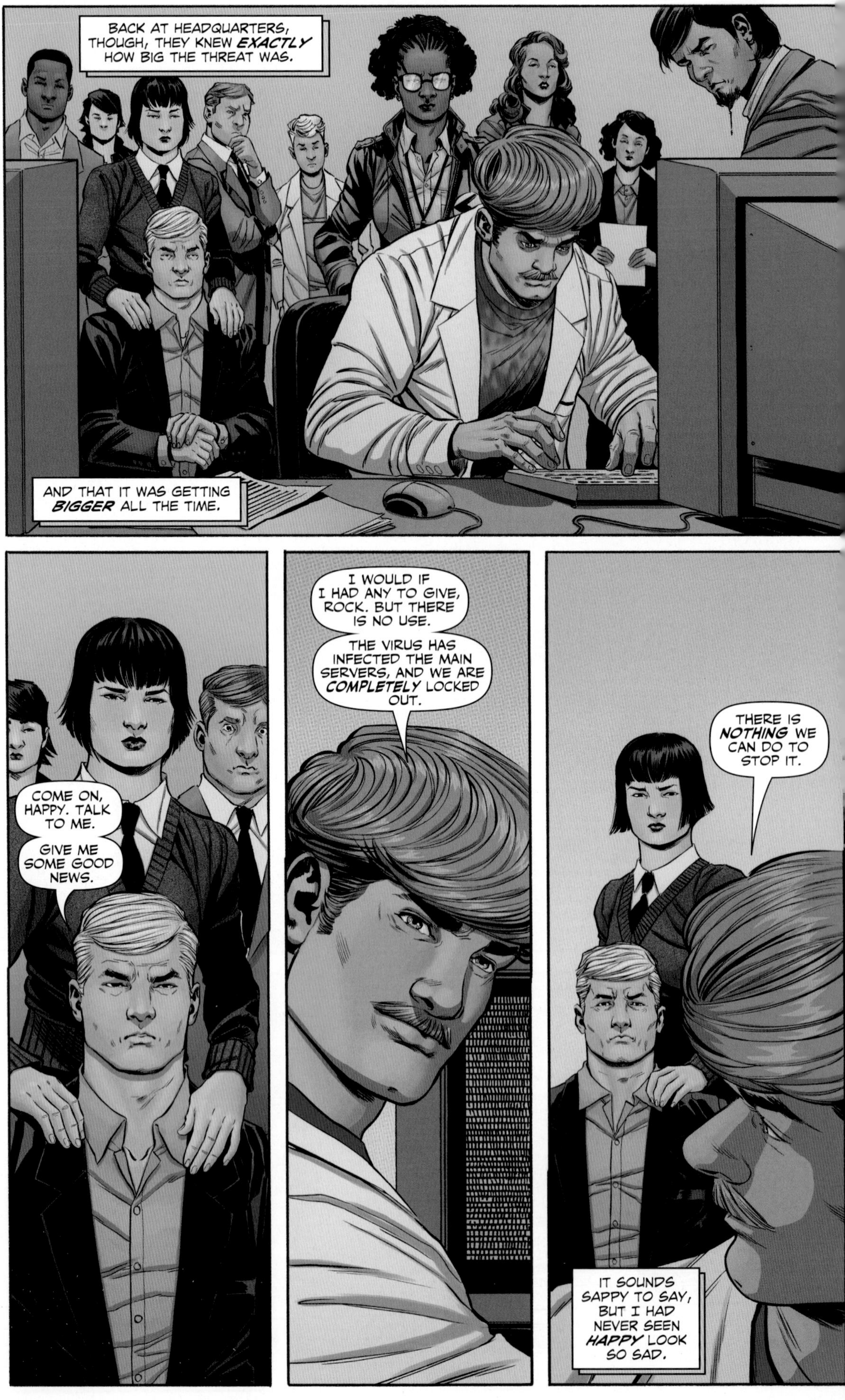
BACK AT HEADQUARTERS, THOUGH, THEY KNEW EXACTLY HOW BIG THE THREAT WAS.
AND THAT IT WAS GETTING BIGGER ALL THE TIME.
COME ON, HAPPY. TALK TO ME.
GIVE ME SOME GOOD NEWS.
I WOULD IF I HAD ANY TO GIVE, ROCK. BUT THERE IS NO USE.
THE VIRUS HAS INFECTED THE MAIN SERVERS, AND WE ARE COMPLETELY LOCKED OUT.
THERE IS NOTHING WE CAN DO TO STOP IT.
IT SOUNDS SAPPY TO SAY, BUT I HAD NEVER SEEN HAPPY LOOK SO SAD.

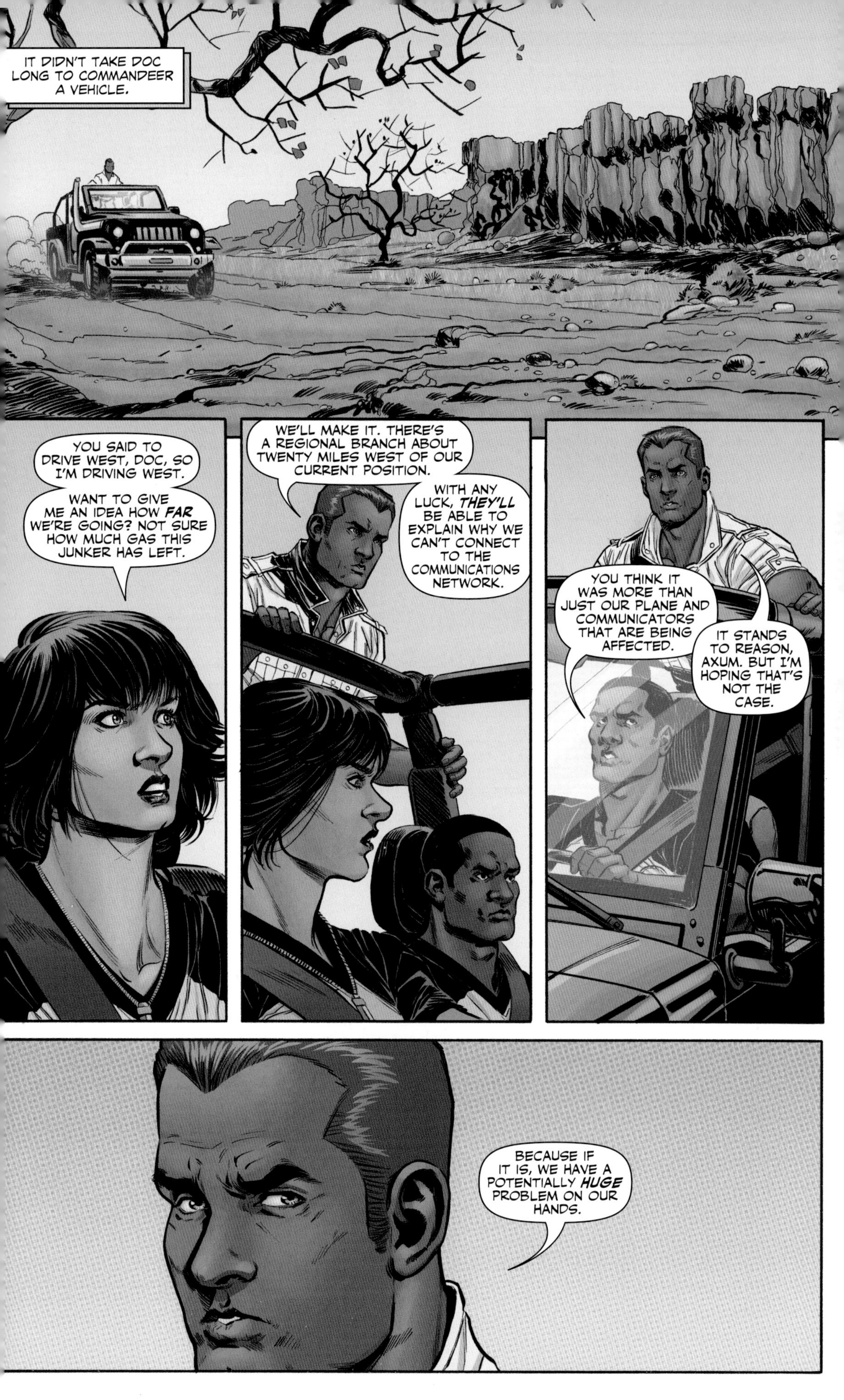
IT DIDN'T TAKE DOC LONG TO COMMANDEER A VEHICLE.
YOU SAID TO DRIVE WEST, DOC, SO I'M DRIVING WEST.
WANT TO GIVE ME AN IDEA HOW FAR WE'RE GOING? NOT SURE HOW MUCH GAS THIS JUNKER HAS LEFT.
WE'LL MAKE IT. THERE'S A REGIONAL BRANCH ABOUT TWENTY MILES WEST OF OUR CURRENT POSITION.
WITH ANY LUCK, THEY'LL BE ABLE TO EXPLAIN WHY WE CAN'T CONNECT TO THE COMMUNICATIONS NETWORK.
YOU THINK IT WAS MORE THAN JUST OUR PLANE AND COMMUNICATORS THAT ARE BEING AFFECTED.
IT STANDS TO REASON, AXUM. BUT I'M HOPING THAT'S NOT THE CASE.
BECAUSE IF IT IS, WE HAVE A POTENTIALLY HUGE PROBLEM ON OUR HANDS.

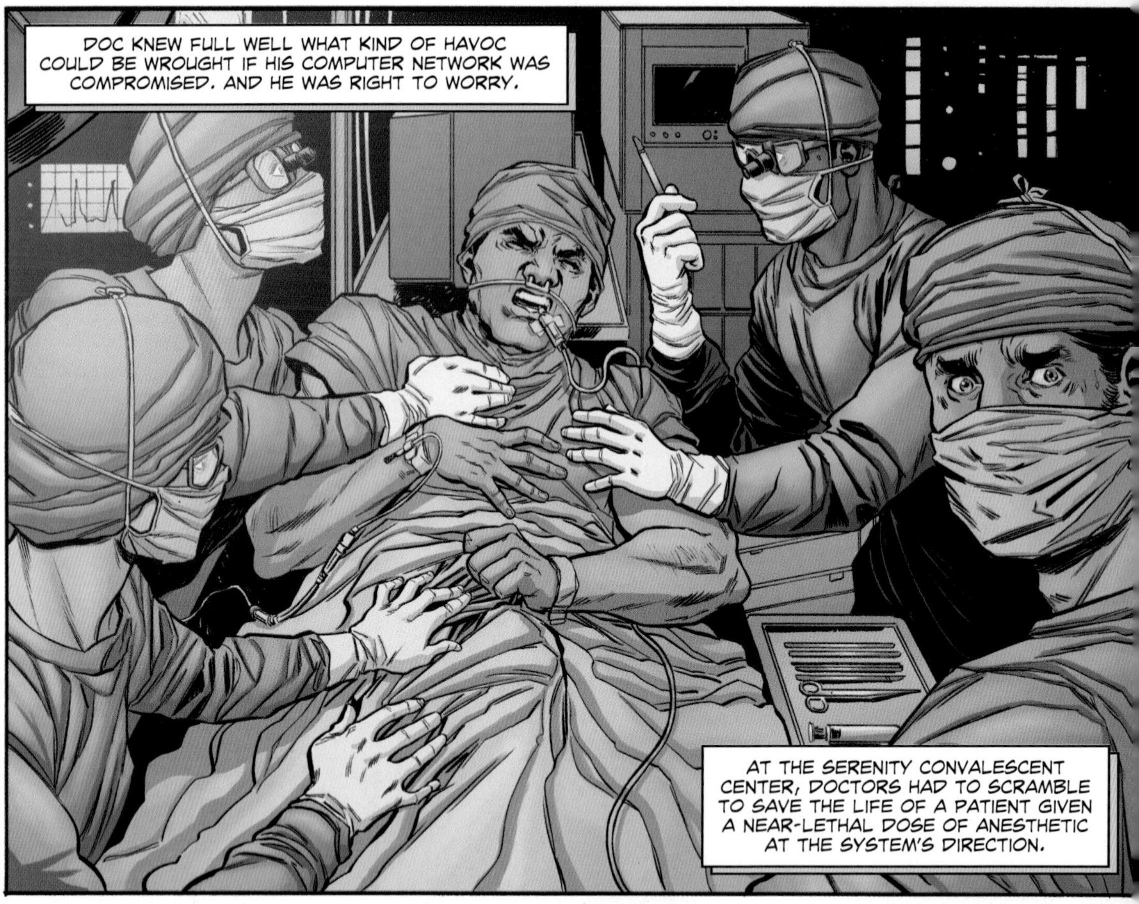
DOC KNEW FULL WELL WHAT KIND OF HAVOC COULD BE WROUGHT IF HIS COMPUTER NETWORK WAS COMPROMISED. AND HE WAS RIGHT TO WORRY.
AT THE SERENITY CONVALESCENT CENTER, DOCTORS HAD TO SCRAMBLE TO SAVE THE LIFE OF A PATIENT GIVEN A NEAR-LETHAL DOSE OF ANESTHETIC AT THE SYSTEM'S DIRECTION.

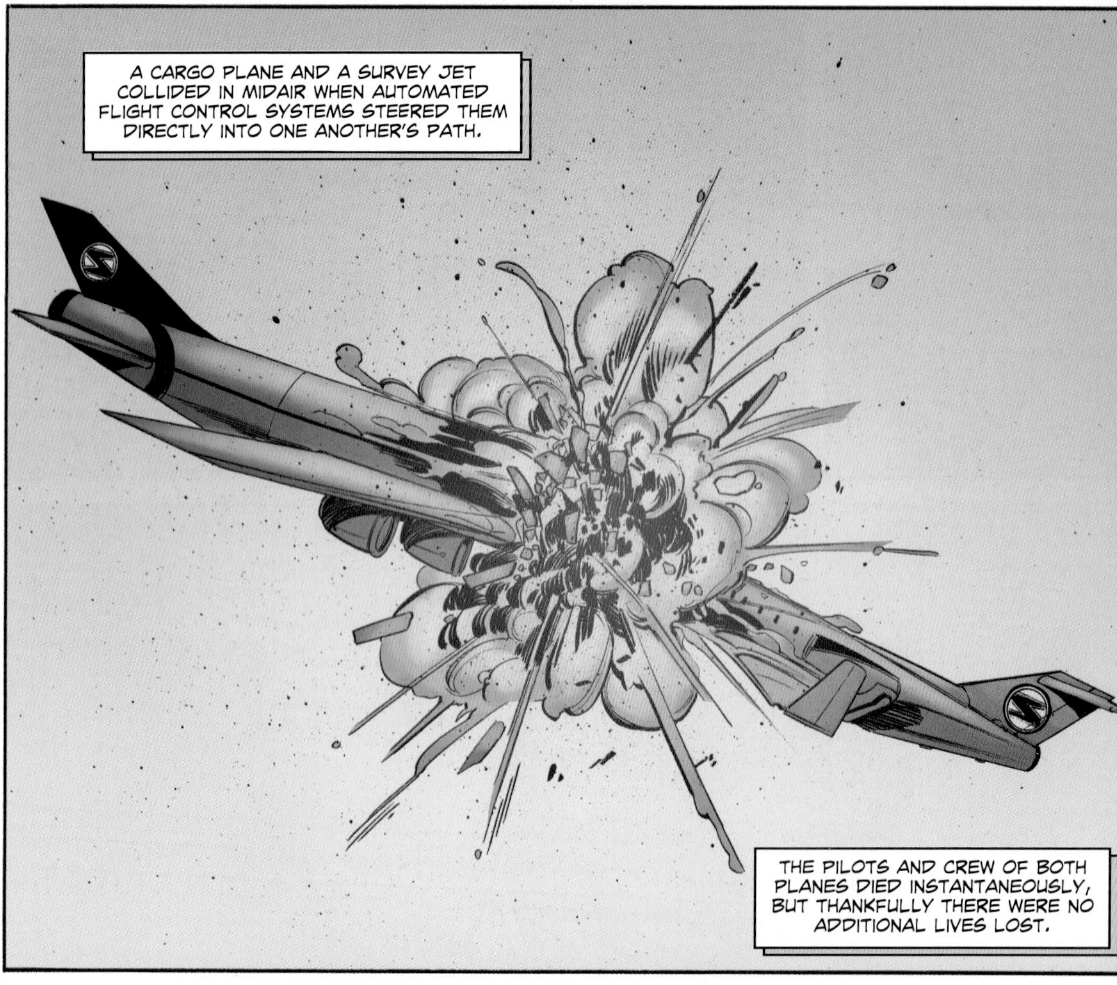
A CARGO PLANE AND A SURVEY JET COLLIDED IN MIDAIR WHEN AUTOMATED FLIGHT CONTROL SYSTEMS STEERED THEM DIRECTLY INTO ONE ANOTHER'S PATH.
THE PILOTS AND CREW OF BOTH PLANES DIED INSTANTANEOUSLY, BUT THANKFULLY THERE WERE NO ADDITIONAL LIVES LOST.

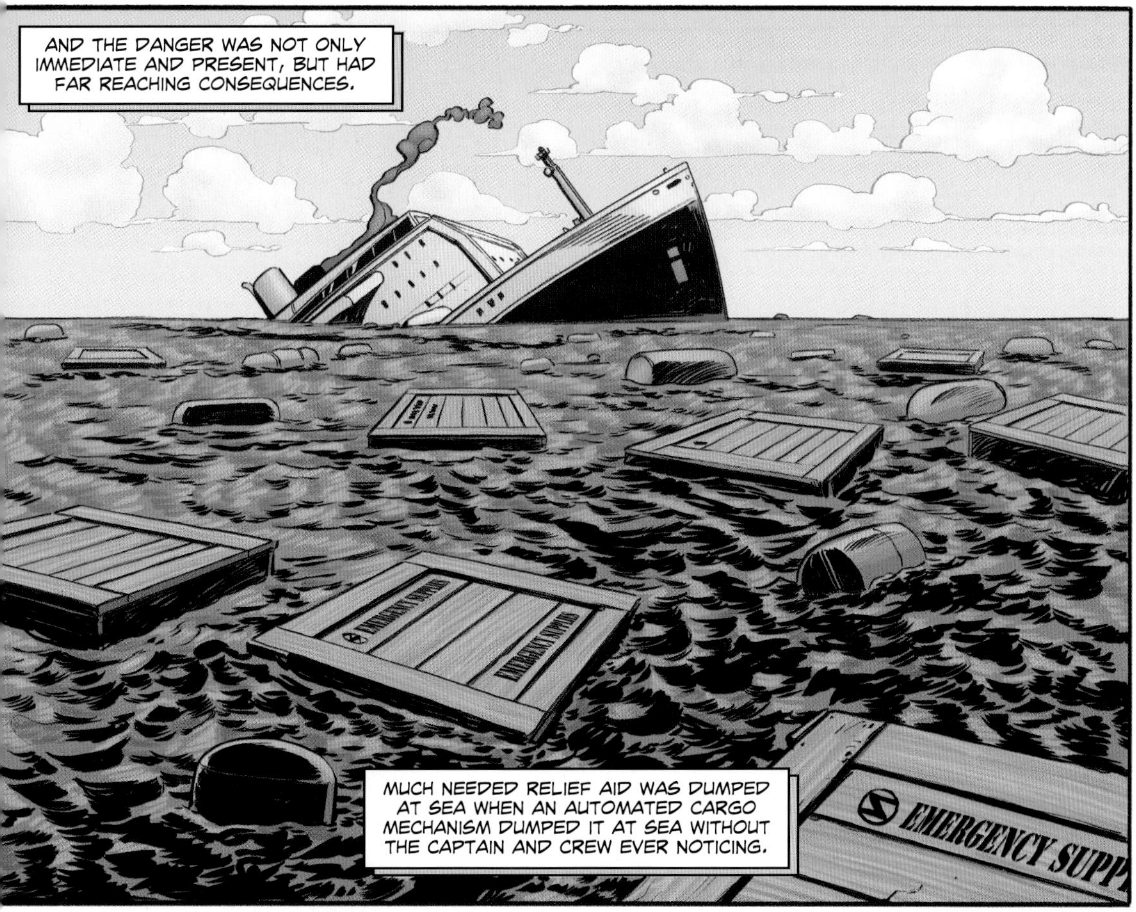
AND THE DANGER WAS NOT ONLY IMMEDIATE AND PRESENT, BUT HAD FAR REACHING CONSEQUENCES.
EMERGENCY SUPPLIES
MUCH NEEDED RELIEF AID WAS DUMPED AT SEA WHEN AN AUTOMATED CARGO MECHANISM DUMPED IT AT SEA WITHOUT THE CAPTAIN AND CREW EVER NOTICING.
EMERGENCY SUPP

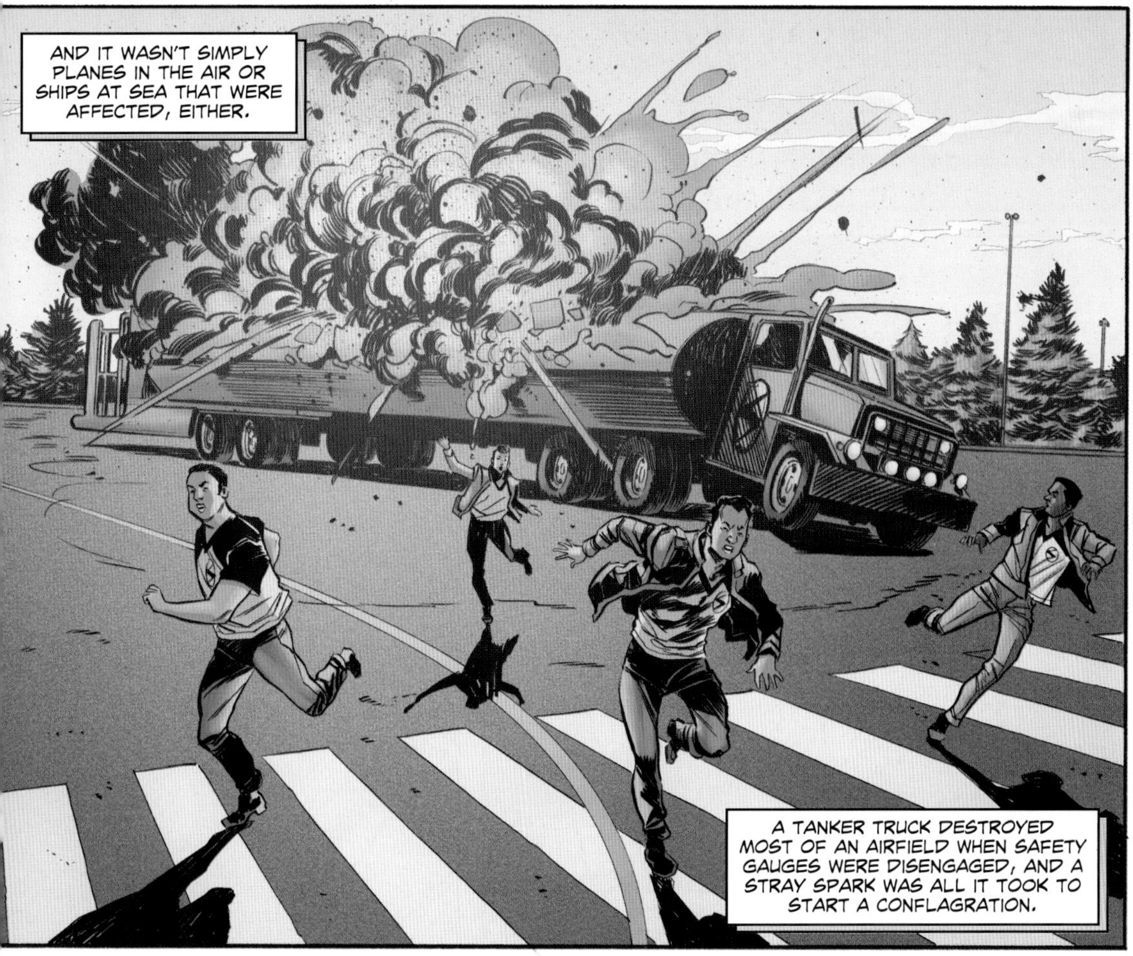
AND IT WASN'T SIMPLY PLANES IN THE AIR OR SHIPS AT SEA THAT WERE AFFECTED, EITHER.
A TANKER TRUCK DESTROYED MOST OF AN AIRFIELD WHEN SAFETY GAUGES WERE DISENGAGED, AND A STRAY SPARK WAS ALL IT TOOK TO START A CONFLAGRATION.

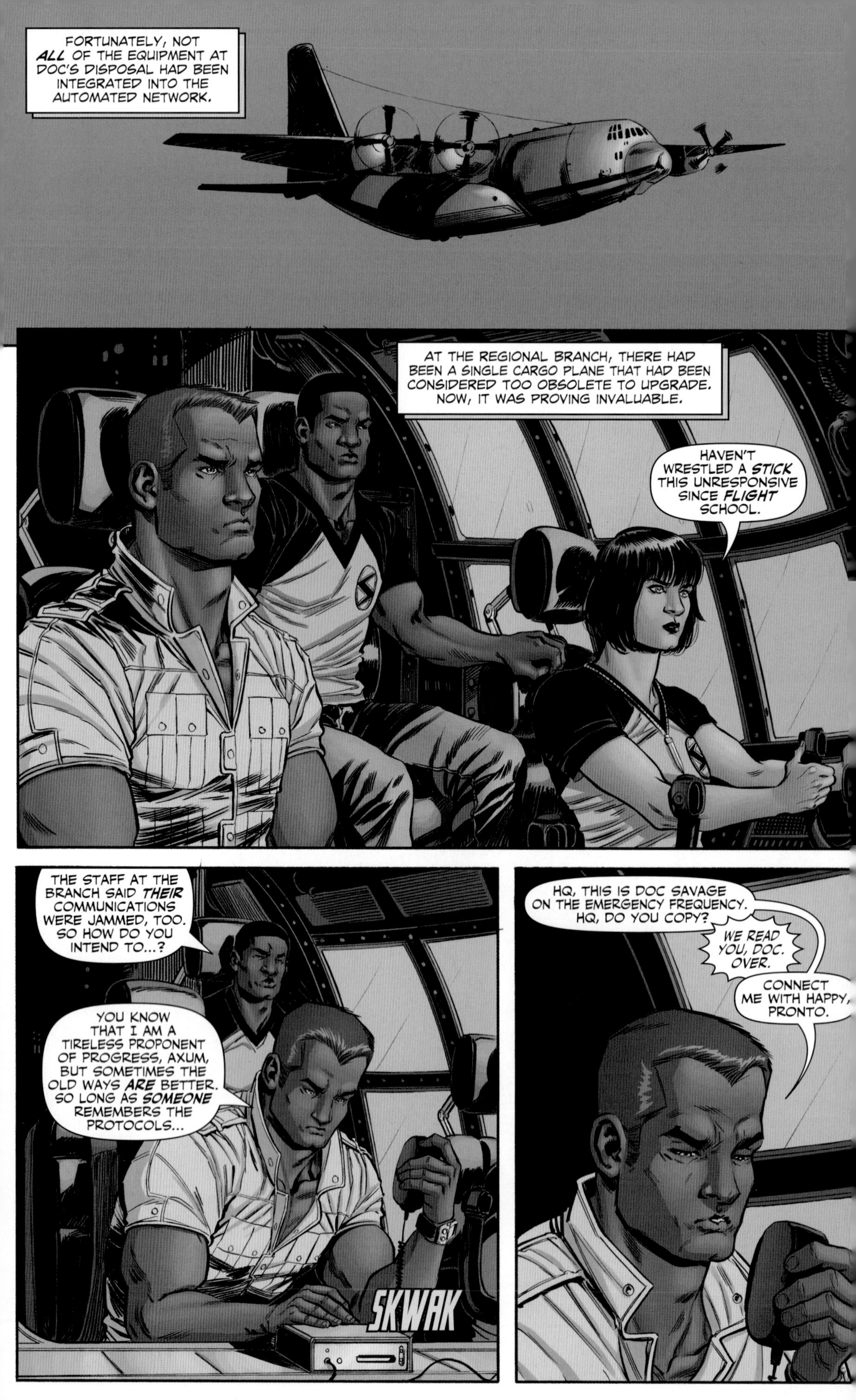
FORTUNATELY, NOT ALL OF THE EQUIPMENT AT DOC'S DISPOSAL HAD BEEN INTEGRATED INTO THE AUTOMATED NETWORK.
AT THE REGIONAL BRANCH, THERE HAD BEEN A SINGLE CARGO PLANE THAT HAD BEEN CONSIDERED TOO OBSOLETE TO UPGRADE. NOW, IT WAS PROVING INVALUABLE.
HAVEN'T WRESTLED A STICK THIS UNRESPONSIVE SINCE FLIGHT SCHOOL.
THE STAFF AT THE BRANCH SAID THEIR COMMUNICATIONS WERE JAMMED, TOO. SO HOW DO YOU INTEND TO...?
YOU KNOW THAT I AM A TIRELESS PROPONENT OF PROGRESS, AXUM, BUT SOMETIMES THE OLD WAYS ARE BETTER. SO LONG AS SOMEONE REMEMBERS THE PROTOCOLS...
SKWAK
HQ, THIS IS DOC SAVAGE ON THE EMERGENCY FREQUENCY. HQ, DO YOU COPY?
WE READ YOU, DOC. OVER.
CONNECT ME WITH HAPPY, PRONTO.

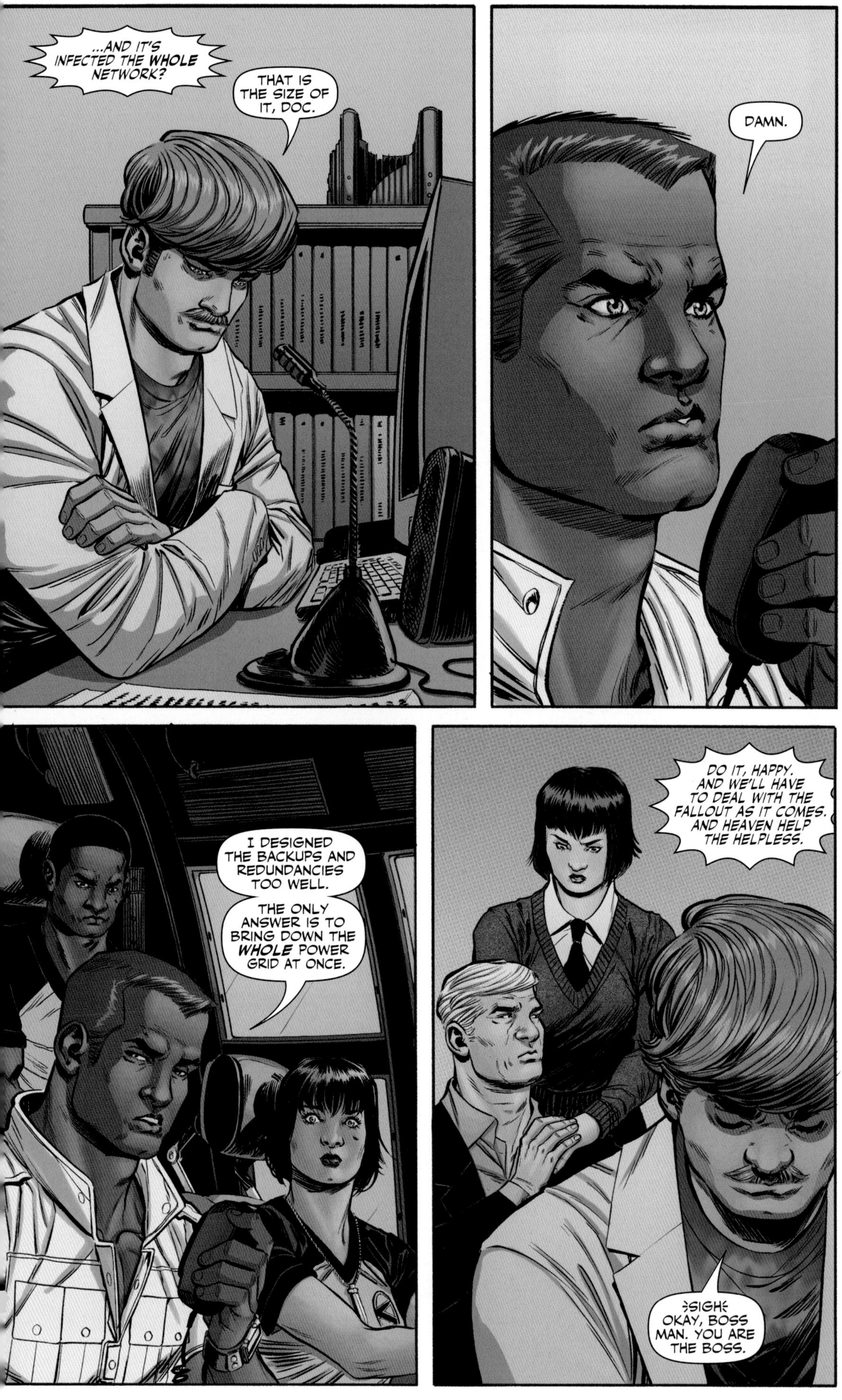

...AND IT'S INFECTED THE WHOLE NETWORK?
THAT IS THE SIZE OF IT, DOC.
DAMN.
I DESIGNED THE BACKUPS AND REDUNDANCIES TOO WELL.
THE ONLY ANSWER IS TO BRING DOWN THE WHOLE POWER GRID AT ONCE.
DO IT, HAPPY. AND WE'LL HAVE TO DEAL WITH THE FALLOUT AS IT COMES. AND HEAVEN HELP THE HELPLESS.
SIGH OKAY, BOSS MAN. YOU ARE THE BOSS.

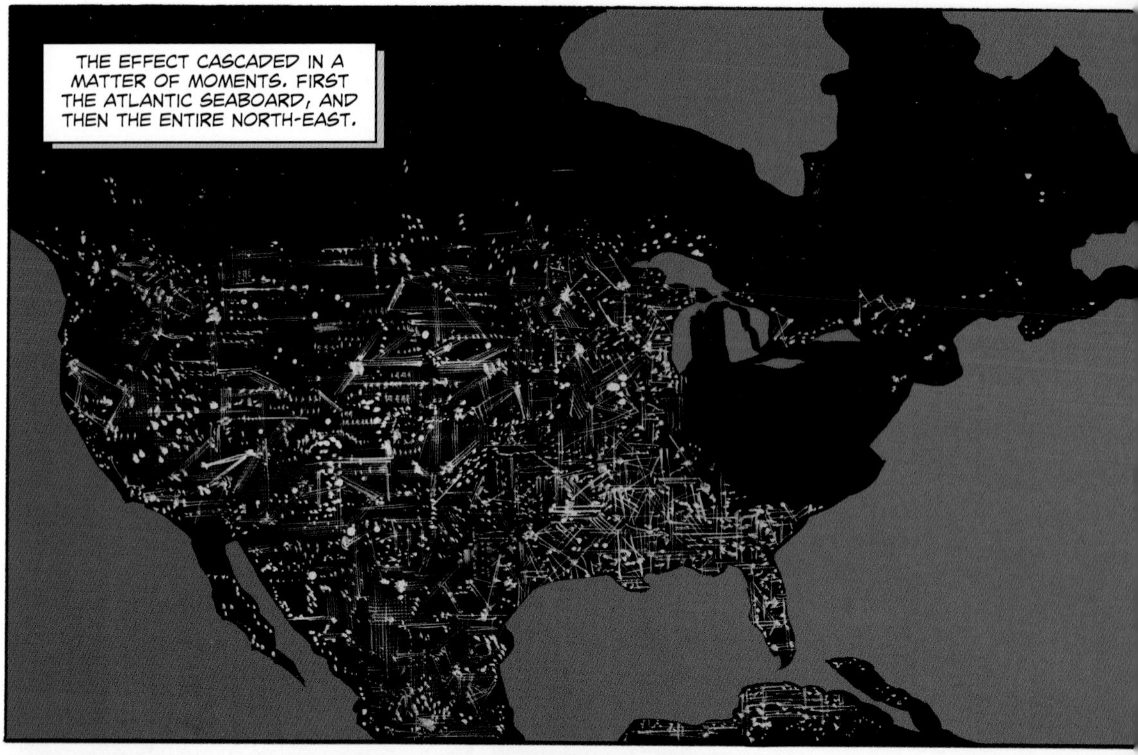
THE EFFECT CASCADED IN A MATTER OF MOMENTS. FIRST THE ATLANTIC SEABOARD, AND THEN THE ENTIRE NORTH-EAST.

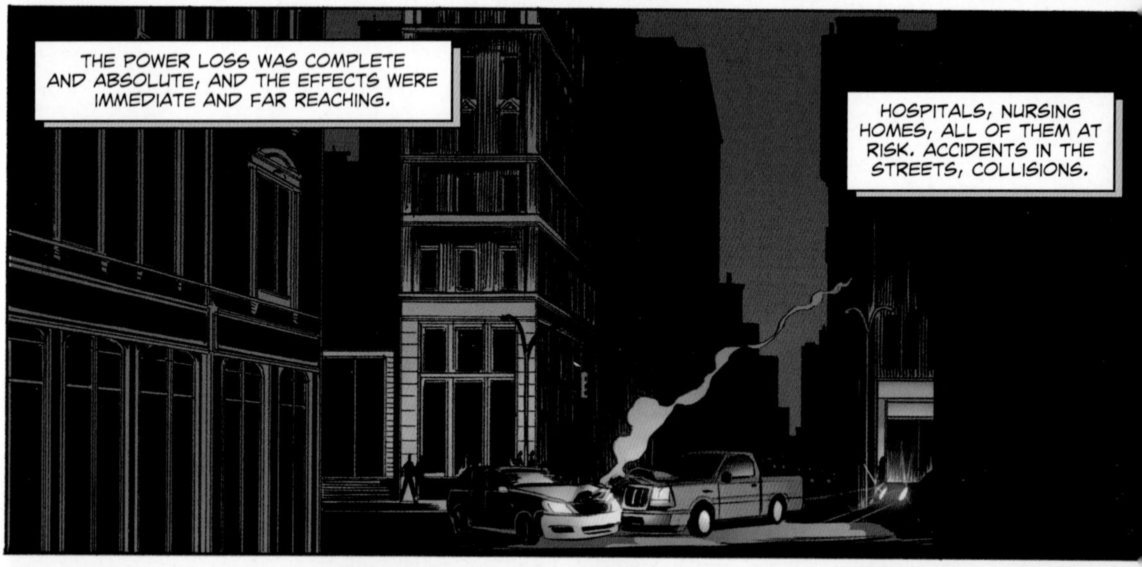
THE POWER LOSS WAS COMPLETE AND ABSOLUTE, AND THE EFFECTS WERE IMMEDIATE AND FAR REACHING.
HOSPITALS, NURSING HOMES, ALL OF THEM AT RISK. ACCIDENTS IN THE STREETS, COLLISIONS.

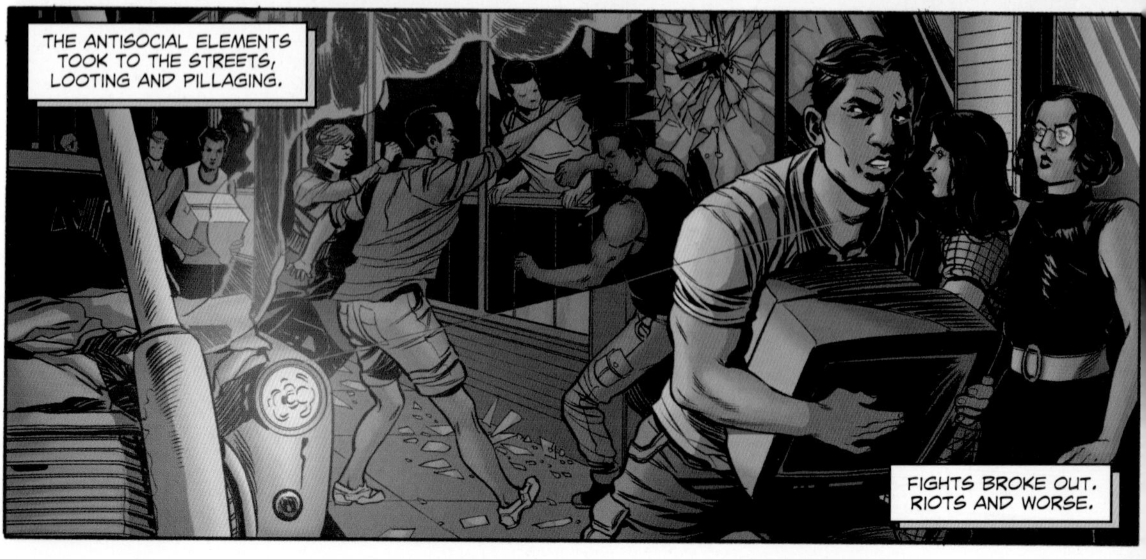
THE ANTISOCIAL ELEMENTS TOOK TO THE STREETS, LOOTING AND PILLAGING.
FIGHTS BROKE OUT. RIOTS AND WORSE.

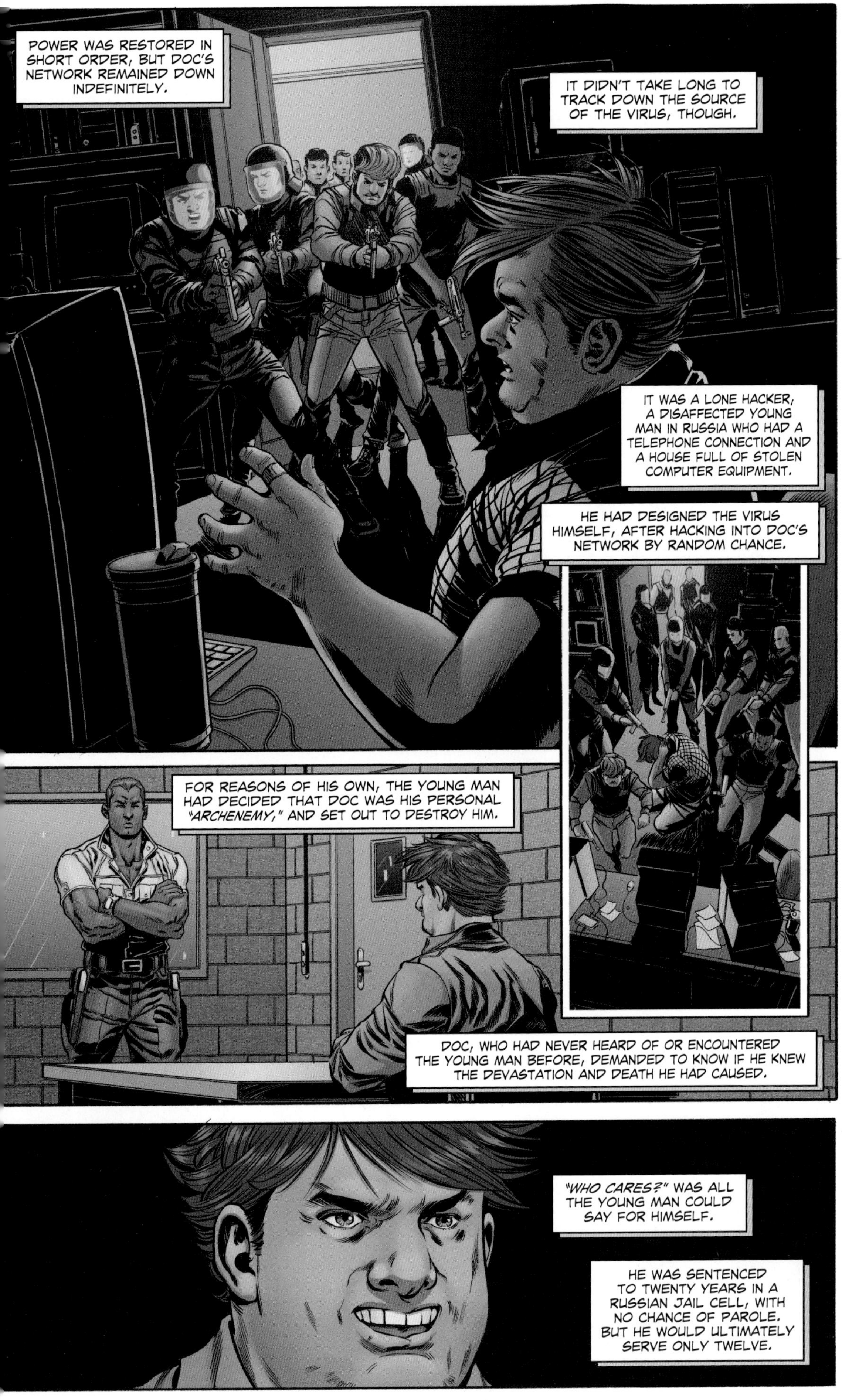
POWER WAS RESTORED IN SHORT ORDER, BUT DOC'S NETWORK REMAINED DOWN INDEFINITELY.
IT DIDN'T TAKE LONG TO TRACK DOWN THE SOURCE OF THE VIRUS, THOUGH.
IT WAS A LONE HACKER, A DISAFFECTED YOUNG MAN IN RUSSIA WHO HAD A TELEPHONE CONNECTION AND A HOUSE FULL OF STOLEN COMPUTER EQUIPMENT.
HE HAD DESIGNED THE VIRUS HIMSELF, AFTER HACKING INTO DOC'S NETWORK BY RANDOM CHANCE.
FOR REASONS OF HIS OWN, THE YOUNG MAN HAD DECIDED THAT DOC WAS HIS PERSONAL *"ARCHENEMY,"* AND SET OUT TO DESTROY HIM.
DOC, WHO HAD NEVER HEARD OF OR ENCOUNTERED THE YOUNG MAN BEFORE, DEMANDED TO KNOW IF HE KNEW THE DEVASTATION AND DEATH HE HAD CAUSED.
"WHO CARES?" WAS ALL THE YOUNG MAN COULD SAY FOR HIMSELF.
HE WAS SENTENCED TO TWENTY YEARS IN A RUSSIAN JAIL CELL, WITH NO CHANCE OF PAROLE. BUT HE WOULD ULTIMATELY SERVE ONLY TWELVE.

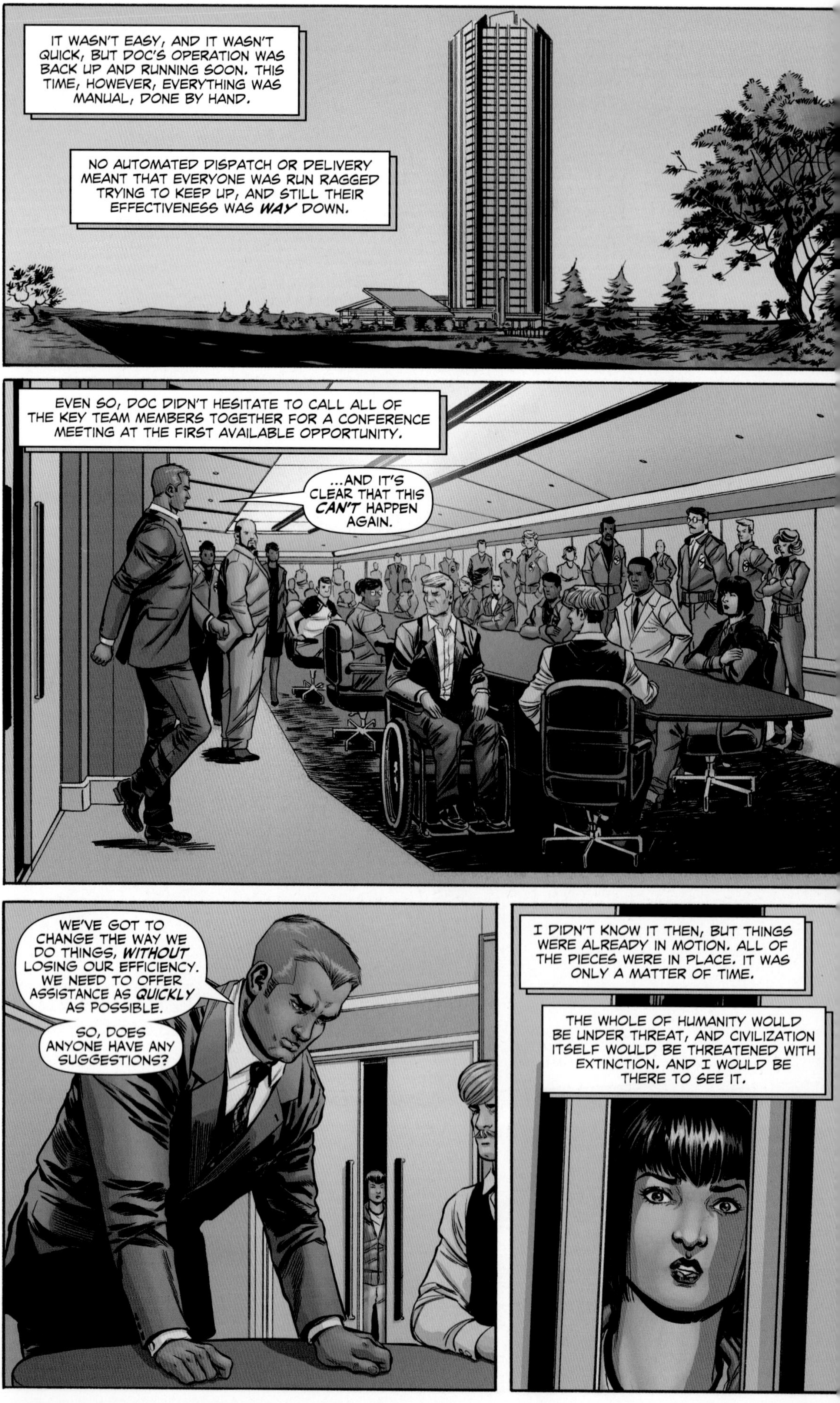
IT WASN'T EASY, AND IT WASN'T QUICK, BUT DOC'S OPERATION WAS BACK UP AND RUNNING SOON. THIS TIME, HOWEVER, EVERYTHING WAS MANUAL, DONE BY HAND.
NO AUTOMATED DISPATCH OR DELIVERY MEANT THAT EVERYONE WAS RUN RAGGED TRYING TO KEEP UP, AND STILL THEIR EFFECTIVENESS WAS WAY DOWN.
EVEN SO, DOC DIDN'T HESITATE TO CALL ALL OF THE KEY TEAM MEMBERS TOGETHER FOR A CONFERENCE MEETING AT THE FIRST AVAILABLE OPPORTUNITY.
...AND IT'S CLEAR THAT THIS CAN'T HAPPEN AGAIN.
WE'VE GOT TO CHANGE THE WAY WE DO THINGS, WITHOUT LOSING OUR EFFICIENCY. WE NEED TO OFFER ASSISTANCE AS QUICKLY AS POSSIBLE.
SO, DOES ANYONE HAVE ANY SUGGESTIONS?
I DIDN'T KNOW IT THEN, BUT THINGS WERE ALREADY IN MOTION. ALL OF THE PIECES WERE IN PLACE. IT WAS ONLY A MATTER OF TIME.
THE WHOLE OF HUMANITY WOULD BE UNDER THREAT, AND CIVILIZATION ITSELF WOULD BE THREATENED WITH EXTINCTION. AND I WOULD BE THERE TO SEE IT.

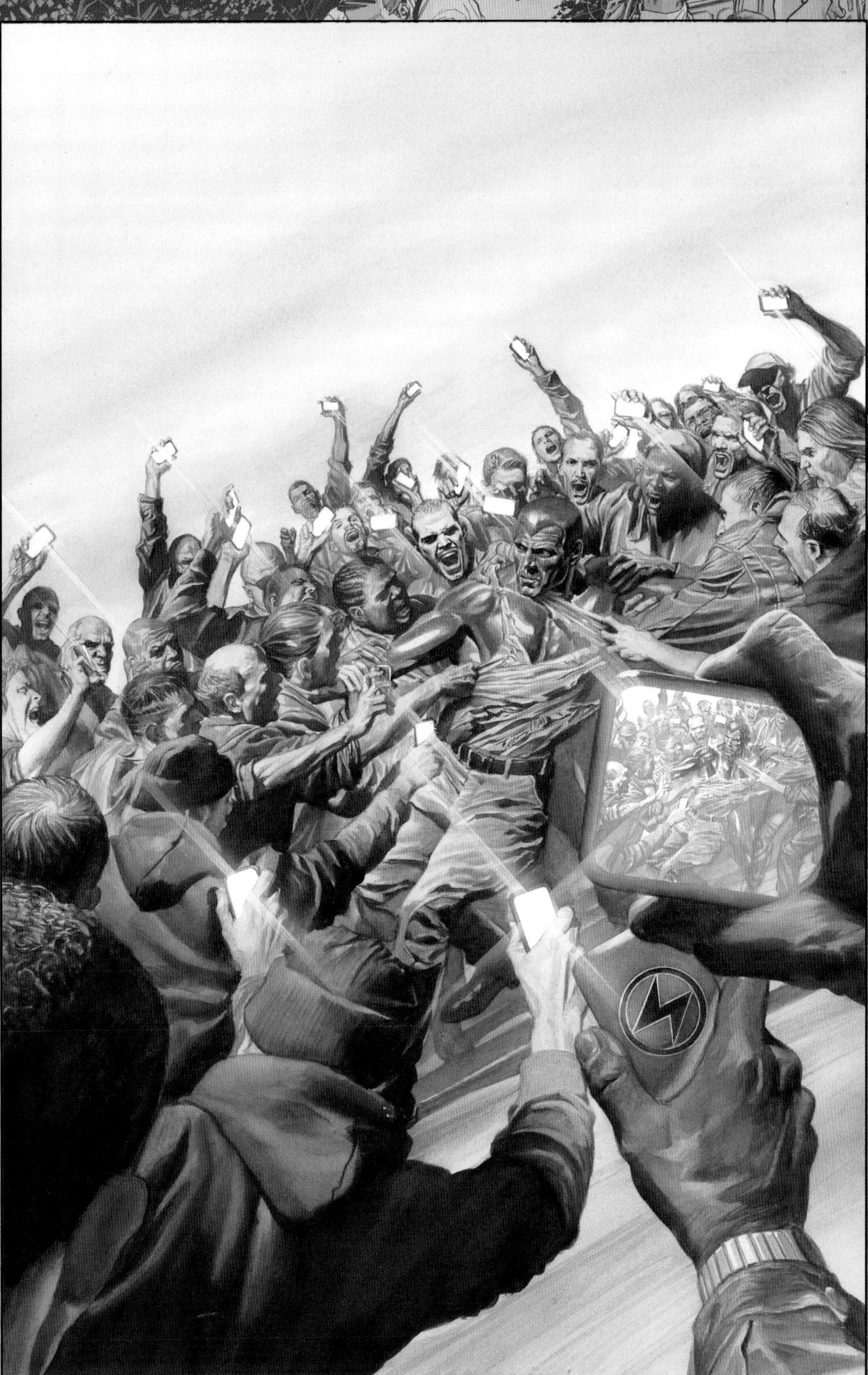

ISSUE **#7** COVER
art by **ALEX ROSS**

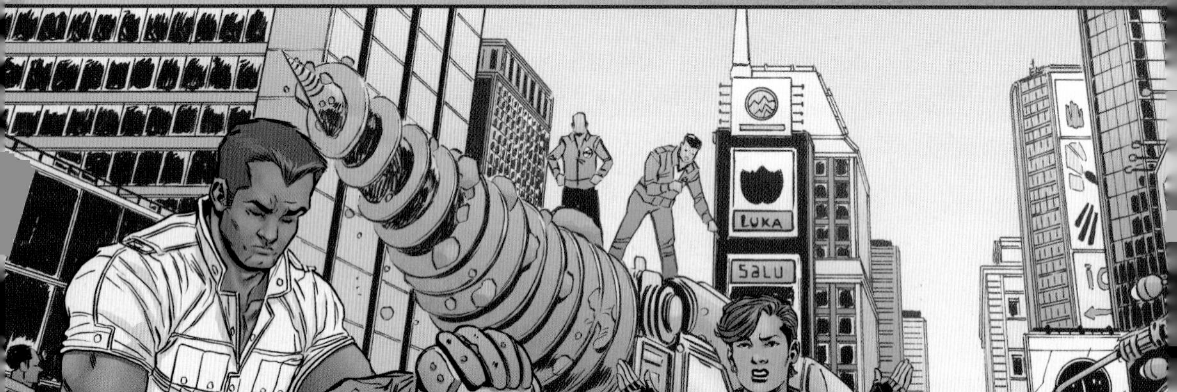

LUKA
SALU
LION

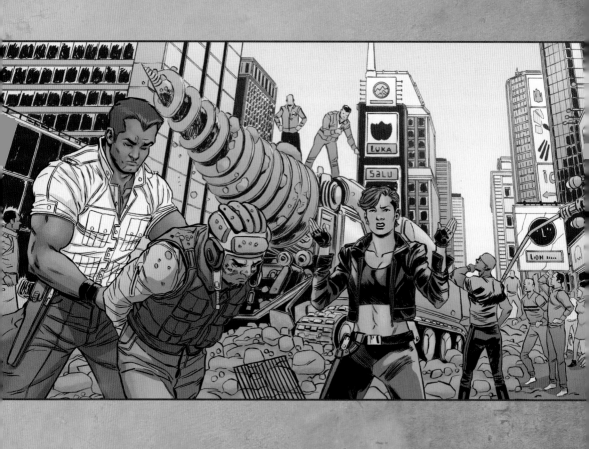

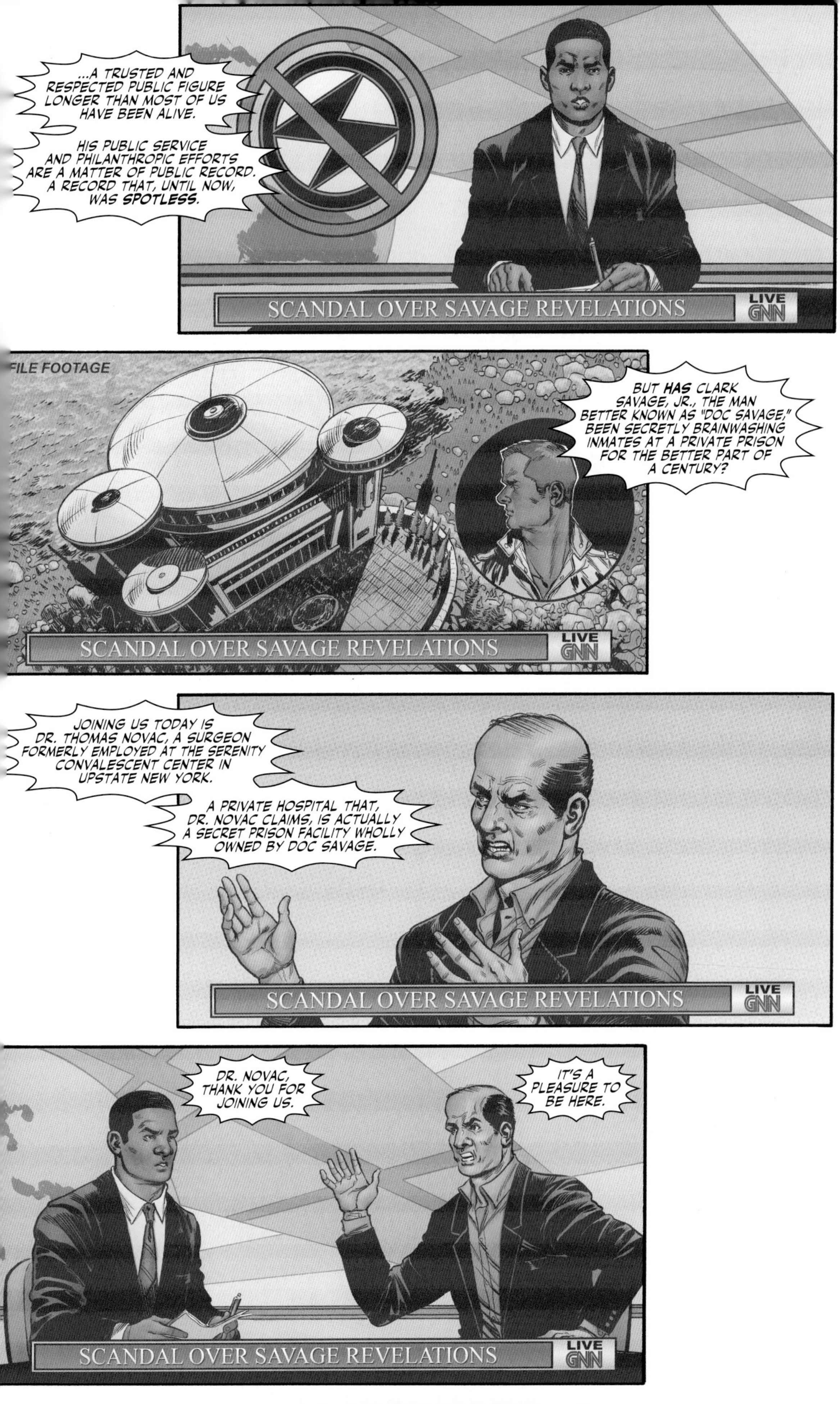
...A TRUSTED AND RESPECTED PUBLIC FIGURE LONGER THAN MOST OF US HAVE BEEN ALIVE.
HIS PUBLIC SERVICE AND PHILANTHROPIC EFFORTS ARE A MATTER OF PUBLIC RECORD. A RECORD THAT, UNTIL NOW, WAS **SPOTLESS**.
SCANDAL OVER SAVAGE REVELATIONS
LIVE
GNN
FILE FOOTAGE
BUT **HAS** CLARK SAVAGE, JR., THE MAN BETTER KNOWN AS "DOC SAVAGE," BEEN SECRETLY BRAINWASHING INMATES AT A PRIVATE PRISON FOR THE BETTER PART OF A CENTURY?
SCANDAL OVER SAVAGE REVELATIONS
LIVE
GNN
JOINING US TODAY IS DR. THOMAS NOVAC, A SURGEON FORMERLY EMPLOYED AT THE SERENITY CONVALESCENT CENTER IN UPSTATE NEW YORK.
A PRIVATE HOSPITAL THAT, DR. NOVAC CLAIMS, IS ACTUALLY A SECRET PRISON FACILITY WHOLLY OWNED BY DOC SAVAGE.
SCANDAL OVER SAVAGE REVELATIONS
LIVE
GNN
DR. NOVAC, THANK YOU FOR JOINING US.
IT'S A PLEASURE TO BE HERE.
SCANDAL OVER SAVAGE REVELATIONS
LIVE
GNN

NOW, THESE ARE PRETTY SERIOUS ALLEGATIONS THAT YOU'VE MADE. YOU SAY DOC SAVAGE *CAPTURES* CRIMINALS AND THEN *BRAINWASHES* THEM?

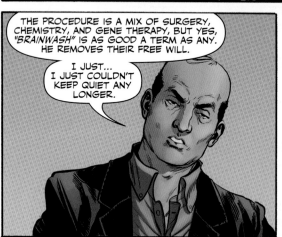

THE PROCEDURE IS A MIX OF SURGERY, CHEMISTRY, AND GENE THERAPY, BUT YES, *"BRAINWASH"* IS AS GOOD A TERM AS ANY. HE REMOVES THEIR FREE WILL.

I JUST... I JUST COULDN'T KEEP QUIET ANY LONGER.

WHEN DR. NOVAC LEFT THE FACILITY, HE DIDN'T LEAVE EMPTY HANDED, BUT TOOK WITH HIM PRIVATE RECORDS WHICH IDENTIFY SEVERAL INDIVIDUALS WHO HAVE RECEIVED THE PROCEDURE.

ONE OF WHOM, STEWART CARTWRIGHT, WAS APPARENTLY TAKEN PRISONER BY SAVAGE IN 1988 AFTER THE *"SUNBEAM"* INCIDENT IN SOUTHERN CALIFORNIA.

OUR INVESTIGATORS LOCATED HIM LIVING UNDER AN ASSUMED NAME IN ANOTHER STATE, WITH VERY LITTLE MEMORY OF HIS PAST LIFE.

WE ATTEMPTED TO GET A RESPONSE FROM CLARK SAVAGE, JR. HIMSELF ON THE MATTER.

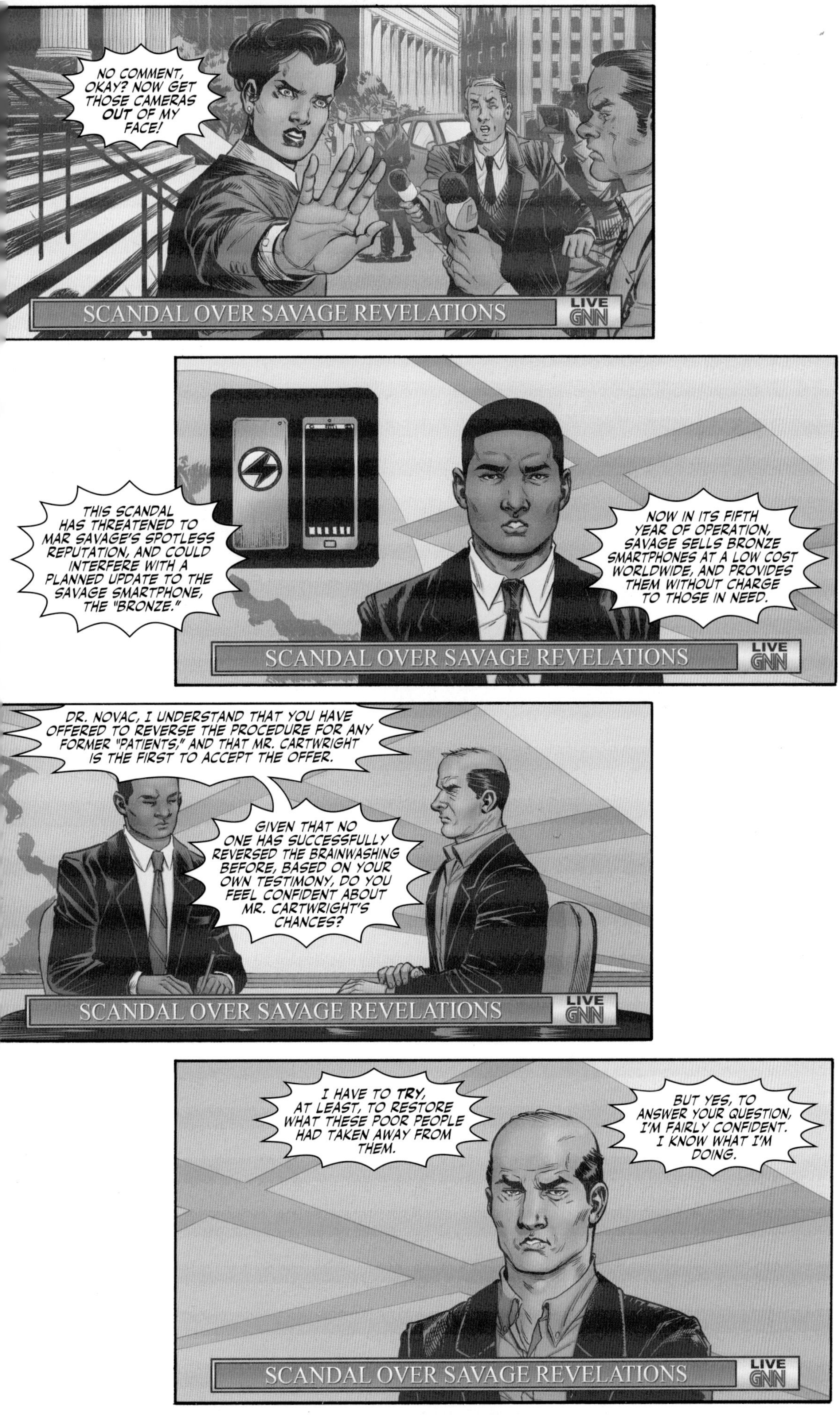
NO COMMENT, OKAY? NOW GET THOSE CAMERAS OUT OF MY FACE!
SCANDAL OVER SAVAGE REVELATIONS
LIVE GNN
THIS SCANDAL HAS THREATENED TO MAR SAVAGE'S SPOTLESS REPUTATION, AND COULD INTERFERE WITH A PLANNED UPDATE TO THE SAVAGE SMARTPHONE, THE "BRONZE."
NOW IN ITS FIFTH YEAR OF OPERATION, SAVAGE SELLS BRONZE SMARTPHONES AT A LOW COST WORLDWIDE, AND PROVIDES THEM WITHOUT CHARGE TO THOSE IN NEED.
SCANDAL OVER SAVAGE REVELATIONS
LIVE GNN
DR. NOVAC, I UNDERSTAND THAT YOU HAVE OFFERED TO REVERSE THE PROCEDURE FOR ANY FORMER "PATIENTS," AND THAT MR. CARTWRIGHT IS THE FIRST TO ACCEPT THE OFFER.
GIVEN THAT NO ONE HAS SUCCESSFULLY REVERSED THE BRAINWASHING BEFORE, BASED ON YOUR OWN TESTIMONY, DO YOU FEEL CONFIDENT ABOUT MR. CARTWRIGHT'S CHANCES?
SCANDAL OVER SAVAGE REVELATIONS
LIVE GNN
I HAVE TO TRY, AT LEAST, TO RESTORE WHAT THESE POOR PEOPLE HAD TAKEN AWAY FROM THEM.
BUT YES, TO ANSWER YOUR QUESTION, I'M FAIRLY CONFIDENT. I KNOW WHAT I'M DOING.
SCANDAL OVER SAVAGE REVELATIONS
LIVE GNN

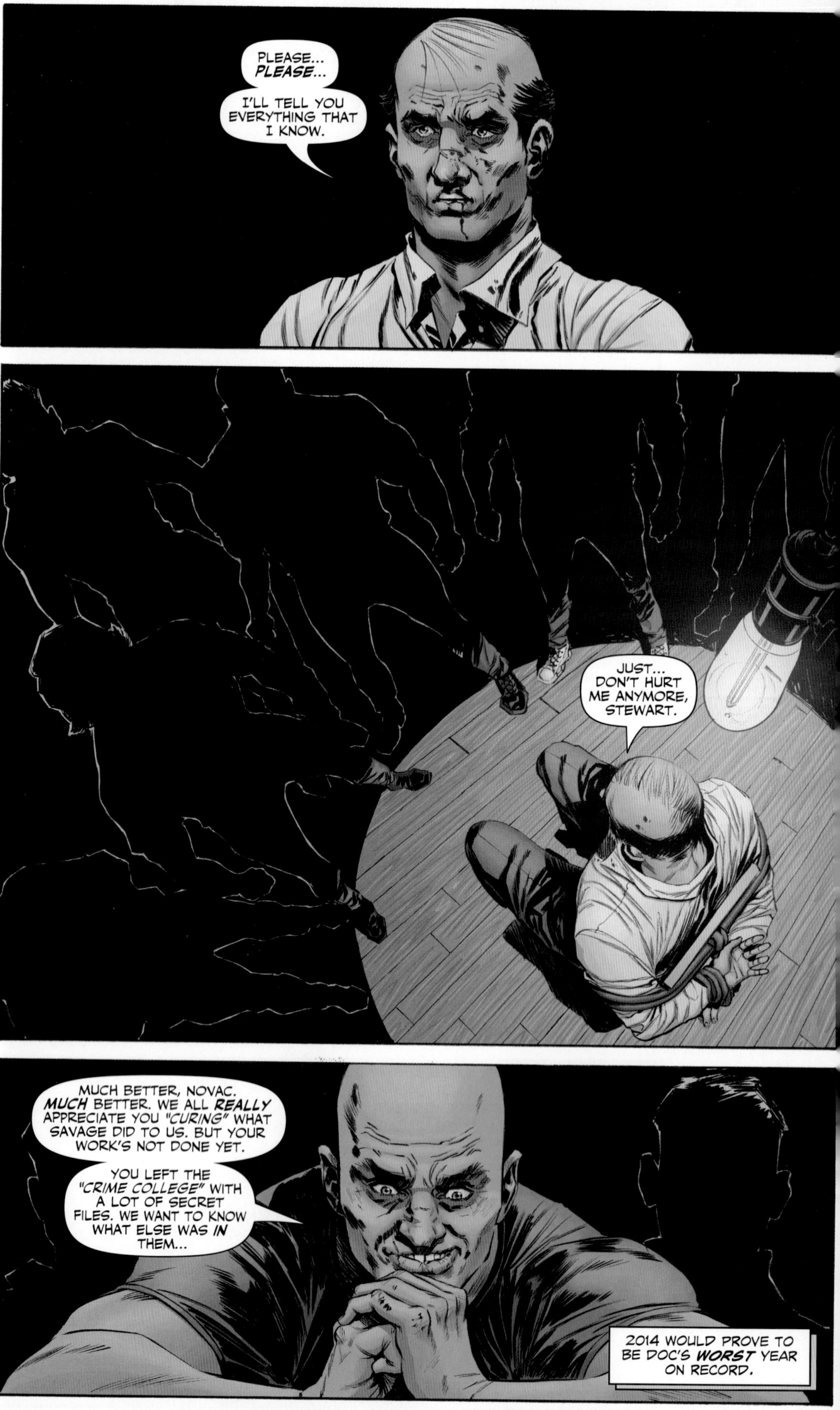
PLEASE... PLEASE...
I'LL TELL YOU EVERYTHING THAT I KNOW.
JUST... DON'T HURT ME ANYMORE, STEWART.
MUCH BETTER, NOVAC. MUCH BETTER. WE ALL REALLY APPRECIATE YOU "CURING" WHAT SAVAGE DID TO US. BUT YOUR WORK'S NOT DONE YET.
YOU LEFT THE "CRIME COLLEGE" WITH A LOT OF SECRET FILES. WE WANT TO KNOW WHAT ELSE WAS IN THEM...
2014 WOULD PROVE TO BE DOC'S WORST YEAR ON RECORD.

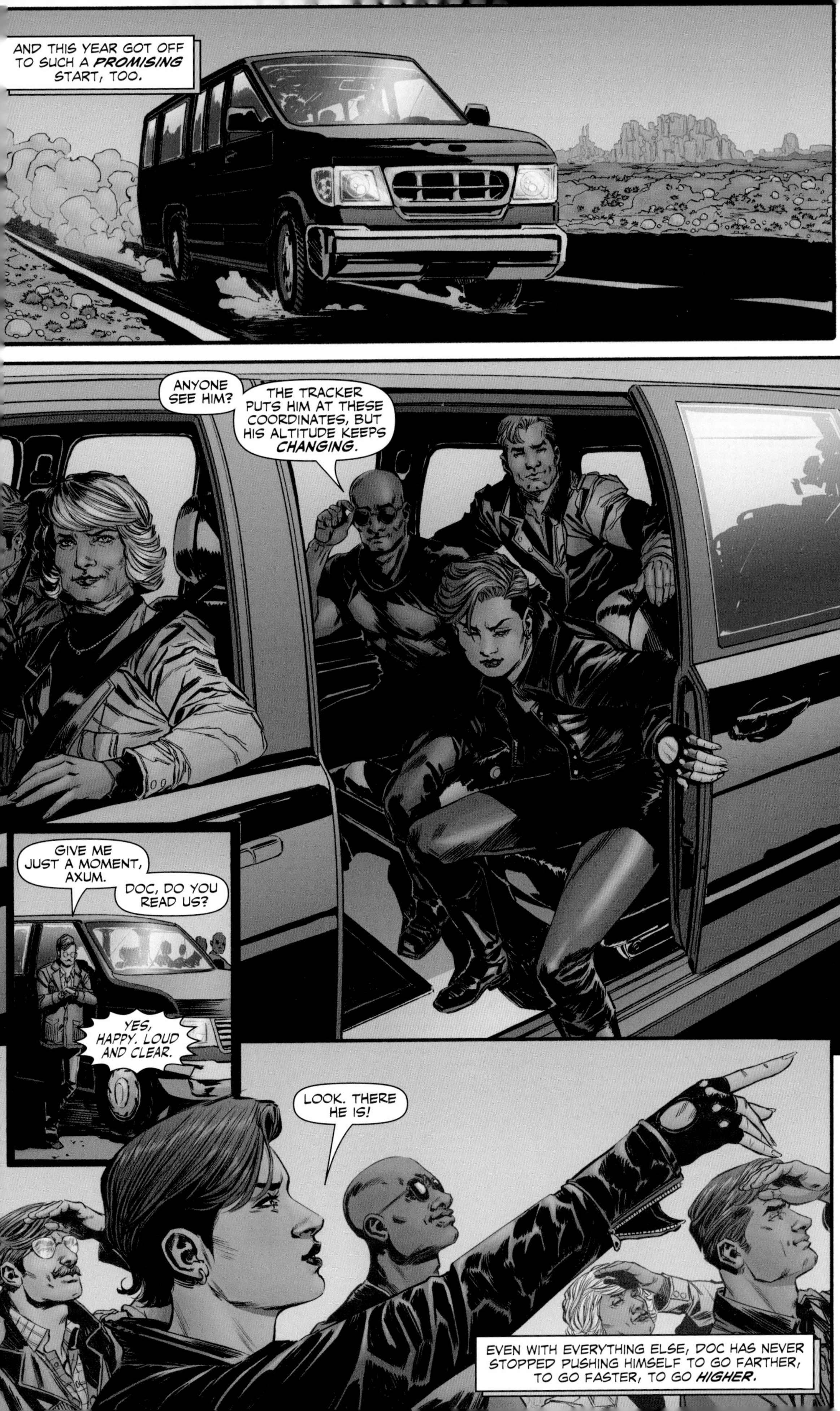
AND THIS YEAR GOT OFF TO SUCH A *PROMISING* START, TOO.
ANYONE SEE HIM?
THE TRACKER PUTS HIM AT THESE COORDINATES, BUT HIS ALTITUDE KEEPS *CHANGING*.
GIVE ME JUST A MOMENT, AXUM.
DOC, DO YOU READ US?
YES, HAPPY. LOUD AND CLEAR.
LOOK. THERE HE IS!
EVEN WITH EVERYTHING ELSE, DOC HAS NEVER STOPPED PUSHING HIMSELF TO GO FARTHER, TO GO FASTER, TO GO *HIGHER*.

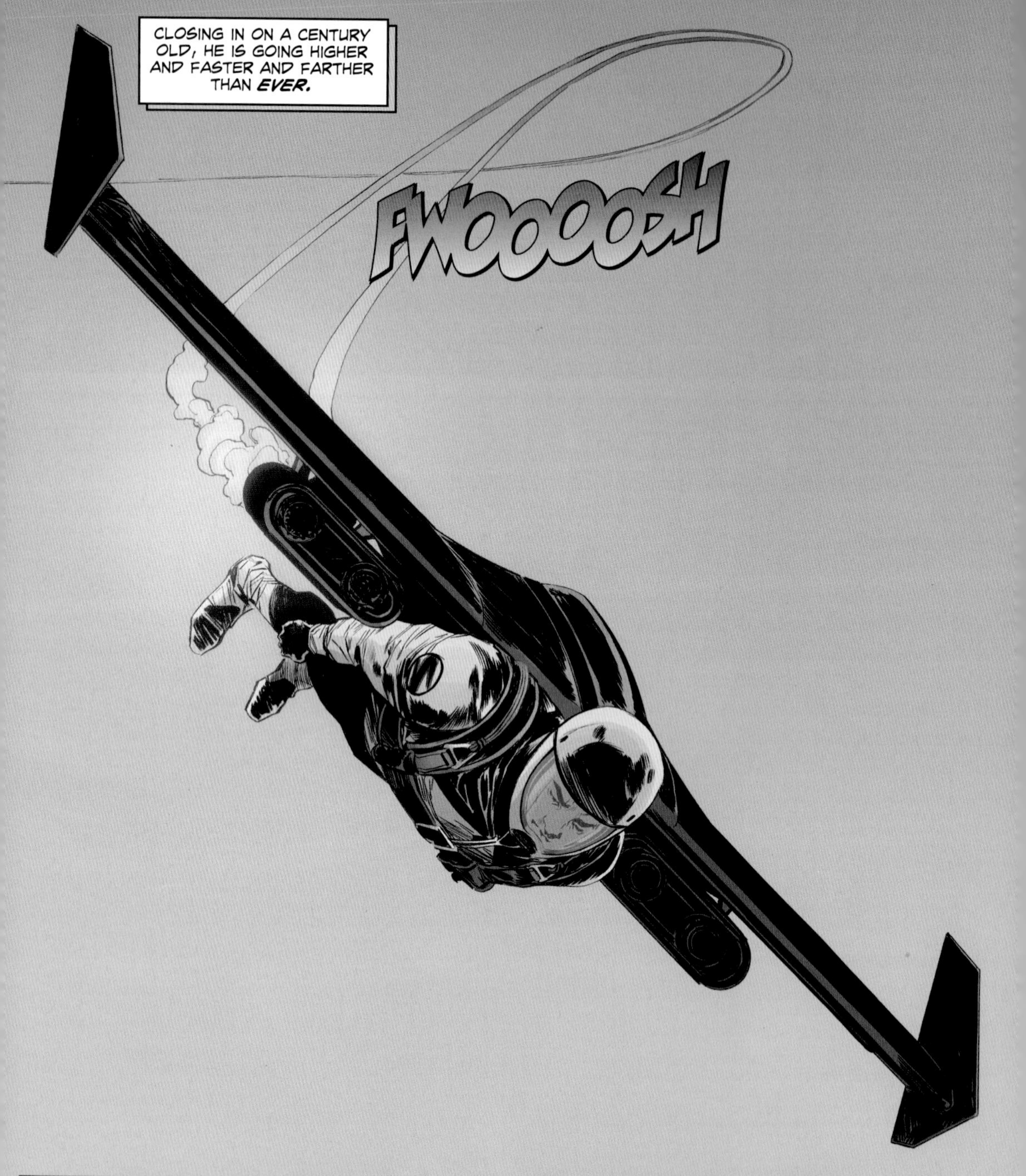
CLOSING IN ON A CENTURY OLD, HE IS GOING HIGHER AND FASTER AND FARTHER THAN *EVER.*
FWOOOOSH

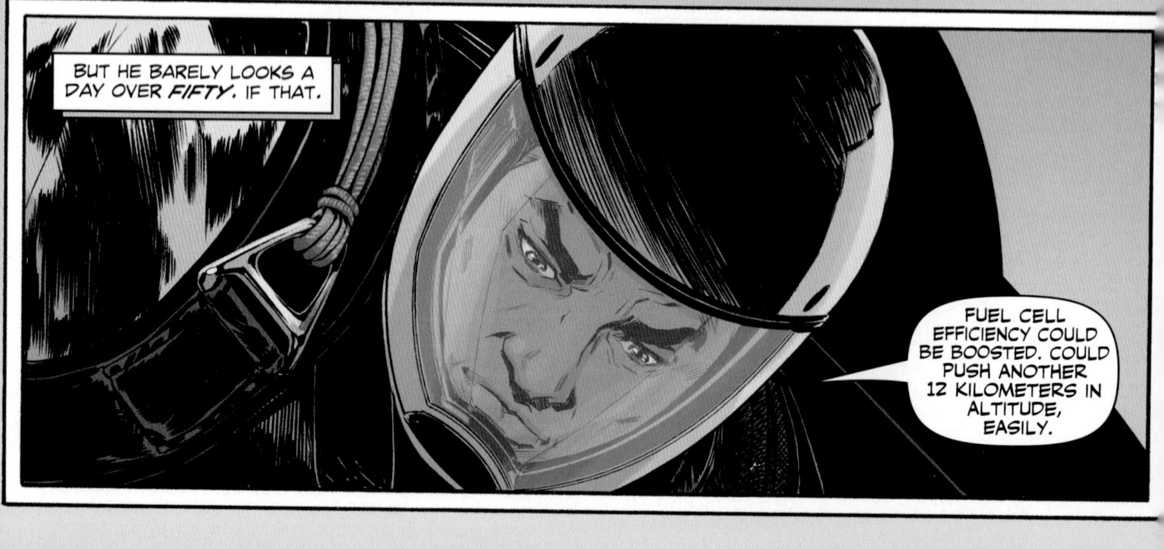
BUT HE BARELY LOOKS A DAY OVER *FIFTY*. IF THAT.
FUEL CELL EFFICIENCY COULD BE BOOSTED. COULD PUSH ANOTHER 12 KILOMETERS IN ALTITUDE, EASILY.

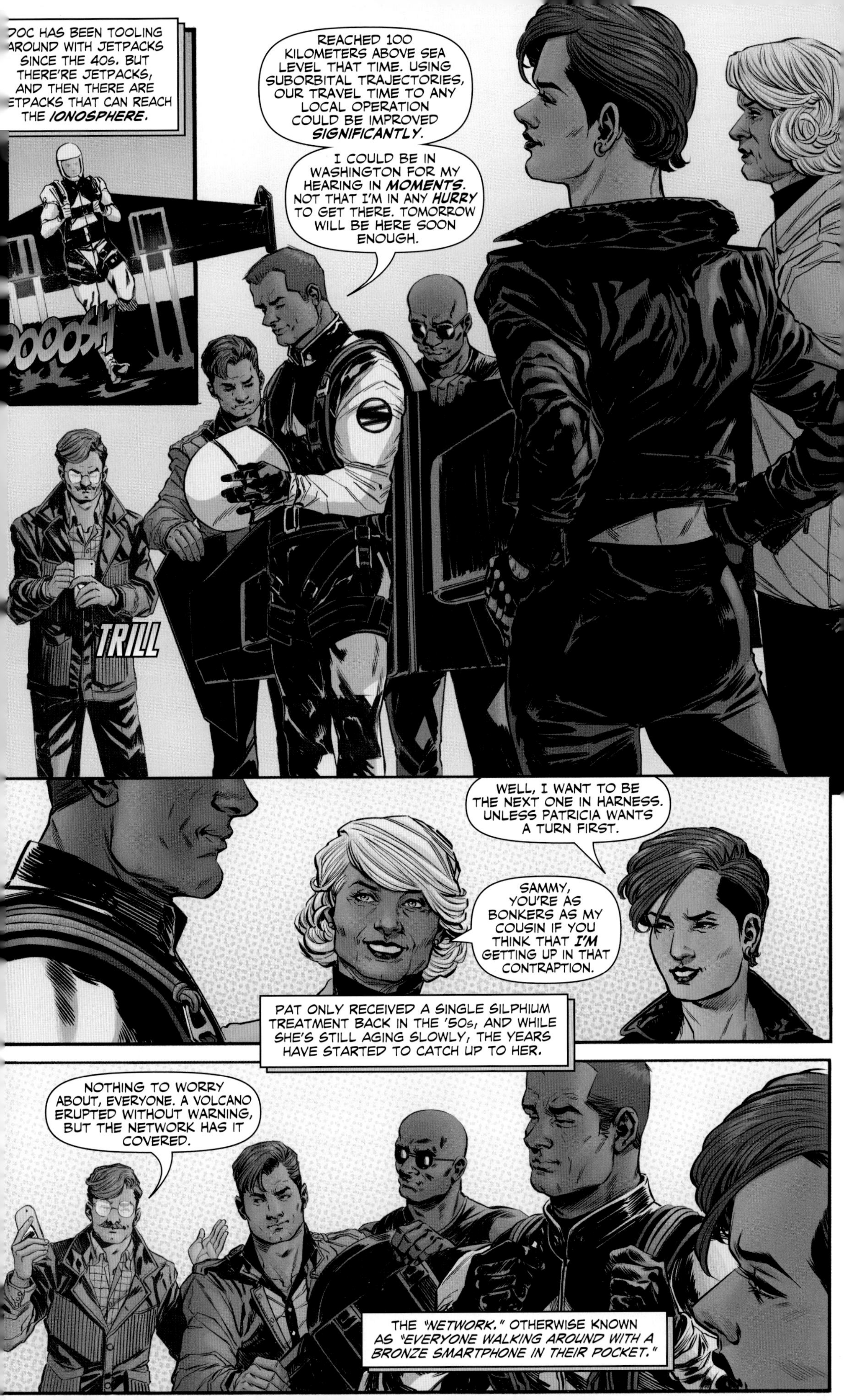
DOC HAS BEEN TOOLING AROUND WITH JETPACKS SINCE THE 40s. BUT THERE'RE JETPACKS, AND THEN THERE ARE JETPACKS THAT CAN REACH THE IONOSPHERE.
REACHED 100 KILOMETERS ABOVE SEA LEVEL THAT TIME. USING SUBORBITAL TRAJECTORIES, OUR TRAVEL TIME TO ANY LOCAL OPERATION COULD BE IMPROVED SIGNIFICANTLY.
I COULD BE IN WASHINGTON FOR MY HEARING IN MOMENTS. NOT THAT I'M IN ANY HURRY TO GET THERE. TOMORROW WILL BE HERE SOON ENOUGH.
OOOOSH
TRILL
WELL, I WANT TO BE THE NEXT ONE IN HARNESS. UNLESS PATRICIA WANTS A TURN FIRST.
SAMMY, YOU'RE AS BONKERS AS MY COUSIN IF YOU THINK THAT I'M GETTING UP IN THAT CONTRAPTION.
PAT ONLY RECEIVED A SINGLE SILPHIUM TREATMENT BACK IN THE '50s, AND WHILE SHE'S STILL AGING SLOWLY, THE YEARS HAVE STARTED TO CATCH UP TO HER.
NOTHING TO WORRY ABOUT, EVERYONE. A VOLCANO ERUPTED WITHOUT WARNING, BUT THE NETWORK HAS IT COVERED.
THE "NETWORK." OTHERWISE KNOWN AS "EVERYONE WALKING AROUND WITH A BRONZE SMARTPHONE IN THEIR POCKET."

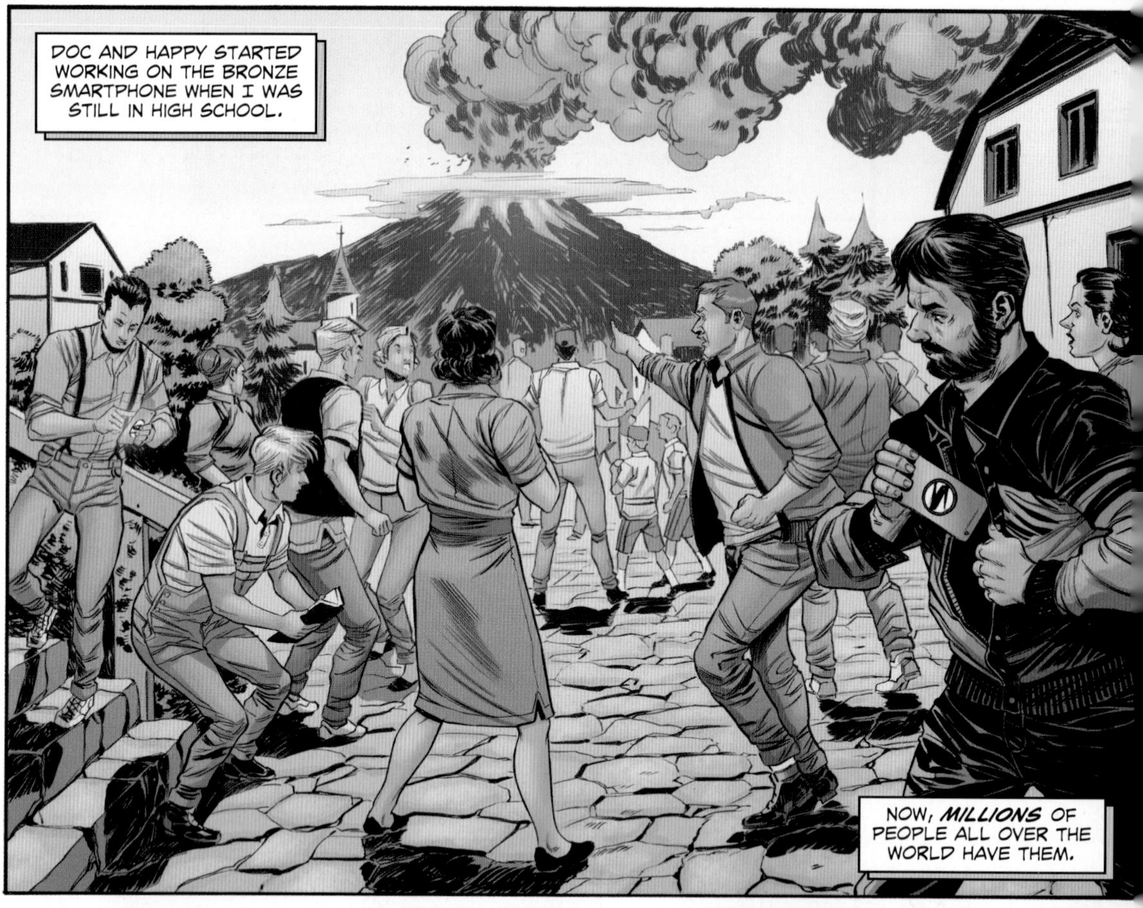
DOC AND HAPPY STARTED WORKING ON THE BRONZE SMARTPHONE WHEN I WAS STILL IN HIGH SCHOOL.
NOW, MILLIONS OF PEOPLE ALL OVER THE WORLD HAVE THEM.

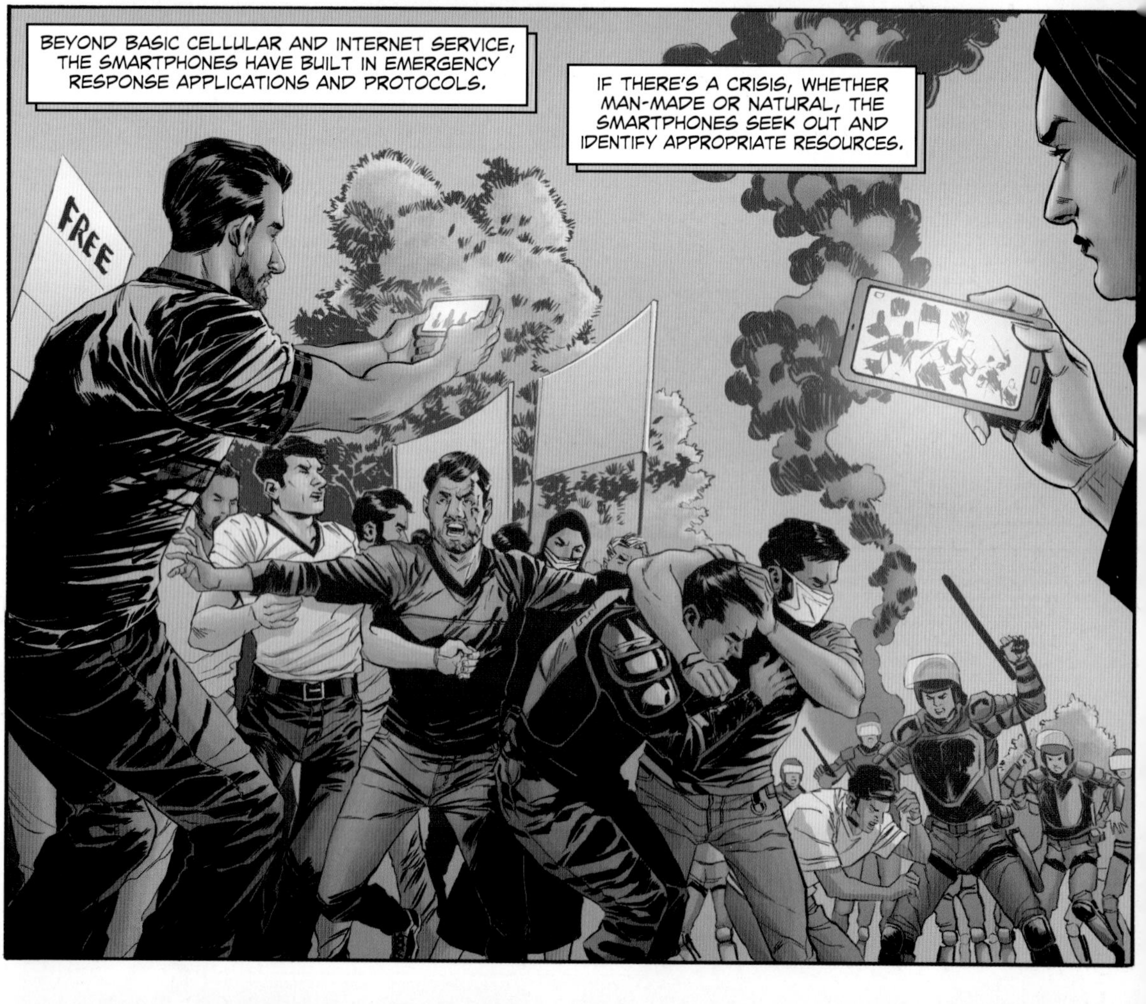
BEYOND BASIC CELLULAR AND INTERNET SERVICE, THE SMARTPHONES HAVE BUILT IN EMERGENCY RESPONSE APPLICATIONS AND PROTOCOLS.
IF THERE'S A CRISIS, WHETHER MAN-MADE OR NATURAL, THE SMARTPHONES SEEK OUT AND IDENTIFY APPROPRIATE RESOURCES.
FREE

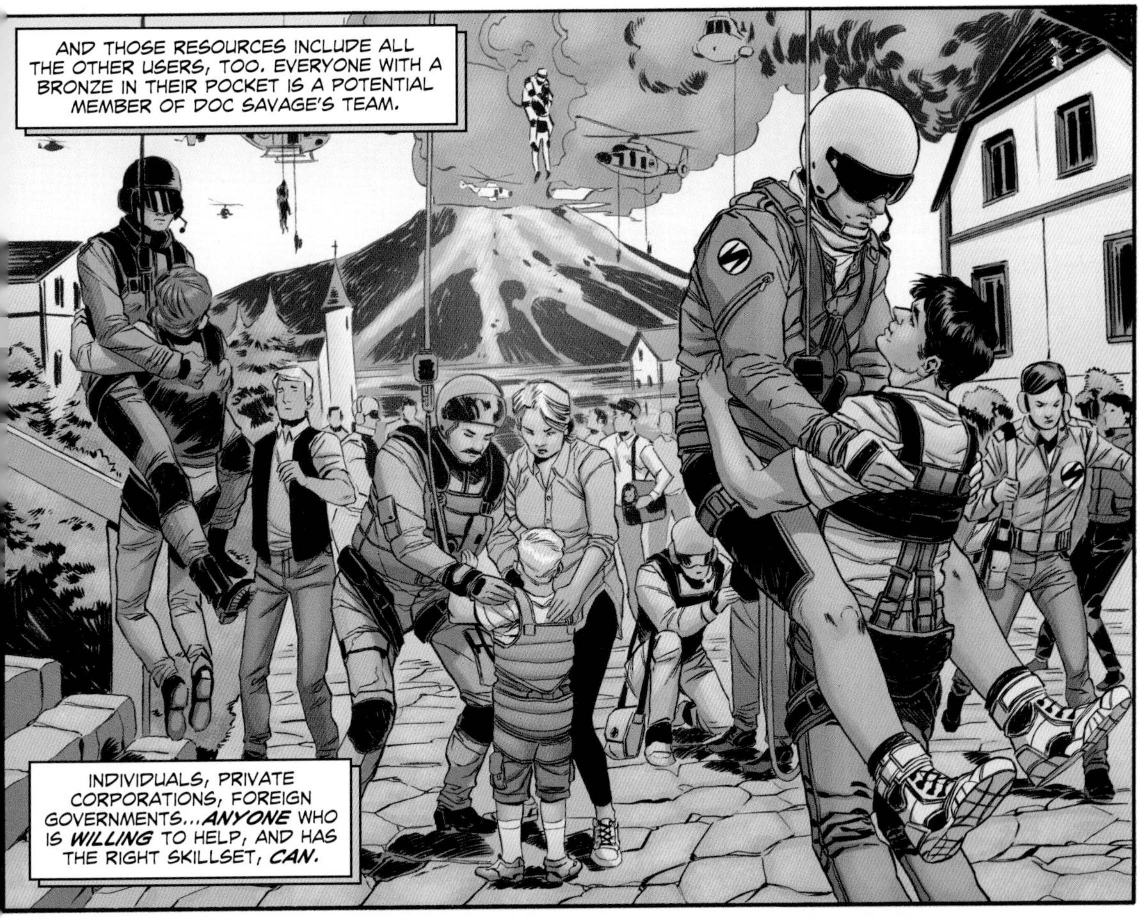
AND THOSE RESOURCES INCLUDE ALL THE OTHER USERS, TOO. EVERYONE WITH A BRONZE IN THEIR POCKET IS A POTENTIAL MEMBER OF DOC SAVAGE'S TEAM.
INDIVIDUALS, PRIVATE CORPORATIONS, FOREIGN GOVERNMENTS...*ANYONE* WHO IS *WILLING* TO HELP, AND HAS THE RIGHT SKILLSET, *CAN.*

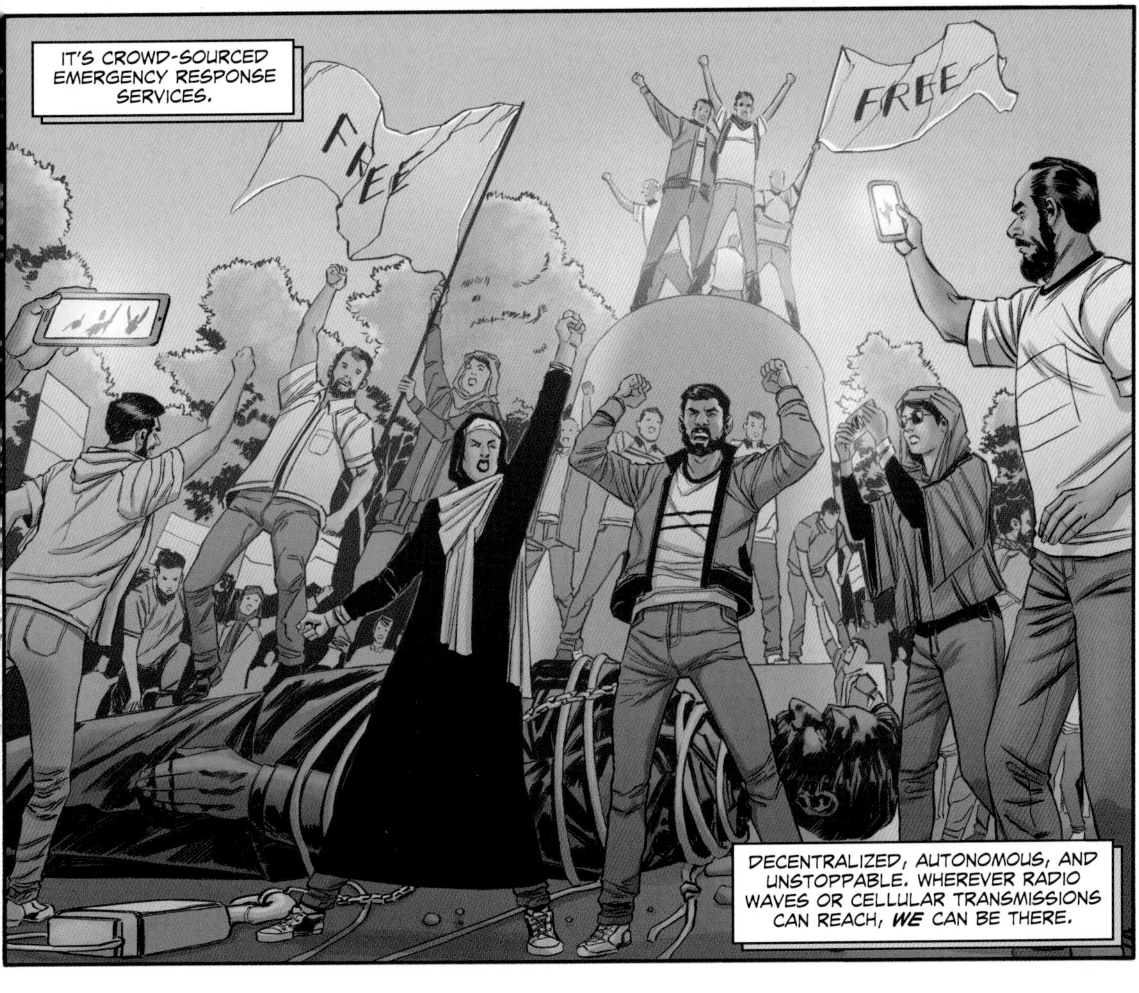
IT'S CROWD-SOURCED EMERGENCY RESPONSE SERVICES.
FREE
FREE
DECENTRALIZED, AUTONOMOUS, AND UNSTOPPABLE. WHEREVER RADIO WAVES OR CELLULAR TRANSMISSIONS CAN REACH, *WE* CAN BE THERE.

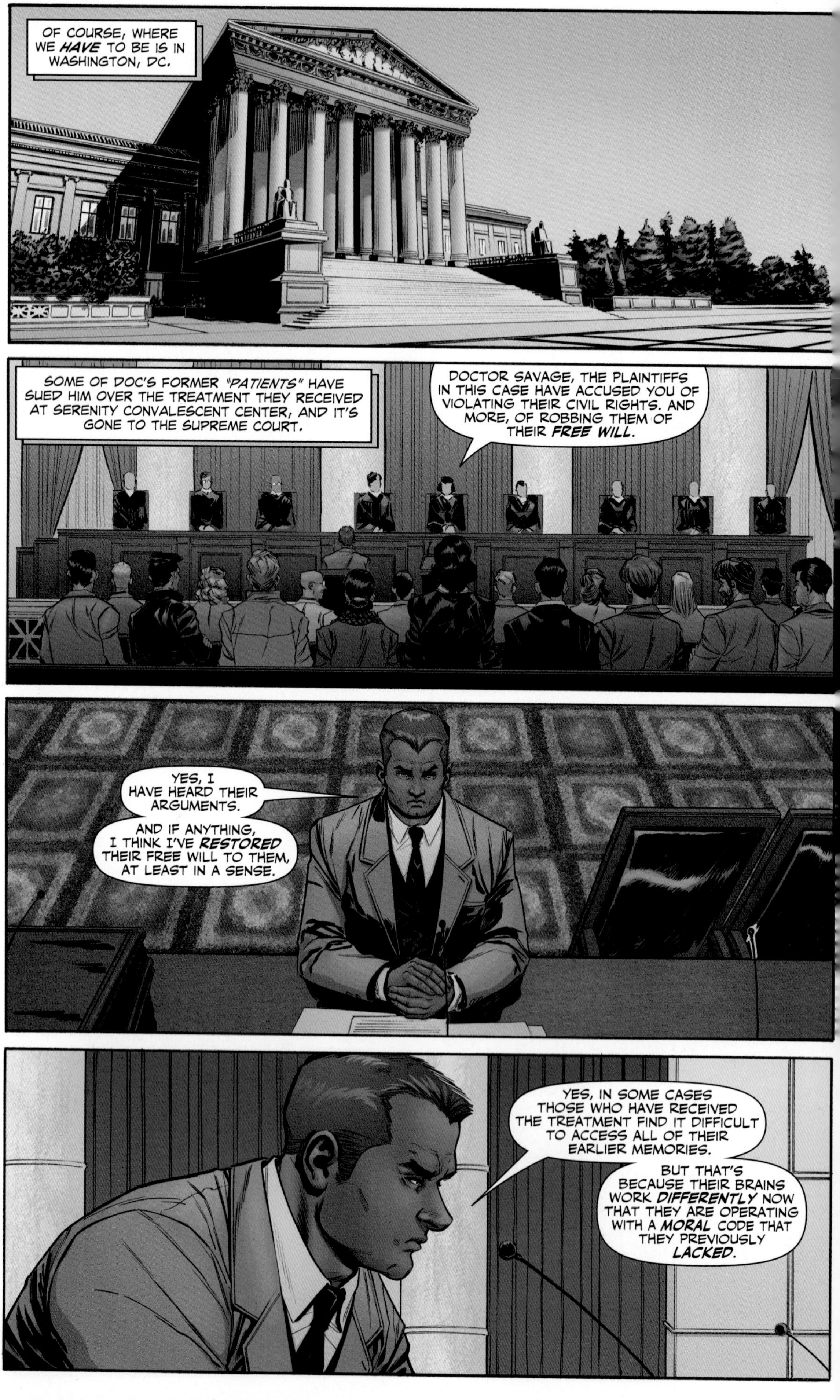
OF COURSE, WHERE WE *HAVE* TO BE IS IN WASHINGTON, DC.
SOME OF DOC'S FORMER "*PATIENTS*" HAVE SUED HIM OVER THE TREATMENT THEY RECEIVED AT SERENITY CONVALESCENT CENTER, AND IT'S GONE TO THE SUPREME COURT.
DOCTOR SAVAGE, THE PLAINTIFFS IN THIS CASE HAVE ACCUSED YOU OF VIOLATING THEIR CIVIL RIGHTS. AND MORE, OF ROBBING THEM OF THEIR *FREE WILL*.
YES, I HAVE HEARD THEIR ARGUMENTS.
AND IF ANYTHING, I THINK I'VE *RESTORED* THEIR FREE WILL TO THEM, AT LEAST IN A SENSE.
YES, IN SOME CASES THOSE WHO HAVE RECEIVED THE TREATMENT FIND IT DIFFICULT TO ACCESS ALL OF THEIR EARLIER MEMORIES.
BUT THAT'S BECAUSE THEIR BRAINS WORK *DIFFERENTLY* NOW THAT THEY ARE OPERATING WITH A *MORAL* CODE THAT THEY PREVIOUSLY *LACKED*.

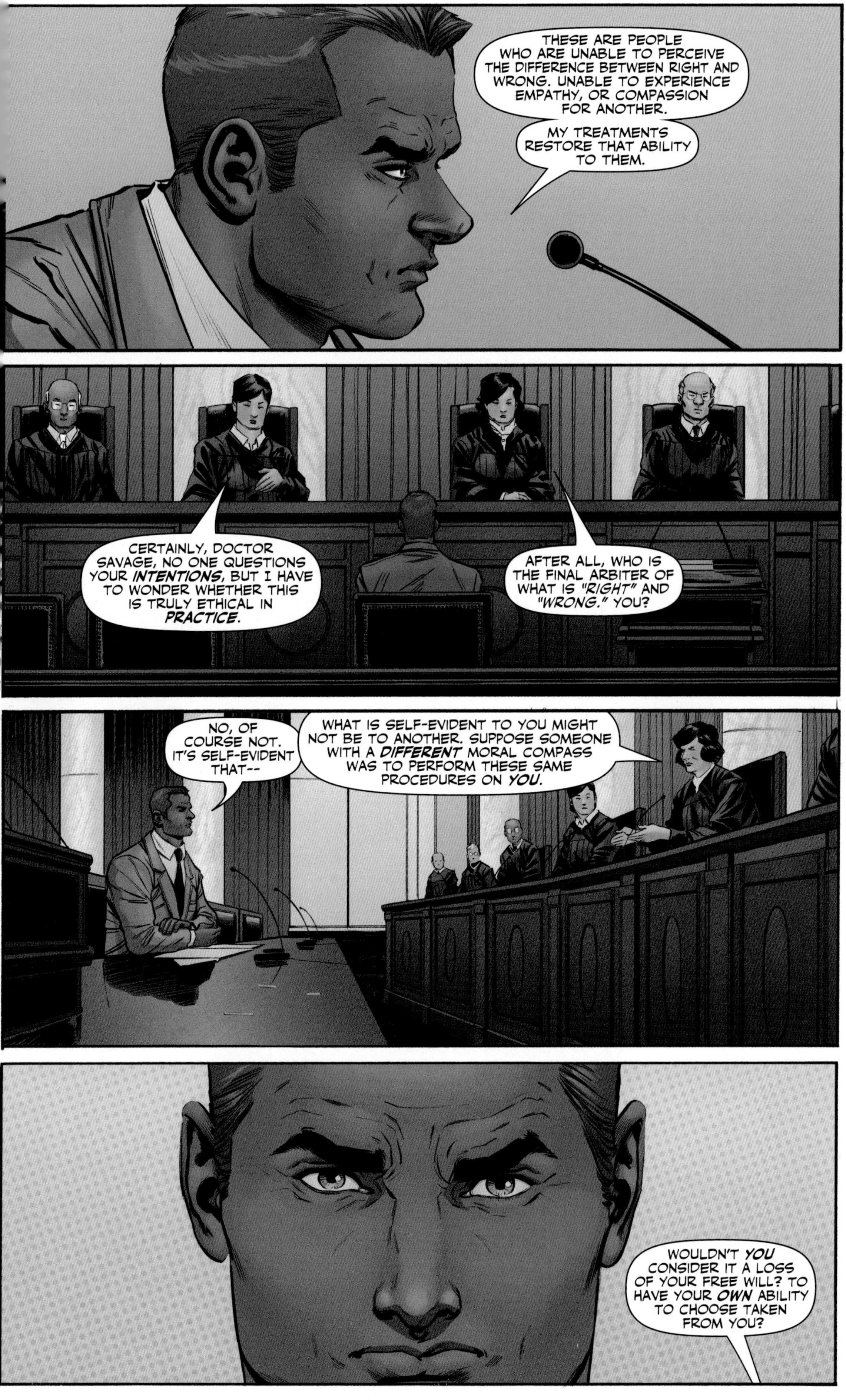
THESE ARE PEOPLE WHO ARE UNABLE TO PERCEIVE THE DIFFERENCE BETWEEN RIGHT AND WRONG. UNABLE TO EXPERIENCE EMPATHY, OR COMPASSION FOR ANOTHER.
MY TREATMENTS RESTORE THAT ABILITY TO THEM.
CERTAINLY, DOCTOR SAVAGE, NO ONE QUESTIONS YOUR *INTENTIONS*, BUT I HAVE TO WONDER WHETHER THIS IS TRULY ETHICAL IN *PRACTICE*.
AFTER ALL, WHO IS THE FINAL ARBITER OF WHAT IS *"RIGHT"* AND *"WRONG."* YOU?
NO, OF COURSE NOT. IT'S SELF-EVIDENT THAT--
WHAT IS SELF-EVIDENT TO YOU MIGHT NOT BE TO ANOTHER. SUPPOSE SOMEONE WITH A *DIFFERENT* MORAL COMPASS WAS TO PERFORM THESE SAME PROCEDURES ON *YOU*.
WOULDN'T *YOU* CONSIDER IT A LOSS OF YOUR FREE WILL? TO HAVE YOUR *OWN* ABILITY TO CHOOSE TAKEN FROM YOU?

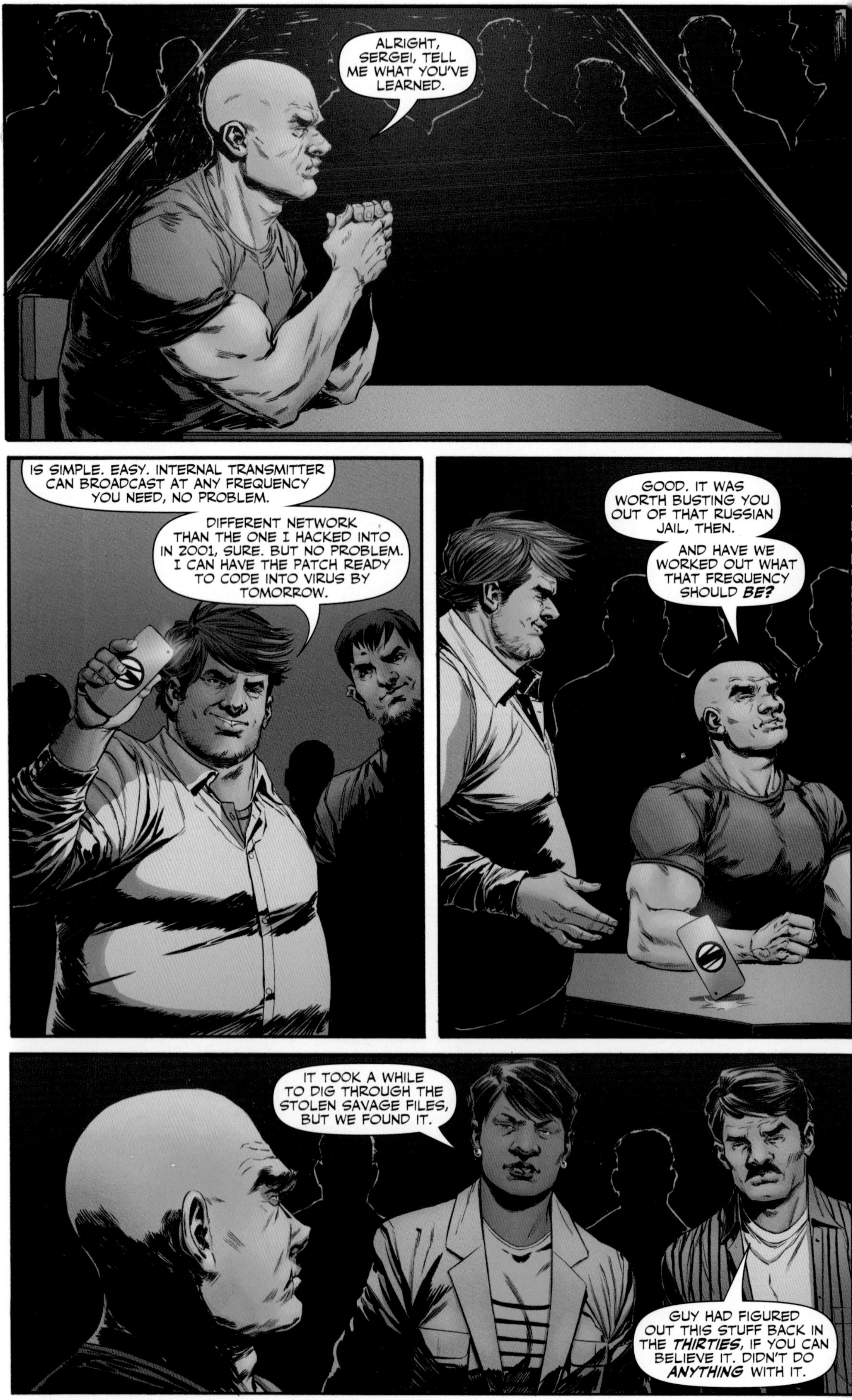
ALRIGHT, SERGEI, TELL ME WHAT YOU'VE LEARNED.
IS SIMPLE. EASY. INTERNAL TRANSMITTER CAN BROADCAST AT ANY FREQUENCY YOU NEED, NO PROBLEM.
DIFFERENT NETWORK THAN THE ONE I HACKED INTO IN 2001, SURE. BUT NO PROBLEM. I CAN HAVE THE PATCH READY TO CODE INTO VIRUS BY TOMORROW.
GOOD. IT WAS WORTH BUSTING YOU OUT OF THAT RUSSIAN JAIL, THEN.
AND HAVE WE WORKED OUT WHAT THAT FREQUENCY SHOULD *BE?*
IT TOOK A WHILE TO DIG THROUGH THE STOLEN SAVAGE FILES, BUT WE FOUND IT.
GUY HAD FIGURED OUT THIS STUFF BACK IN THE *THIRTIES*, IF YOU CAN BELIEVE IT. DIDN'T DO *ANYTHING* WITH IT.

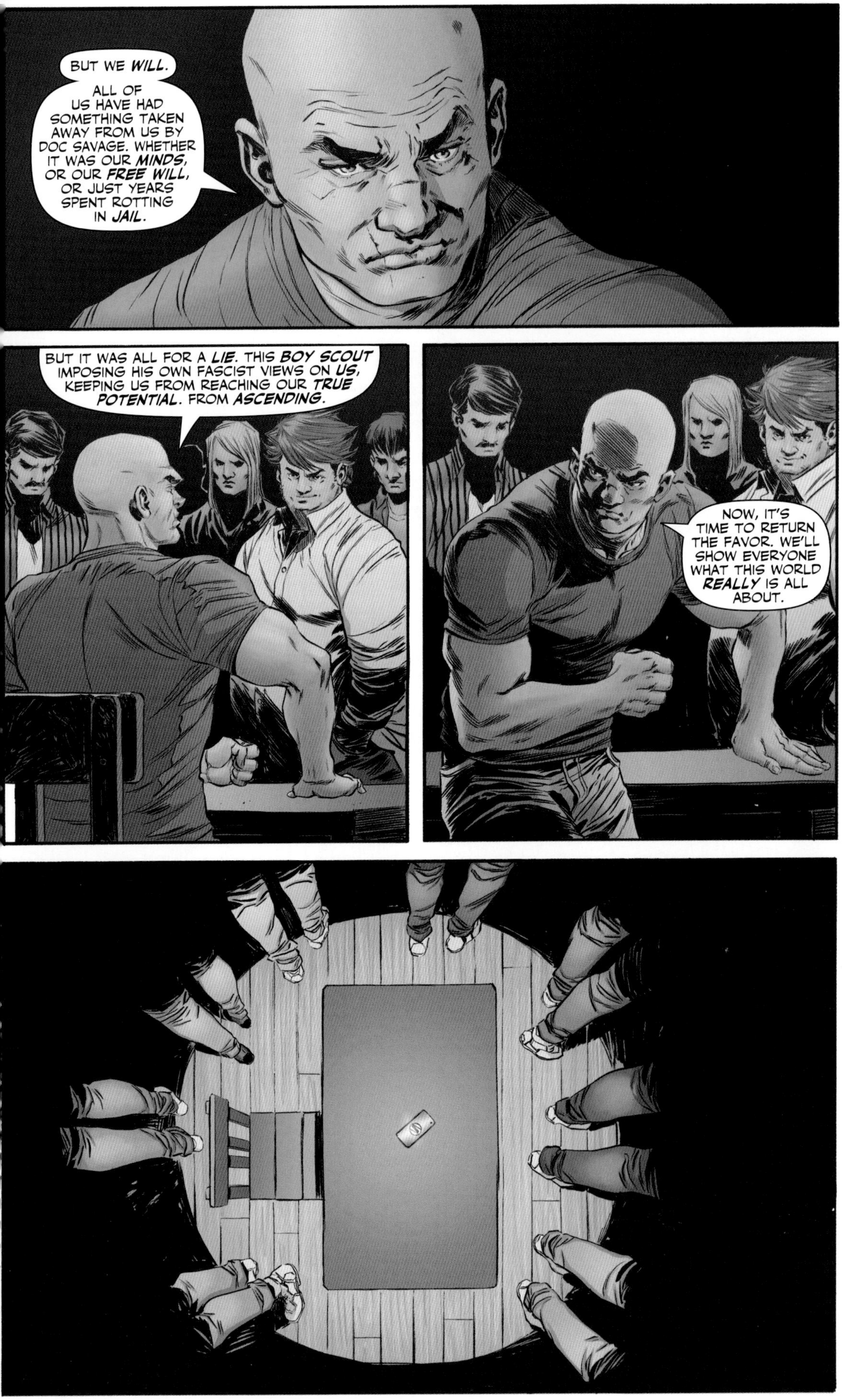
BUT WE WILL.
ALL OF US HAVE HAD SOMETHING TAKEN AWAY FROM US BY DOC SAVAGE. WHETHER IT WAS OUR MINDS, OR OUR FREE WILL, OR JUST YEARS SPENT ROTTING IN JAIL.
BUT IT WAS ALL FOR A LIE. THIS BOY SCOUT IMPOSING HIS OWN FASCIST VIEWS ON US, KEEPING US FROM REACHING OUR TRUE POTENTIAL. FROM ASCENDING.
NOW, IT'S TIME TO RETURN THE FAVOR. WE'LL SHOW EVERYONE WHAT THIS WORLD REALLY IS ALL ABOUT.

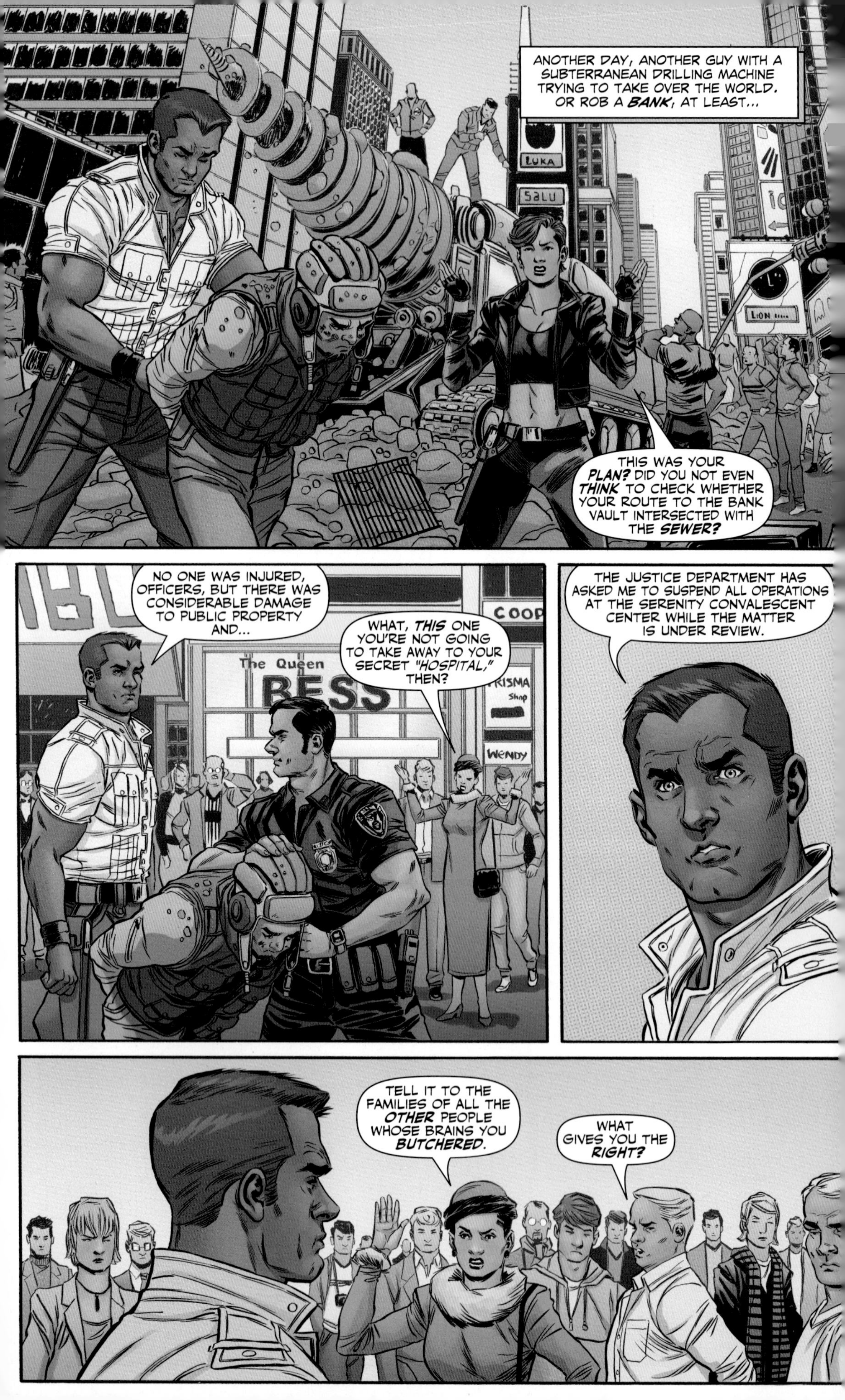
ANOTHER DAY, ANOTHER GUY WITH A SUBTERRANEAN DRILLING MACHINE TRYING TO TAKE OVER THE WORLD. OR ROB A *BANK*, AT LEAST...
THIS WAS YOUR *PLAN?* DID YOU NOT EVEN *THINK* TO CHECK WHETHER YOUR ROUTE TO THE BANK VAULT INTERSECTED WITH THE *SEWER?*
NO ONE WAS INJURED, OFFICERS, BUT THERE WAS CONSIDERABLE DAMAGE TO PUBLIC PROPERTY AND...
WHAT, *THIS* ONE YOU'RE NOT GOING TO TAKE AWAY TO YOUR SECRET *"HOSPITAL,"* THEN?
THE JUSTICE DEPARTMENT HAS ASKED ME TO SUSPEND ALL OPERATIONS AT THE SERENITY CONVALESCENT CENTER WHILE THE MATTER IS UNDER REVIEW.
TELL IT TO THE FAMILIES OF ALL THE *OTHER* PEOPLE WHOSE BRAINS YOU *BUTCHERED*.
WHAT GIVES YOU THE *RIGHT?*

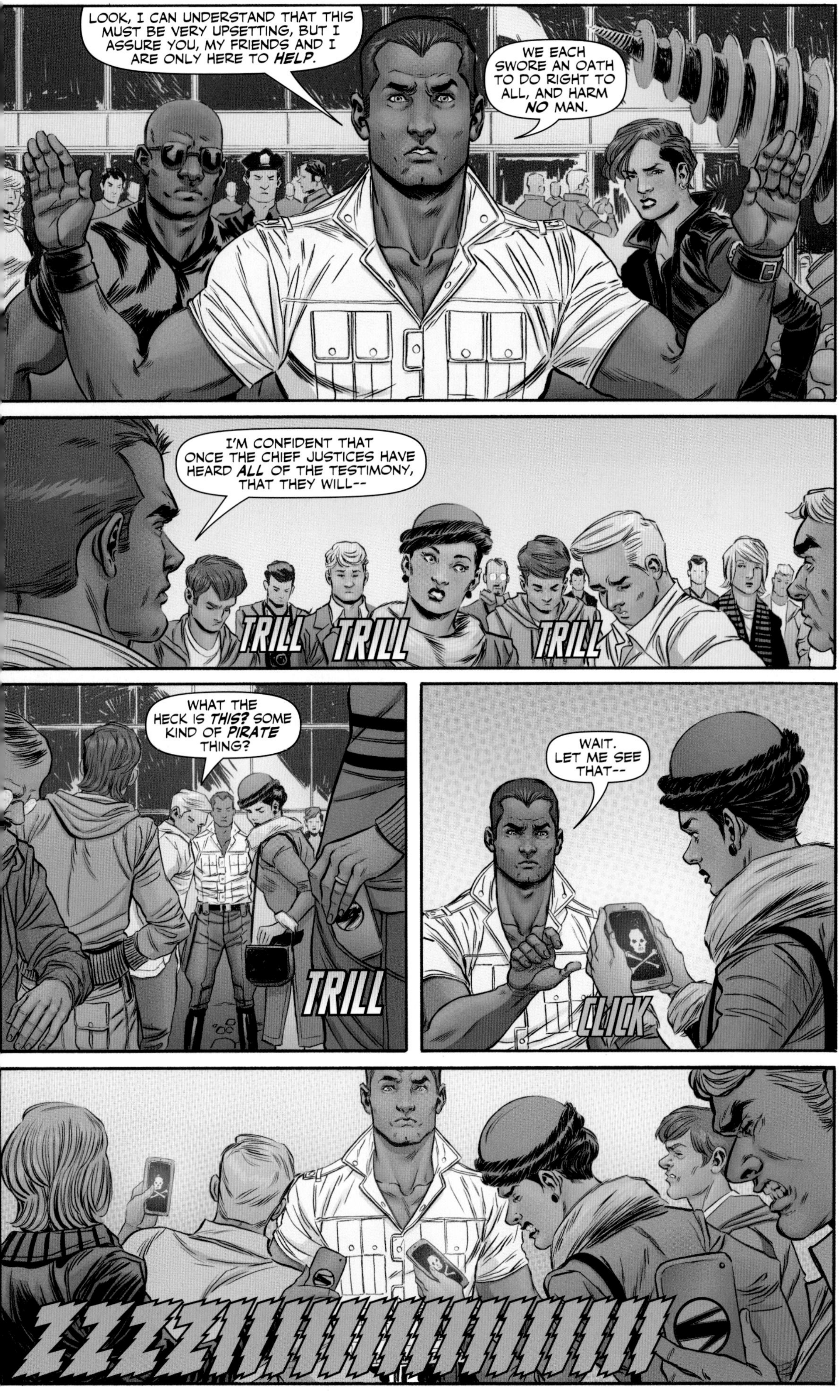
LOOK, I CAN UNDERSTAND THAT THIS MUST BE VERY UPSETTING, BUT I ASSURE YOU, MY FRIENDS AND I ARE ONLY HERE TO *HELP*.
WE EACH SWORE AN OATH TO DO RIGHT TO ALL, AND HARM *NO* MAN.
I'M CONFIDENT THAT ONCE THE CHIEF JUSTICES HAVE HEARD *ALL* OF THE TESTIMONY, THAT THEY WILL--
TRILL
TRILL
TRILL
WHAT THE HECK IS *THIS?* SOME KIND OF *PIRATE* THING?
TRILL
WAIT. LET ME SEE THAT--
CLICK
ZZZZIIIIIIIIIIIIIIII

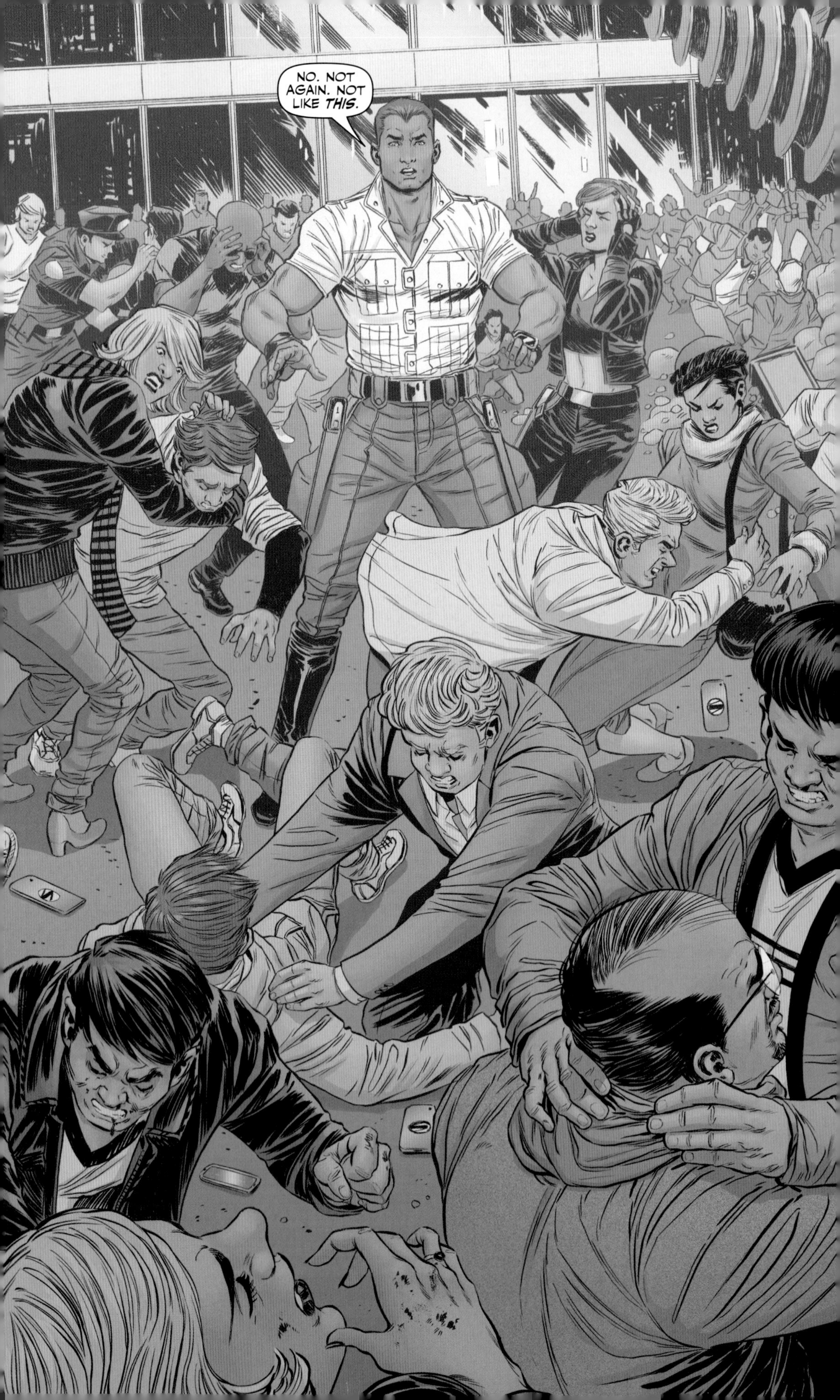
NO. NOT AGAIN. NOT LIKE *THIS*.

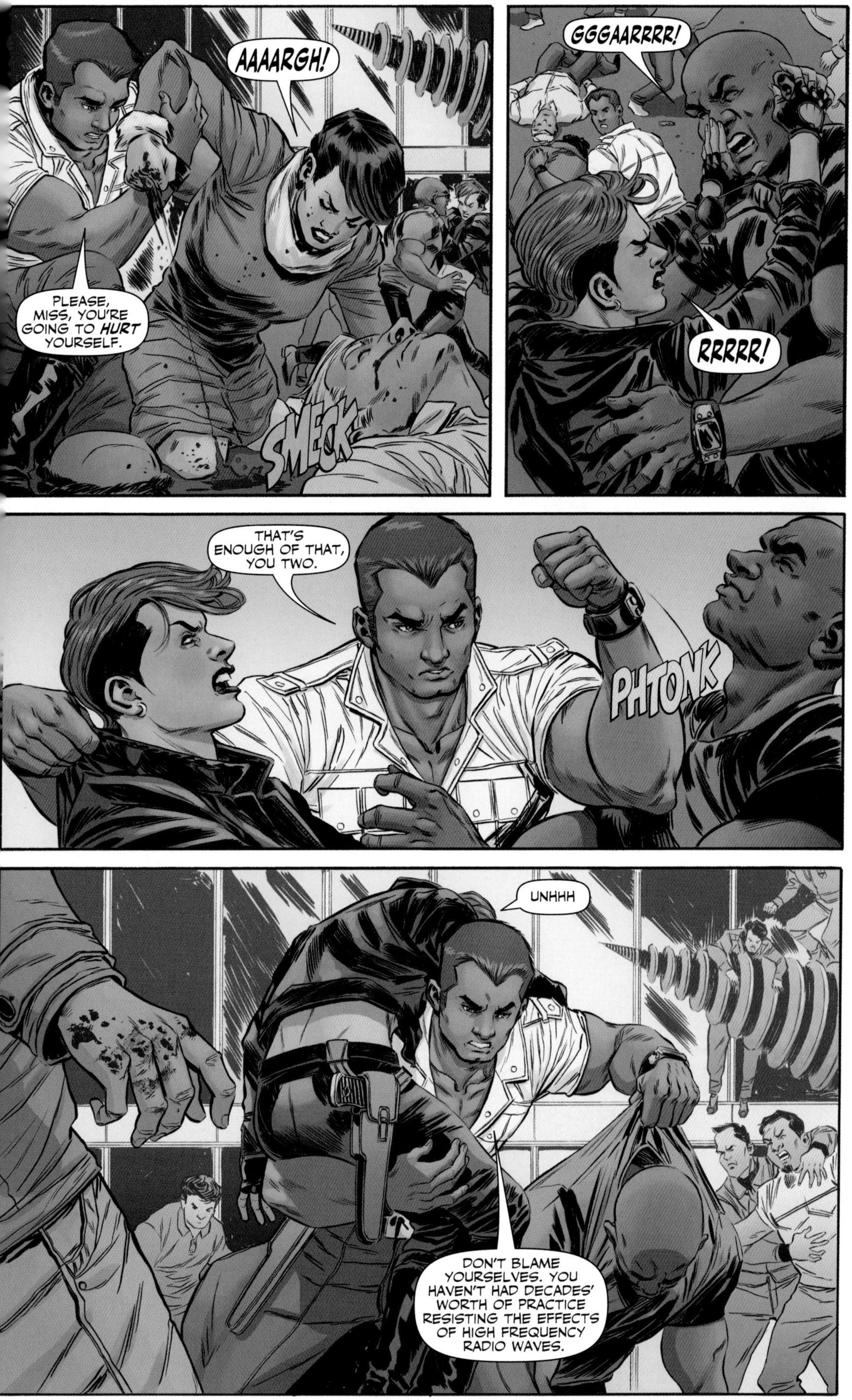
AAAARGH!
PLEASE, MISS, YOU'RE GOING TO HURT YOURSELF.
SMECK
GGGAARRRR!
RRRRR!
THAT'S ENOUGH OF THAT, YOU TWO.
PHTONK
UNHHH
DON'T BLAME YOURSELVES. YOU HAVEN'T HAD DECADES' WORTH OF PRACTICE RESISTING THE EFFECTS OF HIGH FREQUENCY RADIO WAVES.

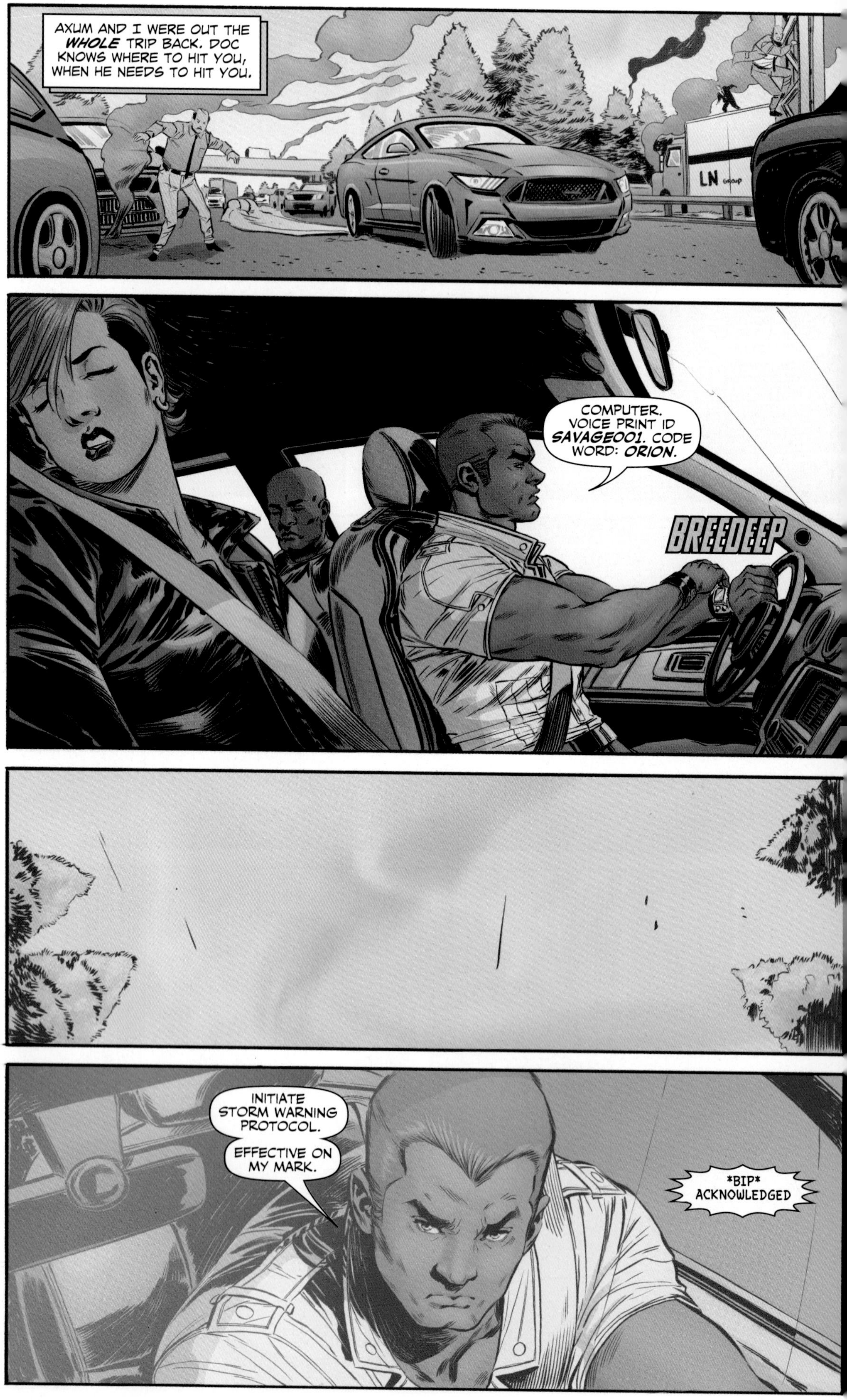
AXUM AND I WERE OUT THE WHOLE TRIP BACK. DOC KNOWS WHERE TO HIT YOU, WHEN HE NEEDS TO HIT YOU.
LN Group
COMPUTER. VOICE PRINT ID SAVAGE001. CODE WORD: ORION.
BREEDEEP
INITIATE STORM WARNING PROTOCOL.
EFFECTIVE ON MY MARK.
BIP ACKNOWLEDGED

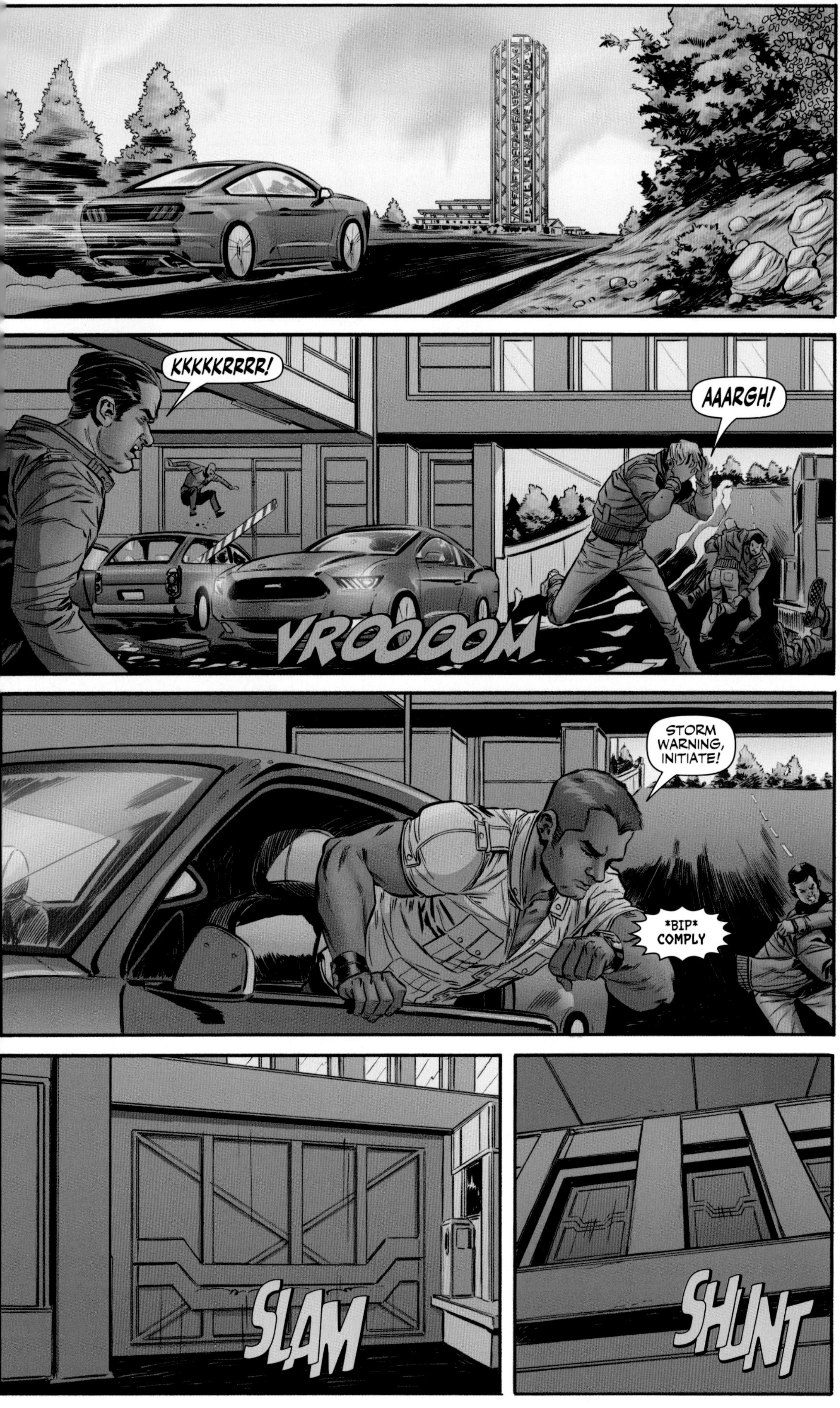
KKKKKRRRR!
AAARGH!
VROOOOM
STORM WARNING, INITIATE!
BIP COMPLY
SLAM
SHUNT

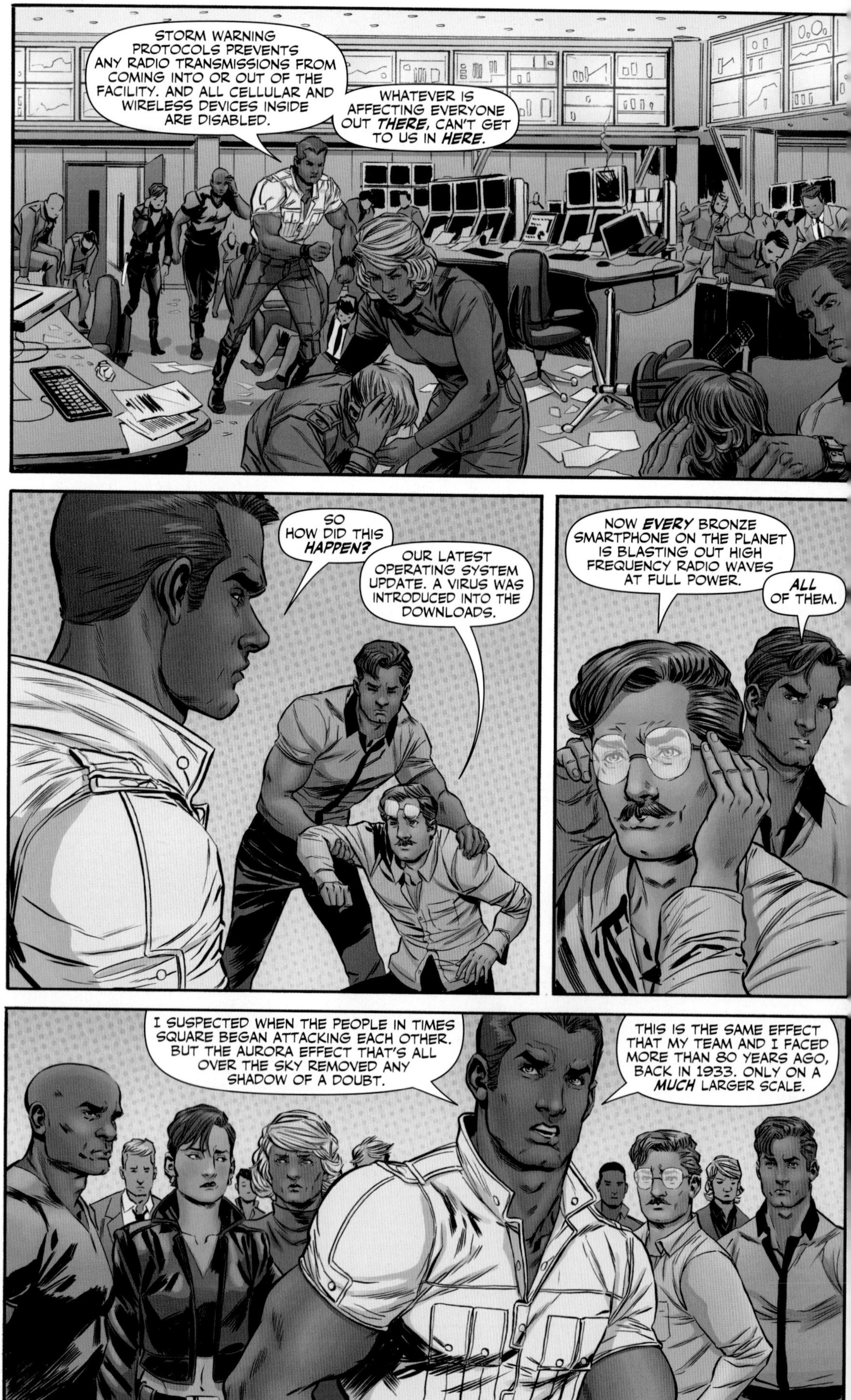
STORM WARNING PROTOCOLS PREVENTS ANY RADIO TRANSMISSIONS FROM COMING INTO OR OUT OF THE FACILITY. AND ALL CELLULAR AND WIRELESS DEVICES INSIDE ARE DISABLED.
WHATEVER IS AFFECTING EVERYONE OUT THERE, CAN'T GET TO US IN HERE.
SO HOW DID THIS HAPPEN?
OUR LATEST OPERATING SYSTEM UPDATE. A VIRUS WAS INTRODUCED INTO THE DOWNLOADS.
NOW EVERY BRONZE SMARTPHONE ON THE PLANET IS BLASTING OUT HIGH FREQUENCY RADIO WAVES AT FULL POWER.
ALL OF THEM.
I SUSPECTED WHEN THE PEOPLE IN TIMES SQUARE BEGAN ATTACKING EACH OTHER. BUT THE AURORA EFFECT THAT'S ALL OVER THE SKY REMOVED ANY SHADOW OF A DOUBT.
THIS IS THE SAME EFFECT THAT MY TEAM AND I FACED MORE THAN 80 YEARS AGO, BACK IN 1933. ONLY ON A MUCH LARGER SCALE.

"THE BRONZE PHONES ARE DESIGNED TO OPERATE AUTONOMOUSLY, SO THAT NO TIN-PLATED DICTATOR OR MADMAN CAN TAKE CONTROL.

"AND EACH HAS **SATELLITE** CAPACITY, AS WELL, IN THE EVENT THAT CELLULAR SYSTEMS ARE INTERFERED WITH.

"AS OF LAST MONTH, ROUGHLY ONE IN EVERY 100 PEOPLE ON THE PLANET POSSESSED A BRONZE PHONE.

"WITH THE BROADCAST RANGE OF EACH INDIVIDUAL PHONE, THAT MEANS THE HIGH FREQUENCY RADIO BLAST IS **BLANKETING** THE PLANET.

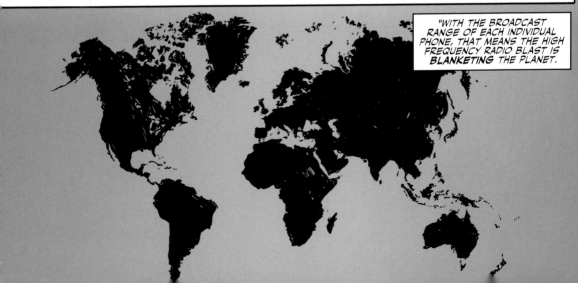

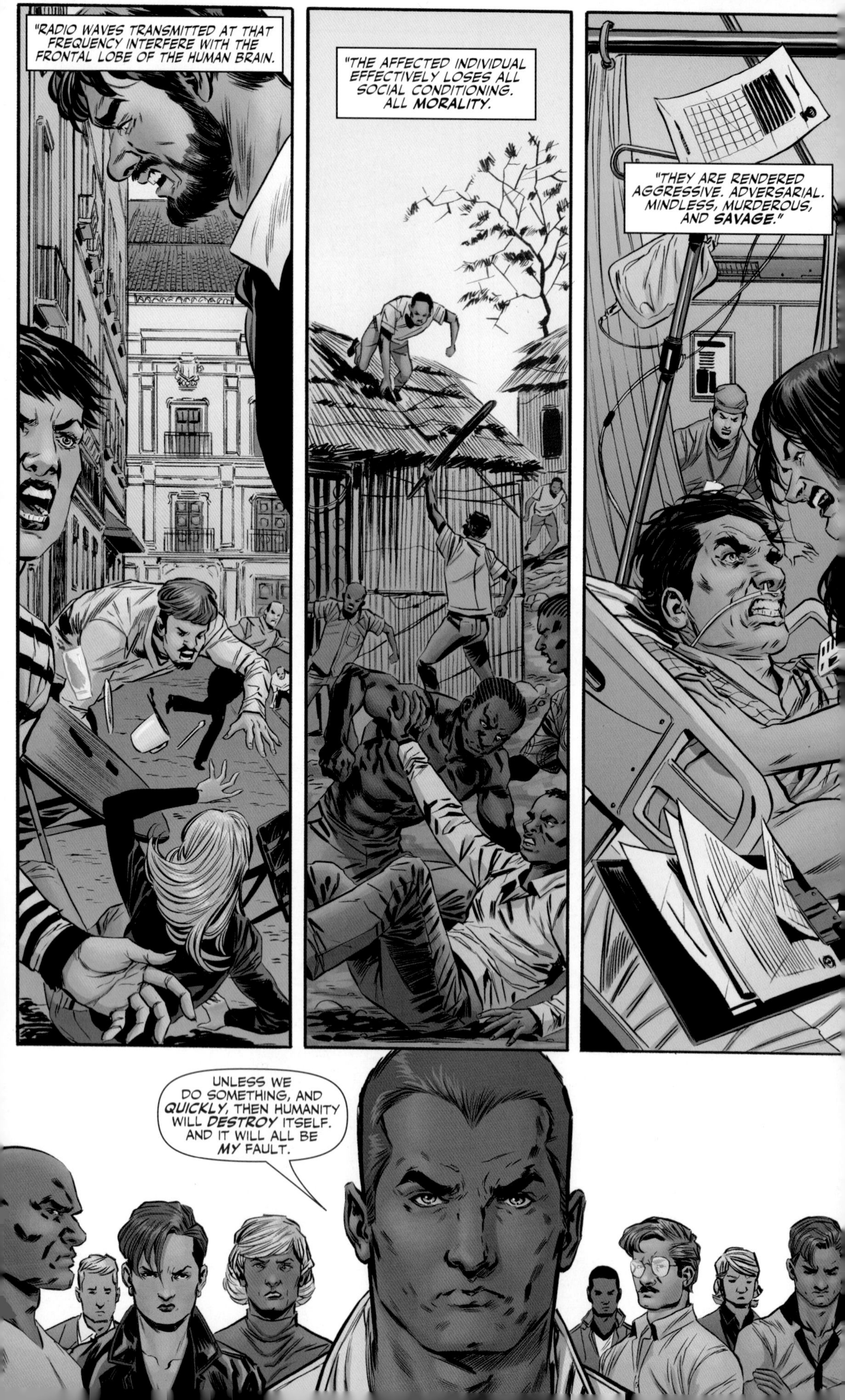
"RADIO WAVES TRANSMITTED AT THAT FREQUENCY INTERFERE WITH THE FRONTAL LOBE OF THE HUMAN BRAIN.
"THE AFFECTED INDIVIDUAL EFFECTIVELY LOSES ALL SOCIAL CONDITIONING. ALL MORALITY.
"THEY ARE RENDERED AGGRESSIVE. ADVERSARIAL. MINDLESS, MURDEROUS, AND SAVAGE."
UNLESS WE DO SOMETHING, AND QUICKLY, THEN HUMANITY WILL DESTROY ITSELF. AND IT WILL ALL BE MY FAULT.

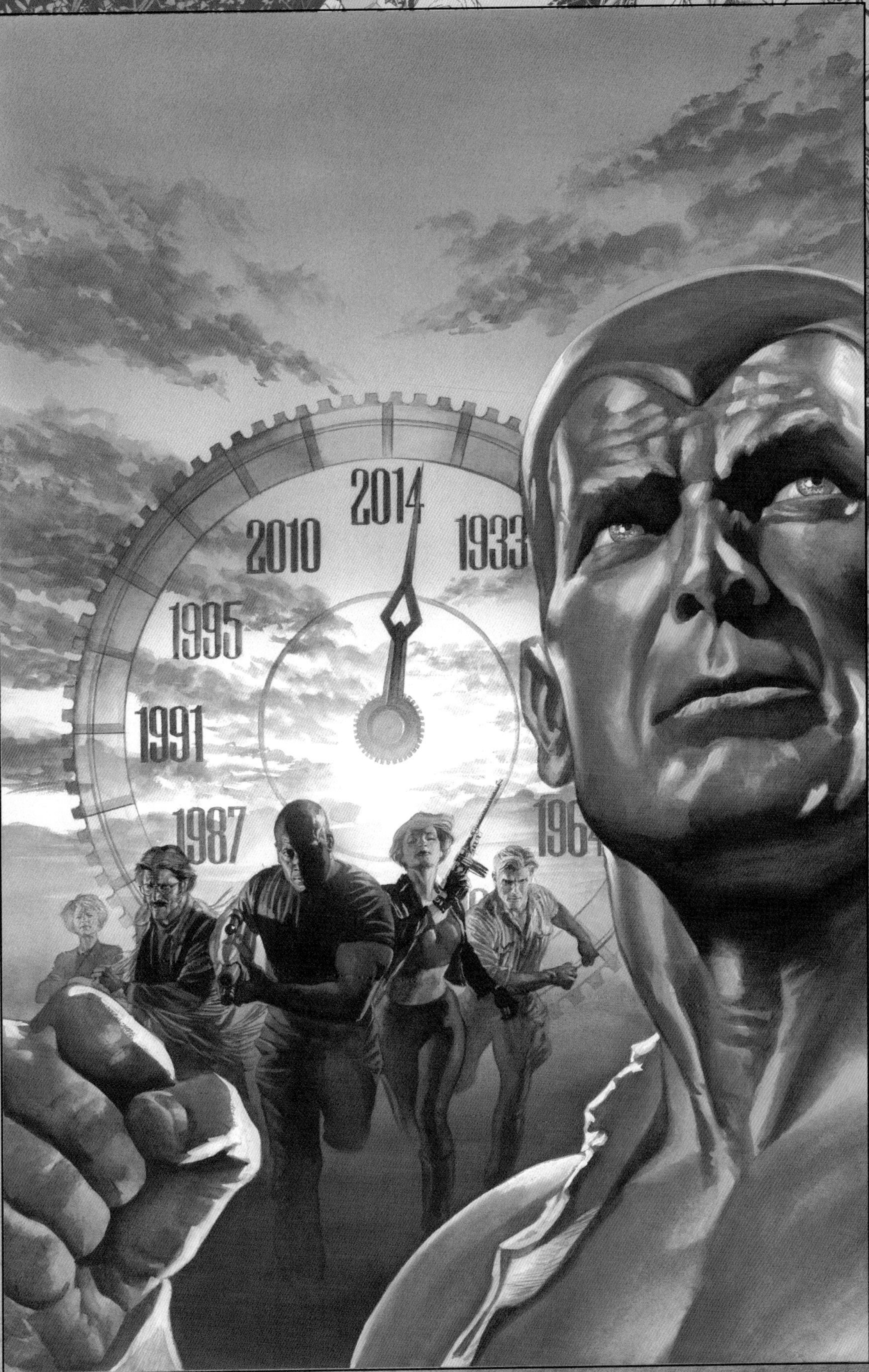
2014
2010
1933
1995
1991
1987
1964

ISSUE **#8** COVER
art by **ALEX ROSS**

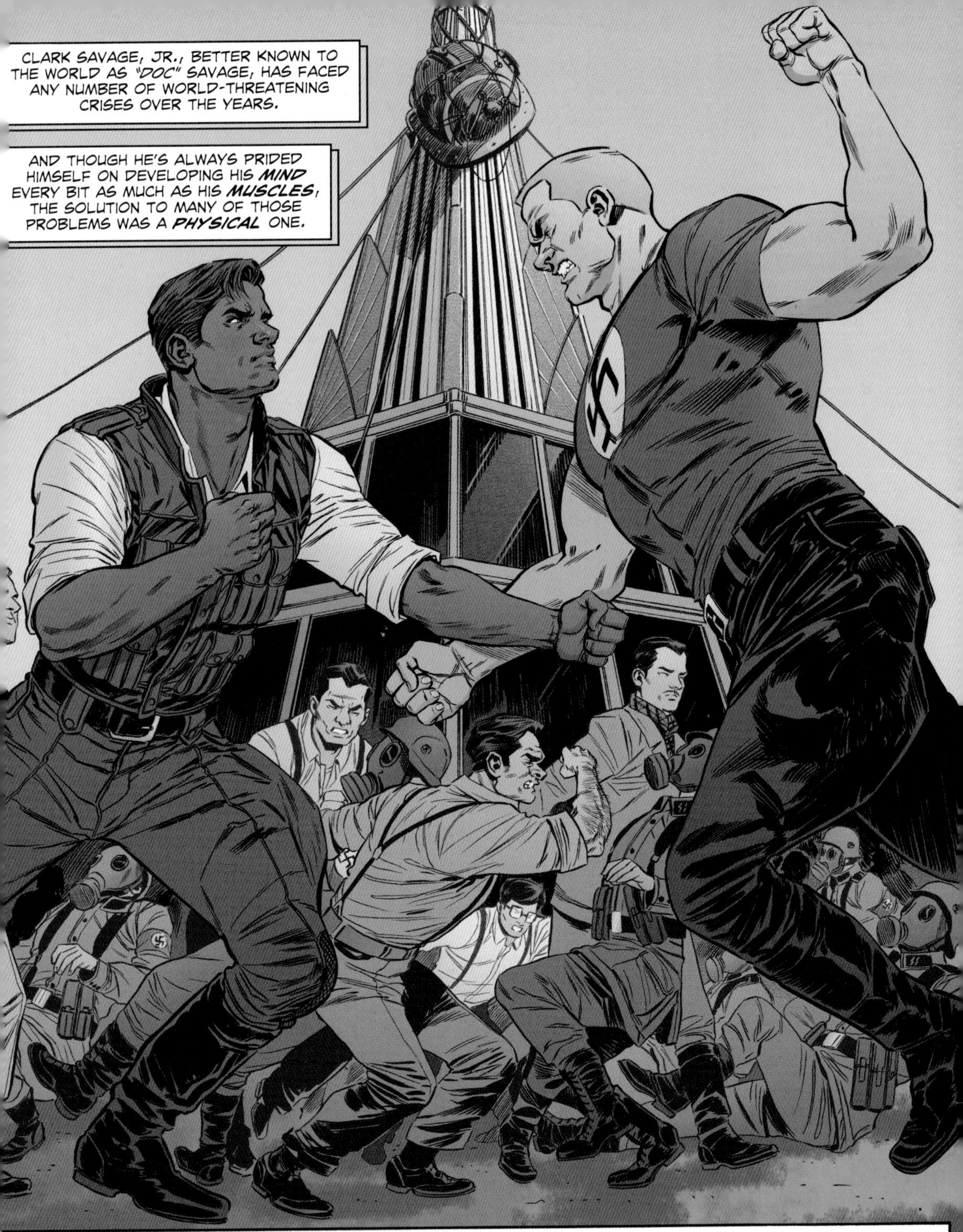
CLARK SAVAGE, JR., BETTER KNOWN TO THE WORLD AS "DOC" SAVAGE, HAS FACED ANY NUMBER OF WORLD-THREATENING CRISES OVER THE YEARS.
AND THOUGH HE'S ALWAYS PRIDED HIMSELF ON DEVELOPING HIS *MIND* EVERY BIT AS MUCH AS HIS *MUSCLES*, THE SOLUTION TO MANY OF THOSE PROBLEMS WAS A *PHYSICAL* ONE.

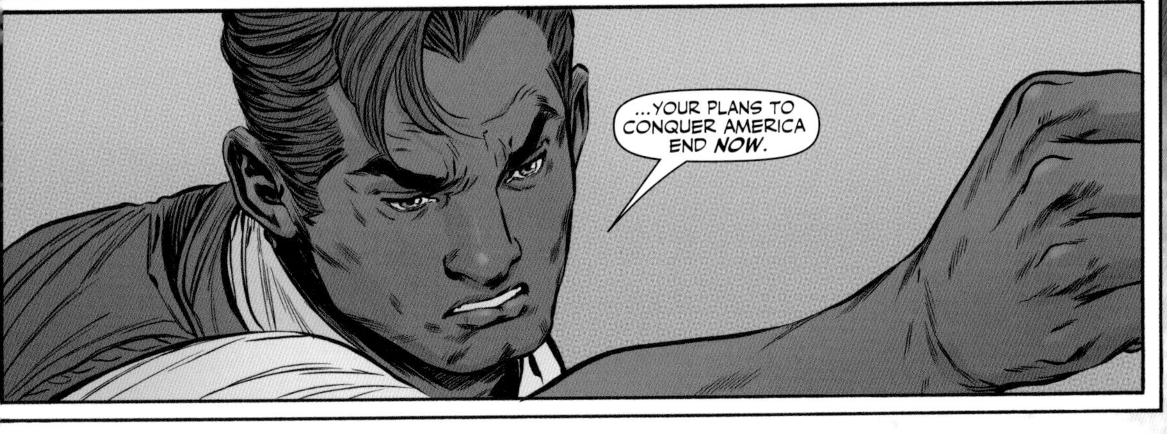
...YOUR PLANS TO CONQUER AMERICA END *NOW*.

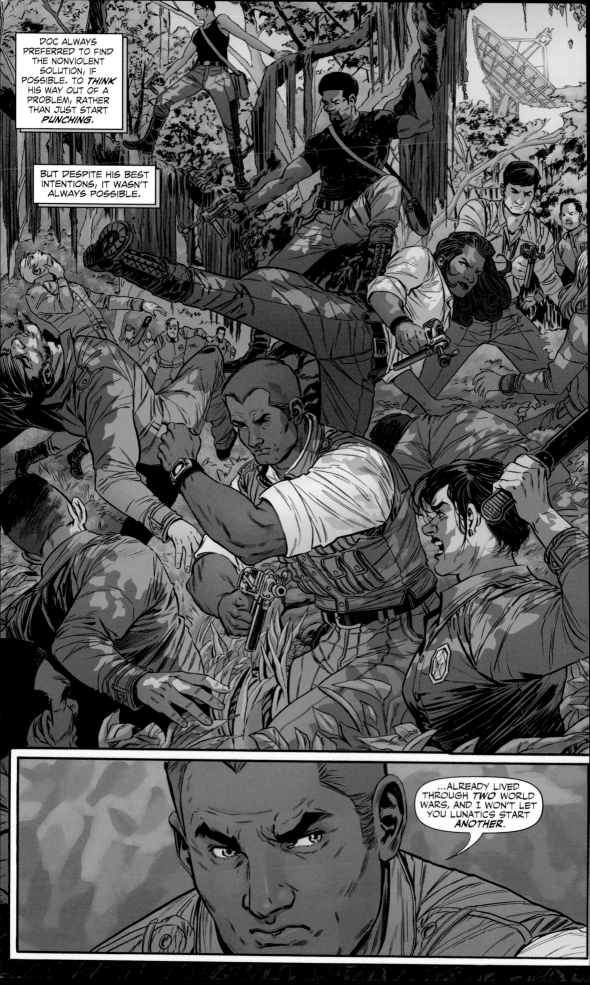

DOC ALWAYS PREFERRED TO FIND THE NONVIOLENT SOLUTION, IF POSSIBLE. TO *THINK* HIS WAY OUT OF A PROBLEM, RATHER THAN JUST START *PUNCHING*.

BUT DESPITE HIS BEST INTENTIONS, IT WASN'T ALWAYS POSSIBLE.

...ALREADY LIVED THROUGH *TWO* WORLD WARS, AND I WON'T LET YOU LUNATICS START *ANOTHER*.

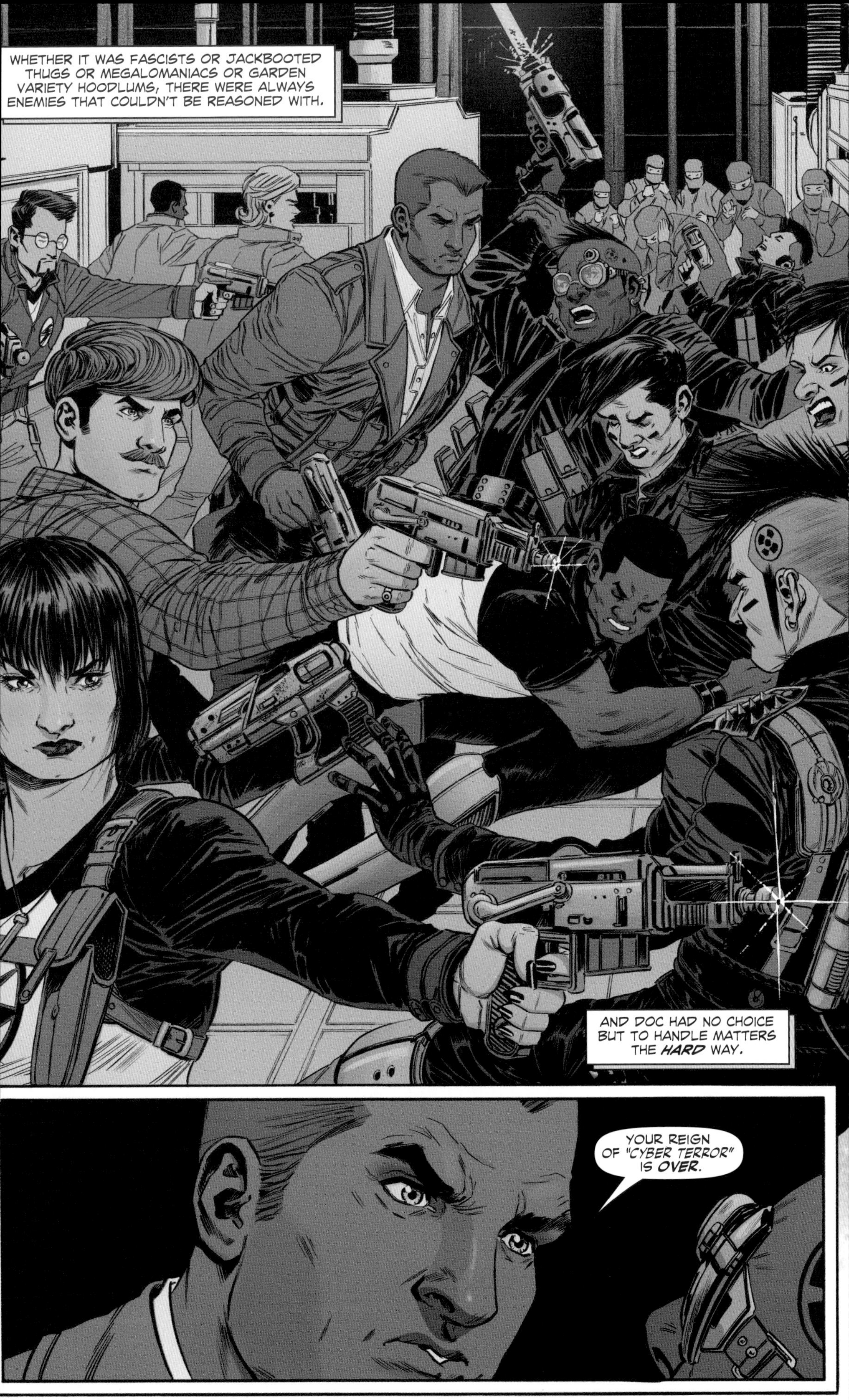
WHETHER IT WAS FASCISTS OR JACKBOOTED THUGS OR MEGALOMANIACS OR GARDEN VARIETY HOODLUMS, THERE WERE ALWAYS ENEMIES THAT COULDN'T BE REASONED WITH.
AND DOC HAD NO CHOICE BUT TO HANDLE MATTERS THE *HARD* WAY.
YOUR REIGN OF *"CYBER TERROR"* IS *OVER*.

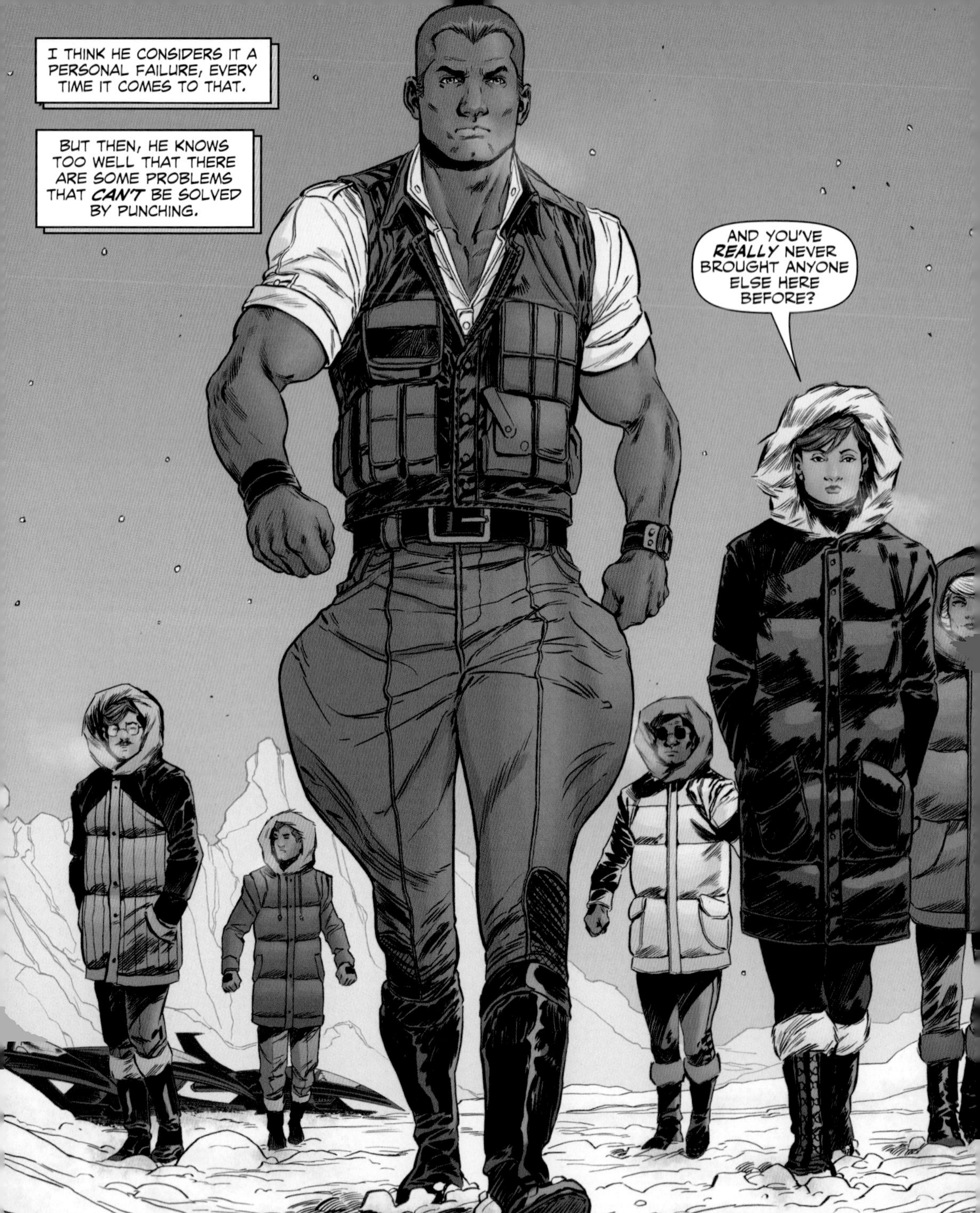
I THINK HE CONSIDERS IT A PERSONAL FAILURE, EVERY TIME IT COMES TO THAT.
BUT THEN, HE KNOWS TOO WELL THAT THERE ARE SOME PROBLEMS THAT *CAN'T* BE SOLVED BY PUNCHING.
AND YOU'VE *REALLY* NEVER BROUGHT ANYONE ELSE HERE BEFORE?

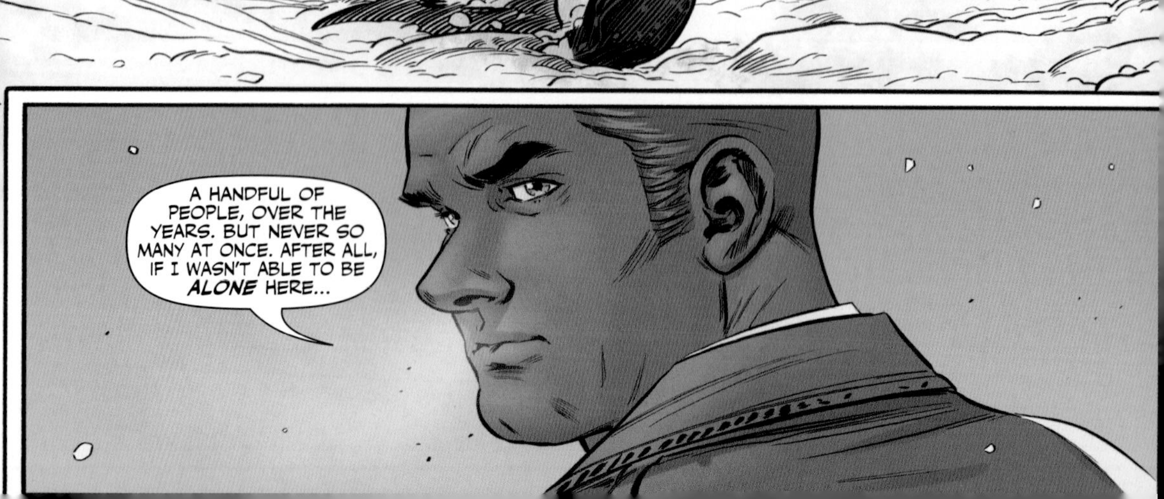
A HANDFUL OF PEOPLE, OVER THE YEARS. BUT NEVER SO MANY AT ONCE. AFTER ALL, IF I WASN'T ABLE TO BE *ALONE* HERE...

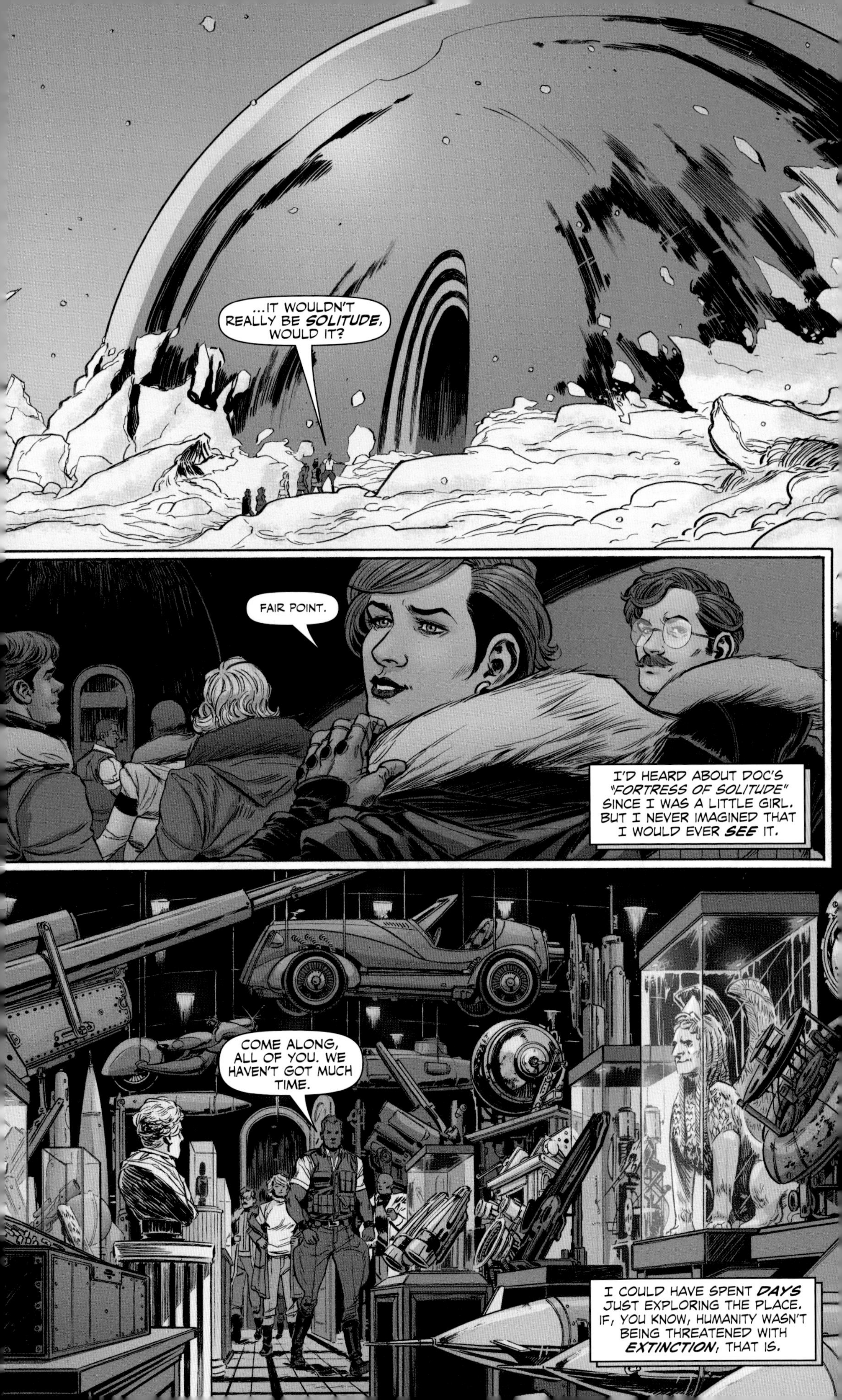
...IT WOULDN'T REALLY BE SOLITUDE, WOULD IT?
FAIR POINT.
I'D HEARD ABOUT DOC'S "FORTRESS OF SOLITUDE" SINCE I WAS A LITTLE GIRL. BUT I NEVER IMAGINED THAT I WOULD EVER SEE IT.
COME ALONG, ALL OF YOU. WE HAVEN'T GOT MUCH TIME.
I COULD HAVE SPENT DAYS JUST EXPLORING THE PLACE. IF, YOU KNOW, HUMANITY WASN'T BEING THREATENED WITH EXTINCTION, THAT IS.

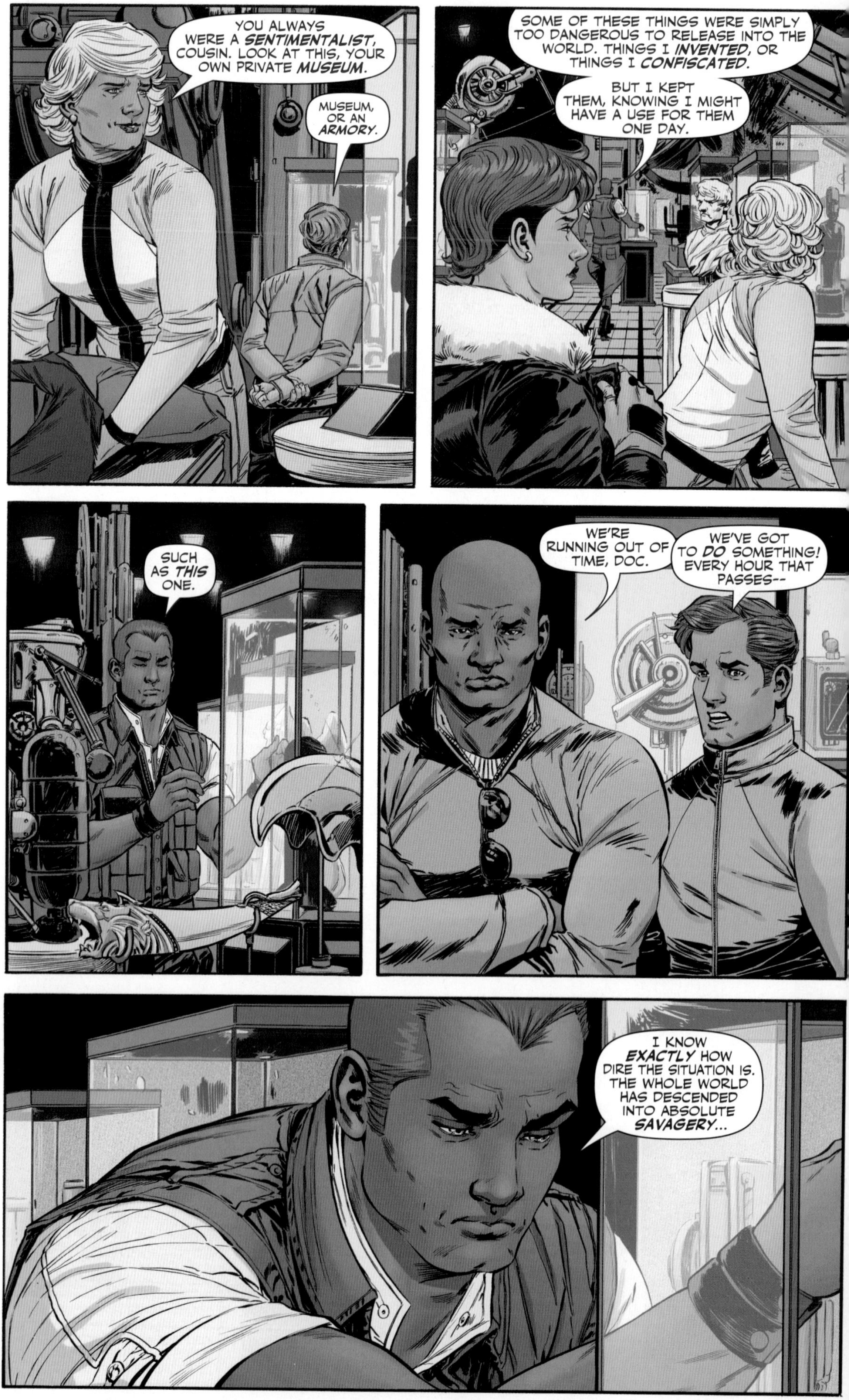
YOU ALWAYS WERE A *SENTIMENTALIST*, COUSIN. LOOK AT THIS, YOUR OWN PRIVATE *MUSEUM*.
MUSEUM, OR AN *ARMORY*.
SOME OF THESE THINGS WERE SIMPLY TOO DANGEROUS TO RELEASE INTO THE WORLD. THINGS I *INVENTED*, OR THINGS I *CONFISCATED*.
BUT I KEPT THEM, KNOWING I MIGHT HAVE A USE FOR THEM ONE DAY.
SUCH AS *THIS* ONE.
WE'RE RUNNING OUT OF TIME, DOC.
WE'VE GOT TO *DO* SOMETHING! EVERY HOUR THAT PASSES--
I KNOW *EXACTLY* HOW DIRE THE SITUATION IS. THE WHOLE WORLD HAS DESCENDED INTO ABSOLUTE *SAVAGERY*...

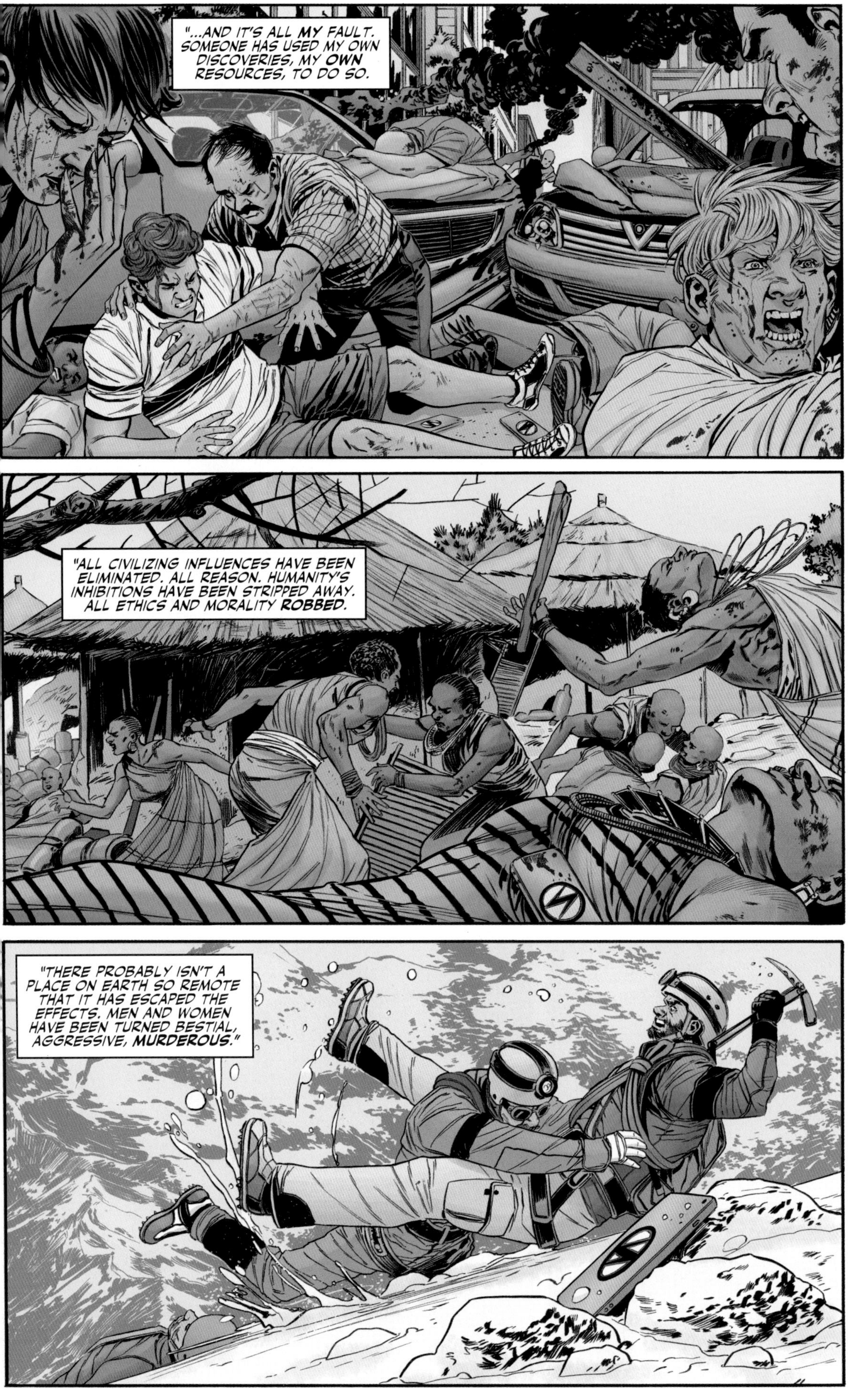
"...AND IT'S ALL MY FAULT. SOMEONE HAS USED MY OWN DISCOVERIES, MY OWN RESOURCES, TO DO SO.
"ALL CIVILIZING INFLUENCES HAVE BEEN ELIMINATED. ALL REASON. HUMANITY'S INHIBITIONS HAVE BEEN STRIPPED AWAY. ALL ETHICS AND MORALITY ROBBED.
"THERE PROBABLY ISN'T A PLACE ON EARTH SO REMOTE THAT IT HAS ESCAPED THE EFFECTS. MEN AND WOMEN HAVE BEEN TURNED BESTIAL, AGGRESSIVE, MURDEROUS."

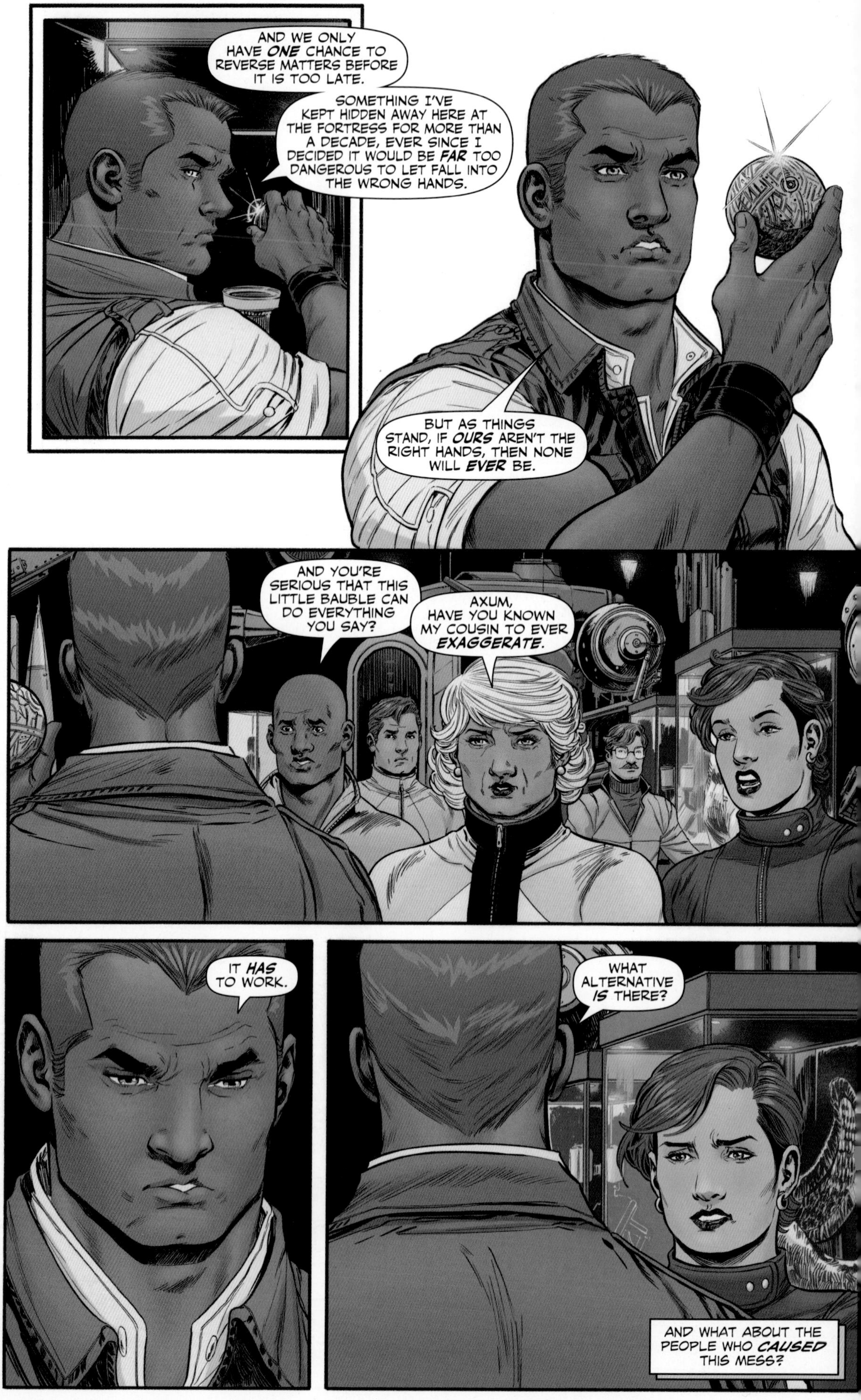
AND WE ONLY HAVE ONE CHANCE TO REVERSE MATTERS BEFORE IT IS TOO LATE.
SOMETHING I'VE KEPT HIDDEN AWAY HERE AT THE FORTRESS FOR MORE THAN A DECADE, EVER SINCE I DECIDED IT WOULD BE FAR TOO DANGEROUS TO LET FALL INTO THE WRONG HANDS.
BUT AS THINGS STAND, IF OURS AREN'T THE RIGHT HANDS, THEN NONE WILL EVER BE.
AND YOU'RE SERIOUS THAT THIS LITTLE BAUBLE CAN DO EVERYTHING YOU SAY?
AXUM, HAVE YOU KNOWN MY COUSIN TO EVER EXAGGERATE.
IT HAS TO WORK.
WHAT ALTERNATIVE IS THERE?
AND WHAT ABOUT THE PEOPLE WHO CAUSED THIS MESS?

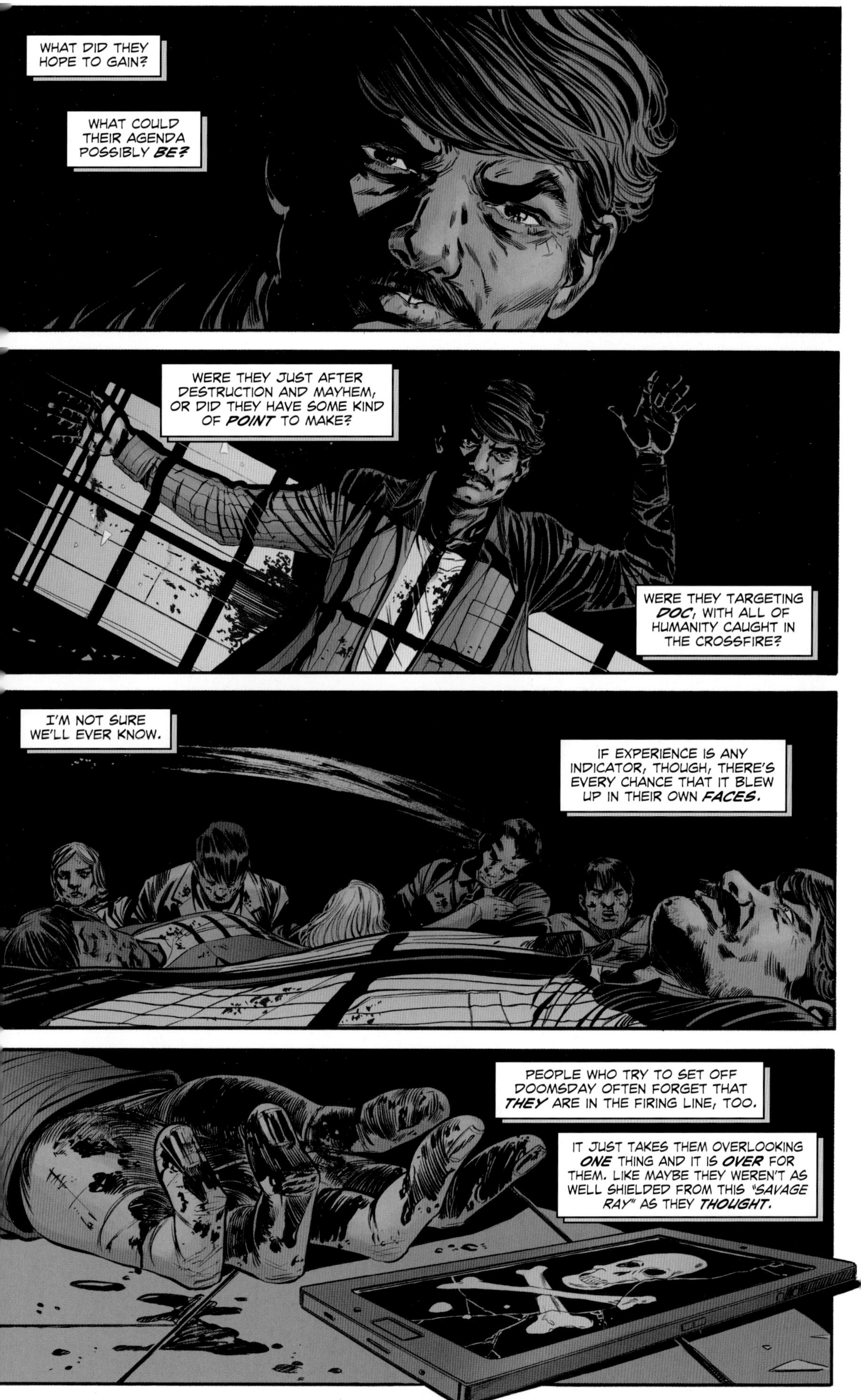
WHAT DID THEY HOPE TO GAIN?
WHAT COULD THEIR AGENDA POSSIBLY BE?
WERE THEY JUST AFTER DESTRUCTION AND MAYHEM, OR DID THEY HAVE SOME KIND OF POINT TO MAKE?
WERE THEY TARGETING DOC, WITH ALL OF HUMANITY CAUGHT IN THE CROSSFIRE?
I'M NOT SURE WE'LL EVER KNOW.
IF EXPERIENCE IS ANY INDICATOR, THOUGH, THERE'S EVERY CHANCE THAT IT BLEW UP IN THEIR OWN FACES.
PEOPLE WHO TRY TO SET OFF DOOMSDAY OFTEN FORGET THAT THEY ARE IN THE FIRING LINE, TOO.
IT JUST TAKES THEM OVERLOOKING ONE THING AND IT IS OVER FOR THEM. LIKE MAYBE THEY WEREN'T AS WELL SHIELDED FROM THIS "SAVAGE RAY" AS THEY THOUGHT.

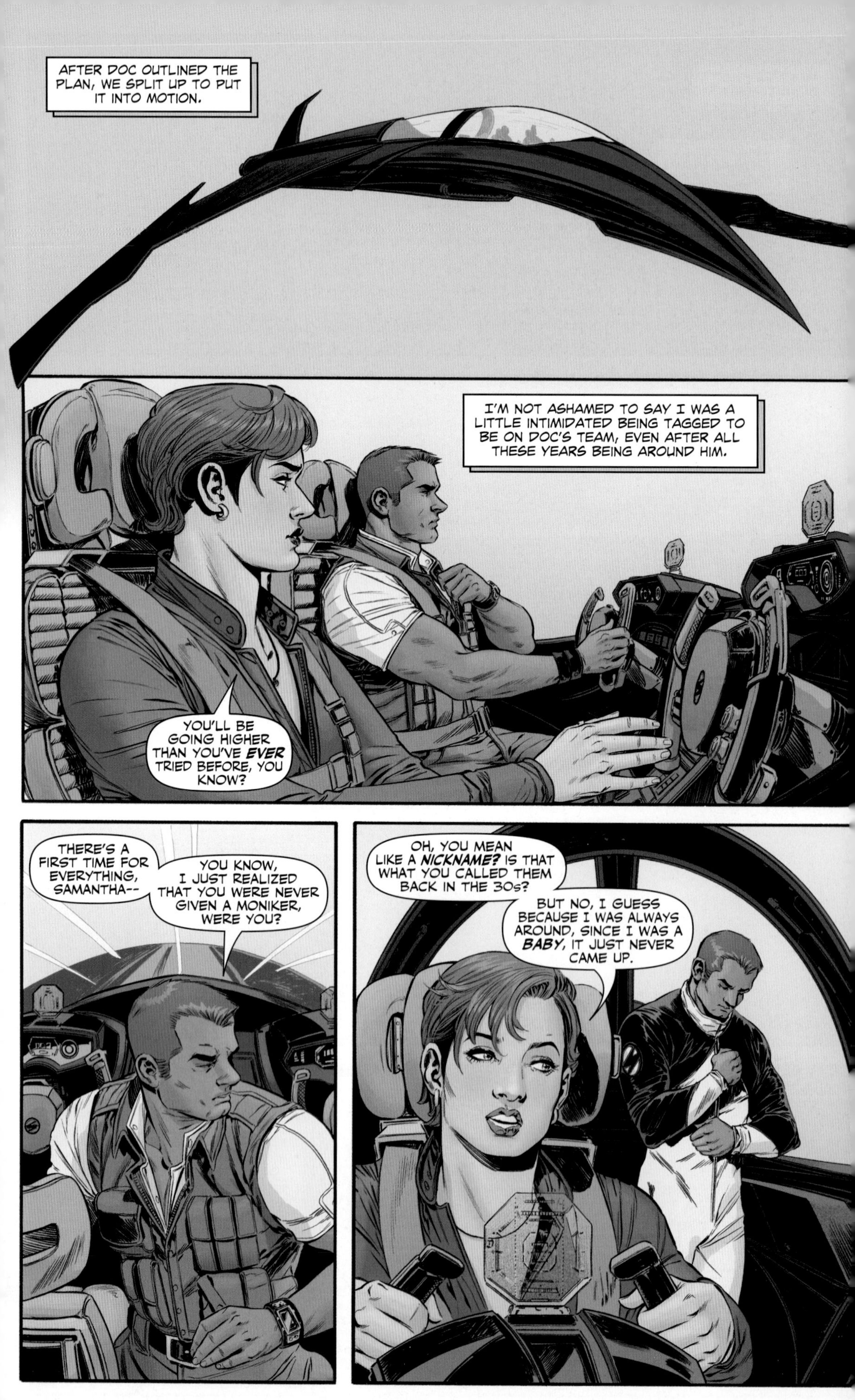

AFTER DOC OUTLINED THE PLAN, WE SPLIT UP TO PUT IT INTO MOTION.
I'M NOT ASHAMED TO SAY I WAS A LITTLE INTIMIDATED BEING TAGGED TO BE ON DOC'S TEAM, EVEN AFTER ALL THESE YEARS BEING AROUND HIM.
YOU'LL BE GOING HIGHER THAN YOU'VE EVER TRIED BEFORE, YOU KNOW?
THERE'S A FIRST TIME FOR EVERYTHING, SAMANTHA--
YOU KNOW, I JUST REALIZED THAT YOU WERE NEVER GIVEN A MONIKER, WERE YOU?
OH, YOU MEAN LIKE A NICKNAME? IS THAT WHAT YOU CALLED THEM BACK IN THE 30s?
BUT NO, I GUESS BECAUSE I WAS ALWAYS AROUND, SINCE I WAS A BABY, IT JUST NEVER CAME UP.

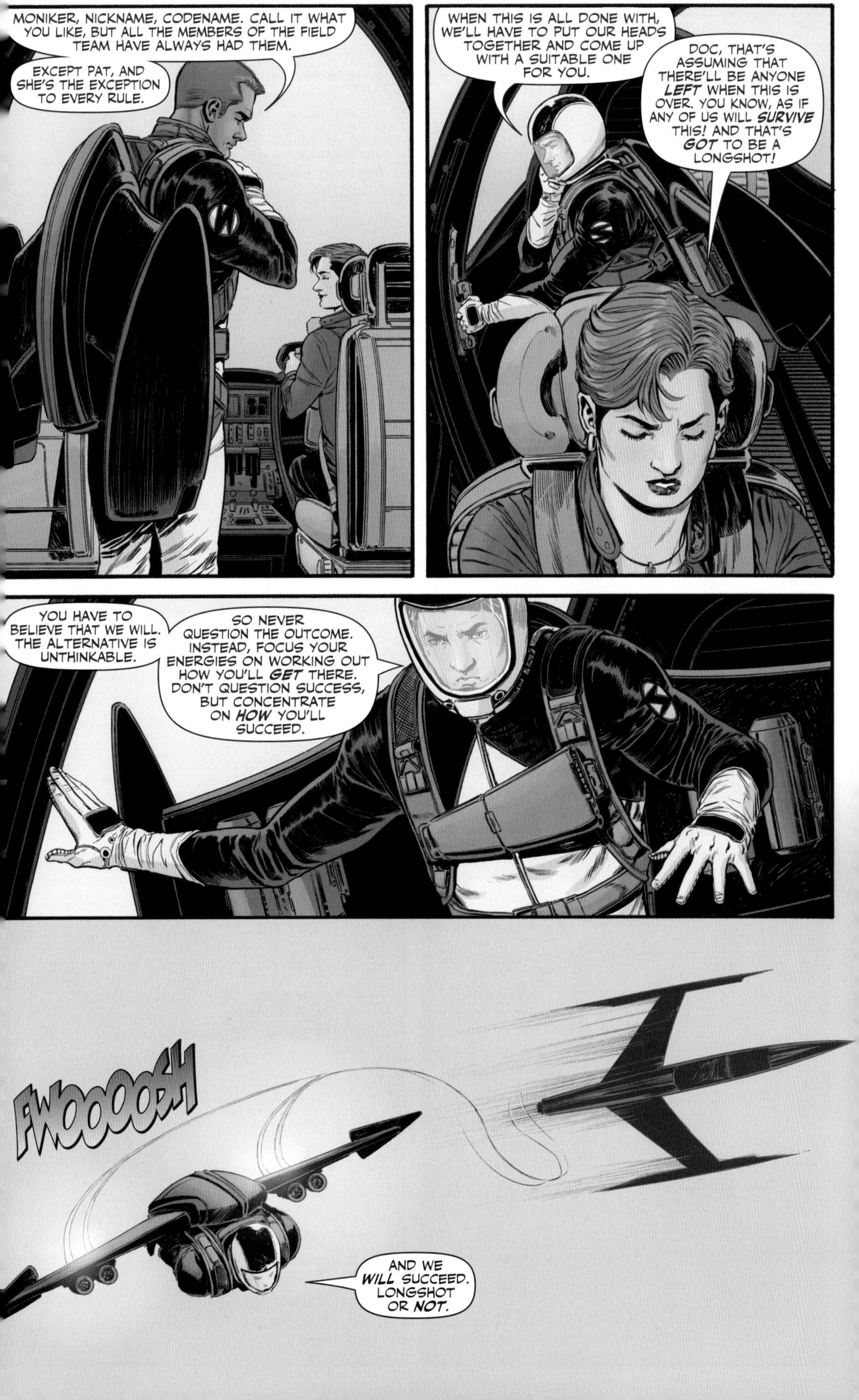
MONIKER, NICKNAME, CODENAME. CALL IT WHAT YOU LIKE, BUT ALL THE MEMBERS OF THE FIELD TEAM HAVE ALWAYS HAD THEM.
EXCEPT PAT, AND SHE'S THE EXCEPTION TO EVERY RULE.
WHEN THIS IS ALL DONE WITH, WE'LL HAVE TO PUT OUR HEADS TOGETHER AND COME UP WITH A SUITABLE ONE FOR YOU.
DOC, THAT'S ASSUMING THAT THERE'LL BE ANYONE *LEFT* WHEN THIS IS OVER. YOU KNOW, AS IF ANY OF US WILL *SURVIVE* THIS! AND THAT'S *GOT* TO BE A LONGSHOT!
YOU HAVE TO BELIEVE THAT WE WILL. THE ALTERNATIVE IS UNTHINKABLE.
SO NEVER QUESTION THE OUTCOME. INSTEAD, FOCUS YOUR ENERGIES ON WORKING OUT HOW YOU'LL *GET* THERE. DON'T QUESTION SUCCESS, BUT CONCENTRATE ON *HOW* YOU'LL SUCCEED.
FWOOOOSH
AND WE *WILL* SUCCEED. LONGSHOT OR *NOT*.

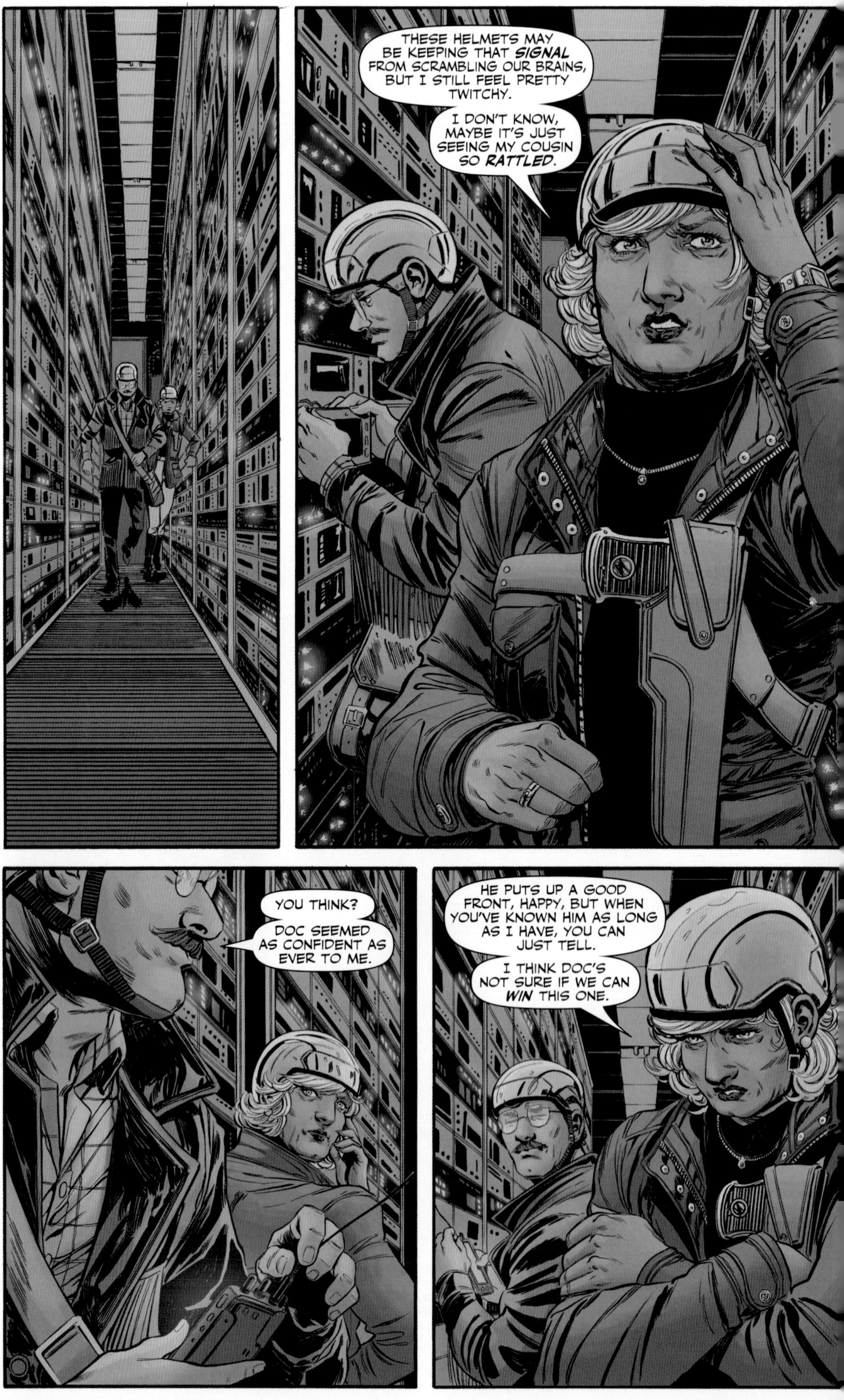
THESE HELMETS MAY BE KEEPING THAT SIGNAL FROM SCRAMBLING OUR BRAINS, BUT I STILL FEEL PRETTY TWITCHY.
I DON'T KNOW, MAYBE IT'S JUST SEEING MY COUSIN SO RATTLED.
YOU THINK?
DOC SEEMED AS CONFIDENT AS EVER TO ME.
HE PUTS UP A GOOD FRONT, HAPPY, BUT WHEN YOU'VE KNOWN HIM AS LONG AS I HAVE, YOU CAN JUST TELL.
I THINK DOC'S NOT SURE IF WE CAN WIN THIS ONE.

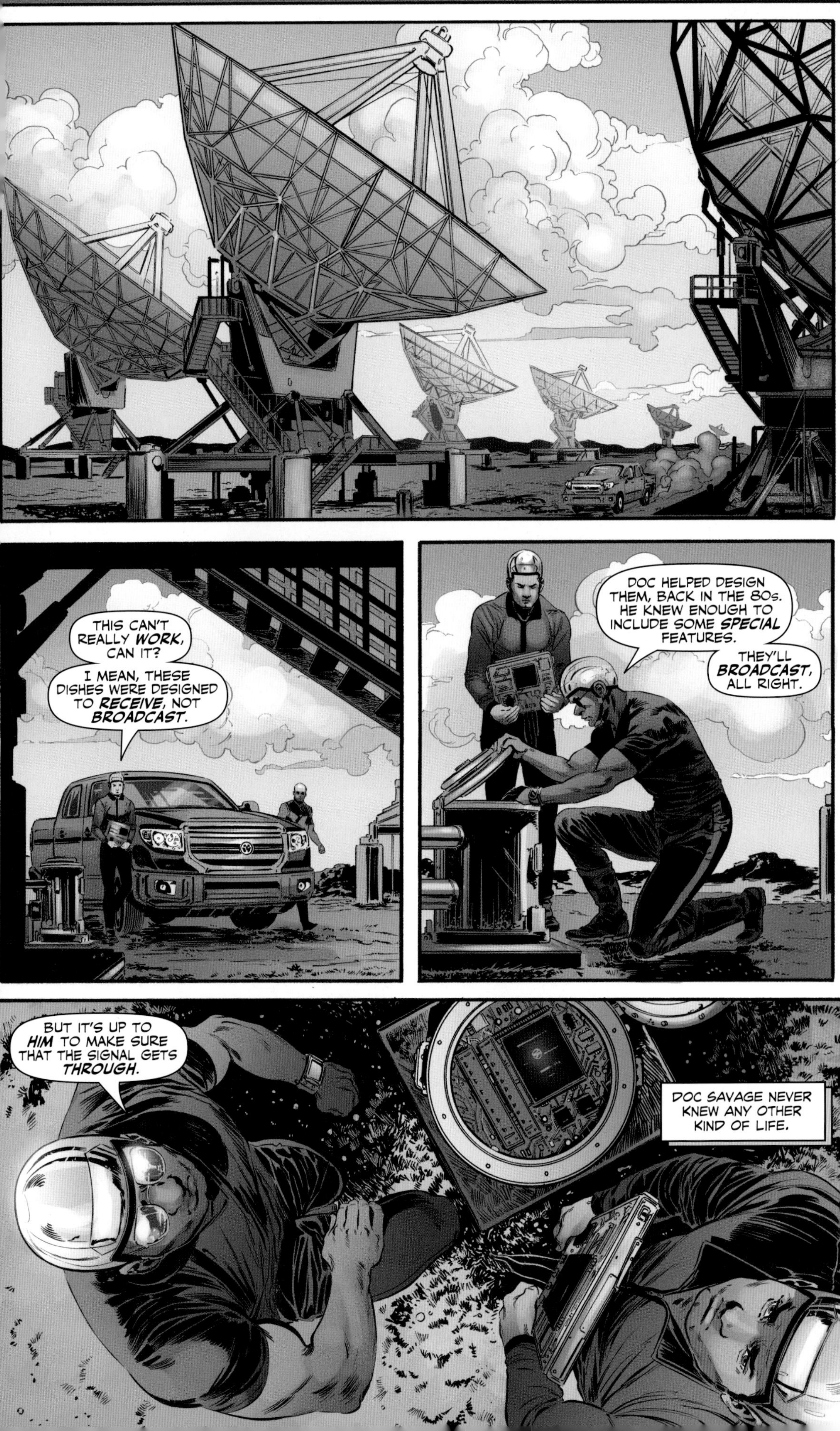

THIS CAN'T REALLY *WORK*, CAN IT?
I MEAN, THESE DISHES WERE DESIGNED TO *RECEIVE*, NOT *BROADCAST*.
DOC HELPED DESIGN THEM, BACK IN THE 80s. HE KNEW ENOUGH TO INCLUDE SOME *SPECIAL* FEATURES.
THEY'LL *BROADCAST*, ALL RIGHT.
BUT IT'S UP TO *HIM* TO MAKE SURE THAT THE SIGNAL GETS *THROUGH*.
DOC SAVAGE NEVER KNEW ANY OTHER KIND OF LIFE.

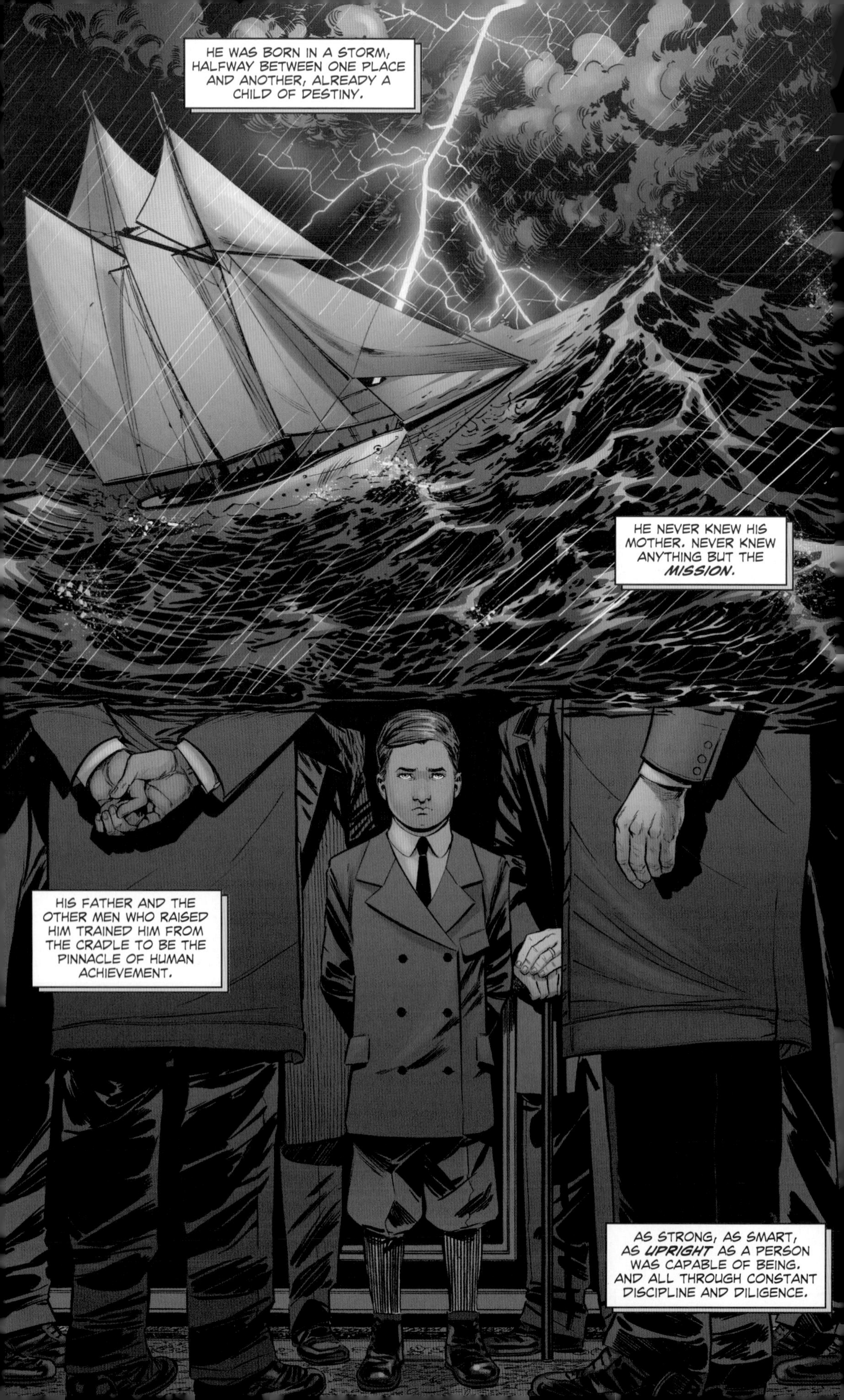
HE WAS BORN IN A STORM, HALFWAY BETWEEN ONE PLACE AND ANOTHER, ALREADY A CHILD OF DESTINY.
HE NEVER KNEW HIS MOTHER. NEVER KNEW ANYTHING BUT THE *MISSION.*
HIS FATHER AND THE OTHER MEN WHO RAISED HIM TRAINED HIM FROM THE CRADLE TO BE THE PINNACLE OF HUMAN ACHIEVEMENT.
AS STRONG, AS SMART, AS *UPRIGHT* AS A PERSON WAS CAPABLE OF BEING. AND ALL THROUGH CONSTANT DISCIPLINE AND DILIGENCE.

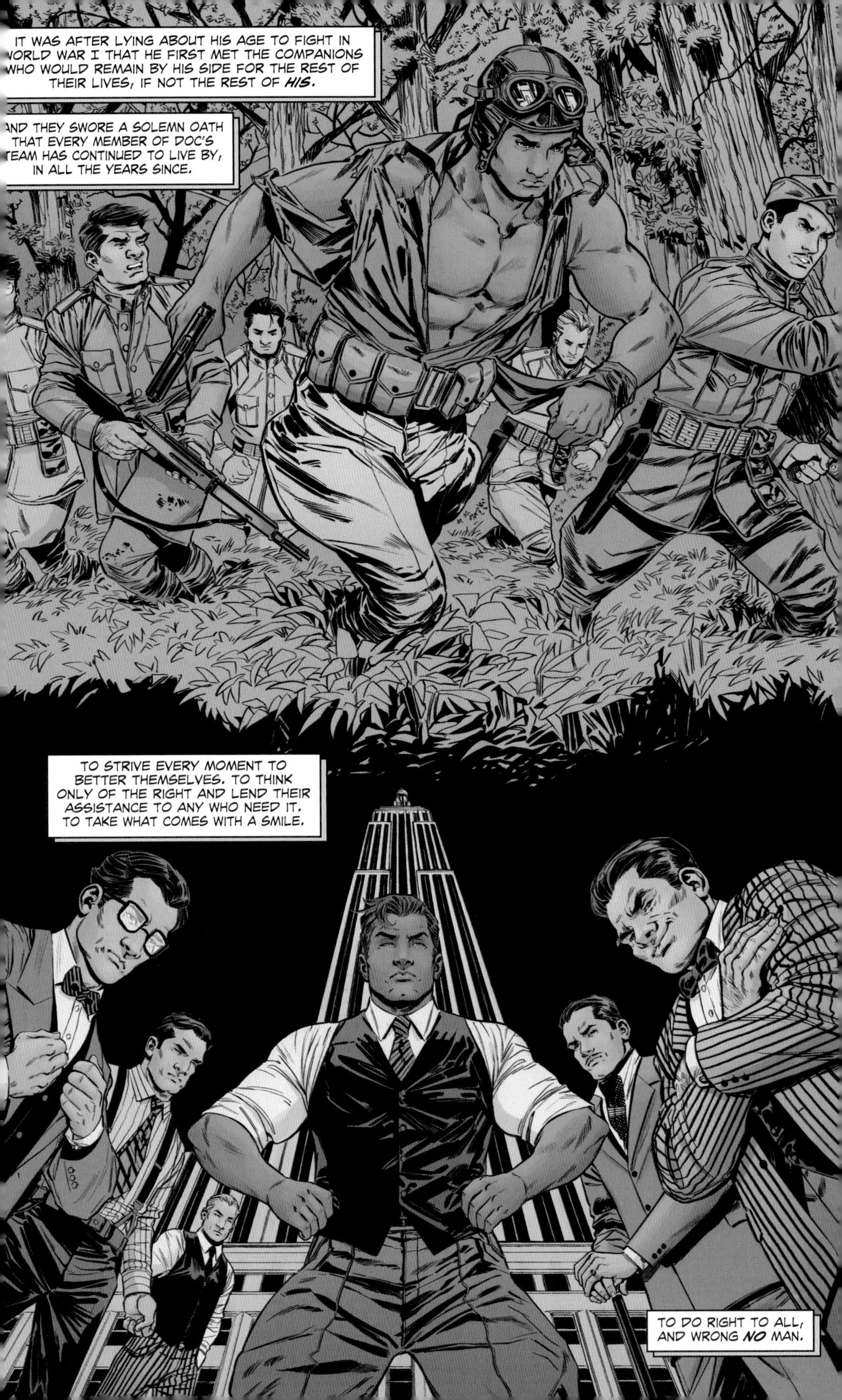
IT WAS AFTER LYING ABOUT HIS AGE TO FIGHT IN WORLD WAR I THAT HE FIRST MET THE COMPANIONS WHO WOULD REMAIN BY HIS SIDE FOR THE REST OF THEIR LIVES, IF NOT THE REST OF *HIS.*
AND THEY SWORE A SOLEMN OATH THAT EVERY MEMBER OF DOC'S TEAM HAS CONTINUED TO LIVE BY, IN ALL THE YEARS SINCE.
TO STRIVE EVERY MOMENT TO BETTER THEMSELVES. TO THINK ONLY OF THE RIGHT AND LEND THEIR ASSISTANCE TO ANY WHO NEED IT. TO TAKE WHAT COMES WITH A SMILE.
TO DO RIGHT TO ALL, AND WRONG *NO* MAN.

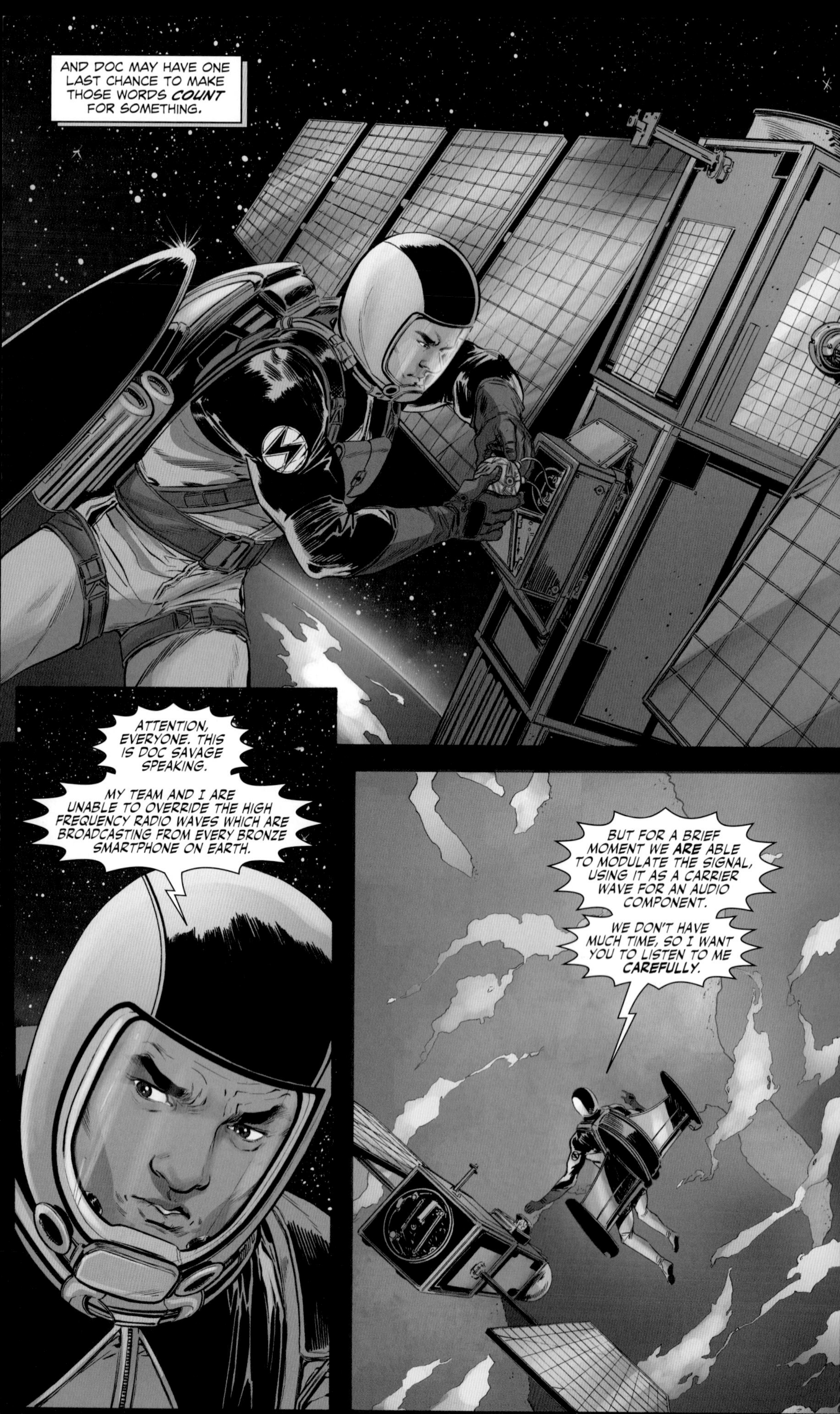
AND DOC MAY HAVE ONE LAST CHANCE TO MAKE THOSE WORDS COUNT FOR SOMETHING.
ATTENTION, EVERYONE. THIS IS DOC SAVAGE SPEAKING.
MY TEAM AND I ARE UNABLE TO OVERRIDE THE HIGH FREQUENCY RADIO WAVES WHICH ARE BROADCASTING FROM EVERY BRONZE SMARTPHONE ON EARTH.
BUT FOR A BRIEF MOMENT WE ARE ABLE TO MODULATE THE SIGNAL, USING IT AS A CARRIER WAVE FOR AN AUDIO COMPONENT.
WE DON'T HAVE MUCH TIME, SO I WANT YOU TO LISTEN TO ME CAREFULLY.

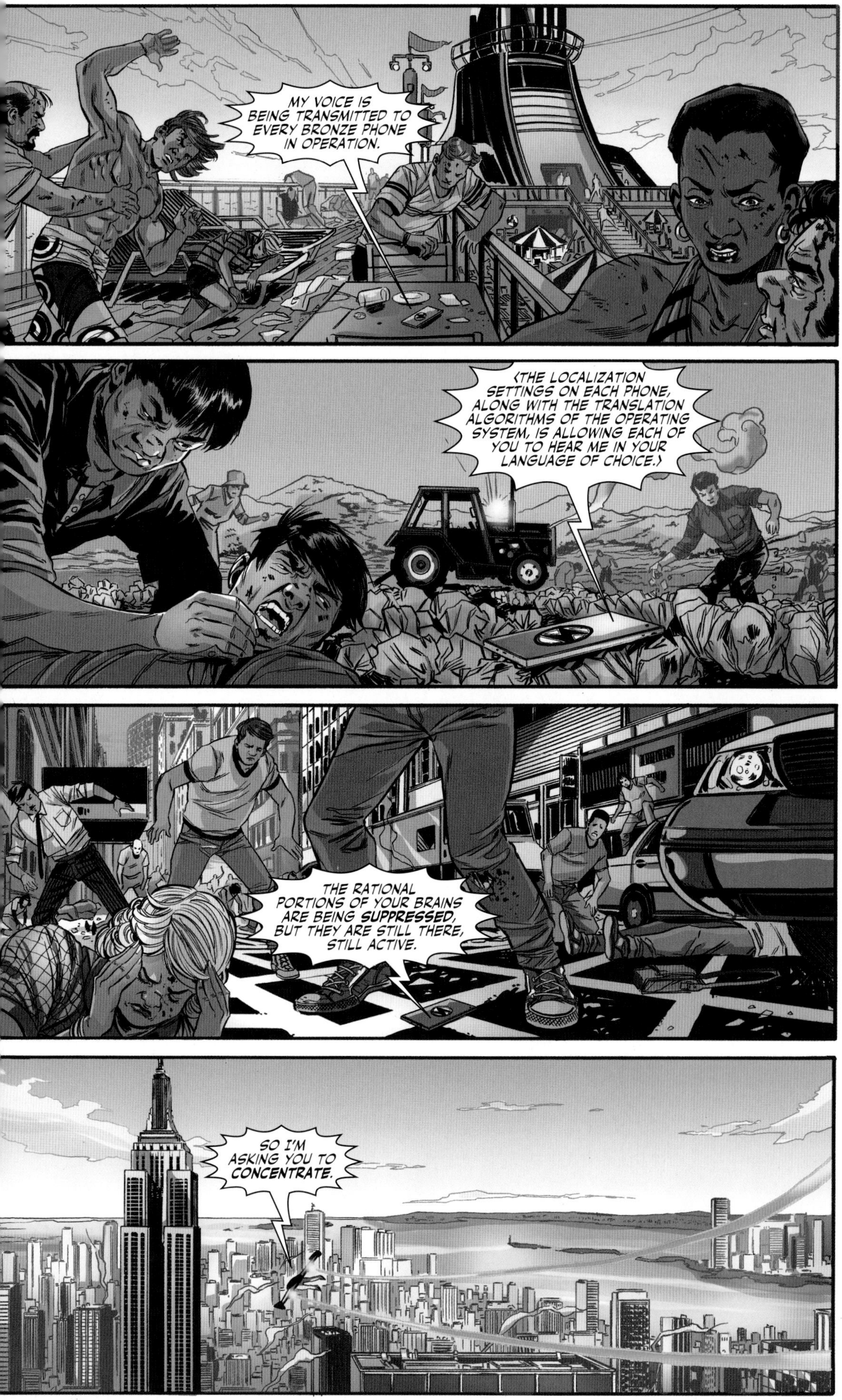
MY VOICE IS BEING TRANSMITTED TO EVERY BRONZE PHONE IN OPERATION.
‹THE LOCALIZATION SETTINGS ON EACH PHONE, ALONG WITH THE TRANSLATION ALGORITHMS OF THE OPERATING SYSTEM, IS ALLOWING EACH OF YOU TO HEAR ME IN YOUR LANGUAGE OF CHOICE.›
THE RATIONAL PORTIONS OF YOUR BRAINS ARE BEING SUPPRESSED, BUT THEY ARE STILL THERE, STILL ACTIVE.
SO I'M ASKING YOU TO CONCENTRATE.

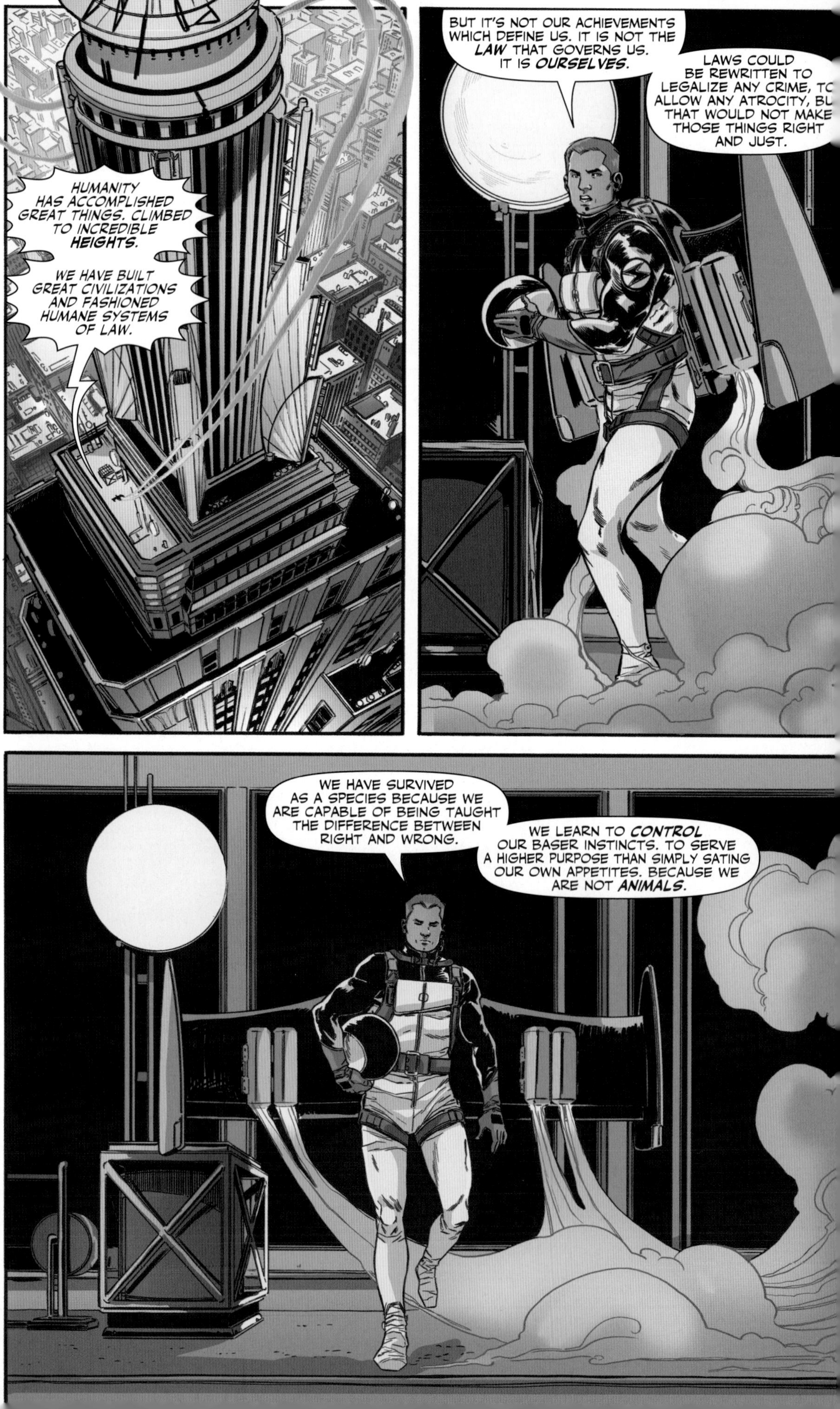

HUMANITY HAS ACCOMPLISHED GREAT THINGS. CLIMBED TO INCREDIBLE HEIGHTS.
WE HAVE BUILT GREAT CIVILIZATIONS AND FASHIONED HUMANE SYSTEMS OF LAW.
BUT IT'S NOT OUR ACHIEVEMENTS WHICH DEFINE US. IT IS NOT THE LAW THAT GOVERNS US. IT IS OURSELVES.
LAWS COULD BE REWRITTEN TO LEGALIZE ANY CRIME, TO ALLOW ANY ATROCITY, BU THAT WOULD NOT MAKE THOSE THINGS RIGHT AND JUST.
WE HAVE SURVIVED AS A SPECIES BECAUSE WE ARE CAPABLE OF BEING TAUGHT THE DIFFERENCE BETWEEN RIGHT AND WRONG.
WE LEARN TO CONTROL OUR BASER INSTINCTS. TO SERVE A HIGHER PURPOSE THAN SIMPLY SATING OUR OWN APPETITES. BECAUSE WE ARE NOT ANIMALS.

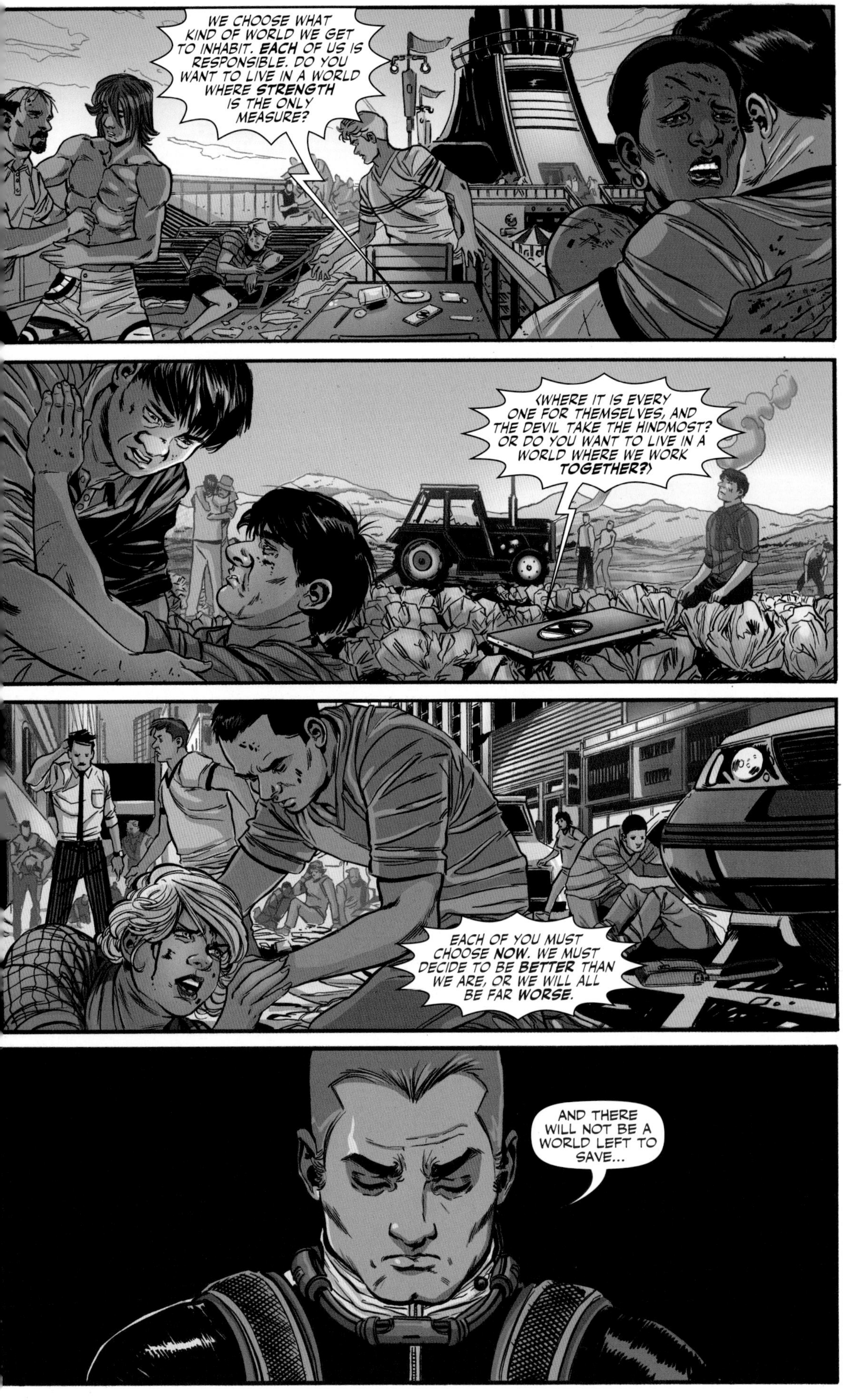
WE CHOOSE WHAT KIND OF WORLD WE GET TO INHABIT. EACH OF US IS RESPONSIBLE. DO YOU WANT TO LIVE IN A WORLD WHERE STRENGTH IS THE ONLY MEASURE?
‹WHERE IT IS EVERY ONE FOR THEMSELVES, AND THE DEVIL TAKE THE HINDMOST? OR DO YOU WANT TO LIVE IN A WORLD WHERE WE WORK TOGETHER?›
EACH OF YOU MUST CHOOSE NOW. WE MUST DECIDE TO BE BETTER THAN WE ARE, OR WE WILL ALL BE FAR WORSE.
AND THERE WILL NOT BE A WORLD LEFT TO SAVE...

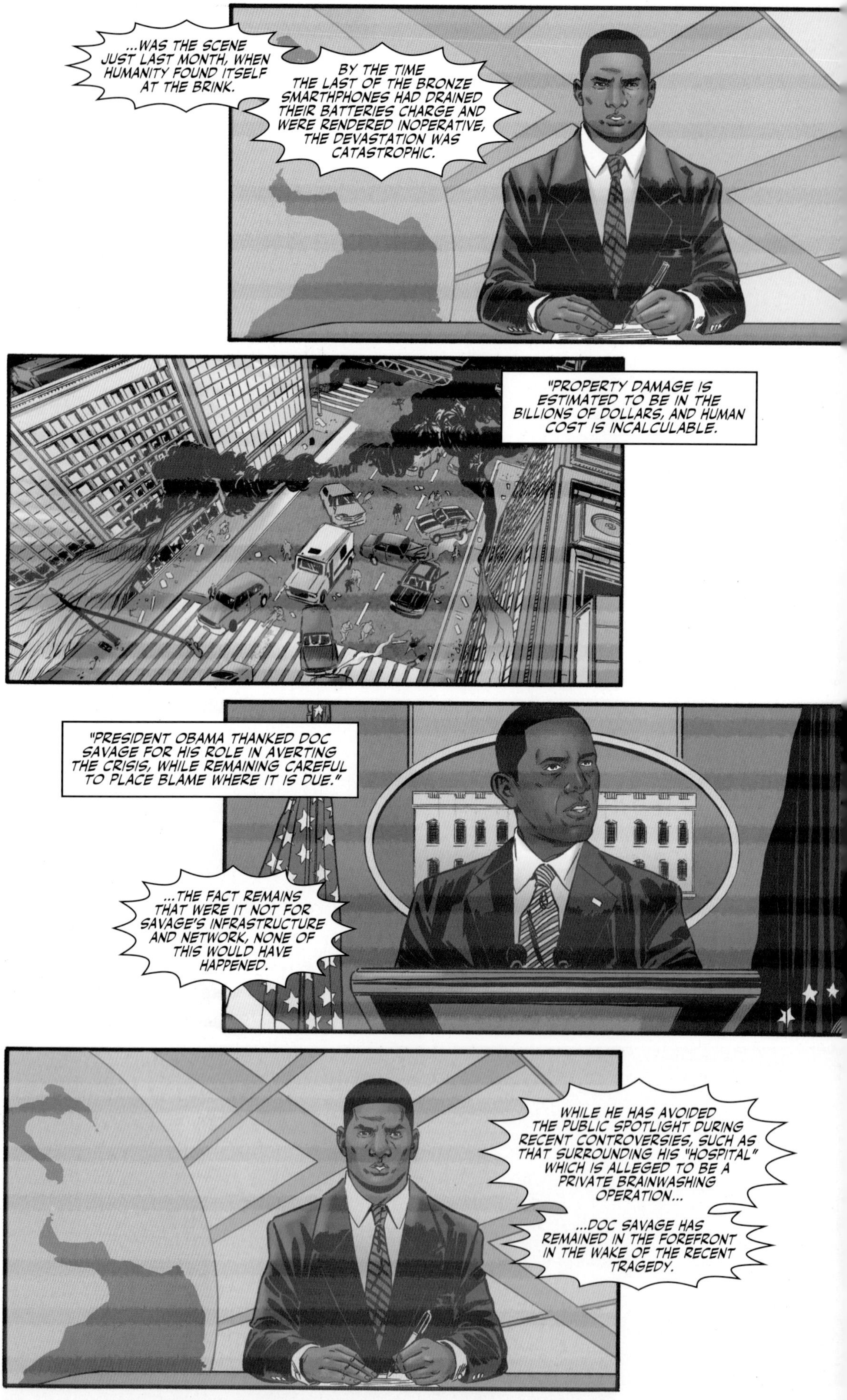
...WAS THE SCENE JUST LAST MONTH, WHEN HUMANITY FOUND ITSELF AT THE BRINK.
BY THE TIME THE LAST OF THE BRONZE SMARTHPHONES HAD DRAINED THEIR BATTERIES CHARGE AND WERE RENDERED INOPERATIVE, THE DEVASTATION WAS CATASTROPHIC.
"PROPERTY DAMAGE IS ESTIMATED TO BE IN THE BILLIONS OF DOLLARS, AND HUMAN COST IS INCALCULABLE.
"PRESIDENT OBAMA THANKED DOC SAVAGE FOR HIS ROLE IN AVERTING THE CRISIS, WHILE REMAINING CAREFUL TO PLACE BLAME WHERE IT IS DUE."
...THE FACT REMAINS THAT WERE IT NOT FOR SAVAGE'S INFRASTRUCTURE AND NETWORK, NONE OF THIS WOULD HAVE HAPPENED.
WHILE HE HAS AVOIDED THE PUBLIC SPOTLIGHT DURING RECENT CONTROVERSIES, SUCH AS THAT SURROUNDING HIS "HOSPITAL" WHICH IS ALLEGED TO BE A PRIVATE BRAINWASHING OPERATION...
...DOC SAVAGE HAS REMAINED IN THE FOREFRONT IN THE WAKE OF THE RECENT TRAGEDY.

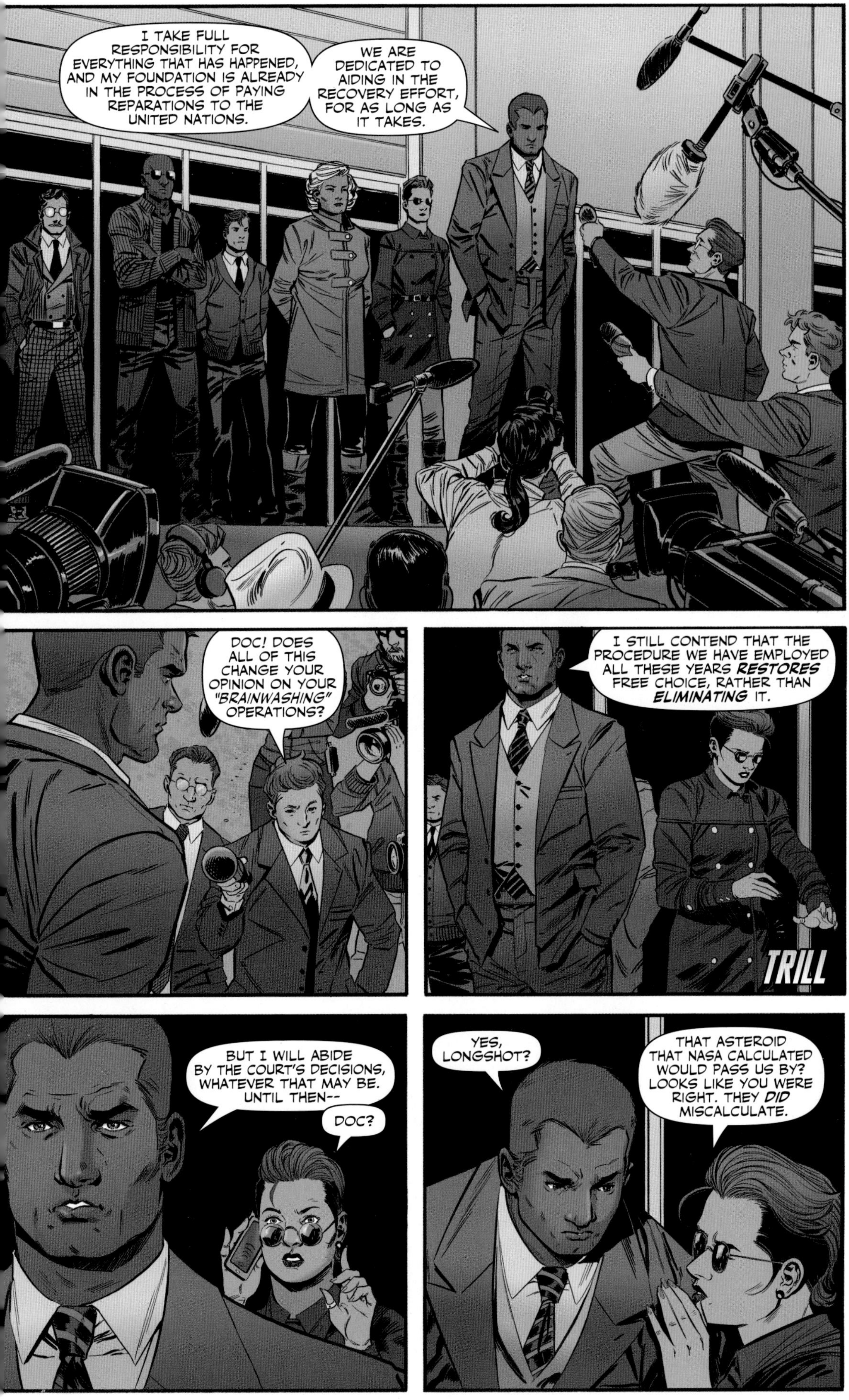
I TAKE FULL RESPONSIBILITY FOR EVERYTHING THAT HAS HAPPENED, AND MY FOUNDATION IS ALREADY IN THE PROCESS OF PAYING REPARATIONS TO THE UNITED NATIONS.
WE ARE DEDICATED TO AIDING IN THE RECOVERY EFFORT, FOR AS LONG AS IT TAKES.
DOC! DOES ALL OF THIS CHANGE YOUR OPINION ON YOUR "BRAINWASHING" OPERATIONS?
I STILL CONTEND THAT THE PROCEDURE WE HAVE EMPLOYED ALL THESE YEARS RESTORES FREE CHOICE, RATHER THAN ELIMINATING IT.
TRILL
BUT I WILL ABIDE BY THE COURT'S DECISIONS, WHATEVER THAT MAY BE. UNTIL THEN--
DOC?
YES, LONGSHOT?
THAT ASTEROID THAT NASA CALCULATED WOULD PASS US BY? LOOKS LIKE YOU WERE RIGHT. THEY DID MISCALCULATE.

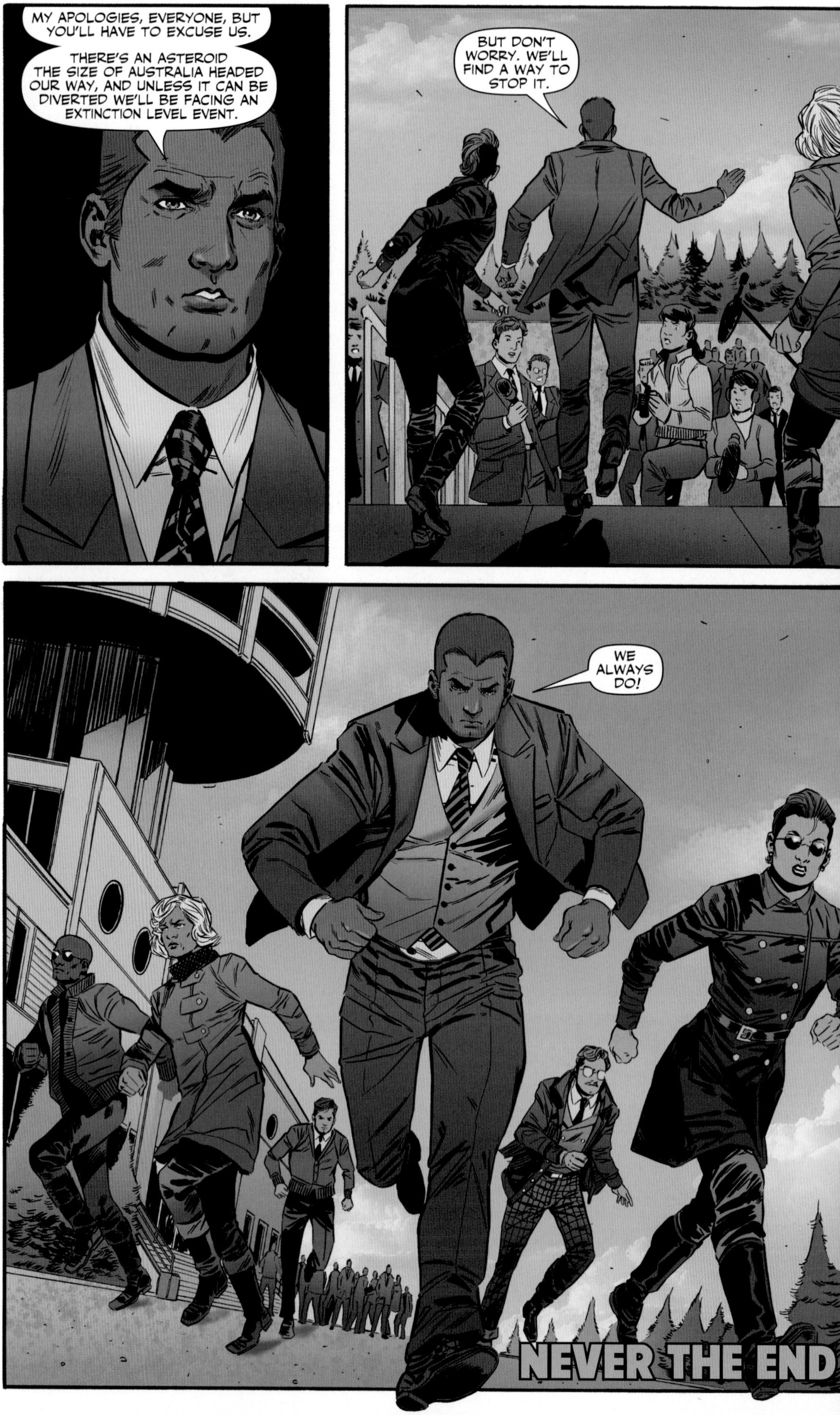
MY APOLOGIES, EVERYONE, BUT YOU'LL HAVE TO EXCUSE US.
THERE'S AN ASTEROID THE SIZE OF AUSTRALIA HEADED OUR WAY, AND UNLESS IT CAN BE DIVERTED WE'LL BE FACING AN EXTINCTION LEVEL EVENT.
BUT DON'T WORRY. WE'LL FIND A WAY TO STOP IT.
WE ALWAYS DO!
NEVER THE END

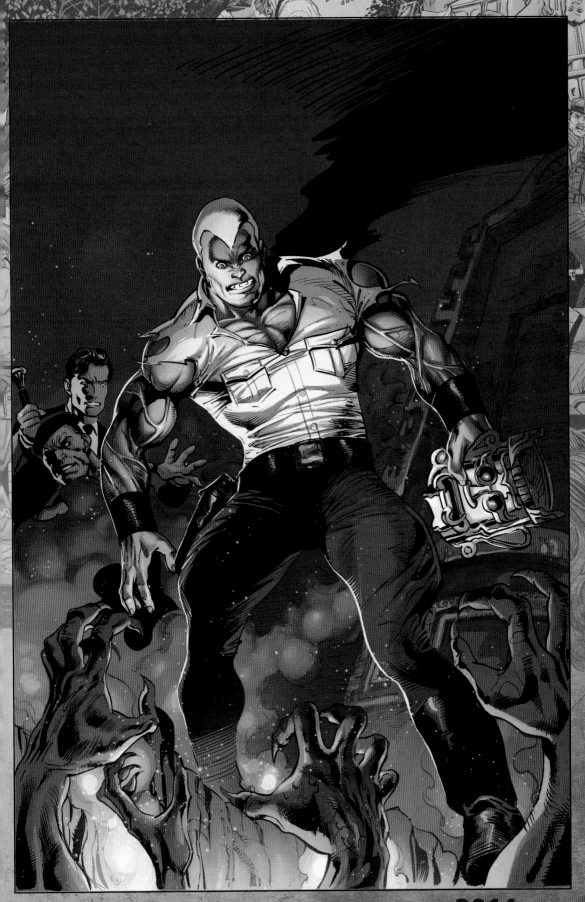

ANNUAL 2014 COVER
art by ROBERTO CASTRO   colors by ADRIANO LUCAS

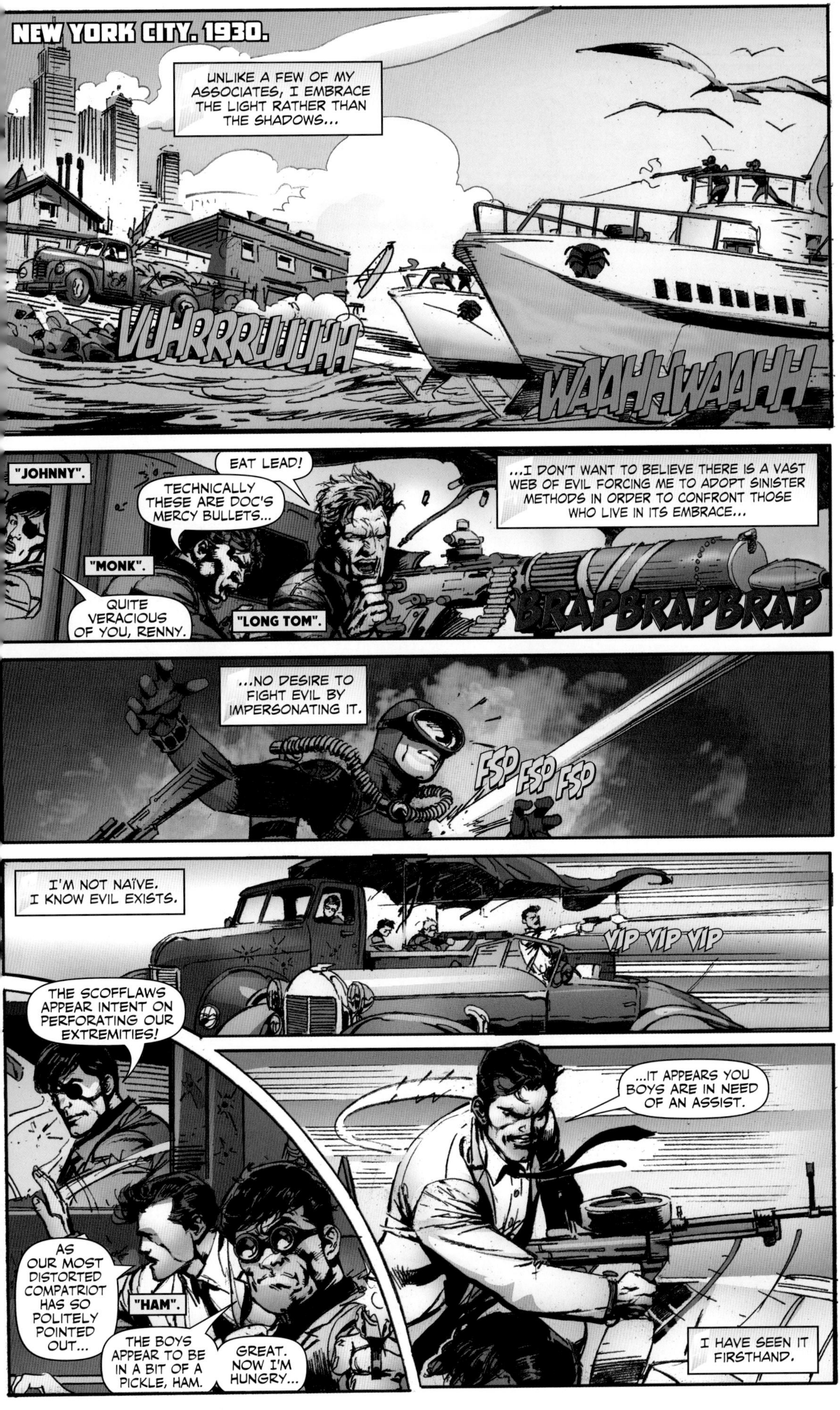

NEW YORK CITY. 1930.
UNLIKE A FEW OF MY ASSOCIATES, I EMBRACE THE LIGHT RATHER THAN THE SHADOWS...
VUHRRRUUUHH
WAAHHWAAHH
"JOHNNY".
EAT LEAD!
TECHNICALLY THESE ARE DOC'S MERCY BULLETS...
...I DON'T WANT TO BELIEVE THERE IS A VAST WEB OF EVIL FORCING ME TO ADOPT SINISTER METHODS IN ORDER TO CONFRONT THOSE WHO LIVE IN ITS EMBRACE...
"MONK".
QUITE VERACIOUS OF YOU, RENNY.
"LONG TOM".
BRAPBRAPBRAP
...NO DESIRE TO FIGHT EVIL BY IMPERSONATING IT.
FSP FSP FSP
I'M NOT NAÏVE. I KNOW EVIL EXISTS.
VIP VIP VIP
THE SCOFFLAWS APPEAR INTENT ON PERFORATING OUR EXTREMITIES!
...IT APPEARS YOU BOYS ARE IN NEED OF AN ASSIST.
AS OUR MOST DISTORTED COMPATRIOT HAS SO POLITELY POINTED OUT...
"HAM".
THE BOYS APPEAR TO BE IN A BIT OF A PICKLE, HAM.
GREAT. NOW I'M HUNGRY...
I HAVE SEEN IT FIRSTHAND.

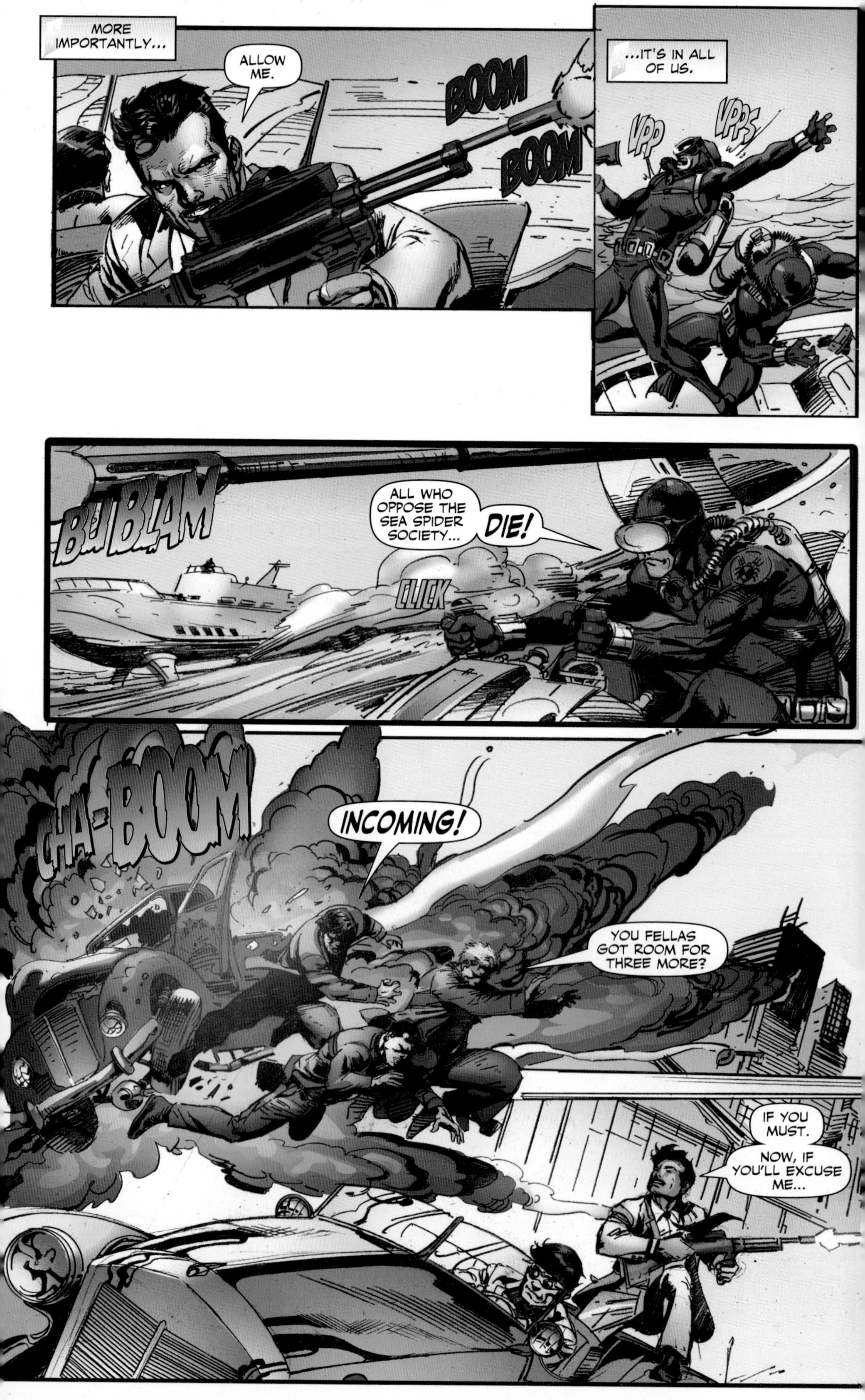
MORE IMPORTANTLY...
ALLOW ME.
BOOM
BOOM
...IT'S IN ALL OF US.
VPP
VPPS
BUBLAM
ALL WHO OPPOSE THE SEA SPIDER SOCIETY... DIE!
CLICK
CHA-BOOM
INCOMING!
YOU FELLAS GOT ROOM FOR THREE MORE?
IF YOU MUST.
NOW, IF YOU'LL EXCUSE ME...

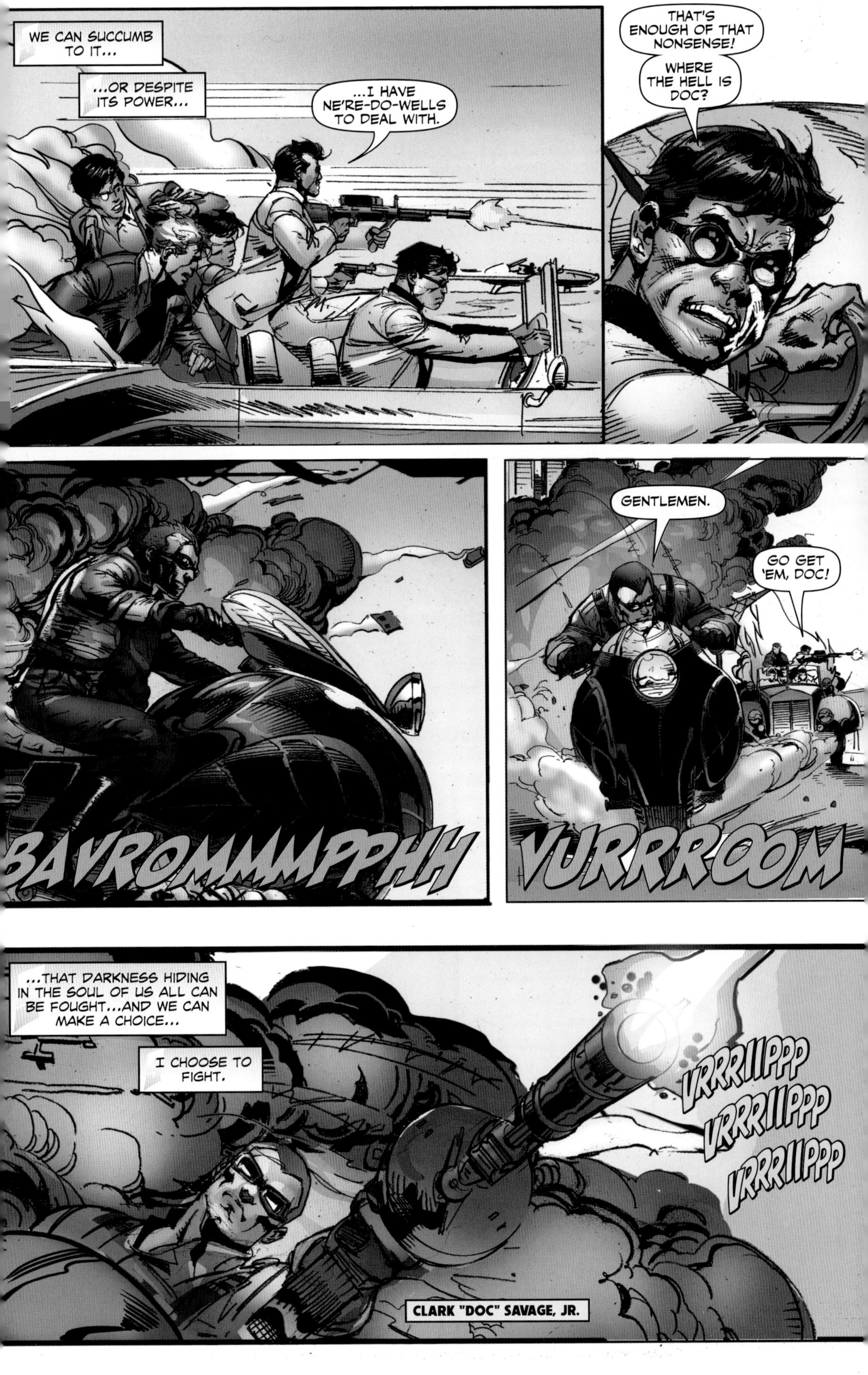
WE CAN SUCCUMB TO IT...
...OR DESPITE ITS POWER...
...I HAVE NE'RE-DO-WELLS TO DEAL WITH.
THAT'S ENOUGH OF THAT NONSENSE!
WHERE THE HELL IS DOC?
BAVROMMMMPPHH
GENTLEMEN.
GO GET 'EM, DOC!
VURRROOM
...THAT DARKNESS HIDING IN THE SOUL OF US ALL CAN BE FOUGHT...AND WE CAN MAKE A CHOICE...
I CHOOSE TO FIGHT.
VRRRIIPPP
VRRRIIPPP
VRRRIIPPP
CLARK "DOC" SAVAGE, JR.

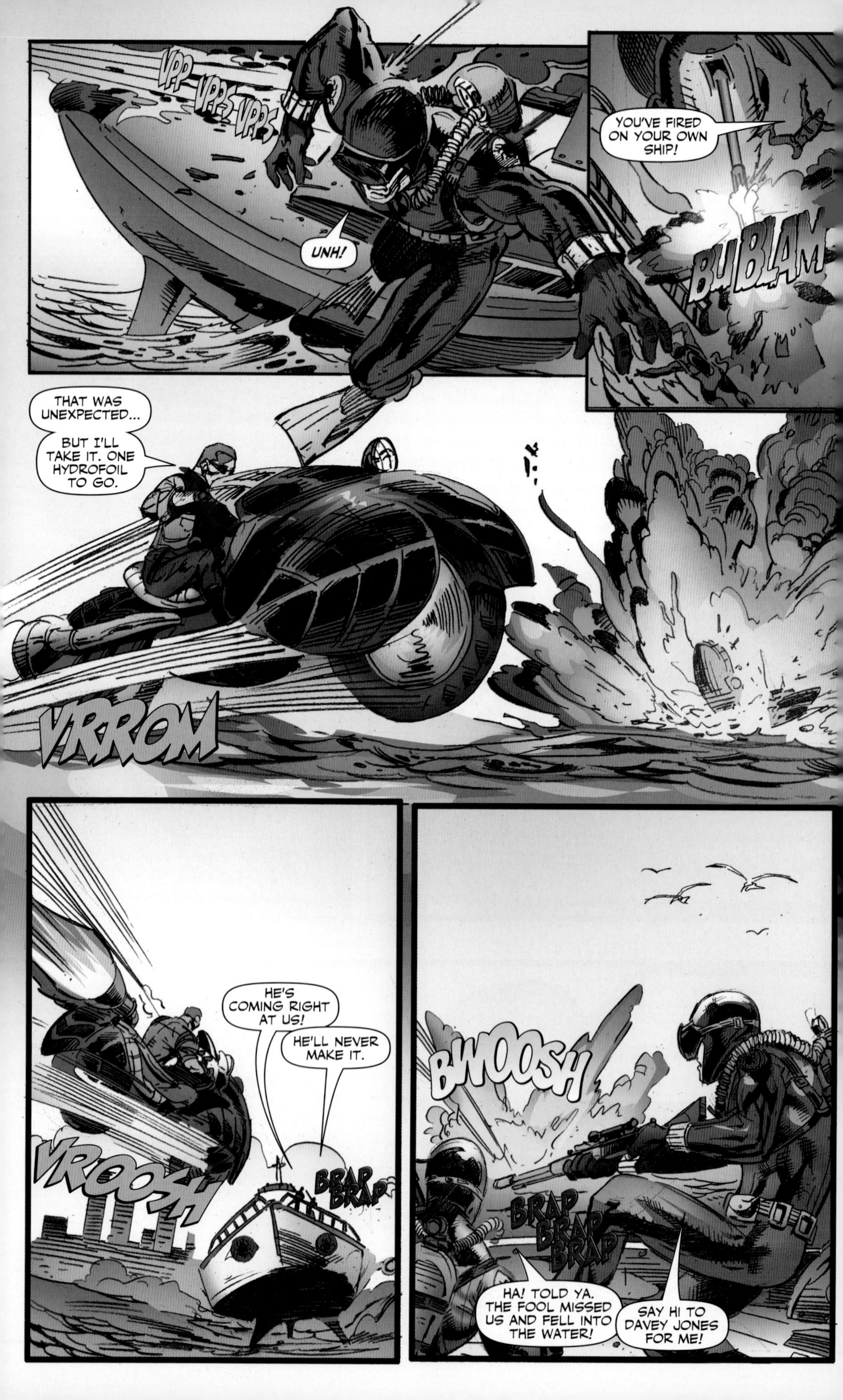
VPP VPPS VPPS
UNH!
YOU'VE FIRED ON YOUR OWN SHIP!
BUBLAM
THAT WAS UNEXPECTED...
BUT I'LL TAKE IT. ONE HYDROFOIL TO GO.
VRROM
HE'S COMING RIGHT AT US!
HE'LL NEVER MAKE IT.
VROOSH
BRAP BRAP
BWOOSH
BRAP BRAP BRAP
HA! TOLD YA. THE FOOL MISSED US AND FELL INTO THE WATER!
SAY HI TO DAVEY JONES FOR ME!

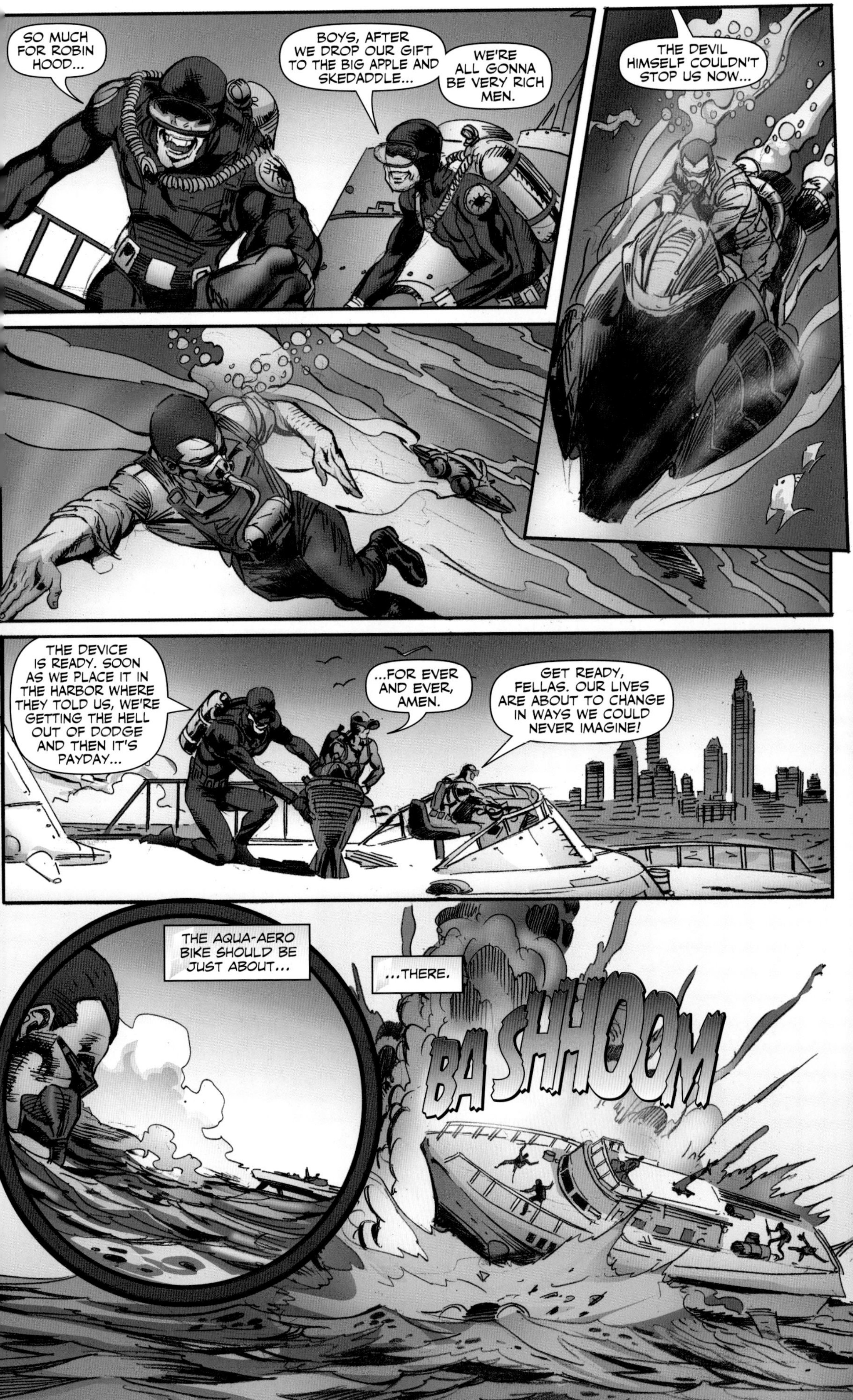
SO MUCH FOR ROBIN HOOD...
BOYS, AFTER WE DROP OUR GIFT TO THE BIG APPLE AND SKEDADDLE...
WE'RE ALL GONNA BE VERY RICH MEN.
THE DEVIL HIMSELF COULDN'T STOP US NOW...
THE DEVICE IS READY. SOON AS WE PLACE IT IN THE HARBOR WHERE THEY TOLD US, WE'RE GETTING THE HELL OUT OF DODGE AND THEN IT'S PAYDAY...
...FOR EVER AND EVER, AMEN.
GET READY, FELLAS. OUR LIVES ARE ABOUT TO CHANGE IN WAYS WE COULD NEVER IMAGINE!
THE AQUA-AERO BIKE SHOULD BE JUST ABOUT...
...THERE.
BA SHHOOM

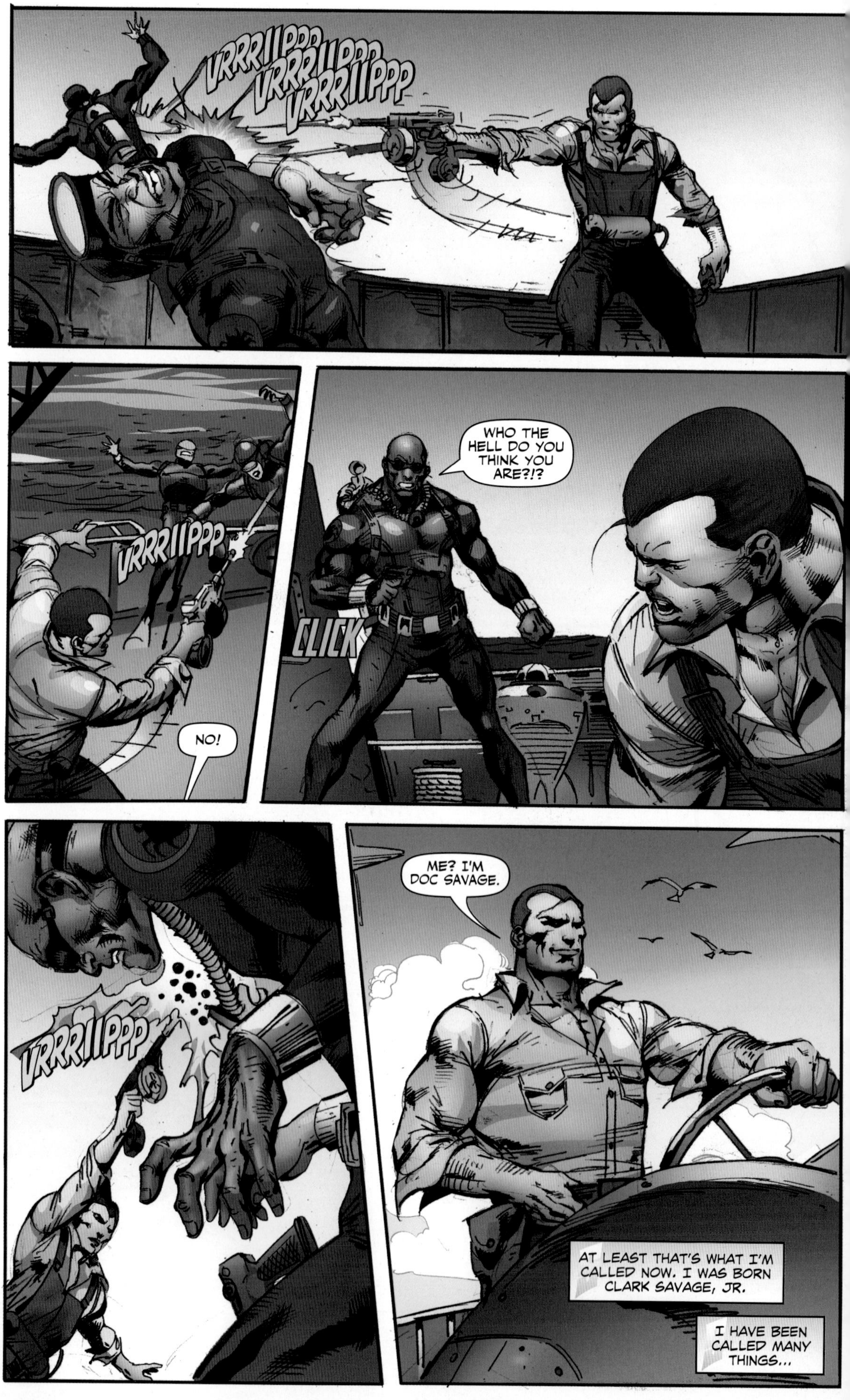

VRRRIIPPP
VRRRIIPPP
VRRRIIPPP
VRRRIIPPP
NO!
WHO THE HELL DO YOU THINK YOU ARE?!?
CLICK
VRRRIIPPP
ME? I'M DOC SAVAGE.
AT LEAST THAT'S WHAT I'M CALLED NOW. I WAS BORN CLARK SAVAGE, JR.
I HAVE BEEN CALLED MANY THINGS...

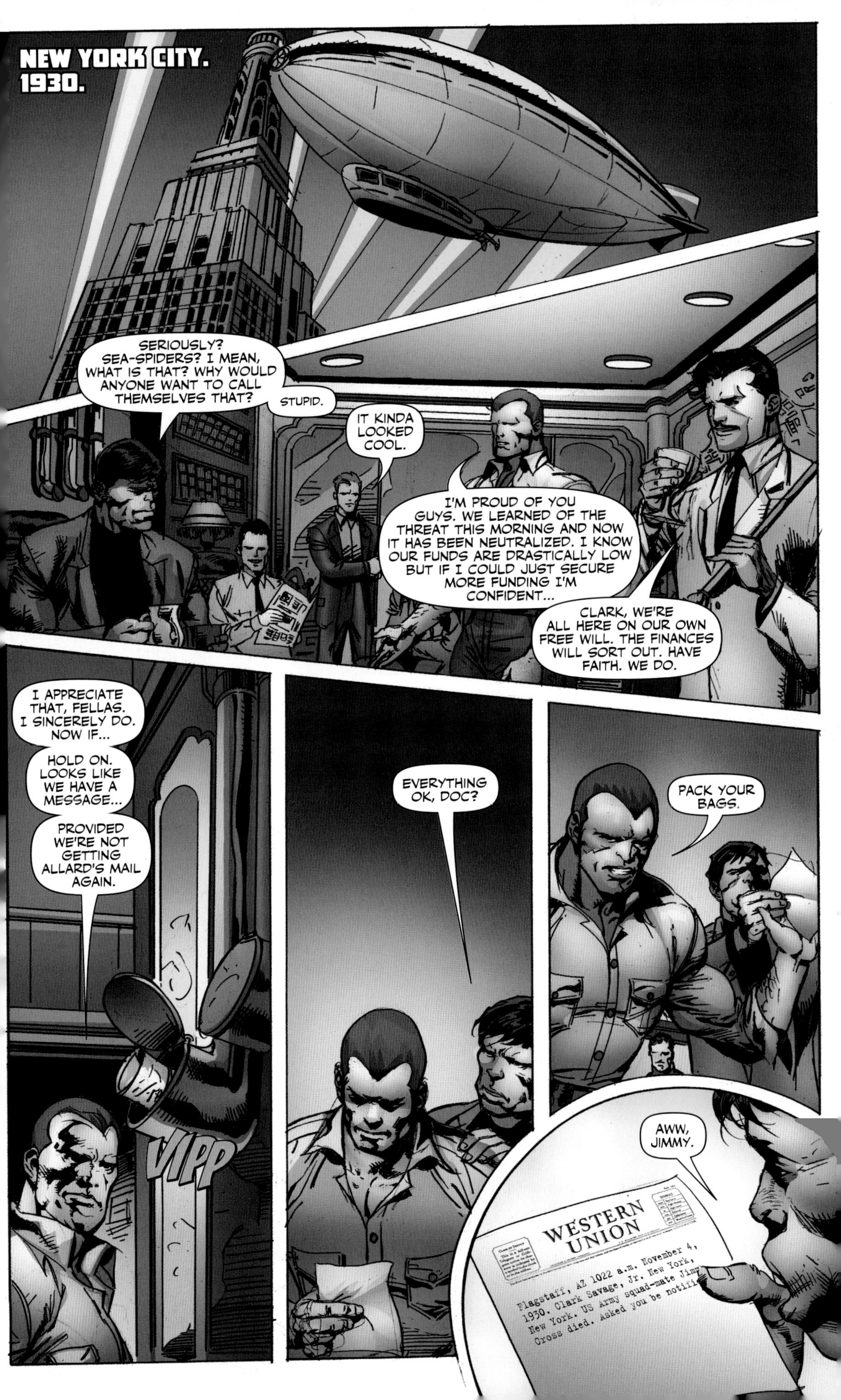
NEW YORK CITY. 1930.
SERIOUSLY? SEA-SPIDERS? I MEAN, WHAT IS THAT? WHY WOULD ANYONE WANT TO CALL THEMSELVES THAT?
STUPID.
IT KINDA LOOKED COOL.
I'M PROUD OF YOU GUYS. WE LEARNED OF THE THREAT THIS MORNING AND NOW IT HAS BEEN NEUTRALIZED. I KNOW OUR FUNDS ARE DRASTICALLY LOW BUT IF I COULD JUST SECURE MORE FUNDING I'M CONFIDENT...
CLARK, WE'RE ALL HERE ON OUR OWN FREE WILL. THE FINANCES WILL SORT OUT. HAVE FAITH. WE DO.
I APPRECIATE THAT, FELLAS. I SINCERELY DO. NOW IF...
HOLD ON. LOOKS LIKE WE HAVE A MESSAGE...
PROVIDED WE'RE NOT GETTING ALLARD'S MAIL AGAIN.
VIPP
EVERYTHING OK, DOC?
PACK YOUR BAGS.
AWW, JIMMY.
WESTERN UNION
Flagstaff, AZ 1022 a.m. November 4, 1930. Clark Savage, Jr. New York, New York. US Army squad-mate Jimmy Cross died. Asked you be notifi

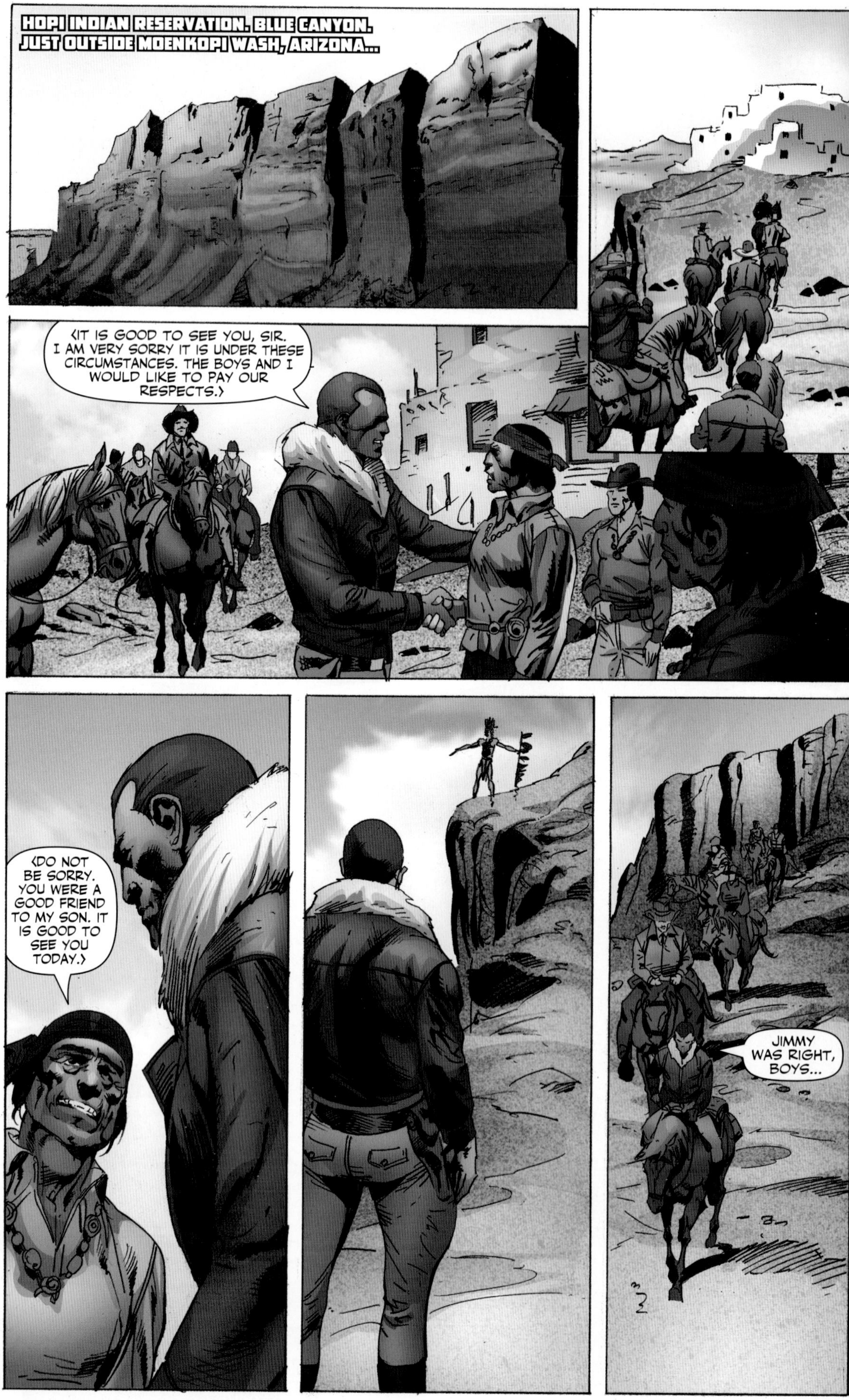

HOPI INDIAN RESERVATION. BLUE CANYON.
JUST OUTSIDE MOENKOPI WASH, ARIZONA...
<IT IS GOOD TO SEE YOU, SIR. I AM VERY SORRY IT IS UNDER THESE CIRCUMSTANCES. THE BOYS AND I WOULD LIKE TO PAY OUR RESPECTS.>
<DO NOT BE SORRY. YOU WERE A GOOD FRIEND TO MY SON. IT IS GOOD TO SEE YOU TODAY.>
JIMMY WAS RIGHT, BOYS...

...SOME THINGS YOU HAVE TO SEE FOR YOURSELF.

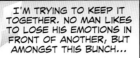

I'M TRYING TO KEEP IT TOGETHER. NO MAN LIKES TO LOSE HIS EMOTIONS IN FRONT OF ANOTHER, BUT AMONGST THIS BUNCH...

...WE'VE ALL SEEN IT BEFORE. YEARS AGO IN THE WAR ON AN UNIMAGINABLE SCALE. BUT DEATH, LIKE MOST THINGS, IS ALL THE MORE POWERFUL WHEN IT'S PERSONAL.

SO MANY EXPECT ME TO BE PERFECT. TO NOT MAKE MISTAKES. NO SUCH MAN EXISTS.

JOHNNY. WOULD YOU CARE TO SAY SOMETHING FOR THE GROUP?

I....I HAVE NO WORDS.

I'M AMONGST FRIENDS...AND AMONGST FRIENDS THERE IS NEVER ANY ASSUMPTION THAT WE'RE ANYTHING OTHER THAN WHO WE ARE. JUST THE BELIEF IN ONE ANOTHER...

IT'S OK. NONE OF US DO.

JIMMY, I'M GONNA MISS YOU.

..TO GET US THROUGH IN THOSE DARKEST MOMENTS WHEN THEIR BELIEF IN YOU IS ALL YOU HAVE LEFT TO HOLD ON TO...

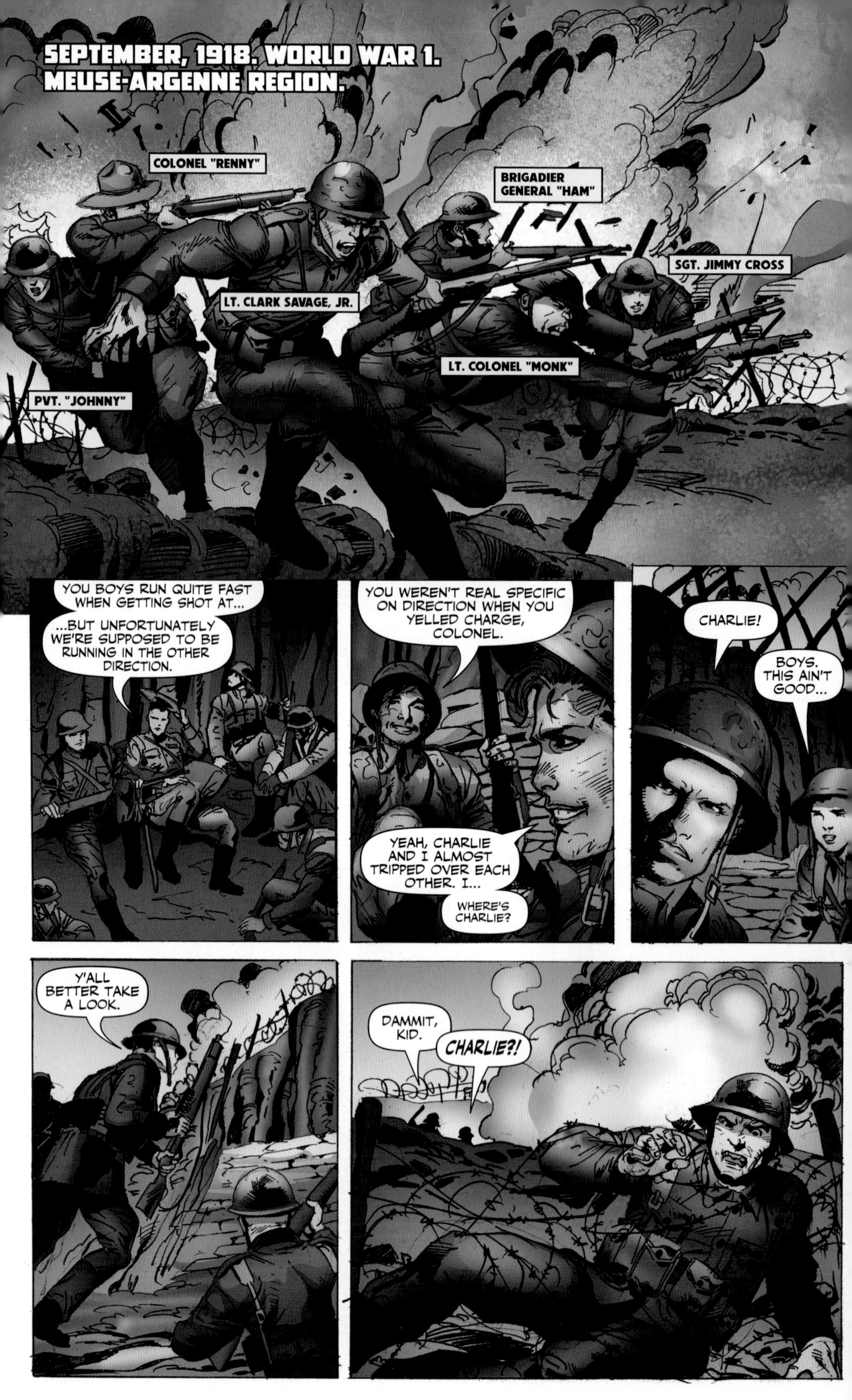
SEPTEMBER, 1918. WORLD WAR 1.
MEUSE-ARGENNE REGION.
COLONEL "RENNY"
BRIGADIER GENERAL "HAM"
SGT. JIMMY CROSS
LT. CLARK SAVAGE, JR.
LT. COLONEL "MONK"
PVT. "JOHNNY"
YOU BOYS RUN QUITE FAST WHEN GETTING SHOT AT...
...BUT UNFORTUNATELY WE'RE SUPPOSED TO BE RUNNING IN THE OTHER DIRECTION.
YOU WEREN'T REAL SPECIFIC ON DIRECTION WHEN YOU YELLED CHARGE, COLONEL.
YEAH, CHARLIE AND I ALMOST TRIPPED OVER EACH OTHER. I...
WHERE'S CHARLIE?
CHARLIE!
BOYS. THIS AIN'T GOOD...
Y'ALL BETTER TAKE A LOOK.
DAMMIT, KID.
CHARLIE?!

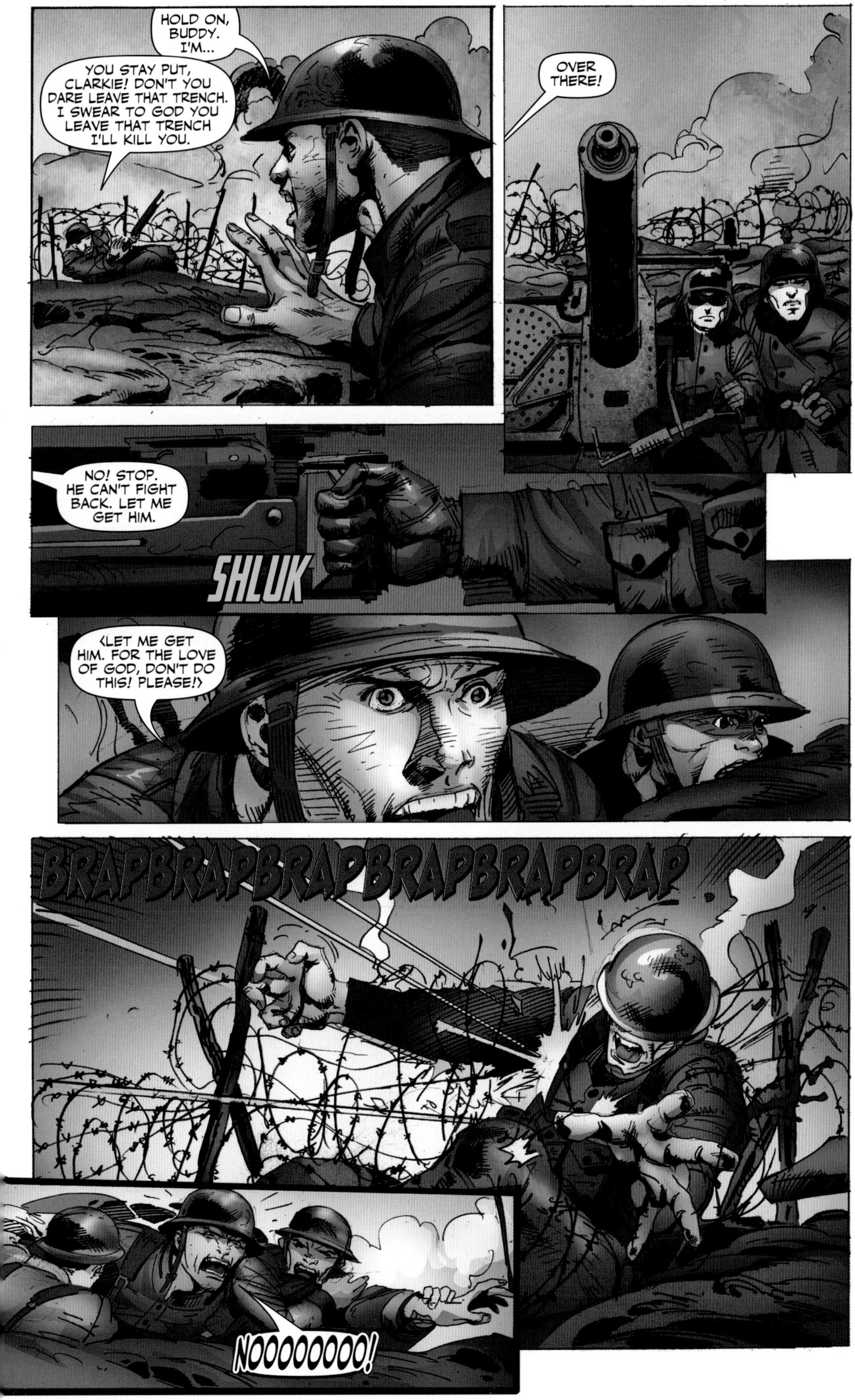
HOLD ON, BUDDY. I'M...
YOU STAY PUT, CLARKIE! DON'T YOU DARE LEAVE THAT TRENCH. I SWEAR TO GOD YOU LEAVE THAT TRENCH I'LL KILL YOU.
OVER THERE!
NO! STOP. HE CAN'T FIGHT BACK. LET ME GET HIM.
SHLUK
<LET ME GET HIM. FOR THE LOVE OF GOD, DON'T DO THIS! PLEASE!>
BRAPBRAPBRAPBRAPBRAPBRAP
NOOOOOOOO!

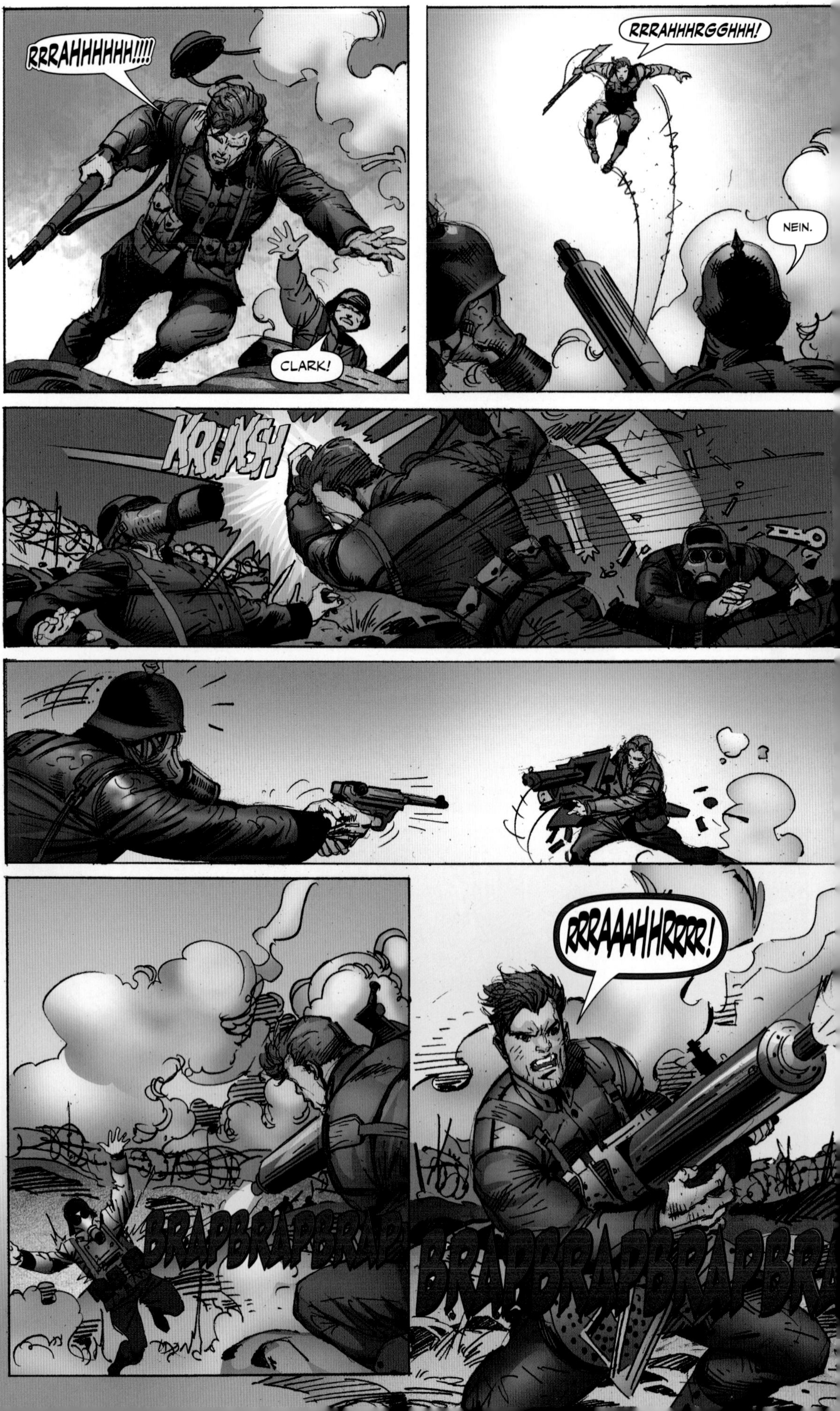
RRRAHHHHHH!!!!
CLARK!
RRRAHHHRGGHHH!
NEIN.
KRUNSH
RRRAAAHHRRRR!
BRAPBRAPBRAP
BRAPBRAPBRAPBRA

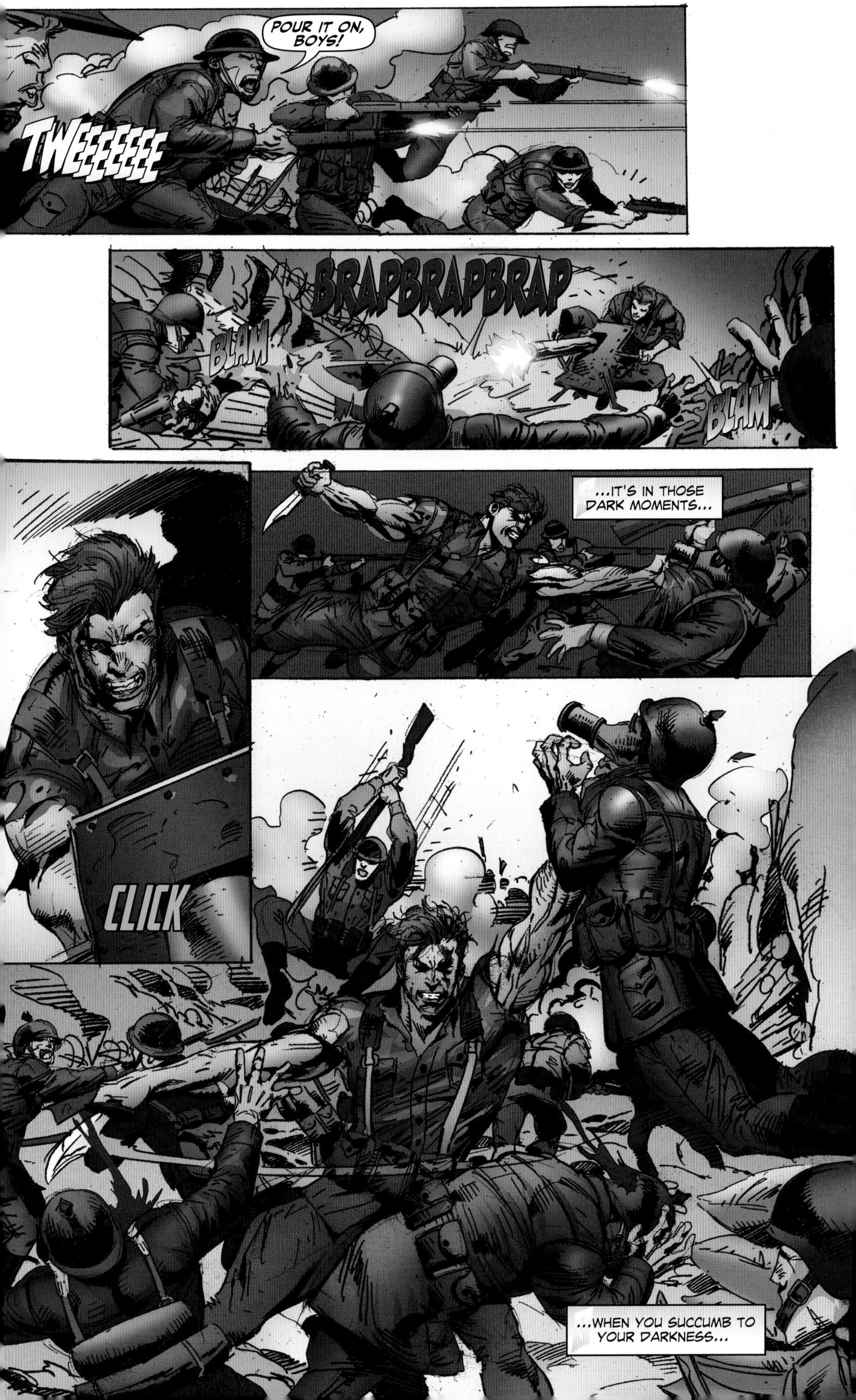
POUR IT ON, BOYS!
TWEEEEEEE
BRAPBRAPBRAP
BLAM
BLAM
CLICK
...IT'S IN THOSE DARK MOMENTS...
...WHEN YOU SUCCUMB TO YOUR DARKNESS...

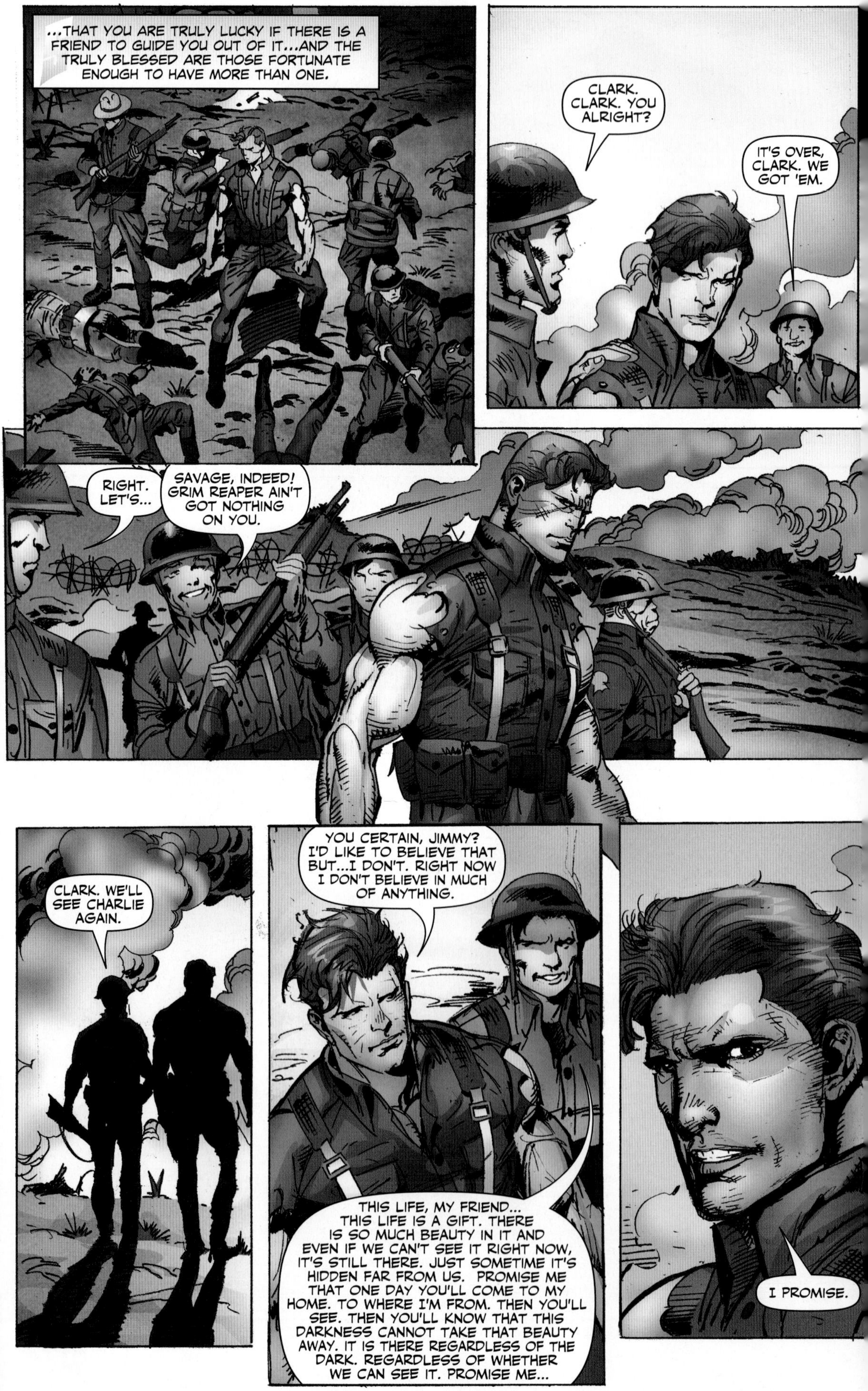
...THAT YOU ARE TRULY LUCKY IF THERE IS A FRIEND TO GUIDE YOU OUT OF IT...AND THE TRULY BLESSED ARE THOSE FORTUNATE ENOUGH TO HAVE MORE THAN ONE.
CLARK. CLARK. YOU ALRIGHT?
IT'S OVER, CLARK. WE GOT 'EM.
RIGHT. LET'S...
SAVAGE, INDEED! GRIM REAPER AIN'T GOT NOTHING ON YOU.
CLARK. WE'LL SEE CHARLIE AGAIN.
YOU CERTAIN, JIMMY? I'D LIKE TO BELIEVE THAT BUT...I DON'T. RIGHT NOW I DON'T BELIEVE IN MUCH OF ANYTHING.
THIS LIFE, MY FRIEND... THIS LIFE IS A GIFT. THERE IS SO MUCH BEAUTY IN IT AND EVEN IF WE CAN'T SEE IT RIGHT NOW, IT'S STILL THERE. JUST SOMETIME IT'S HIDDEN FAR FROM US. PROMISE ME THAT ONE DAY YOU'LL COME TO MY HOME. TO WHERE I'M FROM. THEN YOU'LL SEE. THEN YOU'LL KNOW THAT THIS DARKNESS CANNOT TAKE THAT BEAUTY AWAY. IT IS THERE REGARDLESS OF THE DARK. REGARDLESS OF WHETHER WE CAN SEE IT. PROMISE ME...
I PROMISE.

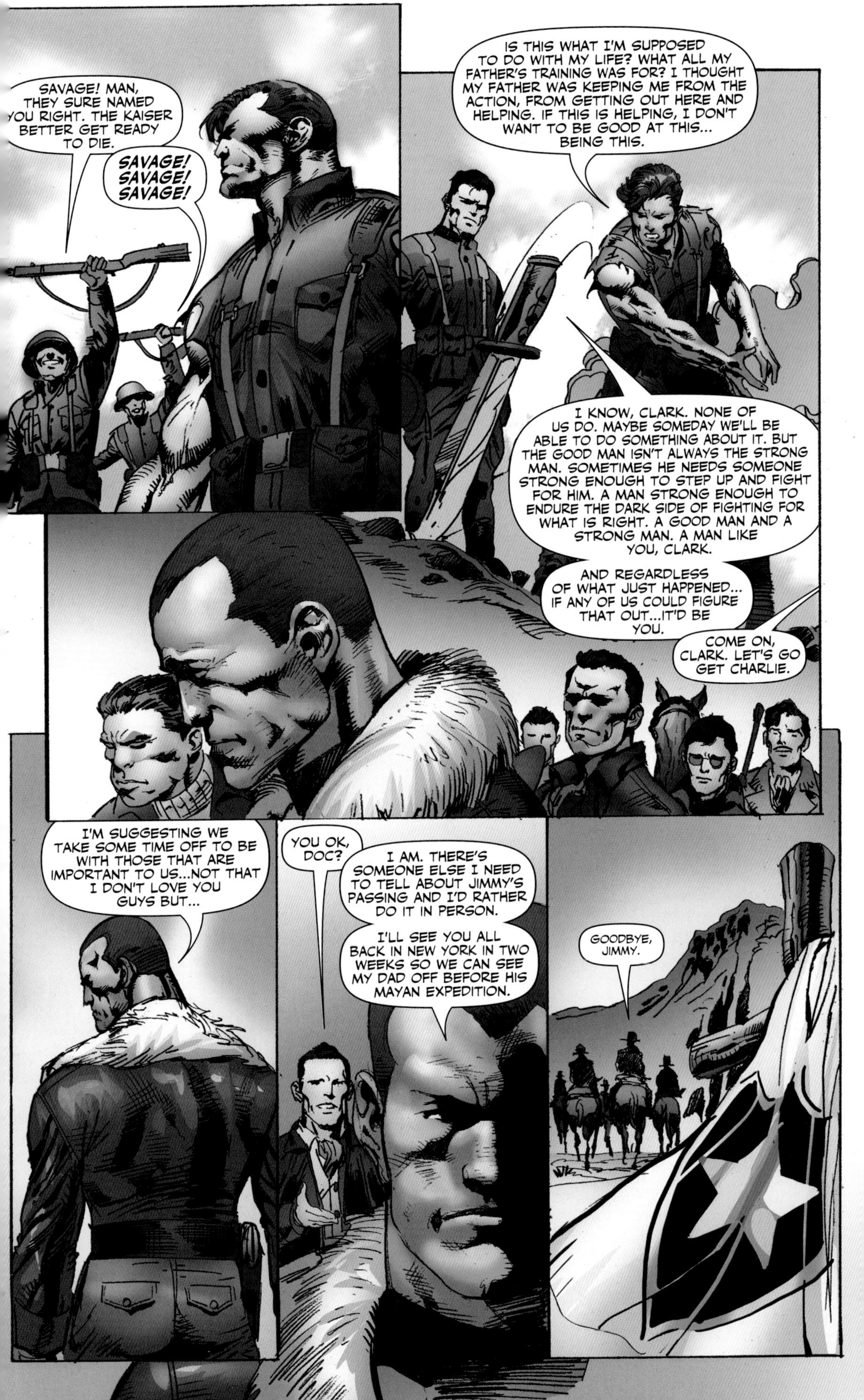
SAVAGE! MAN, THEY SURE NAMED YOU RIGHT. THE KAISER BETTER GET READY TO DIE.
SAVAGE! SAVAGE! SAVAGE!
IS THIS WHAT I'M SUPPOSED TO DO WITH MY LIFE? WHAT ALL MY FATHER'S TRAINING WAS FOR? I THOUGHT MY FATHER WAS KEEPING ME FROM THE ACTION, FROM GETTING OUT HERE AND HELPING. IF THIS IS HELPING, I DON'T WANT TO BE GOOD AT THIS... BEING THIS.
I KNOW, CLARK. NONE OF US DO. MAYBE SOMEDAY WE'LL BE ABLE TO DO SOMETHING ABOUT IT. BUT THE GOOD MAN ISN'T ALWAYS THE STRONG MAN. SOMETIMES HE NEEDS SOMEONE STRONG ENOUGH TO STEP UP AND FIGHT FOR HIM. A MAN STRONG ENOUGH TO ENDURE THE DARK SIDE OF FIGHTING FOR WHAT IS RIGHT. A GOOD MAN AND A STRONG MAN. A MAN LIKE YOU, CLARK.
AND REGARDLESS OF WHAT JUST HAPPENED... IF ANY OF US COULD FIGURE THAT OUT...IT'D BE YOU.
COME ON, CLARK. LET'S GO GET CHARLIE.
I'M SUGGESTING WE TAKE SOME TIME OFF TO BE WITH THOSE THAT ARE IMPORTANT TO US...NOT THAT I DON'T LOVE YOU GUYS BUT...
YOU OK, DOC?
I AM. THERE'S SOMEONE ELSE I NEED TO TELL ABOUT JIMMY'S PASSING AND I'D RATHER DO IT IN PERSON.
I'LL SEE YOU ALL BACK IN NEW YORK IN TWO WEEKS SO WE CAN SEE MY DAD OFF BEFORE HIS MAYAN EXPEDITION.
GOODBYE, JIMMY.

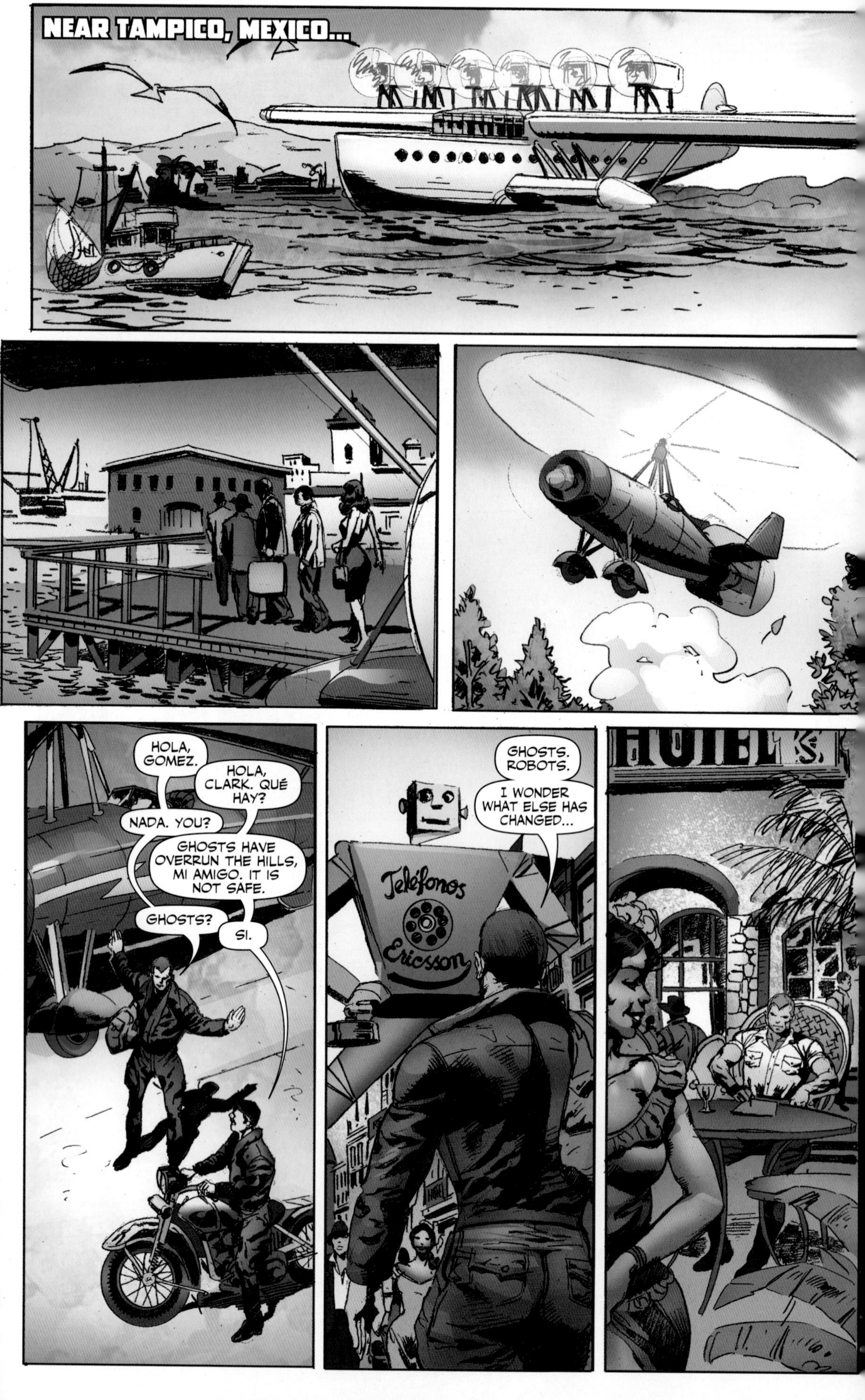
NEAR TAMPICO, MEXICO...
HOLA, GOMEZ.
HOLA, CLARK. QUÉ HAY?
NADA. YOU?
GHOSTS HAVE OVERRUN THE HILLS, MI AMIGO. IT IS NOT SAFE.
GHOSTS?
SI.
Teléfonos
Ericsson
GHOSTS. ROBOTS.
I WONDER WHAT ELSE HAS CHANGED...
HOTEL

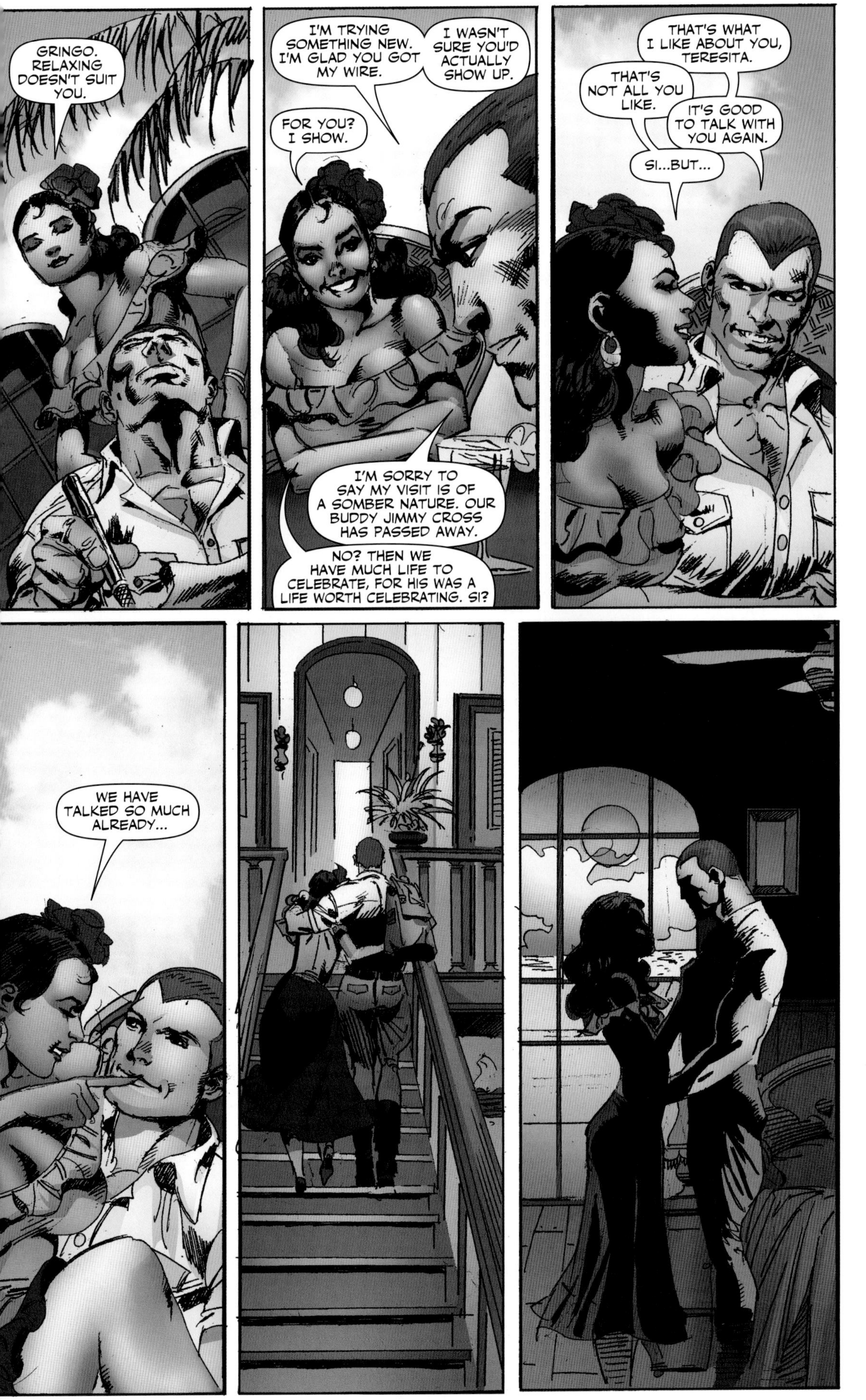
GRINGO. RELAXING DOESN'T SUIT YOU.
I'M TRYING SOMETHING NEW. I'M GLAD YOU GOT MY WIRE.
I WASN'T SURE YOU'D ACTUALLY SHOW UP.
FOR YOU? I SHOW.
I'M SORRY TO SAY MY VISIT IS OF A SOMBER NATURE. OUR BUDDY JIMMY CROSS HAS PASSED AWAY.
NO? THEN WE HAVE MUCH LIFE TO CELEBRATE, FOR HIS WAS A LIFE WORTH CELEBRATING. SI?
THAT'S WHAT I LIKE ABOUT YOU, TERESITA.
THAT'S NOT ALL YOU LIKE.
IT'S GOOD TO TALK WITH YOU AGAIN.
SI...BUT...
WE HAVE TALKED SO MUCH ALREADY...

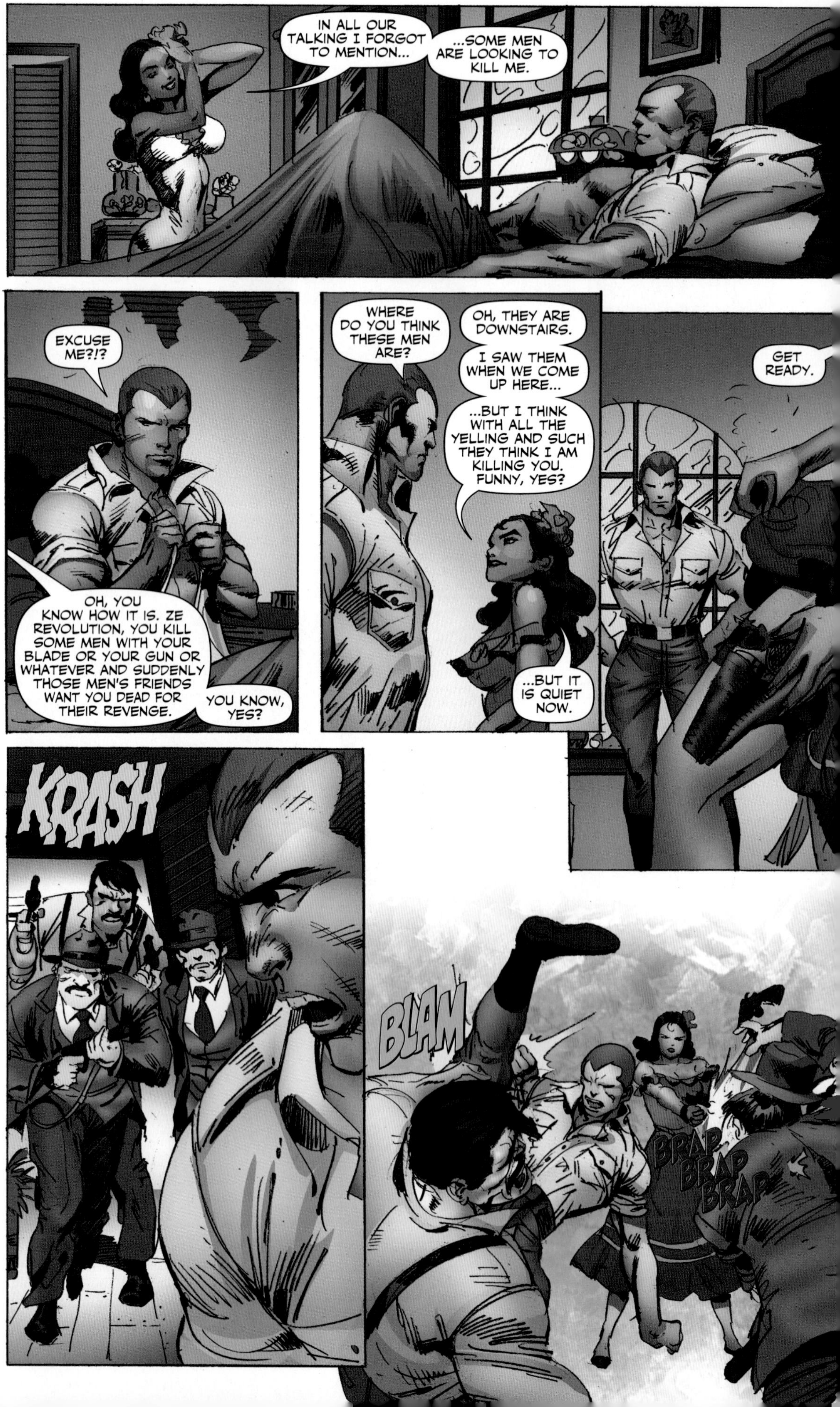
IN ALL OUR TALKING I FORGOT TO MENTION...
...SOME MEN ARE LOOKING TO KILL ME.
EXCUSE ME?!?
OH, YOU KNOW HOW IT IS. ZE REVOLUTION, YOU KILL SOME MEN WITH YOUR BLADE OR YOUR GUN OR WHATEVER AND SUDDENLY THOSE MEN'S FRIENDS WANT YOU DEAD FOR THEIR REVENGE.
YOU KNOW, YES?
WHERE DO YOU THINK THESE MEN ARE?
OH, THEY ARE DOWNSTAIRS.
I SAW THEM WHEN WE COME UP HERE...
...BUT I THINK WITH ALL THE YELLING AND SUCH THEY THINK I AM KILLING YOU. FUNNY, YES?
...BUT IT IS QUIET NOW.
GET READY.
KRASH
BLAM
BRAP BRAP BRAP

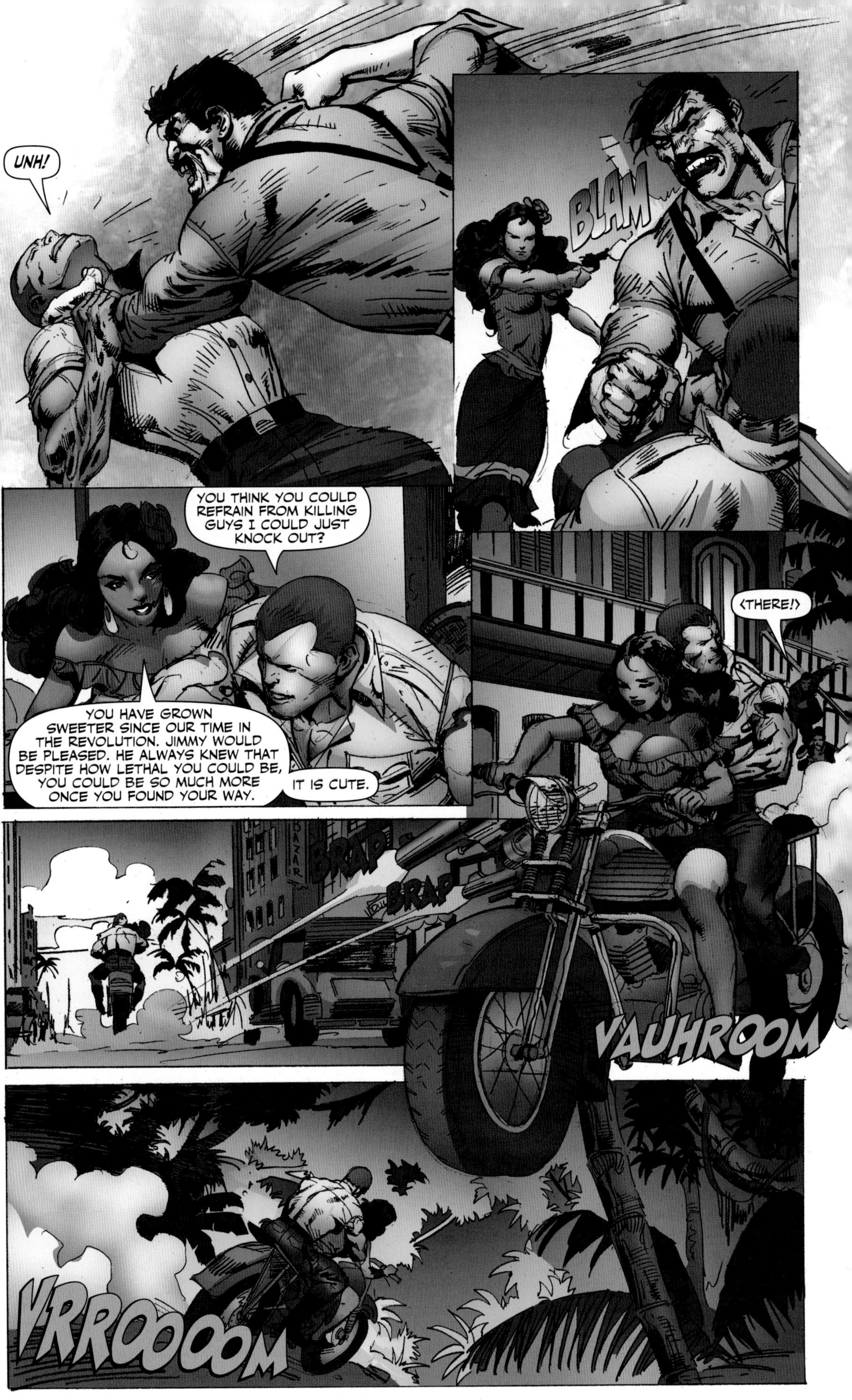
UNH!
BLAM
YOU THINK YOU COULD REFRAIN FROM KILLING GUYS I COULD JUST KNOCK OUT?
YOU HAVE GROWN SWEETER SINCE OUR TIME IN THE REVOLUTION. JIMMY WOULD BE PLEASED. HE ALWAYS KNEW THAT DESPITE HOW LETHAL YOU COULD BE, YOU COULD BE SO MUCH MORE ONCE YOU FOUND YOUR WAY.
IT IS CUTE.
<THERE!>
BRAP
BRAP
VAUHROOM
VRROOOOM

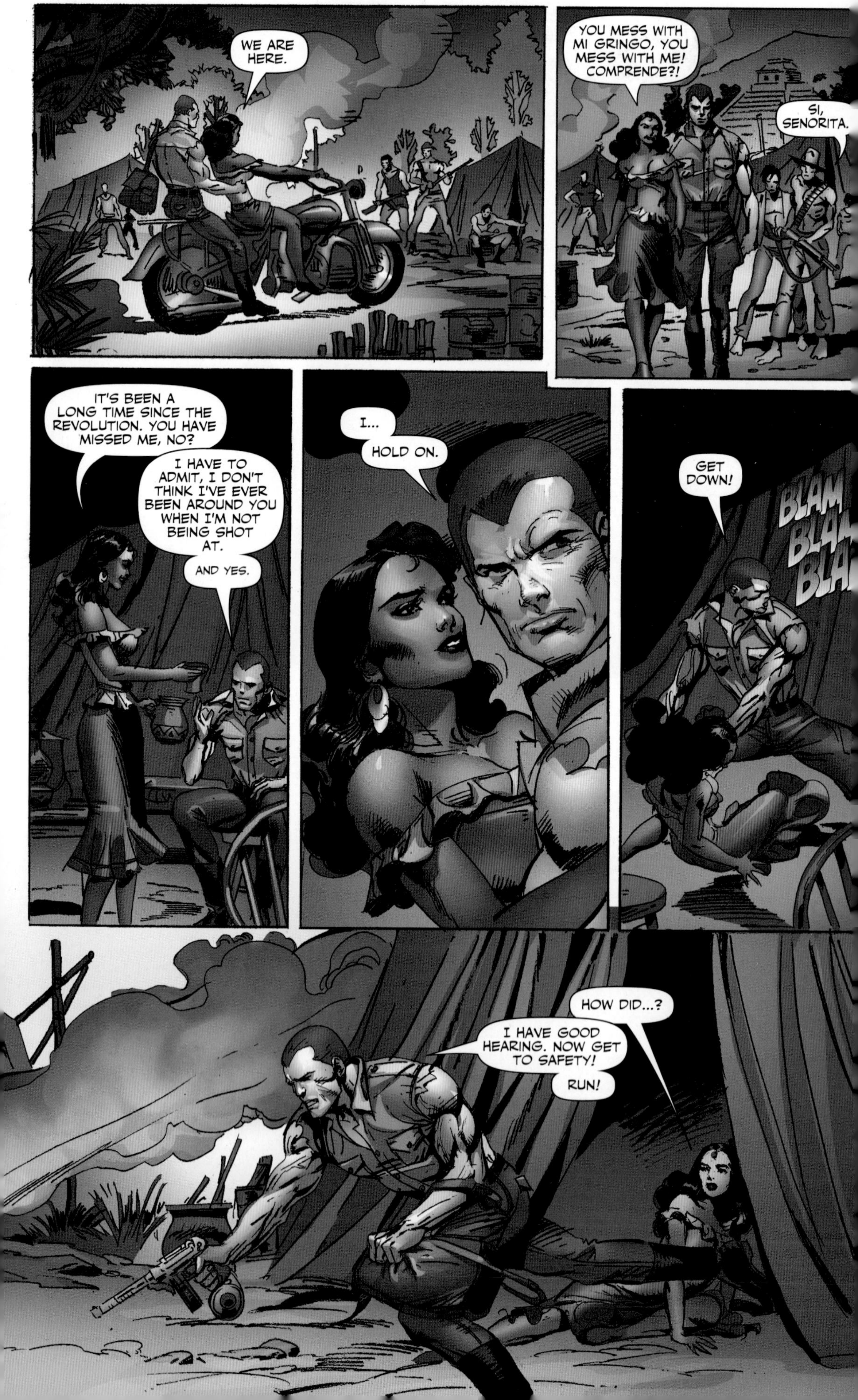
WE ARE HERE.
YOU MESS WITH MI GRINGO, YOU MESS WITH ME! COMPRENDE?!
SI, SENORITA.
IT'S BEEN A LONG TIME SINCE THE REVOLUTION. YOU HAVE MISSED ME, NO?
I HAVE TO ADMIT, I DON'T THINK I'VE EVER BEEN AROUND YOU WHEN I'M NOT BEING SHOT AT.
AND YES.
I...
HOLD ON.
GET DOWN!
HOW DID...?
I HAVE GOOD HEARING. NOW GET TO SAFETY!
RUN!

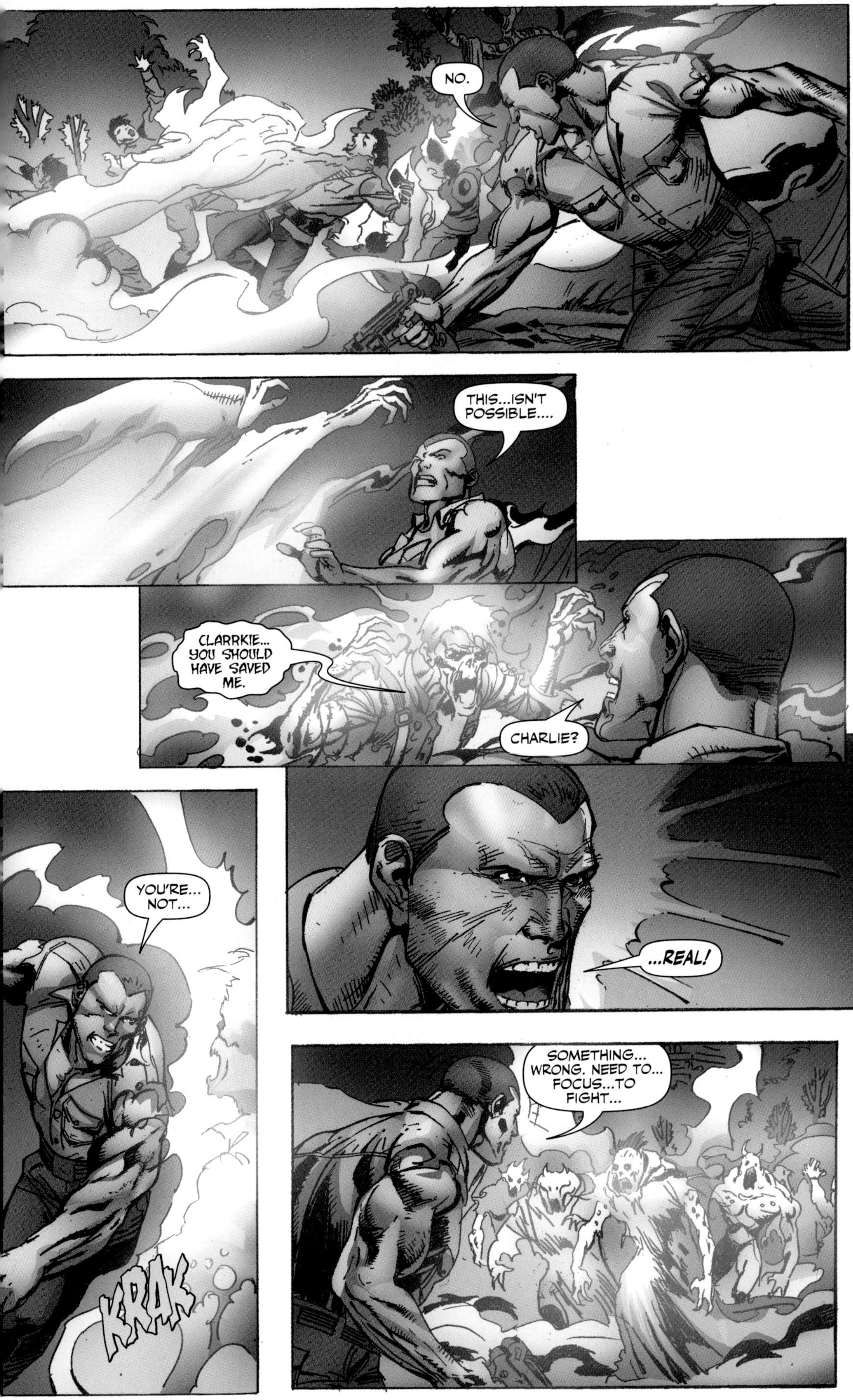

NO.
THIS...ISN'T POSSIBLE....
CLARRKIE... YOU SHOULD HAVE SAVED ME.
CHARLIE?
YOU'RE... NOT...
...REAL!
KRAK
SOMETHING... WRONG. NEED TO... FOCUS...TO FIGHT...

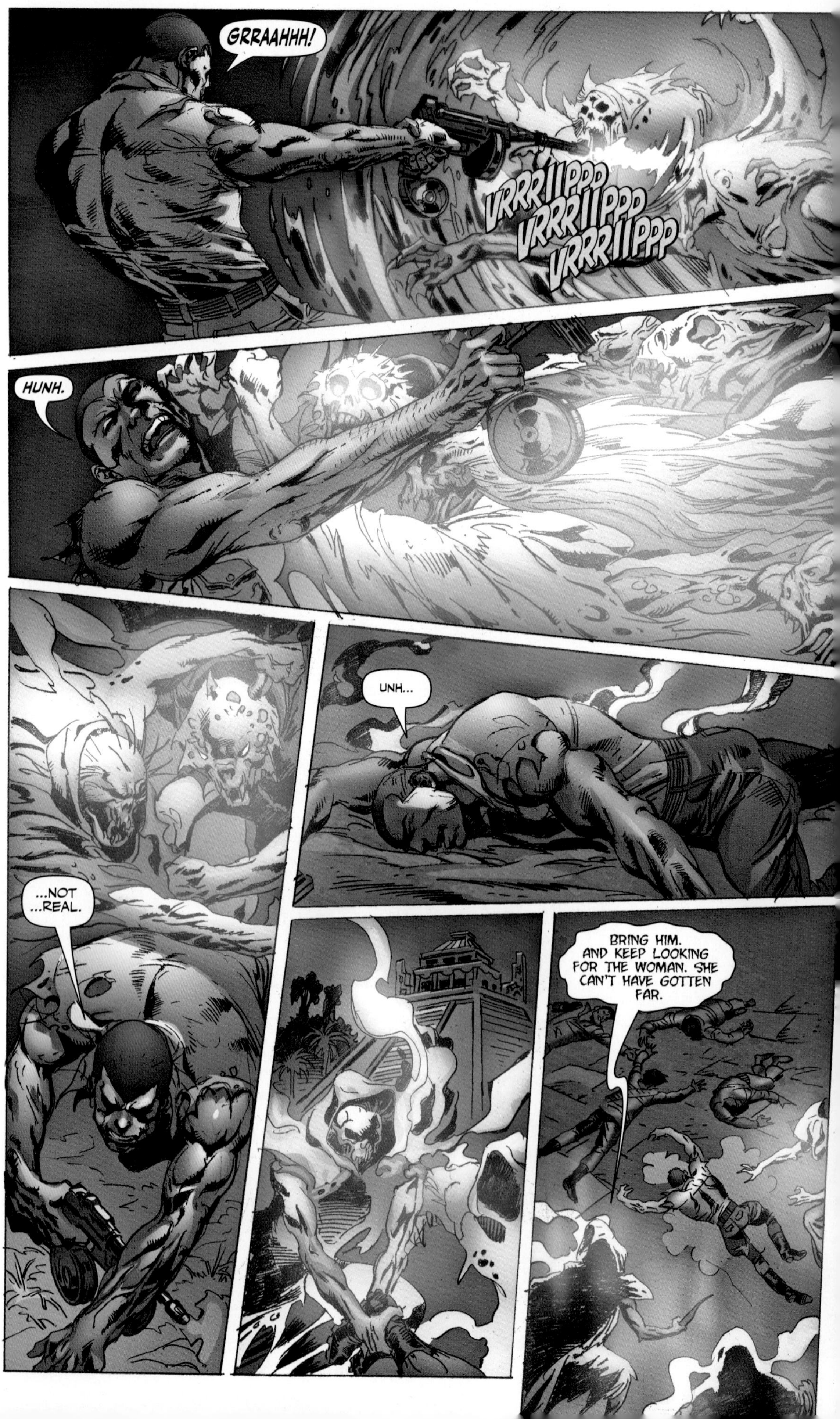
GRRAAHHH!
VRRRIIPPP
VRRRIIPPP
VRRRIIPPP
HUNH.
UNH...
...NOT
...REAL.
BRING HIM. AND KEEP LOOKING FOR THE WOMAN. SHE CAN'T HAVE GOTTEN FAR.

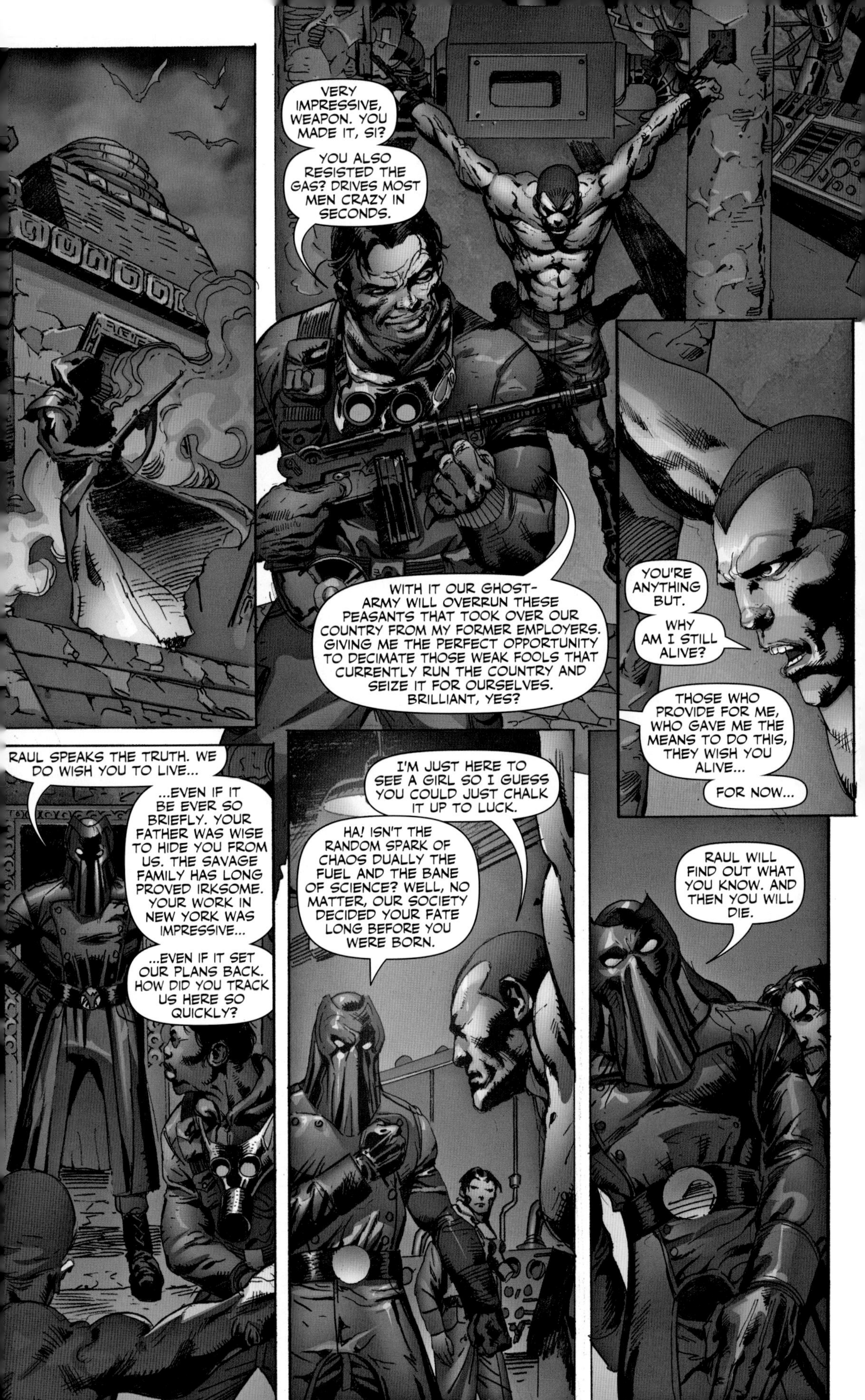
VERY IMPRESSIVE, WEAPON. YOU MADE IT, SI?
YOU ALSO RESISTED THE GAS? DRIVES MOST MEN CRAZY IN SECONDS.
WITH IT OUR GHOST-ARMY WILL OVERRUN THESE PEASANTS THAT TOOK OVER OUR COUNTRY FROM MY FORMER EMPLOYERS. GIVING ME THE PERFECT OPPORTUNITY TO DECIMATE THOSE WEAK FOOLS THAT CURRENTLY RUN THE COUNTRY AND SEIZE IT FOR OURSELVES. BRILLIANT, YES?
YOU'RE ANYTHING BUT.
WHY AM I STILL ALIVE?
THOSE WHO PROVIDE FOR ME, WHO GAVE ME THE MEANS TO DO THIS, THEY WISH YOU ALIVE...
FOR NOW...
RAUL SPEAKS THE TRUTH. WE DO WISH YOU TO LIVE...
...EVEN IF IT BE EVER SO BRIEFLY. YOUR FATHER WAS WISE TO HIDE YOU FROM US. THE SAVAGE FAMILY HAS LONG PROVED IRKSOME. YOUR WORK IN NEW YORK WAS IMPRESSIVE...
...EVEN IF IT SET OUR PLANS BACK. HOW DID YOU TRACK US HERE SO QUICKLY?
I'M JUST HERE TO SEE A GIRL SO I GUESS YOU COULD JUST CHALK IT UP TO LUCK.
HA! ISN'T THE RANDOM SPARK OF CHAOS DUALLY THE FUEL AND THE BANE OF SCIENCE? WELL, NO MATTER, OUR SOCIETY DECIDED YOUR FATE LONG BEFORE YOU WERE BORN.
RAUL WILL FIND OUT WHAT YOU KNOW. AND THEN YOU WILL DIE.

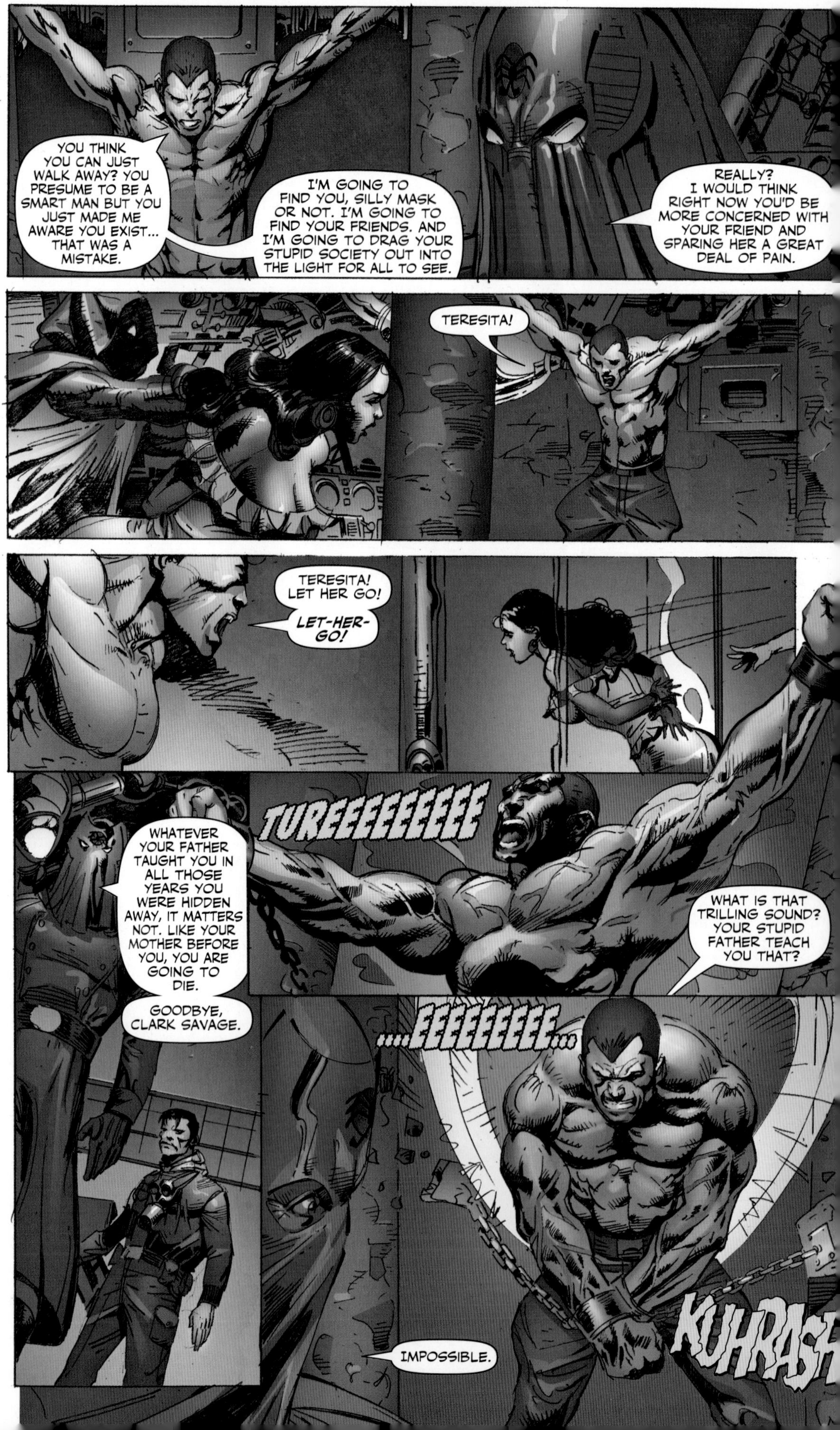
YOU THINK YOU CAN JUST WALK AWAY? YOU PRESUME TO BE A SMART MAN BUT YOU JUST MADE ME AWARE YOU EXIST... THAT WAS A MISTAKE.
I'M GOING TO FIND YOU, SILLY MASK OR NOT. I'M GOING TO FIND YOUR FRIENDS. AND I'M GOING TO DRAG YOUR STUPID SOCIETY OUT INTO THE LIGHT FOR ALL TO SEE.
REALLY? I WOULD THINK RIGHT NOW YOU'D BE MORE CONCERNED WITH YOUR FRIEND AND SPARING HER A GREAT DEAL OF PAIN.
TERESITA!
TERESITA! LET HER GO!
LET-HER-GO!
TUREEEEEEEEEE
WHATEVER YOUR FATHER TAUGHT YOU IN ALL THOSE YEARS YOU WERE HIDDEN AWAY, IT MATTERS NOT. LIKE YOUR MOTHER BEFORE YOU, YOU ARE GOING TO DIE.
WHAT IS THAT TRILLING SOUND? YOUR STUPID FATHER TEACH YOU THAT?
GOODBYE, CLARK SAVAGE.
...EEEEEEEEE...
IMPOSSIBLE.
KUHRASH

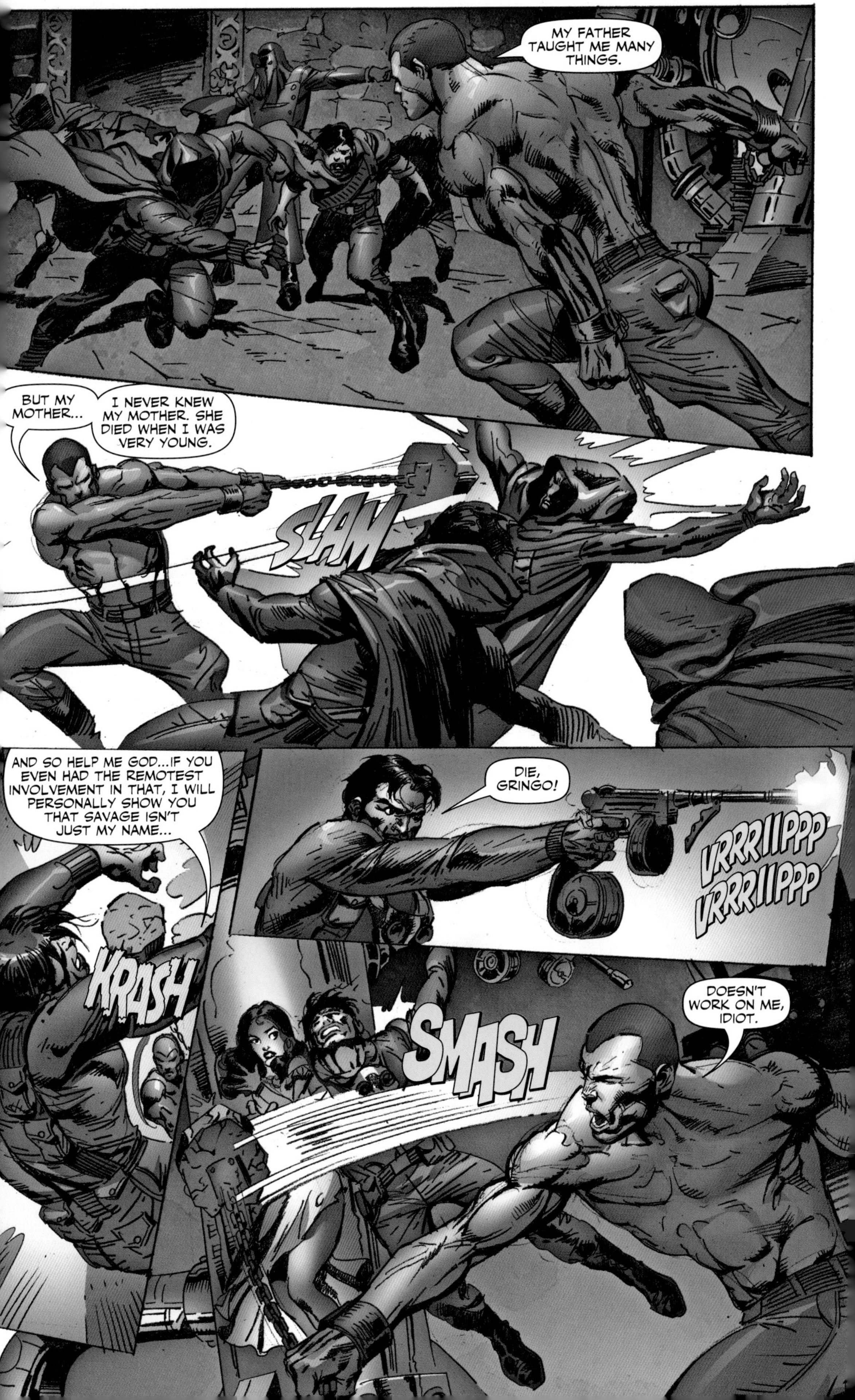
MY FATHER TAUGHT ME MANY THINGS.
BUT MY MOTHER...
I NEVER KNEW MY MOTHER. SHE DIED WHEN I WAS VERY YOUNG.
SLAM
AND SO HELP ME GOD...IF YOU EVEN HAD THE REMOTEST INVOLVEMENT IN THAT, I WILL PERSONALLY SHOW YOU THAT SAVAGE ISN'T JUST MY NAME...
DIE, GRINGO!
VRRRIIPPP
VRRRIIPPP
KRASH
SMASH
DOESN'T WORK ON ME, IDIOT.

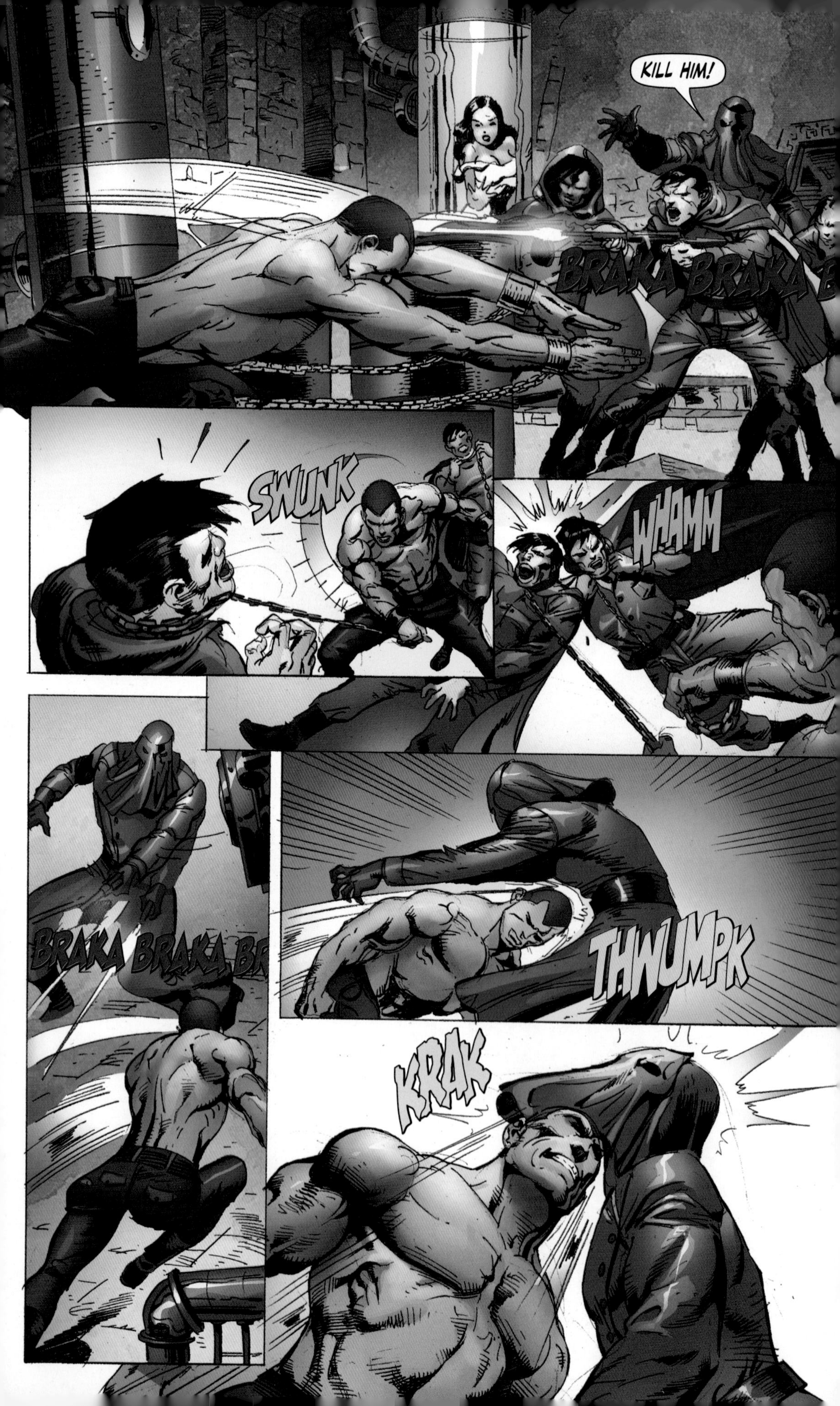
KILL HIM!
BRAKA BRAKA B
SWUNK
WHAMM
BRAKA BRAKA BR
THWUMPK
KRAK

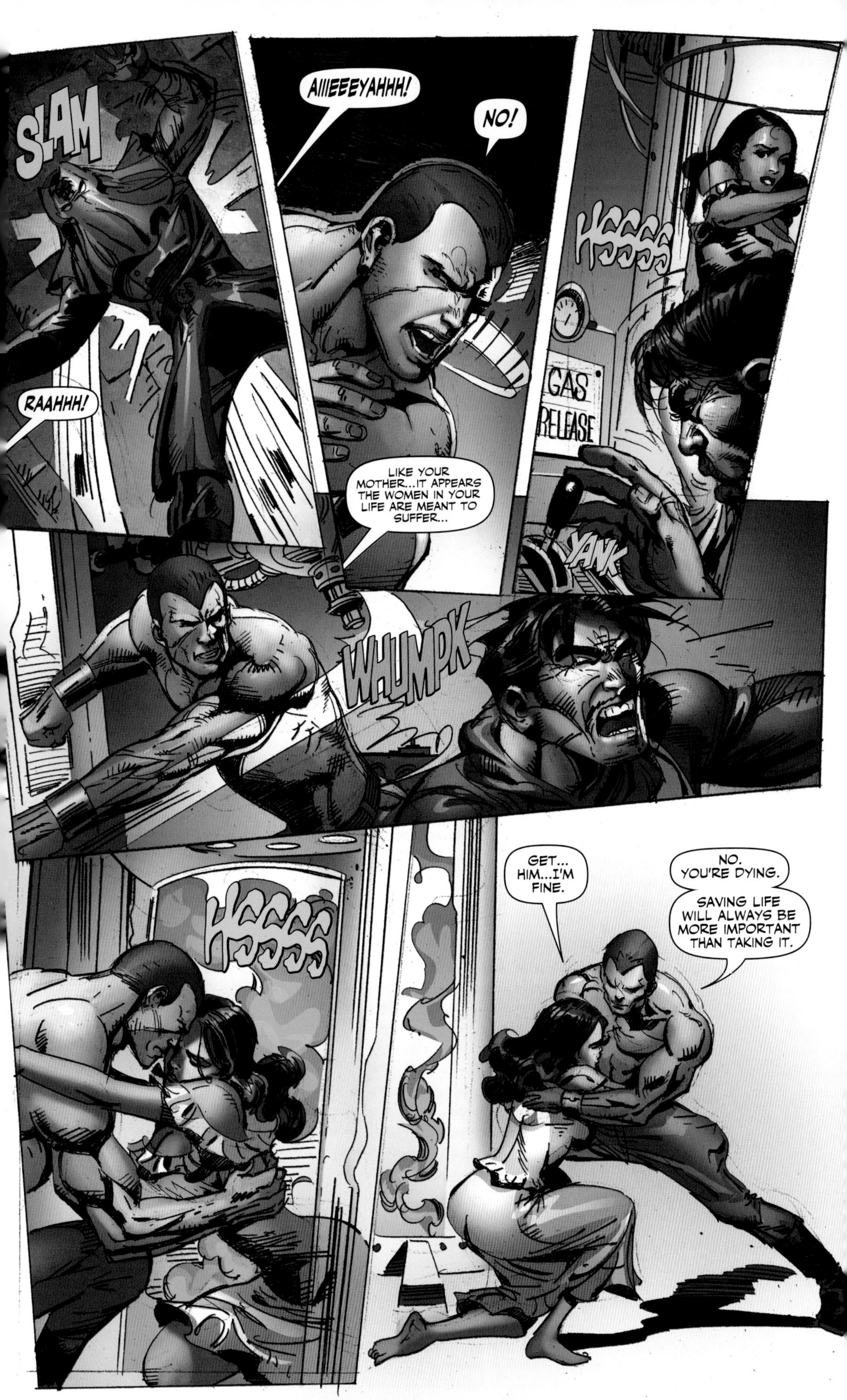
SLAM
RAAHHH!
AIIIEEEYAHHH!
NO!
LIKE YOUR MOTHER...IT APPEARS THE WOMEN IN YOUR LIFE ARE MEANT TO SUFFER...
HSSSS
GAS RELEASE
YANK
WHUMPK
HSSSS
GET... HIM...I'M FINE.
NO. YOU'RE DYING.
SAVING LIFE WILL ALWAYS BE MORE IMPORTANT THAN TAKING IT.

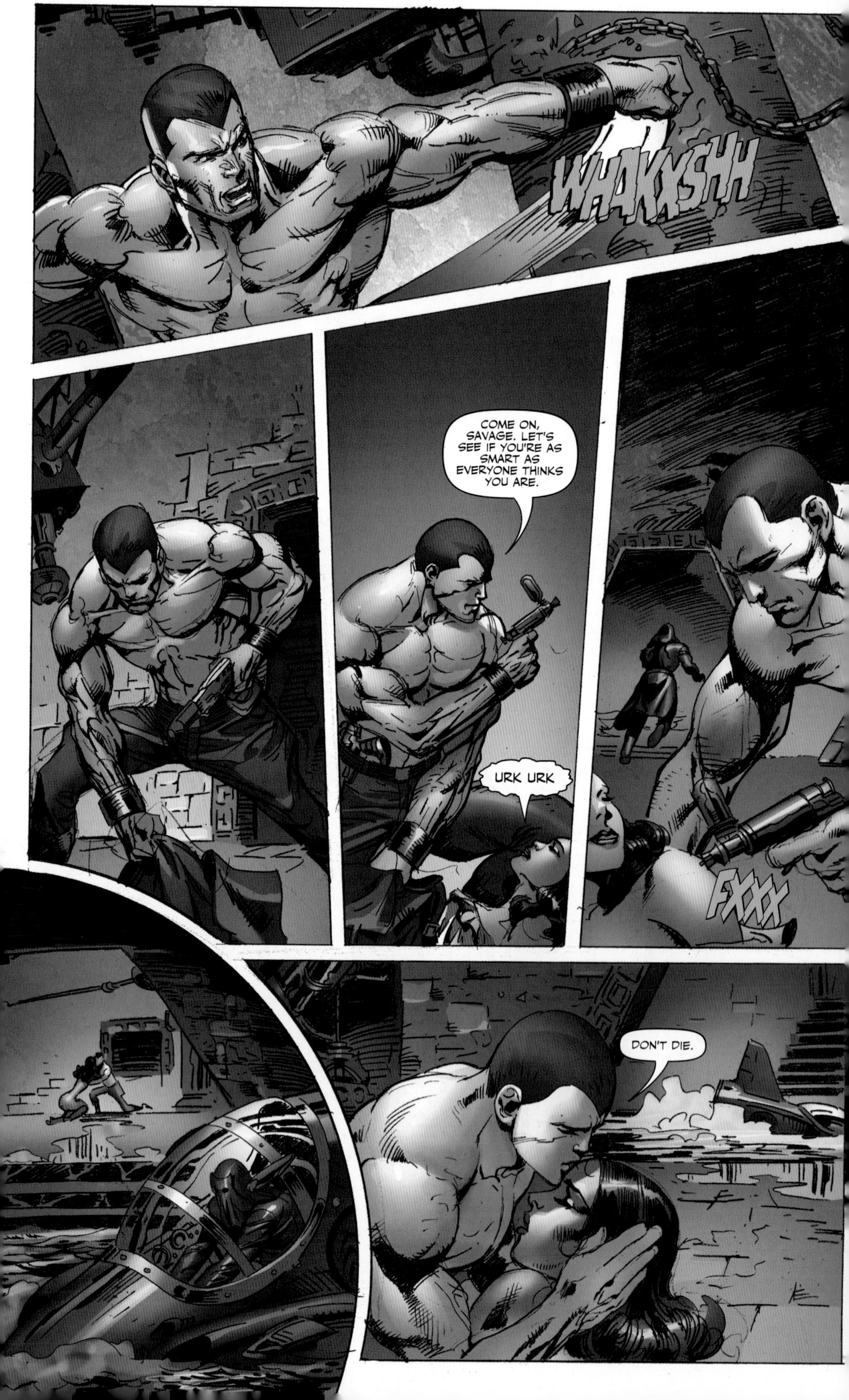
WHAKKSHH
COME ON, SAVAGE. LET'S SEE IF YOU'RE AS SMART AS EVERYONE THINKS YOU ARE.
URK URK
FXXX
DON'T DIE.

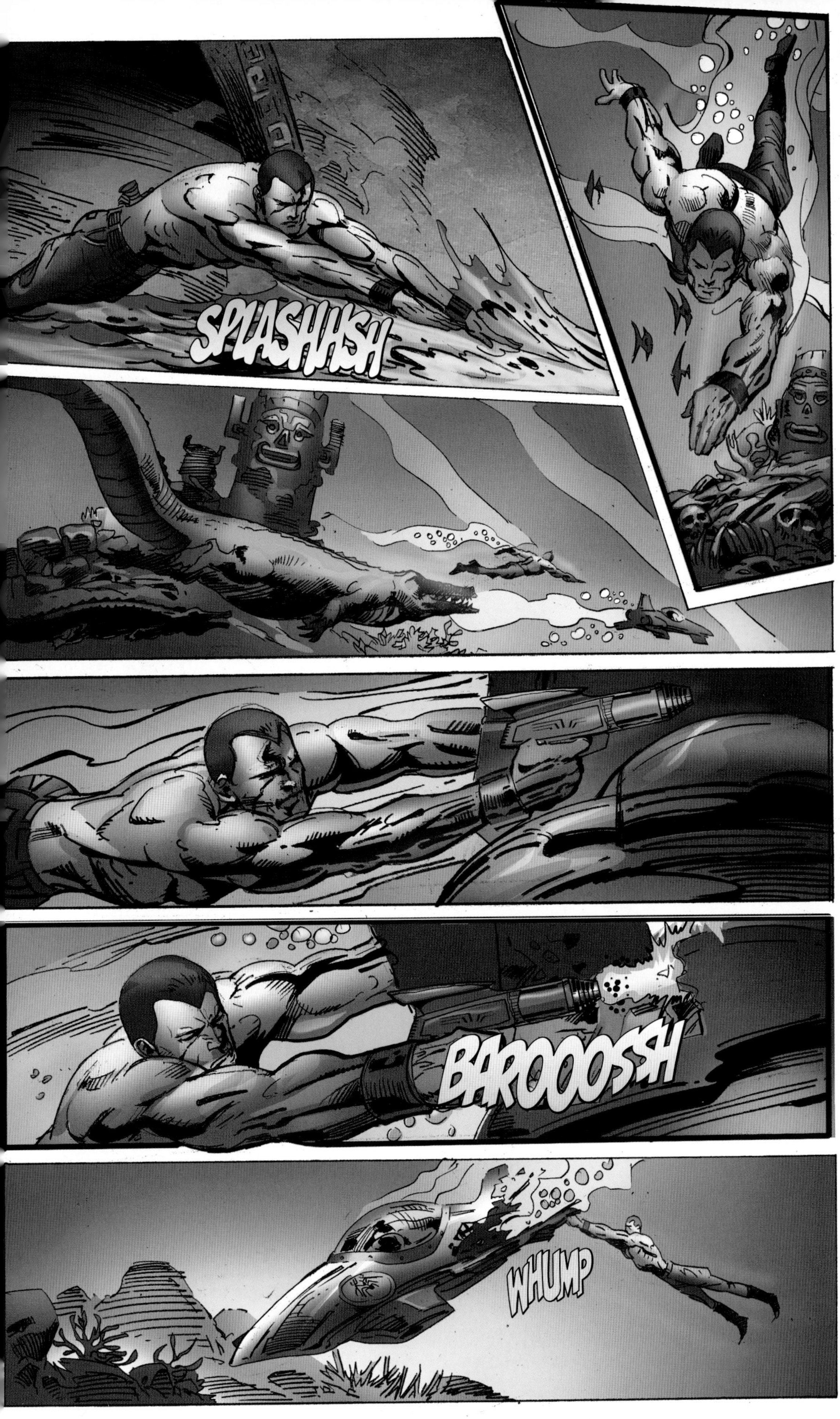
SPLASHHSH
BAROOOSSH
WHUMP

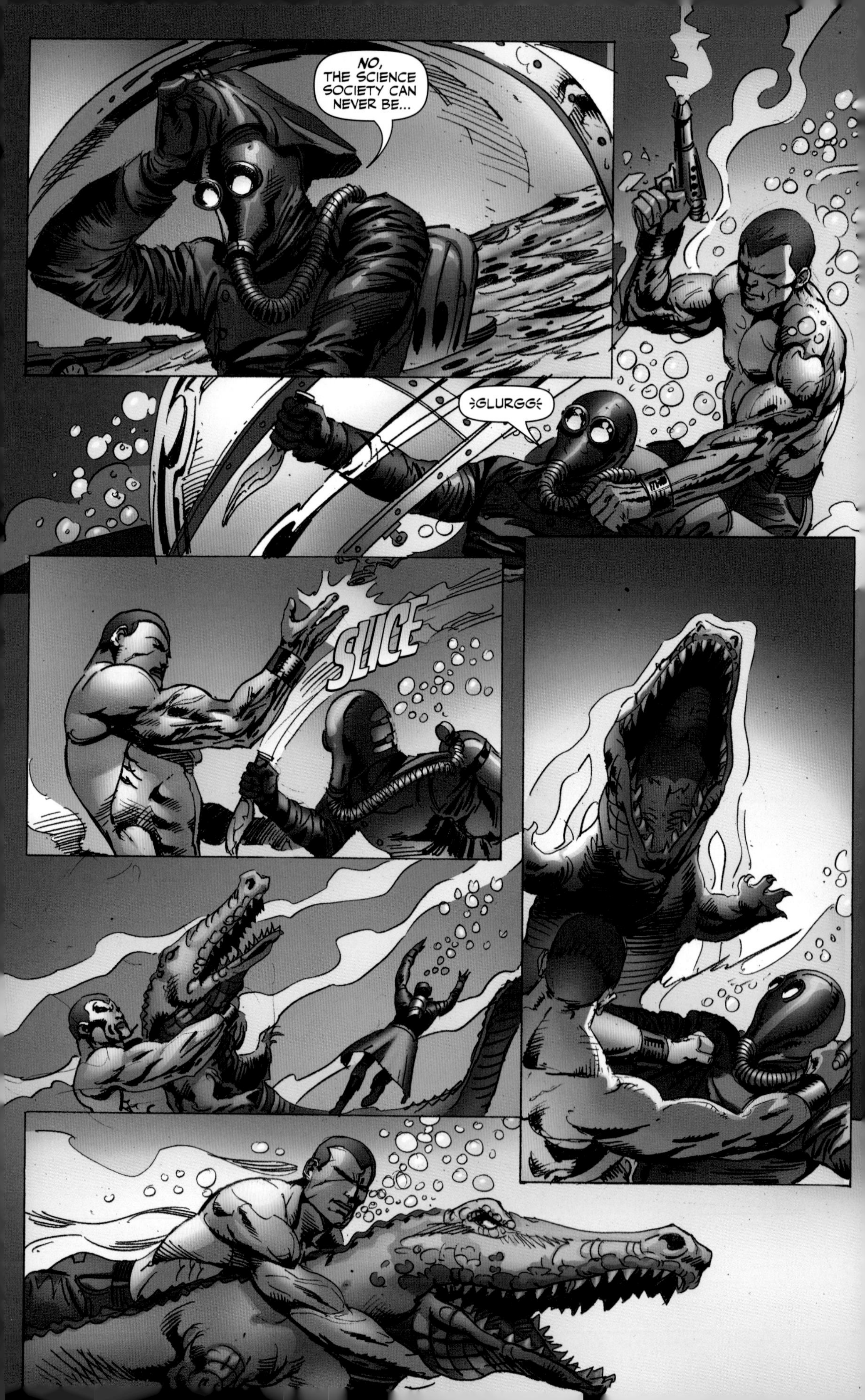
NO, THE SCIENCE SOCIETY CAN NEVER BE...
GLURGG
SLICE

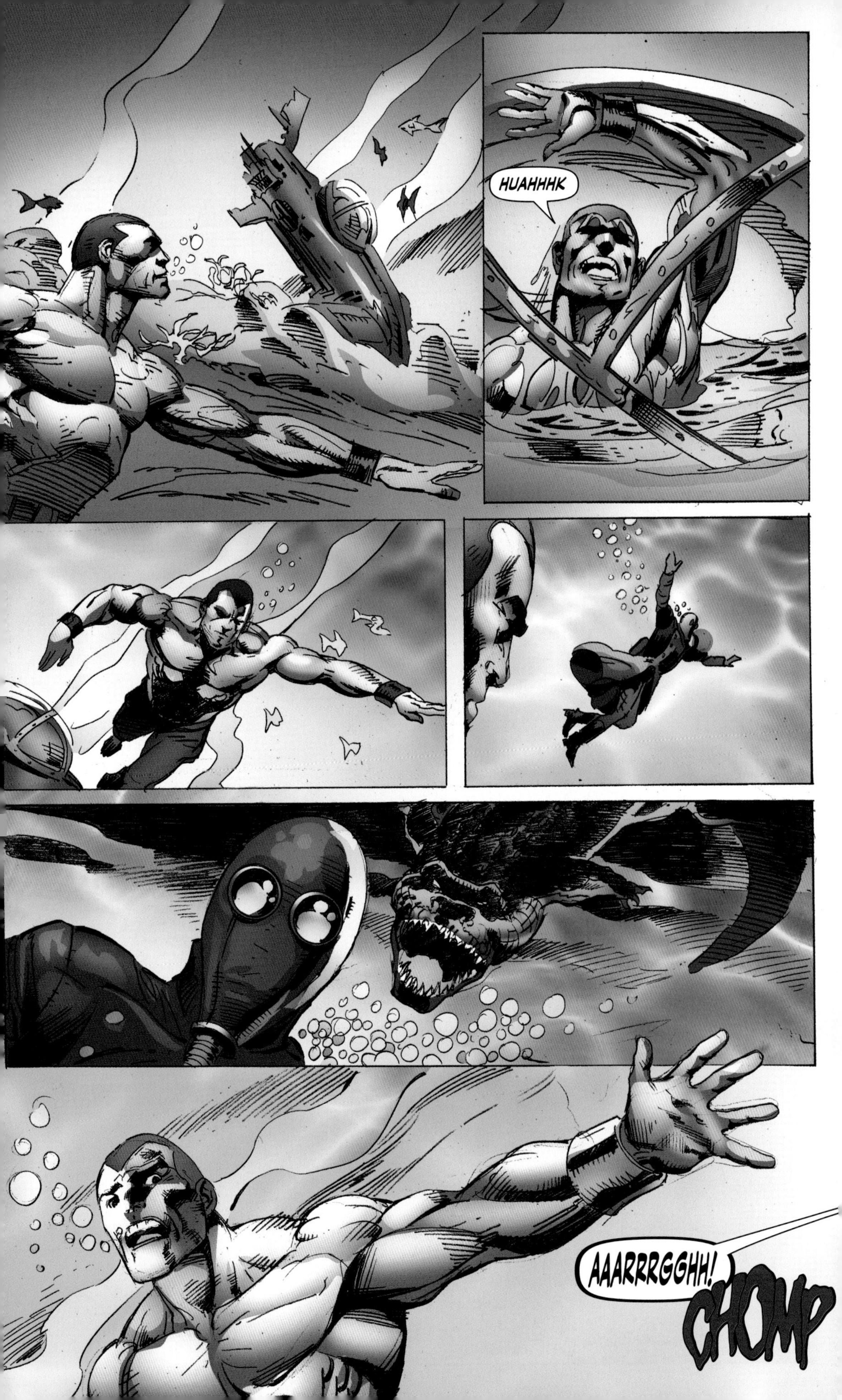
HUAHHHK
AAARRRGGHH!
CHOMP

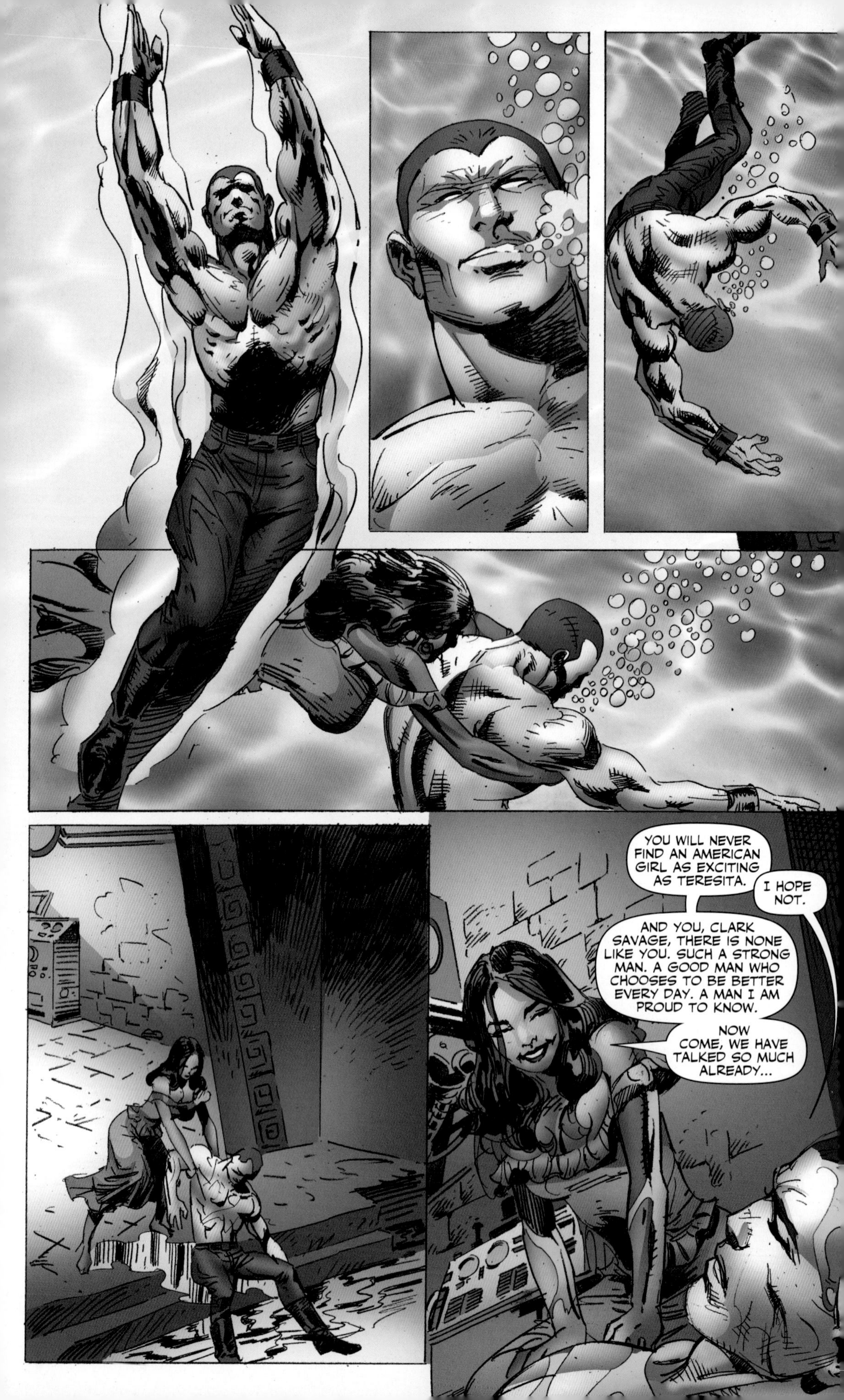
YOU WILL NEVER FIND AN AMERICAN GIRL AS EXCITING AS TERESITA.
I HOPE NOT.
AND YOU, CLARK SAVAGE, THERE IS NONE LIKE YOU. SUCH A STRONG MAN. A GOOD MAN WHO CHOOSES TO BE BETTER EVERY DAY. A MAN I AM PROUD TO KNOW.
NOW COME, WE HAVE TALKED SO MUCH ALREADY...

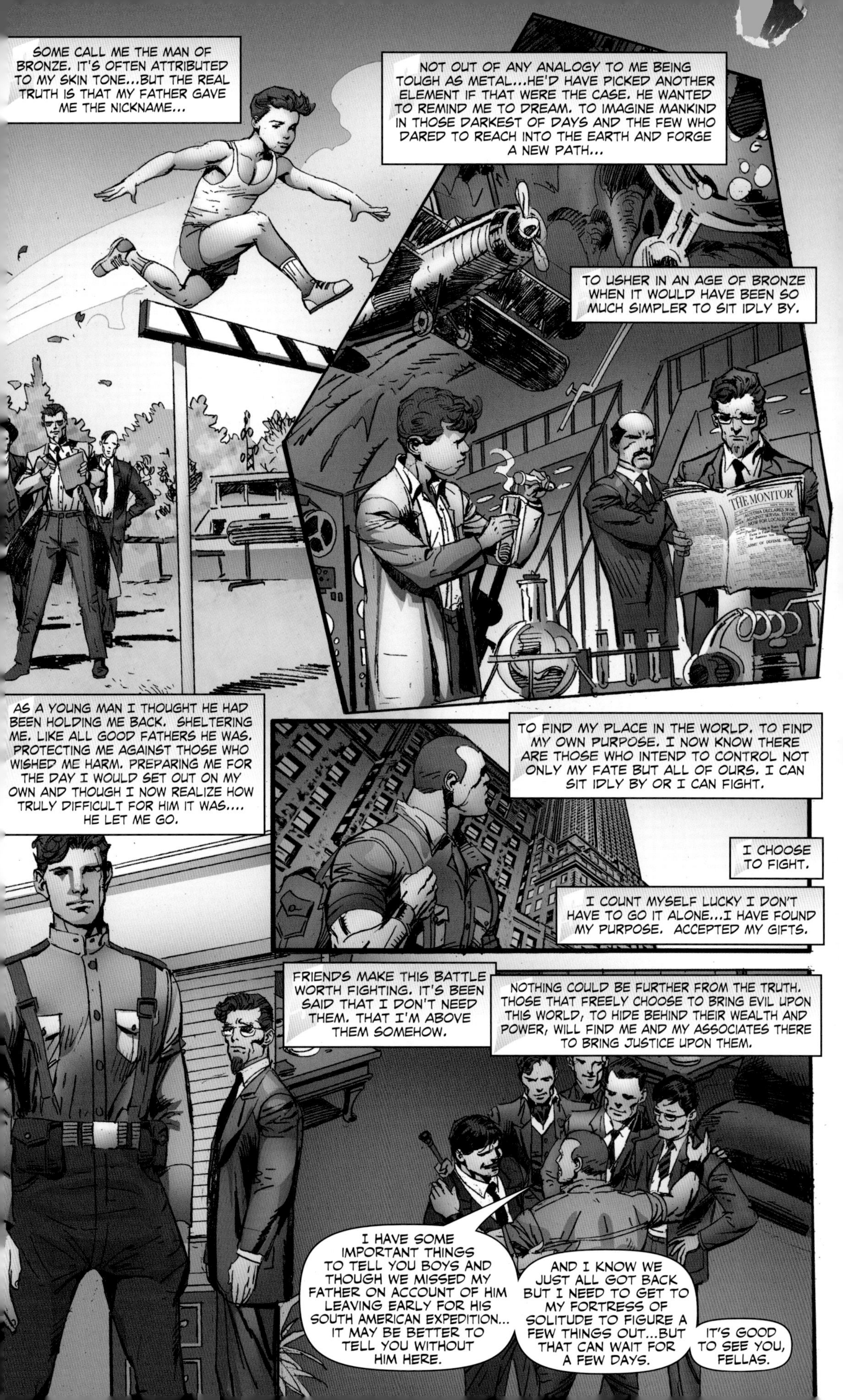

SOME CALL ME THE MAN OF BRONZE. IT'S OFTEN ATTRIBUTED TO MY SKIN TONE...BUT THE REAL TRUTH IS THAT MY FATHER GAVE ME THE NICKNAME...
NOT OUT OF ANY ANALOGY TO ME BEING TOUGH AS METAL...HE'D HAVE PICKED ANOTHER ELEMENT IF THAT WERE THE CASE. HE WANTED TO REMIND ME TO DREAM. TO IMAGINE MANKIND IN THOSE DARKEST OF DAYS AND THE FEW WHO DARED TO REACH INTO THE EARTH AND FORGE A NEW PATH...
TO USHER IN AN AGE OF BRONZE WHEN IT WOULD HAVE BEEN SO MUCH SIMPLER TO SIT IDLY BY.
THE MONITOR
AUSTRIA DECLARES WAR
AS A YOUNG MAN I THOUGHT HE HAD BEEN HOLDING ME BACK. SHELTERING ME. LIKE ALL GOOD FATHERS HE WAS. PROTECTING ME AGAINST THOSE WHO WISHED ME HARM. PREPARING ME FOR THE DAY I WOULD SET OUT ON MY OWN AND THOUGH I NOW REALIZE HOW TRULY DIFFICULT FOR HIM IT WAS.... HE LET ME GO.
TO FIND MY PLACE IN THE WORLD. TO FIND MY OWN PURPOSE. I NOW KNOW THERE ARE THOSE WHO INTEND TO CONTROL NOT ONLY MY FATE BUT ALL OF OURS. I CAN SIT IDLY BY OR I CAN FIGHT.
I CHOOSE TO FIGHT.
I COUNT MYSELF LUCKY I DON'T HAVE TO GO IT ALONE...I HAVE FOUND MY PURPOSE. ACCEPTED MY GIFTS.
FRIENDS MAKE THIS BATTLE WORTH FIGHTING. IT'S BEEN SAID THAT I DON'T NEED THEM. THAT I'M ABOVE THEM SOMEHOW.
NOTHING COULD BE FURTHER FROM THE TRUTH. THOSE THAT FREELY CHOOSE TO BRING EVIL UPON THIS WORLD, TO HIDE BEHIND THEIR WEALTH AND POWER, WILL FIND ME AND MY ASSOCIATES THERE TO BRING JUSTICE UPON THEM.
I HAVE SOME IMPORTANT THINGS TO TELL YOU BOYS AND THOUGH WE MISSED MY FATHER ON ACCOUNT OF HIM LEAVING EARLY FOR HIS SOUTH AMERICAN EXPEDITION... IT MAY BE BETTER TO TELL YOU WITHOUT HIM HERE.
AND I KNOW WE JUST ALL GOT BACK BUT I NEED TO GET TO MY FORTRESS OF SOLITUDE TO FIGURE A FEW THINGS OUT...BUT THAT CAN WAIT FOR A FEW DAYS.
IT'S GOOD TO SEE YOU, FELLAS.

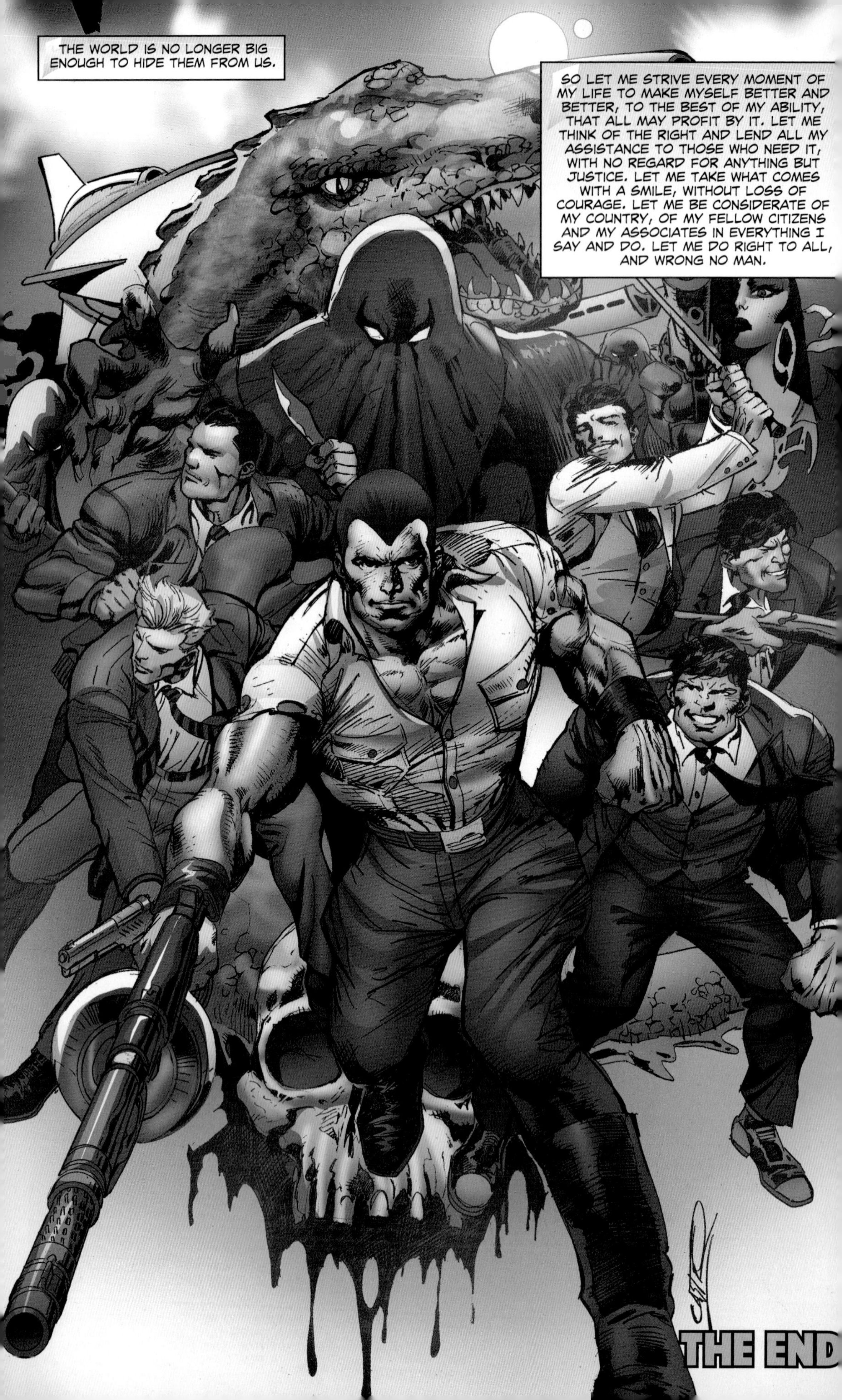
THE WORLD IS NO LONGER BIG ENOUGH TO HIDE THEM FROM US.
SO LET ME STRIVE EVERY MOMENT OF MY LIFE TO MAKE MYSELF BETTER AND BETTER, TO THE BEST OF MY ABILITY, THAT ALL MAY PROFIT BY IT. LET ME THINK OF THE RIGHT AND LEND ALL MY ASSISTANCE TO THOSE WHO NEED IT, WITH NO REGARD FOR ANYTHING BUT JUSTICE. LET ME TAKE WHAT COMES WITH A SMILE, WITHOUT LOSS OF COURAGE. LET ME BE CONSIDERATE OF MY COUNTRY, OF MY FELLOW CITIZENS AND MY ASSOCIATES IN EVERYTHING I SAY AND DO. LET ME DO RIGHT TO ALL, AND WRONG NO MAN.
THE END

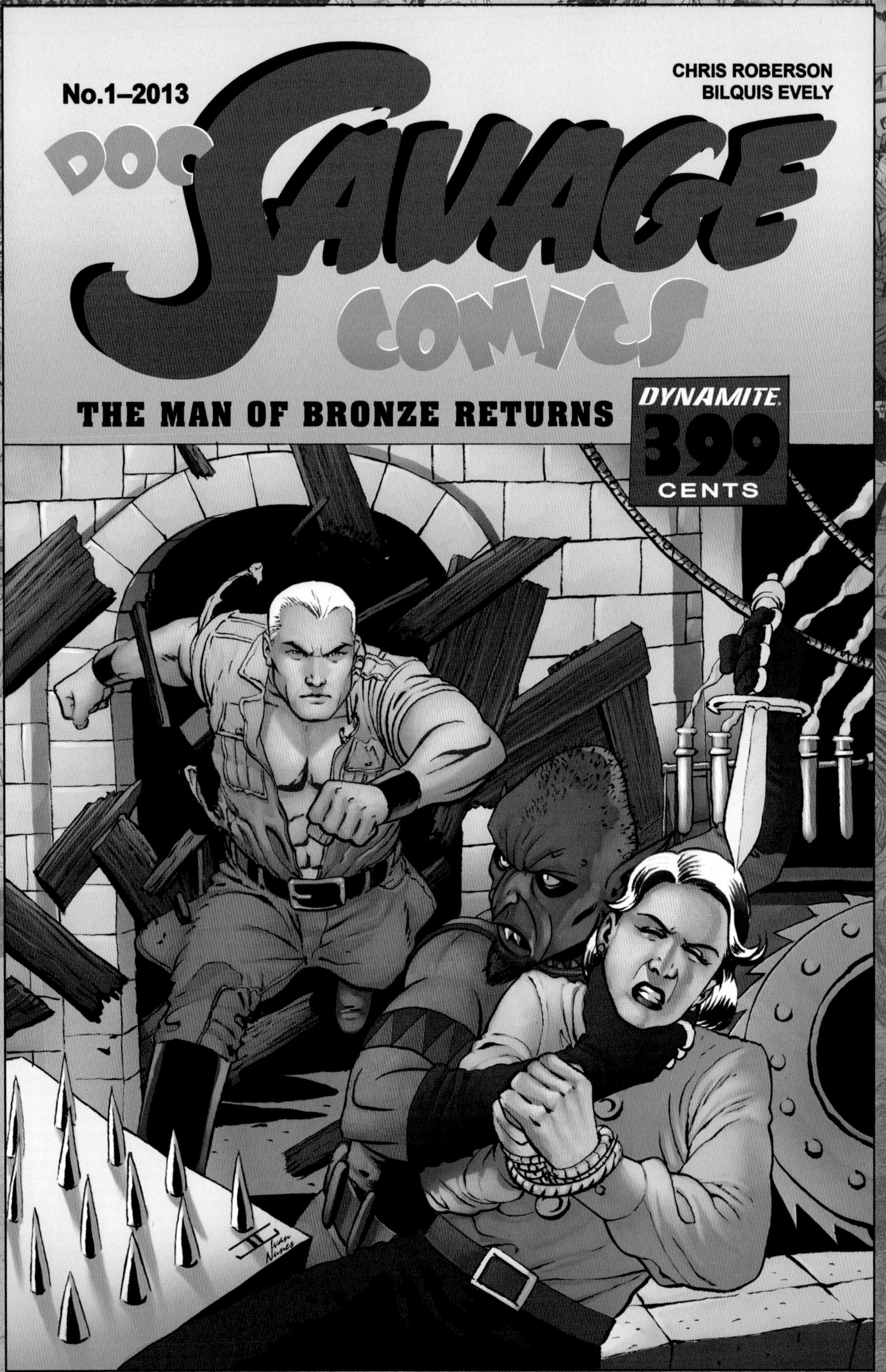

ISSUE #1 ALTERNATE COVER

art by JOHN CASSADAY colors by IVAN NUNES

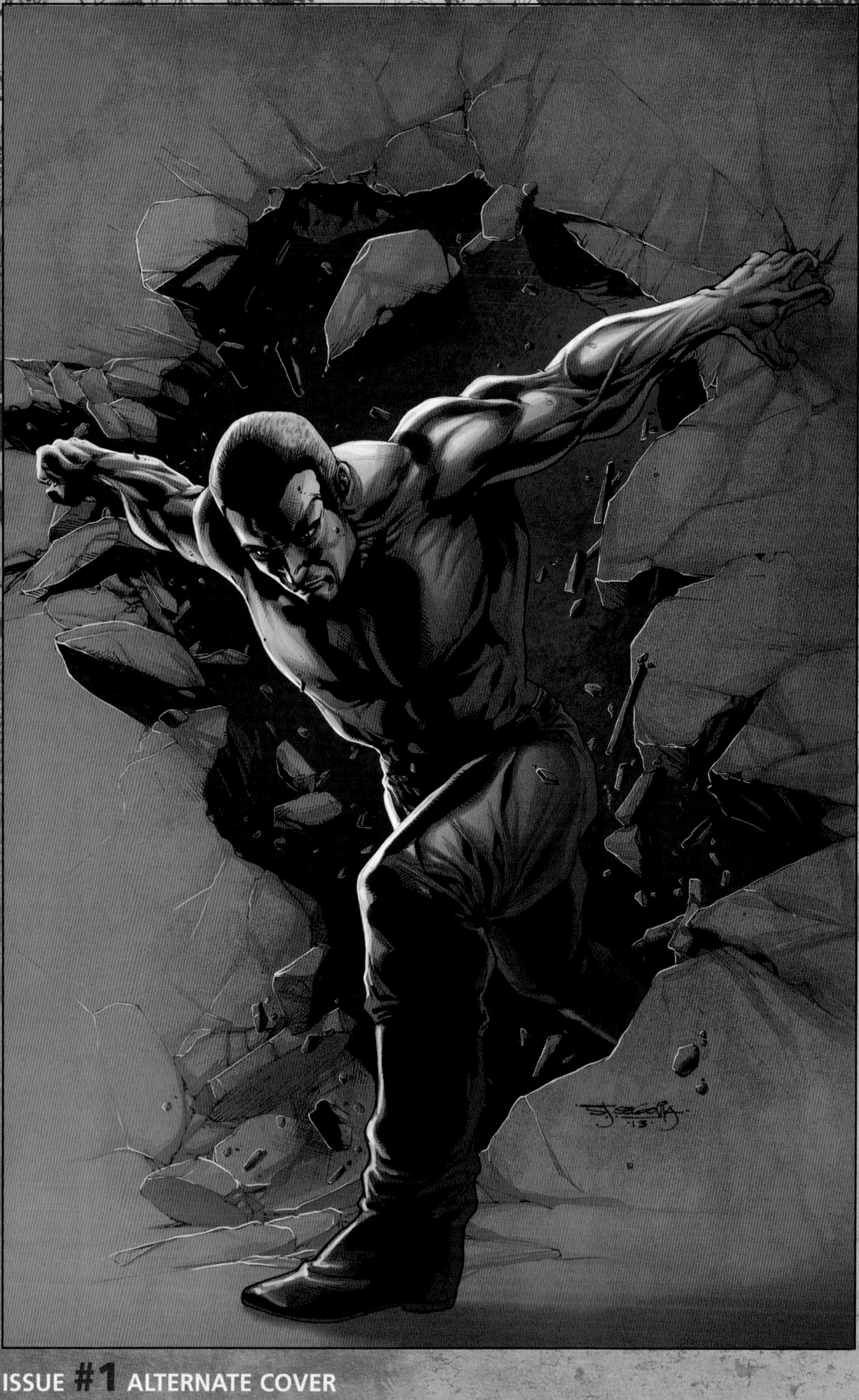
S.J. SEGOVIA '13

ISSUE #1 ALTERNATE COVER
art by STEPHEN SEGOVIA colors by ADRIANO LUCAS

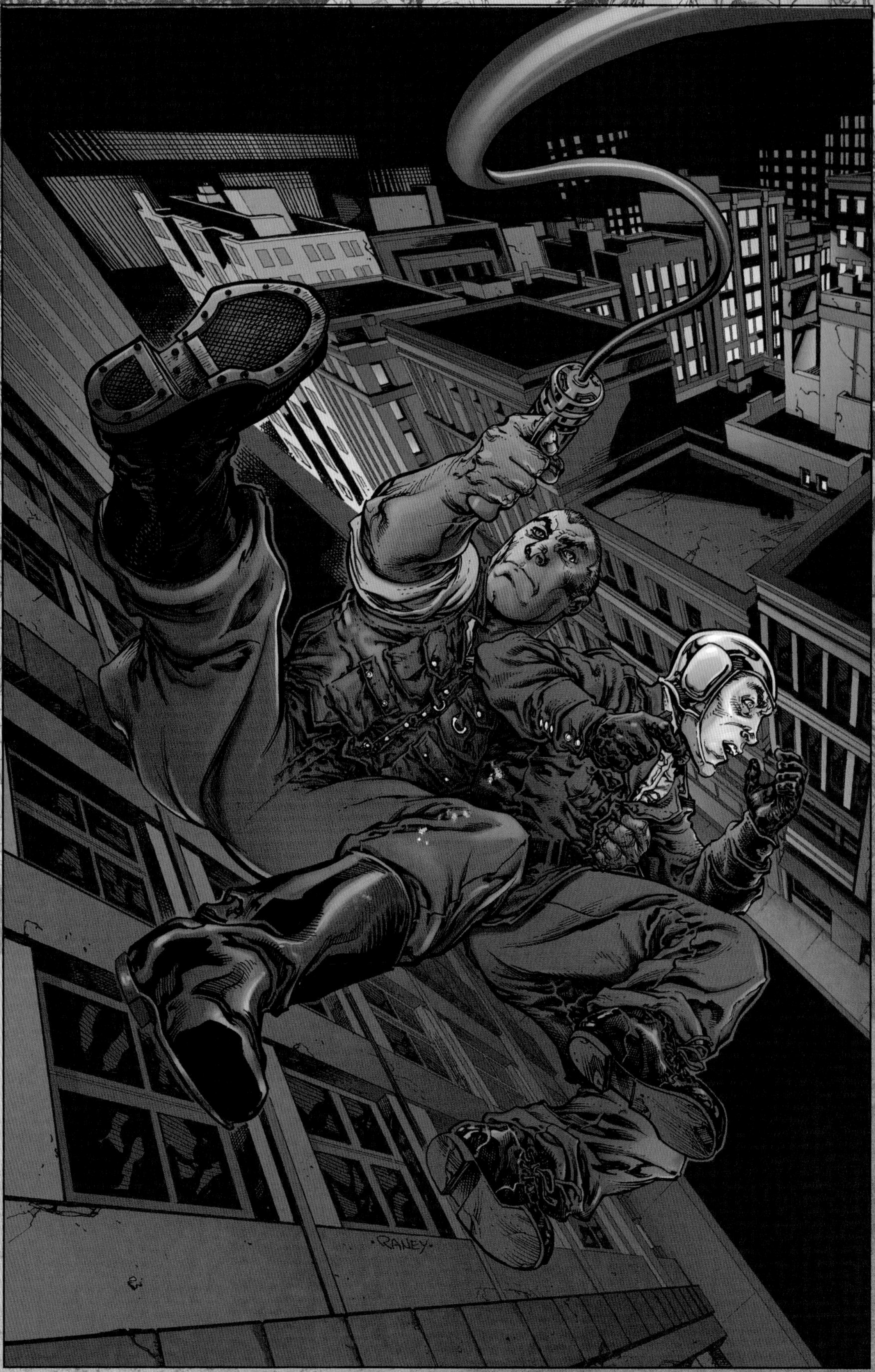
RANEY

ISSUE **#1** CARDS, COMICS, AND COLLECTIBLES EXCLUSIVE COVER
art and colors by **TOM RANEY**

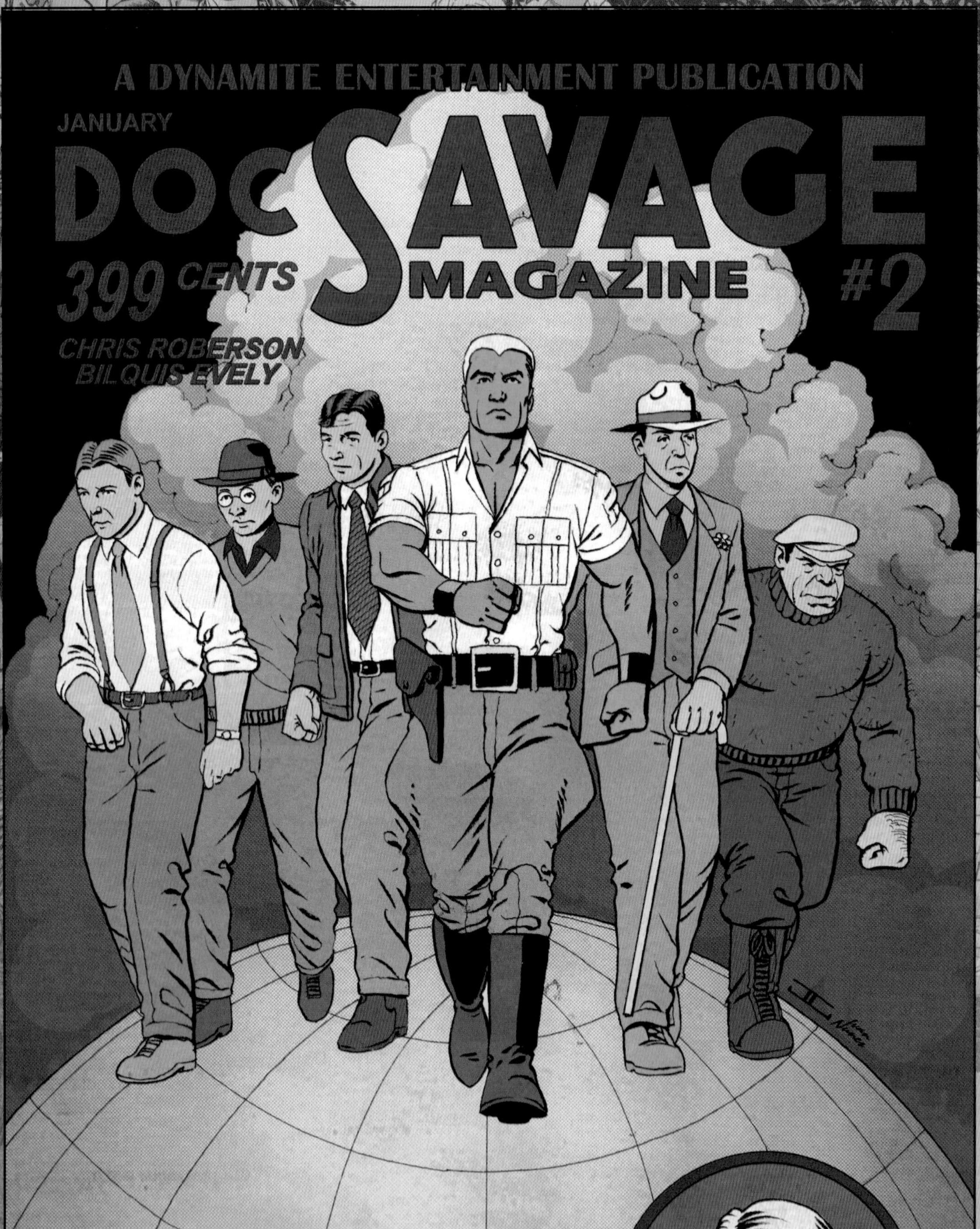
A DYNAMITE ENTERTAINMENT PUBLICATION
JANUARY
DOC SAVAGE MAGAZINE
399 CENTS
#2
CHRIS ROBERSON
BILQUIS EVELY
FEATURING PAT SAVAGE!

ISSUE #2 ALTERNATE COVER

art by JOHN CASSADAY colors by IVAN NUNES

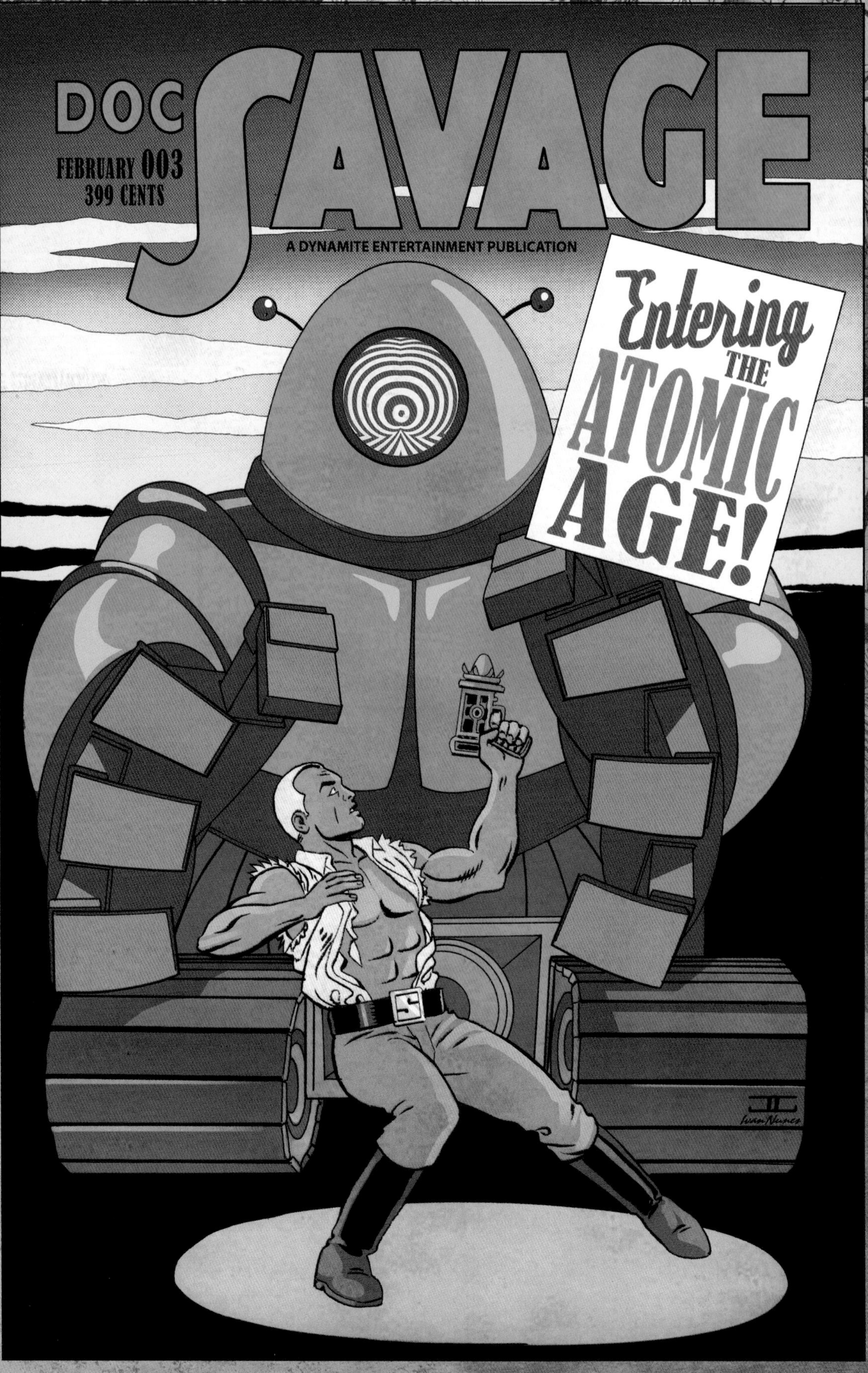
DOC SAVAGE
FEBRUARY 003
399 CENTS
A DYNAMITE ENTERTAINMENT PUBLICATION
Entering THE ATOMIC AGE!

ISSUE #3 ALTERNATE COVER
art by JOHN CASSADAY colors by IVAN NUNES

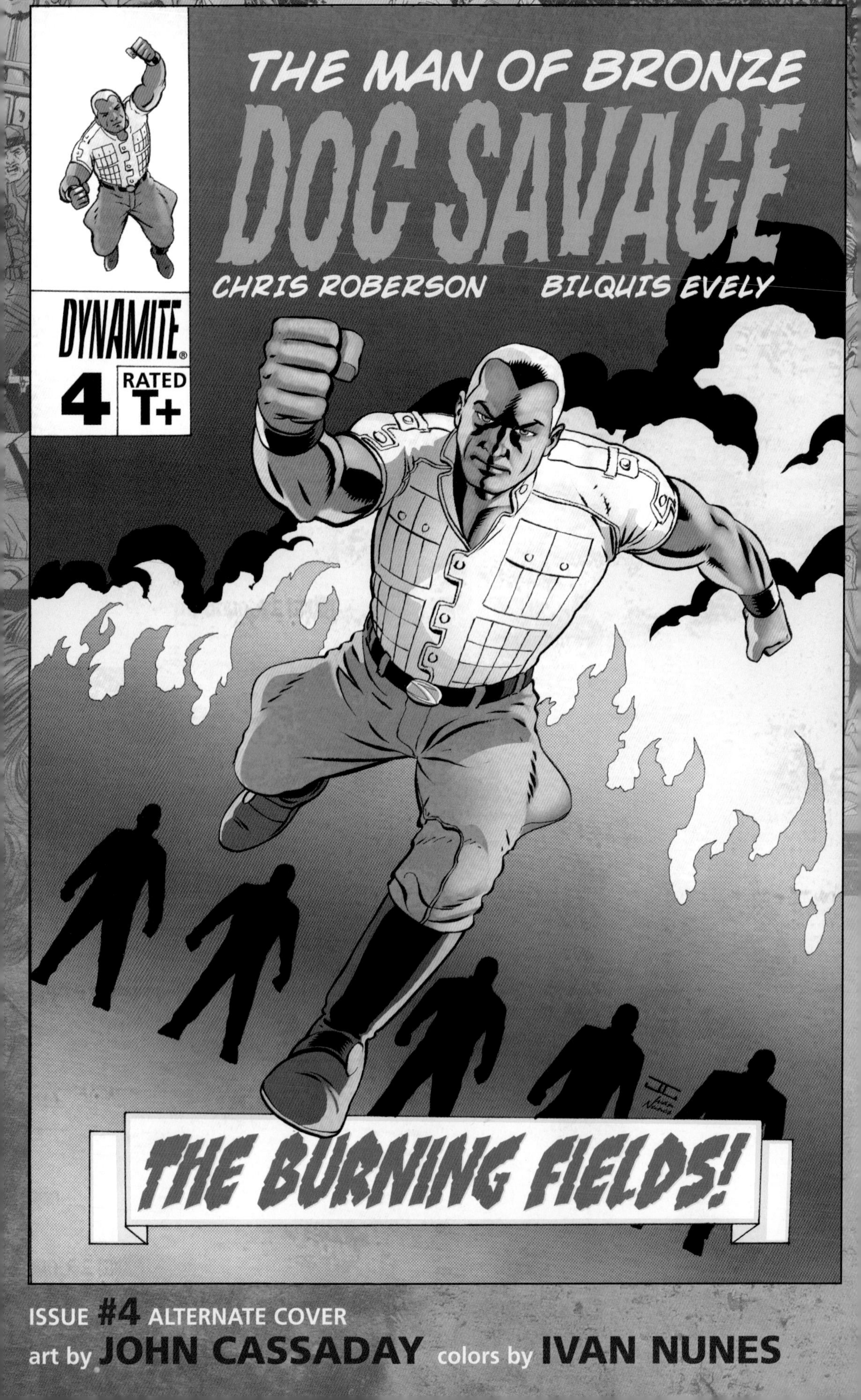
THE MAN OF BRONZE
DOC SAVAGE
CHRIS ROBERSON
BILQUIS EVELY
DYNAMITE
4
RATED T+
THE BURNING FIELDS!

ISSUE #4 ALTERNATE COVER
art by JOHN CASSADAY colors by IVAN NUNES

DYNAMITE COMICS GROUP

DOC
SAVAGE

RATED T+
SUGGESTED FOR
TEENS AND UP

5
APRIL

DOC SAVAGE
THE MAN OF BRONZE

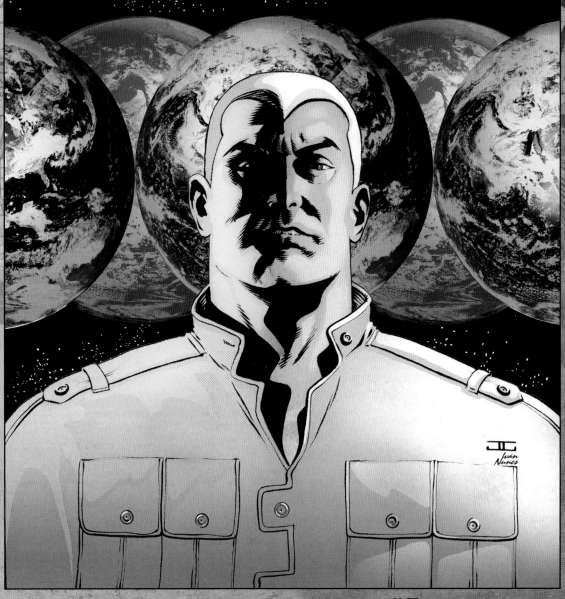

ISSUE **#5** ALTERNATE COVER

art by **JOHN CASSADAY**   colors by **IVAN NUNES**

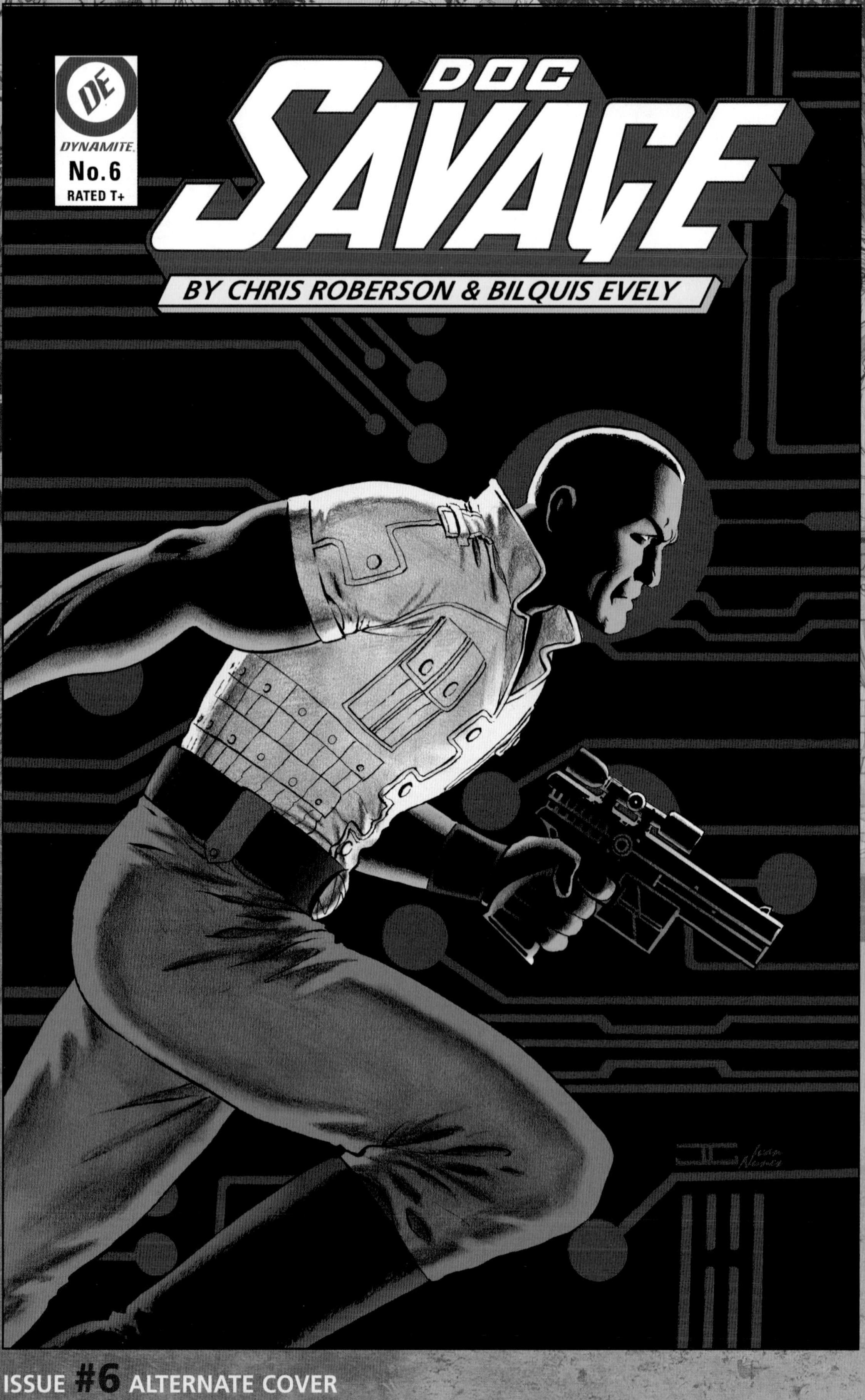
DE
DYNAMITE
No.6
RATED T+
DOC SAVAGE
BY CHRIS ROBERSON & BILQUIS EVELY

ISSUE #6 ALTERNATE COVER
art by JOHN CASSADAY colors by IVAN NUNES

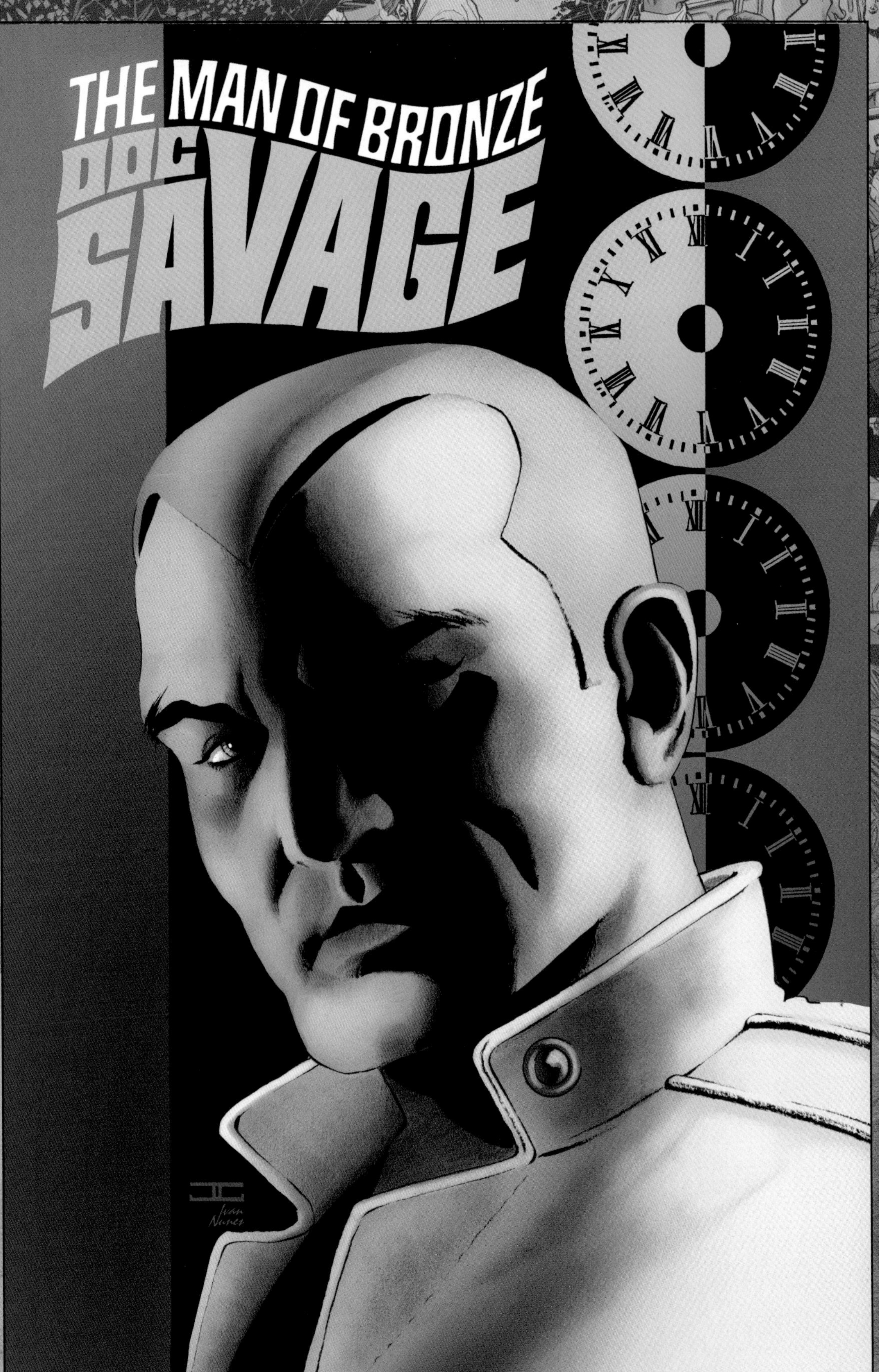
THE MAN OF BRONZE
DOC SAVAGE
Ivan Nunes

ISSUE #7 ALTERNATE COVER
art by **JOHN CASSADAY** colors by **IVAN NUNES**

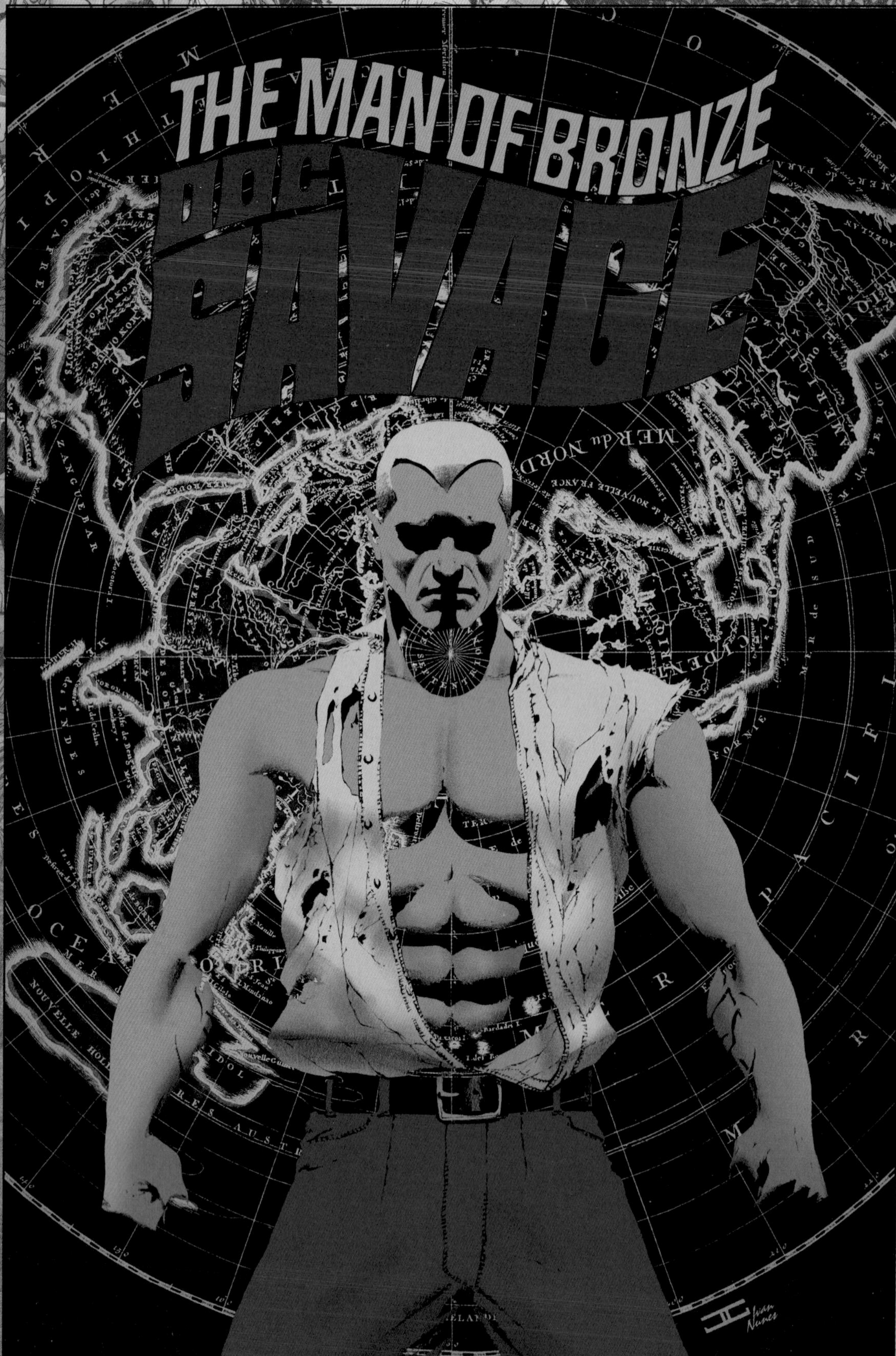
THE MAN OF BRONZE
DOC SAVAGE

ISSUE #8 ALTERNATE COVER
art by JOHN CASSADAY colors by IVAN NUNES